THE HIGH FLYER

SUSAN HOWATCH

THE HIGH FLYER

WHEELER
PUBLISHING, INC.
ROCKLAND, MA
★ AN AMERICAN COMPANY ★

Published in large print by arrangement with Alfred A. Knopf, a division of Random House, Inc., in the United States and Canada.

Wheeler Large Print Book Series.

Set in 16 pt Plantin.

Grateful acknowledgement is made to the following for permission to reprint previously published material:

HarperCollins Publishers Ltd.: Excerpts from *The Shape of Living* by David F. Ford. Reprinted by permission of HarperCollins Publishers Ltd., London.

SPCK Publishing: Excerpts from *The Confessions of a Conservative Liberal* by John Habgood. Reprinted by permission of SPCK Publishing, London.

Library of Congress Cataloging-in-Publication Data

Howatch, Susan
    The high flyer : a novel / Susan Howatch.
        p. (large print) cm.(Wheeler large print book series)
    ISBN 1-58724-211-7 (hardcover)
    1. London (England)—Fiction. 2. Married women—Fiction. 3. Women lawyers—Fiction. 4. Healers—Fiction. 5. Large type books. I. Title.
II. Series.

[PR6058.O912 H5   2002]
823'.914—dc21   2002022317
                                                                                          CIP

Contents

PART ONE

FLIRTING WITH THE ENEMY

There is no shortage of highly individualised beliefs. In fact I am constantly amazed at what people do believe; half-remembered bible stories, odd bits of science fiction, snippets of proverbial wisdom passed on through grandmothers or glossy magazines.

✴   ✴   ✴

We are bombarded with different beliefs, different values, different customs, different interpretations. Experts give us different and incompatible analyses. We are faced with a kaleidoscope of different images. And the overall effect, I suggest, is to reduce all differences to the same level, to make us immune to real distinctions, to imply that the most we can hope for is not truth but mere opinion.

JOHN HABGOOD
Confessions of a Conservative Liberal

ONE

I

When I first saw my temporary secretary it never occurred to me to flirt with him. Even in 1990, when suing for sexual harassment was still considered to be primarily an American activity, an office flirtation would have been considered unwise for a high flyer, and besides, this particular male hardly struck me as being irresistible. He had curly hair, chocolate-coloured eyes and a chunky, cherubic look. My taste in men has never encompassed overgrown choirboys.

Walking into my office I found him stooped over my computer, and since I was not expecting a male secretary I assumed he was someone from the maintenance department. I did notice that he was dressed as an office drone in a grey suit, drab tie and white shirt, but maintenance men often resembled office drones these days; it was a side-effect of the technological revolution.

Abruptly I demanded: "What's the problem?" and added for good measure: "Who the hell are you?" I always feel irritable on Monday mornings.

He glanced up, decided I was just another dumb blonde hired to massage a keyboard and made the big mistake of adopting a patronising manner. "Relax, sweet pea," he said casually, "I'm the temp from PersonPower International! I've been assigned for two weeks to Mr. Carter Graham."

I dropped my bag on the visitor's chair, folded my arms across my chest and dug my high heels into the carpet. Then I said in a voice designed to bend nails: "*I'm* Carter Graham."

The man jumped as if stung by a bee, and as his head jerked up I realised that his square jaw was incompatible with the choirboy image. "I beg your pardon, ma'am," he said at once. "I must have misunderstood the lady in personnel who directed me here."

"The lady in personnel must be suffering from amnesia. She knows I only work with female temps."

"I'm sorry to hear that, ma'am, but let me reassure you by saying—"

"You're gay."

"No, but I can do everything women and gays can do with computers, and I've even taken a course in DTP."

I saw no reason to put up a front by pretending to know what this latest technological time-waster was. "DTP?"

"Desk-Top Publishing, ma'am."

"I don't approve of dubious activities taking place on a desk-top. Are you seriously—*seriously*—trying to tell me that PersonPower International have had the nerve to send a heterosexual white Anglo-Saxon male to work in my office?"

"Maybe they see it as their contribution to multiculturalism, ma'am."

Worried about my ability to keep a straight face I turned aside, tramped to the window and stared at the crowded street four floors below. Only after I had carefully counted to ten did I swing back to face him and say: "All right, so be it. Welcome to Curtis, Towers."

"Thank you, ma'am."

"But now you listen to me, and you listen well. This is a first-names office but you and I are going to use surnames for the duration of your time here. I'm not having all those hormones and pheromones stimulated by any pseuds'-corner office intimacy."

"In that case would you care to be addressed as Miss Graham, Mrs. Graham or Ms. Graham?"

"Well, I certainly didn't go through a wedding ceremony only to be called 'Miss' at the end of it, and I'm not Mrs. Graham, I'm Mrs. Betz. But my marital status is hardly your concern."

"Right, Ms. Graham."

"And your name is—"

"Eric Tucker."

"Okay, Tucker, get me unsugared coffee, black as pitch and strong enough to make an elephant levitate. Then we'll start to flay the fax till it screams for mercy."

He never asked where the coffee machine was or where he could make coffee or whether he would be able to obtain a takeaway from the cafeteria. He just responded smartly: "Yes, ma'am," and zipped out of the room. That impressed me. But I also heard the note of amusement in his voice and knew I was not the only one who had played the scene poker-faced but tongue-in-cheek. That alarmed me. Sharing the same sense of humour can be a snare in an office setting. Humour leads

5

to intimacy which leads to loss of detachment which leads to bad judgement which leads to a mess. I resolved to be on my guard.

I wished he were much younger than I was, but I thought he too was probably in his mid-thirties. Younger men were easier to muzzle and keep on a short leash; younger men were less likely to think a woman's place was not in the boardroom; younger men were easier to intimidate, control and organise. But this smooth-talking item was not a younger man. Nor, I was sure, was he ever again going to remind me of an elderly cherub or an overgrown choirboy.

At that point I spent three seconds wondering why he was working as a temporary secretary and three seconds wondering, in the casual way one does with new acquaintances of the opposite sex, what he was like in bed. Then I said to myself impatiently: "Bloody sex! Why are we all so obsessed with it?" and focused my mind instead on the intricate fiscal affairs of my major clients, the Unipax Transworld Corporation.

II

Arriving home at seven I mixed my first drink of the day and moved out onto the balcony to survey the sky. It was pale blue with puffs of wispy white. The sun was still some way from the horizon, but in the distance the gothic towers and spires of the Palace of Westminster were already forming a shadowy mass streaked with slanting shafts of gold.

I breathed deeply, swallowed a mouthful of my vodka martini and turned my attention from the City of Westminster to its neighbour, the City of

London. The square mile of the capital's financial district stretched to the south and east far below; I saw it as a dense, man-made jungle knifed by skyscrapers which reflected the powerful rays of the setting sun as if they were shards of mirrored glass rising from a dung-heap. Half a mile away the dome of St. Paul's Cathedral appeared to float above the canyons of Cheapside and Old Bailey like an exotic mushroom blooming on an unkempt lawn.

The phone rang.

Stepping back into the living-room I grabbed the receiver. "Hullo?"

There was no reply.

My right hand tightened its grip on my glass. "Hullo?" I repeated sharply, but when the silence remained unbroken I hung up. Immediately the phone rang again. This time, without waiting for the silence, I snarled: "Get a life!" and slammed the receiver into its cradle.

Seconds later, to my disgust, the bell rang yet again, but this time I merely picked up the receiver and waited.

"Sweetheart?"

"Kim! My God, was that you a moment ago?"

"It sure was! What's going on?"

"Just some nutter misdialling—forget it. How's New York?"

"Can't wait to step into Concorde tomorrow! How's life at Curtis, Towers?"

"Lurid as ever—and to cap it all I've got a male temp for two weeks."

"Any good?"

"I hate to admit it, but he's better than any female PA I've ever had."

"Men always outperform women whenever they take on women's jobs."

"So when are they going to take over pregnancy and childbirth? Kim, if you were on this side of the Atlantic I'd—"

"I bet. And while we're on the subject of slappable behaviour, let me tell you this: if the new hired help makes a pass at you I'll have his balls on toast for breakfast."

"If the new hired help makes a pass at me, *I'll* have his balls on toast for breakfast! And talking of sex, darling..." The conversation slid into an exchange of private intimacies.

After I had hung up I returned to the balcony to watch the next stage of the long sunset. Years ago, on my arrival in the capital I had not realised how many Londons there were; the place which I had always thought of as London I had quickly learned to call the West End. That was where the tourists went to see the sights and squander money on shopping. Then there was the East End where, before the Docklands redevelopment schemes, no one from the West End ever went, a huge impoverished territory where fierce indigenous tribes warred with successive waves of immigrants. And finally, between the rich West End and the poor East End, like a jewel wedged between a marble slab and an earthen floor, lay the fabled "City," the oldest London of all, Roman Londinium, sacked by Boadicea, ravaged by the Saxons, plundered by the Vikings, conquered by the Normans, decimated by the Plague, razed by the Great Fire, blitzed by the Luftwaffe, but surviving all this radical pruning to flourish more fiercely than ever. In the 1980s, fired by the Prime Minister whom it revered as a goddess, it had gone mad with excitement and mushroomed into the greatest money-market

on earth. Sparse on regulation, prolific in financial opportunities, it had become a gold-plated
circus stuffed with predators from all over the
globe. Of course the doomsters had said the
money-miracle would never last, but who had had
the time to listen? The great goddess would take
care of the City, that huge jewel in the forefront
of her tiara, and the great goddess had expressed
her intention of being worshipped to the end of
the millennium and beyond.

But there was a chill wind now whispering up
the Thames from the east and laying icy fingers
on all those unsold new developments in Docklands. The great roulette wheel of the property
market had ceased to spin. The 1980s were over,
and an unknown and perhaps very different
decade lay ahead. Mrs. Thatcher, the great goddess, was still behaving as if she could take care
of everything, but her nemesis, the poll tax, was
pushing her deeper and deeper into the political
quicksands, and recently there had even been riots
in Trafalgar Square. Mrs. Thatcher was starting
to look fallible at last, and once confidence in her
was lost, the political predators would tear her
apart. Female high flyers could plummet to earth
faster than any man; the men surrounding them
would always make sure of that. I shuddered as
I thought of that long fall, and as I looked down
on London that evening from the thirty-fifth
floor of Harvey Tower, I noted again that the giant
building cranes were disappearing from the landscape as the economy halted, inflation rose and
darkness began to fall at last on the City.

The river was glowing in the dusk like molten
lava snaking from a volcano. Back in the living-
room I sat at my telescope and focused it on

the Houses of Parliament upstream in West-minster. The towers and spires were now as black and jagged as a tramp's teeth. I decided it was time to think about dinner.

I ate some sardines and a medium-cut slice of wholemeal bread, toasted but unbuttered. It was an austere meal but the very act of eating reminded me of the dinner-party which we were planning to give at the end of the week. To crown Mrs. Thatcher's troubles, the beef market had collapsed. Could I really foist portions of a potentially mad cow on my guests in the manner of the Minister of Agriculture who had recently attempted to proclaim the safety of British beef by ramming a hamburger into the mouth of his four-year-old daughter? No. I tried to console myself by thinking that all over England menus were being reduced to chaos by bovine spongi-form encephalopathy, but this hardly made my ordeal easier to face. It would be the first dinner-party Kim and I had given since our wedding, and although I had researched the subject of eti-quette with a lawyer's attention to detail, I still felt that the whole exercise resembled sitting an exam where one small slip meant total failure.

In addition to the menu I was worrying about the wine. I knew a good claret had to be at least ten years old, but Kim had said we could serve a 1985 St. Julien. I realised that '85 was a good year, possibly the best year for claret in the eighties, but could we really get away with cut-ting such a corner when at least one of the guests was an oenophile? It was all very well for Kim to glide around the conventions; everyone knew he was only a naturalised Englishman and allowances were always made for foreigners, but as a woman I had to get everything not only right but perfect. That was how I had survived in the City among all those sabre-toothed male predators. Survival meant being in control of every single detail of every single project—and I was still a long way from being in control of this dinner-party looming at the end of the week.

Having reached this conclusion I felt so stressed out that I gave way to the urge to binge on cornflakes. Before meeting Kim I had kept my kitchen a cereal-free zone but Kim liked cornflakes and I had fallen into the habit lately of snitching three or four flakes at a time to soothe my nerves. However, at least flake-snitching was an improvement on smoking. I had given up cigarettes two years, six months and fourteen days before.

Still munching I slumped down on the sofa, grabbed the television's remote control and zapped my way into *Panorama* in the hope of diverting myself from any further thoughts about the dinner-party.

The pest who had made the first phone call that evening remained silent but I felt no spasm of curiosity because I knew very well who she was.

I had long since begun to wish that legislation could be introduced to curb ex-wives who turned into stalkers.

III

Before I say more about Sophie I need to say more about Kim.

I had met him seventeen months ago at Heathrow Airport before he had made the move to Graf-Rosen and I had made the switch to Curtis, Towers. In consequence neither of us was travelling first class, but as the airlines had already started to pamper business-class passengers, we were allowed to congregate in a private lounge where even a barman and waiter had been planted to spare us the effort of mixing our own complimentary drinks. Passengers destined for other flights on that airline were also milling around and taking up too much space, but just as I was thinking I would have to drink my vodka martini standing up I noticed a man relaxing alone at a seating arrangement for two on the far side of the lounge.

What happened next may seem hard to believe, but our glances really did meet across that crowded room. I suppose this situation became a cliché simply because it does happen so often, but my first reaction, I have to admit, was to think cynically of those implausible 1950s movies starring Doris Day.

Kim's glance travelled idly over me, moved on, halted and swivelled back. At another time I might have adopted a remote air and gazed at the ceiling, but at home there was a letter from the lover who had just dumped me, and I had certain things to prove to myself in order to heal my bruised self-esteem. Gliding over to this well-dressed stranger, who I at once recognised had the poise of a successful businessman, I indicated the empty chair and said two words. They were: "May I?"

"Make my day."

This response naturally triggered memories of Clint Eastwood, but not for long; I was too busy feeling like Grace Kelly about to vamp Cary Grant, and the next moment I was taking a closer look at this big fish whom I was busy

12

teasing with a shrimping-net. I might have been acting out a romantic cliché, but I was well aware that Kelly and Grant had been directed by Alfred Hitchcock, a genius much admired for his depiction of psychopaths.

But this big fish seemed more like a dolphin than a shark. He had dark hair, silver at the sides, blue eyes, deep grooves at the corners of his wide, subtle mouth, and a furry-purry voice guaranteed to reduce a Rottweiler to a lap-dog. I judged him to be in his late forties, certainly in the prime of middle age, and I knew I had not mistaken the shimmer of success which gave his blunt-featured good looks such a glitzy sheen.

"Going far?" he said as I sat down.

"Only three thousand miles."

"The New York flight?"

"Uh-huh. You too?"

He nodded. "Staying at the Pierre?"

"Not this time."

"Too bad!" He smiled again. His teeth were slightly uneven but I liked that. I was bored with capped teeth which had had all the individuality tortured out of them. By this time I was aware that although he spoke with a faint American accent there had been something European about the way he pronounced "Pierre."

"Business or pleasure?" he was asking idly.

"Both, I hope!"

He finished his Scotch and gestured to my glass. "What are you drinking?"

I told him. He snapped his fingers. The harassed waiter stopped dead in his tracks and took the order for another round.

"Well, thank you," I said, "Mr.—"

"My name's Joachim Betz, but you don't have

to get your tongue around that first name—or the last. Kim will do."

"German?"

"Not exactly. I've been English for a long time now."

"So have I."

"You're not English?"

"Not exactly."

We smiled, savouring our inexactness, before I said: "I'm British but not English. I'm a Scot. My name's Carter Graham, Carter as in President Jimmy."

He asked no questions but accepted the odd first name as if it were commonplace. "I was born in Argentina," he said. "My father was smart enough to escape from the Nazis before the war."

"Your parents were Jewish?"

"Only my father. So by Jewish rules I don't qualify, but I confess that in New York it often suits me to let people assume I'm a Jew."

"I've never found there's much mileage in being a Scot in London."

"How about all those Scots who have made it to the top of the British Establishment?"

"Yes, a great bunch—and all of them men!"

He laughed. "*Res ipsa loquitur?*"

"*Res ipsa loquitur!*"

It was as if we had exchanged the password which signalled membership of a secret confraternity. That Latin tag, "the matter speaks for itself," is one of the first phrases any lawyer learns.

"What's your field?" he demanded.

"Tax. And yours?"

"Investment banking... But is being Scottish

14

really such a handicap for a woman practising law in this enlightened day and age?"

"What enlightened day and age?"

"Well, since we now have a female prime minister—"

"She's a goddess. That's different."

"Explain!"

I sized him up and decided to risk a touch of satire.

IV

"The English dinosaurs who roam the City of London," I said, "divide women into four groups: trash, tarts, girls and goddesses. Trash is anything which fails to speak with a Home Counties accent, and Scots trash, if it aims to be a lawyer, should qualify in Scottish law and stay north of the border. Trash can't be taken seriously. Tarts, on the other hand, can be taken seriously, but dinosaurs only do one kind of business with them—if indeed they do business with them at all. The women in the third category, the girls, speak with a Home Counties accent and are allowed to be businesswomen (a) because they look sweet with their briefcases, and (b) because they can't possibly be a serious threat—they remind the dinosaur of his mother and sister, and all dinosaurs know how to control the females in their families. Goddesses alone are beyond control, but that's all right because they appeal to the dinosaur's primitive need to worship the powerful, and when worshipped the goddess is usually benign towards males and indifferent to females. Very occasionally tarts and trash can be reclassified as girls who may one day be goddesses, but only if their speech is flawless, their manners impeccable and their looks fit to qualify them for the frontispiece of *Country Life*."

My companion was clearly amused. "And how would you define the dinosaurs?"

"They can be any age between forty and ninety, although nowadays they're usually exterminated from the boardrooms before they hit sixty-five. They're in all the major professions, but the law provides them with an ideal environment. The legal dinosaurs talk loudly about modernising attitudes and they make token gestures when it comes to employing women, but this is yet another case of 'the more things change, the more things remain the same.' Even today the dinosaurs with the most power all went to the same schools and they all belong to the same clubs and they all share the same lifestyle—"

"Which is?"

"A pied-à-terre in the Temple or Clifford's Inn or the Barbican. A plush home in leafy Surrey which is serviced by a Home Counties wife encased in pearls and twinsets—"

"You're describing the 1950s!"

"As I said, the more things change, the more things remain the same. Anyone who's truly ambitious soon finds he has to adopt a dinosaur's lifestyle in order to make his dreams come true, so the lifestyle gets passed down intact from one generation to the next."

"But supposing," said Kim, "a dinosaur gets bored with this fossilised English lifestyle? Supposing he wants to ditch the leafy lanes of Surrey and try something new?"

"The desire to ditch would probably be just a passing whim. But there's no reason, of course, why he shouldn't occasionally take a holiday from all those leafy lanes." Raising my glass I paused before saying blandly: "Cheers," and as he smiled again, his eyes now a steamy blue, I knew at once that I'd hooked him.

V

I hardly need say that I was not a goddess. To have accumulated the necessary power, prestige and influence, goddesses had to be over fifty, and for me that milestone was still many years away. But my prospects were good. Having become a partner in my firm of solicitors I had now manoeuvred myself into a position where I could afford to take time out—briefly—for domesticity. According to the life-plan which I had designed for myself before my arrival in London, I had to marry at thirty-five. When I met Kim I was nearly thirty-four and already looking around so that I could complete the assignment on schedule. I supposed it was too much to hope that I would manage to follow Mrs. Thatcher's example of having twins, a move that completed child-bearing in a single nine-month tranche, but I certainly expected to be finished with pregnancies before I was forty. Then I would be free to focus on my career again in what would be the most challenging years of my professional life.

The trouble with life-plans which look so neat on paper is that life itself is always trying to poke holes in them. As soon as I started to look around for a husband I realised there was a big problem: marriageable men were in short supply. My recent lover had spelled this out to me in no uncertain terms before ditching me for a nineteen-year-old fluffette. Unmarried career women in their mid-thirties were pathetic, I was informed, particularly when they were unable to figure out why no man wanted to be stuck with them on a permanent basis. Did they never once realise that there was always a new crop of nubile feminine flesh flowering for the delight of the older male? No man in his right mind, I was informed, wanted the kind of successful woman who had more balls than all the men in the boardroom.

I did manage to laugh as I accused him of whipping himself into a frenzy of jealousy over the penis that I didn't have, but after his departure I found myself fighting a major depression, and although I won through I emerged debilitated. I almost decided not to bother with marriage, but found this was a goal I was unwilling to abandon. The dinosaurs never truly respected a woman unless she had been a wife and mother. Society did appear to have changed in its attitude to unmarried women, but I often suspected the change was no more than a fantasy hyped up by the media while the attitudes of the men in power remained much as they had always been.

A successful woman, it seemed clear to me, had to achieve both a career *and* a faultless domesticity; it was not an either/or situation, and in order to maximise my success I had to stick to my life-plan and net the right husband. Celibacy was just as much for losers as chastity was. That was the dogma. Those were the rules. One conformed or else one was consigned to hell as someone who had failed to make it to the heaven of "having it all." Occasionally, very occasionally, I did think this ideology was as rigorous as the crackpot lifestyle of some fundamentalist religious sect, but I always eliminated that heretical thought by reminding myself what agony it would be to wind up a loser, with everyone breathing contempt on me from all sides.

The irony was that when I first met Kim in that airport lounge I did not see him as a potential husband. I merely saw him as a male who could boost my shattered self-esteem, and besides I had by that time given up hope of marrying a fellow lawyer. Successful lawyers all seemed to gravitate towards the traditional wives who would slot easily into the dinosaur lifestyle, and although I had cast my net wider, trawling among the stockbrokers and the bankers and the various other businessmen who flourished in the City's Square Mile, I had found only the unsuitable and the unavailable.

I had wondered if I was being too fussy, but thought not. It was no good marrying someone unsuitable; I would have been written off as pitifully desperate. It was also no good angling for someone who was already married; that would have been a very unwise move, no matter how desirable the husband was, because people would have said I was reckless, hormone-driven, incapable of ordering my private life properly, and I could not afford to make any move which would have been detrimental to my career.

"My wife's ideal for a dinosaur," said Kim on the flight to New York, "but the trouble is I'm not the dinosaur I appear to be. I've always been the outsider, acting a part in order to get on."

"Me too. So are you saying—"

"I'm saying Sophie and I have recently decided to go our separate ways. There are no children and no other people involved, so the divorce could hardly be easier."

"How civilised," I said politely, but despite this information that he would soon be single I still did not see him as a potential husband. I was too busy massaging my battered ego with erotic thoughts of a one-night stand.

VI

According to romantic convention and modern urban myth a torrid sex-scene should have unfolded when Kim and I went to bed together that same night in New York, but fortunately real life is rather more unpredictable. The last thing I wanted was a torrid sex-scene. Erotic, yes, but not pornographically torrid. In my experience (which was well up to the modern average as established by earnest sociologists) torrid sex-scenes indicated the presence of either male bastards or male perverts or both, and were conducted as if the woman's body were a plastic machine designed for unspeakable experiments. No woman in her right mind could enjoy that kind of rubbish. Torrid sex-scenes might have been fun in the 1960s when everyone was so innocent and the weirdos were still hiding in the woodwork, but now, when everything is not only permitted but expected, they have degenerated into a big bore which is not only repulsive but occasionally frightening.

I sound jaded. I *was* jaded. Sex as a leisure activity is great fun when one's young, but as the years pass, one's horizons alter, one's needs change and one becomes more complex, less easily satisfied. One simply cannot, if one wants to be a mature human being, continue to think of sex as being in the same league as getting drunk in a pub on a Saturday night. The whole subject then becomes murky, fraught with ambiguity and eventually painful. Yes, I was jaded. I was sure too that I was not alone in harbouring jaded feelings, but of course secular society has decreed that one can never admit to feeling less than ecstatic about sex. This is a key dogma, and to deny it is heresy.

However, despite my jaded attitude to sex—despite the fact that I was pursuing Kim not primarily for culturally sanctified thrills but for an ego-boost—despite the fact that I expected little physical pleasure from the encounter but only the emotional satisfaction arising from a power-play successfully executed—despite all these things I had the most welcome surprise. Kim was astonishingly normal. No weirdo came crawling out of the woodwork. No ego-crazed Don Juan treated me as a collection of apertures while watching himself dotingly in the mirror. No tormented masculine psyche worried itself silly about female orgasms. And no flagging middle-aged bodypart flunked consummation amidst a rising tide of embarrassment. He just said casually after we had had a passionate smooch (well worthy of Grace Kelly's famous smooch with Cary Grant in *To Catch a Thief*): "Anything you don't like?" and when I retorted: "Yes—endless foreplay!" he laughed before murmuring: "Sure—why waltz when you can tango?" Then I laughed too and suddenly I thought: this is fun! And I was so surprised because I had quite forgotten how amusing ordinary, straightforward, no-frills sexual intercourse could be if only one had the right partner.

Yet I did not expect afterwards to see him again. I had no illusions; this had been a one-night stand in which I had soothed my damaged pride and he had taken a break from the Home Counties wife whom, I was willing to bet, he had no real intention of divorcing. A woman hardly expects to see a man again after a freakish connection like that, and most of the time she has no desire to see him again either. Sensibly I told myself I had achieved the goal of numbing my pain by means of sophisticated behaviour—although I knew very well that there was nothing particularly sophisticated about using sex in this way. Analgesics, after all, hardly constitute a banner of the beau monde; no one has ever suggested that taking aspirin is the last word in cosmopolitan chic.

On the morning after the night before Kim said: "I'm booked to the hilt for these three days in New York and I'm going to be unconscious every night as soon as I hit the sack, but I'd like to see you again in London. Can I call you at your office?"

But I rejected this suggestion. Personal calls at the office create mess. Word gets around. A woman can never be too careful, particularly when there are male rivals panting to see her bite the dust. "Call me at home," I said and gave him my number, but still I did not expect to see him again.

When he recorded my number carefully in his organiser I noticed again that he was left-handed. I had noticed this earlier when he had made love, and suddenly I had the impression of a mirror image, as if this off-beat outsider who so skilfully played the system was far more like me than I had previously begun to imagine.

He phoned a week later from his City pied-à-terre in Clifford's Inn.

"It's Kim Betz," he said. His faint American accent seemed more noticeable on the phone and so did his even fainter European inflections. "Just checking to see you got home safely from the Big Apple. Still in one piece?"

"Apparently. And you?"

"Very definitely in one piece, all systems go. How do you feel about dinner?"

"I eat it every now and then."

We dined together for three nights in succession and spent the following weekend in Paris.

"What about your wife?" I enquired when this cross-Channel spree was proposed.

"She's visiting a sick friend in Nether Wallop."

"There can't possibly be a place called Nether Wallop!"

"Check the map!"

I was astonished, but the truth was I knew very little of England. Since coming to London I had poured myself into my work, and on my limited time off I had gone abroad to beaches where I could lie on the sand and do nothing. I arrived too exhausted for sight-seeing and left just when I was sufficiently recuperated to fancy it. The idea of expending precious energy on exploring the south of England was one which had never occurred to me. Even my knowledge of the leafy lanes of Surrey was based on hearsay.

I had always lived in cities. I had only bitter memories of Glasgow, but I could remember Newcastle without wincing and later there had been Oxford, beautiful, honey-coloured Oxford, the gateway to another life and another world. I had lost my Scottish accent when my mother had remarried and moved to Newcastle, and I had lost my Geordie accent as quickly as possible after reaching Oxford; I was an old hand at acquiring new identities, and so, I learned in Paris, was Kim. After his father had died in Argentina in 1949, Kim's mother had married an American, a move which had enabled Kim to spend the next four years in New York. When the American husband too had died she had married an Englishman, and at the age of thirteen Kim had finally begun to live in Europe.

As we dined together on our first night in Paris I said sympathetically: "It must have been hard to adapt to yet another culture," but Kim merely said: "I finally got lucky. The English step-father was good news."

"And your mother was happy?"

"Presumably." He thought for a moment before adding: "My mother was the old-fashioned, European type of woman who regarded marriage primarily as a business arrangement."

Cautiously I said: "She didn't mind your father being Jewish? I thought anti-Semitism was rife in Germany before the war."

"He had money, he didn't practise his religion and he was confident when they met in 1935 that he'd never be targeted."

"I see." I found I was unsure what to say next, but Kim remarked easily in his wryest voice: "Although my father died of drink and the American husband got himself shot, my mother finally hit the jackpot with Giles the Brit. He was heavily into money and class but of course, being British, he never discussed them."

"Surely in the 1950s the British were still poor in comparison with the Americans?"

"My mother wanted to get back to Europe."

"But didn't it bother her, marrying a Brit less than ten years after the war?"

"Giles was offering her a beautiful home, a generous dress allowance and an interesting social life. It was obviously time to consign the war to history."

"Sensible lady!" I said, playing safe by mirroring his ironical tone.

"The real problem was that most of the Brits didn't feel quite the same as she did, but she faked a great Swiss accent and was soon living happily ever after."

"How resourceful. But what about you?"

"I was more of a problem, but before I was dumped at public school Giles told me to say I was American. Giles had worked in both Germany and Switzerland before the war, and he realised I'd never succeed in passing myself off as Swiss to anyone who knew anything about the German language. A lot of Americans have German names, and having spent four years in New York I spoke American English anyway."

"But with a German accent."

"Believe me, I toned that down in double-quick time once I was incarcerated with several hundred English boys! And any European inflections I passed off as New York yiddish. That was Giles's idea too."

"He sounds as resourceful as your mother."

"Well, he played his cards close to his chest, and I was never sure what he really thought about being saddled with another man's child, but I realised very early on that I could trust him to do right by me. That was important. It made my life easier because I always knew where I stood with him."

"Did he officially adopt you?"

"Good God, no, we were never on that kind of footing, but he was the kind of old-fashioned, upper-class Brit who was very good at meeting his responsibilities and he saw to it that I had a first-class education. In return I worked like a Trojan and never gave him a spot of bother. After the years with my father, who was a bit of a bastard, and my first stepfather, who was a complete shit, I knew when I was well off, I assure you."

I asked if Giles was still alive, but learned that he had died in 1969. At that point Kim's mother had finally returned to Germany, where she had died of cancer twelve years later.

"Do you have any other German relations?" I asked.

"None survived the war."

"Not even anyone from your mother's family?"

"Cologne was heavily bombed."

I fell silent, glimpsing in that single sentence all the suffering he had glossed over with so little emotion: the exile in foreign lands, the stepfather who had done his duty but refused to adopt him, the ordeal of having to lie at school about his origins, and finally the pragmatic decision to adopt the nationality of the men who had dropped those bombs on Cologne.

I heard myself say: "Did you ever think of settling in Germany with your mother after Giles died?"

"No, by that time I was twenty-nine and my future, thanks to Giles, was quite obviously in England." He refilled our coffee-cups. In the restaurant around us plenty of people were still dining but our corner table was quiet and

26

secluded. "Well, so much for my secret history!" he said with a smile as he set down the coffeepot. "Now let's hear about yours."

But although I had been anticipating this demand for some time, I found I still had not made up my mind what I was going to say.

VIII

"I assume your parents are still alive," said Kim, as I toyed with several opening statements but failed to utter any of them.

"Uh-huh. I check the pulses once a year."

"Surely there's more to them than their pulses?"

"Not a lot. My mother enjoys a very ordinary life with her second husband, who's an electrician. They have two girls, both now married."

"You get on with them?"

"Why not? They're all very nice. It's not their fault that when I visit them every Christmas I feel like an alien dropping in via my private UFO."

"I get the picture... And your father?"

"He's the reason why my mother has this passion for a quiet life in which nothing unpredictable ever happens."

"An adventurer?"

"That's certainly one way of describing him. It would be less glamorous but more truthful to say he's an occasional member of Gamblers Anonymous. He should be a full-time member, but he never gets that far."

"You see him at Christmas too?"

"Sure. I take the UFO up to Glasgow after checking the pulses in Newcastle. He's always delighted to see me."

"Proud of your success?"

"Thrilled."

"And your mother's proud of that too, of course."

"My mother's idea of success," I said, "is marrying a local boy and raising a family. My father's idea of success is living high on the hog. So you can guess which parent comes within a million miles of imagining what sort of life I have."

"Did your father remarry?"

"More than once, like your mother, but it's never worked out. All his wives have found him a walking disaster... And talking of wives—"

I had decided it was time I found out more about Sophie.

IX

"The first thing I have to confess," said Kim, "is that she's not visiting a sick friend in Nether Wallop this weekend. I've no idea where she is. We've been living apart since last February."

From my point of view this was good news but I felt an austere reaction was called for. "Why didn't you come right out and say so on the flight to New York?"

"Sometimes it's wise to be reticent."

"Worried in case I was one of those thirty-somethings hooked on dreams of wedding bells?"

"You'd be surprised what a talent women of all ages have for dreaming!"

"So does this belated confession mean you've decided I'm no dreamer?"

"It means I've decided you're gorgeous enough for me to have a few dreams of my own."

I did not take this remark too seriously, since

lovers do tend to pay that sort of compliment when dining out in Paris, but I appreciated the hint that he was willing for the affair to become more significant. "Okay, Mr. Smoothie," I said. "Let's hear more about this separated wife of yours."

To my relief he then proved more than willing to talk of Sophie, and I learned that they had first met when he had been up at Oxford; she had been the sister of one of his friends there. Her family was both wealthy and well-connected, and having worked out that it would be wonderfully providential if he were to fall in love with her, Kim discovered later, once he was qualified, that he was in love. Surprise! It was an old, old story.

Unlike me Kim was a barrister, not a solicitor, but he had decided from the start that he had no wish to spend a long apprenticeship in chambers, and as the result of his stepfather's influence he had started work as an in-house lawyer at a German bank based in the City. With his bilingual skills and his natural aptitude for business he was soon flourishing, and by the time the marriage took place at St. Paul's Knightsbridge in 1966 he was already earning a good salary.

"So what went wrong?" I demanded, deciding it was time to switch on the pneumatic drill to dig up the truth.

"Isn't it obvious that my marriage was a smart career move but an emotional non-starter? We've stayed together so long only because she really did turn out to be the ideal wife for an ambitious lawyer—and don't think I'm not grateful to Sophie for her support over the years. But in the end a marriage—especially a childless marriage—can't survive on mere gratitude."

"When did you stop having sex with her?"

"About a hundred light-years ago. Naturally I've had other arrangements—"

"Naturally."

"—but last February we had a row when she refused to come to a Livery Company dinner with me and suddenly I thought: screw it. So then I suggested it was finally time we faced reality and talked about divorce."

"How did she take it?"

"She wasn't too keen at first, but in the end she had to concede it would be a relief to end the fiction and live more honestly. I was only showing up at weekends by that time anyway; I always spent Monday through Friday at Clifford's Inn."

"Why was Sophie content to keep the marriage going if she was getting no sex?"

"Sex was never her favourite pastime."

"You're sure about that?"

"Of course I'm sure! Hey, why the cross-examination?"

"Because I want to know exactly where I stand and because I know damn well that even ill-assorted couples can bat around in bed right up to the decree nisi and beyond!"

He said, amused: "I love it when you act tough!" But then he leaned forward across the table, clasped my hands and added as seriously as I could have wished: "There's nothing going on between me and Sophie, Carter. And believe me, this is going to be a friendly, routine, unopposed divorce which will flash through the rubber-stamping process just as soon as we complete the two-year separation in February 1990."

How sad it is that even the most successful lawyers can make massive errors of judgement.

30

X

The main result of these confidential conversations in Paris was that I decided Kim was capable of being the husband I had long wanted but had almost lost hope of finding. He fitted the ideal profile. He was successful enough to earn more money than I did, so this meant a major psychological hurdle was demolished. (Most men feel emasculated if they fail to be king of the bank accounts.) He had the educational background which enabled him to go everywhere and know everyone who needed to be known, yet at the same time he well understood what it was like to be an outsider on the make. He had no parents who might prove tiresome. His marriage was already ending so no one could accuse me of breaking it up, and there were no children about to be deprived of a father. I had, of course, taken care to establish that the absence of children was not his fault; apparently something was wrong with Sophie's Fallopian tubes, and an operation to unblock them had failed. I felt sorry for her. But I also felt very relieved that the absence of children did not disqualify Kim from becoming my husband.

I seemed to have reached the point in my assessment where all I had to do was list his virtues. He had charm, brains, chutzpah, sex appeal, sophistication... I ran out of fingers on my left hand and began to count on my right. He was more than acceptable in bed. I knew he had to be a killer-shark in the boardroom, but he apparently had no trouble leaving this side of his personality at the office and becoming the friendly dolphin in his leisure hours. (This dual-natured temperament is far from unknown in big business, and those who possess it often make devoted family men.) I could think of only one disadvantage: he was a little old. It would have been better if he had been five years younger—but then he would not have been earning so much. However, despite being in his late forties he seemed reasonably fit. He walked to work, swam at weekends, had regular check-ups. He was a fraction overweight, but what's half a stone between friends? He drank, but not to excess. He smoked cigars occasionally but he had given up cigarettes. In short, it seemed reasonable to assume his sperm-count was adequate. (I know this sounds calculating, but a mature woman has to be clear-eyed when assessing middle-aged men as potential fathers, and I was no dewy-eyed fluffette.)

Kim's final virtue was that he had no interest in dewy-eyed fluffettes and made no secret of the fact that he wanted someone who had the brains to share his London life to the hilt. It was true that he was hardly likely to marry a brain-box who looked like the back end of a bus, but fortunately looking like any part of a public conveyance has never been my problem. I took care of myself. Looking good is a weapon when one jousts continually with treacherous males. All the Hitchcock blondes knew that. Hitchcock would have approved of me, even though my big flaw is that I'm two inches too short. Five feet six is the ideal height for a high flyer. Anything taller gets called butch and anything shorter gets stamped on. Many were the men who had tried to stamp on me and wound up with bruised feet... But even the brightest men, as I have already noted, can make massive errors of judgement.

When we were back in London and Kim was telling me about the eminent lawyer who was handling the divorce, I said idly: "It's a pity you can't cite adultery by Sophie to hurry the process along. How can you be sure she hasn't embraced the single life by reversing her anti-sex stance and taking up with some overmuscled hunk twenty years her junior?"

He found that possibility very amusing. "Sweetheart, Sophie wears size twenty clothes and has her grey hair set in corrugated-iron-style waves!"

"For heaven's sake!" I exclaimed, appalled. "Why doesn't she slim down, smarten up, get a life?"

"She thinks she's got a life. She's a pillar of the local church."

"Oh God, are you saying she's one of those ghastly Born-Agains?"

"No, just a member of the mainstream Church of England."

A terrible thought belatedly occurred to me. "Kim, you're not religious, are you?"

"I certainly wouldn't describe myself as a Christian. But I think there's something out there."

"God, you mean?"

"I've never found 'God' a helpful word. But I have my own views on what St. Paul meant when he talked of the Principalities and Powers."

"That sounds like serious fantasy! All I can say is that if you're going to tell me you believe in UFOs, please hand me a large brandy first!"

"I think Jung got it right about UFOs," said Kim astonishingly. "The point is not whether they exist in what we think of as reality, but why people start seeing them. Jung thought they were a *psychic* reality, indicative of profound anxiety in the collective unconscious."

I felt my jaw sag. When I had recovered from my amazement I demanded: "But you're not really interested in all that guff, are you?"

"What guff? Jung? Psychic phenomena? Mysteries of consciousness? Spiritual matters? God? Principalities and Powers? St. Paul?"

"Oh, the whole damn lot! I mean, surely every rational person knows nowadays that there's no God, religion's a crutch for losers and truth which can't be scientifically proved in a laboratory is no truth at all?"

Kim burst out laughing. "Why, what a cute little version of logical positivism! Where did you find that summary—in a Christmas cracker?"

I somehow managed to stop my jaw sagging again. "What on earth do you mean?"

"Sweetheart, logical positivism is an outdated and increasingly discredited philosophy. It reflects the state of mind generated by the Enlightenment, but we're post-Enlightenment now."

I stared at him. I did open my mouth to speak but no words came out because I had no idea what to say. What he was talking about had never featured in any of my law books. I felt like an unbriefed barrister, but the next moment Kim had grasped what had happened and was moving to protect my self-esteem. "Relax!" he said soothingly. "I never read a history of modern thought either until I hit forty—you're much too young to be bothered with that kind of stuff!"

I felt exactly as if a dinosaur had patted me on the arm and said: "Don't you worry your pretty little head about this problem, my dear!" My natural instinct was to punch him on the nose.

34

"I don't give a damn whether you label my views logical positivism, common sense or absolute bullshit," I snapped. "All I know is that I'm going to continue to put my trust in logic and rationality, and no one is ever going to catch *me* dabbling in any kind of philosophical or theological nutterguff!"

"That's fine, sweetheart, but if you're going to be an atheist, do yourself a favour and be an intellectually respectable one, okay? You won't win any brownie points, believe me, by putting a belief in Jesus Christ in the same category as a belief in UFOs... Or are you going to abandon your old-fashioned Enlightenment attitudes and claim that an ill-informed belief is as good as a well-informed one in the post-modern supermarket of ideas?"

I knew at once that all I could now do was concede defeat and change the subject. "No wonder you earn twice as much as I do!" I said good-naturedly. "You've done me up like a kipper! And now if you're in the mood to contemplate me as a late-night snack, why don't we..."

To my relief he was more than willing to adjourn to the bedroom.

XI

Later I decided I should read a book about modern thought and learn how to make an intellectually respectable case for atheism. It would never do to make a gaffe at a future dinner-party.

But the trouble was there was never any time for serious reading. There was never any time for non-serious reading. I even had difficulty in finding time to go with Kim to the theatre and the cinema. Certainly there was never any time to sit and think—in fact the very idea of having enough time to waste time seemed bizarre, even shocking. As a high flyer you bartered your time and energy in exchange for wealth and power and everyone admired you, approved of you, thought you were wonderful, because you were living out the gospel of worldly success and the doctrine of sophisticated salvation. It was a tough life but you could never whinge because you knew you'd got to heaven and therefore, logically and rationally, you had to be happy. To whinge would have been an unforgivable sin. Whingeing was for wimps—who were the sinners, the lost and the damned.

I decided to set aside time on my honeymoon to read a book called *Modern Thought in a Nutshell*. I had no idea whether such a useful précis existed, but it seemed reasonable to hope that it might. The bookshops around the Law Courts always stocked in-a-nutshell summaries of legal subjects for the law students unable to understand their lecturers, and I felt I could cope with even the dottiest aspect of modern thought so long as it was presented nutshelled, preferably on a snow-white beach in the Seychelles...

But in fact my honeymoon, when it came, involved no intellectual reading at all.

I was much too exhausted after the divorce.

XII

Kim and I soon decided that marriage was a viable option, but we also decided to keep both our affair and our marital plans under wraps for a time. There was a good reason for this extreme discretion: by coincidence we were both in the process of changing jobs. Kim had been asked to become Head of Legal at Graf-Rosen, the big international investment bank, while I was being wooed by the partners of Curtis, Towers who were keen for me to shore up their tax department. Obviously it made sense that we should present ourselves as people who had their private lives in immaculate order, and certainly I had no intention of telling my would-be partners that I had marriage plans; they might have felt faint at the thought of maternity leave, even though my life-plan allowed me, if necessary, to work for up to two years after marriage before becoming pregnant.

By that time I had decided that I did not mind waiting another year for Kim's divorce; by the February of 1990 when proceedings could begin I would still be two months short of my thirty-fifth birthday and the year I had earmarked for marriage. I also felt I should welcome the opportunity to get to know Kim as well as possible before tying the knot. The only danger lay in our establishing such a satisfactory relationship that he became too contented with unmarried life, but I reckoned I had the know-how to steer him away from fulfilling this notorious male pipe-dream.

Kim did reconsider the way he was setting about extricating himself from his marriage, but since a year of his separation had already elapsed, it seemed in the end less trouble not to meddle with the wheels which had been set in motion. There is only one ground for divorce: irretrievable marital breakdown. But in order to demonstrate this breakdown it has to be shown that either adultery or unacceptable behaviour (flexibly defined) or one of three different categories involving separation (including desertion) has taken place. Kim and Sophie had agreed last year that they should claim marital breakdown as manifested by the simplest form of separation (two years spent apart, both parties consenting) but if Kim's adultery with me were now to be substituted for the separation, the divorce proceedings could be considerably accelerated.

For a brief moment we were tempted, but we both saw that it was wiser not to play the adultery card. Quite apart from the fact that we were keen to keep our relationship low profile while we were changing jobs, the marriage break-up could so easily be misrepresented. There would have been no drama in court, since uncontested divorces are shunted through so fast that the parties barely have time to hear their names when the list is read out, but word of the adultery could have got around and the truth distorted. People might have thought I had bust up the marriage. Not wanting to be slagged off as hormone-driven or desperate I was keen to avoid this slander, and Kim was equally keen for people not to push the lie that he had junked his wife because he had fancied a much younger woman. People might have thought he was gripped by a midlife crisis and temporarily unreliable.

"And to be honest," said Kim, after we had decided to keep going with the two-year separation, "I'm not sure I would have relished going to Sophie to suggest a quickie divorce based on adultery. Divorce is difficult enough for her as she's a practising Christian in a small, conservative community, but at least the two-year separation route enables her to tell her friends that although the marriage is ending there's no one else involved."

I was not only startled by this comment but disturbed. "Do you mean to say she doesn't know about me yet?"

"Why should she? Since we're both being so discreet—"

"But she's bound to hear eventually!"

"Let's get the job-change out of the way. Then once we're free to be more open about our relationship—"

"Kim, if she hears the truth from someone else, she's going to be miffed as hell. Why don't you go down to Oakshott next weekend and break the news?"

But he said the job-change was creating quite enough stress in his life and Sophie had to be kept on ice until the pressure had eased.

A week later during a rare night out at the Barbican Theatre, we had the disastrous luck to come face to face with Sophie's brother, and the next morning Kim reluctantly phoned Sophie to break the news of my existence. But he was too late. The brother's tongue had already been wagging. Sophie wanted to know if remarriage was being planned and Kim found he could procrastinate no longer.

When he told her the truth she promptly withdrew her consent to the divorce.

XIII

"What the hell's going on?" I said shattered when I heard what had happened.

"She's taking the high moral ground by saying

39

she'd be condoning my adultery if she agreed to a divorce, but I suspect this is really just another case of 'a woman scorn'd' venting her fury."

"But it makes no sense! Surely she realises you've committed adultery before?"

Kim said drily: "It's one thing to turn a blind eye while your husband conducts an ultra-discreet extra-marital sex life; that's all part of being a virtuous long-suffering wife. But it's quite another to find yourself being publicly discarded and replaced."

"But why shouldn't she be discarded and replaced if she's refused to sleep with you for—how long did you say it was?"

"A hundred light-years. Look, sweetheart, I can't tell you how sorry I am about all this but I'm sure it's just a temporary hitch..."

I found no comfort in this assurance. It was true that nowadays no one could delay a divorce indefinitely, but it was also true that Sophie could still make us wait several more years before Kim was able to obtain a divorce without her consent. So horrified was I by this potential derailing of my life-plan that I was beyond speech, and seeing how upset I was Kim redoubled his efforts to reassure me.

"Carter, she's going to abandon this tough line just as soon as she realises I'm determined to marry you—she's going to abandon it just as soon as she realises all her delaying tactics are futile!"

But I was barely listening. Another horrific thought had struck me. "Christ, supposing she takes you to the financial cleaners?"

"She wouldn't," said Kim automatically.

"Why not? If she's got a good lawyer—"

"You're forgetting the law's supposed to avoid punitive settlements. And there's no reason why the financial situation shouldn't result in a standard clean-break arrangement."

My scepticism deepened. "What exactly is the financial situation?"

"Sophie has her own money. Because of this I've always spent freely, with the result that I'm now long on income but short on capital, and that means the crucial asset for me is that house in Oakshott which I bought with my own money and which is registered in my name. When Sophie and I discussed the divorce last year, she offered to buy me out so that she could stay on, and I think that's fair enough as she has more money than I have. So since we're basically in agreement—"

"You're dreaming. Surely under the Matrimonial Causes Act the judge will take your future earnings into account when assessing the assets? And Sophie must be entitled in equity to a share of her home—she's probably even entitled to that under common law!"

"But in cases where both spouses have money, I'm sure they can cut their own deal for rubber-stamping by the judge at the time of the divorce—"

"You're still dreaming. Sophie will now try and screw you over the house."

"No, she won't! She's got too much dignity!"

"Oh yeah? Then what's she doing crashing around in a fury? And incidentally, isn't this vindictive anger of hers immoral for a Christian? Shouldn't she just forgive you and turn the other cheek?"

"Sophie's a good woman but she's not Jesus Christ."

"Then what's the betting that she'll seek revenge and call it justice!"

But Kim was clearly still reluctant to face the worst. "Sweetheart—"

"Look," I said, becoming much milder in the hope of sounding more persuasive, "surely all that counts is that the divorce shouldn't be delayed for years? And since we're both going to be earning megabucks, is it really so disastrous if you emerge from the marriage with less than the ideal amount of capital?"

"But I need every penny that's rightfully mine in order to give you a first-class home in a first-class neighbourhood! Don't you know how much it costs nowadays to buy a decent house in Chelsea or Kensington?"

"But with our joint income we're bound to be able to swing the deal we want! Listen, darling, don't get hung up on that Oakshott house or she'll use it as a weapon against you, and once those lawyers start haggling—"

"My money went into that place," said Kim obstinately, "and I want that money back. If Sophie now starts screaming that any percentage of it should be hers, I'll—"

"Hey, what kind of freak *is* this woman?" I exclaimed, trying to lighten the conversation by injecting a shot of humour. "You keep describing her as if she were two different people! First of all she's meekly agreeing to a divorce and being too dignified to screw you over the house, but the next moment she's ditched her size-twenty housecoat, togged herself up like a Hollywood tragedy queen and dynamited our plans while breathing fire in all directions! Are you sure you're not a bigamist with two wives?"

"Isn't one enough?" Kim retorted acidly, but he did manage to laugh. Then he said: "The discrepancy's an illusion. The truth is that Sophie's what the old-fashioned English still call a 'lady'—someone well-bred, well-mannered, deeply conservative, highly moral and usually well in control of herself. And this sort of woman, who bottles up her emotions, is much more likely to explode with wrath if she feels she's been wronged. She was merely bottled up last year but now she's exploded. *Res ipsa loquitur.*"

I sighed in exasperation. "Okay," I said, "you've convinced me she's just one person, but I still think she's carrying on as if she's fruity-loops. However"—I took a deep breath, knowing I had to concentrate on keeping calm— "I can see now you were right to say her tantrum probably won't last once she realises you're determined to marry me. I'll lie low so as not to inflame her further, your lawyers will wave a magic wand to produce the right financial settlement—after all, what the hell are they being paid for?—and Ms. Fruity-Loops will eventually realise that if she wants to keep her halo twinkling she'll have to abandon the role of avenging harpy. We'll all live happily ever after in the end, I'm sure of it."

But a week later the phone calls began.

TWO

One of the main compulsions of our society is addiction to urgency. This addiction dominates the day with a string of urgent matters... [It] is common in a society whose main criterion for its own health is economic success, and which encourages people to focus their identities through their jobs.

DAVID F. FORD
The Shape of Living

I

She phoned me at my flat in the Barbican. I had just returned from an exhausting day at my new job and was feeling thoroughly creased and cross. Two dinosaurs had tried to stamp on me and two whippets had attempted breast-brushing. Whippets are racy young males with minimal post-qualifying experience who are barely house-trained and who regard a female lawyer as some novel type of inflatable doll.

"Hullo?" I said, taking the call. I was wondering if Kim was phoning to tell me what an idyllic day he had had with all the dinosaurs grovelling before him and all the minimal p.q.e. whippets tiptoeing past in reverent silence.

"Miss Graham?" The woman's voice was a pleasant, educated contralto. I confirmed my identity.

"Miss Graham, this is Sophie Betz."

I hung up. I was still standing there, still too shocked to think clearly, when the phone rang again. I decided the caller was Kim. Bad decision. It was Sophie persisting.

"Miss Graham, please don't hang up. I'd very much like to talk to you, and—"

Slamming down the receiver, I disconnected the phone and mixed myself a double vodka martini.

II

When Kim stopped by at my flat later and heard the news he was even more shocked than I was. He was also far more angry. Now at last the playful dolphin vanished and I saw the boardroom shark. "I'll gut whoever leaked your phone number," he said, "and if the leak came from Milton's office I'll bloody sue him." His distinguished divorce lawyer was in fact a man whom no one in his right mind would sue, but I recognised that Kim needed to let off steam by resorting to violent language.

After I had calmed him down we tried to work out how the leak had occurred. I did have a circle of acquaintances who knew my ex-directory number, but none of them had met Kim, let alone Sophie, and I found it hard to imagine them casually passing my number to a stranger. For a moment I toyed with the idea that the leak had come from someone at the office, but this theory too seemed implausible. My secretary Jacqui, who had accompanied me to Curtis, Towers from my last firm, would never have divulged my home phone number to anyone, and I had given it to none of my new colleagues because I had not been long enough at Curtis, Towers to make friends. The number would be in my personnel file, but I could hardly see Sophie hacking her way into a confidential information system—and how would she have known anyway that I worked for Curtis, Towers?

"She must have hired a private investigator," said Kim abruptly. "A good PI would have ways and means of turning up your unlisted number."

But this plausible explanation only triggered another question: why had Sophie hired a PI? Legally I had no connection with the divorce case. I did find myself wondering if Sophie's lawyers wanted to dredge up information about me in the hope of slinging mud at Kim when the time came to decide who should have the Oakshott house, but I realised at once that since the object of a divorce settlement was not to be punitive but to be equitable, this theory did not make sense. I personally thought the court would order the house to be sold and the proceeds to be divided between the two of them, a decision which would allow Sophie to pay Kim for his half-share if she wanted to stay on in her home. Such a ruling would acknowledge both the fact that Sophie, as a wife of over twenty years' standing, deserved a share of the family home, and the fact that the place had been bought with Kim's money. Of course I was not a divorce lawyer, but as far as I could see mud-slinging would be irrelevant in sorting out this routine separation dispute.

"Let's not forget," I said at last, "that the main result of this PI's work—assuming a PI's been hired—is that Sophie's been able to access me. And that means the next question has to be: why the hell's she calling?"

Kim groaned. "Maybe she sees you as an innocent young woman corrupted by an older man and needing to be saved."

"God! In that case I'll get an answering machine. It's never seemed necessary before, but—"

"No, wait. An answering machine sounds like the obvious solution but I believe it would be a tactical error—Sophie would take it as an invitation to leave message after message. Just keep hanging up on her, and she's bound to get discouraged in the end."

But unfortunately he was underrating his wife's persistence. When she finally realised the phone calls were getting her nowhere, the letters started to arrive at my flat.

III

Since we were both now working in our new jobs and Sophie was aware of the affair, Kim was soon saying that our extreme discretion was no longer necessary, we could let it be known that we were a couple, and why didn't he move in to my Barbican flat.

"Because I haven't invited you to do so," I said, remembering my resolution not to let him become too comfortable before the wedding ring was firmly on my finger. A man's will to marry is a tender plant which needs careful nurturing, and the risk of it dying of inertia is one which needs to be taken seriously. "I agree there's no need to keep the affair under wraps now, but before you move in let's just see what Sophie does next."

"But that's the point!" he protested. "I want to be on hand to screen you from further harassment!"

"If you start to live with me, aren't you much more likely to stimulate it?"

It was on the Saturday morning after this conversation that I received the first letter. It was written on thick cream paper and the engraved address managed to conjure up in every line visions of the leafy lanes of Surrey. "THE LARCHES," proclaimed the print, "ELM DRIVE, OAKSHOTT..." Even the postal code had a T for Tree in it. "Dear Miss Graham," I read queasily, "I am sorry you do not wish to speak to me. I assume you are feeling guilty about committing adultery with my—"

I said aloud: "Oh my God!" and crumpled the letter as I clenched my fist. But then curiosity overwhelmed me and I straightened the paper out again.

"...committing adultery with my husband," the letter continued. "However, I do not write in a spirit of recrimination but out of a desire to save you from—"

My fist reclenched, the paper recrunched and I moved into the kitchen to consign the whole religion-soaked twaddle to oblivion. How dared she talk of "saving" me! These religious nutters were a menace to a free society and to the sacred right of the individual to live as he or she chose.

The flats in Harvey Tower, in common with all the other flats on the Barbican estate, have an extraordinary waste disposal system called the Garchey, which consists of a tube leading from one of the two kitchen sinks in each flat to some unimaginable lower region which connects, I assume, to the sewers. Nothing consigned to the Garchey is ever recovered. Consigning

48

Sophie's letter I turned on the water and flushed the rubbish away, but when Kim heard about the letter he was not only livid with Sophie for sending it but livid with me for destroying it.

"Why didn't you wait to show it to me?"

"Why should I? It was garbage. I junked it. End of story."

"But what did she say?"

"Nutterguff about sin and salvation. I didn't even read beyond the opening lines."

"But of course you did! No woman can resist reading to the end of a letter from her lover's wife!"

"Watch it, buster. I'm not in the mood for being stereotyped and I'm never in the mood to be called a liar."

He apologised at once but was unable to change the subject. "If there are any more letters," he said, "would you please hand them to me unopened?"

"No," I shot back. "I'm a big girl now. I'm allowed to read letters which are addressed to me. For God's sake, Kim, why are you getting your guts in such a twist over this?"

He sighed heavily, apologised a second time but could only add: "I just don't want Sophie upsetting you."

"Fair enough, but I'm hardly a delicate little daisy trembling for fear of being trodden on! Why are you overreacting like this?"

"Who says I'm overreacting?"

"I do. Darling, what's going on? Are you afraid Sophie's going to spill the beans about some vital dimension of the marriage which I don't yet know about?"

"Oh sure! I'm panicking in case she tells you

I'm an unreconstructed male who likes his wife to wait on him hand and foot!"

"God, trying to cross-examine a lawyer like you is worse than trying to pull teeth. Come on, Betz, shape up—I'm not letting you off the hook! Just why are you so livid with Sophie and just why are you so anxious for me to have nothing to do with her?"

He sighed again. He was good at these heavy sighs; I suspected that they gave him time to reorganise his thoughts with lightning speed. But at last he said frankly: "I suppose the rock-bottom truth is that I feel guilty about her—the rock-bottom truth is I feel a bit of a shit. It was okay when the decision to divorce was reached by mutual consent and there was no other party involved, but it does make a difference, I have to admit, that I'm exchanging her for a younger woman. And you know the psychological pattern which guilt so often produces, don't you? You can't face your own self-hatred so you project it onto someone else. If I'm angry at the moment with Sophie it's because I'm actually angry with myself for hurting her; if I'm trying to keep Sophie out of your life it's because I can't stand the effect she's currently having on mine."

After a pause I said: "I like you better for feeling guilty. You'd certainly be a bit of a shit if you didn't. Thanks for being honest with me."

So that was that. But I saw clearly then that the way to help Kim survive this rancorous divorce was not to bother him further with tales of Sophie's harassment. He needed to be cosseted, soothed and supported during this arduous time which was made all the more stressful by the fact that he had just taken on a very high-powered job.

I had read enough pop psychology to know that guilt led to anxiety which led to neurosis which led to melt-down, and I did not want to land my big fish only to discover that I had acquired some sort of piscine blob.

I decided that he should come to live with me at Harvey Tower before guilt could trigger an impotence which might cast a fatal blight on that delicate plant, the male will to marry.

IV

When Kim moved in I was a trifle nervous in case he then revealed unattractive traits which he had so far managed to conceal, but he remained well-behaved and indeed turned out to be superbly house-trained for a man of his age—by which I mean that he did not leave his clothes all over the floor or the bathroom in a mess or dirty dishes stacked outside the dishwasher. He also showed himself capable of doing selected chores, provided that he was the one who did the selecting. Evidently the years of living on his own during the week at his Clifford's Inn pied-à-terre had more than counterbalanced the old-fashioned pampering he would have received from the old-fashioned wife at weekends.

Sophie sent three more letters but I tore them all up unread. And where, it might well be asked, was my natural curiosity? I came to the uneasy conclusion that it had been consigned to a limbo which I was most reluctant to explore. Was I feeling in any way guilty myself? Absolutely not! The marriage had ground to a halt long before I had appeared on the scene. My hands, I told myself fiercely, were as clean as a couple of whistles. My conscience, I told myself even more fiercely, was pristine. I utterly refused, I told myself—now even sweating with fierceness—to feel any degree of guilt whatsoever.

But in that case what was all the fierceness about and why did I feel so sick whenever I received a letter from Sophie that I could hardly wait to flush it down the Garchey?

I decided finally that I should admit the guilt in order to surmount it. Fine. I was experiencing guilt. Not much. Just a bit. And there was no doubt that part of my mind did feel sorry for Sophie. It was no fun for a middle-aged woman to preside over the disintegration of her marriage, but on the other hand so often losers had only themselves to blame for their losses. Why hadn't she shed thirty pounds, smartened herself up, sought therapy for the sex hang-up, made an effort to share Kim's London life? Bearing these failures in mind I decided I could only feel moderately sorry for her—and considering she was currently bent on creating as much trouble for Kim as possible while pestering me with religious nutterguff, I considered I was being extremely magnanimous in feeling sorry for her at all.

Meanwhile Kim and Sophie were communicating only through their lawyers who were enjoying many delicious hours of convoluted negotiations as they attempted to resolve the impasse. Their lavish bills provided lurid proof of what a fine time they were having; as Kim said drily to me once after receiving a bill from Milton, lawyers can be such swine.

I was just thinking in despair that nothing would alter Sophie's determination to make Kim wait the statutory five years in order to obtain a divorce without her consent, when she stunned us by changing course. Maybe she found the legal bills too outrageous to tolerate a moment longer or maybe she finally realised the long-term futility of her stand, but whatever her reason was she agreed to abandon the delaying tactics on two conditions: the first was that Kim should cede her the house at Oakshott, and the second was that they should divorce at once, using Kim's adultery with me as the grounds for establishing the marriage's irretrievable breakdown. No doubt this second condition featured on her agenda precisely because she had realised that Kim was far from keen to go down this route, and she still wanted to cause him as much inconvenience as possible.

Kim was livid. I urged him to grab the divorce, ditch the house and wash his hands once and for all of this revenge-obsessed female, but his macho pride was interfering with his common sense and he hated the thought that Sophie was able to push him around. More time slipped away. More legal costs were incurred. However, this second impasse was again resolved by Sophie herself. She had left me alone ever since changing course earlier, but now she started pestering me again with phone calls and my patience finally snapped.

"GET RID OF THAT WOMAN!" I yelled to Kim. "I don't care how you do it, but if you don't get rid of her right away and grab that divorce I'll—" I was about to say: "I'll climb every wall in this flat!" but I believe he thought I was going to say: "I'll break off our relationship," for he interrupted me so quickly that he stumbled over his words.

"Okay, I'll fix it," he said. "I'm not going to

let Sophie wreck us. I'll call Milton first thing tomorrow morning."

So Sophie had her revenge and Kim lost all the money he had invested in the house at Oakshott, but at least the divorce now rocketed ahead and we were both too exhausted to care that adultery had been substituted for the two-year separation. In the December of 1989, a year after we had first met, Kim and I were free to whip through a registry office wedding before boarding a plane to Germany for the honeymoon, and I could tell myself the nightmare generated by Sophie was finally over.

But I was mistaken.

V

Since I was a sun-and-sand holidaymaker Germany was hardly my first choice as a honeymoon destination, but Kim wanted to relax in an environment he knew well and I could see too that it was an exciting place to be now that the fall of the Berlin Wall was generating talk of German reunification. Realising how keen he was to sample the Deutsch-buzz and acknowledging how frazzled I felt after the divorce-mess, I decided I was more than willing to postpone my dream of a long-haul flight to the Seychelles, and anyway I was so pleased to be Mrs. Betz at last that I found the last thing I wanted to be picky about was the location of the honeymoon.

Fortunately Germany turned out to be fun. What a difference it makes to travel in a foreign country with someone who can speak the language! We visited Cologne, so that Kim could show me his parents' city, and then we withdrew for Christmas to a very grand castle which had been converted into a hotel. It seemed strange not to be trekking north to Newcastle and Glasgow for the annual pulse-check, but I was secretly relieved to delay exhibiting Kim to my family.

"Will they be upset?" Kim had asked in concern when we had been planning the honeymoon, but I had assured him my parents would understand.

In fact it was not until I reached Germany that I wrote to my parents to inform them I was married. After revealing my husband's name I wrote to my mother: "Don't be cross at missing the wedding—it only lasted a couple of minutes, certainly not long enough to justify a trip south, and hardly anyone was present except a few people we've known for years. I'll send you some copies of the honeymoon photos so that you can see how nice-looking he is. He's a forty-nine-year-old lawyer with a top job at an investment bank—" I paused to debate whether I should mention that he was of German descent, but decided this fact was best omitted. I then wondered whether to mention that he was half-Jewish, but decided this fact was best omitted too. Provincial people could be so insular. Finally I concluded: "—and he came to England from America many years ago. He was educated at a famous school and at Oxford, so he's got class as well as brass—all right, I know he's not exactly 'the boy next door,' but I was never going to marry one of those, was I? Love, KATIE."

This letter took me a long time to write and my labours had to be aided by two large glasses of German champagne. But afterwards I dashed off a note which read: "Hi Dad—sorry no Xmas viz this yr—honeymooning in Krautland—Kim's a bank lawyer, surname BETZ, Yankish accent, naturalised Brit, earns megabucks, drives a Mercedes, wears Savile Row suits (like James Bond) and *even has handmade shoes.* Everything totally brill. Love, KITTY. PS. Get the pic? £££ are his business. So don't be dumb enough to dream of fleecing him."

I mailed both these letters with relief.

Then at last I was entirely free to luxuriate in marital bliss.

VI

I noticed that every German we met assumed Kim was a German citizen living only temporarily in London, and Kim never made any attempt to disillusion them. He certainly never mentioned South America, but on the other hand, as I said to myself, why go looking for trouble? Everyone knew South America had been a favourite destination after the war for those Nazis who feared they would have a date with the prosecutors at Nuremberg, and it would have been tedious for Kim to keep explaining that his Jewish father had left Germany in the 1930s. I thought it was very sensible that whenever he was asked where he came from he simply said: "Köln." No one ever expressed any surprise, and it made me realise that his German, unlike his English, was unmarred by any trace of a foreign accent. I had studied German at school so I could speak the language in a limited fashion and understand more than I spoke, but I could not hear the different accents. I only knew Kim was never questioned about his.

"I simply speak as my parents spoke," he said

easily when I raised the subject, "and we always spoke German at home."

I said, thinking of my own past: "Accents can be such a problem."

"The trick is to convert them into an asset by making them all part of playing the system. That's why in Germany I pass myself off as a German, in England I pass myself off as an American and in New York I pass myself off as an Anglicised Jew. That way I can make my background work for me wherever I happen to be."

"Con man! Well, at least my Home Counties accent is better than yours is!"

"You think so?" he said laughing. "You should listen to yourself after a couple of vodka martinis!" And the conversation then concluded as I attempted to wallop him with a pillow and he wrestled the pillow from me in order to put it to a more imaginative use. It was such a luxury to have both the leisure and the stress-free environment to enjoy sex frequently.

Indeed, by the end of the honeymoon we had almost forgotten what stress was, and when we arrived back in London we smooched for some time in my moonlit living-room high above the City before bowling into bed in an ecstasy of happiness. I was such a hardened cynic that I still hardly dared believe such happiness could exist, but the evidence for such a blissful state now seemed incontrovertible. Perhaps I finally dared to ditch my cynicism when I realised Kim was just as stunned by our happiness as I was.

"I feel quite different," he confided that night. "I don't feel dislocated any more."

"What do you mean?"

"I never felt at home anywhere. It was as if some part of me was missing and I was always searching for answers which I was never able to find."

"What answers? What were the questions?"

"It doesn't matter, not any more. This is home, isn't it? You're the missing part of me, and this is where I fit in, here with you."

Pulling him on top of me I said: "I think you fit in here very well."

A satisfying interval passed.

Some time later he said suddenly: "I want to show you the photograph now," and began to scramble out of bed.

As he had told me all his old photographs had been lost during the move to Oakshott many years before, I assumed he was talking of a more recent picture, but the black-and-white snapshot which he pulled from its special place in his wallet was yellow at the edges inside the plastic folder which protected it. "I couldn't show you this before," he said, "because the past seemed so disconnected with the present that I felt there was no way of sharing it, but now that I'm more all of a piece..." Leaving the sentence unfinished he pulled aside the plastic folder and mutely handed me the photograph.

I saw a small boy of perhaps three or four, with dark hair, bright eyes and a radiant, trustful smile. He was wearing long trousers and a short-sleeved shirt. Standing beside him was a large dog, an Alsatian, tail in the middle of a wag, and in the background was a motherly woman with an indulgent expression. All three figures were standing on a lawn by a stone urn planted with flowers.

"That was my nurse who got sacked," said

Kim, "and that was my dog which got lost. I still think of them."

After a pause I said: "When I was small I had a cat which got lost. I still think of him too." There was a silence while I wondered whether this response was adequate, but Kim seemed satisfied by the implied message that I could understand his feelings of bereavement. I wanted to ask questions but was afraid of mishandling the subject when it was still clearly so painful. I merely noted the absence of any equally cherished photograph of his parents.

"I wish I had photos to show you of my own past," I said at last, "but I've never made a hobby of photography."

"Well, I don't need to see pictures of your family, do I? I'll soon be meeting them in person."

"Right." Not for the first time I tried to visualise taking Kim to meet my father, but yet again the scene proved unimaginable.

Meanwhile Kim was saying tentatively: "Will you tell me some day what happened?"

"What happened when?"

"When your parents split up."

"Oh, that! Well, I'll tell you now—it's no big deal. The bailiffs came again and my mother decided that was one visit too many, so she and I took a bus across Glasgow to stay with her sister. In the flat next door lived this old man, and the old man's son used to come up from England twice a month to visit him—the son had gone to Newcastle to find work and he'd actually found it, he was employed. Better still, he was respectable and decent and never went near a gambling shop. The next thing I knew I was being shovelled off to primary school in Newcastle and all the bloody awful little Geordie kids were trying to use me as a football because I spoke broad Glaswegian."

Kim silently slipped his arms around me and pulled me close to him. As I pressed my face against his chest I heard myself add in a rapid voice: "I just wish I'd been allowed to take my cat but my mother said no, she couldn't cope. So I made my father promise to look after it but of course he didn't and it disappeared. He never kept a single promise he ever made. End of story." Raising my face from Kim's chest again I managed to say: "We don't have to talk about the past any more, do we? After all, it's only the present and future which matter now."

But unfortunately this statement proved to be mere wishful thinking.

Less than two months after our return from the honeymoon Sophie's phone calls began again.

VII

I did not tell Kim the trouble had restarted. He was in the midst of a high-powered deal and working morning, noon and night. He did not need any more stress. I was working hard too but I did not find Sophie as upsetting as he did because by this time my prime emotion was neither rage nor nausea but bewilderment. Why was she still calling me even now I was married? Was the woman so obsessed that she had no idea when to stop emoting and face reality? At this point I considered the possibility of labelling her a stalker.

The first time she phoned she said: "This is Sophie Betz. Forgive me for calling again, but—"

I had no intention of forgiving her, not after

her feet-dragging over the divorce. Both my sympathy and my patience had long since been exhausted.

The second time she called she did not announce her name but said in a rush: "I really do think it's my moral duty to—"

I hung up. I was not about to listen to yet another attempt to deliver religious nutterguff.

The third time she said: "Look, I must see you!" and the fourth time she said simply: "Listen!" but I managed to slam down the receiver before she could utter another syllable. After that she rang several times but did not speak; it was as if she hoped to lure me into a conversation by arousing my curiosity. How did I know it was her? Well, who else would it have been? It was hardly likely that a second nutter had started to pester someone who had an ex-directory number.

Naturally I considered the possibilities of either changing my number or having a second line installed, but I did not see how either of these plans could be accomplished without telling Kim the whole story, and I was not yet so desperate that I felt driven to share the bad news with him. Anyway if Sophie's PI could find out unlisted numbers, any changes I might make to my telephone line would be pointless. I did toy once more with the idea of getting an answering machine, a move I could explain merely by saying I wanted to be up to date, but I felt unwilling to risk the chance of Kim pushing the playback button and hearing loony messages from his ex-wife.

By this time we were well into 1990 and my irritation was greatly increased when my much younger half-sisters wrote a joint letter criticising me for not trekking north at Easter to check the pulses and display my husband. What impertinence! I was hardly about to remain soft as Andrex tissues while being lectured by two girls who thought London was some kind of gold-plated cesspit, so I phoned each one up and bawled them both out. Of course I knew I should have trekked north, but I had felt compelled to insist to Kim that we should spend the Easter holiday in Paris.

The basic problem, as I well knew, was that if I took him as far as Newcastle I would be unable to invent a plausible reason for not taking him on to Glasgow and by that time I had realised I could not display him in Glasgow until my father's current situation had improved. On my forward-planning calendar I made a note to sort out the whole mess in September. Then I returned with relief to concentrate on my new life as Mrs. Betz.

After our wedding we had held a reception for a hundred of our better-known acquaintances at the Savoy, and as soon as 1990 dawned many of these people started inviting us out to dinner. It was difficult to fit this active social life into our schedules but we both knew the effort had to be made; all these people were connected in some way with our careers. Neither Kim nor I had close friends—I suppose outsiders often have a chronic difficulty in dropping their masks and being themselves—but we had innumerable acquaintances, some of whom I liked very much and who appeared to like me. I was interested to note that Kim's Jewish acquaintances held him in high esteem. From them I learned that he regularly gave to Jewish charities, and this impressed me, particularly as he had never mentioned making any donations to good causes. It also became clear that he must have studied the Jewish culture in depth; in fact one of his Jewish acquaintances remarked to me how commendable it was that Kim had chosen to honour his father's Jewishness instead of denying it, even though his father had apparently shown no interest in observing his religion.

"But how much of this interest of yours is real," I said unwisely to Kim after this conversation, "and how much is just the result of you playing the system in your usual fashion?" I knew he had always worked for Jewish firms and would have been more than capable of zeroing in on the best ways of demonstrating his solidarity with them.

To my horror Kim took deep offence and became very upset. "If you think for one moment that I'm not a hundred per cent sincere in my commitment to the Jews—"

Secretly cursing myself for such a stupid blunder, I rushed to apologise and swore I admired both his commitment and his sincerity.

That was when I decided that the subject of his Jewish connections was almost as tricky as the subject of what Germany had got up to between 1939 and 1945. Kim himself never talked of the war if he could avoid doing so, and I had only once heard him volunteer a comment on Hitler. He had said: "Too bad no one gassed that shit at birth," and his tone of voice had indicated that the subject of the Third Reich was hardly likely to surface frequently in our conversations.

Anyway, there we were, slaving away at our jobs in the May of 1990 and shimmering away in our social life with our backs firmly turned on the past, when Sophie suddenly abandoned the phone calls to the flat and decided to harass me at work. She could hardly have picked a time which suited me worse. Jacqui, my secretary, had departed for a fortnight's holiday in Greece, PersonPower International had had the nerve to send me a heterosexual male called Eric Tucker to take her place, my chief clients were whingeing, the dinosaurs were stamping, the whippets were breast-brushing, the fluffettes were nicknaming me Slaughter instead of calling me Carter, the crises were constant—and to cap it all my first post-nuptial attempt to host a dinner-party was looming on the horizon. In short, my stress levels were mounting at an alarming rate and I definitely did not need my life to be further complicated by a reappearance of Ms. Fruity-Loops spouting nutterguff. When Tucker the Temp buzzed me with the bad news I wanted to shatter my oak desk with a karate chop.

"Excuse me, Ms. Graham," he said over the intercom, "but there's a call for you from a Mrs. Sophie Betz. I remembered you said Betz was your married name so I figured this could be someone you might want to talk to, but I did say to her that I thought you'd just left for a meeting, so—"

"Terminate her," I said, and severed the connection.

VIII

I sat there, examining the fingernail I had broken by clenching my fists too hard, and thought idly how wonderful it would be to have Tucker as a permanent personal assistant, almost a pseudo-spouse, a male equivalent of Kim's doting long-time PA Mary Waters who had followed him to Graf-Rosen just as Jacqui had followed me to Curtis, Towers. But could I really trust a heterosexual male not to make a sex-mess if he were put in the position of being my chief pamperer, crisis-fixer, gofer and hitman? Probably not. Yet it was becoming increasingly tempting to massage Jacqui out of my life and try.

I hit the intercom. "Hey, Tucker! Get in here."

He was planted on the carpet in front of me in less than ten seconds, white shirt glistening, black shoes gleaming, terminally dull tie toning with his irreproachable charcoal-grey suit. The office serf as male slave, obedient to his lady's every whim—this glorious pipe-dream of every stressed-out female high flyer was now miraculously incarnate in my office. At least something in my life was currently going right.

In a voice mild enough to signal my appreciation I said: "Thank you for handling that call. Mrs. Sophie Betz is my husband's ex-wife and she's been harassing me for some time. If she calls again you can say straight away that I'm not available."

"Right." He thought for a moment. "Is she likely to try to storm your office?"

I respected him for having the intelligence to ask this horrible but necessary question. "Probably not," I said. "I suspect she'd be reluctant to make such a public exhibition of herself, but on the other hand if she's nuts anything's possible."

"Maybe I should know what she looks like so that I can repel any invasion."

"Well, I've never met the woman, but I understand she's fat, fiftyish and frumpish with tightly waved grey hair."

"In that case she'll be easy to spot once she crosses the threshold of Curtis, Towers."

We exchanged poker-faced looks but I knew at once that we were both silently making the same observation. The dinosaurs at Curtis, Towers, unfettered by laws forbidding age discrimination, tended to pressure any female into resigning at the first sign of a varicose vein. No wonder pantsuits were becoming so fashionable.

"Anything else, ma'am?"

"No. Wait a moment—yes. Could you get Mrs. Lake of Blue Lake Catering on the phone? She's booked to do a dinner-party for me on Friday night and as it's now Wednesday afternoon I think it's time I made sure she's not planning to serve mad cow."

He vanished.

By this time Tucker had woven himself seamlessly into his new environment and was proving to be an object of considerable interest to the fluffettes. Later I was to overhear him being discussed passionately in the ladies' loo when an argument broke out about whether his hair should be classified as chestnut brown or darkest red. The freckles visible across the bridge of his nose favoured the darkest-red party, but this faint spattering of pigment was reckoned by the chestnut-brown crowd not to indicate the presence of the red-hair gene unless his forearms were similarly mottled. Speculation then took place about how Tucker could be persuaded to expose his forearms, and Shana, the office shag-queen, was driven to declare rashly that she would discover the colour of his pubic hair, but pride went before a fall and Tucker remained chastely veiled in his white shirts and dark suits. I heard

Shana's excuse for her uncharacteristic failure was that "Slaughter" Graham kept her lad on a tight leash, no doubt to satisfy a craving for sado-masochistic sex-games.

However, these ladies'-loo vignettes took place during the second week of his assignment, and on the day that Sophie called me at work I was still savouring his first week as my pipe-dream incarnate.

I had just finished attending to my broken nail when Tucker slipped back into my room.

"Bad news, Ms. Graham."

"It's the Lake Lady."

"I'm afraid so."

"She's dead?"

"No, departed."

I was outraged. "But that's impossible! She was recommended by two clothes-horses in my building who do nothing but give dinner-parties!"

"I gather the bank manager switched off the business's life-support machine. I just spoke to the bailiff."

"Bloody hell, I don't need this crisis!" I yelled, deciding it was time to do some therapeutic emoting. "For Christ's sake, why didn't the woman let me know she'd be off the map by Friday? This disaster can't have happened overnight!"

"It could be you were low on her list of priorities. She's currently being reassembled in a South London clinic after overgrazing on Valium."

"Okay, that's sad, I'll stop wanting to kill her, but *what am I going to do about my dinner-party*?"

"May I make a suggestion?"

"Yes, but make damn sure it's brilliant."

"I know a cook, cordon bleu, freelance, clean,

sober, respectable and reliable. She lives in Clerkenwell, she's worked for the aristocracy in Belgravia, and she often does Barbican dinner-parties. Shall I call her?"

"Okay, that *is* brilliant—but no, hold it, that type of wonder woman's bound to be booked up for at least six months—"

"Not on Friday nights, not for formal dinner-parties. That's when she cooks dinner for her *cher ami*."

"You?"

"I'm not that lucky. Shall I—"

"Yes, for God's sake eliminate the boyfriend and kidnap her."

An interval followed during which I drew pictures of vodka martinis on my scratchpad, overcame the urge to gnaw my mutilated finger-nail and silently reviewed in my mind's eye all the major chill-food lines in Marks and Spencer's food department.

The intercom buzzed.

"Good news?"

"The best. I've fixed it. She's happy to help you out."

I sagged in my chair, wiped my memory of the chill-food cabinets and said: "Tucker, you should be garlanded with flowers and led through the cheering crowds of the City of London on an elephant. What's this heroine's name and where can I reach her?"

"She's on the line right now and her name's Alice Fletcher. I'll put her through."

I instantly resolved to offer him a permanent job at a salary he would be unable to refuse.

Ms. Fletcher spoke courteously, displaying an effortless mastery of the accent which I called Home Counties and which she probably still called BBC, even though nowadays the BBC prided itself on flaunting regional dialects. She suggested that she call at my flat after work on the following day, Thursday, to inspect the kitchen and discuss the menu. She then said she would do all the shopping afterwards, but when I proved to be too much of a control-freak to let her shop alone she seemed delighted that I was willing to take an interest in the preparations.

At five-thirty on the following evening after a diabolical day which included a fraught partners' meeting, a furious clash with a snooty barrister over his "counsel's opinion," and a ferocious conference with a snotty client who refused to see the difference between tax avoidance and tax evasion, I arrived home to find Alice Fletcher waiting for me in the lobby of Harvey Tower. I eyed her warily but found nothing which set my teeth on edge. She was about my age, dark-eyed with a square, friendly face and brown hair tucked up in a French pleat. She was about twenty pounds overweight but I knew no man would dream of calling her fat; he would be too busy noting that the surplus flesh was distributed in all the right places. As if to play down the voluptuousness and enhance her respectability, she was wearing a decorous black blouse and black skirt beneath her unbuttoned, drab raincoat.

Upstairs in my flat she was polite about my kitchen, which I had not bothered to modernise, and her rigorously neutral expression never changed as she inspected the sparse contents of my storecupboard and refrigerator. Taking a notepad and pen from her bag she asked what food I wanted to serve to my guests.

"That's for you to decide," I said cautiously, "but there must be no beef of any kind."

"I believe Scottish beef is still safe," said Ms. Fletcher, "but of course it would be such a bore for you to have to explain that. Is there any guest who's vegetarian? Or who requires kosher?"

"Not this time."

"All right, but who exactly will be eating this meal? I like to try to anticipate what will appeal to them."

I listed the middle-aged American investment banker, his trophy wife of twenty-eight, the elderly English judge and his worthy spouse who was a prison visitor.

"A bold mix!" said Ms. Fletcher admiringly. "What fun! Anyone else?"

"Just me and my husband. He's a lawyer who's lived all over the world."

"Cosmopolitan," said Ms. Fletcher, classifying him. "He'll adapt to whatever food is set before him. The Americans will want a salad at some stage, and a lo-cal dessert, the judge will be suspicious of any foreign food except French, and Mrs. Judge will be into Tuscan cuisine while secretly hankering for shepherd's pie."

I laughed. "What about me?"

"Ah, I suspect you're not basically a foodie! You're so beautifully slim."

"I might still be obsessed with food. How do you know I'm not bulimic or anorexic?"

"If you were, you'd be too hung up to suggest the possibility to a stranger—in fact you'd probably be in denial and unable to accept you were slim at all."

I was impressed by these deductions, so impressed that I finally dared to believe I was dealing with an intelligent professional. With relief I decided that Ms. Fletcher and I were going to get along.

We were just moseying around the meat cabinets of the nearby supermarket some time later when I became vaguely aware of a woman watching us from the far end of the aisle. I might not have noticed her if she had been less well-dressed, but in her royal-blue coat and matching dress she stood out among the other shoppers, most of whom would have come from the nearby council estates. Her greying dark hair was expensively styled in swirling curves, and as she impulsively darted towards me I saw she had beautiful skin, lined lightly around the mouth and eyes but still very smooth. Her blue eyes were bright with an emotion which might have been anxiety or fear or anger or a potent combination of all three.

"You're Carter, aren't you," she said. It was a statement, not a question.

"That's me." I was trying to think who she was, but such a distinguished-looking woman could have been anyone in the City from a top-grade PA to a key player in a multinational, and it was no easy task to locate her name immediately in my memory.

"I'm sorry," I said, "but I can't quite recall—" Then I broke off as the horrific truth suddenly hit me, and at once the woman said: "I'm Sophie Betz."

THREE

Life is riddled with secrecy. There are secrets in every area—family, politics, business, medicine and all relationships that are about anything important... In intimate relationships it is constantly surprising that the deeper we become involved the more mysterious the other can become.

DAVID F. FORD
The Shape of Living

I

I took a step backwards. I opened my mouth but no words came out. Horror, rage, panic and downright incredulity surged through my brain in an emotional tidal wave.

"I had to see you," she said in a rush. "We have to talk."

"You're Sophie Betz," was all I could say. Then, more stunned than ever, I heard myself repeat with a wholly different emphasis: "*You're* Sophie Betz?"

"Look, I know you don't want to talk to me, but—"

"What the hell are you doing here?"

I was now floundering around trying to make sense of this bizarre appearance, but Sophie was so agitated that I believe she barely heard my question. We were talking across each other, our dialogue out of joint, while around us the shoppers' eyes were glazed and the white lights were glaring and the meat lay in glistening packages on the glacial shelves nearby.

"I tried to spin out the divorce because I thought you might get tired of him, but it all became such a nightmare, so expensive, and then—"

"*How did you know who I was and how did you know I'd be here tonight?*"

"I felt I simply had to make one last effort to save you, so I re-engaged the private detective I used last year. I told him I wanted to know your daily routine and what you looked like, and he took photos and—"

"What a bloody nerve!"

"—and he found out you usually came here at least once during the week after work to pick up things which couldn't wait till the weekly shopping expedition on Saturdays. So when you refused to take my call yesterday I knew I had no choice but to—"

"—haunt Safeway's till I showed up! Wonderful! Okay, now listen to me, Sophie. Don't think I'm entirely without sympathy for you, but the marriage was all over, wasn't it, before I arrived on the scene, so I really don't see why you—"

"I felt called to save you, absolutely *called*, although John—that's my local clergyman—did say after the divorce that maybe it wasn't for me to do that, he said maybe I should now put my trust in God to save you in his own way and in his own time—"

"Sorry, I'm not following you at all, can we keep God out of this?"

"But how can we? We're all utterly dependent on God's grace!"

73

I finally lost patience with her. "I'm not dependent on anyone!" I shouted. "I don't believe in God, and even if I did, I wouldn't need him! I'm a big success entirely due to my own efforts and I've got this life-plan which is panning out beautifully and the last thing I need is a Christian spouting nutterguff in a supermarket when I'm trying to do my shopping!"

"But you're a lawyer—surely you're interested in truth! Listen, Kim's gone down the wrong road. I thought that by staying with him I could save him, but—"

"Christ, you're worse than any American televangelist—"

"Has he told you about Mrs. Mayfield?"

In the profound silence which followed it felt as if the supermarket had been drained of air.

"He's mixed up with the occult," said the woman. "It's dragged him deep into the moral quicksands, so save yourself while you can, move out of his life as quickly as possible—"

"Fuck off," I said, and turned my back on her. I had sucked in some air from somewhere but my heart felt as if it were revving up for a killer thump. My body was clammy with sweat.

"Ask him about Mrs. Mayfield!" she shouted after me. "Ask him about Mrs. Mayfield!"

I blundered away without looking back.

II

I was standing in front of the dairy products cases and staring at the cheeses. I felt as if an hour had passed but the time-lapse was probably no more than two minutes. I was dry-mouthed and feeling nauseous. Some of the cheeses were a suggestive shade of yellow.

Turning away with a shudder I found myself face to face with Alice Fletcher who had followed me silently to the dairy section and was now waiting for me to show signs of recovery.

"Are you okay?" she said, concerned as I registered her presence.

"No, I feel as if I'd had a lobotomy without an anaesthetic. Has that ghastly woman gone?"

"Yes, she walked out."

"Thank God. I'm afraid she's a total nutcase and I'm very sorry indeed that you had to witness such a scene." I started to massage my neck, which was aching with tension. "She's been stalking me at a distance for some time."

"In that case maybe she'll leave you alone now that she's finally managed to speak to you."

"How I wish I could believe that! She's my husband's ex-wife, as you must have realised from the dialogue, and...no, never mind, let's forget her. Can we make a decision now about the meat?"

Alice, brimming over with tact, at once began to talk about the different cuts of lamb.

III

After we had completed the shopping I drove Alice home to her flat in one of the Georgian terrace houses north of Clerkenwell Green and then returned to Harvey Tower. Kim was working late and I did not expect him back until nine. Having put away the shopping I fixed myself a double vodka martini on the rocks and finally acknowledged the magnitude of the shock I had received.

At once I tried to master it by analysing it. I was shocked, I told myself, because Sophie had said hard-headed, well-balanced Kim was mixed up in a nutty activity; I was shocked because my husband had not confided in me about a woman whom Sophie had implied was important to him; but most of all, I knew, I was shocked because there was no way Sophie could be described as fat and frumpish with hair styled to resemble corrugated iron. As I wrestled with this truth I began to see why I was so appalled by it. The talk of Kim being mixed up with the occult was almost certainly the fantasy of a disturbed religious zealot, and Mrs. Mayfield was probably just a past mistress who would prove to be unimportant, but why should Kim have lied to me about Sophie's appearance? I could only suppose that he had described his wife in such unappealing terms in order to reassure me, but I did not need that kind of reassurance—and I did not like him telling me lies.

Having analysed my shock I tried to work out what I should do when he arrived home. Did I or did I not immediately spew out all the vile details of the scene in the supermarket? I reminded myself that he was going to be tired after a long, arduous day; this would not be the best moment to inform him that I had been jousting with his ex-wife in Safeway's. On the other hand (and as a lawyer I knew there was always another hand) what better moment could there be to extract the truth from him than the moment when he was too exhausted to do anything but confess?

Yet this cool insight, which proved that my brain was finally up and running again, failed to calm me. I began to pace around the living-room. I was too tense to eat but I finally managed to sit on the stool by my telescope and gaze out over the blazing lights below. Tuning in to the City in this way always steadied me, made me feel less isolated and more connected with the City's pulse, that driving, thrusting life-force which for me represented the heart of reality. I gazed at the skyscrapers, those temples dedicated to wealth and power, for some time.

Long before Kim's key turned in the lock I had got my act together and resolved not to talk of Sophie when he was exhausted. I did not want to alienate him; the necessary interrogation would have to wait.

I went into the hall.

"Welcome back!" I said brightly, moving into his arms, but no sooner had we kissed than I found myself blurting out: "Who's Mrs. Mayfield?"

IV

All expression vanished from Kim's face. Then he said with superb nonchalance: "She's just someone I don't see any more. Fix me a drink, would you, sweetheart? It's been one hell of a day." And moving past me into the living-room he stretched himself with a yawn before reaching for my unread copy of the *Evening Standard*. I was reminded of a big cat relaxing at last after a busy killing spree in the safari park.

My first reaction was admiration. This was a very cool, tough customer who had taken a blow below the belt almost without flinching. My second reaction was lust. Most women like their men to be cool and tough in a crisis, and I was no exception. My third reaction was relief. Mrs.

Mayfield, just as I had suspected, was a past mistress whom Sophie had cited in an attempt to shock me—as if she thought I would have had no idea that Kim had been unfaithful to her before.

But my fourth reaction was dismay. Why wasn't he asking me where I had heard Mrs. Mayfield's name? Because he was still too shattered to do more than assume a façade of nonchalance was the answer, and it was not an answer I cared for at all. Then I realised there was an answer which was still more unsavoury: perhaps Kim was not shattered but instead operating with maximum skill, putting me on hold with a couple of casual sentences while he quickly designed a satisfactory explanation.

I fixed him a dark Scotch-and-soda, and as I handed it to him he finally asked the question he should have asked in the beginning. "Who told you about Mrs. Mayfield?" he said idly, but before I could reply he was sloughing off the mystery by adding: "I suppose it was either Steve or Mandy Simmons. Where did you bump into them again?"

He was referring to a couple whom we had encountered by chance at a drinks party a month ago. Steve Simmons was a lawyer who worked at Kim's old firm, his wife Mandy had an advertising job in the West End, and they lived in Wapping, east of the City, in a flat which formed part of a converted warehouse overlooking the river. I had never seen this flat because although the Simmonses had been keen to invite us to dinner Kim had told me he had no wish to renew his acquaintance with them. He said that in the past he had become tired of fending off Mandy's advances.

Having no desire to become friendly with a husband-snatcher I had accepted this decision willingly enough, but now it seemed the Simmonses were drifting back into our lives. I stared at Kim. "Mandy and Steve know Mrs. Mayfield?"

"That's another reason why I didn't want to see them again."

Sinking down beside him on the couch I managed to say very mildly: "Do you think you could explain, please, who Mrs. Mayfield is?"

"Sure," said Kim as if surprised that I should think he might want to withhold the information. "But first of all explain how you heard about her. If Mandy and Steve didn't tell you, who did?"

"Take a deep breath," I said, "and prepare to be appalled. It was Sophie."

Kim moved so suddenly that I jumped. One moment he was sprawled on the cushions, the picture of ease, and the next moment he was sitting bolt upright on the sofa's edge. "She called you again?"

"She's called several times."

"Why the hell didn't you tell me?"

"I didn't want to worry you."

"But if I'd known she'd started phoning again—"

"She never achieved a conversation with me! I always hung up before she could get going!"

"But if she told you about Mrs. Mayfield—"

"That wasn't over the phone. She confronted me this evening in the supermarket."

He leaped to his feet. "But what did she—"

"Relax! She was obviously fruity-loops, rambling on about God—it was quite impossible for me to take her seriously!"

He downed the Scotch and moved to the sideboard to fix himself another. All he said was: "I want to know exactly what happened."

I tried to summarise the scene as crisply as possible. "I was shopping with Alice Fletcher for the dinner-party. Eventually a woman approached me. She was British size fourteen, American size twelve, Euro size—but you get the picture. Her hair was styled in a smooth wave. She was wearing a royal-blue coat with a matching dress and looked very smart, very elegant and very stylish. Naturally I failed to recognise her from your description so when she introduced herself I was gobsmacked. I was even more gobsmacked when she said you were mixed up with the occult. She then urged me to ask you about Mrs. Mayfield but at that point I told her to fuck off and went to look at the cheeses... Darling, why on earth did you describe Sophie to me as a size-twenty frump with a corrugated-iron hairstyle?"

"Because it was the truth! She must have lost weight as the result of all the stress and then taken care to smarten herself up before confronting her rival!"

"Well yes, I suppose that *is* just possible, but—"

"How did she know who you were?"

"She admitted rehiring the PI and telling him to take pix. She also said nuttily that she was being called by God to make a new effort to save me, and then she started burbling about moral quicksands and the occult and—"

"Quite. Well, it's plain to see what's happened. Sophie's overreacted, converting a quirky episode in my past—repeat, *past*—into a gothic melodrama which she thinks is still going on."

"She must be totally unhinged!"

Kim shrugged, drank some more Scotch. I noticed that this time he was drinking it neat. "Christians are opposed to the occult," he said flatly, "and nowadays they often confuse it with perfectly reputable New Age practices. Mrs. Mayfield used to get very annoyed with this irrationally hostile stance, so annoyed that she would always refer to Christians as 'the enemy.' She probably still refers to them in that way, but I wouldn't know. I gave up seeing her soon after I met you."

"So Mrs. Mayfield," I said slowly, "is—"

"Mrs. Mayfield's a New Age practitioner."

After a moment I said: "What does she practise?"

"Psychic healing."

There was another pause before I managed to say: "What on earth was a sane, rational man like you doing with an old bag who touted New Age nutterguff?"

"Carter, do you still have no idea how pathetic you sound when you wheel out this dated logical positivism of yours? You sound just as absurd as any religious fanatic who's unable to comprehend anything which falls outside a painfully narrow world-view! How can an intelligent person stand to remain so ignorant of reality?"

"Okay, I'm ignorant. So enlighten me. I still can't understand how you could have got mixed up with this female—unless, of course, you were in the hell of a jam and driven to act out of character."

He finished his neat Scotch and stood looking at his empty glass. "Well," he said when he could play for time no more, "I was certainly in a jam, I concede that."

Then he sank down beside me again on the couch and a very peculiar story began to unfold.

V

"About three years ago," said Kim, "I developed back trouble. The pain wasn't present all the time but when it did strike it was excruciating. However, both the Harley Street specialists I saw failed to help me, although the second one did say he thought the trouble was psychosomatic.

"By this time I was popping painkillers as if they were Smarties and beginning to be afraid all the drugs would affect my work. In desperation I made contact with a healer who advertised in one of the weekend papers, but he was just a quack who took my money and talked rubbish. The only good thing that came out of my meeting with him was that he happened to mention a bookshop which he said was a mine of information about alternative medicine, and it occurred to me that if I was going to emerge from this nightmare with my back cured and my wallet in one piece I was going to have to do some serious research into what was on offer in what you would no doubt call the nutty fringes.

"This bookshop turned out to be crammed with all kinds of esoteric stuff, but nobody was offering palm-readings or gazing into crystal balls or doing anything off-putting so I browsed around for a while. Then I came across a notice-board, and one of the many cards pinned there said: 'MRS ELIZABETH MAYFIELD: PSYCHIC HEALER.' And underneath this title were printed the words: 'CLARIFYING THE PAST, ANALYSING THE PRESENT, ASSESSING THE FUTURE.'

"Well, you can see why the card caught my attention, can't you? If the card had read: 'MADAME ELISAVETA: FORTUNE-TELLER, CRYSTAL-GAZER, MIND-READER' I wouldn't have given it a second glance. But 'Elizabeth Mayfield!' The name sounded so English, so respectable! And 'clarifying,' 'analysing' and 'assessing' were such businesslike words, so down-to-earth and practical! It also occurred to me that if my back trouble really was psychosomatic, a psychic healer could be exactly the kind of person I was looking for."

As he paused to refill his empty glass I said at once: "Right. A very understandable conclusion, particularly as you were so desperate. What happened next?"

"I went to see her. She was a widow, probably in her early fifties, very pleasant, very calm, very serene. She had a little house in Fulham, in that triangle by the Lots Road power station, one of those houses which you could have picked up for a song thirty years ago and would now be worth a very tidy sum indeed. But it was unremarkable inside—there was nothing to indicate that Mrs. Mayfield was making a fortune out of her healing business. I found that reassuring."

"Yes, of course. So how did she approach your problem?"

"Well, there was certainly no crystal ball. After I'd told her about what was going on in my life she asked if I would put my hands on the table, palms upwards. 'I don't read palms,' she said, 'but I like to look at hands. It makes the pictures clearer.' I didn't waste time asking 'What pictures?' because by that time I liked the woman, trusted her. She was such a sympathetic listener—and so sane, you see, so reasonable... Anyway I put my hands on the table and she looked at them and after a while she picked them up, first one and then the other. There were no magic vibrations. Her touch was nothing special. But then—" He broke off.

My heart thumped. "What happened?"

"She told me things she couldn't possibly have known. She knew I was German."

"Well, if you introduced yourself as Joachim Betz—"

"Don't be funny, of course I used a pseudonym! I called myself Jake Barton. But she didn't only know I was German. She knew things about my past."

"Such as?"

"Things about my early life. Things about my father. Things about Argentina... It was uncanny. Then finally, after I'd responded by telling her more about myself, she said: 'You had this deeply traumatic childhood, dragged from one country to another and utterly dependent on the men your mother managed to sleep with. You've never been able to discuss the horror of this early life of yours with anyone, but now you've reached middle age your body's finally breaking down under the strain of suppressing all this past pain—and the trouble's being severely aggravated by your unsympathetic boss and by the wife who doesn't understand you. The road to healing,' said Mrs. Mayfield, 'will take you through four stages. First of all you need to talk freely about the past to someone sympathetic. Second, you must get rid of your wife. Third, you must change your job. And fourth, you must marry again but this time to exactly the right woman.'" He paused to drink before adding: "She said she could guarantee a cure for my back if I took her advice and obeyed her more detailed instructions to the letter."

"How much was all this going to cost?"

"She said that when I was cured I could make a donation to her company, but in the meantime she would only charge her regular fee of twenty-five pounds a session. After my experiences in Harley Street I thought that was a bargain, and I figured that if she cured me I'd be more than happy to make a donation."

"What's all this about a company?"

"That covered her whole business. She ran self-help groups in addition to the one-to-one sessions, and one of these groups featured in the later stages of my cure—it was a form of group therapy with Mrs. Mayfield doing the supervising. That was when I met Steve and Mandy Simmons." More Scotch disappeared.

"How long did the group therapy go on for?"

"Well, after three months I was fine, no more back trouble, but Mrs. Mayfield wouldn't let me quit—she reminded me that my healing had to go through three more stages before I could hope to be permanently cured and that in the meantime I should keep attending the group sessions. 'The trouble will soon come back,' she said, 'unless you get rid of your wife, change your job and remarry.' So I talked to Sophie about a divorce—and when the big job came up at Graf-Rosen I decided to go for it... In fact I wound up taking Mrs. Mayfield's advice all the way along the line until—" He broke off again.

"Until?"

"—until I quarrelled with her. I broke with the

group," he said, "and I washed my hands of that whole scene."

I stared at him. "But why?"

He drained his glass, looked straight into my eyes for the first time since he had begun to describe his meetings with Mrs. Mayfield, and said simply: "I met you."

VI

"You mean—"

"Mrs. Mayfield didn't approve. So the group didn't approve either."

I was outraged. "What a bloody nerve!"

"Mrs. Mayfield said I needed a woman of my own age who had no career and whose chief interests were sex and shopping."

"You've got to be joking!"

"That's exactly what I said, but she took no notice. 'Never trust a woman who calls herself by a masculine name,' she said. 'Never trust a woman who won't introduce you to her family.'"

"But I've every intention of introducing you to my family! And as for my name—"

"I explained why it made good sense to call yourself Carter and why we hadn't yet visited your family, but then she said—"

"This woman's like a runaway tank!"

"—then she said: 'I'm getting a clear picture of her. She's so spiritually ignorant that she'll start flirting with the enemy, and once they've ensnared her they'll try to smash up your marriage.'"

"That's vile!" I was on my feet without knowing how I got there. "It's wicked to make predictions which can only upset people—and predictions for which there isn't a shred of evidence!"

"Sweetheart, I'm sorry"—he too was on his feet—"I shouldn't have told you—"

"Oh yes, you should! And what's more you should have told me about this wicked old cow right from the start, but never mind, I do accept that you wanted to protect me from her bloody awful nonsense." I clenched my right fist, thumped the back of the sofa to relieve my feelings and finally felt calm enough to add: "Of course if what she said wasn't so disgusting it would be funny. You mentioned earlier, didn't you, that she refers to Christians as 'the enemy'? Well, I don't know any Christians! I don't want to know any Christians! There's not a snowball's chance in hell that I'll ever get mixed up with any Christians! So that prediction about how I'll start 'flirting with the enemy' is one hundred per cent total crap!"

"I told her that. In fact that was when I decided that she and I had reached the parting of the ways."

"And not a moment too soon! How did the old bag take the brush-off?"

"Not well. And the group too pestered me not to leave, but everyone went quiet as soon as I married you."

"No wonder you didn't want to see Mandy and Steve again!"

"It was bad luck we bumped into them at that party... Carter"— his arms slipped around me— "I'm just so sorry you've been bothered by all this garbage from the past but at least you can understand now, can't you, why I wanted to protect you from it?"

"I can understand," I said, "but wrapping me in clingfilm is the wrong solution. If there are problems from the past we should share them."

He said yes, he agreed but he didn't foresee any more past problems surfacing. We smooched for a while to express our mutual relief. But of course, as Kim realised sooner than I did, the problem of Sophie's stalking still remained unsolved.

VII

"What am I going to do about Sophie, sweetheart? It's clear she's obsessed, and I can't stand the idea of her harassing you like this."

"You may have to." Criminal law did not cover stalking, and as far as I could see I had no remedy in civil law either; I had insufficient grounds for an injunction.

We mulled over the legal conundrum gloomily. By this time we had eaten some peanut-butter sandwiches, watched the *News At Ten* and were pottering around the kitchen. Kim was pouring himself a glass of Evian water while I was stacking the dishwasher.

"Alice Fletcher suggested," I said as we wandered down the corridor to the bedroom, "that Sophie might leave me alone now that she's achieved a conversation and delivered her warning."

"That theory assumes Sophie's rational." He slumped down on the bed to take off his shoes. "What's this Alice Fletcher like?"

"Oh, definitely a professional. I'm sure she'll do a competent job."

"And she's Tucker's girlfriend?"

"No, there's some other man in the background."

"Does Tucker have a girlfriend?"

"I never, *never* discuss personal matters with Tucker. It's all part of my strategy for keeping the hormones under control."

"You discussed the dinner-party with him—that's personal!"

"He simply came to my rescue, just as a good PA should, when I was tearing my hair and climbing the walls." I refrained from reminding Kim that his devoted PA, Mary Waters, would have slaved through the night, if required, to ensure the success of any dinner-party he had asked her to arrange. "Talking of PAs and PIs," I remarked, "I wonder if Sophie's PI ever tapped Mary for information about me. Maybe Mary would have welcomed the chance to show feminine solidarity with Sophie and demonstrate her disapproval of the second Mrs. Betz." Having been allowed by Sophie to organise every detail of Kim's London life for some years, Mary had experienced a sharp curtailment of her pseudo-spouse role since I had entered his life. I could well imagine her snooping in Kim's organiser and passing on my address and phone number to the PI, but Kim now sprang loyally to her defence and declared that his office paragon was quite incapable of such treachery.

"Tired?" he murmured later as I slipped into bed beside him.

"No, wired. Let's tango."

But although he responded to this invitation with enthusiasm, he eventually had to admit defeat. "It was the Scotch," he said ruefully. "I shouldn't have drunk so much of it at the end of a long hard day."

I snuggled up to him and stroked his chest comfortingly, but half an hour later I was still awake, still remembering all that whisky, still wondering why it had been necessary to drink so very much more than usual.

VIII

When I awoke I resolved to push all thought of fortune-telling old bats and nutty stalkers to the back of my mind in order to focus on the dinner-party. I had been ambivalent from the start about this event not merely because I was nervous of making a *faux pas* which would allow our English guests, the judge and his wife, to classify me as a trashy social climber but because Kim and I were still sorting out our domestic life. It had certainly suited us to begin our marriage at my flat; Kim had needed time to rearrange his financial affairs, and after the strain of changing jobs and surviving the divorce, neither of us had felt immediately inclined to take on the stress of house-hunting. But although the Barbican tower blocks offer many advantages, lavish space is hardly one of them. Of the three bedrooms I possessed, one had been assigned to Kim's junk and one to mine after I had compacted my clobber to give him some space. (Of course we never had time to sort anything out.) All this chaos meant we were conducting a somewhat cramped existence in the living-room and master bedroom, hardly an ideal set-up for grade-A entertaining.

To compound my feelings of disorganisation I had not yet had the time to acquire a reliable cleaner who would also do shopping for me during the week. I had barely managed to find time to track down a caterer, and that move had hardly been an unqualified success. Currently, I told myself that morning, I was neither in the mood nor in the running to be the slickest hostess in town. Indeed the very thought of the dinner-party was making me yearn to add vodka to my morning orange juice.

However, since subsiding in a drunken heap was not a serious option, I rose at five-thirty and put in an hour's deep cleaning of the living-room and main bathroom before I dressed for work, buffed myself to the highest of lustres and arrived at the office for an eight o'clock meeting. The morning rapidly disappeared amidst a rising tide of crises. I had intended to buy flowers at lunch-time and nip back to the flat to put them in water, but that bright idea came to nothing because by one o'clock the fax had gone mad, sending a constant stream of unnecessary documents from Beijing, and I had to try to reach the Beijing partner by phone to demand an explanation. I hated the China office, but as a global law firm we had to buy our clients' land and arrange their leases and draft their contracts and keep their fiscal noses clean even when they were hell-bent on pretending to be clones of Marco Polo.

My success in escaping from the office at five-thirty was entirely due to Tucker the WonderTemp who took control of the fax pandemonium and tracked down the Beijing partner's minion who was sending all the stuff which looked as if it had been drafted in a rice field. It turned out that the Beijing partner was having a nervous breakdown. No one seemed much surprised except the senior partner, who took it as a personal affront and said the man was hardly displaying the spirit which had built the Empire. Some of those old dinosaurs had to be heard to be believed.

In the ladies' loo a small voice in my head said: "I hate this bloody place and I hate this bloody work and I hate never having any time for anything and I hate life being one long crisis and most of all I hate giving dinner-parties for people I don't care if I never see again." But of course this stream of heresies was only erupting because I was stressed almost out of my skull, and I knew I had to shape up straight away before someone decided I was a wimp and tried to stamp on me.

Taking a cab to the florist in Moorfields, I told the woman to give me thirty pounds' worth of yellow and white stuff plus a slice of jungle, and staggered back into the cab with what felt like half a rain forest in my arms. At Harvey Tower I had trouble working out how I could push the lift button but luckily some helpful resident arrived before I could try to kick-box the panel.

On my arrival in the flat I found there was a mess in the living-room. A picture had fallen, slamming into the sideboard, knocking over a lamp and hitting the floor with a force which had shattered the glass in the frame. Muttering curses I dumped the flowers in the bath and returned to the living-room to survey the damage more closely but concluded the mess could be eliminated without too much trouble. I was relieved to see that although the picture—a print of Kim's Oxford college—would need reframing, the print itself was undamaged. Wasting no more time I bagged the broken frame and swept up the glass.

I should perhaps state that I was neither amazed nor incredulous that the picture should have fallen from the wall. When one lives thirty-five floors above the Barbican podium, which is itself on average two and a half floors above street level, one expects one's living quarters to shift fractionally from time to time; tall buildings need to have a certain flexibility built into them and I was accustomed to the hairline cracks which occasionally appeared in the plasterwork. My prime emotion on discovering the mess had been annoyance that I had used a mere nail instead of a Rawlplug to fix the picture to the wall.

It was not until Alice arrived minutes later that I thought of Sophie. No doubt Alice's presence conjured up the memory of Sophie in the supermarket, but I suddenly found myself remembering my past comment that Sophie would take her revenge and call it justice. It then occurred to me that although Sophie had achieved her aim of a confrontation, I had repulsed her in no uncertain terms. Could she have felt that God was now commanding her to give me hell by invading my living-space and trashing a picture which she would know had sentimental value for Kim? This was a deeply unnerving theory, but fortunately I soon grasped it had to be wrong; it would have been impossible for her to gain entry to the flat. The lobby at podium level was manned twenty-four hours a day, and at street level there was always someone on duty in the car park to repel intruders.

Thrusting all thought of Sophie from my mind I arranged most of the flowers into two vases, one for the living-room and one for the bedroom, where the guests would be leaving their coats. I was then faced with the challenge of designing the remaining flowers into a small, supremely tasteful table arrangement, but I soon decided this would take more time and talent than I possessed so I dumped the floral surplus in my junk-room. Better to have no table arrangement at all than one which failed to be perfect.

Struggling at last into my favourite black dress, I told myself fiercely that dinner-parties should be banned by law.

IX

Words can barely describe the relief I experienced when the evening proved to be a success. This triumph was perhaps hardly a surprise, since I can go to enormous lengths to avoid failure, but honesty compels me to admit the occasion was a success not because I had the flat looking like a dream-pad in a property magazine but because Alice produced a meal worthy of a multistar Michelin restaurant. How she did it in my cramped unmodernised kitchen must remain one of the culinary wonders of 1990.

She had chosen a Basque recipe; roast saddle of lamb was accompanied by almonds, potatoes and a sauce Béarnaise in which mint replaced the usual tarragon. The first course consisted of an elaborate salad, designed to seduce the American guests, and as it was in the Tuscan style it also entranced the judge's wife, who, just as Alice had suspected, was keen to display her knowledge of Chiantishire cuisine. After the main course a lemon sorbet kept down the cholesterol count for those who cared about such things and provided an acerbic contrast to the luscious lamb, but following the sorbet a board of mouth-watering Stilton, Cheddar and Brie circulated for those who still yearned to kick their diets in the teeth. A large bowl of grapes accompanied the cheeseboard in its wanderings.

Moving into the kitchen to check the progress of the coffee I murmured to Alice: "Magnificent! Well done!" and Alice's plump cheeks became pink with pleasure. This evening she was wearing glasses because, she said, she had only recently taken to trying contact lenses and she was still unable to wear them for long periods. In keeping with her professionalism she was dressed in a plain black dress with black stockings and flat black shoes; a white apron billowed over her resplendent bosom. I was reminded incongruously of a certain kind of card seen in West End phone booths, the card advertising the services of prostitutes who gratify the weirdos by dressing up in uniforms to provide kinky sex.

The coffee circulated. Liqueur chocolates were passed around. Behind the closed door of the kitchen Alice began the next phase of clearing up. On his way to fetch the box of cigars Kim murmured to me: "How's she getting home?"

"Her partner or fiancé or whatever he is will come and pick her up. She'll call him from the bedroom when she's ready to leave."

"Great cook, great dinner—and great uniform!" He winked at me.

I gave him a mild cuff and turned my attention to the non-smokers who were regrouping around the telescope as the cigar-fiends headed for the balcony. To my relief the night was fine. The guests spent ages drooling over the view.

When I next checked on Alice I found she had finished clearing up and had called the boyfriend, but he had been delayed; was it all right

95

if she waited for him in the flat or would I prefer her to go downstairs? She knew he would appear eventually. There was no question of him not showing up.

"Well, of course you must stay in the flat!" I exclaimed. "Switch on the bedroom TV and make yourself at home!" Being so excessively hospitable to strangers was hardly my style, but I was more than keen to display my gratitude to her.

The porter eventually buzzed from the lobby just as we had closed the front door on the last guest. "Mike in the garage says someone's come to pick up your cook, Mrs. Betz."

"Thanks." I hung up the intercom's receiver and floated into the bedroom where Alice was watching an old black-and-white film on TV; I caught a glimpse of Joan Crawford emoting beneath eyebrows thick enough to support a row of dinner-plates. "Your pal's arrived," I announced. "Hey, let's invite him up here for a drink—why didn't I think of that earlier? If anyone deserves a drink you do!" It need hardly be said that I was in that expansive mood which follows a period of sustained stress. Huge relief had produced a euphoria hyped up by vodka, port and claret. (Kim had succeeded in passing off the '85 St. Julien as a much older vintage; everyone had been too pie-eyed after the generous pre-dinner drinks to notice the date on the label.)

Alice was saying to me: "I wouldn't dream of troubling you," but she was overruled by Kim.

I recalled the porter on the intercom. "Could you ask Mike to tell the gentleman he's invited up to the thirty-fifth floor for a drink?"

But the gentleman declined to come. It was very kind of Mr. and Mrs. Betz, but he would just collect Ms. Fletcher and disappear.

"He needs the personal touch!" I declared, determined to draw this shy wallflower into the centre of the action. "Come on, Alice, we'll go downstairs and get him. Kim, stay here and open a bottle of champagne to celebrate the best dinner ever cooked in Harvey Tower!"

Poor Alice, who of course was stone-cold sober, tried to protest but was quelled by the Betz brigade radiating drunken imperiousness. We rode down past the podium and emerged into the car park to find a very clean white Peugeot parked directly in front of the door which led to the lift shafts. As we appeared the driver sprang out. He was a tall, slim man in his forties with brown hair, neatly cut, and an unusual face, all strong bones and hard angles and taut pale skin. He wore jeans and a black leather jacket. As he came to greet us I noticed that he moved with a grace almost liquid in its fluency, a grace which made me wonder if he was an accomplished actor well used to inhabiting the best stages in town.

Alice said to me: "This is Nicholas Darrow. Nicholas, may I introduce—" She paused, tripped up by the conundrum of alternative surnames.

"Carter Graham," I said, automatically serving up the name I gave to everyone I met through my work, and as the stranger held out his hand the facings of his jacket parted so that I could see not only the blue shirt beneath but also the telltale strip of white plastic at his neck.

He was a clergyman.

X

I was so struck by the coincidence that I was face to face with a Christian only a day after I had sworn that Christians would never play a part in my life that for a moment I was immobilised. I had to remind myself very sharply that this was a man I was unlikely to see again.

"Hi," Darrow was saying perfunctorily while I was still wrestling with my amazement, and the next moment I found myself clasping his outstretched hand. He had long, slim fingers which wrapped themselves firmly around mine.

All I could say when my hand was released was: "Alice didn't tell me you were a clergyman."

"Well, I shouldn't imagine the subject came up," he said neatly. "After all, I wasn't on the menu." He turned to Alice. "Everything okay?"

"Fine!" She smiled at him radiantly.

"Then we'll be on our way. Ms. Graham, forgive me for turning down your kind invitation, but I have to be up early tomorrow."

I muttered some civility before Alice said goodbye and volunteered to help me out with any future dinner-parties. Having thanked her, I watched them depart and then rode back to the thirty-fifth floor.

"So you failed to lure him upstairs!" commented Kim who had wisely avoided opening the champagne. "How did he resist you?"

"No idea." I wandered into the bedroom and started shedding my jewellery.

"Nice guy?"

"Not my type." I glanced at my reflection in the mirror and decided I looked like a Hitchcock heroine who had survived some peculiarly sinister encounter. (Grace Kelly after her escape from Raymond Burr in *Rear Window*?) I wondered why I found myself unable to say to Kim: "You'll never believe this, but the boyfriend turned out to be a clergyman! How about that for a laugh?" But perhaps a sinister encounter could not, by definition, ever be considered amusing.

Fortunately I was too drunk to meditate further on Mrs. Mayfield's prediction that I would start "flirting with the enemy." Having knocked back the maximum dose of Alka-Seltzer I removed my make-up, stripped off my clothes and sank into oblivion as fast as a concrete block disappearing into quicksands.

XI

I needed to give full recognition to my hangover the next morning, although officially there was no time; on Saturdays I had to operate to a tight schedule in order to complete all my chores. I had to clean the flat, do the wash, pick up the cleaning, raid the supermarket, visit the hairdresser, manicure my nails, replenish my make-up supplies, sort out the mail I had been too busy to open during the week, balance my cheque-book and run a couple of miles on the treadmill I kept among my clobber in the second bedroom. The bonus this weekend was that I had already done a deep clean of the living-room, which now only required tidying, and Alice had left the kitchen pristine except for the floor, an area I could usually wash in less than a minute.

Being house-trained (though not quite so house-trained as he had managed to be before the wedding), Kim had his own chores to do. He did his own wash and picked up his own cleaning. We had tried to merge our washes and amalgamate our pick-ups, but somehow we always required different settings on the washing machine, and as for the cleaning, there was usually too much for one person to collect in a single visit. Kim raided the supermarket for me sometimes but was unreliable as he always deviated from my list and imposed his own choices, most of which I disliked on principle. He refused to do any housework—a perfectly valid line to take, but until I could find the time to hire a cleaner I was unable to refuse too. As the result of the divorce he had more correspondence than I did to tackle at weekends, and on this particular Saturday he was going to have to take his shattered picture to be reframed after his swim at the health club. Often he had to walk over to his office and work for a couple of hours. In short, we were busy, busy, busy on Saturdays, and waking hung over was definitely not the best way to start the weekend.

We were still slumped in bed, still drinking black coffee and feeling as if we ought to be hooked up to life-support machines, when the phone rang.

"Our doting guests are calling to shower us with compliments," I said.

"Already? You seriously think they're conscious? Hey, kill that noise before my head splits open!"

I picked up the receiver and succeeded in uttering a monosyllable. It was: "Yep?"

A woman's voice said with awful brightness: "Hullo, is Jake there, please?"

"Wrong number. Sorry."

"Wait, is that Carter?"

I was so startled that I said: "Yes, it is," instead of demanding to know who was calling.

"Oh Carter, it's Mandy Simmons—remember me? We met recently at that super party in Mayfair, and—"

"I remember. Who's Jake?"

"Oh, isn't that silly of me, I quite forgot, he's usually known as Kim, isn't he? We always called him Jake in the group... Have you heard about our little group, by any chance?"

"You bet," I said, wishing my brain was less soaked in chemicals. "I just loved the way you all told Kim not to marry me."

I was aware of Kim sitting bolt upright. "Give that to me," he ordered, reaching for the receiver, but I clung on. Meanwhile Mandy was bubbling away, frothy as a shaken carbonated drink. "Goodness me, don't take offence just because we made a silly mistake! We realise now we overreacted, and that's exactly why I'm calling! Tell Kim we'd really love to see him again, and— is he there by any chance? Can I speak to him?"

"In your dreams, sister," I said and tried to slam down the receiver but Kim caught my wrist and took over the call.

"Mandy?"

"Jake!" I could hear her very clearly. I was pressed against Kim, my ear inches from his. "Sweetie, what on earth have you been saying about us to Carter? She sounded absolutely ferocious!"

"Mandy, let's get this straight. I'm grateful to the group for all the help I received, but—"

"Elizabeth's missing you terribly!"

"Elizabeth's a tough lady. She'll survive."

"It's *your* survival we're all worried about,

sweetie! I say, did you tell Carter about your Nazi past?"

Kim slammed down the receiver. Then he hurled the phone at the wall so violently that the plastic casing split, and blundered from the bed to the bathroom.

FOUR

We feel that the weave of our self with others is unravelling or being torn...habits of trusting communication are betrayed.

D A V I D F. F O R D
The Shape of Living

I

I remained where I was, propped against the pillows. I had never realised before that a person can be literally shocked rigid. Finally my brain kicked in and I was able to unlock my limbs, retrieve the shattered phone and replace the receiver. Padding to the bathroom door I listened, holding my breath, but there was no sound. In the shower-room nearby I dowsed my face with cold water but when I came up for air I still found lucid thought impossible. I only knew that I now possessed knowledge that Kim had been very determined I should never acquire and that if I failed to play my cards correctly Mandy's dyna-mite might well have a devastating effect on the marriage. I needed to be sympathetic and supportive, not angry and shocked.

Yet I *was* angry and shocked. In the kitchen I drank two glasses of water to drown my hangover and then moved to my telescope in the living-room. Outside the rain was falling and it was too misty to see far, but I followed the river east from its south-north twist at Westminster until I wound up staring at the golden figure of Justice, holding her sword aloft, above the criminal courts of the Old Bailey. I was still sitting at my telescope, still thinking of how justice had been meted out to the Nazi war criminals at Nuremberg, when I heard Kim moving about in the kitchen.

I did not turn around but merely called: "Sorry—I should have put some fresh coffee on."

"That's okay." He sounded calm. I assumed he too had been fiercely willing himself to regain his equilibrium, and suddenly the likeness between us gave me strength. I felt that the scene I now had to handle required no elaborate strategy but only the faith that the relationship would survive.

Idly I heard myself say: "I know that type of woman. She usually works in glamour-mills famous for bloodbath turnovers, and she'll simper and coo in her little-girl frock right up to the moment when she's whipping out the knife to disembowel you. Of course she knew, didn't she, that even after you came on the line I'd be listening in to every word she said."

"Right." He emerged from the kitchen with a tall glass of milk in his hand and drifted over to me.

"Have a look," I said, patting the telescope. "It's very therapeutic, puts everything in perspective."

But he shook his head. "I'd be too afraid I'd see the City bombed to pieces."

At once I said: "That was a very long time ago and you were only a baby at the time."

"True. Only a baby...but not, I'm afraid, in Argentina. Did you never suspect?"

I could only say with great difficulty: "I trusted you." Somehow I managed to add: "When did life in Argentina begin?"

"Nineteen forty-seven. I was born in Cologne in 1940 and my father, of course, wasn't Jewish. He joined the Nazi Party in 1929, the year Hans Frank became its legal adviser... Have you ever heard of Hans Frank?"

I shook my head, so shattered by this rapid recital of facts that the name barely registered, and at once Kim added, as if driven to speak before his nerve failed him: "My father was a lawyer, well-educated, from a good family. I mean, he wasn't just some robot in the OKH who put his brains on ice while he obeyed orders—"

Mechanically I repeated: "OKH?"

"The German Army High Command. The OKH and the OKW were...no, forget that. It's enough to say that my father found the military types very boring. Before the war he worked with Hans Frank on the *Gleichschaltung* legal system and became a member of the German Academy of Law when Frank founded it. He and Frank were good friends. Frank was famous for saying: 'Love of the Führer has become a concept in law.' Frank...well, Frank became famous for a lot of things... He was hanged at Nuremberg after the war."

He paused but I was too numb to respond, and at last he began to talk again, still using the flattest possible voice. "Frank became Governor-General of occupied Poland," he said, "and operated from Wavel Castle in Krakow. He initiated the policy of destroying and degrading the Poles until they were reduced to a slave society—oh, and he murdered Jews, of course. Masses of them. More people died in Poland than anywhere else during the war... Well, I don't need to say anything further, do I, except that my father worked in Krakow alongside Frank. And he did business with a man named Reinhard Heydrich... Ever heard of him? No? He never made it to Nuremberg because he was assassinated in 1942. He formed the *Sicherheitsdienst*—the SD—which was an intelligence and security service for the SS, and he was the principal Nazi agent in the campaign against the Jews. The SD was closely allied to the Gestapo."

He paused again, and the next moment I felt his fingers tentatively brushing my shoulder. Perhaps he needed to see if I would recoil, but by this time I had managed to focus on the fact that Kim, born in 1940, was hardly responsible for his father's choice of friends.

Forcing myself to cover his hand briefly with mine I was able to ask: "Were you in Krakow with your father?"

"No, no, Poland was dangerous territory, blighted, filled with people whom my father regarded as subhuman. But he arranged for me and my mother to live near the border in eastern Germany so that he could often come and see us. Sometimes my mother managed to visit him in Krakow but she never took me with her.

I was always left behind with my nurse and the dog."

"So that photograph you showed me—"

"That was taken at our house in eastern Germany."

I began to fidget with my telescope as if compelled to pretend the conversation was so mundane that I could still play with my favourite toy. "How did it all end?"

"In chaos." Seconds passed before he could speak again. He was shuddering, setting down his half-empty glass of milk. "Frank fled to Germany before the Russian advance in 1944," he said, "but my father stayed on for a while—the Russians didn't make their final push into Poland until the January of 1945. When he did leave Poland he was ordered to stay in eastern Germany, and I'm sure he would have sent me and my mother back to Cologne at that point if it had been feasible, but Cologne was rubble and the Allies were advancing on the other front and my mother was frightened, so...we stayed on. But naturally my father knew the end was coming and he made his plans for when the time came to escape."

"What happened when the time came?"

"My father had had to go to Berlin, but he had allowed for that in the plan. When my mother got his message to leave she sacked my nurse, turned the dog loose and dragged me onto what must have been one of the last trains out of our town. To shut me up she said the Russians were coming and they killed all children under five. I was still a few months short of my fifth birthday... But the worst thing she did was not allowing me to say goodbye to my nurse or my dog." He hesitated before saying carefully: "My nurse's name was Helga and my dog's name was Wotan. I think of them always, every year, on that day."

"Maybe Helga was all right. Maybe—"

"No, you don't understand. The Russians were coming."

I swallowed and said: "Well, at least someone would have looked after the dog."

"No, no, you're not on the same planet, you've no idea. Everyone was starving. The dog would have been dead in twenty-four hours."

I had ceased to fidget with my telescope. "What happened to you and your mother?"

"We had to take a succession of trains—my father hadn't allowed sufficiently for the chaos—but I can't remember much about the journey now except that I had nothing to eat for three days and the lavatories didn't work. Finally we reached Italy. There was some sort of *Schloss*— a castle. We had to wait there for my father. Fortunately he had plenty of money because he'd built up a secret stash in Switzerland."

I remembered stories of confiscated wealth. Faintly I repeated: "Secret—" but he did not allow me to finish.

"When he joined us at the *Schloss* we all went down to Rome," he said. "By that time the whole place was seething with refugees—all Europe was a shambles and it was easy to get lost in the crowd. After that we had to wait for a while but by this time we were in the so-called 'rat-run,' the pipeline to freedom, so we knew the right papers would turn up in the end. We finally got out of Italy on a ship stuffed with emigrants from every nation in Europe. I remember my mother throwing a tantrum because she had to eat at the same table as Jews. Typical. She never changed. Neither of them ever changed."

He suddenly sat down on the arm of the sofa, set his glass on the coffee table and leaned forward, pressing the palms of his hands on his knees. There was a sheen of sweat on his forehead and he was staring down at the carpet as if the neutral colour helped him to concentrate.

"No," he was saying, "my parents never changed. There was no remorse, no regret of the Nazi excesses, nothing. They hated Argentina, all they could do was talk of Germany. My father took to drink. My mother...well, never mind what my mother got up to. They were hopeless, no use to me whatsoever. Finally my father died of liver trouble. Good news, I thought. But then my mother hooked the Yank to get herself American nationality—everyone wanted to get to America in those days, it was the land of milk and honey and Europe was still a wasteland, but Christ, what a nightmare those years in America were. The Yank was even more of a shit than my father—thank God someone finally blew his brains out... Then the Brit showed up. Of course my mother would never normally have considered pulling a Brit—in her eyes the Brits were far lower than the Yanks—but she was desperate because the Yank had spent what remained of the Swiss stash. So we wound up living in England. Big irony. Did Giles know the truth about us when he married her or did she con him by saying, as she always did by that time, that her first husband had been a Jewish refugee? Don't know. But he was nobody's fool and I think he probably married her knowing the truth but not giving a damn. She was very decorative... He only ever said one thing to me about my early life. He said: 'I don't believe the sins of the fathers should be visited on the children. That's not what we in England call "playing the game."'"

He stood up, wiping the sweat from his forehead, and moved to the sideboard. To my horror I saw him add a shot of brandy to his half-empty glass of milk.

"When my mother was dying I did ask the vital questions," he was saying. "You mustn't think I chickened out. I said: 'What exactly did my father do?' but all she said was: 'How should I know? He never spoke of his work,' and when I pressed her she only answered: 'He was in administration. He was a good German. He loved his country.' She'd long since closed her mind against the truth, but because of my father's connections with Reinhard Heydrich I was sure his 'administration' concerned the Jews... I said to my mother: 'We wouldn't have needed false papers to get out of Europe unless he'd been on the wanted list,' but she just insisted: 'He was never on any list, he never killed anyone, all he did was paperwork, and who cares now anyway? Only a bunch of Jews!' She was always in denial, just as so many Germans were... Did you know that after the war the Allies forced the Germans into cinemas to watch films of the camps? Did you know that, Carter?"

I said stiff-lipped: "No, I didn't."

"Well, they did. And the Germans came out of the cinemas and said: 'That was a propaganda film made in Hollywood.' I uncovered that story during my researches. I uncovered a lot of facts during my researches, and I never once kidded myself they were fiction. I wasn't going to be like my parents—and in particular I was never, never going to be anti-Semitic... Of course I'm sure now that the Swiss stash was confiscated Jewish money."

I whispered: "All your Jewish friends... All those Jewish firms you worked for..."

"Well, naturally I've always gone out of my way to put my talents, such as they were, at their disposal, and naturally every penny I give to charity goes to their good causes. What the hell else do you expect me to do?" As he turned abruptly to face me I saw his hand tremble as he pushed back his hair. "During that bloody war," he said, "little kids the same age as I was died in the camps. I saw pictures of their bodies. And those pictures weren't manufactured in Hollywood."

I was on my feet, moving towards him, but he had already turned away. I heard him say: "After my mother died I broke down and told Sophie everything. Big mistake. She couldn't handle it. We never slept together again."

Without hesitation I slipped my arms around him to signal how different I was from my predecessor.

II

After we had embraced fiercely he said in the same unemotional voice he had used earlier: "It was the deception which shattered her. Of course she minded about the background but she could forgive me that. What she found impossible to forget was that I had never confided in her."

At once I said: "What the lucky people of this world fail to realise is that for those who are less lucky there are some subjects which really are unspeakable."

He was so relieved by my understanding that it took him a moment to murmur: "Your father?"

I nodded, hugging him again.

"Tell me."

"The stupid thing is it won't seem bad because my father did nothing bestial—he didn't sexually abuse me or beat me up or lock me in a cupboard. There must be thousands of kids who have to cope with fathers who are gambling addicts, but the point is, isn't it, that when one's a kid the problem seems uniquely frightful because you feel no one else could possibly be going through what you're going through. It's a delusion but it's such a powerful one that it makes the whole subject taboo."

He looked more relieved than ever, and at last we sat down together on the couch. "There must be thousands of men today in Germany who had Nazi fathers," I said, "and those fathers can't all have been monsters like Hans Frank. Maybe your father really was just a good lawyer who got too deeply entangled with a nightmare regime and then had to conform to stay alive."

"No doubt that was the defence he would have offered at Nuremberg."

"But you can't be sure he would have wound up there!"

"Maybe he wouldn't have wound up with the big boys at the major trial. But there were many trials at Nuremberg...and all the evidence points to the fact that he knew he had to get out of Europe. We took the rat-run; we disappeared into Argentina; it was the classic mode of escape for the Nazis who couldn't face the Allies."

"And for a lot of refugees, surely, who just wanted to start a new life overseas?" I argued, but he was no longer listening.

"After Sophie had rejected me," he was saying, "I had a—well, no, it wasn't a breakdown, high flyers don't have breakdowns, but I became a workaholic to try to stop myself thinking of the past, and when I couldn't stop thinking about it I found I had to start researching, it was compulsive—in the end I wound up researching that whole bloody war...But I never found out exactly what my father had done, and I reckon he seized the chance to burn the worst of his 'paperwork' after Frank left Krakow in 1944. God, how much I wanted to uncover the truth! At one stage I was so desperate that I even visited Auschwitz to see if it produced a memory of my parents talking about the death-camps...but it didn't. Have you ever been there?"

"No."

"It was appalling but in some way which defies rational analysis it was also spiritual, it spoke to the spirit—and then I got interested in God and tried to research him too, but I wasn't impressed by what I turned up, I couldn't relate to it. But I could relate to the idea that there were Principalities and Powers of Darkness—I could relate to the whole concept of demonic levels of reality—because I knew I had experienced them in my early life. In fact all my life I seem to have been struggling with the demons—wrestling with the Powers—"

"Darling, don't say any more—you don't have to talk about this stuff—"

"But that was my problem, can't you see? I couldn't talk about it! I just went on and on researching until my back hurt so much I had to stop—it was my body telling my mind to rest, I can see that now, but at the time I couldn't rest, couldn't, I was obsessed. God, I was so afraid of breaking down—I was literally living from one day to the next—and that was where I was when I saw Mrs. Mayfield's advertisement. Of course I'd never have gone near her if I'd been well, but I was drinking in the last-chance saloon, absolutely on my uppers—"

"Yes, I understand now—it all makes sense—"

"—and she helped me, she fixed the pain, she knew what to do. She was a psychic healer and she healed my psyche—and that should have been the end of the matter, but it wasn't. It wasn't the end of the matter at all."

"I'm not sure I follow."

"Well, if you go to a doctor and he cures you, you don't hang around his office afterwards, do you? You get on with your life and the doctor gets on with his. But it's not like that once you've supped with Mrs. Mayfield. You're expected to make a regular habit of turning up for dinner, and then one day you find you're clean out of all your long spoons."

"Clean out of...sorry, I'm still not following this—"

"Forget it, let's just say it's not so easy to shake off Mrs. Mayfield as I thought it would be. For instance, I'm sure she's now decided the time's right to use Mandy to try to draw me back into the group."

I was appalled. "But why can't you just tell Mrs. Mayfield to get lost?"

"I wish I could but I have to tread carefully."

"For God's sake, why?"

"Because she knows too much about me," said Kim, "and having been blackmailed once in my life I can tell you it's not an experience I'd care to repeat."

III

I was too shocked to speak. I was hardly even aware of him kissing the top of my head as he hauled himself to his feet. I just continued to sit on the couch as if paralysed.

"It's okay," said Kim wryly over his shoulder from the kitchen threshold. "No need to panic— I'm not being blackmailed at the moment! All I'm saying is that I'm sensitive to the possibility of a recurrence."

I finally managed to follow him.

"I'm going to make some more coffee," he said. "Want some?"

"The only thing I want is more information. What the hell happened when you were blackmailed?"

"What do you think? Someone found out who I was and threatened to tell my Jewish colleagues that I was the son of a Nazi war criminal."

"But how did this person—"

"It was sheer bad luck. I met this German-American who was working in the London office of his New York firm. It turned out not only that he'd lived in Argentina after the war but that he'd actually travelled out there on that same ship in 1947. I'd been seven then and he'd been twelve, so it was hardly surprising we failed to recognise each other when we met again, and in fact at first we thought we'd never met at all; as I told you, there'd been hundreds of people aboard. Then he said: 'What did you say your name was?' and when I told him he said: 'No, I didn't mean Betz—what was your first name?' I explained that I called myself Kim nowadays because English-speakers found 'Joachim' tricky to pronounce, and at once he said: 'Were you the little kid who called himself Joachim Lange once by mistake and got slapped by his mother?' Well, I didn't hesitate. He'd never mentioned he was Jewish. He'd never mentioned that he'd spent most of the war in hiding. So I said: 'Yes, Betz was the name on our new papers, but I was born Joachim Lange. No doubt you had a new name too.' Then to my horror he answered: 'I didn't change my name till later. My name then was Goldfarb and I well remember the fuss when your mother refused to eat with Jews.'"

"Oh my God—"

"Well, he would have had no concrete proof if I'd later denied the story, but of course his word would have been enough to the Nazi-hunters. They'd have unmasked me to my Jewish friends and colleagues without any hesitation at all, and we both knew that."

"But how in God's name did it all end?"

"I wound up paying him for three years. That was an additional source of stress and the whole disaster made a big dent in my capital, which is the real reason why I don't have as much money today as I should have. But finally, just when I was at my wits' end, he fell under a train—and before you start to remember your favourite Hitchcock movies, let me assure you that I was in a meeting with eight other people at the time he died, and he wasn't murdered anyway; numerous witnesses saw him fling himself onto the line. It turned out his mistress had just ditched him."

"Did the police—"

"Yes, they did question me as I had an appointment with him later that day, but I just said he was a business acquaintance."

"You didn't tell them about—"

"No, of course not, and as the death was a suicide there was no need for them to pry into his financial affairs once they found out about the mistress."

"But Kim..." I was so shattered by this time that I had to struggle to find the right words. "With that kind of incident in your past, why on earth did you disclose the truth about your early life to Mrs. Mayfield and make yourself vulnerable all over again?"

"I told you. I had to talk to someone. And I trusted Mrs. Mayfield."

"But that group—"

"I wasn't worried about the members because she controlled them, and as we all made disclosures to each other in the name of group therapy we knew nobody would break ranks for fear of reprisals."

"But what happens if you now refuse to rejoin the group? Look how Mandy spewed out your secret when she knew I was listening in!"

"She'll claim she had no idea you could hear what was being said, but don't worry about Mandy, I'll fix her. I'll talk to Mrs. Mayfield."

"I don't want you talking to Mrs. Mayfield!" I cried, unable to control myself any longer, and running all the way down the corridor to the bedroom I shed my robe and took refuge beneath the duvet.

I was dry-eyed but aching with tension. Curling myself into a foetal ball I pulled the duvet over my head and shuddered in the darkness.

He slid into bed beside me. He too had shed his robe, and when he pulled me into his arms I uncurled myself and pressed my face against his chest, a move I often made when I wanted to escape deep feelings of insecurity. But this time the insecurity stayed with me. I rubbed my clammy palms against his dry back and drew his face to mine so that I could blot out the horror by kissing him, but I was too aware of his unshaved skin and the repellent reek of brandy.

I drew back.

"My darling," he said, "sweetheart—"

Shoving the duvet aside I sat up. "Let's get dressed," I said abruptly. "Let's get everything under control. *Let's get ourselves in order.*"

He laughed and pulled me back on the pillows. "You sound like a German!" he said amused, trying to kiss me, but again I drew back.

Violently I said: "What I can't stand here is you being so damn casual and jokey. I was okay when you were talking of your parents and your researches and the sheer bloody hell you went through trying to come to terms with the past. You were real then. But once you started talking about Mrs. Mayfield you seemed to become someone phoney, someone I don't know, someone—"

"I'm sorry. I was only trying to—"

"How *could* you talk of being blackmailed as if it were a mere passing inconvenience? How *could* you try and gloss over it as if—"

"I was only trying to spare you from the full horror of it all. You'd already had to absorb so much."

"That's patronising. I'm the one who decides how much I can or can't absorb. I don't need you making that kind of decision for me."

"Okay, but—"

"I want you to be genuine, I want you to be truthful! How else can I trust you and feel secure?"

"I understand. Yes, of course. Look, I only went for the gloss when I saw you were becoming upset—"

"Okay, we got our wires crossed, but now be honest and answer me this: why didn't you go to the police?"

"I didn't trust them."

I stared at him. "You think all coppers are bent?"

"No, of course not. But I didn't trust them not to remember the Blitz."

"*The Blitz?*"

"Okay, I go to the police. I say: 'Excuse me, I'm the son of a Nazi and I'm in a real jam because—'"

"But none of the police today would have been old enough to have fought in the war!"

"You think the British don't remember? My God, haven't you been reading the papers properly this month? Was mad cow disease the only news item which got through to you?"

"Oh, you mean—"

"I mean there's a big debate coming up in the House of Lords on the issue of whether or not old Nazis living in England should be prosecuted for their war crimes, so don't try and tell me the war's a dead issue!"

"Okay, I concede the wrinklies still bang on about it, but I for one don't spend my time thinking about—"

"You don't spend your time thinking about anything except your job!"

"That's a bloody awful thing to say!"

"You told me to be truthful!"

I tried to hit him but he grabbed my wrist and swung his body on top of me. I struggled but it was useless. He was too heavy, too strong.

When I was still he said gently: "I love you, I'm sorry for everything, you've been wonderful... So we don't really have to quarrel now, do we?"

I shook my head, no longer able to speak, and allowed him to make love to me.

V

I thought all the drink would ensure that he stopped short of penetration, but he was fresh from several hours' sleep and charged up by all the black coffee. The act did not last long and he seemed neither to expect nor require a response, so I just lay there and waited for the ejaculation.

After we had showered and dressed he announced that protein was good for hangovers and embarked on producing a platter of ham and scrambled eggs. I ate a little to please him, and eventually he said: "Now I want you to promise me not to worry about Mrs. Mayfield. I can handle her."

"But if she wants to blackmail you—"

"I think the danger's more theoretical than real, and to be frank I'm more worried about Sophie continuing to pester you."

I was surprised what a relief it was to focus on

Sophie again, and as soon as I did focus on her I saw at last what had been going on.

"Of course!" I exclaimed. "Now I understand! What Sophie really wants to do is bust up our relationship by spilling the beans about your Nazi past—she thinks I'll be as incapable of handling that as she was!"

"Exactly. She's saying she wants to save you because I'm 'mixed up with the occult,' as she puts it so inaccurately, but in actual fact—"

"—in actual fact that's just her way of justifying her behaviour to herself when the bottom line is she's mad as hell at being junked for a younger woman and can't stand the thought of me being Mrs. Betz!"

"That makes sense, certainly."

"Well, I know everything now, don't I, so Sophie's automatically defused. Unless—" I stopped. I had remembered the fallen picture and my nightmare vision of Sophie trashing the flat.

"—unless she's got so hooked on revenge in her unbalanced state," said Kim, finishing the sentence for me, "that she'll want to continue giving you a hard time just for the hell of it."

I decided to talk to him about my nightmare vision.

VI

"No, no, no," said Kim reassuringly when I had finished. "That theory can't be right. How could she have got into the flat?"

"Well, she'd only need one key, wouldn't she, since the lobby door at podium level is always unlocked unless there's a temporary porter on duty. Maybe Mary Waters snitched your key and had it copied."

"*Mary?* You've got to be kidding!"

"Look, I know you won't hear a word against your devoted slave, but it's not impossible that she's sided with Sophie here, and if she has—"

"Sweetheart, you've let your passion for old movies get the better of you! It's only in old movies that the virgin secretary sublimates her love for her boss by siding with the spurned ex-wife against the blonde glamour-girl! In real life Mary just sees wives as patterns of information to be logged on the computer so that she can remind me when their birthdays come up, what their favourite flowers are, where they like to eat and whether or not they're allergic to choco-late—"

"I don't believe I'm hearing this. How many wives do you have and who's allergic to choco-late?"

We finally started to laugh.

Sick with relief I realised the crisis was on the wane.

VII

Before we left the subject of Sophie I said: "Maybe now's the time to get an answerphone. I would have insisted on one when she started calling again, but I didn't want you to know the trouble had recurred."

He hesitated fractionally but said: "Okay, let's do it but I still hate the thought of you being bothered by recorded messages."

"I understand why you disliked the idea of an answering machine when you wanted to stop

Sophie telling me the truth about your past, but now I know the whole truth that worry of yours no longer exists, does it?"

"True... But I still think the machine would only encourage her to annoy you."

"You can play back the tapes to save me from annoyance!" I glanced at my watch. "I've got to get going," I said, and at that point we parted, I leaving for the hairdresser, he promising to clear up the breakfast debris before putting in a couple of hours' work at the office.

Later, as my hair was being coaxed to the exact shade of muted gold which toned so perfectly with my austere office suits, I found it hard to decide which of the lacerating dialogues had undermined me most; my perspective was changing as my sodden brain dried out enough to process the information properly. Now the blackmail, though still a horrific story, seemed less important than the picture I had acquired of a disturbed, damaged man who had teetered on the brink of breakdown before reeling into the orbit of a fraudster. I did not want Kim to be disturbed and damaged. I wanted him to be hardheaded and tough-minded, absolutely in control of his life and his world. I wanted him to be the man I thought I had married.

I recalled the tormented ramblings, the driving obsessions, the weird metaphysical references to the Principalities and Powers of Darkness—even to demons—and as I instinctively recoiled from such abnormality, I was conscious of Mrs. Mayfield's name hanging over the whole mess like some monstrous moon shedding light on a blighted landscape from a black and blasted sky.

It was not until I was picking up my cleaning some time later that I began to feel unpleasantly bewildered. Surely I should have managed to uncover Kim's neurotic side before I married him? After all, I had done everything right. I had approached the marriage rationally and sensibly, even considering such essential details as his sperm-count. I had loved him, of course, but I had not been whirling around in a frenzy of romantic illusions, hell-bent on proving love was blind. I had analysed all his pros and cons— or so I had thought. I had talked to him, wined and dined with him, travelled with him, tried him out in bed and lived with him. Surely after fulfilling all these requirements, just as the modern dogmas demanded, I should not now be feeling gutted by a string of revelations which I had never in my wildest premarital dreams begun to imagine? My predicament baffled me. It was not at all in accordance with my life-plan.

Returning to the flat I hung up my clean suits and set off for the supermarket. In the garage I found the Mercedes gone, a fact which meant Kim had finished his overtime at Graf-Rosen and taken his picture to be reframed. It also meant that I was stuck with the Porsche, not the best car for doing the weekly shopping, but today I thought that was probably the least of my problems.

I felt unexpectedly nervous in the supermarket, but there was no sign of Sophie. The place was packed. I hated shopping on Saturday afternoons and felt furious with myself for wasting so much of the morning being hung over. Plunging into the heaving throng I tried to concentrate on filling the cart with the necessary items but eventually I found myself coming to a halt in one of the aisles like a train which had run out of steam. I gazed at the vast display of toilet rolls, all packaged in a variety of pastel shades. Did we need to stock up on lavatory paper? I could not remember, and for once I had made no list. I could remember only the morning's revelations.

But now I found myself approaching them from another angle. This was not a conscious decision. It was merely my trained legal mind kicking in to try to help me break out of the emotional roller-coaster I was riding. Recalling the crucial scenes as if Kim were my client, I realised that various questions were lining themselves up in my mind. They were: had this man still been lying at any point during the morning's conversations, and if so, what had the lie been and what had it meant? And even if there had been no more lies, had he in fact been telling the whole truth? Were there yet more dimensions to the truth waiting to be uncovered? And was there a subtext in all these revelations, meanings which were implied rather than openly expressed?

It was restful looking at the toilet rolls, assembled in their pretty colours. Selecting a four-pack I moved on slowly while my mind once more began to replay the morning's dialogues.

I reviewed the German reminiscences but decided they rang painfully true. I considered his compulsion to make amends to the Jews, but on this point I had found him wholly convincing. And as for all that obsessive research... I paused by the snack racks. Mountains of revolting junk food stretched down the aisle into the distance—but suddenly I was no longer seeing the garish packaging. A voice in my head was saying: "The

Nazi-hunters would know what his father had done and whether his father should have ended up at Nuremberg. Surely Kim could have adopted a pseudonym, concocted a cover story and tapped in to their information systems if he had really wanted to find out what had happened?"

However, even the Nazi-hunters could not know everything. Europe had been in chaos. Records had been destroyed. Probably many horror stories would never now be known.

I moved on, still thinking of Kim's father, and the next moment I was seeing the subtext of Kim's monologue about his parents. He had hated them. He had never actually said so, but every word he had spoken on the subject had revealed his anger and contempt.

This was chilling. I did not hate my own parents. I just had nothing to say to them. If I were to be informed that my mother was at death's door I would not exclaim: "Good news!" I would be on the next train to Newcastle to show her that although I was a rotten daughter in many ways I did care when the chips were down. I would go to see my father too in similar circumstances— after making sure the sob-story was not just a scam to extract money from me. But the only woman Kim had spoken of with warmth had been his nurse and the only man Kim had spoken of with respect had been his English stepfather—and even when Kim had been talking of Giles there had been a curious dearth of affectionate remarks.

Strange things could happen to children who were not loved properly when they were young. They could grow up emotionally stunted and not fit to become parents themselves, but on the other hand—and yes, thank God for the other hand—Kim had had his nurse caring for him until he was nearly five and he was obviously unstunted now in his love for me.

I moved slowly on around the supermarket.

In front of the meat cabinets I paused again, remembering Sophie, and it was then that I had my most horrific moment of the entire morning.

I had been operating all the time on the assumption that Sophie was emotionally disturbed and Kim was well-balanced. But supposing it was Kim who was nuts and Sophie who was sanity personified? And supposing Sophie's warning about "the occult" had been not an unconscious attempt to justify her stalking when her real motive was so far from benign, but instead a desperate effort to convince me that her concern was rooted in reason and good sense?

Aloud I said: "I've lost it. I'm fruity-loops." Various people turned to give me a quick glance but no one looked surprised. One met nutters in London all the time nowadays, particularly since the government had started closing down the mental hospitals.

Completing the shopping as quickly as possible I snaked back to Harvey Tower in the Porsche. The Mercedes was back in its slot, and when I called the flat from the lobby Kim came down to the car park to help me with the bags.

Later in the kitchen when we were unpacking he said startled: "Why have you bought bacon when we never eat it?"

"Oh, is it bacon? I thought it was ham."

"And why did you buy Special K instead of corn-flakes? And my God, are those *flowers* decorating the lavatory paper?"

I laughed at his expression but felt my eyes sting

with tears. Turning away at once I managed to say: "I was discombobulated."

He heard the catch in my voice. "Carter—"

"I'm all right," I insisted fiercely. I hated crying and firmly believed that crying in front of another person represented a loss of control which could only lead to disorder. Flaking out's for the fluffettes.

I heard him say gently: "I can't tell you how sorry I am. You've been so brave, so—"

"Can it." I tried to study the flowers on the borders of the lavatory paper, but when he touched me I hurtled into his arms and stuck there. His clasp tightened. For a while he said nothing, allowing me to recover my composure, but after I had raised my face to his he kissed me on the mouth and said: "I hate myself for upsetting you."

"It's okay, I've assimilated it all now." I kissed him back. He had shaved, the alcohol fumes had been vanquished; he was kissable. His eyes were a clear hot sexy blue. His dark hair was slightly ruffled by the exertion with the shopping bags, but that just made him look sexier. His minimal sideburns, the perfect shade of grey and immaculately trimmed, jacked up his good looks to film-star standards. He smelled strongly of aftershave, faintly of soap and alluringly of Macleans toothpaste, the peppermint kind which always made me salivate. The turgid memory of the morning's hung-over sex vanished. I wanted only to rip off his clothes, pin him down on the bed and ravish him.

But I didn't. I said instead: "Kim, there's one last thing I want to say about this morning's revelations."

"Sure! If there's anything more you want to ask—"

"I want you to listen—and make sure you listen well." Stepping backwards away from him I put the box of Special K away in the storecupboard. That gave me additional time to psych myself up. Then I said: "I love you and I truly sympathise with you over all those past traumas. But I too have my past traumas and this means there could be a serious problem for us in future unless you recognise that I can't stand being lied to by someone I love. Silly of me, isn't it, to be so influenced still by the fact that my father's lies destroyed my trust in him, but there we are, that's life, and I suspect a lot of us are stupid in some way or other as the result of being booted around by a loved one when we were small." I began to open a packet of biscuits with a steady hand to demonstrate how calm I was. "Well," I said, pulling out a stick of shortbread, "I've nothing else to say except that if you've got any further confessions to make I'll hear them now, if you don't mind, and not later as the result of further chats with Mandy Simmons."

There was a silence. I bit into the shortbread and chewed quietly while I watched the electric clock marking the seconds as it hung on the wall nearby.

At last Kim said: "I couldn't have done that better myself!" He sounded both amused and admiring.

"What do you mean?"

"Well, the speech had to be made, didn't it? Although for a moment I thought you were going to flunk it in favour of sex."

"Was that what you intended when you kissed me?"

"I kissed you because you were looking like a million dollars after your visit to the hairdresser—naturally I wanted to seduce you rather than listen to you! What kind of a husband do you think I am?"

"A master of the delaying tactic." I looked him straight in the eyes. "Can I have your response now, please, to the issue I've just raised?"

"Message received and understood."

"Any further confessions?"

"None."

"Are you sure?"

"You have a confession in mind?"

"Just a question. Why didn't you go to the Nazi-hunters to find out what your father had done?"

"I'd have thought that was obvious. I didn't seek their help because I was terrified they would check any cover story I chose to use and find out who I was. And because I was sure I'd be able to uncover the facts for myself. And because I was ashamed, because I felt guilty, because I was horribly and hopelessly hung up over the whole bloody mess."

There was another pause before I said abruptly: "Thank you. I'm sorry, but I had to know." Closing the packet of shortbread I put it away alongside the Special K, and as I did so he ran a finger lightly down my spine.

"Do I get to seduce you now?"

"No," I said. "I get to seduce you."

He laughed.

We went to bed.

129

Afterwards as I lay in his arms I felt faint with relief. The crisis had finally been surmounted and the marriage was now in apple-pie order again ...
   Or was it?

FIVE

It is probable that in practice the religion of many in our society could be described as a form of polytheism: there are many shifting objects of esteem and desire, many beliefs, many "gods" demanding "worship" in explicit or implicit forms, and time and energy are divided among these "cults"... Even a claim to impartiality, neutrality or flexibility in the face of religious options is itself a definite and controversial option. The great questions about life-shaping truth, beauty and practice do not allow for neutral treatments. Everybody stands somewhere!

D A V I D   F.   F O R D
The Shape of Living

I

"I trust it's permissible for me to express the hope, Ms. Graham," said Tucker on Monday morning, "that the dinner-party was a success?"
   "Tucker, you're beginning to sound exactly like

130

Bunter the Valet in those televised Lord Peter Wimsey mysteries!"

"Thank you, ma'am. May I reassure you that you sound nothing like Lord Peter?"

"How sweet of you to think I need reassuring—but what I really need is the chance to thank you for producing that white rabbit out of your hat. The party was a big success."

"Good food?"

"To swoon for. By the way, what's the story on that slimline number called Darrow who picked Alice up afterwards?"

"He's the Rector of St. Benet's-by-the-Wall in Egg Street."

"Ah, one of those City churches! I thought English Heritage just kept them open for their architecture... Hey, how did you and Alice meet?"

"Through mutual acquaintances. My brother knows Nick Darrow."

"How original to know a clergyman! You don't see many of them around these days, do you?"

"That's because most of them choose not to wear their dog-collars outside their churches."

"But that's cheating!"

"Do doctors wear white coats outside their hospitals?"

"But are you saying there's a whole secret army of clergymen out there and no one knows who they are?"

"Maybe you should write to *The Times*, ma'am, and suggest that they should be electronically tagged. It might make you feel the situation was less alarming."

"Why can't they just wear their dog-collars? Oh, and talking of alarming situations, what's the latest news from Beijing?"

With sighs we abandoned our now well-established routine of swapping quips while remaining poker-faced, and settled down to yet another day of routine legal mayhem.

II

The week wore on in unremarkable fashion, by which I mean there were no more crises, panics, balls-ups and melt-downs than usual at the office while at home I found that Kim and I had slipped back into our former ease with each other. On Monday and Tuesday night he had to work late but I did not mind that as I felt I needed a touch of solitude to complete my recovery. On Wednesday and Thursday we were very cosy and watched videos of old Hitchcock movies. Kim liked Hitchcock's work almost as much as I did. We debated whether James Stewart was a better leading man than Cary Grant and which one of them should have replaced Sean Connery in *Marnie*.

Tucker bought an answerphone for me but Sophie never called and the supermarket remained a Sophie-free zone. There was no further word from Mandy Simmons. I began to feel very much better.

On Friday morning I said to Kim as he ate his Special K: "I'll be back late tonight. The time's come to make Tucker a permanent fixture at Curtis, Towers so I'm going to make him an offer he can't refuse."

"Lucky man!" commented Kim drily, setting aside his empty cereal bowl. "But I'm not sure I approve of you having a heterosexual PA."

"I'm not sure I approve of you having one either."

132

"Well, if you're quite sure he's not going to be trouble—"

"I can handle Tucker. He respects the boundaries."

"Just make sure Jacqui doesn't sue you for wrongful dismissal!"

"Relax—another partner wants her! I plan to have her moved sideways with a pay increase."

"Fixer!"

We kissed and he departed for his office in Moorgate, five minutes' walk away.

I hurried away shortly afterwards. I was much looking forward to propositioning Tucker.

III

"Tucker," I said half an hour later at the office, "as this is the last day of your assignment I intend to take you out for a drink tonight. Please don't even think of refusing."

"Thank you, ma'am. You'll be relieved to hear that the idea of refusing a drink is one which never normally crosses my mind."

Tucker was wearing a navy-blue suit, the one which fitted better than his charcoal-grey or black outfits, and yet another of his office-serf ties which looked as if they had been designed by a dozy robot. His black shoes were shining. His socks were dark and sedate. His forearms, which had given rise to such animated speculation in the ladies' loo, were as usual chastely swathed in virgin white. I wondered if I was beginning to resemble one of those fabled Victorian gentlemen who vibrated with lust at the thought of an exposed feminine ankle.

I took Tucker to the Lord Mayor's Cat, a

wine bar which specialised in champagne. Folded into one of those alleys between Cornhill and Lombard Street east of Bank, it was a dark, antiquated establishment, only partially modernised, which had somehow survived the German bombs. Its recent metamorphosis from a pub to a wine bar had been marked by a change of name and a new signboard which hung low over the entrance. The picture on the board showed that famous medieval Lord Mayor of London, Dick Whittington, with his equally famous feline friend; the cat, firmly in the foreground of the painting, was standing on his booted hind legs and clasping a bottle of champagne to his furry bosom.

Inside I elbowed my way through the yuppies at the bar and found the booth which the landlord had reserved for me in the back room. The landlord himself quickly appeared, giving us the red-carpet treatment and enquiring what we wanted to drink.

"Bring us two tankards of the Widow, maximum bubbles, minimum froth, and cold enough to chill hell," I said. That took care of the order, and if Tucker disliked Veuve Clicquot that was just too bad.

As soon as our drinks arrived I terminated the chitchat and got down to business.

"Let me be quite frank with you," I said, "and say that you're the best PA I've ever had. Now that we're out of the office and your assignment is finished I feel free to apologise for all the feminist chill, but the truth is a woman in my position can't be too careful and I always had to bear in mind the possibility that you might be a tiger-thumper."

"How thrilling! What's that?"

"A woman-hater who likes to sabotage female executives, and it's not a thrill, it's a bore. Now Tucker, because you've proved you're not a tiger-thumper, I want to make you an offer. In fact I want to play you the financial music of the spheres, I want to make you a proposition that'll blow your socks off, I want—"

I told him what I wanted. He looked at me with his bright dark eyes and an expression of deep concentration, as if he were memorising every word I said in order to record it later for posterity. I began to feel like Dr. Johnson in the presence of Boswell. Then I began to feel like Queen Victoria in the presence of Disraeli, that charming and cunning political operator who knew exactly how to deal with powerful women. But finally I began to feel like a leopard advancing on a tourist who breathed: "What a pretty pussy-cat!" before running a mile in the opposite direction.

Breaking off in the middle of outlining the bonus scheme for employees I said abruptly: "Okay, your socks are still glued to your feet and you're waiting for me to shut up so that you can kick my proposal in the teeth. But before you boot it over the Bank of England, just tell me this: have you secretly hated every minute of the last two weeks?"

"Absolutely not!" He looked shocked.

"Is the problem in any way connected with gender?"

"In no way at all!" He cleared his throat. "It's been most interesting to observe you at close quarters. I don't often meet someone of your particular talents, so I've regarded this assignment as a valuable learning curve."

The odd part was that although these words

sounded as if he might be mocking me he spoke so earnestly that I had no trouble believing he was sincere. But what did this mean? What kind of oddball liked to observe people at close quarters and classify the experience as a valuable learning curve? I wondered in alarm if he was about to be unmasked as a kinky voyeur.

"Okay," I said tersely, "it's cards-on-the-table time. Just who are you, Tucker, and how did you come to wind up in my office?"

"May I respond first of all to your extremely kind, flattering and generous offer of a permanent job?"

"You've already done so by not rolling over in ecstasy, waving all four paws in the air and waiting for me to tickle your chest."

"On second thoughts maybe I'll accept the offer after all. I rather like the idea of—"

"Oh no, you don't!"

"Okay, forget the chest-tickling. The truth is, Ms. G, that I'm not in the market for a permanent job. I just use my office skills to boost my income when my real work doesn't bring in enough money."

"What's your real work?"

"I'm a novelist."

"A *novelist*?" I could hardly have sounded more horrified if he had confessed to being an undertaker.

"You must have heard of novelists! They're the nutters who shut themselves up in solitary confinement for pleasure!"

"But are you published?"

"Yes, I've had a couple of WWII novels accepted."

"Double-you double-you—"

"That's what the Americans call the Second World War. WWII novels are a subdivision of the Adventure Genre, and all novelists who don't earn millions have to submit work which can be placed in an accepted category for marketing purposes."

"What name do you write under?"

He told me.

"I don't recall seeing—"

"No, you wouldn't have come across my books. They have a short shelf-life because I'm not in the big time."

"But of course you'll make it big eventually!"

"All I hope for," said Tucker, "is to improve. Very few novelists write anything worthwhile before they're forty. I'm thirty-five. I'm learning all the time and working whenever I can and one day, I hope, I'll be able to write something worthwhile, but in the meantime—"

"—in the meantime you have to wait for the megabucks, yes, I see. But later there'll be the Aston Martin and the trophy wife and the manor house in the Cotswolds and the villa in Chiantishire and—"

"I'm not interested in all that."

"Don't be funny, of course you are! You must be!"

"No, I assure you that my idea of success has nothing to do with wealth and status symbols."

I stared at him. "I don't get it. Why not?"

"I don't think they have much to do with reality."

I boggled. "But Tucker, you can't just sit here in the heart of the City of London, where wealth and status symbols are worshipped as gods, and voice those kinds of sentiments! I mean, this is very subversive propaganda you're spouting, it's quite contrary to mainstream thinking, it's in total defiance of the *Zeitgeist*!"

"Ah, I'm a real fifth columnist, aren't I, Ms. G!" said Tucker amused. "Little did you think, when you invited me out for a drink tonight, that you'd be socialising with an anarchist—or as they used to say in the war, flirting with the enemy!"

I knocked my tankard clean off the table.

IV

"God, I can't believe I did that!"

"Hang on, let's grab a waiter—"

"Jesus, my new suit!"

"Hey, could we have help here, please?"

A cloth arrived. So did Mine Host, tut-tutting and wringing his hands sympathetically as he supervised the mopping-up operation.

"More fizz for the lady, please," said Tucker, suddenly becoming an assertive male instead of a docile faux-eunuch, and added to me as Mine Host zipped off and the waiter withdrew with the cloth: "Do you usually jump as if electrocuted after half a tankard of Veuve Clicquot?"

"Not normally, no, I just felt skittish. Where were we?"

"We'd just established that we worshipped different gods."

"I don't worship anything," I said, patting a stray strand of hair back into place and smoothing my sodden skirt. "I'm ideologically neutral."

"I doubt if that's either ontologically or epistemologically possible."

I forgot my ruined suit. "Huh?"

"I doubt if it's possible to have a mode of

being which is ideologically neutral, and I doubt too if such a concept is recognised as valid by any modern theory of knowledge. No judgement is value-free."

I blinked. "I'm sorry, but could you just run all that past me again?"

He repeated the sentences before explaining: "It's impossible to step completely outside the influences of one's culture, environment, genes and upbringing to adopt a stance which could accurately be described as neutral. In other words we all subscribe, either consciously or unconsciously, to ideologies and religions, even though we may not always recognise them as such."

"But I'm not religious! I not only don't believe but I just don't care—I can get along fine without any kind of god or religion!"

Mine Host arrived with another foaming tankard of Veuve Clicquot.

"Let's keep our consumption equal," I said to Tucker as I poured him a share.

"Thanks. Ms. G, may I make a few observations based on my time spent working with you?"

"If I feature in your next novel I'll sue you."

"If you feature in my next novel you probably wouldn't recognise yourself. Look, you do have a religion, and I think you're deeply religious. Shall I tell you what your religion is?"

"The law."

"No, no, that's just the means you've chosen to achieve your ends. Your religion, Ms. G, is Order."

"Order?"

"Yes, that's the god you worship. That's what your life's about. You live in a chaotic jungle, the financial killing-fields of the City of London, but your whole life is dedicated to bringing Order out of chaos. You're like one of those nuns who fearlessly, day after day, brings Christ to the teeming hordes of Calcutta."

I started to laugh. "I've never heard such—"

"Wait, I haven't finished yet! Your devotion to Order was the first thing I noticed about you. Your appearance is immaculate. No hair is ever out of place. No skirt is ever creased. Your filing systems are things of rational, logical beauty. Your reports, your memoranda, your letters all shine with the most well-ordered intelligence. Your clients find you indestructibly well-organised and utterly in control—and that's what it's all about, isn't it? If you reduce chaos to order, you're in control. And how do you reduce chaos to order? You exercise your reason, your logic and your intelligence to make an enormous success of your profession. And what does this success generate? Money, power and status—but you don't want these things for the usual greedy, self-indulgent reasons, Ms. G, and that's what's so endearing about you; I think that deep down you're not a natural free-spender dedicated to conspicuous consumption—that's not your game at all. But money, power and status combine to give you a lot of control over your life, and the more control you have the easier it is for you to luxuriate in Order—to commune regularly with your god. Ah yes, Ms. G, never doubt that you're deeply religious! You go to worship every day for hours on end at your office, your Holy Trinity is money, power and status, and over and above your trinity is the godhead, Order, the ground of your being, the fount of all goodness, your *raison d'être*, your love, your life."

I swallowed some champagne. The bubbles danced in my throat. Finally I was able to remark coolly: "You're saying I'm fruity-loops."

"Not at all! I'm just saying that you're not ideologically neutral, and that far from having no need of a god you need Order as much as the very air you breathe. The really interesting question, of course, is why. Just what is it about this god of yours that has your soul enslaved?"

"But surely everyone likes order and having control over their lives?"

"On the contrary, a lot of people love a bit of chaos—they find it stimulating. And how far do we ever really have control over our lives, particularly when we get booted around by forces over which we have no power at all?"

I drank some more champagne. Or rather, I took several large gulps. "But some degree of organisation is always possible. If one draws up a life-plan—"

"A life-plan!"

"Provided one draws up a highly organised life-plan dictated by reason and logic," I insisted hotly as he started to laugh, "there's no reason why the future shouldn't be brought satisfactorily under control!"

"I concede we all need goals to aim for, but 'a highly organised life-plan dictated by reason and logic' is bound to get derailed eventually! The future's too unpredictable!"

"Not my future!"

"Ms. G, what are you so afraid of here? Why is your idea of hell a future open to change and chance and the unexpected—to innovation and creativity? By locking the door against any future you can't foresee you're restricting yourself intolerably, can't you see that? How on earth can God use you to play an exciting part in his creation if you just see creation as a big mess and refuse to come out of your immaculately well-ordered shell?"

By this time I was actively guzzling my champagne. When I came up for air I said: "This conversation's way out of control!"

He laughed. "No, the control's all here but I'm exercising it, not you—and I bet that was a future you didn't predict when you invited me for a drink this evening!" He drank too before adding briskly: "Okay, so much for religion. Now, Ms. G, before we go any further I yearn to satisfy a burning curiosity. Will you slap my face if I ask you a personal question?"

"I think I can just about control my itching fingers."

"Then I'll chance it, here goes: no British parents ever called their daughter Carter. What's your real name?"

Regarding my fingers with interest to see if they developed a life and will of their own, I said flatly: "Catriona."

"But that's pretty! Why don't you use it?"

I curled my fingers into the palms of my hands and thumped my right fist hard on the table. "*You* just try using it!" I hissed. "You just try! You'll find that in no time at all you'll get called Cat or Catty or Kitty or Kit-Kat or even—*even*"— I sucked in my breath before spitting out the syllables—"*Pussykins*. Finally I rearranged the letters and came up with CARTA. I adopted a more familiar spelling for the sake of convenience."

"But 'Catriona Graham' sounds so attractive—like the heroine of a gothic novel—"

"—which was exactly why I flushed it down the john. I was pissed off with being an underrated fluffette... What do you think of your own name?"

"I'm better off than my brothers."

"What names did they get lumbered with?"

"Athelstan and Gilbert. As my father's a professor of early English history, he couldn't resist naming Athel for the Saxons, Gil for the Normans and me for the Vikings."

"Did your mother have no say in these brutal decisions?"

"She was supposed to name the daughters but she never had any."

"God, how women get short-changed! What do these brothers of yours do?"

"Athel's an accountant, married with three kids and living near my parents in Winchester; he's spent a lifetime rebelling against that name by being as conventional as possible. In contrast Gil's a gay activist."

"Help!"

"You're anti-gay?"

"No, no—I've just never been able to see the point of homosexuality, that's all. I mean, it's never been on my list of things to do. I mean—"

"You mean you're heterosexual."

"Yes, but—"

"—you don't want me to think you're a queer-basher. Quite. I'm not anti-gay either, but activists of any sort always drive me bananas and sometimes after a row with Gil I feel like the worst homophobe in town... Do you have brothers?"

"Just two much younger half-sisters." I told him briefly about my family. Then the conversation changed course again, zig-zagging in and out of our life-histories and spinning off at various tangents as if we were engaged in an elaborate dance which we had to compose from an enormous variety of steps.

"Let's have some more fizz," said Tucker. "My round this time, but I'll let you order because I want to write down the wording you used. I might put it in a book one day."

So I said to the waiter: "Two more tankards of the Widow, please—maximum bubbles, minimum froth and cold enough to chill hell," while Tucker scribbled in a notebook, and afterwards we snuffled and giggled like two teenagers and agreed what a relief it was that we no longer had to swap quips with straight faces in the name of office propriety.

"Tell me about this big jungle-cat you're married to," demanded Tucker when the champagne arrived. "The rumour mills at Curtis, Towers say he's some kind of American who's purred his way to power at a global investment bank."

"He's a British subject but you're right about him being a big cat. He's king of the legal jungle at Graf-Rosen... Are you married?"

"Not with my breadline income, no."

"You might have married a rich wife! No, wait a minute—if you had a rich wife, you wouldn't be hacking it in temporary work, would you?"

"Oh yes, I would! I'd never consent to being kept!"

"But have you never been married?"

"I've never been in a position to keep the kind of woman I like in the style to which she would long since have become accustomed."

"Well, of course if you just want some fluffette who expects to be feather-nested—"

"Not all women have your brains and earning capacity, Ms. G! Spare a thought for the weaker sisters who need plenty of male support when they're making a home and bringing up the kids!"

"Well, sure. But—"

"As a matter of fact I gave up fluffettes years ago."

"What do you chase now? Married sizzlerinas?"

"No, I've abandoned them too—although I must say I'm sometimes tempted to take them up again. What's left on the singles' shelf isn't so hot."

"God, that's a sexist remark!"

"Yes, isn't it? But I was suddenly overcome with the urge to dynamite all that cool control of yours and see you get wildly, heart-stoppingly angry—"

"Dream on, buster! Listen, how do you know so much about people?"

"I'm a novelist. People are my business."

"Yes, but to penetrate as far as you did just now when you were analysing me surely requires—"

"I'm into penetration."

"Tucker, I feel a slap coming on—"

"I feel all kinds of things coming on! Ms. G, if you weren't newly married and if I hadn't given up married sizzlerinas—"

"Every finger of my right hand is now flexed!"

"—but since you're still virtually on your honeymoon and I'm about to live a life of rigorous austerity in order to write my new WWII book—"

"I'm the ship you pass in the night, Tucker. No question about that."

"But such a ship! And such a night!"

"Cool it, fireball!" I knew then how right I had been to keep our relationship at the office within strictly formal limits. The trouble with men is that once you give them an inch they're panting all over everywhere. What can it be like to live with all those unpredictable surges of testosterone? No wonder boardroom debates are so often littered with impulsive judgements and rash decisions.

"Shall we go?" I suggested politely in my most businesslike voice, but I was unable to avoid a small sigh of reluctance.

"I think the question is can we stand."

"Perhaps we'd better pay the bill first."

"Good thinking. I always feel weak at the knees whenever I see a bill for champagne."

"You're not paying."

"Yes, I am!"

"Oh, don't be so macho, Tucker!"

"But you love it! You've no time for wimps, have you? You like backbone, you like balls, you like—"

"Okay, bring me the head of the waiter on a silver salver but make sure the bill's attached."

We continued to joust over the bill but finally agreed to split it fifty-fifty.

Then we floated outside into the golden light of that May evening.

V

"I'll walk you home," said my squire, resurrecting an era of feminist pre-history.

"No, this is 1990," I said. "I'll walk *you* home—or rather, to your tube station. Which one is it?"

"No tube, Ms. G! I too live in the City."

I was most surprised. The City is not primarily a residential area. "You live in the Barbican?" I said puzzled. The Barbican is a huge complex which contains over twenty blocks of flats as well as offices, schools and the Arts Centre, so it would have been quite possible for both of us to live there without encountering each other, but I thought it strange I had never seen him if for two weeks we had been pounding the same path to work.

"No, I live in Fleetside," he said. "My brother Gilbert, the gay activist, lets me have a room and bath on the top floor of his house there."

"Fleetside... I can't quite remember where—"

"It's one of those lanes off New Bridge Street between Ludgate Circus and the river."

I could not recall any houses in that area but my knowledge of the western reaches of the City was not as comprehensive as it might have been. I worked in the eastern reaches, lived on the northern boundary and seldom roamed west or south of St. Paul's.

We drifted down Cornhill to Bank, that throbbing heart of the City where several roads meet by the Bank of England, and crossed the junction into Queen Victoria Street. To escape the traffic fumes we eventually veered into the maze of streets south of the Cathedral before moving down into the valley where the Fleet River had once flowed above ground into the Thames. Neither of us was bothering to talk much by this time. Gliding along on our tide of champagne we savoured the warmth of the evening and occasionally exchanged idle remarks.

"Did Shana the Shag-Queen ever get you to expose your forearms?"

"Hell, she wanted me to expose a good deal more than that!"

"But you didn't."

"No, I'm allergic to silicone. What's all this about my forearms?"

"The fluffettes thought the skin there might decide whether you were a true redhead or just a brownhead with auburn aspirations."

"Well, I can tell you that I'm quite definitely not a redhead! I made up my mind about that at a very early age."

We reached New Bridge Street and paused to cross the road. To the right the traffic roared across Ludgate Circus and to our left the statue of Queen Victoria, another high flyer with a superb record of reducing the world to order, presided over the approach to Blackfriars Bridge.

"Do you ever expose your forearms in public, Tucker?"

"Why are you so mesmerised by these forearms of mine?"

"Well…always encased in those snow-white shirts…always so mysterious, so fascinating, so suggestive—"

"'Clothed in white samite, mystic, wonderful'?"

"How well you put it!"

"That wasn't me, that was Alfred, Lord Tennyson."

"Oh."

We reached the lane called Fleetside and immediately stepped out of the golden sunlight into deep shadow. Out-dated office buildings crying out for demolition rose on either side of us, and towards the end of this forlorn canyon stood a blackened Victorian church, probably some folly built by a religion-crazed City dignitary and long since closed. I was still gazing vaguely at the building when I noticed that next door there stood a house, a tall, dreary pile with steps which led up to the front door and railings which were set in the pavement above the basement. The house was the only one in the street.

"So this is where you hang out!" I exclaimed intrigued. "Your brother must be doing well if he can afford such a huge place!"

"It comes with the job."

"What job?"

"He's the vicar of St. Eadred's Fleetside."

I stopped dead. I was still staring at the house. I stared and stared until I realised I was staring at the plaque which proclaimed: "THE VICARAGE." Beyond the house the church now seemed to be towering aggressively over the narrow street.

"You look fascinated, Ms. G! Have you never seen a vicarage before?"

I turned to face him. I took a deep breath. And I finally managed to state the obvious. "You're a Christian."

"Yes, but don't let it bother you, I'm not a very good one yet."

"I suppose I'd already realised...you mentioned God earlier...when you were talking about..." My voice trailed away.

"When I was talking about embracing the chaos and living dynamically—yes, we had a great talk about our religions, didn't we? I enjoyed that. Hey, come on in and meet my brother!"

"Thanks, but I've got to be getting back," I said automatically. However, I was still so bemused that I stayed rooted to the spot. "How can a gay activist be a clergyman?" I asked. "Isn't that breaking the rules?"

"Well, Gil's certainly not the Bishop of London's favourite poodle, but he's a good priest and he believes in God, which is more than some of the Church of England's employees do these days, so the difficulty isn't as severe as you might think... Come on, change your mind—let me fix you some coffee!"

"No, I've really got to go—"

"You think Gil's going to do a Dracula and sink some fangs into your neck? Or are you just allergic to Christianity?"

"Of course not—on both counts! After all, everyone can believe what they like now, can't they, since absolute truth's been abolished and each truth's considered to be as valid as any other truth—"

"—as the trendy nihilist said, laughing all the way to the asylum! Okay, Ms. G, if the moment to part has finally arrived may I thank you for the champagne, the job offer and the raising of my masculine consciousness, and say how much I've enjoyed working with you?"

I at last succeeded in pulling myself together. Achieving my warmest smile I said graciously: "You may! Many thanks for all your help, and good luck with the new novel. May I sign off by finally using your first name?"

"Only if you'll allow me to do likewise! So long, Pussykins," he said poker-faced, and then ran laughing up the steps to the front door before I could leap forward to commit assault and battery.

VI

Having taken a cab from Fleetside I reached Harvey Tower and soared up to the thirty-fifth floor shortly before eight-thirty. The effects of the champagne were still so potent that I felt I hardly needed the help of the lift.

"I called up for a pizza," said Kim on my arrival, "when I discovered the fridge contained nothing but a dead radish."

"But I had a wonderful meal planned from the freezer!"

"Forget it, we're eating pizza. It's keeping warm in the oven."

I had to confess I was happy to abandon my plan to cook.

"So how was Tucker?"

"He turned me down."

"I don't believe it! He was trying to jack up the pay!"

"No, he's not interested in money."

"Everyone's interested in money! What is he, some kind of nutcase?"

"He's a novelist."

"Well, there you are. He's a nutcase."

"No, he's not! He's clever and amusing and tough and brave—it takes guts to fly in the face of convention!" I retorted hotly, still too spaced out to be as careful as I should have been when commenting on my heterosexual male office companion of the last two weeks.

Kim finished his Scotch and said in a voice designed to chill a boardroom: "What's so gutsy about being a failure and a drop-out?"

"He's not a failure and a drop-out! He's a damned good secretary and he's also a published novelist!"

"If he was any good as a novelist he wouldn't have to hire himself out as an office drone! What kind of a life does he have? What are his prospects?

And why are you getting so dewy-eyed all of a sudden about some guy who's obviously a natural-born loser?"

Automatically I reacted as I would have done if I had been attacked by a dinosaur at the office. The first stage always consisted of holding my ground and continuing to push my case in the firmest possible voice, but if this approach failed to work I moved with lightning speed into the second stage which I called "the slammer": I bawled the offender out as if I were a sergeant-major addressing a raw recruit on the parade ground. Men are usually so dumbfounded when a woman exhibits this kind of behaviour that they lose their momentum, and during this moment of stupefaction I can step in and gut them with a short, sharp, silken put-down. Some female high flyers, I know, like to turn on the tears in order to achieve this wrong-footing of the male aggressor, but I think they run too great a risk of being dubbed "hysterical"—the favourite word in the tiger-thumpers' vocabulary when dealing with a woman who gets the better of them.

Launching myself into stage one I held my ground and said politely but in the firmest possible voice: "Tucker doesn't see things the way we do because he marches to a different drum. He's a Christian."

"Ah well, that explains it—Christians invert everything! Success is failure and death is life and poverty is riches and—"

"Why have you suddenly got so hostile?"

"Maybe because I'm damned hungry and want to eat. Maybe because I'm pissed off because you've spent half the evening getting drunk with some jerk you obviously find cute. Maybe because—"

I wasted no more time but launched straight into the slammer. "You're being a real pain, Betz! Shape up, wise up and grow up, for God's sake, before someone gives you a one-way ticket back to kindergarten!"

"—maybe because I'm remembering that prophecy about flirting with the enemy!" Kim hurled back, not only outshouting me but slickly side-stepping my attack by ignoring it. "And maybe because I've just been having a meeting with Mrs. Mayfield!"

Wholly outflanked I slumped down on the stool by my telescope and listened to the shattering silence which followed.

VII

"Okay," said Kim abruptly at last. "We've had our spat. Let's eat."

"But Kim—"

"I said let's eat." He moved into the kitchen, took the pizza out of the oven and began to carve it up. As I joined him I was aware that my champagne high had vanished with the speed of Cinderella's coach at the stroke of midnight. I felt taut with shock.

"It's the pizza de luxe," said Kim, dissecting the pizza with surgical precision. "I ordered extra mushrooms for your half and extra salami for mine."

Managing to keep my voice level I said: "If you were lodging a complaint against Mandy Simmons, why couldn't you just ring up?"

"I want five minutes of absolute quiet while I eat this."

"But—"

153

"Five minutes. Absolute silence. Or I'm going to start getting really angry."

I knew I had to take a stand. There was no choice. This was a crucial moment in our relationship because if I gave way to him this time there would be other times, each one more serious than the last. "I'm sorry," I said, perfectly polite though using my hardest voice, "but I'm not going to stand for being bossed around like that in my own home."

"I'll do what I damn well like! It's my home too!"

"Not legally."

He went white. I myself was white already but with fright, not rage. We froze, each willing the other to back down, until finally he exclaimed: "Well, *shit*!" and flung the dirty carving knife on the carpet so violently that it pierced the pile and rang out on the concrete below.

Once more I cannoned into the slammer. "Shut up!" I yelled. "Knock it off! I don't take violence, verbal or physical, from any man, so don't even think of carrying this bloody unpleasant behaviour any further! And now I'll give you your five minutes of absolute silence—I'll give you five minutes to calm down, unscramble your brains and get your act together before I boot you out into the street!" Then I walked to the door before turning to gut him with the short, sharp, silken put-down. "There's no room in this home, I assure you," I said, "for the spirit which built the Third Reich."

I walked out. In the passage I stumbled but righted myself. On reaching the bedroom I went out onto the balcony and stood taking huge gulps of air while the cold sweat trickled down my spine and the unshed tears burned my eyes.

He arrived exactly five minutes later with a slice of pizza wrapped in a strip of paper towel. "I've brought you a peace offering," he said.

"I'm not hungry."

"Ah, come on, sweetheart, give me a break! I'm sorry—very sorry—that I upset you."

"That sounds more like a sentence I can get along with." I took the slice and nibbled the thin end.

"It's cold out here," he said. "Let's go in. I'll bring the pizza into the bedroom so that we can have a picnic."

We retired indoors. The pizza was good but I found I was still unable to do more than pretend to eat. My stomach had started to hurt, reacting to the extreme tension. In the end I abandoned my slice and just drank the Evian water which Kim had brought from the kitchen.

Eventually I said: "I apologise for that remark about the Third Reich."

"You were upset. I'd upset you. Let's just draw a line beneath the entire scene and move on."

I nodded thankfully, not looking at him. I did not want him to see the tears which had sprung back into my eyes.

Soon after that he returned to the kitchen to make coffee, and later, when we were sitting together on the sofa with the steaming mugs in our hands, I at last began to relax.

But I knew my relaxation was premature. I had yet to hear about his meeting with Mrs. Mayfield.

SIX

Communication in intimacy takes on a great urgency and even risk. When and how should I say what I feel? What questions should I ask? What are the limits, in physical or emotional intimacy, or in commitment? What should be shared with others? But surrounding and underlying all those is the central mystery of the other person and what is happening between us.

DAVID F. FORD
The Shape of Living

I

"I called her earlier this week," Kim said when I eventually nerved myself to reintroduce the subject of Mrs. Mayfield. "She was very apologetic when I told her about Mandy's disastrous phone call. She did admit, though, that she'd asked Mandy and Steve to make a special effort to lure me back into the group, and that was when I realised I had to set up a face-to-face meeting with her."

"I still don't see why!"

"But you must know how it is when one's trying to brush people off—personal contact can be vital in ensuring a permanent parting with no unpleasant consequences!"

"Well yes, but—"

"Anyway to butter her up I bought her a couple of drinks in that rooftop cocktail lounge

156

of the Park Lane Hilton. She likes that sort of place."

"And?"

"I managed to persuade her that it was pointless for me to keep on with the group when I finally had my life in order and didn't need therapy any more. We did argue about whether I had my life in order, but I got her to concede group therapy wasn't now necessary. So that's the first step accomplished. The second step is to part from Mrs. Mayfield herself, and that'll take longer, but I'll get there in the end."

"Are you telling me you're planning to see her again?"

"Just once a month, yes. Okay, I know that's not the news you want to hear, but—"

I decided to smother my anger. I was feeling too emotionally bruised to do otherwise, and besides, I thought I should recognise he was doing his best to dislodge these parasites who were clinging to him. "At least you've succeeded in ditching the group," I said, trying to be supportive, but I was unable to stop myself adding: "When are you seeing Mrs. Mayfield again?"

"Soon, but the next meeting's got nothing to do with the monthly sessions—she suggested I come to the Simmonses' flat this coming Tuesday in order to say goodbye to the group. It'll be a brief visit, but Mrs. Mayfield thought it was important that my association with the group should end on a friendly note."

"Uh-huh." Moving to the stool I began to peer through my telescope at the multiple patterns of light beyond the window.

"Carter?" I was aware that he too was leaving the couch, and as his fingers brushed my shoulder

I knew he was inviting me to be honest with him.

Taking a deep breath I demanded: "Why didn't you tell me earlier that you were seeing her tonight? And why didn't you even tell me you'd spoken to her earlier this week to complain about Mandy Simmons?"

"I didn't want to upset you. After that scene last Saturday when I had to talk about my past—"

"I appreciate your concern," I said carefully. "Thank you. But as I've already said, the best way forward is not to wrap me in clingfilm to protect me from your problems, but to share them with me so that I can give you the proper support. To be frank, I hate the idea of you going back to that group for even a farewell visit, and I hate the idea of you continuing to see that woman for even a single session, but I do understand that the kid-glove treatment is the way to go in this case, so you mustn't think I'm not willing to back you up... Did Mrs. Mayfield ask after me?"

"Yes, she did." He moved away again, picking up his coffee-mug and sitting on the arm of the sofa. "She asked if you'd been flirting with the enemy."

"Bloody hell!"

"Forget it," he said drily. "The flirting's finished, hasn't it? You're not seeing Tucker again."

"Right." I swivelled back on my stool to face the telescope and took another look through the lens.

"You didn't really find him attractive, did you?"

For the second time I found the telescope had to be abandoned. "Kim, why are you suddenly behaving like someone who's insecure with women?"

"I'm not! It's just that you're my wife and I'm not about to tolerate some smart-aleck no-hoper sashaying around on my territory!"

In a moment of revelation I suddenly saw how Mrs. Mayfield was undermining our marriage. First she had told Kim, who respected her opinions, that I was the wrong wife for him. Then she had thrown out a prediction about my future conduct which had made him anxious. And finally, now that her prediction had by sheer bad luck come true, she was twisting the knife by reminding him of her warning and encouraging the anxiety in his mind to mutate into anger and suspicion.

I was appalled, but I realised at once where the best course of action lay. Moving to the sofa I gently transferred his coffee-mug from his hand to the table and then gave him the steamiest of kisses before murmuring in an amused voice: "Darling, Tucker's in love with his pen, not his penis—the entire relationship was platonic from start to finish, I promise you!"

Kim somehow avoided sagging with relief, and we wandered off to share a shower.

But I did not care for the way he had tried to trash Tucker.

I did not care for it at all.

II

Some time later, during a leisurely moment in our intimacy, he said suddenly: "You were terrific tonight."

I was startled, not so much by the words themselves but by the fact that I had misread his reason for pausing. I thought he had been concentrating on holding back. I had been motionless, not wishing to trigger any abrupt ending, but as soon as he spoke I knew the pause had nothing to do with any concern about control. It was as if now that he was indisputably the man in possession he had paused to reflect on his conquest with satisfaction and pay the appropriate compliment. At the same time I could not help but think the compliment was odd. What had I done that was so terrific? As far as I could see I had merely survived a fearful marital row.

"Terrific?" I repeated mildly, glad I did not have to be motionless any longer; I shifted fractionally beneath him.

At once he shoved himself all the way into me and cut off my gasp by kissing me hard on the mouth. "Yeah," he said, finally lifting his face from mine. "Terrific." Unexpectedly he laughed and released me. I felt him slide out as he let his left hand trail down my body. "Hey," he said, "let's do this a little differently," and the next moment his left arm had slipped around my body to flip me over onto my side so that I had my back to him.

"Wait a minute," I said quickly, "what—"

"Relax!" he said at once. "Same destination."

"Oh, fine..." But for some reason I felt ill at ease. It occurred to me that perhaps I was not finding it so easy to slough off the memory of that fraught conversation earlier. I had been keen to make love but I had visualised the reconciliation as a brisk blast of passion which knocked all the painful memories flat, not as a lengthy, leisurely coupling which seemed to imply our row had never taken place.

"You're really turned on, aren't you?" I said lightly when he slid out again and flipped me onto my back before returning by the familiar route. "This may seem a dumb question, but what exactly did I do to pull the switch?"

He did not answer. He was busy rolling us both over so that I ended up on top and he could relax against the pillows. He was still so revved up that the angle of the connection was now awkward for me. I bent over, trying to get comfortable and not altogether succeeding. "Kim?"

"Yeah."

"Tell me."

"Later," he said, and spun out the intercourse for a long time from a variety of different positions.

III

My bewilderment created tension when I least wanted it, and the tension exacerbated the discomfort where I least needed it. This was deeply frustrating; I felt my body was letting me down, but in fact, as I now realise, my body was faithfully transmitting the message that all was not emotionally well. In the end I faked the orgasm to try to encourage him to finish, but he took no notice—or at least he paused to allow me to go to the lavatory but then resumed as if nothing had happened. By this time I was more than confused and uncomfortable. I was unnerved. I had become accustomed to intercourse which was passionate and not infrequent but also straightforward and seldom prolonged. I always found this comforting and occasionally I found it satisfying. Certainly I was not discontented, and I often reflected how well Kim suited me. If we were now, for no apparent reason, embarking on a more extensive form of intimacy, I was delighted to match the different pace he was setting, but did this exciting new development mean he had been secretly bored for months? Why had he resisted turning up the heat before? And why had he suddenly changed?

The change was in no way frightening. No nasty practice oozed out of the closet, and the shark, who had appeared during our searing row, had quite vanished. I was playing with the dolphin again, and this time the dolphin was more affectionate and friendly than he had ever been before—and more gentle too when it was all over and he could stroke my hair and kiss my cheek before enfolding me in his arms. If I had not been so baffled—and so worried that he might have found our previous sexual relationship inadequate—I would have been very happy indeed.

Later when we were drinking Evian water to quench our thirst he said: "You're perfect. I'm so lucky."

I kissed him and responded with similar compliments before I was finally able to ask: "Why have you never made love to me like that before?"

"Maybe it required a special set of circumstances... God, that was one hell of a row we had earlier!"

"You're not saying—" I broke off.

"No, I'm not saying I enjoyed the row! But it gave me such a charge to see you punch your way out of that tight corner!"

I was astounded. "Well, I hope you're not looking forward to further rows in the same style!"

"No, but I just love it when you act tough!"

I could not help saying: "Most men don't."

"Most men are wimps," he said with contempt, and turned out the bedside light with a yawn of contentment.

So one of us at least had converted the evening's nightmare into a positive experience. But I was left feeling more puzzled than ever.

I felt I had understood nothing.

IV

The next morning at breakfast I felt driven to mention my bewilderment to him, and at once he moved to reassure me. "Look," he said, "don't start thinking that the sex up till now has been somehow insincere on my part just because I chose to keep things basic! I've always enjoyed myself in bed with you, but to tell the truth I found last year so stressful, thanks to the divorce and the job change, that I didn't feel up to being more than basic anyway—so the no-frills sex suited me as much as I was sure it suited you."

"But why were you so sure it suited me?"

"Well, you told me your previous lover had made himself very unwelcome in that department when the relationship was going to pieces, so naturally I was anxious to give you all the time you needed to readjust."

"Ah, I see!" I said, much relieved by the simplicity of this explanation, but then I became conscious of its implausibility. "But we've been sleeping together for nearly eighteen months," I said, trying to keep my voice casual. "Wasn't that rather a long time to wait before you cast your worries about me aside?"

"I guess I was scared of alienating you by

making a wrong move. I felt I had to wait until you demonstrated that you were finally able to be yourself with me—and that moment finally came during the row last night."

I stared at him. "But that wasn't me at all! That was just me playing the high flyer in order to survive!"

"Well, whatever you were doing you were great." He pushed away his empty cereal bowl, drank some coffee and glanced at his watch. "I must get going."

"But Kim—"

"What is it, sweetheart? You're not still feeling muddled, are you?"

"Not exactly, but...well, you're very confident and experienced, aren't you, and it must have been obvious that I'd consigned my previous affair to history within days of our first meeting. So why on earth should you have been scared of alienating me by making a wrong move?"

"You were just so special," he said, "that I was willing to go to any lengths to avoid losing you." But even before he had completed this glib explanation the penny had dropped.

"My God!" I exclaimed in horror. "This was another of Mrs. Mayfield's prophecies, wasn't it? She not only said you were marrying the wrong woman—she told you our sex-life would go down the drain!"

I saw him decide that denial was not a viable response. With a shrug of his shoulders he said: "I admit she forecast sexual trouble, but surely all that matters now is that we've proved her wrong?"

"I'd like to shoot that old bat from six different positions! What exactly did she say?"

"Oh, just that far too much of your energy would be channelled into your work and that this would give you problems with your sex-drive and your ability to relax in bed—"

"Okay, I won't shoot the old bat immediately—I'll sue her for slander first! How dare she say such things about a woman she's never met!"

Kim murmured very mildly: "You're saying there's no grain of truth in that assessment?"

I did a double take. "What's that supposed to mean?"

"Well, of course anyone can have a problem with sex occasionally if they've got too much on their mind—"

"*What are you talking about?*"

"Maybe you think I don't know when you're faking it."

"I never fake it!"

"No? When did you last have a genuine orgasm?"

"Last night! You want a detailed report of my symptoms?"

"What symptoms? Your breasts never changed colour!"

"What the hell do you think my breasts are— a set of bloody traffic lights?"

He started to laugh. "How about twin beacons on a pedestrian crossing?"

At once I saw that humour would provide me with an escape route. Laughing too I slipped my arms around his neck, gave him a quick kiss and said firmly: "No more silly questions, okay? And next time you see that witch Mayfield, do me a favour and slip arsenic in her herb tea!"

Then I slipped rapidly towards the shower-room.

It was a Saturday, and to make amends for his Neanderthal behaviour during the previous night's row, Kim volunteered to come with me to the supermarket after he had put in a couple of hours' work at the office that morning. We were just standing in a check-out queue after a long interval spent plundering the shelves when Kim said suddenly: "There's Sophie."

I felt exactly as if I were in a plummeting lift. "Where, where, where—"

"Over there—walking to the exit." He shot away, weaving in and out of the crowds, and left me standing paralysed by the shopping cart. By this time I had spotted the royal-blue coat, but a second later more departing shoppers had blocked my view. The far doors opened. When they closed again the blue coat had disappeared.

Seconds later Kim dodged the last person in his way and plunged outside in pursuit.

I was so rattled that I failed to pack the bags quickly as each item was charged, and I was just scrabbling to find my cheque card even though half the shopping remained unpacked, when Kim returned to my side.

"Did you catch her?"

"No, I can't think how she got away."

"Those shops which front the street and back onto the mall have two exits. If she went in from the mall and exited into the street—and if her car was nearby—"

"Get a move on, ducky!" said the woman behind me in the queue. "I ain't got all day."

Kim started shovelling the remaining items into bags. I found the cheque card and peeled off a cheque. A minute later we had succeeded in extricating ourselves from the chaos.

"Damn the woman!" I still felt shaken. "She was obviously going to accost me again before she saw you and fled!"

Kim promised to threaten her with an injunction, but later he told me Sophie had refused to talk to him when he had called.

VI

The next development in the Sophie saga came— after an unexpectedly quiet weekend—on Monday. The quiet was unexpected because I had thought Kim would be keen for more high-octane sex, but either he himself was temporarily satiated or he thought I was, and neither of us made any attempt to seduce the other. Perhaps he sensed I was feeling uneasy as the result of our explicit conversation about matters which are, I believe, better not discussed. I say this not to be Victorian, not to be prudish, not to be hung up but merely to be practical. Sexual blips—I refuse to call them problems and thus give them an importance they should never possess—are always tiresome but it's no good whingeing about them or getting in a panic. In the past I had always kept calm and waited for them to go away; I always told myself I never had a sexual problem which a vodka martini was unable to solve. The idea of talking about such matters has always struck me as being a very risky, ill-judged, self-indulgent way of carrying on and not at all consonant with being a female high flyer who has to be one hundred per cent perfect in every venture she undertakes. I knew I was good at sex. I had researched it, studied it and regularly practised it, so nobody was now going to tell me I was ever less than competent at it, least of all an old bat who made wild guesses while trying to pass herself off as a psychic. As for Kim I had to admit I was nervous in case he dragged up the subject again, but if he did I was more than ready to swear I had enjoyed the torrid scenes of Friday night immensely and that no one, not even my husband, had the right to tell me otherwise.

I had just finished mentally making speeches to myself in this fashion when Sophie reappeared in my life for another stalking session.

I left the office on Monday at my usual time, around half-past six, and following my long-established custom I walked home to the Barbican. I worked in a street called Bevis Marks on the eastern side of the City's Square Mile, and I found it soothing always to follow the same route home to Harvey Tower which, like all the Barbican tower blocks, knifes the sky on the north of the estate where the City borders Islington and Clerkenwell.

Leaving the office I walked up St. Mary Axe into Houndsditch, crossed the noisy thoroughfare of Bishopsgate and hurried out of the diesel fumes into the extensive gardens surrounding St. Botolph's church. The church reminded me of Tucker. I found I was noticing all the churches in the City now, all those mementos of its long history, and on the previous day when sitting at my telescope I had stared not at the skyscrapers but at the spires sown among the jumbled streets as if scattered by a careless, profligate hand.

Beyond the churchyard I headed for Finsbury Circus, a green area where in summer games of bowls were played on the immaculate lawn, and office workers wandered in the lunch-hour past huge trees and borders bright with flowers. Beyond the Circus lay another roaring main road, Moorgate, where Kim worked, and at the tube station nearby in Moorfields I took the escalator up to the Barbican podium, that vast maze of walkways and terraces which connected all the different areas of the thirty-eight-acre Barbican estate. There were twelve entrances, called "gates," up onto the podium, and the Moorfields escalator was known as Gate Three.

Along the podium I padded, under the pillars which supported one of the low-rise apartment blocks, Willoughby House, past the palm trees which lined the rooftops of Brandon Mews— the slim terrace houses which faced the water- falls and lakes below the podium—and finally into the Speed Highwalk which overlooked Silk Street on the northern edge of the estate. As I turned the corner into the Highwalk I could see, many yards ahead of me, the steps which led up to another level of the podium, the level which passed the main entrance of Harvey Tower. The evening breeze blew coolly on my face, and I was just lifting a hand to tuck a stray strand of hair back into position when I saw a woman pausing at the foot of the distant steps. She was too far away for me to see her clearly, but I recognised the royal blue of her coat.

I was wearing the flat shoes I always wore for the walk to and from the office, but they were hardly designed for sprinting and anyway for a long moment I was unable to do more than stare. When I did rush forward I stopped almost at once. I found I was recoiling from the prospect of another confrontation with Sophie, and meanwhile Sophie herself was hurrying away down the covered walkway which led to the Arts Centre. I watched her until she disappeared into the gloom at the far end. Then I ran down the Highwalk, raced up the steps and rushed across the podium to the lobby of Harvey Tower.

VII

I knew something was wrong as soon as I reached the flat. The bedroom door, which I had left ajar, was wide open.

"Kim?" I called, thinking that his late meeting had been cancelled, but there was no reply.

Cautiously I moved into the living-room. On the floor with its frame broken was another picture, a modern oil-painting called *Paradox in Aquamarine* which Kim had given me for my birthday. In utter silence I knelt down to inspect the damage. By some miracle the canvas had survived intact but the frame was clearly beyond repair.

I sucked in some air, clambered to my feet and went into the kitchen to get some ice for my evening drink, but as soon as I reached the threshold I stopped dead. Kim's cereal bowl was lying smashed on the floor. The garbage bag, which should have been put out for collection, had fallen on its side and most of the contents had spewed out across the floor.

I suddenly found I had to sit down.

I had left earlier than Kim that morning in order to review some papers for a meeting at eight. Kim did occasionally abandon his cereal bowl on the counter instead of slotting it into the dishwasher, and he might have forgotten to put out the garbage, but he would not have left the cereal bowl so near the edge of the counter that it fell off, and if he had accidentally kicked over the garbage bag he would not have left its contents strewn over the floor.

Standing up again I took a wary look around the flat but there was no other sign of disorder. Having swept up the fragments of the cereal bowl I rebagged the garbage, but long before I had finished I was again trying to work out how Sophie had gained access to the flat.

VIII

"It's impossible," said Kim when he returned home.

"But *somebody* was in this flat! And since I saw Sophie on the podium—"

"How sure are you that it was her?"

"Well, I admit I was a long way away, but since we know she was flitting around this area in a royal-blue coat on Saturday—"

"If she came here to trash the flat, why not do it earlier when there was no risk of being seen by either one of us on the podium?"

"She probably figured it would be easiest to slip unaccosted through the lobby at a time when people were returning to the Tower from work," I said promptly. I had already worked this out. "The porter wouldn't pay her the same attention then as he would have done if she'd turned up earlier."

"True. Okay, she swans into the lobby, she jingles her own house-keys to give the impression she's either a resident or staying with a resident—"

"And she gets past the porter into the lift-lobby. Up she goes to the thirty-fifth floor, and—"

"—waves a magic wand to unlock the front door. Back we come to that same big question: how did she get the key? And please, sweetheart—no scenarios involving my loyal PA!"

I emitted that sound which resembles "Arrrgh!" and ran my fingers through my hair.

"Let's tackle the problem systematically," said Kim, deciding at last to take it seriously. "There are three sets of keys. You have a set, I have a set and the porters have a set which they're forbidden to dole out without our permission. No one currently has our permission, not even the window-cleaners—who don't need the keys anyway as they can access our balconies via the fire-escape staircase."

"And the access door's always kept locked, isn't it? Besides, even if Sophie got through that, she couldn't unlock the balcony doors of the flat, so—"

"—so the most likely explanation is that she has a copy of the front door key."

"If only I'd had an extra lock put on!" I exclaimed futilely. "But when one lives thirty-five floors up in a building with twenty-four-hour porterage, a building in a part of London where the crime rate is low—"

"Where do you keep your keys when you're at the office?"

"In my bag which I lock in my desk. What about you?"

"I keep my keys on my person, and I assure you Mary never gets close enough to steal them. But wait a moment...yes, I've got an idea! There was a time, wasn't there, when we were having an affair and Sophie had learned of your existence but I still wasn't living at Harvey Tower."

Instantly I grasped his line of thought. "You were still living at your old pied-à-terre in Clifford's Inn. Did Sophie—"

"Yes, as my wife she had access to the spare keys at the porters' desk there—I never got around to cancelling my permission because after we separated I couldn't imagine her ever wanting to come to the flat. So that means she and her PI could have searched the place for information about you, found the Barbican keys and then copied and returned them all on one day so that I'd have been none the wiser. I never kept the Barbican keys on my person until we started living together, but you did give me a set earlier in order to cover those times when—"

"—when we agreed to meet here after work and I wasn't sure exactly when I'd be back," I concluded in triumph, delighted that the mystery had been finally solved. "Congratulations! Well, at least there's no problem figuring out the remedy. I'll arrange for the lock to be changed first thing tomorrow morning."

"No, wait—let's first give her enough rope to hang herself. Remember, nothing's proven. Defending counsel could argue that a mouse did the damage."

I snorted in disgust. "Now, that *is* far-fetched! How does a mouse climb up thirty-five floors without being spotted?"

"They can travel up the ducts. A mouse could have tipped the bowl off the counter and upended the garbage."

"Well, if it lifted *Paradox in Aquamarine* off the wall, it must have been genetically engineered."

We finally managed to laugh. Rising to his feet Kim examined the wall and although the screw which had supported the picture was still in position, I heard myself say: "This incident has to be connected to the other smashed picture, doesn't it?"

"Not necessarily."

"But you've got to admit it's quite a coincidence!"

"Life's littered with coincidences." He started to examine the damaged frame of *Paradox in Aquamarine*. "The best way forward," he said, "is to warn the porters and car park attendants to watch out for a woman in a royal-blue coat and make a note of the times she enters and leaves the building. Then if she creates more havoc we'll have witnesses to prove that she was on the site, and we'll be able to back up our testimonies by the evidence of the video cameras in the car park or the lobby. I'll check with Milton but I'm sure that'll give us the means to slap an injunction on her."

"Oughtn't we to instal a video camera in the flat to catch her in the act of trashing?"

"Sure, if we're looking for proof to convict her of a criminal offence, but I don't want that kind of scandal. Let's go for the injunction—I'm sure it requires a lesser burden of proof, and it would be a much more civilised way of restraining her."

"Well, one thing at least is proved beyond doubt," I commented, relaxing at last. "She's totally loony-tunes. A fruity-loop basket-case. Very sad."

He made no attempt to argue with me.

IX

I hoped he might initiate sex that night, but when the ITV News finished at ten-thirty he made no secret of the fact that he was tired. I lay awake for a while, trying not to worry about sexual blips which always passed so long as one did not lie awake worrying about them, and was relieved when I started to feel drowsy, but sleep that night brought no peace and I awoke with a gasp at two. My heart was pounding and my body was sweating with fear. Forcing myself to breathe evenly, I was unable to stop recalling the dream scene for scene.

Actual past events had been bizarrely mingled with fantasy. The bailiffs had arrived to take away the furniture and one of them had dropped my mother's best teapot so that it smashed to pieces on the floor; that was an actual past event. Then the bailiffs had produced clubs and instead of taking the furniture away they had smashed it to pieces; that was fantasy. I was running around trying to find my cat, known by me as Hamish and by everyone else as Wee Hamish, and had found him hiding under the sink; that was an actual event. Then Hamish shrank in my arms to the size of a matchbox; that was fantasy. The next moment I was making my father promise to look after Hamish; that was an actual event. But then the bailiffs were smashing my father to pieces and preparing to blow up the house; that, of course, was fantasy, and I awoke at the moment when the largest of the bailiffs was on the point of decapitating me. No wonder my awakening was violent.

Moving carefully so as not to wake Kim, I slid

out of bed, grabbed my robe and slipped down the corridor to the living-room. By the time I had managed to calm down I was wide awake so I decided to make myself some hot milk, but as soon as I entered the kitchen the memory returned of the smashed cereal bowl and the scattered garbage. The violation of my home, that tower-fortress which no bailiff would ever invade, suddenly seemed unbearable. Taking the bucket from the cupboard below the sink I began to perform a ritual cleansing by washing the kitchen floor.

Then I realised this was just the beginning of the task. I had to wash the surfaces of the cabinets and counters. I had to clean the electric rings of the hob. I even had to clean the oven. I cleaned and cleaned, every atom of my being focused on wiping out the memory of the disorder, but when the kitchen was pristine I still could not rest. The vacuum cleaner was too noisy to use at that hour but I dusted all the surfaces in the living-room and polished the brass trim on my telescope. Only when this last chore was accomplished did I sit down and have a drink. But it was Scotch I drank, not milk.

I knew by this time that I was deeply disturbed and I knew too that I was disturbed because something had threatened my security; I never dreamed of the bailiffs unless I was fearful of being overwhelmed by some force beyond my control. At first I blamed Sophie's stalking, but gradually it dawned on me that this obvious explanation of my anxiety could not be correct. After all, Kim had proposed a feasible plan of action for bringing Sophie under control. So if I was now cleaning my flat in the early hours of the morning like some obsessive-compulsive drone-ette, I needed to identify some other threat to my security, a threat which I unconsciously sensed would be far more difficult to defuse.

As I tried in vain to make sense of this mystery I found myself staring at the fallen picture propped against the wall nearby. Not for the first time I wished Kim had bought me a different present. He had paid a great deal of money for the painting so it had to be good, but the fact that it had been expensive did not make me like it any better. Against an aquamarine background three parallel white tubes, like cricket stumps, occupied the centre of the canvas. That was it. That was *Paradox in Aquamarine*. I failed to see the point of it, but how little I knew about art! There had never been time to learn because at school I had had to concentrate solely on mastering the academic subjects which would take me to Oxford and at Oxford I had chosen to concentrate solely on getting the best possible law degree. Art was just one of many subjects I had ignored in order to fulfil my life-plan. My knowledge of English literature was confined to the set books I had been obliged to study at school—and what could Tucker have thought of my failure to recognise that line of poetry by Tennyson? He must have judged me to be as ignorant as a computer nerd.

As I finished the Scotch it occurred to me that I needed to reduce my alcoholic intake if I wanted to avoid the disaster of weight gain. Perhaps too I needed to evolve a longer route to and from work in order to provide myself with more daily exercise—and the next moment, as I remembered my journey home that night, I started thinking of Sophie again.

But this time my thoughts were travelling along a different track. I was realising that if I were Sophie, wanting to sneak into Harvey Tower, I would hardly wear a smart royal-blue coat which would make me stand out from the crowd. And if I were Sophie, wanting to trash the flat in an orgy of revenge, I would hardly just smash a bowl, upend a garbage bag and crack a picture-frame. I would rampage through the whole flat and wind up slashing the suits in Kim's half of the bedroom closet.

I began to roam around the room. I was now asking myself whether Sophie's behaviour in the supermarket on the night she had accosted me was in any way compatible with this new image of the wild-eyed harridan who was sufficiently out of control to blitz her way into my flat yet sufficiently restrained to cause only a token amount of damage. It had dawned on me that I was knee-deep in a scenario which made no sense at all.

I decided I needed to speak to Alice Fletcher, the detached observer of that supermarket scene. What had been Alice's private opinion of Sophie, and was it in any way compatible with this new role of trespassing harpy? I wanted to talk to her immediately, but it was no good calling her up in the middle of the night.

I sat down at the telescope to watch the dawn break. The City was emerging from the darkness into the misty morning so that I was reminded of the cone of a smouldering volcano; a mass of dark, jumbled shapes were waiting for the yellow-orange glare which would bring them to life. The church spires were barely visible but I could see one or two slicing through the mist, and as

I watched, the dome of St. Paul's, perfectly curved, began to emerge above Ludgate Hill. To the east the pale sky was turning tawny, and seconds later the first rays of the morning sun touched the gold cross on the summit of the Cathedral.

"Sweetheart."

I jumped so violently that I nearly slipped from my stool.

"Sorry!" Kim had the grace to look abashed. He was standing on the threshold, leaning against the doorframe. I wondered how long he had been watching me. "I woke up," he said, "and when I saw you were missing I wondered if you were all right."

"I was fine until you almost gave me a stroke!" I retorted, trying to speak lightly, but I was aware of a knot of dread inexplicably tightening in the pit of my stomach.

He wandered across the room to join me. "What a sight!" he exclaimed as his gaze absorbed the view, and at once I responded: "Isn't it great?" but I was now having trouble breathing evenly. In fact I even wondered if I might be on the brink of hyperventilating because I had finally identified the threat to my security, the threat which had converted me into a cleaning-obsessed insomniac. I was facing the vile possibility that Kim himself had disarranged the flat before he had left for work that morning. This was the cleanest, neatest, most obvious solution to the mystery—yet as I could think of no sane reason why Kim should have done such a thing, the theory seemed almost unbearably sinister.

"Are you sure you're all right, sweetheart?"

"Uh-huh. Just mesmerised by the dawn."

"Mesmerised by the City, you mean! How am I going to tear you away when it's time to buy our house in Chelsea?"

I seized the chance he was offering me to divert my mind from frightening thoughts which made no sense. "I wish we didn't have to move west!" I exclaimed impulsively. "Is it really so essential that we go?"

"Well, it's a question of status, isn't it? Anyone who's anyone has a house in Chelsea or Knightsbridge or Kensington or Belgravia."

"Yes, but..." I was having to make a huge effort to sustain this conversation. "I do accept," I said in a rush, "that this flat is much too small for us, but to be quite honest I've never been keen on this plan of yours to go upmarket. Couldn't we stay on at the Barbican by getting a house? The Brandon Mews houses would be too small as well, I realise that, but the houses on Wallside and the Postern are large and have those wonderful views over the Roman Wall and St. Giles Cripplegate—"

"I don't want to look out on any damned church."

"Then what about the houses in Lambert Jones Mews? They look out over those beautiful gardens! And really, the Barbican's got everything, hasn't it—the Arts Centre, the restaurants, the library, the schools, the gardens, the playgrounds... I keep thinking it would be such a great place to bring up children!"

He swung to face me. I heard him say sharply: "What children?" and suddenly I knew not only that he had arranged the disorder in the flat but that he was conning me in ways I had not even begun to imagine.

180

PART TWO

WRESTLING WITH
THE POWERS

And in any case the big religious and philosophical questions refuse to go away. Human beings can't simply abandon the search for meaning in life without losing something essential to our humanness. And that is why the kind of agnosticism which tries to put these questions on one side is in my view a form of escapism.

It is not for nothing that intimate relationships have usually been hedged around with conventions, ceremonies and taboos. They involve dangerous moments of exposure, both physically and psychologically. The most intense emotions of shame, rage and hatred can be aroused when intimacy is abused... The fragile personality is most at risk when engaged in the self-exposure which intimacy demands.

JOHN HABGOOD
Confessions of a Conservative Liberal

SEVEN

The wounds which most cruelly disfigure the heart are given and received between lovers, husbands and wives, parents and children, friends, long-term colleagues and partners—any relationship where deep trust and loyalty create potentially tragic vulnerability.

DAVID F. FORD
The Shape of Living

I

I can now see how strange it was that Kim and I had never previously discussed the possibility of having children, but I can also see exactly how this non-communication occurred. He had told me early on in our acquaintance that Sophie's childlessness had been a disappointment, and so I had assumed, in my opinion not unreasonably, that he had been sorry not to become a father. This had also led me to assume, again in my opinion not unreasonably, that one of his motives for marrying a much younger woman was to give himself a second opportunity to father a family. Many middle-aged men did this; it was not an unusual situation.

Similarly, I had made no secret to Kim in the early stages of our affair that I was a modern woman with modern aspirations. It was true that I had avoided a detailed discussion of my life-plan, since experience had taught me that women waving life-plans were a sexual turn-off, but I had hardly thought it necessary to spell out the aspirations of the dedicated female high flyer, determined to "have it all."

The whole matter might have surfaced earlier if we had not been in such a transitional stage of our lives, but because we were not yet established in a more permanent home I had never been tempted to bring up the subject of children; I had always felt that this was a topic best discussed when pregnancy was finally a viable option and my contraceptive routine could be abandoned. Certainly waiting had been made easier by my belief that Kim would welcome the chance for a family when the time was right. The knowledge that not only had I utterly misread him but that he had utterly failed to understand me came as such a shock that for a long moment I was speechless, unable to express any emotion whatsoever. I merely sat there on my stool by the telescope as dawn broke over the City, and as I stared at him he stared back, equally shocked, equally unable to express his feelings.

He was the first to attempt a sentence. It was: "But you're a career woman."

I could make neither head nor tail of this. "So?"

"You're not interested in domesticity."

"Not at the moment, no."

"But... I'm sorry, I seem to have missed a trick somewhere, let me start again. Carter, how was I supposed to know you wanted children?"

"Because I'm a woman. Women have babies."

"But you have this completely masculine lifestyle!"

"Well, I have to, don't I? How else am I supposed to keep my career in order?"

"But—"

"Wasn't it obvious that I wanted children? I mean, I only want to do what all successful women do nowadays! You do the career number, you reach a certain stage, you move sideways in your life to do the domestic number, you produce the children, you move sideways back again after each pregnancy and finally you have both your lives, professional and private, absolutely in order by the time you're forty. It's the current creed for women like me."

Kim ran his hand distractedly through his hair. "I hardly know whether to laugh or cry! Sweetheart, how many female high flyers do you know who can actually achieve these ridiculously demanding goals without neglecting their husbands, short-changing their children and teetering on the brink of a major nervous breakdown?"

I did not answer. The shock was reaching me afresh. I tried to refocus the telescope but the lens seemed to be permanently blurred.

"Carter, I don't think you know the first thing about yourself, I really don't. You're not in the least interested in domesticity and you're not truly interested in motherhood either. If you were you would have brought up both subjects long ago."

"But you see, I thought—"

"You're just taking this line because it's fashionable, but, sweetheart, you don't have to pretend to be what you're not—at least, you don't have to pretend to me! I love you for what you are, not for what the spirit of the age says you ought to be, and when I married you I quite accepted that we would be a childless couple."

"Ah."

"I admit that long ago when Sophie and I were first married I did want a family, but when that didn't happen I discovered I was relieved. I was far from sure that I would have made a good parent. No one ever set me much of an example."

"I see." I gave up trying to focus the telescope and sat looking at my neatly folded hands.

"I'm sorry," I heard Kim say, his voice genuinely kind, "I'm making a hash of this conversation, aren't I? Let me try and do better. You want kids? Fine. I'm not saying no. But I'd like time to get used to the idea, and forgive me, but I think you too need time to take a cool, tough look at exactly who you are and what you want. You don't want to make a big mistake just because you've failed to face up to reality."

"Uh-huh," I said. "Well, I wasn't planning to get pregnant anyway until we were settled in our new home."

"Wise decision! Once we're settled we'll discuss the subject again." He stooped to kiss the top of my head. "Come back to bed—you'll feel like hell later unless you get some more sleep."

"I want to watch the dawn for a bit longer."

"It's wonderful how you can keep your eyes open..." He kissed me again and drifted away.

As soon as I was alone I rubbed the tears from my eyes and succeeded in focusing the telescope. St. Paul's was radiant now, bathed in a brilliant golden light, and when I looked up from the lens I saw that all over the City the towers and spires of the churches were shining beneath a cloudless sky of duck-egg blue. I thought: why am I seeing only the churches? Why am I no longer seeing the City's glittering, gutsy modernism

185

but only the beautiful relics of its vibrant, haunting past? And as my eyes filled again with tears which distorted my vision, I seemed to see all those spires bend towards me, as if I were recognised and cherished and yearned for by a stranger whose name I did not know.

I went to the kitchen to tear off a strip of paper towel which I could use as a handkerchief. Then I lay down on the sofa with my eyes squeezed shut and wondered when the world had last seemed so disordered, so utterly beyond my control.

II

I recovered from that moment of despair. It took an enormous effort but I blotted out all thought of the future and willed myself to escape into unconsciousness. I was woken by Kim an hour later at seven.

"How are you feeling?"

"Don't ask." The last thing I wanted was a day which had begun at two in the morning.

On arrival at the office I managed to focus solely on my work. Never had the rubbishy meetings and the routine melt-downs been more welcome. It was not until I came up for air after a morning of total immersion in my clients' problems that I remembered a decision I had made earlier to phone Alice Fletcher.

An answering machine picked up the call at her flat in Clerkenwell. Maybe she was cooking lunch somewhere. Unable to accept being thwarted in my quest I grabbed the phone book, looked up St. Benet's-by-the-Wall and discovered to my surprise that there were three listings, one for the

186

Rectory, one for the vestry and one for something called a Healing Centre, a designation which drummed up unpleasant images of charlatans like Mrs. Mayfield. With a shudder I dialled the first number, and after the third ring a man's voice said briskly: "Rectory."

"Is that Nicholas Darrow?"

"No, it's Lewis Hall. Can I help you?"

"I'm trying to track down Alice Fletcher. Do you have any idea where she is?"

"She's ten feet away and dishing up lunch. Give me your number and she'll call you back."

"I'll wait," I said, interested to discover how this bossy specimen would react to a woman who refused to be ordered around.

"Who's this calling?" Mr. Macho was turning shirty.

"Carter Graham, Carter as in—"

"—President Jimmy. Hold on," said the stranger, ordering me around again, and plonked down the receiver on a hard surface.

I was astonished that he had used the reference to President Carter which I always produced when clarifying my name, but before I could speculate whether this was the result of chance or of Alice meditating to him on the odd names of her clients, Alice herself picked up the receiver.

"Carter?"

"Alice, I know this is a bad time and I apologise, but I need to see you urgently on a confidential matter. Do you have a fifteen-minute slot which you can give me later today?"

Alice seemed bemused, perhaps by the thought of her day being divided into fifteen-minute slots. "After work?" she suggested tentatively. "About six-thirty?"

"Fine. Can I buy you a drink somewhere?"

"Oh!" She seemed amazed by this suggestion, as if no one had ever come up with such an idea before. "How very nice of you but I've two people coming over for dinner at seven, and—"

"Never mind, I'll be at your flat at six-thirty and be gone by six-forty-five," I said, concluding the call.

At that point I might have started thinking of Kim again, but fortunately there was no time as I was due to attend a business lunch upstairs in one of the private dining-rooms. Willing myself to ignore my increasing tiredness I checked my appearance to reassure myself my resemblance to a hag in need of a face-lift was still minimal, and hurried off to keep my next appointment on time.

III

"It's about that scene in the supermarket," I said as I accepted the glass of sherry Alice handed me. I had left the office early and stopped off for a quick flip of champagne to keep my eyes open, so I was able to face the sherry without wincing. Alice's basement flat was surprisingly light, the walls a bright cream, the wood floor lacquered and glowing, the windows curtained by a material in which earth-brown mingled with sunshine-yellow. In the living-room were parked some items of furniture which looked like genuine antiques. I guessed these had been inherited, and for a moment I envied Alice that stable, middle-class background from which she obviously came.

"I really appreciated your tact at the time," I

188

was saying as I explained the purpose of our meeting, "but for various reasons I now want to hear exactly what you thought of the scene—and please be quite frank. I need to have the honest opinion of an independent witness."

Alice seemed untroubled by this challenge and only asked: "Where shall I start?" As she spoke, a ginger cat came through the cat-flap from the garden.

"Begin: 'We were standing by the meat cabinets.'"

Alice launched herself into her narrative. As she talked the ginger cat leaped onto her lap and made a great business of revolving on it as if he hoped to knead the flesh into an orthopaedic mattress. He made me think of lost Hamish. My mother had meanly refused to acquire another cat for me, but later she had given a cat to her other daughters and told me I could share it with them. I had never bothered. I had been too old by that time to want to share anything with my half-sisters, and anyway the cat had been a slobbish creature, spoiled and overfed almost to death in that dull home where nothing ever happened. I had never liked it.

"...and so the scene made quite an impression on me," Alice was saying, summing up. "One doesn't usually see such high drama in the supermarket."

"One certainly doesn't. Now, Alice, how did this woman seem to you? What kind of a person do you think she was?"

"Rich," said Alice promptly. "I'm sure her clothes were custom-made because they fitted so beautifully. And she was upper class—there was no mistaking that accent. She also struck me as

189

a confident person, someone who would organise charity events or sit on the local hospital committee."

"And how would you describe her mood?"

"Agitated. Deeply concerned. But in control."

"In control?"

"Well, I mean she didn't grab you by the lapels of your jacket or hiss in your face or scream or shriek or give any indication that she was in urgent need of a psychiatrist. I once saw someone undergo a psychotic episode," said Alice helpfully, "and I can tell you that Sophie's behaviour in the supermarket wasn't remotely in that category... Are you still wedded to the idea that she's nuts?"

Having extracted the vital evidence I decided that the interrogation could now drift into a chat. "It's tempting for me to assume she's nuts," I said, "but the trouble is I'm not an unbiased witness here. Sophie gave us a lot of trouble over the divorce after assuring Kim she wouldn't make trouble at all." This statement did not explain why I was now so keen to establish whether or not Sophie was unbalanced, but I was hoping Alice would be sufficiently diverted by the word "divorce."

She was. "Oh, I do sympathise!" she exclaimed. "We're currently battling with just that problem— the wife who first said she wanted a divorce but who's now clinging on and causing chaos!"

"Your fiancé's in the throes of divorce? But I thought clergymen didn't do that kind of thing!"

"Mostly they don't but it does happen nowadays and it's so difficult for Nicholas because the Healing Centre's trustees disapprove and that's why our engagement has to be a secret—that's why I never refer to him as my fiancé—that's why—"

"—that's why your life's currently damn tough. But why's the wife playing the limpet?"

"Well, their elder son got involved in a drug-bust, and Rosalind feels she can't cope on her own, so—"

"The situation's obviously a nightmare. Are you sure you want to marry this man? After all, you've got plenty of sex-appeal—you can't be short of admirers."

Alice boggled. "*Me?*"

I suddenly saw the problem. I never cease to be amazed how many attractive women have such low self-esteem that they crucify themselves over unsuitable men. "Yes, you!" I barked, unable to resist trying to drill some sense into her. "Hey, don't waste time over this man if he's too much of a wimp over the wife to give you a square deal!"

"Oh, Nicholas could never be described as a wimp! I know he loves me and I know he wants to marry me, but—"

"Listen, sister, you've got to take a much tougher line with this ditherer if you don't want to wind up trashed! Abandon the stiff upper lip, stop being so damned nice and kick in a door or two to let him know you're getting restless!"

"Oh, but—"

"Is he one of your dinner-party guests tonight?"

"No, he's gone down to Surrey to see his wife."

"Well, all I can say is it's damned lucky it's not me he's engaged to! I'd smash his teeth in!"

The doorbell rang.

"I've outstayed my welcome," I said, rising to my feet, "and been bloody rude into the bargain, but I like you, Alice, and I think you deserve all the support you can get."

"Well, as a matter of fact, I do appreciate the sympathy. I've been feeling a bit down lately, and—"

"*A bit?* God, you're brave! Most women would be in a depression as deep as the Grand Canyon by this time and pigging out on Prozac!"

The doorbell rang a second time.

"Wait there," said Alice, who was now looking not merely dazed by my volubility but enthralled. "Just wait. Don't go away." She darted from the room.

I poured myself another finger of sherry to keep my brain synapses firing and knocked it back while she was opening the front door.

"Hullo, my dear..." I instantly recognised the voice I had heard during my lunchtime call to the Rectory; there was no mistaking those crisp, bossy tones coupled with that old-fashioned public-school accent. Realising I was about to meet a tiger-thumper I checked my appearance in the mirror above the fireplace and prepared to give him a memory which would make his flesh creep.

"Carter Graham's here," Alice was saying to him over her shoulder as she led the way into the living-room, and added to me: "Carter, this is Lewis Hall who works with Nicholas at St. Benet's."

Shattered to see that the tiger-thumper was yet another clergyman, I took a moment to absorb the fact that he was very different from Nicholas Darrow. For a start he was old. He had silver hair, black eyes with bags underneath, a hawkish nose and a streetwise look, as if he had seen everything there was to see and done everything there was to do not just once but at least three times. His thuggish build was incongruously encased in the traditional clerical gear which was topped off by a thick white collar and garnished with a glitzy little pectoral cross.

"How do you do, Miss Graham," he said, holding out his hand with professional ease. "I've been hearing about you."

"It's Ms. Graham," I said, certain this would infuriate him. "How do you do, Mr. Hall."

"It's Father Hall," he said without missing a beat, "and I'm delighted to make your acquaintance."

What a tiger-thumper, immediately trying to chop me down to size by flaunting a paternalistic authority! But I always respected the thumpers who kept their cool.

"Carter," Alice was saying, "I don't have to introduce my second guest, do I?"

I looked past her and saw Eric Tucker.

IV

Tucker was wearing an eye-zapping shirt—sky-blue but with wide cream stripes—and a silver-buckled belt which slunk sinuously around the waistband of his tight black trousers. The open neck of the shirt revealed curly dark hair which might or might not have had a reddish tinge when exposed to strong sunlight, and his sleeves were demurely buttoned at the wrists, a fashion statement which would no doubt have sent all the office fluffettes into a fresh frenzy of speculation. I almost felt fluffy myself but decided this was just the result of drinking Alice's sherry.

"Greetings, Ms. G!"

"Hey, Tucker! Why aren't you in seclusion, toiling away on your book?"

"I got hungry. We starving authors are notoriously reliant on good women who throw us a crust every now and then in the name of Christian charity!"

I said poker-faced: "So glad you're getting a change from champagne."

"Talking of crusts," said Alice, "do stay to dinner, Carter! There's plenty to eat and you'd balance the numbers so beautifully—do say you'll stay!"

For one long moment I thought how pleasant it would be to remain in that warm, welcoming room while I jousted with the tiger-thumper and traded quips with Tucker and displayed feminine solidarity with Alice, but I knew I had to go. I could not bear to keep fulfilling Mrs. Mayfield's prophecy—or rather, her outrageously lucky guess—and anyway there was no point in being drawn further into a world which had no place in my life-plan.

"Thanks, Alice," I said, "but my husband's expecting me. I've got to get back."

"I've a feeling we'll meet again," said the tiger-thumper, giving me a very straight look with his sharp black eyes, "but meanwhile I wish you well."

Another prophet! Repressing a shudder I murmured a politeness and edged away.

"Drop in at the St. Benet's Healing Centre some time!" said Tucker impulsively. "I'm there every Thursday evening as a Befriender, doing the late shift!"

"Befriender?"

"Trained listener for people in trouble. We're like the Samaritans."

I was quite unable to stop myself lingering. "You mean you do voluntary work?"

"It's the condition I have to fulfil in order to live at my brother's vicarage... By the way, how's the chap who went native in Beijing?"

"Still faxing quotes from Confucius."

I heard him laugh. I longed to stay. My hand even faltered before it reached the catch which opened the front door.

"Thanks for your help, Alice," I said in the hall. "If ever you want moral support, just give me a call."

Alice seemed delighted by this offer. Indeed it was touching how grateful she was. I found it amazing that a London woman could reach her mid-thirties and still appear so unspoiled by the sheer nastiness of so much urban life, and I wondered if she had spent her twenties being a nun, marooned in some place where life had passed her by. She had the air of a Cinderella who had not been too long at the ball, and I felt unexpectedly protective of her, as if she were in some strange way a reflection of my younger self, the self who had arrived in Oxford to play Cinderella in the 1970s.

Having grabbed a cab in Farringdon Road I cruised south to the Barbican. The slim, sharp-edged tower-blocks were visible ahead, conjuring up images of sharks' teeth, and the thought of sharks reminded me with a shiver of Kim. I had lied to Alice. My husband was not waiting for me at home. It was Tuesday evening and he had gone to the Simmonses' flat in Wapping to say goodbye to the group. He had told me he would be home by nine and I knew I had to spend the intervening time figuring out what I was going to say to him, but the trouble was my mind was now shying away from Alice's firm opinion that Sophie was sane. I could not face the implications. I was too tired—and too shell-shocked still from the revelation that Kim had no desire for children. My mind now only wanted to close down.

I was half afraid I would find the flat in disarray again, but to my relief everything was in order. Suddenly my exhaustion overwhelmed me. Stumbling into the bedroom I flaked out on top of the duvet.

When Kim woke me later by shutting the front door, the darkness at once made me wonder what time it was, and remembering his promise to be home by nine I glanced at the luminous figures of the bedside clock.

The hands pointed to twelve minutes past midnight.

V

I shot off the bed, flicked on the lights in the passage which led from the hall to the living-room and caught him as he padded noiselessly away across the thick carpet.

"What the hell's going on?"

He swung to face me but remained calm. "Didn't you get my message?"

"What message?" I said before remembering that I had flaked out without checking the new answering machine. "Sorry," I said confused. "I goofed." Following him down the corridor I entered the living-room and played back the message. He had said: "I'll be leaving the group early, as promised, but I'll be back later than I anticipated. I'll explain later."

"So explain," I said, resetting the machine.

"I had to take Mrs. Mayfield home."

"Damn the woman! Okay, you had to go all the way from Wapping in the east to Fulham in the west and then double back as far as the City, but in the evening you could do that journey without getting stuck in traffic jams. Why the long delay?"

"Mrs. Mayfield asked me in."

"What for?"

"A cup of tea."

"You sat drinking tea for"—I did a quick calculation—"well over two hours? What on earth were you talking about?"

"This and that." He yawned, wandered into the kitchen and filled a glass with Evian water. I stared at him. The mildness of his reactions and the languor of his movements made me wonder if he was drunk. It was as if someone had put a stifling hand on his personality and caused it to blur at the edges.

"How did the parting with the group go?" I said sharply, changing tack to give myself more time to analyse his behaviour.

"Fine. No problem. Mrs. Mayfield saw to that." He yawned again before drinking more water.

"Excuse me asking," I said, keeping my voice as calm as his as I followed him to the bedroom, "but what exactly did you discuss with Mrs. Mayfield?"

"What I always discuss with her: my problems. I hadn't realised how steeply my stress levels had been rising as the result of Sophie acting up and Mandy spilling the beans and you

197

saying you wanted children, but as soon as I started talking—"

"For Christ's sake!" I was shocked to the core. "Kim, that conversation of ours was private! How dare you go repeating it to that woman!"

"But she was great! She made me feel laid-back. I'm fine now."

A horrific thought struck me as I watched him clumsily unknot his tie. "Kim, have you been taking drugs?"

Instantly he sharpened up. Now it was his turn to sound shocked. "Not unless you count Mrs. Mayfield's herb tea! Give me a break, Carter—you know I'd never do such a thing!"

I was silent. I did indeed know we had identical views on the subject of drug-taking, a practice which was becoming increasingly frequent among the City's white-collar workers, although only a lawyer with a yearning to self-destruct broke the law by toking up at work. Curtis, Towers had a policy of instant dismissal if anyone was caught abusing illegal substances, and Graf-Rosen's rules were similarly tough. What the whippets and fluffettes did outside the office was their own affair, but no high flyer who wanted to stay aloft risked ruin for a drug habit, just as no high flyer risked becoming too dependent on alcohol. One needed to keep one's wits razor-sharp. At work I never even drank in the lunch-hour. My drinking was strictly an after-hours activity.

I heard myself say levelly: "Nevertheless you're giving the impression you've taken a hit. Just what was in Mrs. Mayfield's herb tea?"

"Sweetheart, you're being paranoid about Mrs. Mayfield!"

"Look," I said, trying hard to stay calm but not altogether succeeding, "this woman makes no secret of the fact that she thinks I'm bad news. Can't you understand how hurtful it is to me to know you've consulted her behind my back and told her about that very private conversation we had this morning?"

"I'm sorry, but I felt I just had to get advice about how to put things right—"

"But we'd have worked everything out! I still don't see why you—"

"I've got to go to the bathroom," he interrupted, and escaped.

I shed my clothes, pulled on my robe and sat bolt upright on the edge of the bed. My brain, soothed by several hours of deep sleep, was now firing on all cylinders, but in contrast Kim's brain was clearly cobwebbed. If I was going to hit him hard for crucial information this was the time to do it, and although the thought of another row was appalling, I felt I had to know what the truth was about Sophie and the disorder in the flat.

To psych myself up I pictured Kim confiding in Mrs. Mayfield. That certainly triggered the adrenaline rush I needed, and as I took a deep breath to prepare for blast-off, Kim wandered back from the bathroom. "My pupils look normal," he commented. "I think we can exonerate Mrs. Mayfield's herb tea."

"Well, ain't that grand!" I snapped. "But it's you I'm interested in exonerating! Now just you tell me this: did you make that mess in the flat yesterday and encourage me to blame Sophie?"

His eyes widened. I could see him struggling to work out first if he had heard me correctly, second how I could have come up with such a theory and third how he should react, but unfortunately this sequence was proof of neither innocence nor guilt, only of the fact that I had stunned him. I decided to twist the knife.

"You could have made that mess yesterday morning before you left for the office," I said. "In fact that's the most obvious explanation."

He said flatly: "You're out of your mind," and slumped down on the bed before demanding: "What was my motivation, for God's sake?"

"You tell me."

He groaned and began to unbutton his shirt. "All I'm going to say is that I'm dead beat and in twenty seconds from now I'm going to be unconscious. We'll talk tomorrow."

"It *is* tomorrow. Kim, if I didn't love you so much, I'd let this ride, but—"

"You can't be serious about such a grotesque theory!"

"I'm certainly serious in thinking there's something profoundly off-key going on and that it's all connected with Mrs. Mayfield!"

He flung his shirt on the floor and stood up again. "Let's try and get this straight. You're upset because you feel I've betrayed you by talking to Mrs. Mayfield about a private matter. But my conversations with her are entirely confidential, and if she were a qualified therapist you wouldn't think twice about what I've done!"

"But she's not a qualified therapist! And how can she possibly give you objective advice about your marriage anyway when she's admitted she's utterly opposed to it?"

"I think she'll come round to the marriage. I think that in time—"

"What time? You told me you were going to break with her as soon as possible!"

"Yes, I know I told you that, but if she comes to accept the marriage—"

"My God, she's been trying to make you go back on your decision to junk her! Kim, can't you see how she's manipulating you? Can't you understand what's happening?"

"It's you who can't understand!" Suddenly he had sloughed off his sleepiness as easily as he had stripped off his shirt, and had fired himself up to counter-attack. "The trouble with you," he said exasperated, "is that you refuse to acknowledge the spiritual dimension of life—you're so keen to escape reality that you're like a horse in blinkers, only able to see the scenery straight ahead and missing the view on either side!"

"Well, if the view on either side encompasses horrors like Mrs. Mayfield, thank God for blinkers, that's all I can say! Too bad you don't have any blinkers of your own!"

"Shut up and listen," he said seizing control of the conversation, but I hadn't lost the game, not yet, not by a long chalk, because he was now so annoyed that he might commit an indiscretion which I could use to open him up and drag the truth kicking and screaming into the light of day.

Sensing the conversation was about to move into an even more disturbing phase, I leaned back against the wall to fake an air of relaxation and waited for the chance to move in for the kill.

VI

"I may have given you the impression I don't believe in God," Kim was saying strongly, "but

201

in fact what I meant, when I was telling you about my spiritual quest after my visit to Auschwitz, was: 'He wasn't there for me.' I do think God exists somewhere, but he's a very second-rate deity—he's withdrawn from the world after making a mess of it, and so the forces we have to deal with on a day-to-day basis are the Powers and Principalities. Mrs. Mayfield just calls them the Powers.

"I lived with those Powers when I was growing up. I saw them all around me, I saw what they did to people, I saw what they did to my parents, but I had no power over the Powers, I had no more power than the little kids who died in the camps. I was regularly beaten up by the Powers, but there was nothing I could do except promise myself that one day—*one day*—I'd get the power to beat them back. And that was why I started chasing money and success. I worked and I worked and I worked and I did get power, but the power was never enough—the Powers still pursued me, I couldn't throw them off, and finally there came a time, the time of the blackmail, when I thought I was done for, but Mrs. Mayfield saved me. She saved me because she had *real* power—she had power over the Powers, she could manipulate them, bend them to her will because she could access that Supreme Power, that primeval force, which ultimately controls them. So don't ever ask me again what I see in Mrs. Mayfield, because when I'm wrestling with the Powers, she's the one who knows how to rescue me. She's the one who can send them back to their source, that primeval source from which they come."

He slumped down on the bed as if exhausted by this outburst, but a second later he was on his feet again, too strung up to keep still.

"It's evil which constitutes reality in this world," he said, pacing up and down, "and what human beings long for most is to escape pain and suffering. Schopenhauer got that right—but of course you wouldn't have read Schopenhauer. You never read anything except the latest laws on tax!"

"I may be very ignorant," I managed to say, "but there's one thing I do know and I didn't need to read a book in order to find it out. What people want most of all is to love and be loved."

"Don't hand me that romantic rubbish! Love's nothing but a built-in biological imperative to perpetuate the human race!"

Without hesitation I said: "That's the nastiest speech I've heard for a long time, and to make matters worse it's absolute crap!"

"But there are plenty of people who think as I do!"

"Yeah—people like Mrs. Mayfield! Power-junkies hooked on domination! Kim, can't you honestly see that once you downgrade love like that you downgrade human beings, and once you downgrade human beings you're squarely on the road to Auschwitz?"

"If you're calling me a Nazi, I swear I'll—"

"I know you hate the Nazis!" I cried. "But that's exactly what makes this conversation so appalling! You're talking as if your next line of dialogue is going to be: '*Heil Hitler!*'"

"Bullshit!" he shouted. "You don't understand a single thing I've said! The Third Reich was generated by the Powers and Hitler abused his power to go along with them—he did everything he could to help them win! But my aim is always to defuse the Powers by controlling them and subjugating them. That's the only way to feel safe and secure! That's the only way to ensure a decent, normal life!"

"All right," I said rapidly, recognising that his distress was genuine, "you're basically one of the good guys. But I still think there's something unreal about this world-view of yours. There's a sort of nothingness about it...a sort of absence of something...an absence of the good perhaps, yes, that's it; you're concentrating all the time on the darkness of evil, but what about the light? What about beauty and joy and all the experiences which make one feel it's great to be alive? For instance, what about that terrific sex we had last Friday? That was such a great way of expressing our love for each other—are you seriously trying to tell me it was nothing but a manifestation of a biological drive?"

All his aggression vanished. Painfully he said: "I was unsure how well you liked that."

"My darling Kim—"

"You shouldn't have faked it."

"Okay, I'll come clean: I was getting sore. But that doesn't alter the fact that it was great sex! I felt really guilty that I needed to call a halt—I felt you didn't deserve to be disappointed by a partner who was less than perfect, and that was another reason why I—"

"For God's sake, you were making love, not sitting the Law Society examinations!" he said, still too upset to laugh but struggling for a humorous response to end the quarrel, and a second later we had blundered into each other's arms.

"Surely you can admit now," I said at last after we had embraced fiercely, "that love's more important than power?"

"But love's dependent on power."

"What do you mean?"

"When I watched my father go to pieces after the war I realised that a man's got to be macho and he's got to have power if he wants a woman to keep on loving him. Otherwise she just goes off and screws someone else."

I was appalled. "Not if she loves him!"

"Now you're being romantic and sentimental again. Admit it—it was the power which first attracted you to me! I could see how the power turned you on as soon as you found out what I did and could figure out how much I earned!"

I forced myself to answer steadily: "In the beginning I wasn't looking for love, just for sex. But our relationship's travelled a very, very long way since then."

"If I lost my job tomorrow you'd leave me."

"Don't be absurd!"

"If you found out I was powerless you'd be gone. That's the way of the world. That's rock-bottom reality."

"No," I said stubbornly. "You're wrong. Rock-bottom reality is that I love you. Rock-bottom reality is love."

He moved blindly back into my arms again and I hugged him with all my strength. For a while neither of us spoke but when he released me at last he whispered: "I'd like to believe that. I really would."

"Can't you at least believe that I love you?"

"Yes, but I'm afraid the Powers will smash your love up unless I've got the means to beat them back. I've got to have the strength," he said, turning away from me, "to keep wrestling with the Powers, and at the moment Mrs. Mayfield's the one who ensures I have that strength, Mrs. Mayfield's the one who can control the Powers so that they don't overwhelm me. One day," he said, "I believe I'll be strong enough to do without Mrs. Mayfield, but I'm not quite strong enough yet. I've been through so much. I need more time."

There was a long silence. Finally I said: "Okay, let's leave it at that for now," and standing on tiptoe I kissed him on the cheek.

But he barely heard me. "Carter, you don't really think, do you, that I arranged that mess in the flat yesterday?"

"No, that was just a forensic trick to get you to open up. Let's forget it," I said, unable to summon either the nerve or the energy to return to the subject, but later I lay awake haunted by all my anxieties until dawn began to break again over the City.

VII

I knew he had outplayed me, not only sidestepping the confession I had sought about the disordered flat but even persuading me to acquiesce in his desire to maintain contact with Mrs. Mayfield, but nevertheless I felt I had succeeded in gaining a much clearer picture of what was going on. I now had a better understanding not only of his hang-ups—all much worse than I had ever imagined—but of his relationship with Mrs. Mayfield; I could see that she had managed to exploit his profound emotional damage so that he had become psychologically dependent on her. I had assumed Kim was being inexcusably perverse in keeping the relationship going, but now I realised that this behaviour sprang from an irrational fixation, not from a rational choice. This did not justify his association with a woman opposed to his marriage, but it did allow me to reclassify his actions as neurotic instead of deliberately hurtful, and this in turn made it possible for me to forgive him.

It seemed plain he needed some form of psychiatric help to sort out his emotional problems and wean him from Mrs. Mayfield, but I knew he would refuse to consult a psychiatrist. As I once more sat on the couch in the early hours of the morning and sipped Scotch, I tried to calm myself by listing the good points which still existed alongside the crisis. We loved each other; the sex was good and getting better; when he was being the dolphin instead of the shark he was fine; we had much in common, we got on well, we were certainly capable of making each other happy. The problem of children was tricky but not, I now decided, insuperable. I was confident that I could win him over, perhaps by giving way on the decision about where we were going to live, and I told myself I should no longer see the reproduction issue as a long-term anxiety.

The real long-term anxiety was Mrs. Mayfield. She would have to be dynamited out of his life, I could see that, and I would just have to hope that Kim's natural toughness would ensure his survival once his psychological prop was removed, but how did I manoeuvre myself into a position where I could light the fuse?

Suddenly I thought of Sophie, issuing her warning in the supermarket. Sophie was sane, I was sure of that now, just as I was sure that Kim had created the mess in the flat and encouraged me to attribute it to Sophie because it was vital to him that I should write her off as someone who had no credibility at all. This in turn meant that Sophie knew still more unpalatable facts which Kim was determined to keep from me, and I was sure that at least some of these unpalatable facts must relate to Mrs. Mayfield.

"He's mixed up with the occult..." It occurred to me now that I had never taken this allegation seriously. I had been too busy dismissing Sophie as demented, and besides, whenever the word "occult" cropped up I always thought: nutterguff! and switched off. But what exactly was the occult? Supposing it consisted not just of ludicrous ladies reading crystal balls and silly students messing around with Ouija boards, but of something very much more dangerous? The Witchcraft Act, I knew, had been repealed earlier in the century. Maybe all kinds of creepy-crawlies had sidled out of the woodwork by this time and were busy battening on vulnerable people.

I had no idea whether witchcraft and the occult were the same thing, but suspected that even if they were not, both had been covered by the Act. The fact that these activities were no longer illegal certainly restricted my opportunities to dynamite Mrs. Mayfield, but shady activities could often lead to law-breaking. Instantly I thought of blackmail. If I could prove Mrs. Mayfield was a criminal I could gut her. All I needed was the necessary information—a conclusion which meant I had no choice now but to seek out Sophie.

This was hardly a pleasant prospect but desperate situations called for desperate measures. I could not continue to share Kim with Mrs. Mayfield. Of that I was quite sure.

Returning to bed I wondered if he had lied to me when he had denied taking drugs that evening. But I managed to dismiss that anxiety by focusing on the fact that at least he had ditched that dire group.

Making an enormous effort I at last succeeded in willing myself into unconsciousness.

VIII

The persistent tension was reaching me, seeping deep into my body and stealthily infiltrating my mind. Again I tried to shut out my anxieties by concentrating on my work, but this time I failed. The lack of sleep was undermining me too, and by three o'clock I was totalled. Telling Jacqui to hold all calls I tried a power-nap, but my brain instantly accelerated, keeping me awake with thoughts of the neurotic stranger I had married. My head started to ache. I took aspirin to no effect. At last, seriously worried in case I started making bad decisions, I realised the smart thing to do was to withdraw from the scene.

I found a taxi in Bishopsgate and reached the car park on the street level of Harvey Tower minutes later. The attendant on duty nodded sociably to me but I was hardly in the mood for conversation. Stumbling into the lift I sagged back against the panels.

In the thirty-fifth-floor lobby I suddenly felt I was going to pass out and I had to lean against the wall to steady myself, but fortunately the dizziness soon passed. I unlocked the front door—and immediately felt sure something was wrong. Kim had been the first to leave that morning and

I knew the flat should be immaculate, but nevertheless I was convinced I was going to find more disorder. I checked the master bedroom nearby and heard the breath rasp in my throat. The wardrobe doors were yawning wide. The floor was strewn with Kim's suits, but although I examined them I found no sign of damage, and meanwhile my own clothes were still suspended from the rail. I stood breathing rapidly as I surveyed this bizarre scene, but before I could start rehanging the suits, which I had picked up from the floor and placed carefully on the bed, it dawned on me that the rest of the flat needed checking. At once I raced down the corridor to the living-room.

The cushions from the sofa had been tossed onto the floor and the stool by the telescope had been upturned but the telescope itself was untouched and all the pictures were still on the walls. A weird feature of the disorder was that the television was on, the volume mute. Grabbing the remote control I zapped the picture, and it was then that I heard the sound of dripping in the kitchen.

The refrigerator door was open, prevented from swinging shut by a carton of milk which had fallen on its side and was leaking stealthily from its closed but unsealed flap. The carton was protruding from the shelf at an angle which allowed the milk to drip straight onto the vinyl floor below.

I stared at this evidence that the disorder was recent. Then I tipped the carton upright, slammed shut the fridge door and shot back into the living-room to call the office of Graf-Rosen.

I knew it was possible that Kim had sneaked home during the lunch-hour.

"Mary, it's Carter," I said as Kim's PA came on the line. "Is Kim there?"

Ms. Waters immediately assumed the hon-eyed tones which masked her dislike. "I'm afraid he's in a meeting, Carter."

"How long's the meeting been going on?"

"Since two."

It was now twenty past four and I doubted if the milk could have been leaking from the carton for more than five minutes. But maybe the carton had not started to leak straight away; maybe the unsealed but closed flap had at first proved an effective dam.

Abruptly I said: "Did he have a lunch-date?"

"Yes, upstairs with two partners."

"He hasn't been out of the building?"

"Oh, there wouldn't have been time! Carter, is something wrong?"

I pulled myself together. "I was confused because I thought I spotted him just now on the Barbican podium. Okay, Mary, don't mention this call to him—obviously I saw a look-alike." I hung up, aware of an enormous relief. Whoever the culprit was, Kim was in the clear.

But a second later I was deep in confusion again. If Kim was innocent then all my deductions based on his guilt were wrong and Sophie was still Ms. Fruity-Loops, stomping around my flat and creating havoc. Moreover if the disorder was recent Sophie might still be in the area. Heaving open the sliding door I rushed onto the bal-cony.

The Barbican flats all have wraparound bal-conies which double as fire-escapes and make life easy for the window-cleaners. My views east and north were restricted, but the area of the podium to the south and west of the Tower was clearly visible to me and when I rapidly scanned the landscape I caught sight of a fleck of royal blue far below. It was adorning one of the seats which overlooked the gardens at the western end of the podium.

I dived indoors, slid into a pair of flat shoes, grabbed my bag and shot out of the front door. By a miracle the lift arrived instantly. At podium level I tore past the astonished porter and raced outside. All weariness had now vanished, killed by the adrenaline which was surging through my veins. Across the podium I ran, with Shakespeare Tower on my left and Ben Jonson House soaring above its forest of columns on my right. Ahead were the gardens framed on three sides by the low-rise blocks which stood on the north-western edge of the estate, and there, looking out over this tranquil scene with her back to me was Sophie, sitting placidly in her royal-blue coat as if she were savouring a well-earned rest after her bout of destruction. Well, why shouldn't she spend a little time relaxing? I was supposed to be at the office and she would have thought herself as safe as an escaped criminal sunbathing on the Costa del Sol.

When I drew closer I saw she was wearing a hat, a nasty piece of black felt which surprised me because I knew Sophie dressed with good taste. But my surprise barely registered. I was too busy relishing my triumph.

I slowed to a walk to recover my breath; now that she was grabbable I could afford to take a moment to ensure I was ice-cool for the dénouement, but suddenly she wrong-footed me by sensing my presence. I saw her shoulders stiffen. The next moment she was rising to her feet, but when she turned to face me I found myself staring at her without comprehension.

This woman was a stranger. But she knew me. She was smiling radiantly. Beneath the heavy powder on her face she was pink-cheeked, as if something had delighted her. Her lips were slightly parted; she looked as if she had seen a luxury item which she could hardly wait to purchase. Her blue eyes were serene but moist, as if the delight was almost too much for her to bear. Grey curls peeped from under the cheap hat. She looked like an old-fashioned grandmother viewing the latest addition to a far-flung but peculiarly close-knit family.

"Why, what a lovely surprise!" she said cosily in a creamy voice. "It's Carter, isn't it, dear? I recognise you from your photographs. Do I have to introduce myself or can you guess who I am?"

My voice said: "You're Mrs. Mayfield," and as I spoke I felt the repulsion ripple down my spine.

EIGHT

When someone deeply hurts us it is one of the worst forms of overwhelming.

DAVID F. FORD
The Shape of Living

I

"I'm ever so pleased to meet you, dear," said the woman, and I could feel her strong, sinuous personality wrapping itself around me as efficiently as an anaconda busy domesticating some unfortunate tree. Meanwhile her creamy contralto with its south London accent was calling to mind images of a suburban matron pouring out tea in a lace-curtained parlour. I could see now that the royal-blue coat was not in the least like Sophie's. It was loosely cut, shoddy, perhaps even something she might have run up on a sewing machine in double-quick time when the idea of masquerading as Sophie had first surfaced. The coat was unbuttoned, sagging open to reveal a floral dress topped by a thin grey cardigan. The weather hardly justified the wearing of a cardigan in addition to the coat, but that sort of person was always wedded to her cardigan. It was like part of a uniform.

I tried to estimate how old she was. She had good legs and her narrow, elegant feet were jacked up by high-heeled shoes as if she wanted to distract attention from the bulky upper half of her body. She was certainly dressed to look sixty, but the grey curls seemed like a wig and her skin was good. In the end I decided she could have been any age between forty-five and seventy, and a member of any number of professions ranging from chartered accountancy to hooking.

"Shall we sit down for a moment?" she was saying. "It's so lovely here by the gardens, isn't it, and they've even got goldfish, I see, in that pond, although I don't suppose they'll last long, poor little loves, they're bound to be kidnapped for cat-food. Well, I was just on my way to see a friend of mine who lives in Ben Jonson House"—she indicated the long block of low-rise flats nearby—"but I found I was early so I thought I'd pause to admire the beauties of nature, somehow managing to flourish even in the most peculiar places, and you can't get anywhere more peculiar than the Barbican, can you, nearly forty acres of brutish concrete dreamed up, I'm sure, by a bunch of men entirely unaided by women—women would have softened all those straight lines and put the whole thing on street level, much more practical for shopping, but men never think of the needs of housewives, do they, which is why they designed a huge housing estate two floors above the ground—or is it three?—and then finished off their fantasy by putting all the low-rise blocks on legs. What *did* they think they were doing, I ask myself, but that's men all over, isn't it—minimum self-knowledge and maximum capacity to cause trouble!"

As she paused for breath I was finally able to say in my hardest voice: "You've been messing up my flat."

"Well, I heard about the trouble you've been having, but—"

"I mean today. Just now. You bust in and blitzed around."

"Not me, dear, although I admit I've just come from Harvey Tower. Harvey Tower! Named after William Harvey, I'm told, who made all those discoveries about the circulation of blood when he was working nearby at Bart's Hospital—I love the way the Barbican blocks are called after historic City celebrities, I really do, but why are all these celebrities men? Lauderdale, Shakespeare, Cromwell, Ben Jonson, Defoe, Thomas More—"

"If you didn't trash my flat what the hell were you doing at Harvey Tower?" I was finding her rambling, elliptical style curiously exhausting; I began to feel as if I were wrestling with toffee.

"Your husband left his organiser at my house last night, dear, and when he rang me this morning to check it was there I said I'd be visiting my friend Pauline this afternoon and could drop the organiser off at the porters' desk."

I said very clearly: "I put it to you that you talked your way past the porter. I put it to you that you then entered my flat with a key which my husband had given you last night. I put it to you—"

"Put it where you like, pet. It's a fantasy."

"But—"

"Here's what happened. I arrived at the Barbican tube station. I trotted down the Beech Street tunnel, which runs under this lovely, lovely garden where we're busy enjoying the beauties of nature. Your husband had already phoned the lobby porter to tell him I'd be coming, but of course Harvey Tower, being designed by men and therefore hugely unpractical, has its entrance at podium level, so I had to go in from

216

Beech Street through the car park, explain my errand to the attendant there and wait while he phoned the lobby porter to check I wasn't some nasty IRA terrorist. What a kerfuffle! But at least you can tell yourself the security's excellent. Anyway, once the attendant heard I was expected he allowed me to take the lift up to the porters' desk, and then—"

"You went straight up to the thirty-fifth floor without pausing at podium level!"

"No, dear, I went straight to the lobby where I left the organiser, snug in its little Jiffy bag, with the porter, and then I went straight out into the gardens. If your flat's been disturbed again, the culprit wasn't me."

"I don't believe you!"

"Well, suit yourself, dear," said the woman serenely, "but you really should calm down—your stress levels are much too high and I'm not surprised you were driven to leave work early. Suffering from a tension headache, were you? Feeling groggy from lack of sleep?"

"Now look here, Mrs. Mayfield—"

"I see big health problems ahead if you go on like this, pet, I really do, and I said as much to Jake last night. I hope you don't mind me calling your husband Jake, but that was the name he used when he first came to see me and I always thought he instinctively knew it suited him better than Kim. 'Jake' sounds so strong and tough, and of course he's ever so keen on the macho."

"Stuff that—what I want to talk to you about is—"

"Names are so important, aren't they?" continued Mrs. Mayfield, effortlessly ironing out my interruption. "For instance I never allow myself to be called 'Betty' or 'Lizzie' or 'Ellie' or any of those other nasty abbreviations, I'm always 'Elizabeth'! It's a question of tone, a question of class. 'Elizabeth Mayfield' sounds so pretty, doesn't it, so elegant, so English—oh, I just love my name, I really do, it makes me so happy just to listen to it! But *your* name, dear, if you'll pardon me saying so, is a mistake. Flaunting a masculine name to conform to a masculine lifestyle means that a large part of your true nature's being suppressed, and I think poor Jake is just beginning to realise this. 'Carter Graham'—no, no, no, dear, it won't do—it won't do at all! Have you ever thought of calling yourself Kate?"

"Mrs. Mayfield," I said, so infuriated by this time that I could cheerfully have consigned her to an acid bath, "let's cut the crap and get down to business. I know for a fact—"

"Pardon me, dear, but I don't think you know anything for a fact, you're absolutely out of your depth—which is why you're mishandling this conversation. I'm perfectly willing to be friendly! Why do you keep jumping down my throat?"

"Because you told Kim not to marry me! Because you spun him all that guff about how I'd start 'flirting with the enemy'! Because you forecast sexual problems in an attempt to bust up my marriage!"

"Well, pet, I never think it's a good idea for people to rush into a second marriage the moment they get their divorce, and as for flirting with the enemy, well, it wasn't guff, was it? You fancied that young man who came to work for you! You fancied him and you flirted with him and—"

"I absolutely, categorically deny—"

"—and I'll tell you something else, my love.

You're not through with the enemy yet, not by a long chalk."

"Look, it's no good trying to pull this psychic stunt on me because I just don't believe in—"

"It was quite dark," she said dreamily, gazing out over the flowerbeds. "It was a lovely, plush, velvety darkness, not inky, not grimy, but *voluptuous*. I loved it, I was entranced by it, I was *luxuriating* in it, and as I watched I saw you running down this dark, dark street. But you didn't like the dark at all—silly, ignorant little girl that you are beneath all that pseudo-masculine, pseudo-sophisticated, pseudo-intelligent modern nonsense—and when you got to the house you started banging on the front door in hysterics. I couldn't see the house properly because everywhere was so dark, but I knew there was a church nearby because the next moment...well, it was all symbols, dear, you wouldn't understand, but I read the symbols and I knew you were knocking at the closed door, the one with no handle, and I knew that the next moment *he* would be there—you know who I mean, I won't say his name—"

"I don't know who you mean, I don't want to know who you mean, and all I can say is—"

"A clergyman answered the door but of course he was just standing in for that other person, and then I saw beyond the symbols and realised you'd be sucked up by the enemy, absorbed by them, eaten alive by them—"

"You're certifiable." I started to struggle to my feet. "You ought to be locked up."

"Really, dear? Are you sure you're not projecting onto me all the worries about your own mental health which you never dare to acknowledge?"

"What the hell do you mean?"

"You're breaking down under the strain of maintaining this masculine lifestyle, pet—the disorder in the flat is just mirroring the disorder in your mind, and I predict there'll be other signs of derangement too before long. That flat must have ever such a lovely view, but you're very high up, aren't you, and one day soon you're going to go out onto that balcony and you're going to look down on that concrete podium thirty-five floors below and you're going to want to smash yourself on it—SMASH yourself on it—you'll long to smash yourself on it, long to, it'll be an urge you'll never, never be able to resist—oh, you'll try to resist, of course, you'll fight and fight against it, but in the end you'll go out on that balcony and you'll move to that rail and you'll—"

"You're evil," said my voice as every drop of blood in my body seemed to turn to ice. "You're wicked. You're obscene."

"Rattled you, have I? Well, it's about time someone did! You're living in a state of illusion, my girl, and if you don't shape up soon and realise that Jake's quite the wrong husband for you, I promise that one day you're going to step out on that balcony and—"

I shouted her down. I was sweating and faint but I drummed up the strength to yell: "Fuck off! You leave me and my husband alone or I'll get the police to arrest you!"

"I've broken no law, dear, and as for your husband, why shouldn't he see me if he wants to? I can do him more good than any doctor!"

"The right osteopath would have fixed his back trouble without battening on him afterwards like a bloody vampire!"

"Pardon me, pet," said Mrs. Mayfield in a

voice oily enough to undulate under all my defences, "but did you say back trouble?"

I sank down abruptly on the bench.

II

There was a vile silence. I knew I should end it at once but no words came.

"Fancy!" said Mrs. Mayfield placidly at last, reverting to her cosier manner. "Well, if he wants you to think his problem was back trouble, far be it from me to interfere!" She glanced at her watch. "Gracious me, look at the time—I must fly!"

"Wait." I was fatally entangled at last, and suddenly I saw I had been wrestling not with toffee but with a tarantula who had now trussed me up in its web. "What was really wrong with him?"

"Oh, nothing serious," said Mrs. Mayfield, daintily adjusting the cuff of her coat after the glance at her watch. "Just the usual masculine trouble, but I knew Jake would be fine once I'd introduced him to the right group to restore his confidence." She produced some skin-tight gloves from her handbag and slowly drew them on while making sure every wrinkle in the material was smoothed away. I was reminded of a pathologist preparing to disembowel a corpse.

My voice said numbly again: "I don't believe you."

"That's because I did such a good job of curing the impotence, dear, but of course the problem could recur if his relationship with you were to get as fraught as his relationship with Sophie— and that reminds me, pet, do stop talking about having children! He doesn't want them, never has,

221

never will, and once he thinks you only want him for fertilisation purposes he'll never get an erection and you can guarantee he'll be looking elsewhere for sex in no time flat. After all, that's what happened before."

"You're saying—you mean—"

"Well, of course he doesn't want you to know that his first marriage was far more of a mess than he ever told you it was! No wonder Sophie's panting for revenge now that he's ditched her—she stuck by him all those years when she could have been having children by someone else! No wonder she can't wait to tell you about his impotence and his efforts to cure himself with other women and finally about all the lovely, healing, fun-times he's had with my group! No wonder she's bursting with the desire to tell you that unless you agree to do without children your marriage will be on the rocks in no time!"

"But he's told me he's willing to consider having children!"

"Well, he would, wouldn't he? He's ever so keen on you at the moment, but it won't last, can't last, because your sex-life's inevitably going to go to pieces—well, of course I could see this problem coming a long way off! He thought you were so wedded to your career that you wouldn't want children, but I said: 'Don't make me laugh! That girl's suppressing a huge part of her femininity and one day she's going to get fed up with being a pseudo-man. She'll go domestic, take cooking courses, fall in love with a Hoover and—naturally!—want a baby. It'll be nature reasserting itself,' I said, 'and she'll not only hear the biological clock ticking but she'll ditch the job, shed the masculine identity and get pregnant faster than you can say "mother's milk." You mark my words,' I said, 'this is *not* the kind of girl you want to marry. You want a woman who married young and got all the maternity stuff done at an early age.' But he couldn't see it! The silly little love was so infatuated that he took you at face value! I could hardly believe he was capable of being so naïve!"

I levered myself to my feet. My legs felt as if they were only flimsily attached to my body and I had to grip the edge of the bench to steady myself. Stiff-lipped I said: "What happened last night when he said goodbye to the group?"

"Oh, was he planning to say goodbye? That's news to me... And now I really *must* be on my way! Lovely to have met you, dear, although I'm sorry you were so edgy and under the weather. Don't hesitate to contact me in future, will you, if you decide you want help in curing that little orgasm problem you have—I've got another group you'd do very well with, and I'm sure they'd be ever so happy to meet you!"

And smiling radiantly she gave a little wave in the style of the Queen Mother before tip-tapping away across the podium in her elegant high-heeled shoes.

The sun was still shining on all the flowers nearby but I felt as if I were suffocating in a cloud of darkness. Slumping down on the bench again I buried my face in my hands.

III

I felt butchered. Indeed I felt so beaten up that I could barely believe my clothes remained untorn and my body unmarked. My entire per-

223

sonality felt as if it had been slashed to ribbons and spat upon—and not just my everyday personality which I had become so accustomed to projecting but also the secret self which I kept safe, tucked away behind hard-hitting Carter who could wipe floors with whippets and dynamite every dinosaur in sight. Dimly I understood what had happened. Carter had been shredded, and now, with my prime line of defence destroyed, I was exposed, fragility personified, on the edge of a cliff overlooking a bottomless void. And who was this mysterious "I" who could look at the ruins of Carter and experience unprecedented terror? I knew it was me, but it was not an "I" who could survive except behind the walls of a heavily defended fortress.

I set to work to rebuild Carter. What would she do next? I thought she would say: "Shit!" in fury or: "Screw the bitch!" in order to generate the adrenaline necessary for survival, but although I gave the words a try they merely sounded pathetic. Apparently Carter was still out to lunch. I found myself crying. This was pathetic too—pathetic, shaming and horrifying. I was going to pieces, fulfilling the woman's vile predictions... Terror overwhelmed me again. I pictured myself plummeting from the balcony and being smashed to death, but before I could pass out at the thought of how I had been programmed to self-destruct, Carter's voice said shakily: "Get lost, nutter-person!" and I knew she was announcing her return.

I wiped the tears away and when I opened my eyes again I was Carter. I clenched my fists to test the power of my will and at once a vital sentence surfaced in my mangled brain to give me additional hope that I was on the road to recovery. I said aloud to myself: "That was the Mayfield story. But I don't have to be stuck with it."

My thoughts became more organised. I staunched the wounds which had been bleeding from the devastating knowledge that Kim's deception had extended much further than I had ever suspected; I taped up the deep gash I had sustained on learning that he had discussed with Mrs. Mayfield even the most transient of my sexual shortcomings; I dug out the shards of shock which had speared me after I had learned that Mrs. Mayfield's group was sexual in nature and purpose; I wiped from my mind the consequent possibility that Kim had been unfaithful to me last night, perhaps after toking up on drugs. The healing words: "That was the Mayfield story. But I don't have to be stuck with it" gave me the strength to put the worst of her allegations on hold. There were only two facts, it seemed to me, that I had to face in order to avoid sliding into a state of denial. The first was that Mrs. Mayfield was determined to destroy Kim's second marriage as ably as she had destroyed his first, and the other was that I had severely underestimated the lethal nature of the corrupt mess from which Kim was now trying to extricate himself.

Or from which I hoped Kim was trying to extricate himself. I thought Mrs. Mayfield had probably been lying out of spite when she claimed to have no knowledge of his intention to part from the group, but of course I only had Kim's word that a parting had ever figured on his agenda.

I decided that in order to keep sane I had to operate on the assumption that Kim really did want to extract himself both from the group and, ultimately, from Mrs. Mayfield. Kim had revealed some unpalatable facts about himself the previous evening, but as the result of the pressure I had put on him I thought he had been telling the truth about his activities: he had said goodbye to the group, and although he had wanted to give up Mrs. Mayfield he did not yet feel strong enough to do so.

A number of observations then became clear, and I was relieved to find that they were a lawyer's observations, cool and rational. The first was that as a healer she had committed an appalling breach of confidence by talking of a patient's case-history; even if she had invented the story about Kim's impotence in order to undermine me, she had gone through the motions of violating confidentiality. The second observation was that by attempting to plant a compulsion to self-destruct in my mind Mrs. Mayfield had committed an act of psychological warfare which any right-thinking person would consider deeply malign. And the third observation was that it was now more important than ever that I should find out the true facts from Sophie.

Having repaired my make-up I struggled to my feet. By this time I was remembering Kim's talk about "wrestling with the Powers," and it occurred to me that he had made a fundamental mistake. He had said Mrs. Mayfield had the power to control the Powers, as if she were no more than a magician using secret knowledge, but Mrs. Mayfield was the face of that Primeval Power which generated the Powers, I knew that now. In her that Primeval Power was embodied. In her it lived and moved and had its being.

This sounded like metaphysical nutterguff, but I had to believe my own experience and these were the only words I could find which described it. I had to face the fact that I had been mentally brutalised, battered, humiliated, trounced and trashed by a force far beyond anything which normally emanated from middle-aged suburban bitches who wore cardigans. I had wrestled with the Primeval Power and been decked, that was the truth of it. But I was not about to quit the ring.

I decided that my next task, before phoning Sophie, was to prove that Mrs. Mayfield could have slithered into my flat before delivering Kim's organiser.

Taking a deep breath I headed back at last across the podium to the lobby of Harvey Tower.

IV

"Yes, that's quite correct, Mrs. Betz," said the porter on duty. "Your husband called earlier to say a lady would be delivering a package for him, so when she arrived in the car park I gave the okay for her to come up to podium level."

"And did she reach you straight away?"

"I think so...more or less. I was dealing with some removal men at the time and as one of the lifts had to be set aside for them she might have had to wait for a couple of minutes in the basement, but I remember her coming into the lobby. She wore a royal-blue coat, which made me do a double take as Mr. Betz had warned us all to be on the look-out for ladies in royal blue, but obviously that was just a coincidence."

"Did she go back down to the car park after she'd left the package with you?"

"No, she went straight out onto the podium."

This was not the clear-cut evidence I had hoped to hear, but I still thought it probable that Mrs. Mayfield had gone straight from the car park to the thirty-fifth floor and taken a couple of minutes to mess up the flat before riding down to the lobby to deliver the organiser. I was now sure she had come to Harvey Tower expressly for the trashing because otherwise her appearance there made no sense. If Kim had really left his organiser behind at her house he would have sent a messenger to Fulham on a retrieval mission as soon as he had arrived at Graf-Rosen that morning. He would not have wanted to be deprived of his organiser for a moment longer than was necessary.

I speculated that the Jiffy bag contained not the organiser at all but paper wadding tucked around Kim's key to the flat, the key he would have left with her the previous evening. On arriving home he would have let himself into the flat by borrowing the spare set of keys, and on leaving for work early that morning he would have returned those keys to the porters' desk. There was no way I could check this theory yet, since the porter now on duty was not the one who would have been on duty early in the morning, but it seemed a plausible hypothesis, as plausible as the hypothesis that Mrs. Mayfield had used his key to enter the flat that afternoon and afterwards popped the key in the Jiffy bag for him to collect later.

At that point I cast a sharper eye over the conspiracy between Kim and Mrs. Mayfield, the conspiracy to destroy Sophie's credibility by making it seem as if she were unbalanced enough to blitz around my flat. If I had not met Mrs. Mayfield on the podium, what deductions would I have drawn from today's disturbances? I would have heard from the porter that a woman in a royal-blue coat had been to the building after a man claiming to be Kim and speaking with a slight American accent had phoned to ensure her admittance; Kim would have denied it was him and told me the package contained nothing but paper wadding; and I would have jumped to the conclusion that Ms. Fruity-Loops had been hard at work again, this time assisted by her friendly PI.

I had been riding up in the lift while these thoughts flickered through my brain, but as soon as I reached the thirty-fifth floor it dawned on me that I had to go down again.

It was essential that I intercepted that Jiffy bag to confirm my suspicions.

V

The only reason why I had not demanded the Jiffy bag immediately was that I was unsure how willing the porter would be to relinquish it. I thought there would probably be some rule about never handing over a package to anyone except the addressee or an authorised agent, but I had now psyched myself up to play my least favourite role: the blonde fluffette.

"Hi, it's me again!" I said winningly, slinking out of the lift-lobby and draping myself against the porters' desk. "Oh, I do hope you can help me! It's about that package the lady in blue delivered. My husband called as soon as I got to the flat just now and—oh wow!—he says the bag contains his Psion organiser and he wants me to phone through some information logged there for a meeting he has in ten minutes' time! Isn't it awful how much people depend on technology these days? One really does wonder where it will all end..." The porter, who was over sixty and hated technology almost as much as he loved fluffy little wide-eyed blondes, immediately became voluble and I spared a full minute to listen enrapt to his reminiscences about the good old days before I escaped to the lift, the Jiffy bag tucked beneath my arm.

I experienced a shudder of fear when I finally entered the flat and thought of the balcony, but fortunately I was so keen to open the bag that I was able to wipe the image of a smashed corpse the instant it flashed into my brain. I was diverted further by the discovery that the bag really did contain the organiser. I stared at it, wondering if my conspiracy theory was adrift, but almost at once I realised that the presence of the organiser proved nothing; it could just mean that Kim had genuinely forgotten it and decided he could wait to get it back. I also realised that the only question which truly mattered was whether the bag contained Kim's key to the flat. If it did, then Mrs. Mayfield had had the means to enter the flat that afternoon.

I upended the bag and shook it.

Out dropped the key.

VI

I opened my mouth to utter a string of expletives but not one word came out because I was so shocked. It is one thing to devise a thoroughly upsetting theory. It is quite another to see that theory proved true.

I realised I had to have a drink and that the drink had to be a double vodka martini on the rocks. I went into the kitchen. The small pool of milk was still lying on the floor but I was in such a state that I made no attempt to wipe it up. I just grabbed the ice-tray from the fridge and got on with the job of mixing my tranquilliser. With the glass in my hand I returned to the living-room, but the large windows there were so numerous and the wraparound balcony so extensive that I knew at once that this was not a place where I could focus on regaining my nerve. I withdrew to the bedroom. The wraparound balcony extended there too, but the room had fewer windows and at least I could bolt out of the nearby front door into the windowless lift-lobby if Mrs. Mayfield's predictions became too insistent.

I knocked back my drink in less than two minutes. However, I felt that after being beaten up by Mrs. Mayfield a rapid infusion of alcohol was the least I deserved. I decided to have another. After all, these were exceptional circumstances.

When I returned to the bedroom with my refilled glass I found not only that I was thinking clearly again but that I had reached the point where I was wondering afresh what Sophie knew that Kim was still so anxious to conceal. The impotence seemed at first to fit the bill; if I were to believe Mrs. Mayfield, Kim had lied to me about Sophie's sterility, Sophie had wanted children which she was perfectly capable of having, and Kim had been so unwilling to father them that he had been smitten by an impotence which

Mrs. Mayfield had cured by introducing him to other women and the joys of group sex. But, as I now saw, there was a hole in this story. Kim might well have consulted Mrs. Mayfield if he had been suffering from impotence, but he had told me he had met Mrs. Mayfield only three years ago and by then he and Sophie had been living separate lives for a long time. If he really had suffered from impotence at that point it could have had nothing to do with Sophie's desire for children, a topic which would have surfaced much earlier in the marriage.

On the other hand I only had Kim's word that he had met Mrs. Mayfield three years ago.

And on yet another hand, how far could I believe Mrs. Mayfield anyway?

As I gulped down my drink I began to feel as if I were drowning in lies and that if I did not take active steps to uncover the truth without delay I was going to go under. I seemed to be encountering the lie as a killer—not just a harmless fib which could be shrugged off but a towering edifice of deceit which could result in derangement and destruction.

By the time I had finished my drink my mind was made up. My first task was to phone Kim to say I would be out for the evening and my second task was to see Sophie.

I set down my glass and reached for the bedside phone.

VII

It was now after six, a time when most of the officedrones were on their way home and the big cats were calculating how much longer they needed to stay at their desks in order to stop their power-bases being cracked by any charge of lack of commitment. When I dialled Kim on his private line he picked up the receiver halfway through the first ring.

My heart queasily skipped a beat. "Hi," I said, making a huge effort to sound normal. "How are you doing?"

"That's exactly the question I've been wanting to ask you!" he said concerned. "I called Curtis, Towers and found you'd gone home early with a migraine."

"I'm better now. Look, I'm calling to say I'll be out tonight. Sarah's just phoned in tears so I said I'd take her out to dinner and help her drown her sorrows." Sarah was a solicitor who had worked at my last firm.

"Sacked?" he said sympathetically.

"Dumped. The lover's gone back to his wife, just as I always thought he would... Why were you trying to get in touch with me?" I was sure it was because he had heard from Mrs. Mayfield of my encounter with her, but all he said in reply was: "Warren Schaeffer's in town unexpectedly and as he wants to discuss strategy with me before he flies on to Tokyo tomorrow morning I said I'd meet him at the Savoy tonight, but God knows when I'll be back. You know how peppy people are when they arrive after a west-east flight across the Atlantic— he'll probably still be going strong at midnight."

"Dope his Perrier water at dinner!" I said, wondering if Mrs. Mayfield had failed to get through to him; he sounded so natural that I was tempted to believe he really was going to meet that American colleague at the Savoy. "Okay, darling, tell Warren hullo from me—"

"I sure will—and give my best to Sarah—" He told me he loved me, and hung up.

Instantly I dragged the telephone directory from the hall closet and looked up the number of the Savoy.

"Mr. Warren Schaeffer, please," I said when the operator answered, but although she rang the room for some time no one took the call.

I consoled myself with the thought that at least Kim had told the truth when he had said Warren was in town. Then I dialled directory enquiries to track down Sophie's number.

VIII

At that point I had a setback: there was no Betz listed at Oakshott. Sophie had evidently elected to have an unlisted number after Kim had left home, a wise decision for a woman living on her own but not a helpful one to a person who wanted to contact her urgently.

I was just beginning to think I was fatally stymied when I remembered the organiser. Gasping with relief I retrieved it from the living-room, took a long, hard look at the keyboard and willed myself to keep calm. I never admitted it to anyone, but I was far from keen on technotoys. I did have an organiser—it was vital not to be judged a Luddite—but I still relied on my Filofax and only kept the organiser for show. Tucker had deduced this early in our acquaintance and had tried to give me a helping hand by programming my organiser with an amazing array of information, but although I had been gracious in thanking him I had remained unconverted. I was always afraid of wiping some vital detail by mistake or winding up with a dead battery. In contrast there was never any question that I might fail to keep my Filofax in perfect order.

Kim's organiser was the Psion LZ, a terrifying little item which, he had boasted, contained filing systems, a diary, a notepad, a password facility, a clock plus timer with information about time all over the world, and, last but not least, a telephone/address directory. It could even, if properly wired, talk to printers and computers, but now all I wanted was for it to talk to me. I tried to convince myself that any organiser was basically simple to operate, but I was gripped by my fear of being a technodumbo and only my desperation drove me on to dice with disaster. I was sure that Kim would have recorded the new unlisted number, and although he would know the address so well that logging it would have been unnecessary I thought he would have recorded it to round off the entry. Kim liked well-ordered information as much as I did.

I finally took the plunge and hit the keyboard. Within seconds the telephone/address facility showed up and I paused to congratulate myself, but although I scrolled rapidly through the B-section I found no entry under Betz.

I wondered if the entry could be under S for Sophie. I tapped the keys—and hit the jackpot. There on the screen before me was the address which I half remembered from the first letter she had written me, the address with a different tree in every line, and below the postal code was the phone number.

I dialled it. After two rings an answering machine cut in, and this surprised me because I had not thought Sophie was the kind of woman

235

who would be modern enough to have one. But I knew so little about Sophie. My knowledge of her was a mess of preconceived notions, casual prejudice and downright lies.

The message consisted of Sophie's voice saying pleasantly: "You have reached Oakshott 346157. Please leave your message after the tone," but I had no time to be disappointed by this lack of originality because I had to devise my own message. When the tone had blared I said: "Sophie, it's Carter. I've got to talk to you about Kim, Mrs. Mayfield and that bloody group. I apologise for all the times I kicked you in the teeth. Sophie, if you're listening to this, please, please pick up." I waited but when nothing happened I concluded: "Okay, I'll be leaving London for Oakshott at seven and I hope to be with you by eight."

I made a note of the address and phone number. I was tempted to check the entries under MAYFIELD but I restrained myself. Better to quit the organiser before I made a mess and betrayed my presence, and besides, I was prepared to bet that any information about Mrs. Mayfield would be impossible to access without a password.

Returning to the living-room I replaced the organiser on the coffee-table alongside Kim's front door key, and withdrew to the kitchen to make myself some black coffee. I was already regretting the double vodka martinis.

While I was dosing myself with coffee I changed into a sweatshirt and jeans. In the bathroom I saw my make-up needed attention again but I merely washed off the remnants and ran a comb through my hair. Normally I would never have faced my predecessor without make-up, but now I was in such a state that I no longer cared. In the mirror my reflection looked younger and also curiously naked as if it had been stripped of an inner confidence I had long taken for granted.

For a moment I stood shuddering at the memory of Mrs. Mayfield. Then before I could remember the balcony I fled to the garage, and minutes later I was at the wheel of my Porsche.

IX

I knew Oakshott lay only a mile from the A3, one of the main arteries leading out of London to the south, but I had never been there. How was I going to find "The Larches" in Elm Drive? I might wander around in the deepening twilight until I was thoroughly lost. On the Kingston bypass I pulled into a petrol station and called Sophie again from my carphone, but the machine was still picking up so I severed the connection without leaving a message.

Traffic was still heavy on the A3 even though the rush hour was past, and it was after eight when I reached the Oakshott exit. The sun had set, and as I coasted along through thick woods I was conscious of feeling the town-dweller's old, old distrust of the countryside's creepy loneliness and chilling examples of nature in the raw. I did not like the look of those dark woods. They reminded me of German fairy-tales in which revolting things happened to children who strayed too far into the forest. Nor did I care for the lack of streetlamps. I was relieved when I saw lights ahead, but although I was prepared to stop in the village to ask the way every shop was closed, the petrol station was in darkness and there appeared to be no pub. Surely every English village had a pub! I coasted on, but the pub must have been tucked away down some lane because I never saw it, and the next moment I was back in the forest again with no streetlamps. I decided this was a truly repulsive part of the world, and I was still meditating moodily on this unproductive judgement when I saw not only a turning to the left ahead of me but also a large signboard listing various streets. Halting the car so that my headlights cut through the thickening dusk to the names, I read: "SANDHURST ROAD leading to WOODVILLE PLACE, THE SPINNEY and ELM DRIVE."

Swinging the car to the left I began to trickle down Sandhurst Road. Numerous houses, some already floodlit to repel invaders, lurked on relatively small plots amidst an oppressive number of trees on either side of the road. In the glare of the floodlighting I also saw dense undergrowth featuring garish flowers which I suspected were rhododendrons, Surrey's classy version of the triffid. The journey was getting nastier and nastier. By the time I reached Elm Drive there was such a nervous knot in the pit of my stomach that I decided to stop the car and take some deep breaths.

But once the engine had died, the silence was so overpowering that I felt more rattled than ever. I told myself it was absurd to be demoralised merely because the environment was so different from the one I was used to, but I was dimly beginning to realise that the problem lay not just in the unfamiliarity of my surroundings but in the fact that my disorientation was enabling all the horrors of the past few hours to crawl closer to the surface of my mind. I knew then that the only way to fight off a complete flashback of the scene with Mrs. Mayfield was to move on.

Setting off again I angled the car slowly from side to side so that I could read the names on the gates of the houses. Fortunately Elm Drive was not long, so although "The Larches" was at the end it only took me a couple of minutes to locate it. Parking the car a few feet past the open gates I cut the engine again and crawled out reluctantly into the damp, chilly evening air.

The drive turned out to be much longer than I thought it would be; that was the bad news. The good news was that someone appeared to be at home. The curtains were already drawn but lights glowed on the ground floor.

I padded along, my trainers crunching on the gravel and my eyes focused on the house ahead. It was enormous, possibly even more enormous than the monsters I had passed earlier. There was a three-car garage but all the doors were shut. The walls of the house were covered with ivy—or was it Virginia creeper? Whatever it was, it was sinister, conjuring up memories of all the wrong fairy-tales again. The dusk was becoming more opaque, obscuring my view of the garden, but the lawn on my right was visible; in the subdued light emanating from the house I could see the shaven grass shining as if it were not grass at all but an expanse of water reflecting the light of the moon.

I finally reached the front door and rang the bell.

There was no response. I tried peeking in through the windows but the curtains were too closely drawn for me to see into the rooms beyond. I rang the bell again but when there was still no reply I decided I had nothing to lose by moseying around the back before the darkness drowned the last of the twilight. Padding past the corner of the three-car garage I entered a small paved yard containing dustbins and saw a door which I guessed led into the kitchen.

I tried the handle. To my amazement the door opened. I had heard of places in the country where doors could be left unlocked, but I had never imagined myself encountering such a phenomenon. I waited for a moment. Surely an alarm would go off? But nothing broke that vast silence and in the end, my curiosity overcoming my nervousness, I stepped into the house.

"Sophie?" I called sharply. "Are you there?"

But there was no reply.

The door at the far end of the kitchen was open and from the light in the passage beyond I was able to see the room clearly. There was a large amount of space, suggesting that some interior decorator in the not-too-distant past had done a radical make-over. I doubted that the house was more than sixty years old but the 1930s architect would still have designed sculleries and larders and all manner of poky little nooks where the servants could sweat away preparing the food. Now there was just this big room stuffed with oak fittings where every modern appliance was concealed and only the Aga was exposed to convey its ghastly image of non-urban life.

In the middle of the room was a long wooden table and sitting on top of it was a wide-brimmed straw hat. Next to the hat was an object which I thought at first was a tray bearing entrails, but this deduction only showed how ready I was by that time to jump to melodramatic conclusions. The object was an unusual wooden basket, so flat that it was almost without sides, and lying in this basket lay some dirty gardening gloves and a pair of secateurs. Perhaps the lady of the house had been busy snipping the triffids before vanishing into thin air.

I was now sure I was alone, but as I walked down the passage towards a distant cavern which I assumed to be the hall, I did call Sophie's name again, just in case she was upstairs and had failed to hear my call from the kitchen. But again there was no reply. Obviously she was out and obviously I had no right to intrude on her territory, but people who leave their backdoors unlocked and their burglar alarms switched off are almost begging for a passing stranger to tour their stately homes.

It suddenly occurred to me that if Kim had been accustomed to this kind of grandiose environment it was odd that he should have been willing to settle even temporarily for the cramped quarters of my Barbican flat. Even though he knew how fond I was of my home, I thought he might well have been tempted to suggest that we rent a bigger property while we waited to start house-hunting, particularly as he was now earning so much money. Had the blackmail taken an even bigger toll on his capital than he had admitted? Was there perhaps some other drain on his income? With a sinking heart I realised I knew nothing for certain about his financial affairs, and in an effort to blot this uncomfortable fact from my mind I once more refocused on my surroundings.

I was now reaching the double-height hall, a

magnificent waste of space, where a staircase rose in a curve to the first floor beneath a central chandelier. The latter hung in massive splendour from the ceiling far above, and its multiple lights streamed down upon the glowing colours of the circular carpet below. As my glance travelled beyond the far edge of the carpet I saw that the lights were also picking out the colour of a dark red suit which was lying casually at the foot of the stairs.

A split second later my mind registered the fact that someone was inside the suit. Sophie was lying coiled on the floor, her head at a hideous angle to her neck.

I knew at once she was dead.

NINE

We often fail to cope, at least by the standards of success set up by us or by our families or by others. The failure itself becomes a complex event in our lives. We may end up in psychiatric care ...

DAVID F. FORD
The Shape of Living

I

One of her shoes had come off and was lying nearby. As my feet carried me closer to the corpse my mind registered the fact that the high heel was missing, and a second later I saw it lying some feet away. At once I visualised Sophie stumbling on the stairs, snapping the heel and fatally losing her balance, but even while this devastating sequence of events was flashing through my mind I found myself hoping she was still alive. Kneeling by her body I reached for her wrist, but there was no pulse and her skin was unnaturally cool.

I wondered how long it took dead bodies to chill. Maybe Sophie had even been dead when I had phoned from London, although the evidence of the straw hat and that odd horticultural accessory, the wooden basket, suggested she might have been in the garden at the time.

The shock finally hit me. I was suddenly so frightened that I could hardly breathe. I tried to move but found myself paralysed while the words of the classic question—"Did she fall or was she pushed?"—ricocheted around and around in my brain. Who would have thought that a cliché could trigger such a gush of raw, undiluted terror? My stomach wanted to heave but fortunately the muscles there had gone on strike. I began to pant. I had never panted with fear before. For one long moment I stood listening to this harsh, alien sound, but then I rushed from the house and hared down the dark drive to my car beyond the gates.

II

Once I had ensured I was safe from any murderer who might be lingering on the premises I rapidly got a grip on my panic. My loss of nerve was certainly humiliating, but I told myself that in the circumstances this was forgivable behaviour.

Scrambling out of the car I moved back to

the open gateway. The house looked exactly the same. No additional lights had been turned on and no Hitchcock psychopath (Bruno in *Strangers on a Train*?) was sauntering down the drive to kill me. Therefore it seemed reasonable to assume I was in no danger, but unfortunately by this time my mind was again so clouded by panic that I was no longer in the mood to be convinced by rational assumptions.

I had realised that I was going to have to return to that house.

III

I had to wipe the message I had left on the answerphone. There was going to be an inquest. The police would ask questions. The coroner would ask more. Even if Sophie had died as the result of an accident and no other person had been involved, I hardly fancied being hauled up in court to explain a voice-message which not only put me at the scene but raised all kinds of questions about why I had been so keen to see my husband's ex-wife. Once the investigators began to trawl through the murky waters of Kim's private life God only knew what they might uncover, and although I longed to see Mrs. Mayfield in trouble with the police I did not want the trouble to engulf either me or Kim.

On the other hand, if Kim had killed her I had a duty to co-operate with the police. Indeed if Kim had killed her I would want to co-operate with the police. But as matters stood I had no proof either that Sophie had been murdered or that Kim had done the killing.

I had to break off to do some more shuddering

244

but once I had recovered I was able to think more incisively. Kim was a cool, tough customer. I could see him racing down to Oakshott ahead of me in order to negotiate with Sophie, but I had difficulty visualising him making such a mess of the negotiations that she wound up dead, especially when he had such a first-class motive for silencing her.

I decided I was going to act on the assumption that Sophie had died accidentally when Kim was miles from Oakshott, but I did wish the idea of him preceding me to the house was less plausible. If he had left the office as soon as we had spoken on the phone he could have had a head start on me of at least half an hour if not longer, as I tried to get in touch with Sophie, drank black coffee and changed into casual clothes. And if he had arrived on the scene, could his presence and Sophie's fall have formed nothing but a big coincidence?

I decided that I should not attempt to answer this question in case I started to pant again, but the next moment I had a brainwave which made me feel much better. Mrs. Mayfield could have killed Sophie after instructing Kim to set himself up with an alibi. I had no trouble whatsoever imagining Mrs. Mayfield pushing Sophie downstairs.

I suddenly became aware that I was still standing by the gates, still looking at the house, still listening to the alien silence—although the silence was in reality not empty at all but filled with the scufflings in the undergrowth of nocturnal creatures busy snaking around among last autumn's leaves. An owl hooted somewhere. Without doubt the countryside was the stuff of nightmares. I pined futilely for my urban tower.

Driven on by the need to act before I fluffed out again I forced myself to return to the back door. There was still no sign of a smiling psychopath. Feeling more confident I padded once more into the kitchen and when I saw the gardening gloves, lying in the wooden basket, it occurred to me to think of fingerprints. The gardening gloves were too thick to be anything but a hindrance indoors, but there were some rubber gloves by the sink and I thought Sophie had probably been a good enough housewife to keep a spare pair in stock. I did not want to use the gloves by the sink in case the police started wondering who had taken them—and I would have to remove any gloves I used because they would contain my fingerprints.

I found a spare pair in a cupboard below the counter and stuffed the plastic wrapper in my bag. Once I was gloved I used a tea-towel to wipe the knob on the cupboard, the handle of the back door and the panel of the light-switch. I tried to remember if I had touched anything else. I had grasped Sophie's wrist in my search for a pulse but I did not think fingerprints could be lifted from skin—or maybe nowadays they could. That meant I would have to—but I chopped off that thought. First things first. I had to wipe that tape.

There was an extension in the kitchen but this was just an ordinary phone. Tiptoeing into the hall I found the door which led into the living-room and switched on the lights. I saw what I wanted at once. An answering machine was hooked up to a phone on a table by the sofa, and I was just heaving a sigh of relief when I realised something was wrong. There was no beep signalling that a message had been left, and no flashing red light either.

I checked the tape.

It had been wiped.

IV

I stood staring at it. I was thinking that although Kim would have wanted to wipe the tape to protect me, Mrs. Mayfield would have felt under no such obligation.

That meant it had been Kim, not Mrs. Mayfield, who had visited Oakshott—but no, not necessarily; there was yet another possibility. Sophie herself could have wiped the tape. She could have returned to the house from the garden, played back all the messages and reset the machine before Mrs. Mayfield arrived.

Returning to the hall I saw the corpse and fetched the tea-towel from the kitchen so that I could wipe the wrist I had held. Afterwards I finally suffered a physical reaction to all the shock but I managed to find the downstairs lavatory before I threw up. This well-ordered evacuation of my stomach contents came as a relief to me, not just because I felt better afterwards but because the mess could be flushed away without trace. Having drunk some water by using my hands as a cup I dragged myself back into the kitchen to replace the tea-towel.

Here an important thought occurred to me. This was my one and only chance to search Sophie's territory for an explanation of the mysteries which had driven me to Oakshott. Returning to the living-room I found that the antique desk was almost empty, a fact that suggested it was kept merely for its ornamental value, but the desk in the study on the other side of the hall looked more promising. This desk was modern and functional. It contained not only stationery but also files, some hanging from a rail in the deep bottom drawer and some stacked flat in the drawers above. There was no typewriter or word processor, but I noticed a small Xerox machine on the table by the window and guessed that Sophie was efficient enough to keep copies of all her handwritten business letters.

The files presented a striking array of colours: terracotta brown, pillar-box red, sea-green, sky-blue—and there was even a nauseating shade of yellow which reminded me of my recent session in the lavatory. It did not take me long to work out that the reds related to the house and car, the browns to the garden (much correspondence with a landscape architect), the blues to her work connected with the local church and other charities, and the pukish yellows to correspondence with lawyers. I reflected that it was probably not without significance that she had allotted the lawyers in her life such a disgusting shade.

I removed the yellow files. There was one relating to the death of her mother and matters arising from probate. Another contained correspondence relating to a trust of which she was a trustee, and there was a similar file relating to a trust under which she was a beneficiary. I also found correspondence relating to employment legislation. Apparently her gardener had been in trouble with the Inland Revenue because... I stopped reading.

There was no file relating to the divorce.

Replacing the yellow files I checked the contents of the drawers above, but they were entirely devoted to beige files containing correspondence with her stockbroker and accountant. I flipped through but it was just the usual guff spawned by accountants and stockbrokers hired to feather-nest a wealthy client.

Searching the rest of the desk I discovered that the bottom drawer on the other side of the knee-hole was locked. This made me sit up. I deduced that although Sophie had trusted her cleaner not to snoop in boring files, there was at least one file which had to be kept under lock and key.

I returned to the living-room, where I had previously noted Sophie's handbag lying on a chair. In a zipped compartment I found her key-ring and saw that one of the keys was a small modern item which looked as if it might fit a drawer of a large modern desk.

It did.

I opened the drawer but found it empty.

Someone had been there before me.

V

Again I reminded myself that I still had not proved Kim had been in the house. Sophie herself could have removed the contents of the drawer and absent-mindedly relocked it, even though there were no contents left to safeguard; perhaps she had decided to keep the contents somewhere which was still more secure. I wondered if she had a safe, but there was no sign of one on the ground floor and I found I was unable to face going upstairs. My courage was on the ebb. It was time to go.

As soon as I had reached this decision I could

hardly wait to hurl myself from the house. It took a huge effort to backtrack through the rooms I had visited to make sure I had left no trace of myself behind, but once this safety-check had been completed I hurried outside.

Closing the back door I stripped off my gloves, shoved them deep into my bag alongside their Cellophane wrapper, and fled down the drive to my car.

VI

I thought it best not to stop on the A3 but as soon as I reached London I found a quiet sidestreet and used the carphone. At my flat the new machine picked up the call but I did not leave a message; it was enough to know Kim was still out. It occurred to me that if he had gone down to Surrey the Mercedes would be missing from its slot in the garage, but if he had merely gone to the Savoy he would probably have taken a cab, particularly as he and Warren were going to be drinking.

I tried to remember whether the Mercedes had been in its slot when I had set off earlier from the garage in my Porsche, but our slots were some way apart and I found I was unable to picture whether or not Kim's had been empty.

I called the Savoy again but was told Mr. Warren Schaeffer was still not answering the phone in his room. Glancing at my watch I realised he could be lingering over dinner but I decided not to have him paged. Eventually he would return to his room and eventually I would get to speak to him. Driving east along the south side of the river I finally crossed Blackfriars

Bridge into the City just before ten and five minutes later I was back in the garage of Harvey Tower.

The Mercedes was missing. Moreover the parking attendant was able to remember that Kim had taken it out at around six-fifteen. "He came in from the street," I was told, "so it looked as if he'd come straight from work."

This evidence certainly suggested a man in a hurry following a warning call from Mrs. Mayfield that the conspiracy was shot and I would inevitably be Surrey-bound in pursuit of the truth. But again, nothing was proved. Kim could have been in a rush to get down to Surrey but he could equally have been keen to get to the Savoy for his first drink of the evening, and maybe he was old enough not to be bothered by the prospect of driving home after plenty of alcohol. It did occur to me that he would have wanted to stop off at home to shower and change if he had been planning to dine at the Savoy, but then I recalled that he could have done that at the office; he always kept a clean shirt there.

I was just on the point of convincing myself that he had gone to the Savoy when I realised he would be very reluctant to face a top-level business meeting without his organiser.

I rode up to the lobby to talk to the porter who had come on duty at six. "Excuse me," I said, "but did my husband stop by earlier to try to collect a package?" But the porter said he had not seen Kim that evening.

I withdrew to the lift-lobby. I was now sure that there had been no business meeting with Warren Schaeffer and that Kim had headed straight for Oakshott after we had spoken on the phone.

The lift arrived. I stumbled inside, stabbed the button and slumped against the far wall. It seemed as if I was being jacked up to a new level of tension, and when I opened my front door a moment later I found I had plunged into yet another nightmare.

The flat was a shambles.

VII

Before I opened the front door I was delayed because I was unable to find my keys; I had reached such a pitch of stressed-out exhaustion that when I found they were not in their usual compartment I proved incapable of tracking them down until I had knelt on the floor, turned my bag upside down and picked over the contents. With the key-ring at last in my hand I wanted to get up but I was too debilitated to do more than slump back on my heels, and it was then that I heard a sequence of banging, clattering sounds in the distance, as if someone were slamming doors in between flinging saucepans around the kitchen. From my position in the centre of the lift-lobby I was equidistant from all three front doors of the thirty-fifth-floor flats. Too dazed to identify which flat the sounds were coming from but knowing that my flat had to be empty, I waited zombie-like for the noise to cease. Only then did I succeed in hauling myself to my feet and opening the front door.

The moment I stepped into the hall I saw that the door of the master bedroom, the door which faced down the long corridor to the living-room, was closed even though I was sure I had left it open, but I was distracted from this discrepancy by the fact that all the pictures lining the walls of the corridor were askew. Moreover when I glanced through the open door into the second bathroom I saw that the shower-curtain had been derailed from the pole which was sagging from one of its holders. Too stupefied to stop I moved on towards the living-room.

Here the furniture was wildly awry, the sofa now slanting at a crazy angle and both armchairs tipped on their sides. The étagère had crashed to the floor, and not only all its ornaments but all its glass shelves were broken, the fragments scattered over the carpet. The stack of magazines on the coffee-table had been pitched sideways as if buffeted by a gale-force wind, and again the stool by the telescope had been upturned. But the telescope itself was still standing unharmed.

Dumbfounded by all this fragmentation I backed away, but when I glanced into the kitchen I saw more mess. The mug which I had used for my black coffee earlier was lying broken on the floor, the kettle had fallen into the sink and the toaster, hanging over the counter, was only saved from falling by its cord, which was still plugged into the outlet on the wall. As I stared in utter disbelief at this incomprehensible scene the lights flickered as if the electrical supply were about to fail, but before I had time to cringe at the thought of a power cut, the disruption ended.

I rescued the toaster from its dangling position and turned back into the living-room. On the carpet among the slew of magazines and smashed ornaments lay not only Kim's organiser, which I had left on the coffee-table, but also his key, the key which had dropped out of the Jiffy bag, the key to the flat.

I stared at that key.

Because of the porter's testimony less than five minutes ago I knew Kim had not been in the flat since I had left it earlier; to get in he would have had to borrow the spare set of keys again from the porters' desk, but the porter had firmly stated that he had not seen Kim that evening. The spare keys would never have been doled out to Mrs. Mayfield—unless, of course, Kim had phoned earlier to give his permission, but the porter had made no mention of such a call and in the context of our conversation I felt he would have told me if he and Kim had spoken to each other. So if the spare keys had not been handed over to Mrs. Mayfield, then Mrs. Mayfield could not have entered the flat.

But if Kim had not been in the flat and Mrs. Mayfield had not been in the flat and Sophie had not been in the flat, who—

My brain seemed to give a strange lurch, like a defective car slipping gears. I could not work out this conundrum which defied reason and common sense. I could only stand amidst the mess and say to myself: this cannot have happened so therefore it has not happened. Yet it had happened. I told myself there had to be a rational explanation. But there was none.

Fear swept through me, and the rush of adrenaline seemed to explode in my mind, wiping out my exhaustion and firing me up to an unprecedented pitch of nervous tension. Again my brain lurched, and suddenly I was seeing the scene before my eyes so clearly that it was as if the rim of every object was edged in black. All the colours seemed to be abnormally bright, even garish. I felt as if someone had injected LSD straight into my head to scramble my brains.

I looked back at the kitchen and found everything was strange there too, particularly the red rubber gloves by the sink. I knew they were a pale, pinkish red but now they were scarlet. Rubbing my eyes in a futile attempt to clear my vision, I remembered the yellow gloves I had taken from Sophie's kitchen and knew I should now transfer them from my bag to the garbage. By eliminating this untidy detail I could start the task of reducing the chaos to order, but I did not move. I said aloud: "Order," but I could only think what a strange sound those syllables made and how senseless they seemed. Order. The word was just five letters of the alphabet arranged in a certain way, and the arrangement was now obsolete. There was no meaning there any more.

I had just completed this thought when I realised that the balcony's sliding door must be ajar.

The curtain was drawn to one side still but even so it partially concealed the door and it was this hidden section which was obviously adrift from the frame; the curtain was shifting in the breeze, and the moment I noticed this I realised for the first time that the room was abnormally cold.

I picked my way slowly across the littered carpet. The door had to be closed at once because otherwise I might want to go outside, and once I was standing on the balcony I would without doubt want to climb over the rail. In an ordered world I would not want to throw myself off a balcony, but there was no order any more and I felt I was predestined to fall from a great height. Hadn't there been another high flyer long ago who had flown too close to the sun and fallen to earth when his wax wings had started to melt? My wings were melting now—I could feel the wax dripping down my back—but so long as I shut the door and stayed in the ice-cold room the wax would harden again and I would be safe. Even so I could feel the balcony luring me on to fulfil my destiny. It was beckoning me forward, compelling me to—

I drew back the curtain and bumped into the glass. The door was closed. Yet it could not be closed because I had seen the curtain shuddering in the breeze. So—

I stopped. A sound had reached me from the far end of the flat. Someone was behind that closed door of the master bedroom, but of course this was impossible because no one could have entered the flat. So rationally, logically, that meant... But I could not think what it meant. All I could think was that those words "rationally" and "logically" were so fragile, so utterly irrelevant in this chaotic world which was driving me inexorably into melt-down. The god Order had been destroyed, and into the vacuum created in my consciousness poured the Principalities and Powers, huge cosmic forces over which I had no control and against which no frail unarmed human being could hope to survive undamaged.

I heard the sound again. I knew the intruder had to be Mrs. Mayfield, even though I could not understand how she had got in. By this time I was so frightened that I was temporarily beyond displaying fear. With my body on autopilot and my brain still fried as if by chemicals which I myself was manufacturing, I moved like a robot to the threshold of the living-room and stared down the corridor to the door facing me at the far end. For a moment I thought I was too terrified to speak.

Then I heard myself call with a bizarre, stilted politeness: "Mrs. Mayfield, could you come out, please, because I don't like you hiding in there."

Instantly the door flew open. It flew open so fast that it hit the wall behind with a bang.

Beyond the threshold but nowhere near the door a woman stood facing me. I saw the glow of royal blue but I never paused to stare at her clothes because I was so stunned by her face. There was no mistaking her. Every feature was sharply outlined, my enhanced perception ensuring that I saw her with abnormal clarity.

It was Sophie.

For one long moment we stared at each other. Then as the door slammed shut to enclose her again, I began to scream and scream as if a madman were butchering me with an axe.

PART THREE

FRAGMENTING IN THE DARK

The open door; and the closed door. It is a profoundly religious theme, because religion has always dealt with what anthropologists call "thresholds," those periods of significant transitions in life, the passing through a new door into the unknown... They are potentially dangerous moments... And the question of who stands at the door, and whether doors are perceived as open or closed, and what we expect to find on the other side of them, is more than a nice piece of religious imagery. It has to do with our capacity to change, and with the kind of security needed to cross some major threshold.

JOHN HABGOOD
Confessions of a Conservative Liberal

TEN

*Our defences and securities vary... But under-
lying them all is the fact of agonised fragility.
Just facing this truth of our own fragility is a
major step in the formation of a heart.*

D A V I D   F .   F O R D
The Shape of Living

I

The world had been turned inside out. It had been
blasted off its axis and rendered incomprehensible. No words could have described the abyss
into which I was now falling, the abyss where my
intellect and my will no longer operated, the
abyss where the saving power of my hard-won inde-
pendence and my proud self-sufficiency was
exposed as a grand illusion. The high flyer's
wings had melted. I was in free fall, plummeting
not only to earth but to an earth which was so
chaotic, so entirely devoid of familiar landmarks,
that it resembled an alien planet.

I screamed until I ran out of breath. Then I
found myself hurtling out of the flat, slamming
the front door and racing down the emergency
staircase. I was too terrified to wait for the lift.
Down and down the stairs I pounded but eventually my knees trembled, my calves ached and
I had to sit down. I was still about twenty floors
above the podium. Finally I staggered to the
nearest lift-lobby. Still breathing hard I watched

the door to the stairs in case Sophie burst through it in pursuit of me, but no one came and at last I remembered I had to summon the lift. I went to the wall by the nearest shaft but there were no buttons. Belatedly my brain served up the memory that in a Barbican tower block the lifts were summoned by buttons placed on top of a cylinder which stood in the centre of the floor.

The lift came. I pressed the lowest button for the car park, but when I reached my Porsche I realised numbly that I could go no farther. I had no car-keys. I had no keys of any kind. I had no money. I had no charge cards. I had rushed out of the flat in such a state that I had forgotten my bag, and now I had nothing, nothing at all. I felt as if I were stark naked and staked to an anthill.

I leaned panting against the Porsche, and with that same eerie clarity of vision which had allowed me to see every feature of Sophie's face, I saw how fragile my world was and how insignificant. It was as if after focusing on my heavily defended fortress, a camera had pulled back to reveal that the fortress was no more than a grain of sand in a desert, while beyond the desert lay a vast multicoloured landscape which I had never even begun to imagine.

I tried to think. I could get the spare keys from the porters' desk, return to the flat and retrieve my bag. That was the logical, sensible thing to do. But I couldn't do it. I couldn't go back to that flat in case Sophie was waiting to drive me off the balcony. So that meant...

I suddenly realised that if I lingered in the garage much longer Sophie might give up waiting in the flat and come after me. Immediately I began stumbling towards the entrance of the car park. I passed the attendant, who looked at me strangely, and emerged into the Beech Street tunnel which was brightly lit. There I saw cars travelling between Aldersgate Street in the west and Finsbury Pavement in the east as if life were still continuing normally in some dimension to which I no longer had access. I walked west out of the tunnel, and when I saw the Barbican tube station ahead of me at the junction I longed to escape into the Underground but of course I had no money for the fare. All I could do was walk, and I knew I had to keep moving because when I looked up at the night sky I saw the velvety darkness, the *voluptuous* darkness which had made Mrs. Mayfield salivate, and I knew it was waiting to suffocate me if I failed to find a safe place to hide.

Turning left into Aldersgate Street I hurried down the west side of the Barbican, the side where the ramparts and turrets and slit windows of the walkways rose high above the street like the walls of a medieval castle.

I was trying to think whom I could approach for help. I pictured several acquaintances who would at least start by showing sympathy, but the sympathy would certainly be short-lived if I were to turn up late at night and say: "My flat keeps getting wrecked and I think my husband killed his ex-wife—oh, and by the way, I've just seen her ghost." That was the road to the asylum, and once word got around that I was suffering a breakdown of some kind I'd be finished. Obviously I'd fallen through a black hole into another universe but I had to believe I could crawl back. The only trouble was that I could not crawl back on my own. I was lost, shredded, wiped. I needed a fixer whom nothing would faze.

Immediately I thought of Tucker and remembered his part-time voluntary work listening to people in trouble. He would listen to me. He would know what to do. He would cope with the fact that I was calling at such a preposterous hour and in such a pathetic condition.

Giving a sob of relief I broke into a run for a few yards before slowing to a reasonable pace. I had some way to go. I had to conserve my energy.

Aldersgate Street was a drab place by day and a dingy place by night, but the City was quiet at that hour and at least I did not have to endure the kerb-crawlers who would now be hard at work in the West End. I began to feel calmer. The weird clarity of vision had ebbed, and as I moved through the neon glow it was possible to forget that above the glow was the dark, waiting to drop on me the instant I lost my nerve.

I felt like losing my nerve when I saw ahead of me the dark tower of the Museum of London, a circle surrounded by high buildings where Aldersgate Street met London Wall. Here too there were neon lights, but the high buildings seemed as if poised to crush me and the sinister tower of the Museum reminded me of Kim, talking neurotically of the Powers.

I began to increase my pace. I was now horribly afraid of breaking down, but I felt that if only I could get past that circle I might still succeed in holding myself together.

I found it helped to pretend I had an invisible companion. I said aloud to him: "Please beat back the Powers. Please lighten the darkness," and the strange thing was that when I spoke these words I felt that someone was indeed falling into step beside me. I told myself this was mere wish-fulfilment—how could it be anything else?—but I was puzzled by the fact that my invisible companion was not at all as I would have wished him to be. Given the choice I would have hired a muscleman pumped high on steroids and toting a Kalashnikov, someone who could respond to violence with violence, but I knew this stranger was quite unarmed. Moreover he was helping me not because he had been hired to do so but because he had been where I now was and he knew that what I needed most at that moment was companionship, encouragement and the inspiration just to keep on keeping on when my world was in ruins, my body was exhausted and my mind was so bruised that I hardly recognised it as my own.

Yet although the stranger had no weapon of any kind, the darkness parted before him as he escorted me to the first exit out of that sanity-splitting circle, and when I finally rounded the long curve of the road which led into King Edward Street I saw ahead of me, high on Ludgate Hill, a great explosion of light. The dome of St. Paul's was floodlit. The sky around it was pitch-black, so black that the grey dome seemed white, and the cross on the summit shone like molten gold on a slab of jet.

I hurried uphill, past the old graveyard called Postman's Park, past the rose-garden in the ruins of Christ Church Greyfriars, until finally I veered left towards the parallel street of St. Martin's Le Grand which linked Aldersgate Street with Cheapside. So many of the City's streets had ancient names, far more ancient than Wren's version of the Cathedral which was now so close that it seemed to be erupting above the drab modern office buildings which still separated me from it. I remembered all the times I had glanced casually at that floodlit dome through my telescope. I had been so remote from it, so sealed off from its powerful reality, yet now, dragged from my ivory tower and flung out into the dark, I felt as if I were seeing not just the dome but the whole Cathedral for the first time. How vast it was, rising so high above all those acres rebuilt after the war and linking the resurrected City with a past which was still vibrating in the names of the streets—and as my companion steered me on towards the light I knew that if I were to recite those names the sound would soothe my mind and keep me sane.

"St. Martin's Le Grand," I heard myself say aloud, "Little Britain, Cheapside, Poultry, Milk Street, Egg Street, Love Lane, Old Jewry, Cornhill, Threadneedle Street, Bishopsgate, Moorgate, London Wall, Houndsditch, Bevis Marks..." On and on rolled the names as I remembered that when terrorists were arrested in Northern Ireland they survived interrogation by endlessly naming the streets of Belfast. And it seemed to me then that I too had fallen into the hands of an enemy, though it was an enemy who was as invisible as the compassionate stranger who had fallen into step by my side.

I was very close to the Cathedral now; I was crossing the street towards Paternoster Row. Paternoster Row! I could remember when I had first arrived in the City and studied the map. Several of the streets around St. Paul's had religious names: Paternoster Row, Ave Maria Lane, Amen Court... How quaint I had thought, that

265

those echoes of a dead culture should still survive, but the culture was not dead at all, I could see that now; it was vibrantly alive, and as I entered the pedestrian precinct on the north side of the churchyard, all the names were chiming in unison so that every past and present particle of that brilliant landscape was fused in some eternal Now which was beyond my ability to understand.

The precinct was deserted, and for a moment as I hurried along it I was cut off from the noise of the traffic but the silence did not frighten me because everywhere was bathed in light. The Cathedral towered above me as I struggled around its perimeter and emerged at last at the top of Ludgate Hill.

I began the journey down to Ludgate Circus, the main junction at the bottom of the valley, but as soon as the floodlit Cathedral lay behind me I began to be afraid again of the dark. I could feel the fear expanding but my companion was hustling me forward at an increased pace as if determined to snatch me from the suffocating net spread by my enemy. "Keep naming the names!" I heard him urge, so I started reciting them again, muttering like some pathetic old bag lady who was living on the streets after being turned out of her mental hospital. "Paternoster Row, Ave Maria Lane, Amen Court... Paternoster Row, Ave Maria Lane, Amen Court..." I reached the Circus, crossed New Bridge Street and hurried on downhill towards the river.

At the top of Fleetside I paused, my nerve finally failing me. The streetlights were out. Just some electrical fault, of course, but... How dark it looked down there, how very dark, even though there was a light still burning above the front door of the house by the church. "Keep naming the names!" cried my companion, knowing I was flagging, and in his determination to save me I knew just how much I was cherished. "Keep naming the names!" But my powers of speech were ebbing fast and all I could do was whisper: "Paternoster... Ave Maria... Amen," over and over again as I groped my way into the dark towards the light at the end of the street.

I was within ten yards of the Vicarage when the light went out.

"*Run!*" shouted my companion before I could waste breath on a scream, and I did run. The adrenaline generated by terror gave my body such a boost that I covered the last yards in a flash and vaulted up the steps to the front door.

It was too dark to see where the bell was. I started to bang on the panels.

"Help me!" I shouted. "Help me! Let me in!"

At once the porch light flicked on again as someone unhooked a chain and reversed the locks. The next moment the door swung wide and I saw a man's tall figure silhouetted against the lighted hall.

I was still shouting: "Help me, help me—" but I did not have to shout any longer. It was as if my invisible companion had finally materialised, pouring himself into the man in front of me so that the man himself, though a stranger, seemed known to me through and through. A hand reached out, drawing me firmly across the threshold, and as I stumbled at last out of the dark I heard him say in the gentlest and kindest of voices: "It's all right. You're safe here. Come on in."

II

I sank down on the nearest chair in a large hall at the point where an ornate wrought-iron staircase rose to the floor above. The front door closed. My rescuer stooped over me. "Have you been attacked?"

I shook my head. I knew I had been attacked over and over again, but I knew too that it would be wiser not to talk about wrestling with the Powers and being vanquished, of struggling through the darkness with an unseen companion who had given me the strength to survive. Yet at the same time, because I knew that in some mysterious way this man *was* my unseen companion, I found myself addressing him as if he had been with me on the journey. I felt I had to make at least some attempt to tell him how grateful I was, how amazed, how overwhelmed.

In a rush I said: "I'm not sure how to thank you because what you did was so extraordinary that I can hardly put it into words, but I know the Powers were powerless against you, they couldn't break into that circle you created around me, you cared enough to make sure they couldn't break in. I didn't know there could be such caring by a stranger but it happened, I experienced it—yet at the same time I can hardly believe it because the caring was so undeserved, so unmerited, so unlike anything I've ever experienced before."

There were tears streaming down my face but I was barely aware of them. I was more aware of him squatting down by my side so that we could converse more easily, but he made no attempt to speak. He simply went on holding my hand, being there, caring for me although I had done nothing to earn such care. However, as the seconds passed and my mind began to slip back from its heightened state of consciousness into its normal mode of perceiving reality, I began to grasp that this was a man who in the ordinary course of my daily life I had never previously met. He was dark, about forty, with straight hair, brown eyes and a sensitive mouth. Only his square chin seemed familiar. He was clearly troubled by my distress but in no way embarrassed by it. The expression in his eyes was as kind as his voice, and cautiously I reached out to touch his clerical collar. I think I wanted to make sure he was real and not the hallucination of a disturbed mind.

"Odd how we still wear these collars, isn't it?" he said casually. "Sometimes I think the Church is far too wedded to tradition."

I decided he was real. It was the wry, humorous tone which convinced me. Tentatively I said: "I'm looking for Tucker."

The clergyman said startled: "*I'm* Tucker. How can I help?"

"No, I don't mean you." I tried to explain but it was too difficult. I started to cry again.

"Ah," said the clergyman, having put two and two together, "you want my brother. Just a moment." And he moved into a room on the other side of the hall. As I watched he flicked a switch on a box which stood on a large, untidy desk and said a moment later: "A friend of yours is here. She seems a little distressed, so if you could come down straight away... Thanks." He cut the connection but even before he could return to the hall I heard a door banging shut at the top of the house. Wiping my eyes with the back of my

269

hand I looked down at my jeans and wondered if Tucker would recognise me.

Footsteps clattered down the stairs and came to an abrupt halt on the half-landing above the hall. Tucker's voice exclaimed amazed: "God Almighty, Ms. G, whatever have you been up to?" and a second later he was bounding down the remaining stairs two at a time to eliminate the gap which separated us.

I tried so hard to be Carter Graham. I tried so hard to produce a snappy response worthy of a smart high flyer. But in the end all I said was: "Oh Tucker, I'm so glad to see you!" And hurtling into his arms I collapsed sobbing against his chest like some flaked-out fluffette floundering around in another era, in another world, long ago.

III

"Hey, it's okay, it's all right—I'm here—I'll listen—I won't go away..." Tucker was soothing me with old-fashioned gestures and modern platitudes; I was being enfolded in a solid, respectable clasp and my back was being patted gently, moves which kept his hands occupied in a suitably asexual manner. I was dimly aware that he was wearing a sweatshirt devoid of a logo, and white jeans. The sweatshirt smelled of fabric softener, as if it had just been laundered. His curly hair seemed longer than when I had last seen it, brushed and subdued, at Alice's flat, and this hint of Bohemianism was enhanced by the designer stubble which was darkening his jaw. His eyes were bright with concern, astonishment and something else, something very friendly which I could not immediately define. It was as if my extreme vulnerability had touched him in ways which he had never anticipated but was far from finding unwelcome.

Meanwhile my disintegration into total fluffiness was so appalling me that I was struggling to stand up straight and switch off the waterworks. As I feebly mopped my face again I managed to say: "Sorry, Tucker, not quite myself. Just been to hell. Didn't like it."

"Come up to my room and tell me everything!"

"Eric," said the older Tucker, "I think Ms. Graham, who's clearly very shocked, might prefer more neutral surroundings. Why don't you take her into the reception room down here while I make some tea?"

"I'll handle this, if you don't mind, Gil."

"I do mind. I'm responsible for strangers who come to this house in distress and I'm entitled to say how they should be received."

"Oh, don't be so damned pompous!"

"Better pompous than irresponsible!"

I seemed to be reviving ancient nursery feuds. Quickly I said: "I don't want to cause trouble. I'll just sit here in the hall."

"No need for that," said the younger Tucker quickly, shaping up. "We'll do as Gil suggests," but at once his brother said to me: "Is that acceptable to you, Ms. Graham? You're the one who's important here."

I was so surprised by this unusual and imaginative consideration that at first I could only mutter an assent, but curiosity soon surfaced. "How did you know who I was?"

Gilbert Tucker gave a fleeting, ironical smile before saying drily: "You've been mentioned now and then during the past few weeks." He turned aside. "Let me make that tea I mentioned."

"This way, Carter," said his brother bossily, piloting me across a nearby threshold into a small, shabby room where two battered leather armchairs faced each other beside an elderly gas fire. Above the fireplace hung a crucifix consisting of a light brown wooden cross and a figure made of pewter-coloured metal.

"Do you want to wait for the tea to arrive or do you want to plunge into your story straight away?" said Tucker, parking himself in the chair opposite me.

But I did not know. All I could say was: "God, I can't believe I fluffed out against your chest like that!"

"I assure you my chest was happy to be of service."

"I bet. Hey, Tucker..." My voice trailed away.

"Yes, Ms. G?"

"Something's wired a computer virus directly into my brain. I've been hacked."

"I'll fix it."

My eyes yet again filled with tears.

"Ah, Ms. G, Ms. G—"

"Can it, Tucker. I've got to think," I said feverishly. "I must *think*."

For by that time my battered powers of reason were telling me that I had to stop myself dumping him in deep trouble.

IV

The problem was my behaviour at Oakshott.

When lawyers find someone who may or may not have been murdered but who has without doubt died in a manner which requires investigation, they don't go poncing around in rubber gloves while wiping fingerprints off doorhandles and snooping among private files. They call the police. Or at the very least they call for an ambulance. If Sophie had died by accident I might get away even now with pleading mere unprofessional behaviour, but if Sophie had been murdered I risked being charged as an accessory after the fact. In retrospect I was appalled that I had behaved so idiotically but at the same time I could see just how it had happened. Shock had knocked me off balance, and it was worth remembering too that the events at Oakshott were only the latest in a series of blows to my equilibrium. If I had finally freaked out in that silent, sinister house amidst those silent, sinister woods, it was hardly surprising. But it did leave me in a difficult position as I struggled to clamber back onto an even keel.

Obviously the most important task I now had to undertake was to protect Tucker from being dragged into the Oakshott débâcle. If Sophie had been murdered and I confided in him, he too could be classed as an accessory after the fact unless he confided in the police immediately. So I could not tell him Sophie was dead. But if I could not tell him Sophie was dead, how could I tell him that I had seen her ghost—and would he believe me even if I did tell him? I thought he might quixotically try to believe me, but I did not want someone being quixotic. I wanted someone who could accept my story and come up with some practical suggestions for sorting out my life. Or in other words, I was beyond being helped by a mere trained listener, no matter how sympathetic and delightful he was. I needed an expert—and not just some whimsical old ghostbuster from the nutty fringes. I wanted a professional who was protected by the rules relating to confidentiality.

I had just reached this rational though baffling conclusion when the Reverend Gilbert Tucker entered the room with a mug of tea.

V

Gilbert seemed alarmed by the deep silence, and as he set the tea down on the lamp-table by my chair he said quickly to me: "How are you feeling?"

"Banjaxed. But not brain-dead, not any more." I turned to his brother. "Tucker," I said, "don't go ballistic, but I've got to talk to Gilbert on his own. I've just worked out that I need a priest."

"It can happen to the best of us, Ms. G, but at least the clerical white rabbit is right here and I don't even have to pull him out of a hat." He stood up.

"No need to go too far away—"

"I'll be in the kitchen." He smiled encouragingly at me before he left the room.

As Gilbert took his place in the armchair opposite I said: "How far does clerical confidentiality run nowadays?" but he was reassuring.

"Nothing you tell me now will be repeated by me to anyone else."

I listened to my shallow breathing for several seconds before saying: "Truthfully?"

"Truthfully. I deal in trust, not betrayal."

I swallowed. "All the time?"

"It has to be all the time. After all, you can't be half trustworthy any more than you can be half pregnant. You're either trustworthy or you're not."

I mentally pawed these sentences as if they were pieces in a complicated jigsaw which needed rearranging, but finally decided no rearrangement was necessary for the picture to make sense. I reminded myself that I was not about to confess to murder. My misdeeds, terrible though they were when committed by a lawyer, were almost certainly not sufficient to drive a clergyman to wash his hands of me and phone the police. I decided some sort of confession could now be risked. But I also decided to be as sparing as possible in my references to the Oakshott horrors.

"All right," I said. "I trust you not to shop me but I wonder if I can trust you not to laugh. I've seen a ghost."

Gilbert looked startled but not, so far as I could tell, disbelieving. "Where?"

"In my flat just now. It was my husband's ex-wife."

"When did she die?"

"Earlier this evening in Surrey. I found the body."

Somehow Gilbert kept calm and continued to ask sensible questions. "How sure are you that she was dead?"

"There was no pulse. She had fallen downstairs. Her neck was broken."

"An accident?"

"Probably."

"But you didn't call the police?"

"Too worried about the possibility of murder."

"I understand, but let me just get this absolutely straight. You found this woman dead in Surrey. You then drove home to your flat—"

"—and found she was already there, waiting for me, yes, except of course she couldn't have been. I don't believe in ghosts so I couldn't have seen what I know I did see. But on the other hand—"

"—you did see what you know you did see."

"Yes—and I can't deal with that, can't get any kind of handle on it at all." I paused to suck in some air before adding: "All I know now is that I can't go back to the flat until this has been sorted out, but how can I get rid of this thing? How can I be sure it's gone away? How can I be sure it won't try to kill me by dragging me out onto the balcony and tipping me over the rail? I met a vile woman this afternoon who calls herself a psychic healer and she tried to make me believe I'd want to throw myself off the balcony, so what I'm afraid of is—"

"You must have the best possible help," said Gilbert Tucker at once, not even waiting for me to finish this sentence, "and you must have it without delay. Now, I'm not an expert in this area, but I certainly know a man who is. He's another priest here in the City, and his name is Nicholas Darrow..."

VI

The church of St. Benet near London Wall—St. Benet's-by-the-Wall, as it was known in late twentieth-century London—was a striking little number designed by the architect of St. Paul's, Sir Christopher Wren, in the seventeenth century after the Great Fire had devastated the City; I learned later that St. Benet's had been damaged in the Second World War but restored in the 1950s. Unlike Gilbert Tucker's gloomy gothic anomaly in Fleetside, this church was

276

floodlit, white and sleek. It stood in a little graveyard where flowers and shrubs had been cultivated, and beyond the graveyard Egg Street ran north to London Wall, the road which ran parallel to the south side of the Barbican. I knew Egg Street but I had barely noticed the church; I had barely noticed any of those City churches before I had arrived with Tucker at St. Eadred's Fleetside after our champagne farewell at the Lord Mayor's Cat.

I had previously paid little attention to the Rectory of St. Benet's either. Its high handsome Georgian façade was familiar to me but I had thought the house merely contained the offices of some old-fashioned firm willing to endure the inconveniences of an antique building. I looked at the house now with new eyes as Tucker halted Gilbert's car in the forecourt and switched off the engine.

The time was almost eleven, but I still felt I was travelling in a dimension where the ordinary rules relating to time had blurred. For a moment I remembered my life-plan, mapped out in the days when the past could be ignored, the present was under control and the future was always subject to the power of my will, and as I saw how efficiently this vision had been hacked to pieces I wanted to scream with rage and despair.

"Okay, Ms. G?"

"No, but never mind."

"Want to fluff out against my chest again?"

"Maybe I could save that for later. I feel in urgent need of something to look forward to."

He laughed as he unbuckled his safety belt, and I groped my way out of the car.

Nicholas Darrow, the pale, bony, smooth-talking

item who was currently giving that nice Alice such a tricky time, opened the door before we could ring the bell. Evidently he had been watching out for us from his study, an austere room into which he ushered us as soon as we entered the house. I was surprised to see a computer standing on the modern desk; I had assumed all clergymen would still be living a pretechnological existence.

The study walls were painted an unpleasantly stark shade of white and there were no pictures, only a modern crucifix quite different from the one in Gilbert's reception room. This one looked as if it had been specially commissioned from a talented artist; carved out of a single piece of wood it was all flowing lines and unusual angles, rather like Nicholas himself. As my gaze returned to his face I tried to concentrate on what he was saying.

"Lewis has gone to fetch Alice," he was informing us, "so why don't you stay until they get back, Eric? Carter, take a seat in this chair here"—I was installed in a tub-like arrangement of hard wood laced with foam rubber—"and, Eric, if you want to bring that chair closer..."

I was so glad to be in the presence of the necessary expert that I was prepared to be uncharacteristically meek, but there was something about this man which set my teeth on edge. It was perhaps unfair to label him arrogant; he was merely exuding the self-confidence which all successful professionals display when in action on their own turf, but nevertheless he had the air of a man who deep down thinks himself the cat's whiskers. I still did not find him attractive, but I could see now that he had the kind of off-beat sex-appeal which would keep the females mewing in the pews if not raving in the nave.

"Let me just touch on a couple of practical details before we go any further," he said, sitting down near me at his desk and swivelling his chair so that he was directly facing the tub where I was installed. "Gil mentioned that your flat was currently uninhabitable, so I want to offer you the option of staying here tonight. That's why Alice is coming—to be with you in the flat at the top of the house if you want to stay. Of course you may prefer to go to a hotel, but you're very welcome to stay here if you wish."

I realised he was trying to beat back his natural bossiness and avoid imposing solutions on me; this was good. But the idea of him being able to summon Alice so easily from Clerkenwell at such a late hour was one which made me want to hiss; this was bad. Instantly I found it much harder to suppress my twinge of hostility.

"How kind of you," I said, very cool. "I would indeed like to stay. But I'm sorry Alice has been inconvenienced."

"Oh, she's more than capable of saying no to me, I assure you!" he replied at once. "But you made a big impression on her recently, and she said she'd be only too willing to help."

This was a slick sentence but it had the ring of truth, and when I allowed myself to look mollified he gave me a brief professional smile as if he quite understood that I was not the kind of female who would ever mew in a pew. "The next practical matter we need to touch upon," he said, "concerns your husband. As you're on your own I assume he's engaged elsewhere this evening, but when is he due to surface? He'll want to know where you are."

This was certainly an angle I had failed to

consider. I stared at him as I tried to work out how to respond.

"It's not urgent," he said as he saw I was baffled. "If you told him you were going to be out for the evening he's not going to start worrying about you just yet. On the other hand, if you disappear for the whole night without warning—"

"Yes." I could see the problem but the solution still eluded me, probably because I was finding it increasingly hard to cope with the thought of what Kim might have been doing.

"Do you have an answering machine?"

"I do, yes, but I can't think what message I could leave on it."

"Oh, I'll leave the message," said Nicholas. "No need to worry about that. Would you object if I were to tell him where you are?"

"Uh..."

"Has he been showing a pattern of violent behaviour?"

"Oh no!" I said at once. "He loves me!" But then the words "violent behaviour" sank deeper into my mind and I remembered Sophie's crumpled body. "Oh my God," I heard myself mutter. "Oh my God..." Tears began to stream down my face again.

"Eric," said Nicholas, "pass that box of Kleenex, would you? Thanks. Now Carter, we'll get to all the tough stuff later when Lewis returns, but meanwhile let's just focus on clearing up this practical detail. As I see it, this is the situation: you don't have to talk to Kim at this point and you don't have to see him, but I do think it might be a good idea to feed him some basic information. Otherwise even if he doesn't call the police to report you missing, he's going to be angry and upset tomorrow morning, and angry, upset people are always harder to deal with than people who are merely puzzled and concerned."

"Yes. Right." I could understand this. "Okay."

"Shall I make the call?"

"Please."

"Number?"

"Oh God, I can't remember, I'm so banjaxed—no, wait a minute, it's coming—" I reeled off the numbers and he started to dial.

As the machine picked up the call he said neutrally: "Mr. Betz, this is Nicholas Darrow, the Rector of St. Benet's Church in Egg Street. I'm calling to let you know that your wife's safe and that she'll be staying tonight with Alice Fletcher here at my Rectory." He gave his phone number, repeated it and hung up. "Now on to the next question," he said to me. "When did you last eat?"

"I think I had lunch. Or did I? I can't quite—"

"Have you had any alcohol during the last twelve hours?"

"Yes, but that was ages ago."

"How much did you have? I'm sorry, that sounds as if I'm about to criticise you, but I'm not—I'm just trying to get an accurate picture of your physical condition."

"I drank two double vodka martinis. I'd had the hell of a shock, and—"

"You don't need to justify yourself. What you do need to do is eat. When Alice arrives—"

A car door slammed outside.

"Good timing!" said Tucker wryly, and went out into the hall to open the front door.

VII

Alice came right up to me and said: "I'm so sorry if things are awful for you at the moment, Carter," but I could only grab her hand to signal my thanks. Meanwhile Nicholas was saying: "Alice, Carter needs to eat. Maybe some cold meat—a bit of salad—nothing too heavy—"

"Leave it to me." She withdrew just as Lewis Hall, the silver-haired tiger-thumper, cruised into the room.

"I told you, didn't I, Ms. Graham, that we'd meet again," he said as soon as he saw me, "but I'm sorry the circumstances apparently leave so much to be desired... Good evening, young Tucker! How very stimulated you look—playing the white knight evidently agrees with you!"

Tucker shifted uneasily from one foot to the other but said with the air of a man determined to hold his ground: "I know the interview's about to become confidential, but I thought I'd wait in the kitchen in case I'm needed later."

Hall merely turned to his colleague. "Do we need a white knight in the kitchen at this point, Nicholas?"

"I think not," said Nicholas, completing the mopping-up operation, "but thanks for your help, Eric. I'll call you first thing tomorrow."

This dismissal was accepted without protest but as Nicholas sat down again in his swivel-chair and Hall began to clear a space amidst the files and books which were stacked on the round table in the centre of the room, Tucker moved over to me to signal his reluctance to leave. "If you want me," he said, slipping a business card into my hand, "just whistle."

Hall cleared his throat. "Nicholas, do you have a block of A4 I could use?"

Nicholas extracted the notepad from a drawer of his desk and handed it over without a word. Neither of the clergymen looked at me, and I realised then, as Tucker left the room, that they probably knew rather more than I did about that past of his to which he had alluded at the end of our champagne session, the Bohemian past in which he had bobtailed around with married women after yawning himself loose from all the fluffettes.

I glanced at the business card. Gilbert's printed details had been crossed out, and on the back below a handwritten telephone number Tucker had scrawled: "MY PRIVATE LINE," and underlined the words three times.

"While we're waiting for your food to arrive," said Nicholas, as I slid the card into the back-pocket of my jeans, "let me just take a moment to give you an idea where we're coming from and how we operate. Do you know anything about my ministry at St. Benet's?"

Sinking back again into the tub-chair I said cautiously: "I know you operate something called a Healing Centre."

"In that case let me put the Healing Centre in its context before you start worrying that we're quacks operating a medical rip-off. St. Benet's is one of the City's Guild Churches, a fact which means we're open during the week and closed on weekends. Many of these churches have special ministries, and when I took over St. Benet's in 1981 I was already a specialist in the Christian ministry of healing. Christians have traditionally been interested in healing not just because Jesus was a very great healer but because the importance of healing and wholeness in body, mind and spirit is implicit in his teaching about how to get a top-quality life. This means I work alongside a doctor, because I see my ministry as complementing orthodox medicine and not acting as an alternative to it. The Healing Centre's in the crypt of the church. I also work there with a psychologist, and we have access to other medical specialists."

He paused as if to allow me the opportunity to voice objections but when I remained silent he added: "One of the most reassuring facts, some outsiders find, is that there are a number of checks and balances in place to make sure I don't turn into a phoney wonder worker who gets his kicks out of manipulating people. If I turn dishonest, the medical profession withdraws its support, the Bishop's troubleshooter drops down on me like a ton of bricks and the trustees of the Healing Centre, which is a registered charity, demand my resignation."

As I at once thought of Mrs. Mayfield I heard my voice repeat: "A phoney wonder worker... manipulating people..."

"I'm afraid the whole field of healing is rife with fraud, so let me explain what I mean by dishonesty. If I'm dishonest I forget I'm here to serve people, not to dominate or exploit them. If I'm dishonest, I lose sight of Jesus Christ who preached a gospel of faith, hope and love, not a manifesto of power and profiteering. If I'm dishonest I forget there's no place for self-centredness in a Christ-centred ministry of healing. The healer's got to be a person of integrity whom people are justified in trusting."

He paused again. This time I managed to say: "I think I should tell you I'm not a Christian."

284

"I appreciate your honesty, but in fact we have no policy of exclusion here. We operate on the principle that every individual is created by God for a purpose in his scheme of things, and that therefore every individual should be treated with respect and cared for accordingly."

"Sometimes," said Hall, "we have to deal with troublemakers who try to infiltrate the Centre, but we never turn away those in genuine need." He was now sitting at the round table with his notepad open in front of him, and as he spoke he began to doodle on the blank page.

"We get all kinds of cases, of course," said Nicholas, "including the kind of case which I believe you yourself are presenting... Now, Gil didn't go into detail about what kind of paranormal problem this is, but let me reassure you by saying that although the media love to hype up paranormal incidents and deck them out in all kinds of fancy trimmings, the reality is usually far less preposterous and far more interesting than the media would have us all believe."

"All we're really talking about here are unusual pastoral situations," said Hall, doodling away busily. "That's why priests get involved. The majority of cases involve distressed people who need pastoral help."

"Or in other words," said Nicholas, following on so smoothly that the dialogue began to seem like a monologue, "the paranormal is usually grounded in the normal and remains closely linked to it—one can even say that it's just a level of the normal which we don't often encounter."

"Like a whistle pitched so high that only a dog can hear it," said Hall helpfully. He began to draw a dog on his notepad. "The whistle exists in reality but humans can't hear it unless their normal hearing is somehow enhanced."

"I think it's also worth pointing out," remarked Nicholas, "that there's nothing particularly spiritual about the paranormal. What we're really talking about is a phenomenon of consciousness which produces mysteries, but these mysteries can usually by solved by a combination of reason and logic allied to insight and experience."

"The symptoms of the disorder can be extremely disturbing, of course," added Hall, "but once the underlying disorder is treated the symptoms soon disappear, so—"

"—so the important task for us now," said Nicholas, again producing a seamless follow-on, "is to try to uncover the basic problem which is generating the unpleasant symptoms. That's why I'll need to ask you questions about your background so that I can get a full picture of what's been going on. Lewis will be taking notes because in this sort of case I always work with someone who can take a careful record of the evidence; it protects the client and it protects me too. I promise you we're scrupulous in applying security procedures—the notes will be kept under lock and key—but if at any stage of your story you want Lewis to stop writing all you have to do is say so."

"Normally Nicholas works with a layman on these cases," said Hall, who by this time had given the dog a clown's hat and was busy sketching in a circus background, "but since Gilbert Tucker mentioned that clerical confidentiality was essential here I decided to fill the role of note-taker and corroborating witness. I hope that's acceptable to you. I'm very old but not, thank God, senile."

"He's still only sixty-nine," said Nicholas to me, "but for some reason he often talks as if he's ninety-six."

I had just managed to stop myself trotting out that 1960s' mantra: "Sixty-nine is Divine," when Alice re-entered the room with a tray of food.

VIII

"Now," said Nicholas, pouring out a cup of tea for me as I began to nibble a raw carrot, "let's make a start on your story while you eat. I'm hoping that the more you unburden yourself the more you'll feel like eating."

Alice had withdrawn again after telling me she was going upstairs to prepare our bedrooms. Meanwhile Hall had stripped the top sheet from his notepad to expose a blank page and was making a heading in a handwriting which was too eccentric for me to read from where I was sitting.

Returning to his swivel-chair Nicholas added: "Before I ask you questions about the background, would you like to have a shot at summarising in a couple of sentences what the paranormal trouble is? It might help to ease the stress, but on the other hand if you feel this is too difficult at present—"

Waving this sentence away before he could finish it I said rapidly: "This evening my flat was disarranged—it keeps getting disarranged, but this time no one could possibly have done it. And I saw a ghost. And—am I allowed a third sentence?"

"By all means."

"I keep having hellish thoughts about throwing myself off my thirty-fifth-floor balcony because a psychic healer planted the idea in my mind this afternoon and now I can't get it out again." I faltered but managed to add: "I don't know whether this balcony phobia is paranormal activity or just me going nuts, but my husband's mixed up with this woman—she's determined to break up our marriage, and—" But at this point I was unable to continue.

At once Nicholas demanded: "What's her name?" and as I answered: "Mrs. Elizabeth Mayfield," I saw both men wince before they looked at each other in silence.

ELEVEN

When someone has compassion on us we find ourselves really seen, heard, attended to... If someone's attention is genuinely compassionate it does not stop at attentiveness: he or she is willing to speak, act and even suffer with us and for us. It is in such passivity, as we receive their compassion, that the most powerful dynamics of our own feeling and activity are shaped. Amazed gratitude for such compassion can last a lifetime.

DAVID F. FORD
The Shape of Living

I

I was the one who broke the silence. I said: "You know her."

"Oh yes, we know Mrs. Mayfield!" agreed Hall sardonically. "Or rather I should say we know of her. We've never actually met the woman. We just meet the casualties she leaves behind."

Nicholas merely said as he examined his thumbnail: "She keeps her distance from us. People like that usually do."

"People like what?"

"Prime manipulators in cults or groups which are not just antipathetic to Christianity but actively hostile to it."

At once I said: "She told Kim I'd start 'flirting with the enemy.' That was her exact phrase. But I didn't know any Christians when she said that. She couldn't possibly have known—foreseen—"

"Such people often have psychic gifts," said Nicholas, clearly quite unimpressed by Mrs. Mayfield's clairvoyance. "That's all part of the problem. They don't offer their gifts to God so that the gifts can be used for serving others. They offer the gifts up elsewhere and then abuse them to serve themselves." He turned to Hall. "It looks as if we have three problems to consider. One: the recurring disorder in the flat. Two: the ghost. And three: the presence of Mrs. Mayfield."

"They're probably all linked," said Lewis, writing busily, "but of course one mustn't jump to conclusions, so—"

"—so let's now take a look at the background. Carter, can you fill us in, please, about who you are, where you come from and how long you've been married?"

I somehow succeeded in embarking on my narrative in a calm and steady voice.

By this time I had realised I was going to tell them the whole story. This was not just because I had seen it might hamper their investigation if I started withholding facts; it was because they were both so professional, so patently men of integrity and so obviously at ease in this foreign country where I was a complete stranger that I knew I would be mad not to put my trust in them. Neither of them had batted an eyelid when I had mentioned the ghost. Neither of them had appeared to find the disturbances in the flat in any way remarkable. But most of all I was reassured by their reaction to Mrs. Mayfield. Here were two people who not only had her measure but were able to make her seem less powerful. She was a dangerous woman but not uniquely so; they had come across her type before; she had never had the nerve to seek them out; her clairvoyance was run-of-the-mill stuff, nothing remarkable, just a gift she had chosen to abuse. I felt enormously relieved that they had not only grasped the situation at once but were able to reinterpret it for me in a way which made it easier to cope with the nightmare which Mrs. Mayfield presented.

As I told my story they asked questions to clarify details. Nicholas asked questions about the keys and about the Barbican's security arrangements. Hall cross-questioned me about the earlier disturbances in the flat; he was not hostile, but in paying great attention to detail he was very persistent and some of the questions he asked were extraordinary. ("Did you see any of the objects move of their own accord?" "Did you see any object sail through the air and make a sharp-angled turn?" "Did any of the electrical appliances turn themselves on unaided?" "Did the lights go on and off without any switches being touched?") In the beginning my responses were sarcastic, reflecting my incredulity that he should believe me capable of inventing such possibilities, but after a while I was too exhausted to give anything but straight replies. "The lights did flicker tonight," I said finally, "and earlier the television was showing a picture although it had been left on stand-by, but those were obviously just electrical blips. So why are you throwing out all these mad suggestions which no one but a nutter would take seriously?"

At that point Hall said to Nicholas: "The case is quite obviously genuine," and Nicholas said apologetically to me: "I'm sorry, but we have to be sure. It's all part of the routine, just a normal procedure, nothing personal."

I had broken off my narrative so that Hall could focus on the disturbances, but now I resumed it. When I reached the point where I had to describe my visit to Oakshott neither man made any attempt to interrupt me.

"...and coming home on the A3," I heard myself say, "I stopped at a petrol station and used a public phone to give the police an anonymous tip-off." Why did I tell this lie? I regretted it instantly but knew I had been driven by an acute desire to avoid any discussion about whether or not we should inform the police of Sophie's death. I could no more cope with the subject of the police at this stage than I could cope with the memory of my unprofessional behaviour in that horrible house.

However, having slipped in the little lie to

make the narrative more palatable, I saw Hall's pen falter on the paper. He never looked up but I knew the lie had been detected; perhaps my voice had changed fractionally. I glanced at Nicholas but he immediately looked away and examined his thumbnail again.

Having lost the thread of my narrative I floundered around trying to recapture it.

"You resumed your journey along the A3," said Nicholas, helping me along but addressing the thumbnail. "You reached London—"

"I reached London and tried calling the Savoy again but Warren still wasn't in his room. I then drove on to the Barbican..." My voice had levelled out but I remained rigid with discomfort. I could not remember when I had last made such a hash of telling a lie.

Fortunately my listeners were soon diverted by my account of my return to Harvey Tower. To compensate for the lie I now put in every detail, even describing how I had been so exhausted that I could barely get to my feet after finding my keys.

Nicholas said casually: "Did you feel similarly exhausted before when you were on the brink of discovering a disturbance?"

"I was knackered when I came home for the first time today after leaving the office early. But I wasn't grovelling around on the floor and feeling too zonked to get up."

"Let's hear more about the final disturbances now," said Hall. "You gave us a preview when you mentioned the flickering lights, but can we have a step-by-step account of what happened?"

So I completed my narrative, struggling hard to maintain a steady voice, but when I had finished describing with deep embarrassment the

292

irrational events which had occurred, Hall merely said: "Was the telescope smashed?"

"The telescope? No, it was still standing."

"Always untouched, wasn't it, although it would have been easy to knock over. After all, here you have a situation where the sofa and armchairs were being tossed around, a display-stand over-turned, glass shelves broken—"

"What are you suggesting?"

"I'm not suggesting, merely observing. It's a curious detail." He made another note and turned the page of his notepad.

"Let's just recap for a moment," said Nicholas quickly. "Carter, you said the door of the bed-room flew open and cracked against the wall. Are we to assume that no one could have been standing behind the door and manipulating it?"

"I suppose so." I struggled to concentrate again. "If someone had been standing behind the door it wouldn't have crashed into the wall because it would have hit that someone first."

"That needn't be the case, surely," said Hall, looking over the top of his reading glasses. "It would depend how much space there was between the hinges and the wall, the wall which would be hit by the unchecked door."

I was getting confused. "Yes, that's true."

"I'd like to clarify the lay-out of this flat," said Nicholas, diverting me with a practical question. "I've been in the Barbican tower blocks on enough occasions to know that although the flats may differ in the internal lay-out, each con-sists of a rectangle bisected by a corridor. Where's your living-room in relation to your bedroom? I'm trying to picture the geography of the scene when you saw Sophie."

I explained how the master bedroom stood on the right of the front door and faced down the long corridor to the living-room at the far end. "That's how I was able to stand on the living-room threshold and look straight at her."

"What kind of distance are we talking about here?"

"At least thirty feet."

"And how well lit was the corridor?"

"There are two lights in the corridor and one in the hall and they all work off the same switch which I turned on as soon as I entered the flat."

"Do you wear glasses?"

"No."

"All right, you have good sight, the location was well-lit, the door flew open and you saw this woman whom you instantly recognised. How long did the moment last before the door slammed shut again?"

"It's hard to say. Probably around five seconds."

"And you saw her clearly."

"Unusually clearly. As I mentioned, I was experiencing this weird, heightened perception which I suppose was some sort of reaction to all the stress."

"Was she transparent?" asked Hall with interest.

"No, of course not!" I was appalled by the question and also embarrassed, as if it represented a social blunder.

"And you say she was wearing Sophie's royal-blue outfit," persisted Nicholas, apparently not interested in transparency. "But are you sure about this? There's no possibility that it was Mrs.

Mayfield's downmarket attempt to mimic the coat?"

"None... Wait a minute, are you suggesting..." My voice trailed away.

"We have to consider every possibility," said Nicholas comfortably. "That's routine. Lewis used to say long ago when he was training me in this ministry that when dealing with the paranormal one first has to consider the normal, rational explanation because nine out of ten times it's the normal, rational explanation which is correct."

"Well, of course," I said, stimulated by the words "normal" and "rational," "the obvious explanation is that this was all rigged by Mrs. Mayfield, but I just can't see how she did it. Quite apart from the fact that I'm positive in my identification of Sophie, Mrs. Mayfield couldn't have had access to my flat tonight. She had no key."

"I can think of a way round that one," said Hall, taking off his glasses and giving them a polish. "When your husband loaned her his key earlier she could have had a copy made before returning the original in the Jiffy bag."

I stared before saying to him with increased respect: "That never occurred to me."

"You had other things on your mind. However, despite floating that idea, I have to say that I'm always very suspicious of conspiracy theories."

Nicholas said: "Lewis prefers to follow the principle of Occam's razor."

"What's that?"

"The principle that when there are competing theories the one closest to the truth is likely to be the one which is the simplest, the one which is shorn of fancy embellishments." He glanced across at Hall. "I'm tempted to think that both the disturbances in the flat and the appearance of the ghost represent phenomena which are easy to classify."

"I'm so glad," I said drily, "because I'm still completely at sea. Is it too much to hope that you can give me a rational explanation of what's been going on?"

"We can offer you what we believe to be a rational conclusion based on our experience in this field," said Nicholas politely, "but whether you yourself will find it rational is another matter altogether. Have you ever heard of poltergeist activity?"

III

"Sure," I said without hesitation. "It's nutter-guff spawned by horror movies and no sane person could possibly believe in such a thing."

Nicholas appeared untroubled by my furious incredulity. "If you've been relying on horror movies for your information," he said, "you may well have no idea what a poltergeist really is. For a start, it's not a ghost. It's got nothing to do with ghosts at all."

Feeling more furious than ever as I realised I had a lawyer's duty to give him a fair hearing I said crossly: "Okay, I'll bite. If it's not a ghost, what is it?"

"Evidence of a disturbed household."

I stared at him.

He stared back.

Then as my anger faded I realised I was hor-rified.

Sensing how unnerved I was Nicholas moved at once to calm me. "It's no big deal," he said. "We don't know yet how the phenomenon works, but we know why it happens and we know what we can offer in the way of effective remedies."

I said stiff-lipped: "Sorry. Can't believe, won't believe. But I respect you enough to keep listening."

"In that case let me say that the hallmark of the poltergeist case is that objects get disturbed or broken, apparently without human intervention. In fact there always is a human involved, but the human is operating at a distance—the theory is that the human acts involuntarily and unconsciously to generate a certain form of energy which moves these objects. We refer to this person as the owner of the poltergeist, and it seems clear that the purpose of the poltergeist activity is to relieve a stress which is building to intolerable levels... Have you ever heard of cases where adolescents cut themselves to relieve unbearable tension?"

I nodded, unable to speak.

"The poltergeist phenomenon seems to be similar, particularly since most cases occur in households where there's a disturbed adolescent; one of the problems adolescents have is that they often don't possess the ability to get rid of their tensions by expressing them verbally."

"What about the households without adolescents?"

"In those cases the owner of the poltergeist is usually someone who's repressing emotion on a large scale, possibly someone who's never come to terms properly with a traumatic past and who's refusing to deal with it even though memories of the trauma are invading the present."

With enormous relief I said: "That's Kim." Fascination was now mingling with my scepticism. "So how do you fix this problem?"

"It sometimes helps to bless each room of the house or flat, and I would always offer to pray on the premises with those afflicted, but the solution to aim for is counselling. The underlying tensions have to be uncovered, examined and healed—and then once the stress has been eased, the disturbances will cease."

"Poltergeist activity usually burns itself out anyway after nine months or so," remarked Hall, producing a packet of cigarettes. "Life moves on; tensions ebb and flow. But of course the activity is so tiresome that it's always desirable to end it as soon as possible... Nicholas, what happened to that ashtray you used to keep here?"

"I finally got tired of it."

"How intolerant! Do you smoke, Ms. Graham?"

"I gave it up."

"Really? I wish you'd teach me how!"

"Something tells me, Father Hall, that you're far too much of a tiger-thumper to welcome instruction from a woman!"

"My dear Ms. Graham, I can't think where you got that idea from! And let me stress that I'm most exceedingly partial to tigers!"

Nicholas remarked mildly: "I always enjoy feminist strip-cartoons, but why don't you two start calling each other by your first names while we focus on the matter in hand? Lewis, do you want to make any further comment about the disturbances in the flat?"

"No—except to explain to Carter that paranormal activity can feed upon itself in a spiralling crescendo of unpleasantness, and this seems to be what happened tonight."

"I agree." Nicholas turned back to me before embarking on a summing up. "My theory runs like this: you arrived back at the flat shattered by Sophie's death; your experiences at Oakshott had triggered intolerable tensions; you knelt on the floor to retrieve your keys, and at that point the kinetic energy generated by the tension was released, causing the fresh disturbance in the flat; after the release you were so exhausted you could hardly get up, but once you entered the flat the sight of the disorder heightened the tension again and this in turn resulted in a fresh bout of poltergeist activity: the flickering of the lights, the shifting of the curtains—and finally the violent opening and slamming of the bedroom door, the movements which framed the sighting of the ghost."

At once I said strongly: "I dispute every word you've said. I still don't believe in poltergeist activity, and even if I did the owner of the poltergeist wouldn't be me."

Again Nicholas remained tranquil. "I thought it was important that I should be upfront and honest with you about what I suspect," he said, "but you're under no obligation to agree with my theory. We have a saying in this type of case: 'The facts are sacred but interpretation is free'—or in other words, you can adopt any theory you like so long as it doesn't do violence to the facts... Now, are we ready to move on and discuss the ghost?"

Having snitched the saucer below my teacup to use as an ashtray, Lewis was busy smoking his filthy cigarette while Nicholas himself, casually crossing one long leg over the other, was leaning back in his swivel-chair. For a moment I longed to yell in exasperation, but I knew such idiotic behaviour would solve nothing and anyway by this time I had been seduced by their low-key style and laid-back authority which allowed me to disagree with them as violently as I chose.

I decided I had to grit my teeth and go on.

V

"What I want to do," said Nicholas, "is to work out why you saw this ghost and what this sighting means."

Fear drove me into maintaining a defiant response. "Surely the only conclusion a sane person could reach is that when I saw the ghost I was mad?"

"Lewis," said Nicholas, "you worked for several years in a mental hospital. Would you care to comment on Carter's question?"

"The possibility of mental illness has to be considered, of course," said Lewis, busily sketching a cat on his notepad, "but in the absence of florid ramblings and other bizarre behaviour, and in the presence of careful narration coupled with an exhausting preoccupation with rationality, I suggest we can only declare the lady sane." The cat he was sketching had turned into a tiger with a curvy body and bared teeth.

"But surely," I argued, "seeing a ghost must be classified as a hallucination?"

"Not much of a hallucination, was it?" said Lewis unimpressed. "All you saw was a woman in a royal-blue coat. If she'd been foaming at the mouth,

300

waving an inverted cross or dancing stark naked with a brace of satyrs, I'd be more inclined to take your claim of a hallucination seriously." He had begun to draw a caveman standing over the tiger with a raised club.

"May I," said Nicholas courteously, "intervene? Carter, you're in difficulties here because you're asking yourself the wrong question. The question is not whether or not you saw a ghost; we know you saw one. But why did you see it? And what does this experience mean?"

I said confused: "You both think this wasn't a hallucination?"

"I prefer to use the word 'hallucination' when mental illness is present. In a case like this I would call the incident a 'sighting,' and I think you yourself stumbled across the key to the mystery earlier when you talked of being in an altered state of consciousness as the result of your fear and stress. Normally in the Western world we associate an altered state of consciousness with drug-taking, but in certain circumstances the brain itself can generate the chemicals which heighten perception and enable an unusual level of reality to be experienced."

"It's as if you hear the whistle which normally only a dog can hear," said Lewis, now working on a background to his sketch.

"It doesn't make the experience less real," said Nicholas carefully. "It just means that the experience is different from an everyday experience. It's also different from a hallucination, which would draw heavily on the imagination and usually include bizarre features. In this case your mind was drawing on an incident which actually took place—this was your memory of Sophie as she looked in the supermarket. But why was your unconscious mind serving up this memory in such a very vivid and frightening way?"

With great reluctance I had to admit I was intrigued. "But surely," I said, trying hard to remain rational, "in scientific terms this was nothing but a psychological projection?"

"Scientific reductionists would indeed say that, just as religious reductionists would say it was nothing but a departed soul detained on its journey back to God. But I'm always very suspicious of 'nothing but' theories because I think life is a good deal more complex and subtle than they allow. It was certainly a psychological projection in the sense that it was a memory projected from your mind, but I think it was a long way from being 'nothing but' a psychological projection. That's why we have to ask the questions which fall outside the provenance of science, the questions relating to meaning and value, because only then, in my opinion, will we reach the truth about what happened here."

"I agree," said Lewis, shading in the vegetation he had drawn around the tiger, but before I could comment Nicholas added swiftly to me: "The point to grasp is that although this psychological projection served up an image which the rational side of your brain knew to be impossible, this is actually no big deal. This is just you operating in an altered state of consciousness and seeing a psychic level of reality."

"You saw a ghost," said Lewis, effortlessly reactivating the double-act. "But so what? Lots of people see ghosts. There are even lots of different kinds of ghost which people see. Some are ghosts like your ghost, some are place-ghosts, some are—"

"I don't want to know."

"Fine," said Nicholas. "In that case let's—"

"What's a place-ghost?"

"There!" said Lewis smugly. "I knew you'd never be able to resist your feminine curiosity in the end!"

"And I might have known you'd never be able to resist a tiger-thumper's put-down!"

"Surely it should be 'tigress-thumper'? Why are you desexing yourself?"

"The feminising of male nouns by the addition of the letters E-double-S has been classified as representing an unjust discrimation against women by a patriarchal society."

"Well, if you believe that, you'll believe anything!"

Nicholas said: "I hate to interrupt when I can see you're both busy enjoying this curiously old-fashioned repartee, but can I just answer Carter's question about what a place-ghost is? It might provide a break-through about what happened tonight."

"Go ahead," said Lewis, "but whatever you do don't call the ghost a ghostess."

"A place-ghost," said Nicholas before I could draw breath to hiss, "is, as the name implies, a ghost attached to a certain place, and it tends to go through the same actions again and again, like a short video which gets repeatedly replayed. It's quite harmless and seldom interesting, and it can be seen either by one person or by a group of people, none of whom necessarily has any connection with either the ghost or the place. Now obviously Sophie wasn't a place-ghost, because she had no connection with your flat and she wasn't performing any routine action. If she was going to be a place-ghost she'd be seen at the house at Oakshott."

"So what kind of a ghost did I see tonight?"

"Well, I'm bound to say," said Nicholas, "that this sounds like a bereavement ghost. When people suffer a bereavement—and particularly a bereavement which is a great shock—they sometimes do experience, very clearly, the presence of the person they've lost. They don't always see the dead person, but visual projections are far from unknown, and unlike the place-ghost this phenomenon always reveals a powerful connection between the viewer and the viewed. How did you really feel about Sophie, Carter? Beneath all the shock, what emotions did you experience when you found her dead?"

Tears again began to stream down my face.

VI

I heard myself say: "I'd been such a shit to her. I thought she was just a brainless old cow mainlining on an outdated morality, but she wasn't like that, she was dignified and intelligent—and sort of brave and committed—a woman of principle—and I was just a rude, arrogant, ignorant coward, always running away from her and never having the guts to face up to what she represented—and what she represented was that I'd been bloody to another woman—me, with my belief in showing solidarity with the sisterhood! Okay, I'm not really an activist who gets high on spouting feminist nutterguff, I admit I had my tongue in my cheek just now, but if some woman's being rubbished by a man I like to show sympathy because God knows I get plenty of men trying to rubbish me, but there was Sophie, being rubbished by this man I'd nicked from her, and I treated her as if she were trash. I can't believe I behaved like that. It was vile.

"I didn't set out to nick him from her. He told me the marriage was over, but maybe that was just another lie. Certainly if I'd believed that the marriage was still viable I'd have settled for a one-night stand. My last lover junked me for a nineteen-year-old fluffette. I wouldn't have wanted to do to any woman what that flea-brained fluffette did to me.

"If only I'd wised up earlier, but I was always in denial where Sophie was concerned, and it wasn't until Mrs. Mayfield gutted me that I had any real insight into how Sophie must have been brutalised by Kim's association with that hag—so brutalised that she'd wanted to stop me being brutalised too. Talk about feminine solidarity! Sophie knew what all that was about, but I knew less than a tiger-thumper, I can see that now.

"So when I got to Oakshott and found her in that disgusting house I...well, I couldn't believe she was dead—oh, I went onto autopilot and did what had to be done, but part of my mind was sort of bleeding, I thought no, no, no, she can't be dead because I have to talk to her—and I had to talk to her not just to find out the truth about this shark who's bedded down in my flat but to say to her: 'I'm sorry. I was a real slag. Please forgive me.' But then she wasn't there so I couldn't say that and I couldn't bear not being able to say it, and all the way back to London there was a part of my brain saying: 'Come back, Sophie, I want to say I'm sorry. Come back, Sophie, I want to ask you to forgive me. Come back, Sophie, I need to talk to you, I need to hear what you have to say. Sophie, Sophie, Sophie,' this voice in my head was saying, 'I've got to see you, I've got to see you, I've got to see you...'"

VII

I destroyed the last Kleenex. Immediately Nicholas reached down into the bottom drawer of his desk and produced another box. As I mopped and snuffled I kept thinking how furious my mother would have been with me. She had never shed tears, no matter what my father had done. Tears were for women who deserved to be losers. "Big girls don't cry," she had said whenever I had started to whimper, yet now here I was, shaming her by being so feeble... I somehow got the tears under control.

"Sorry about that," I said at last. "You must be thinking I'm pathetic."

"On the contrary," said Nicholas. "I was thinking how brave you were, able to face up to such hard painful truths in the presence of strangers."

I repressed the urge to weep all over again and somehow succeeded in whispering: "If only I could feel that Sophie would have forgiven me."

"I'm sure she would have wanted to. Possibly she might not have succeeded straight away—you might have had to allow her time to be angry—but Christians make a practice of praying for the grace to forgive those who have wronged them."

"It's part of a spiritual dynamic," said Lewis, who had lit another disgusting cigarette. "We need to forgive others as we need to be forgiven ourselves... Nicholas, should we take a break here to allow Carter more time to recover?"

"I don't need more time," I said, snapping back to normal in a flash, "and why are you asking Nicholas a question which should be addressed to me? Why are you treating me as a non-person who can be organised without her permission?"

Lewis said to Nicholas: "The lady's clearly recovered. Shall we proceed?"

"How do you feel about that, Carter?" said Nicholas, asking the right question.

"Oh, for God's sake let's go on," I said irritably. "I'm afraid of Kim arriving before we've discussed Mrs. Mayfield." But the next moment I was asking stricken: "Will I be likely to see the ghost again?"

"I don't believe so," said Nicholas firmly. "Now that you've vented your grief and guilt, your psyche is unlikely to serve up Sophie in the form of a bereavement ghost. There's still a possibility that her journey back to God has been delayed, particularly if she was murdered, but if that's the case she'd appear at Oakshott."

"She could appear there as a place-ghost," said Lewis briskly, "or she could appear as another type of ghost, the 'unquiet dead' type. Unlike the place-ghost, this type can interact with humans and isn't confined to a video-replay form of routine."

"The dead person doesn't have to have been murdered," added Nicholas. "Any sudden death might have the same effect, because what we're really talking about here is unfinished business. Sometimes the dead don't find it easy to move on—particularly if the living are trying to hold them in place."

I opened my mouth to say I did not believe in any kind of afterlife, but then realised I would sound exactly like a flat-earther busy asserting her convictions to two sailors who had circumnavigated the globe. Instead I mumbled: "Are you saying my flat will be all right now?"

"I think we need to reclaim it formally for you," said Nicholas, sounding more businesslike as he switched from commenting on ghosts to outlining a plan of action. "May I make some practical suggestions?"

"Please."

"The trouble is they probably won't seem practical to you, but I promise they're usually effective. What I'd like to do, with your permission, is to go to your flat with you and Lewis at, say, nine o'clock tomorrow morning. We'd straighten everything out and then I'd bless each room before celebrating mass on the spot where Sophie appeared—I always believe in celebrating mass when a ghost has been seen. We'd pray for Sophie, of course, and for you too. Now, you needn't join in; I respect the fact that you have other beliefs, but if you could be there as a benign presence this would be helpful."

"But as I'm not a believer, how will all this make a difference to my feelings about the flat?"

"That's a good question, but God's healing activity isn't dependent on whether or not you believe in him."

"All healing comes from God," murmured Lewis. "What Nicholas is really saying, Carter, is that you can't limit the power of God by your unbelief."

"But why should I believe that statement?"

"All right," said Nicholas quickly, "let's try and

meet you where you are—let's try to explain the rationale behind my proposals without mentioning God at all. This is the way I see it: as far as the ghost is concerned, I think you've now got your conscious mind around this phenomenon, but the ritual and the prayers will be helpful in speaking to your unconscious mind—they'll allow your confession about Sophie to be processed there in a non-verbal form so that you can finally come to terms with her death and be healed of the psychological pain you feel in relation to her. So in my opinion you won't need therapy afterwards to help you overcome this particular trauma; the prayers and ritual will complete the progress you've already made."

"You're saying they're for ironing out the unconscious?"

"I'm saying they should help you assimilate the experience in a positive way. Please note that I'm not guaranteeing a cure, but usually some form of healing is possible."

"Nicholas's job as a healer is to line himself up with God through prayer and the sacraments," said Lewis, who apparently had no inhibitions about reintroducing God into the conversation. "The aim is to allow the healing power of God to flow as effectively as possible into the situation which requires healing, but although the power can override your unbelief, there's always the chance that the power may be withheld, either wholly or partially, and that's why we never promise miracles."

"But if all goes well I'll get a ghost-free flat without having to bat around with a therapist?"

"Yes, but don't forget we're not writing off therapy as a useful tool in the healing process. Once we turn to the poltergeist activity—"

"Let me make it clear that Lewis and I could be wrong about our poltergeist diagnosis and you could be right about your conspiracy theory," interrupted Nicholas. "We don't yet have enough information to come to a firm conclusion, but this much at least seems clear: whatever the explanation is, you need counselling to deal with the extreme stress of your current situation."

"If Nicholas and I are right," resumed Lewis, "the poltergeist activity will now go into abeyance. By the very act of confiding in us you'll have 'lanced the boil,' as it were, and relieved the intolerable tension which was generating the energy. But unfortunately the tension will only build up again unless the root cause of the problem is tackled."

Nicholas added before I could comment: "The psychologist who works with us at the Healing Centre has a lot of experience in counselling City executives who are under stress. Do you think Kim could be persuaded to join you in some counselling sessions here?"

"Good God, no!" I said automatically, but again Nicholas remained tranquil.

"That's a pity," he said, "because there's no way Kim can be detached from this problem. He's probably under heavy stress himself, he's certainly contributed to your own stress, and we know his past troubles are seriously interfering with his present life. So—"

"I'm not saying he doesn't need counselling," I interrupted hastily. "If you ask me, he needs a psychiatrist. But what I'm saying is that Kim would never, never cross the threshold of anything which calls itself a Christian Healing Centre."

"Back we come to Mrs. Mayfield," murmured Lewis, and picked up his pen again.

VIII

"How long has Kim been anti-Christian?" asked Nicholas neutrally after I had talked for some time about the deterioration of my relationship with Kim as the result of the miasma generated by Mrs. Mayfield.

I thought hard. "When I first knew him," I said at last, "he seemed reasonably tolerant of Christianity—he certainly made me conscious of my ignorance about religious matters and gave me the impression that Christianity was a belief system which only the ignorant slagged off."

"And later?"

"Later...after he started seeing Mrs. Mayfield again...yes, he was actively hostile."

"I'm afraid that's a sign that he's drifted back into her control." Unexpectedly he swivelled his chair to face the computer. "Let's see what the latest update is on her activities."

I was amazed. "She's on your computer?"

"There's an organisation which makes a study of all these cults and groups, particularly the ones which can be destructive to the personality and result in mental breakdown. It's an organisation we work with closely—they keep us abreast of the latest developments and we pick up the casualties they uncover." He typed in an order while adding: "The occult scene is fragmented—there's no great overarching organisation complete with master-mind, but some of the individual manipulators can do a lot of damage, particularly to poorly integrated personalities."

I heard my voice ask: "What exactly is the occult?"

"Literally it's something hidden. It describes

311

belief systems which are built on special knowledge which is only available to the select few—as opposed to Christianity, which is based on God's revelation in Jesus Christ and available to all."

"The word 'occult' is used very loosely and inaccurately nowadays," remarked Lewis, sketching a witch on his notepad. "People use it to describe anything from Wicca practices to Satanism, but strictly speaking, occultists are devotees of Gnostic ideas propounded in various esoteric books which have been enjoying a revival in recent times."

"But surely this is all quite harmless?"

"Certainly it can feature eccentrics who are more pathetic than dangerous. But unfortunately these societies can be infiltrated and corrupted by a wide range of undesirables: people who get their kicks out of power, people who are addicted to manipulating others and people who are dedicated to destroying things as painfully and nastily as possible."

"But why can't the police be involved?"

"They are," said Nicholas, tapping the keys again with a new instruction. "We often work with them, but people like Mrs. Mayfield are usually skilled at operating just within the law... Ah, here we go. Mrs. Elizabeth Mayfield, aged fifty-one, nationality British, no husband, an address in Fulham, currently operating as a psychic healer, no professional qualifications, runs groups in Hendon, Hammersmith and Wapping—"

"Wapping's where Kim went last night."

"—possible links with a pornography ring but nothing proven...associated with past sex-groups but nothing criminal proven...questioned by police over distribution of obscene videos but no charges brought. However, if we go further back we find a criminal record. We have soliciting, procuring, perjury, indecent assault on a minor—"

"Christ!" I exclaimed before remembering where I was. In embarrassment I muttered: "Excuse me."

"Colourful stuff, isn't it?" said Nicholas, gaze still on the screen. "But all that was back in the 1960s. She did time and emerged wise enough to set herself up behind a respectable façade. She disappeared for a while in the late seventies and early eighties, but she wasn't in prison and the police suspect she may have been operating under another identity for reasons which aren't clear but which could be consonant with criminal activity and/or occult involvement—and I'm now using the word 'occult' in its strict sense."

"That's why Sophie's mention of the occult is so interesting to us," said Lewis abruptly to me. "Was Sophie using the word loosely, as so many people do nowadays, or was she talking specifically about an occult society?"

Nicholas added in explanation: "We've never known for a fact that Mrs. Mayfield is involved in any occult society. We know she's a psychic who advertises as a healer and makes money out of vulnerable people; we know she runs sex-groups under the guise of group therapy; we suspect that in these areas she stays within the law by never dabbling in extortion and always dealing with consenting adults—though we know she does a great deal of psychological damage and can bring those adults to breakdown. But we've never been able to connect her with any corrupt

313

occult society which would inevitably be involved in criminal activity."

I swallowed with difficulty. "What kind of criminal activity?"

"Blackmail. Offences with minors," said Nicholas colourlessly, "and animals."

"The groups usually start off by operating within certain parameters in order to obtain what they believe to be enlightenment," said Lewis, who I was beginning to realise had no hesitation in calling a spade a spade, "but they never stay within those parameters because when people get their kicks out of perversions they always wind up needing a bigger and better fix to maintain the level of satisfaction. Usually the group divides into different levels of initiates—and there's always an inner circle where just about anything goes."

I slid my tongue around my lips. "Such as Satanism?"

"Not necessarily," said Nicholas before Lewis could give another blunt reply. "The media hype up Satanism, but most of these people like Mrs. Mayfield wouldn't call themselves Satanists and wouldn't practise any Satanic rituals."

Lewis said severely to him: "That doesn't mean they're not capable of being far more destructive than a bunch of misfits who get together to celebrate a black mass for kicks! You shouldn't play this down, Nicholas—you shouldn't gloss over the degradation and defilement, the abuse of the human spirit, the dismantling of personalities, the—"

"I've no wish to gloss over anything," said Nicholas, "but I think we should remember we've no proof that Mrs. Mayfield's involved in criminal activity, we've no proof that Sophie used the word 'occult' in a sense which might imply a corrupt society, and we've no proof that Kim's secret life has ever extended beyond visits to Mrs. Mayfield in Fulham and to the group in Wapping."

Gripping the arms of the tub-chair so hard that my fingers hurt I managed to say: "I still can't understand how Kim, who's a very tough, sophisticated man, could ever have got involved with someone like Mrs. Mayfield."

But Lewis had no trouble explaining this. "You can be outwardly very tough and sophisticated," he said, "but inwardly poorly integrated. Mrs. Mayfield has probably been exploiting an inner vulnerability which drove him to seek help originally from a strong-willed woman who would win his trust and make him feel secure."

Nicholas added: "It would be this inner vulnerability which would make it difficult for him to leave her, and you can be sure that Mrs. Mayfield would want him to stay—she'd use all her skills in psychological manipulation to undermine his will. As a successful businessman with a wide range of wealthy contacts Kim would be a great prize for her, even if she's not involved in the kind of occult society which always seeks such people."

My throat began to ache. I whispered: "I'm sure he's a good man deep down," but as I spoke I realised I was sure of nothing now which related to Kim.

"Time to remind ourselves again about what we know and what we don't know," said Nicholas, instantly detecting the rise in my distress. "We know Kim's involved with Mrs. Mayfield and at least one of her groups. But his story is that he quarrelled with her on his marriage and this could well be true—and if it *is* true this would support Carter's belief that he's a good man keen to make a fresh start. We don't know for a fact that he was conspiring with Mrs. Mayfield to fake the disturbances at the flat. (All right, I haven't forgotten the contents of the Jiffy bag but maybe he really did leave both the key and the organiser behind by mistake at Mrs. Mayfield's house.) We also don't know for a fact that he was in Oakshott tonight, and we certainly don't know for a fact that he was responsible for Sophie's death. Let's try to keep our minds prised open an inch here."

"What really bothers me," I said, grateful for this reassuring perspective but still feeling distressed, "is that I keep thinking I've found out the whole truth but there always turns out to be more. What actually was it that Sophie wanted to tell me? At first I thought she just wanted to tip me off about his secret life with Mrs. Mayfield. Then I thought she wanted to tell me about Kim's Nazi past and the blackmail. And finally, thanks to Mrs. Mayfield, I'm facing a story about impotence, but there's a hole in this story, and—"

"Mrs. Mayfield was out to undermine you," said Lewis. "Be sceptical."

"But even if I don't believe her, how do I avoid suspecting there's more truth still to come out? If Kim went to Oakshott tonight to beg Sophie to keep quiet—"

"But we don't know yet he went to Oakshott, do we?"

Nicholas, who seemed to have drifted off into

a reverie during this exchange, now interrupted us. "The part I'm getting odd vibes about," he said, "is this whole business of Kim's Nazi past. I feel there's something off-key here... Could Kim really have worked alongside Jews for years, mixed with them socially and never been detected as a fake?"

I said at once: "You misunderstand. He never claimed to be Jewish and he never claimed to have been brought up in the Jewish religion. He just represented himself as a sympathetic fellow-traveller, someone with a Jewish father but no real Jewish background."

"But if he's taken great care to pass himself off as a fellow-traveller for years, doesn't this black-mail story of his make him seem uncharacteristically foolhardy? He was very cavalier in divulging potentially fatal information to this stranger who could just as easily have been a Jew as a gentile!"

"I thought that too," I said, "but I'm sure the blackmail happened. Why invent such a story when he could blame a stockmarket disaster for his lack of capital?"

"Maybe his pride told him he wasn't the kind of man to have a stockmarket disaster. And maybe he needed to cover up the fact that he'd been paying large sums to Mrs. Mayfield."

"But he said how reasonable her charges were!"

"There'd inevitably be donations as well, probably to an offshore account."

"Wait a minute," said Lewis suddenly. "Let's assume he really has been blackmailed; I doubt if the donations to Mrs. Mayfield would explain a major hole in his capital, because she wouldn't want to alienate him by being extortionate. But let's also assume that the true story of the black-mail is something he's still covering up. If you were Kim, Nicholas, and you had a very unpleasant secret in your past which had ultimately resulted in blackmail, how do you prevent your second wife from learning about it when your first wife is dead keen to spill the beans? Answer: You keep the two women apart, you destroy your first wife's credibility and finally you dredge up for your second wife another very unpleasant secret, such as your Nazi past, to act as a red herring."

"No, that won't wash," I said promptly. "He didn't tell me about the Nazi past voluntarily. Unless..." My voice trailed away.

"The disclosure by Mandy Simmons could have been staged," said Nicholas with reluctance. "He'd need an excuse to bring such a secret out into the open."

"Playing the Nazi card would have had several advantages," pursued Lewis. "He not only makes it look as if *this* is the secret Sophie's trying to divulge and thus kills Carter's curiosity; the admission encourages Carter to show additional sympathy for him by revealing that he too was a victim of the Nazi madness, and it also allows him to show Sophie in an unsympathetic light by claiming she rejected him when he confided in her. And finally the story enables the blackmail to be plausibly relocated in a different set of circumstances in order to explain the hole in his capital. The only slip-up he made was not making the blackmail story more convincing, but on the whole I think he was very clever."

"Time to rein ourselves in again," said Nicholas, seeing my appalled expression. "This is just speculation. In fact all this conversation proves,

Carter, is that Lewis and I are having a hard time building up a clear picture of Kim and that it's vital we should meet him as soon as possible."

As if on cue a bell jangled in the distance and a thunderous knocking broke out on the front door.

TWELVE

An immense amount of energy, ingenuity and money is devoted to keeping secrets, and also to uncovering them.

DAVID F. FORD
The Shape of Living

I

"Remember," said Nicholas swiftly as the shock made me leap to my feet, "you don't have to see him. But a meeting might be helpful in resolving the unanswered questions."

"So long as you two are here I don't mind."

Nicholas moved at once towards the hall. As he passed Lewis he said: "You play Mr. Nice-Guy," and Lewis gave a grunt of assent before slipping his notepad beneath a pile of files.

I heard Nicholas open the front door. By this time Lewis was standing very close to me as if he were a bodyguard whose client needed the highest level of protection.

In the hall Nicholas was saying politely: "Mr. Betz?" and Kim was demanding: "What the hell's going on?" before shouting at the top of his voice: "Carter, where are you?"

"What a way to behave!" I muttered furiously, but I was sweating with fright and dread.

Lewis muttered: "If the worst comes to the worst there's a panic button which connects us to the Wood Street police station," but before I could ask him where the button was I heard Nicholas say, still faultlessly courteous: "Your wife's in my study. If you'd like to come this way—"

Kim erupted into the room but stopped dead when he saw I was screened by a bodyguard.

"Mr. Betz!" exclaimed Lewis in delight. "We're so glad you're finally here!"

"Fuck off," said Kim brutally, and swung to face me. "Carter—"

I made the split-second decision that attack was the best defence. "For God's sake, Betz!" I yelled, launching straight into "the slammer." "Shape up before these guys decide you need a head transplant! Where the hell have you been and what the hell's going on?"

"That's exactly what I was going to ask you! Listen, sweetheart—"

"Shut up! I've had the worst evening of my entire life, I've been scared out of my skull, I'm absolutely on the ropes—and now, to cap it all, I have to cope with you behaving like a bloody stormtrooper!"

"I'm sorry, but I'm appalled that you should be hiding out here with these two fakers, and what I want to know is—"

"These two *gentlemen*—repeat, GENTLEMEN—have been telling me all about Mrs. Mayfield! They know—"

"I don't give a shit what they know! What *I* want

to know is what the fuck's been going on at the flat!"

"Your evil old cow trashed it! She's bored with your plan to discredit Sophie and she's now trying to terminate your second marriage by driving me out of my mind!"

"Don't be ridiculous! Look, we have to talk right away, and if you think I'm going to spill my guts out in front of—"

"I've already told them everything."

"You've *what*?" He was so shocked that he swayed on his feet. He even reached out for the edge of the table to steady himself, and I felt the balance of power shift between us as his anger dissolved into confusion.

"It's all right," I said automatically, "there's confidentiality. If you could just stop playing the stormtrooper for a moment—"

"Okay, okay, okay." He finally came to his senses and tried to remodel the tough line. "I'm sure we can work this out," he said, "but please—let's have a couple of minutes together on our own." And before I could reply he was adding to the men: "I'm sorry. Excuse me. I've been out of my mind with worry and stress."

At once Lewis said sympathetically: "Of course," and it was left to Nicholas to ask in a neutral voice: "How do you feel about this suggestion, Carter?"

"I'll go along with it," I said, "because I think it'll be the quickest route to achieving a discussion between the four of us, but I want to remain within sight of you and Lewis."

We rearranged ourselves. Nicholas and Lewis stayed in the study but the door was left wide open so that they could see me as I withdrew with Kim to the far side of the hall. Leaning against the banisters at the foot of the stairs I glanced past Kim to Nicholas, who was standing with his right hand resting on his desk. I was suddenly sure his fingers were inches from the panic button; feeling more secure I turned to Kim but before I could utter a word he was saying in a low voice: "I love you. No matter what's happened, that hasn't changed."

This was so very much the last thing I expected him to say that I was disarmed. The balance of power shifted again, hovering in an uncertain equilibrium.

"Hell, you're sexy when you act tough!" he murmured, capitalising on the moment of intimacy. "If we were alone now—"

"Skip the gloss, buster. You were at Oakshott tonight, weren't you?"

Instantly he abandoned the attempt to sweet-talk me. "No, I was with Warren at the Savoy. Why should you think—"

"Did you kill her?"

He was stunned, so stunned that he was unable to rewrite his script. All he could do was whisper incredulously: "How on earth did you know she was dead?"

"You think I didn't go through that unlocked back door and look for her?"

"But I figured you'd just ring the front doorbell a couple of times, hang around for a few minutes and then go away! You mean you actually went round to the back and—"

"Kim, did you kill her?"

"For Christ's sake, no, of course not!"

"But you were there. Who else would have wiped my message from the answering machine?"

"Okay, I was there, but—"

"Was the death an accident?"

"God knows! When I found her dead I panicked—I know you'll find that hard to believe, but—"

"No, I panicked too—I went around wiping away my fingerprints. I must have been out of my mind."

"Then that makes two of us. God, if we both tinkered around with what may prove to be a crime scene—"

"—we'll be in deep professional shit. But listen, Kim, what the hell do you think happened?"

"It did look like an accident." He ran his fingers distractedly through his hair. "But on the other hand—"

"A nutter could have got in. If she was out gardening with the back door unlocked and the alarm not set—"

"I noticed the gardening gear on the kitchen table."

"But would she have been gardening while wearing that rather smart red suit?"

"Oh, that was as old as the hills, strictly for pottering around in. Sophie didn't like trousers. Her idea of casualwear was old clothes."

"Okay, so if we assume she was gardening—no, let's hold this discussion right there and go back to the clerics. I want them to hear this."

"But I don't understand—why involve them? In fact how on earth did you manage to wind up here?"

"I'll explain later."

"But Carter, listen—I don't think we should discuss this mess with anyone right now—"

"I told you—I've already done it. Oh, and by the way, you should know about my one lie. I told the clerics I made an anonymous call to tip off the police once I was on my way back to London. I didn't want them getting hung up on the morality of—"

"Of course not. But why continue to confide in these guys? After all, what can two clergymen possibly know about the world you and I move in?"

"More than you can begin to imagine," I said drily, and headed back into the study.

He followed more slowly, trailing behind, his fists shoved deep into his pockets and reluctance engraved in every line of his tense, shadowed face.

II

"Have a seat here at the table with me," said Lewis sociably to Kim. "By the way, may I offer you some whisky?"

Kim was so surprised that it took him a moment to say: "Thank you. With soda, please."

Lewis disappeared. When Kim and I were both sitting down I said to Nicholas: "We've decided to have an exchange of information."

Kim said abruptly: "You mean you've decided. I'm only going along with this because—" But he clearly could not think of a reason which did not look like a loss of face.

"I expect," said Nicholas peacefully, "you want to make a gesture of support to your wife."

Kim looked relieved to have his behaviour explained in a way which showed him in a passable light, but he was still shifting uneasily in his chair when Lewis returned with a glass of whisky and soda.

"What you two have to take on board," said Kim after he had taken a sip, "is that I love my wife. I know it must be looking to you as if we're going through a rough patch, but we're going to win through. My marriage means everything to me."

Lewis murmured: "I understand you haven't been married long."

"Just a few months."

Lewis took out his packet of cigarettes. "Smoke?"

"I gave up. Except for the occasional cigar."

"Congratulations! That's a feat I've never been able to achieve. Will it bother you if I—"

"No, go ahead."

This odd little social exchange, reminiscent of the early stages of a cocktail party before the drink had started to flow, somehow seemed to lighten the atmosphere, normalising it, finally achieving the conversion of a violent scene into a business meeting.

"Carter," said Nicholas, slipping effortlessly into the role of chairman, "since Kim's made his gesture of support, would you care to reciprocate by giving him a summary of what happened tonight up to the moment when you reached the flat?"

Well accustomed to performing at business meetings, I found myself embarking on a workmanlike narrative.

III

My monologue was only derailed when I revealed my decision to search Sophie's desk.

"But what did you think you'd find?" demanded Kim, apparently astonished.

"The truth, of course! What else? The truth about your past, the truth about your first marriage—"

"But I'd told you the truth!"

"Let's just pass that up for now," said Nicholas, "and stick to the narrative. Go on, Carter."

"Don't try and con me," I said fiercely to Kim. "I'm no whippet with minimal p.q.e. who can't figure out a fluffed-up contract! If you didn't have more unpleasant truths to hide, why did you rush to Oakshott to get to Sophie before I did?"

"Hold it," said Nicholas, determined to rein me in. "We'll find out exactly what Kim did in a minute. Let's just complete your story."

"I rifled the desk," I said, willing enough to continue now that I had warned Kim not to mess me around, "and found the files which related to legal matters, but the divorce file was missing. There was also a locked drawer which proved to be empty. I then left the house and returned to London. End of story." I swung back to Kim. "What did you remove from that locked drawer?"

He sighed but admitted willingly enough: "Love-letters. Apparently she'd had an affair some years ago but the man had broken it off."

"But she was so moral! She was a Christian!"

"Not all Christians are saints." He gestured to the clerics. "Ask them."

"I'm afraid that's true," said Lewis. "Human nature being what it is, we can't always live up to our ideals."

I said to Kim: "I don't understand your motivation for taking this file."

"As a matter of fact it was a large brown envelope, not a file. I took it because...well, this may sound odd but I felt it was something I could do for Sophie. I didn't want that piece of gossip to get out into the community where she was respected."

"I'm sure I'd have felt the same if I'd been you," said Lewis sympathetically, and added: "I was married once myself."

"Then you'll understand my second reason for not wanting the letters to become public: I didn't want anyone to know my wife had been unfaithful. It was a question of what the feminists call 'macho pride.'"

"Ah well," said Lewis with a thin little smile and a shrug of his shoulders, "feminists..."

Nicholas cleared his throat, as if he felt all this male bonding might prove excessive, and said crisply before I could unleash a response: "Thank you, Carter, for that summary. Now, Kim, perhaps you could start your own narrative by telling us when you made the decision to go down to Surrey."

Kim drained his glass and held it out to Lewis. "Can I please cadge some more of this stuff?"

The manoeuvre gave him extra time to think, of course. To my dismay I realised he could still be deciding to lie to the back teeth.

IV

"I came out of a long meeting," said Kim when Lewis returned with the refilled glass, "and was told that Mrs. Mayfield had called." He paused. "I'm not sure how far I should backtrack to explain about the disturbances in the flat."

"We'll get to the disturbances later. Keep going."

"Well, when I called her back she said Carter had caught her on the podium and accused her of trespass and malicious damage. Carter had already accused me of trashing the place earlier. I said to Elizabeth—to Mrs. Mayfield—that it sounded to me as if Carter would see her presence near Harvey Tower as proof we were engaged in a conspiracy to discredit Sophie, and that Carter was now going to want to see Sophie to find out why she needed to be discredited. I said to Mrs. Mayfield that I'd go straight down to Surrey to work something out, but she advised me against that and offered to see Sophie herself."

"Obviously the hag got straight into her car and drove down to Oakshott," I said. "I think—"

"Yes, I can imagine what you think, but you're wrong. Carter, when I phoned Elizabeth back from my office at ten to six this evening I was calling a number in north London which she had given Mary earlier—after leaving the Barbican she'd gone out to Hendon where she had an engagement tonight."

"Where she planned to prance around with another of her bloody groups, you mean!"

"I take your point," said Nicholas swiftly to Kim to keep the narration on track. "You're saying that if Mrs. Mayfield was in Hendon, not Fulham, she couldn't have killed Sophie before you arrived on the scene. But how do you know when Sophie died?"

"The body was still warm when I found her, so she couldn't have been dead long. And incidentally I really didn't want Elizabeth to go to Oakshott. By that time I was sure appeasement, not intimidation, was my only hope of neutral-ising Sophie."

"Would you mind not calling Mayfield Eliz-abeth?" I said. "It makes me want to puke."

"Let's just recap for a moment," said Nicholas, making another skilful intervention. "You talked to Mrs. Mayfield. She advised you not to go to Oakshott and offered to go herself, but—"

"—I refused the offer and ignored her advice. After this phone call I immediately tried to get hold of Carter but she wasn't at the office, and I was just considering the horrific possibility that she'd already left for Oakshott when she rang from the flat and said she was going to be dining out with a friend. (Of course I didn't believe her.) I then said I was going to be spending the evening at the Savoy with an American colleague of mine, but as soon as the call ended I took a cab to the garage at Harvey Tower. When I saw Carter's Porsche was still there I was enormously relieved because I knew I'd have that vital head-start on the journey to Oakshott."

"So you left London."

"Yes, but I didn't call ahead to warn Sophie I was coming until I'd taken the Oakshott exit off the A3. I hadn't intended to call her at all, but then I realised that if I just turned up on her doorstep she might be intimidated and I didn't want the meeting getting off to a bad start. When there was no reply to my call from the car-phone I was surprised as I didn't think she went out much in the evenings, but I was confident she wouldn't be late back. I left a message and drove on."

"Did you have a key?"

"No, Sophie had the locks changed after I left home. We used to leave a spare key in the outside lavatory, but she'd changed that hiding-place too along with the locks—as I discovered when there was no response to the front doorbell. At that point I tried the handle of the back door more out of frustration than any real hope of finding it unlocked, and lo and behold, it opened. When I found the alarm was off I was concerned because I felt sure Sophie wouldn't normally have gone out without leaving the house locked and the alarm set, so even before I found the body I was prepared for something bad to have happened."

"What did you do when you found her?"

"Made sure she was dead. After that I saw the broken heel of her shoe and decided the death was probably an accident, but at the same time I knew she could have been killed by a madman. There was evidence that she'd been gardening...someone could have slipped into the house...anyway, when I considered the possibility of murder I'm ashamed to say I lost my nerve, so..." He hesitated.

"So you took evasive action," said Lewis, still exuding sympathy.

"Right. I found the answering machine and played back the tape. To my horror I heard Carter had also left a message to say she was on her way, and I certainly didn't want her involved in the mess. I wiped the tape."

"Were you worried that Carter might arrive at any moment?"

"No, on the tape she'd said when she was leaving London and I figured I was safe for at least another twenty minutes, particularly since she had to find the house."

"Was it then that you searched the desk?"

"No, I then drew the ground-floor curtains to give Carter the impression that Sophie had gone out, leaving a few lights on and the curtains closed to await her return after dark. But after I'd done that, yes, I went to the desk and removed the large brown envelope along with the divorce file. I knew her lawyers would have copies of all the divorce correspondence, but I didn't want her relatives paddling through letters which could have contained very private and personal information."

"I don't suppose you were keen on me doing any paddling either," I said.

"Sweetheart, I told you—I never thought you'd enter the house!"

"Obviously there was no time to read the file at that moment," said Nicholas, "but did you take a look later?"

"Yes, on the way home I pulled off the A3 and had a quick flick through, but as far as I could see it was all standard stuff, nothing dramatic at all."

"Sez you," I muttered before demanding sharply: "Where's that file now—outside in your car?"

"No, when I finally got back to the Barbican after dining with Warren I took both the file and the envelope of love-letters up to the flat so that I could examine them properly, but as soon as I got inside and saw the mess—"

"Hold it," said Nicholas. "We've skipped a bit. What did you do after your quick flick through the divorce file in the car?"

"I called Mrs. Mayfield—or at least, I tried to but I didn't succeed because I couldn't remember all the digits of that Hendon number. I then called my New York colleague, Warren Schaeffer, at the Savoy, and told him I wanted to stop by— I'd actually called him earlier, before I left the office, to ask him to cover for me if Carter rang up to check where I was, and he'd promised to tell the switchboard not to put through any calls made by a woman. I'd done the same thing for him once in New York when he was in a tight marital corner, so I knew he'd be happy to oblige."

"I'd realised you were lying about having a business meeting with Warren," I said. "If that had been true, you'd have picked up your organiser."

Before Kim could attempt a reply Nicholas asked: "What time did you get to the Savoy?"

"Not long after eight-thirty. But when I reached the Savoy I didn't go to the reception desk to ask for Warren because I didn't want any of the staff there remembering when I'd arrived; I thought I should make at least some attempt to set up an alibi. So I parked the car down by the river and slipped in the Embankment entrance when the doorman was busy hailing a taxi. Then I went straight up to Warren's suite—he'd already told me the number."

"And you dined with him."

"In the Grill, yes, at around nine-thirty—his stomach was still on New York time. We had drinks in his room first and also in the bar afterwards."

"Did you try calling Mrs. Mayfield again?"

"I tried the Fulham number when I got back to my car but she was still out. I left a message and drove on to the Barbican."

"And at Harvey Tower—"

"I found no Carter, the flat a shambles and your message on the answerphone." He turned to me again in what appeared to be genuine bewilderment. "Why on earth did you smash up the flat?"

"*Me?*" I cried. "But it was that arch-cow Mayfield!"

"I'm certain that's not true."

"Well, if I didn't," I said heatedly, "and you didn't and she didn't, who the hell did?"

"Perhaps this is the moment," said Nicholas, "to try to establish with Kim's help exactly who caused these disturbances."

I said at once to Kim: "It was a conspiracy, wasn't it?"

"Well, yes and no," said Kim confused. "Certainly nothing could have happened this evening. You must have done it yourself in some kind of trance—what do the psychologists call it? A fugue."

"I damn well did not!"

"May I intervene," said Nicholas, "before this argument gets too circular? Let's start at the beginning. Now, the first incident, if I remember correctly, was the smashing of the print of Kim's Oxford college. Can you both agree on who did that?"

"It was an accident caused by the vibrations of the building," said Kim without hesitation, but I answered: "It could have been an accident. But it could also have been the first act of a conspiracy."

"No, it was a genuine accident," insisted Kim, "but it did give me the idea about how I could destroy Sophie's credibility by suggesting she was demented."

"You see?" I said triumphantly to Nicholas and Lewis. "He's confessing to a conspiracy!"

"But it wasn't operating today," said Kim, deflating me. "Mrs. Mayfield dropped out."

My automatic response was: "I don't believe you."

Before Kim could answer Nicholas suggested: "Let's just look at the second incident, the smashing of the painting, the breaking of the cereal bowl and the spilling of the garbage bag," but he had barely finished speaking when Kim said: "Okay, that was me. I did it, just as you suspected, Carter, before I left for work. Mrs. Mayfield told me how much to disarrange because she said it was important not to go over the top. She also agreed to be visible on the podium at the far end of the Speed Highwalk when you came home from work that day. By coincidence she had a royal-blue coat, so—"

"What about that time when we saw the woman in royal blue leaving the supermarket?"

"Yes, that was Mrs. Mayfield. I wanted to give you the impression that Sophie was lurking around like the mistress in *Fatal Attraction*."

"And after that we get to the first disturbance today," said Nicholas, allowing me no time to comment. "This was the disturbance Carter found when she returned home early from work. Did you at least plan that, Kim, even if you didn't do it?"

He admitted that the plan had been in place. "Carter had asked me if I'd created the earlier disturbance," he said, "and that gave me a bad jolt because I realised my scheme was about to backfire—and once it backfired I knew she'd want to talk to Sophie. So I said to Elizabeth— to Mrs. Mayfield—that she had to help me by creating a disturbance at a time when I had a cast-iron alibi. When I saw her last night we worked out the plan. I gave her my front door key; then we designed her way into the building by using the excuse that she was dropping off my organiser. But when I called her back after my meeting this afternoon she said she'd changed her mind— she'd dropped off the package at the porters' desk but she'd never gone up to the flat. She said she didn't want to get into any situation where she ran the risk of being arrested for damaging property."

I said stubbornly: "I don't believe her. She had the key of the flat copied this morning and then went to the flat this afternoon to do the first round of damage. After that she dropped off your key with the organiser in the Jiffy bag, returned tonight with the copy of the key and—"

"No, I'm sure that's not right," said Kim firmly. "She said she'd come out against the conspiracy not just because it was too damn risky but because ultimately the impression we were trying to give of Sophie slickly whisking past all the porters time after time was too implausible."

"Mrs. Mayfield was lying to put you off the scent! She's determined to destroy our marriage and destroy me too!"

"Sweetheart, listen to yourself! You're paranoid!"

"Oh no, I'm not! She wants me to throw myself off the balcony. She's planted this vile idea in my head and now I can't get it out again—"

"You're sick." He turned to Lewis. "All this stress has pushed her over the edge."

"I work with a doctor," said Nicholas subtly before Lewis could speak. "Do you think I should contact her?"

"No, no!" said Kim, backtracking rapidly as he realised he had no desire for anyone else to be involved in the crisis. "No, I'm sure we can sort this out without additional professional help. Carter, is this why you intend to spend the night here—because you've developed a phobia about the balcony?"

"I'm spending the night here because the flat's totally uninhabitable! And by the way, I don't want you going back there at present."

"What do you mean?"

"You've polluted my beautiful home with your lies—you've lied and lied and lied—and worst of all you've collaborated with that disgusting woman in a plan to trick and trash me! Damn it, it's not because of her but because of *you* that I've wound up scared out of my skull tonight!"

"But I swear I had nothing to do with the damage to the flat this evening—"

"You can swear till you're blue in the face but you're not going back to that flat yet so you can give me your keys! I know you've got the spare set—you'd have collected them from the porter in order to get into the flat just now!"

"Sweetheart—please! What do I have to do in order to get you to be reasonable?"

"TELL THE TRUTH!" I yelled. "What was it that drove you to go to Oakshott tonight? What was it that Sophie knew and never managed to tell me?"

He tried to play for time. "I'm not sure I can talk about that right now," he said, but I snapped back straight away: "Get real! It was all to do with that occult society, wasn't it?"

"What occult society?" he said astonished.

VI

I struggled to maintain my momentum. "Sophie said you were mixed up with the occult."

"Obviously she was just referring to Mrs. Mayfield's psychic healing. People often use the word 'occult' today to describe a whole range of activities which have nothing to do with the occult at all."

"Very true!" said Lewis, seizing the opportunity to exude sympathy again.

"But is that the whole picture?" murmured Nicholas vaguely. "Isn't the reality a little more complex than that? In my experience the milder forms of so-called 'occult' involvement can lead insidiously to more dangerous forms, including corrupt versions of Gnosticism. People can easily be drawn out of their depth."

"Not people like me," said Kim. "And if I wanted to join a society which specialised in weird rituals I'd take up Freemasonry. The business contacts would be a lot more useful."

These statements were so rational, so drenched in common sense, that I decided I had taken a wrong turn. I tried to get back on course. "So the stuff which Sophie never managed to tell me about had nothing to do with your occult involvement?"

"I've never been involved with the occult."

"I mean—"

"No, it had nothing to do with my involvement in New Age healing. It was about something which happened before I ever met Mrs. Mayfield."

"So what the hell was it?"

Unexpectedly he rose to his feet and moved to the window as if his tension was so great that he

337

could no longer remain still. Without looking at me he said: "Mrs. Mayfield gave you a hint during that conversation you had with her this afternoon. But she served it up with a twist which wasn't true because she wanted you to abandon the idea of having children."

My heart began to beat very fast. "You mean the impotence story?"

"Yes." He turned to face me again. "It was true that there was a period early on in my marriage when I did suffer from a prolonged bout of impotence," he said, "but that wasn't because Sophie wanted children and I didn't."

"Then what caused the impotence?"

"Guilt. It was my fault that Sophie became sterile," he said, exhausted, and slumped down on the window-seat as if the confession had taken his last ounce of energy.

VII

Stiff-lipped I said: "What happened?" By that time I was starting to feel sick.

He leaned forward, elbows on his knees, and screened his face with his hands. "I picked up gonorrhoea during the first months of the marriage. I thought I hadn't passed it on to Sophie but I had. She just showed no symptoms."

I was silenced. Nobody moved. Finally Kim wiped the sweat from his forehead, let his hands fall and said in a rapid, uneven voice: "The truth came out in the end—when the damage had been done. If I'd told her at the start...but I didn't. We did try to set the tragedy behind us but the marriage never recovered and after a while the guilt hit me. That was when I became

338

impotent and that was the problem Mrs. May-field cured and yes, I've known Mrs. Mayfield for very much longer than I chose to disclose to you. So the rock-bottom truth is that there was no back trouble three years ago, no stress-related medical problem which arose out of an increasing obsession with my Nazi background...and no fidelity to Sophie even before she and I started sleeping apart. I'm afraid my first marriage was very far from being the uneventful, painless arrangement that I led you to believe it was."

I was still beyond speech. I could only listen as he added desperately to Lewis, the assigned sympathiser: "I just couldn't bear the idea of Carter learning about this disaster which showed me in the worst possible light as a husband. I love Carter, I've been faithful to her, she's the most wonderful thing that's ever happened to me—and that's why I've been so determined to make a fresh start, that's why I've tried so hard to prevent Carter hearing about the Kim Betz whom Sophie knew. I wanted Carter to love me for the man I really was, deep down, the man I now feel I can claim and become. I wanted to keep her quite separate from that other person, the shit who'd mis-treated Sophie and messed around in the world of Mrs. Mayfield."

There was a pause. To my horror I found there was a lump in my throat and tears were burning my eyes again. I stared down at my clenched fists.

Lewis said at last, choosing his words with care: "Thank you, Kim. How hard it is, isn't it, to speak frankly of very painful matters."

"Just a moment," I said. I was still struggling with the urge to cry but I was determined to force my emotions out of sight. "There's something I still don't understand. Why did Mrs. Mayfield agree to help you keep me and Sophie apart? You acted to protect our marriage but Mrs. Mayfield obviously wants to bust it up."

"Her main aim is to draw me back into her world. She'll help me now in order to soften me up and then she'll take care of the marriage later—or so she thinks. But of course I'll never let her do such a thing." He turned to Lewis again. "You understand what I've been saying, don't you?" he said urgently. "I'm sorry for what I've done, I want to start afresh, I want to live very differently in future. Surely as Christians you and your colleague can only give me your support?"

"Wrong move!" I cried at once, my tears forgotten. Shooting to my feet I said strongly to Nicholas: "It's time to switch on the scepticism—he's just using Christian doctrine to manipulate you."

VIII

Kim shouted: "That's not true!" but Nicholas was already standing up. The swift grace of the movement reminded me again of an actor, confidently dominating his chosen stage.

"Wait!" he said with an authority impossible to ignore. "We've clearly reached the stage where we need to take a break and get some sleep. Kim, you can be sure that we take very seriously everything you've said and that we're anxious to give you and your wife every support. Carter, let me assure you that we always consider the possibility of manipulation in these cases."

"Oh, spare me the butter-smooth diplomacy!"

I said angrily. "Why don't you come right out and condemn him for what he did to Sophie?"

"I'm not in the business of passing judgement," said Nicholas evenly. "I leave that to God. What I will say is that in my opinion Kim's revelations need no further comment. He committed adultery. The innocent suffered. There were tragic consequences. Doesn't this very painful morality tale speak for itself?"

I opened my mouth only to find I had nothing to say. Meanwhile Nicholas had turned to Kim.

"We plan to go to the flat at nine tomorrow morning," he said. "Is it possible for you to join us there so that we can all work together to ensure there are no further disturbances at the flat?"

"Excuse me!" I said in fury. "What right have you to invite any person to my flat, particularly a person I don't want to see there at present?"

"I'm sorry," said Nicholas at once. "That was insensitive of me, but—"

"Yes, it damn well was!"

"—but since Kim has admitted his part in the disturbances I think it makes sense to enlist his help in setting the flat right. It's an opportunity to involve him in the healing process."

"Well, of course I'll do anything I can to help," said Kim immediately. "Carter—sweetheart—give me a break, can't you? I really, truly hate being cut off from you like this—"

"I'm sorry," I said. "I know I'm being vile to you but I can't stop myself, I'm still too upset. Could you hand over those keys now, please?"

"But sweetheart—"

"To be frank, Kim," said Lewis, "I wouldn't want to return to that flat tonight, if I were you.

There's nothing more depressing than returning to a home that's been vandalised, as any victim of burglary will tell you, and if you choose to spend the rest of the night in a hotel I'm sure you'll be doing yourself a favour."

I saw Kim again seize the opportunity to climb down without losing face. "That makes sense," he said. "Okay, I'll go to a hotel now and join you at the flat tomorrow at nine." And to me he added: "Don't forget that you're the most important person in my life and I love you."

I grabbed his arm as he turned towards the door. "You still haven't given me the keys!"

"Look, I've agreed to go to a hotel—"

"*Give me the keys!*"

He sighed heavily but produced the ring holding the key to the Tower and the key to the flat. "I don't want to fight with you, sweetheart. It cuts me up to see you so upset. I'm very, very sorry."

Once more I murdered the desire to cry as Kim said civilly to the clerics: "Thanks for your patience. Sorry I beat up on you in the beginning."

"Don't worry about that. I'll see you out," said Nicholas before Lewis could volunteer, and led the way into the hall.

Lewis immediately retrieved his notepad and began to write his summary of the interview.

IX

"He would never have given you permission to take notes," I said. "I suppose that was why you never bothered to ask for it. Do you think he killed her?"

"We don't know for a fact that she was killed by anyone." He looked up as Nicholas returned to the room.

"What did you think of him?" I persisted. "I know you were slobbering over him in order to play Mr. Nice-Guy, softening him up, but what were you thinking while you slobbered?"

"I thought he was a clever man," said Lewis, "and he certainly seems to be very involved with you, but beyond that I don't care to venture an opinion at present."

"Why not? I suppose you think I might have hysterics!"

"If I did, I assure you I'd know better than to say so."

"God, you're such a tiger-thumper! How did your wife stand you?"

"She didn't. We got divorced."

"Carter," said Nicholas, resuming his role of diplomat, "can I take you upstairs to join Alice? I'm sure you're keen to get some sleep."

"Wait a minute. What's *your* opinion of Kim?"

"Some of his statements struck me as being more truthful than others, but that's par for the course in this kind of case."

"But what I want to know is—"

"You're desperate to know where the truth lies, but Lewis and I need time to think carefully about what we've heard. So if you'd now like to get some rest—"

"No, don't try to kick me upstairs again!" I exclaimed, hyping up my annoyance to divert myself from the knowledge that I was feeling increasingly upset. "I refuse to be shovelled off to bed like a small child who's behaving badly! Anyway I don't want to sleep upstairs in case I

343

feel driven to fling myself out of a window. Do you have a ground-floor sofa I can use?"

The two men exchanged swift glances before Nicholas said with unexpected gentleness: "I'm sorry, I'd quite forgotten Mrs. Mayfield's psychological warfare, but let me now take steps to deal with that. The first thing to stress is—"

"Forget it," I said. "You're like Lewis. You just think I'm overwrought and hysterical."

"I assure you—"

"And now you're being smarmy, trying to handle me with kid gloves as if I were some rubbishy Victorian maidenette—damn it, it's so arrogant and patronising that I don't know how Alice stands it! And incidentally, I don't like the way you're treating Alice. You're not playing straight with her, probably because you think you're the cat's whiskers and can get away with anything where women are concerned, but let me tell you this, Mr. Whiskers: *I* don't find you attractive, so don't expect *me* to go mewing in the pews of your church! I can see through you just like *that*!" I tried to snap my fingers and failed. That was when I realised I was raving. I frowned and rubbed my eyes. "Bloody hell," I muttered, "I'm traumatised. Excuse me."

"I'm extremely sorry," said Nicholas concerned, "that I've made such a bad impression on you, but please believe me when I say—"

"I'll take the tiger-thumper," I interrupted, unable to stand the butter-smooth diplomacy a moment longer. "He'll lay it on the line about how to beat the arch-cow's psycho-crap. Tell him to hang up his thumper and get down to business."

Nicholas removed Lewis's pen and notepad. "I'll finish this in the kitchen," he said. "You help Carter."

344

The moment he left the room I burst into tears.

X

"This proves you're both right," I muttered when I could speak. "I *am* overwrought and hysterical."

"I don't recall either of us applying those adjectives to you. Have a Kleenex."

I grabbed a couple of tissues from the box he held out. "But you're *thinking* I'm overwrought and hysterical."

"I can't answer for Nicholas, but I'll tell you what I'm thinking. I'm thinking that you've just emerged from an extremely upsetting scene during which your husband made a confession which no newly married woman should be expected to listen to without experiencing a very deep distress. If anyone's entitled to shed tears at this moment, you are."

"I despise tears," I said. "Tears are for losers who haven't the guts to fight back when life kicks them into the gutter and stamps on them."

"On the contrary, tears are for everyone, winners and losers alike. Tears serve a very useful function in alleviating emotional stress, and since the subject of stress has come up more than once tonight—"

"I absolutely refuse to believe that poltergeist theory!"

"That's fine. We accept your refusal. What we're primarily worried about is how we can help you ease your undeniable stress both now and in the future. That's why Nicholas was so keen for you to get some rest. After all you've been through

345

tonight, rest is essential before we tackle the next phase of the problem tomorrow."

"But how can I rest when you two refuse to tell me what you thought of Kim, how can I? The whole nightmare's going round and round and round in my head—"

"My dear—no, I'm sorry, I mustn't call you that, must I, modern women don't like it. Carter, Nicholas and I probably feel much as you do. We want to believe Kim was being straight with us. But because of his association with Mrs. Mayfield we have to consider the possibility that his testimony tonight contained lies. Now, a lot of people cherish the fairy-tale that liars are easy to spot because they blush or look shifty, but as a businesswoman you'll know, just as Nicholas and I know, that a really accomplished liar always sounds like a truth-teller. That's why we have to think so carefully about what we've heard tonight. That's why we have to avoid jumping to false conclusions. It's the only professional way to proceed... Have another Kleenex."

Having snuffled into a fresh tissue I said: "I loved him so much when he said he wanted to be his real self with me. But I'm going mad not knowing when he's lying and when he's telling the truth."

"Did you believe his confession about infecting Sophie?"

"Yes, that I did believe. It had the vilest possible ring of truth, and I certainly believe he'd go to extreme lengths to prevent me hearing about the disaster."

"I wonder what the police are making of it all."

There was a silence. I wanted to confess my

lie about tipping off the police, but I found this was beyond me. I could not cope with the thought of the police at all. I had to have more time.

"Even if there's no evidence that either of you were at Oakshott tonight," said Lewis, and I could feel him watching me closely, "the police are going to want to talk to Kim as the ex-husband."

"Sure... Hey, can you go ahead and fix my balcony phobia, please?"

"I can certainly try." To my relief he abandoned the subject of the police and extracted from Nicholas's desk what appeared to be a handful of necklaces. But when he detached one I saw a little crucifix dangling at the end of a thin chain. "No, it's not a lucky charm," he said briskly. "Christians don't believe in magic amulets. But it's a device for centring the mind in times of prayer. It reminds us that no demon can withstand the power of Christ."

I experienced a sharp disappointment. In despair I said: "But I don't believe in all that stuff!"

"I'm sure you'll understand what I'm driving at if I translate it into a language which is more accessible to you. Each profession spawns its own language, doesn't it? For instance, you lawyers often talk to one another in jargon a layman can't understand."

"Quite. But—"

"Priests are just the same. We have our special language and catch-phrases. 'No demon can withstand the power of Christ,' I said. But now listen to this: 'No urge to self-destruct can withstand the power of the drive to integration when that drive is properly channelled.' How does that sound?"

I stared at him. "Well, I can understand that sentence, of course. But do you mean—"

"I'll tell you what I mean. Christ is a symbol of integration and wholeness. Demons are symbols of fragmentation and sickness. Human beings have an inbuilt capacity to repair themselves (which is always so useful to doctors) and an inbuilt drive to achieve what Jung called 'individuation' (which today we'd see as a state of well-integrated wholeness, a state of realised potential). This inbuilt capacity for repair and this inbuilt drive to be integrated have the power to triumph over damage and fragmentation."

"Not when people die!"

"Even death can be redeemed, but what I'm primarily talking about now is the dynamic of being fully alive. I'm saying that if we can tap into this great inbuilt desire for healing and integration we'll win out over the compulsion to fragment. Or to put the situation in religious language: there's no darkness so dark that it can't be redeemed in some way by the light, and no willed wickedness (such as Mrs. Mayfield's attempt at mind-control) which can't be beaten back by prayer to God in the name of Jesus Christ."

"But I can't pray!"

"Nonsense, it's easy, children do it without thinking twice. It's just talking to God—or to Christ. (Humans find it easier to talk to a man than to a great big indescribable entity called God.) All you do is—"

"But I couldn't!"

"Oh, don't be so feeble—surely a tough woman like you can talk to anyone? All you do is this: hold this little crucifix in order to centre yourself on what you're doing, and then shoot off prayers like

348

arrows. You'll be tuning in to the great integrating principle in your unconscious mind and thus lining yourself up with the power which sustains all life everywhere. Just say: 'Lord Jesus Christ, help me,' or simply: 'Jesus—help!' He'll get the message. He's the integrating principle. Tune in to him—connect with your inbuilt drive to wholeness in the right way—and Mrs. Mayfield's power to split you into fragments doesn't stand a chance."

I was silent. Lewis waited. I went on being silent and Lewis went on waiting, but at last I said slowly: "When I talk to him...will I feel a sort of presence?"

"You might."

"A sort of unseen companion?"

"Possibly."

"How would I know he wasn't wish-fulfilment?"

"He'd surprise you in some way. He wouldn't be quite what you thought you wanted. Maybe he'd even be very different from what you thought you wanted. But you'd recognise him 'in the breaking of the bread,' as we say. There'd be something about him which would ring a vital bell."

"Such as?"

"It varies, but usually there's a powerful sense of wholeness, the kind of completeness you feel when you're deeply cared for and cherished. Love is the most powerful integrating force on earth." He opened another drawer of the desk and pulled out a postcard with a printed inscription. "Here," he said, "have one of these to help you along."

"What is it?"

"A famous prayer called 'St. Patrick's Breastplate,' which is excellent for concentrating the mind to repel malign attack. Read it in the night if you're feeling anxious—oh, and make sure Alice shows you how to work the intercom. You can buzz me at any time during the night if you feel the need for reinforcements."

"So that gets me through tonight. But what about all the nights after that?"

"Tomorrow we'll do our stuff at the flat, and I think you'll find not only that the atmosphere will be much improved but that the balcony will be a safe place again. However, to keep up the level of protection I'll get our prayer-group to pray for you until you feel the danger's passed. We often pray for those under psychic attack from people like Mrs. Mayfield."

I was silent again, fingering the crucifix, but finally I slipped the chain around my neck and said: "I like straight talkers. If you could just remember never to treat me as some kind of ape who flunked a 'homo sapiens' rating, you and I could get along."

"I'll crank up my ancient memory straight away."

"And tell Nicholas I'm sorry I zapped him just now. I do realise I was only dumping on him all the anger and frustration I was feeling about Kim..." I destroyed another Kleenex and held up the box. "Can I take this upstairs?"

"Let me give you a new one."

"I've never known a house so stuffed with Kleenex!"

"Well, it certainly beats ironing handker-chiefs."

He produced another box for me from some cache on the other side of the desk.

Then he took me upstairs to join Alice.

XI

The attic flat was large, freshly painted in that dreary colour magnolia, and carpeted with a boring beige woolly nylon product, but the modern furniture was brightly upholstered so the atmosphere was far from downbeat. I was hardly in the mood to spare much thought to the interior decoration but I was relieved to find I hadn't been billeted in a slum.

"We refurbished the flat eighteen months ago," said Alice after Lewis had departed. "It had seen a lot of sadness but Nicholas held a service of blessing in it and it got better. The curate used to live here but we don't have a curate at present."

"The flat's been unoccupied for eighteen months?"

"No, there was a woman deacon who stayed for a time but she and Lewis didn't hit it off so she left."

I was shown a clean, neat bedroom with sloping ceilings, and when we moved back to the living-room she demonstrated how to work the intercom.

"I expect you're sick of tea by now," she said. "Nicholas is always pouring tea into his clients, but would you like some hot chocolate? I've got some delicious stuff which is only forty calories a sachet..."

It was a relief to postpone the moment when I had to be on my own, trying to sleep, and although I was too tired to talk much the silences were not uncomfortable. In her cherry-red dressing-gown Alice seemed cosy and comforting, effortlessly exuding the non-intrusive attentiveness of a skilled nurse with an ailing patient.

"Thanks for being here," I said at last. "I

should have thanked Nicholas too for his hospitality but I was too busy bucketing around like a menopausal harpy on uppers."

"People *in extremis* often behave out of character," said Alice with supreme tact. "I'm sure Nicholas understood."

I put down my empty mug and started to fidget with the keys Kim had given me. Eventually I said: "What do you think of Eric Tucker?"

"Oh, he's much improved! I like him now."

"What was wrong with him?"

"Well…" There was a pause while Alice worked out how to continue being supremely tactful. "He had some financial problems which made him unhappy, and unhappy people are often quite difficult, aren't they? But last year he went back to live at Gil's vicarage—he'd lived there before—and that was such a good thing because Gil makes rules and creates structures for him, and I think that deep down this is what Eric wants. He needs order."

"Order?"

"Yes, just like a spoiled child secretly does after being allowed to run wild. I suppose you could say Gil's completing Eric's upbringing."

"Gil must be some kind of saint!"

"Oh no!" said Alice with enthusiasm. "He's very controversial and always getting into trouble with the bishop!" She hesitated before confiding: "Gil's gay."

"Yeah. Too bad for us women."

"Never mind, we've got Eric. Gil says Eric's so heterosexual he ought to be adopted as a mascot by the anti-gay lobby at the Church of England's General Synod."

I stared at Kim's keys and thought of Tucker.

Of course I had already worked out that I had to go back to the flat well before nine on the following morning. But I had worked out too that I was incapable of going on my own.

THIRTEEN

There is an added twist to the agony (of suffering) when, as so often happens, the suffering is connected with malice, selfishness, indifference, injustice, or some other form of evil.

DAVID F. FORD
The Shape of Living

I

Once I was in bed I grabbed the crucifix like a baby clutching a rattle and read the prayer called "St. Patrick's Breastplate," but I was so tired that the words made no sense. I turned the light off but immediately switched it on again.

I decided I might try praying—but not just yet. That extreme measure could wait until I was desperate. Meanwhile I was hoping that my unseen companion would make himself known again, but although I did summon the nerve to close my eyes nothing happened so I assumed he was attending to people far needier than I was. I told myself I was fine, lying on the bed with my eyes shut. Sleep was out of the question, but people could survive without sleep for some time before they had to be removed to a mental hospital. Surviving the next few hours should be well within my abilities.

I wondered if Lewis was praying for me or whether he was now asleep. I thought he was probably asleep but gradually, as time passed, I became obsessed with the thought that someone was praying for me somewhere. Maybe it was Gilbert Tucker over in Fleetside... I thought of Gil saying: "It's all right. You're safe here. Come on in," and the next moment, as I began to traverse the rim of consciousness, I knew that in the replayed memory lay the prayer which I had been too inhibited to articulate. I knew too, the split second before my companion fell into step by my side, that my prayer was going to be answered by someone who felt I was far too valuable to be neglected—and then as I once more rounded the curve into King Edward Street, my companion took my hand to lead me uphill again to the Cathedral, where the brilliant light blasted apart the darkness of Mrs. Mayfield's velvety, voluptuous night sky.

II

I had set the alarm on my watch for six o'clock and the moment I awoke I sat upright, knowing I had a vital task to accomplish. I had to see those papers which Kim had been desperate enough to remove from the house at Oakshott. By this time I had realised that although I believed his horrific confession about Sophie, it did not relate in any way to the mystery of the blackmail story which both Nicholas and Lewis had found unconvincing.

I had already spent time worrying in case Kim had gone to Mrs. Mayfield to obtain the copy of his front door key, but I reasoned that he would not want to give me proof that she had had the means to achieve the final trashing of the flat. I thought that no matter how much he wanted to re-annex the files he would not turn up at the flat until nine when we had all agreed to meet there.

Tiptoeing to the bathroom I removed the crucifix from around my neck and washed myself all over as I stood at the basin. There was no shower and I did not want to wake Alice by running a bath. Later I borrowed her deodorant, which she had obligingly left on the bathroom shelf along with her other overnight essentials, but I was unable to use her make-up as her skin-tones were different from mine. However, I felt this misfortune had to rank as the least of my worries. Pulling Tucker's card from the hip pocket of my jeans I padded into the living-room to the phone.

He answered on the first ring. "Yep?"

"It's me. Are you asleep?"

"Don't be funny, this is prime time! I'm working."

"Oh God, I'm sorry—"

"It's okay, just let me mentally climb out of my Spitfire—"

"I'm about to offer you another ride into the sky but not in a WWII plane. Can you face taking the lift with me to the thirty-fifth floor of Harvey Tower?"

"With exceptional ease. When?"

"Now. The trouble is I'm still too fluffed out to face that place on my own but I've got to go there to retrieve some vital papers. Can you borrow Gil's car again?"

"Your chauffeur will be at the Rectory in ten minutes. Do I need to shave?"

"I'm asking you to be a pillar of strength, Tucker, not a snogger's delight."

"Too bad," he said, and hung up.

III

In the kitchen I found a ballpoint pen attached to a block of paper inscribed "SHOPPING LIST," and scribbled on the top page: "Alice—Gone home to pick up some stuff. Back soon. Love, C." Having attached the note to the door of the fridge with a butterfly magnet I then withdrew to the living-room to watch for Tucker.

The elderly white Ford trickled over the cobbles of Egg Street a few minutes later. Noiselessly I crept downstairs. I was worried in case there was an alarm which I would not know how to deactivate, but to my relief I discovered in the hall that Nicholas was already up, a fact which probably meant the alarm, if one existed, had been switched off. There was a light shining beneath the closed door of his study. What could he be doing at such an early hour? But perhaps the mysterious activity was part of some clerical routine.

Noiselessly easing the latch away from the lock I stepped outside and shut the front door behind me with only the smallest of clicks before I paused to glance at my watch.

The time was twenty minutes to seven.

IV

"Let me give you a briefing," I said to Tucker, the business language surfacing in my mind with a comforting familiarity. "There's a problem with my flat. It keeps getting disarranged. The clerics have diagnosed poltergeist activity but I don't accept this, (a) because it doesn't accord with my world-view, and (b) because my husband admitted last night during a hellish conference at the Rectory that he was at least partly responsible. He also admitted he was aided and abetted by a truly revolting number who calls herself Mrs. Mayfield and who uses up people as fast as I've recently been using up Kleenex. Don't ask me how my husband got involved with this old crone, who Nicholas tells me has a criminal record; it's sufficient to state that he—Kim—refuses at present to give her up. Now, before joining me at the Rectory last night, Kim left two files at the trashed flat—or, to be accurate, a bilious-yellow file and a large brown envelope—and it's those files I have to retrieve, but before you start worrying about the prospect of facing my husband in his pyjamas, let me set your mind at rest by saying he won't be there. I insisted on taking his keys to stop him going back to the flat and destroying the files, so he'll have spent the night in a hotel."

Tucker made no comment on Kim but asked with interest: "What are the clerics proposing to do about the alleged poltergeist activity?"

"Various things. But there's also another weird happening they have to take care of, and to do this they're turning up at the flat at nine to stage some kind of religious production. I wasn't too keen when this idea was first mooted, but the truth is the flat's currently so uninhabitable that anything seems worth a try, even a procedure which doesn't accord with my rational world-view."

Tucker said carefully: "Does Nick know what you're up to at this moment?"

"I left a note for Alice."

"Okay, but when we get to the flat, let's give him a call to say what's going on. If this is a tricky case I'm sure he'd want to be kept informed."

"It's not worth a call, Tucker! We'll be in and out of that flat in a couple of minutes!"

"Wonderful, but I don't like the sound of Mother Mayfield."

"Right now she'll be tucked up in her dinky little villa in Fulham with her grey wig hung up on the bedpost."

Unfortunately I was by this time so relieved to have survived the night and so pleased to be junketing around with Tucker again that I never paused long enough to visualise an alternative programme for Mrs. Mayfield. If I had, I would hardly have pictured her snoozing in bed. I would have imagined her fully dressed and drinking herb tea as she plotted Kim's next move.

V

In the garage below Harvey Tower I said to the attendant: "We won't be long—where can my guest leave his car?" and the attendant directed us to an empty bay right by his booth. "That's handy!" I said to him as I got out. "Can I have it again later?" And I explained how I would be returning with two clergymen. The attendant, suitably impressed, printed in his book for the attendant who would be taking over from him at eight: "BAY 12 RESERVED FOR TWO CLERGYMEN VISITING FLAT 353 (BETZ)."

358

"My stock's gone up," I murmured amused as I led the way to the lift-lobby, but Tucker's attention had been diverted.

"Hey, look at all this!" he exclaimed. "What an evocative use of concrete—it makes me think of a WWII bunker!"

"That's probably the nicest thing anyone's ever said about the car-park level of Harvey Tower."

Tucker was wearing blue jeans and a black leather jacket which was open to reveal a fresh-looking white T-shirt. The crotch of his jeans seemed to present a more worn shade of blue than was visible elsewhere, but jeans often look patchy in interesting areas, particularly when viewed in artificial light. His curls crept below the collar at the nape of his neck but were tucked tidily behind his ears, while his facial hair, which was busy converting itself from a designer stubble to an undesigned beard, seemed dark at a distance but more ambiguous in colouring when seen close up in the lift. The faint aroma of the T-shirt's fabric softener reached me. It was mingling with the smell of macho mouthwash combined with something which might once have been extra-strong coffee.

"Ready for take-off?" I said as the lift-doors closed.

"Do they have those oxygen masks which come down from the ceiling?"

"No, we just gasp for air like hard-pressed goldfish."

"I kind of like the idea of you and me being hard-pressed together, Ms. G."

"I bet... I've missed your humour, Tucker."

"Then I must take care not to get too serious, mustn't I?"

The lift started to zip skywards. As usual it moaned and hummed as if it were aching to mate with the lift in the nearest shaft.

"Hell, this is sexy!" said Tucker suddenly. "Do you do this every day?"

"Every day. Sometimes several times."

"How long does it take?"

"Not long enough for what you obviously have in mind. Unless, of course, you favour what Shana at the office calls a quick shag."

"Forget it," said Tucker. "I like to take my time."

The lift began to slow down.

"Tucker," I said with what I hoped was a clinical interest, "did we actually exchange those last remarks or was I hallucinating?"

"No hallucination, Ms. G. Just sheer nervous tension on your part and sheer yobbish manners on mine. Shall we revert to being Lord Peter Wimsey and Bunter?"

"I hardly think we need go that far."

The lift doors rolled open. I stepped out onto the carpeted concrete floor which lay thirty-five floors above the podium and at once I started to feel queasy. As my hand flew upwards to clasp the little crucifix I realised to my acute dismay that there was no thin chain around my neck.

"What's the matter?" demanded Tucker, seeing my expression change.

I told him and added, trying not to panic: "I took the thing off this morning in order to wash but I forgot to put it back on again."

I half-expected him to make a humorous remark but instead he became serious. "Let's go back to retrieve it," he said quickly. "Egg Street's so near—going back's no big deal."

But I was already telling myself not to treat the

crucifix as a lucky charm. "No, let's be rational about this," I insisted. "Let's keep a sense of proportion. All we need to do is go into the flat, grab the files and get out again. I don't have to go anywhere near the—" I broke off, trying to distract myself by producing the key-ring. "Tucker," I heard myself say, "if I open the balcony door in any room, please could you yank me back and ram the door shut again?"

"Your wish is my command, Ms. G. Here, give me those keys before you drop them and I'll fit the right one in the lock for you."

I passed over the key-ring. "I suppose you're not wearing a mini-cross yourself under that T-shirt?"

"I'm sorry to say I'm not." Unlocking the door he held it open for me so that I could move past him into the flat.

But the files, we discovered, were nowhere to be seen.

VI

As soon as I crossed the threshold I called out Kim's name in case he had used Mrs. Mayfield's key after all, but to my enormous relief there was no response. Gingerly I glanced into the master bedroom. Logic told me I would not see Sophie there again, but I feared suffering a flashback which might send me tripping out into a heightened state of consciousness. However, nothing happened and gradually I became aware of the disorder which I had been too frightened to note when the ghost had appeared. Kim's suits were on the floor again, the bedroom chair was askew and both the bedside lights had been knocked over. Auto-

matically I moved forward to straighten the bedroom chair but wound up much too close to the
window.

I fled back into the hall.

This unpleasant excursion to the bedroom
was the first reason why it took me longer than
it should have done to realise that the files were
nowhere to be seen. The second reason was that
I then became preoccupied with my balcony
phobia and had to open the front door again so
that I could make a quick exit if my nerve
snapped. Unfortunately the wraparound balcony passed not only two sides of the living-
room but all three bedrooms. The kitchen, utility
room and two bathrooms on the other side of the
central corridor were windowless, but I felt that
if madness struck they might not seem far enough
from the abyss.

By the time I had left the front door ajar,
Tucker had moved down the corridor and was
exclaiming at the mess in the living-room. Responding to his reaction also delayed me in my
quest for the files, and as my attention was
drawn back to the disorder I became aware that
the flat had a heavy, oppressive atmosphere; I told
myself I was letting my imagination get the
better of me, but I soon felt queasier than ever.

"This is truly weird," said Tucker appalled as
I entered the living-room. "The whole flat feels
as sick as a dog."

It occurred to me that this cliché summed up
the atmosphere very well. There was even a
smell reminiscent of vomit, but I solved that
mystery when I moved into the kitchen and
rediscovered the pool of milk which I had never
wiped from the floor.

Backing away with a shudder I said: "Let's grab the files and go," but Tucker had started staring at the view.

"It's a great sight," I heard him murmur, "but aren't you a little cut off from the real world down there on the ground?"

A second later I was not only looking past him at the balcony but picturing the long drop on the other side of the rail.

"Excuse me," I said and bolted to the kitchen sink, but no retching ensued. I just stood there, trembling like a leaf, until I became aware that Tucker had followed me to the kitchen threshold. "Sorry," I mumbled. "Temporarily incapacitated. Balcony."

"That sour milk's enough to make anyone puke—you've picked the wrong room to recover in... Why the balcony phobia?"

"Mrs. Mayfield said I'd throw myself off it."

Tucker immediately assumed an expression of amazement and demanded: "Why would you want to do that when there are three lifts outside your front door?" And as I achieved a shaky smile he added encouragingly: "But forget all that—just watch me. I've got something to show you that'll wipe out all thought of balconies in double-quick time... Are you watching?"

"Avidly." By this time he had withdrawn a couple of paces into the dining-area and I had been lured forward to the kitchen threshold.

"*Voilà!*" said Tucker, apparently bent on dramatising himself. Shrugging off his leather jacket he slung it over the nearest chair and clenched his fists to harden his muscles. My mouth opened as I reacted to the short sleeves of his T-shirt.

"Your forearms!"

He held them out for my inspection. "Aren't they magnificent?"

"Wondrous," I said poker-faced, all nausea forgotten.

"You're stunned?"

"Overwhelmed."

Tucker faked narcissistic delight and flexed his muscles again like a bodybuilder. His forearms were in fact exactly the shape and size one would expect to see on a thirty-five-year-old male in good health, but they were sparsely covered with a rust-coloured fleece, and beneath this eye-catching attribute I saw what appeared at first glance to be sunburned flesh. But I was mistaken. It was freckled skin, the kind of skin a certain segment of the population acquires in lieu of suntan. The freckles would fade in winter and flower in summer. Their significance was undeniable.

"So now I know how to classify the colour of your hair!"

"You see?" said Tucker triumphantly. "I always told you I wasn't a redhead!"

We started to laugh. Eventually I managed to say: "I know how you feel. I've always believed I wasn't a brunette. The only difference between us is that I have to resort to a bottle to sustain my belief and you don't."

"As a novelist I pride myself on my imagination! So of course I'll always see you as a blonde, even if you give up the bottle."

I laughed again, pushing back my hair in an unexpected moment of self-consciousness. I did not look at him.

"Feeling better?"

"Much." It was then that I finally remembered what we were supposed to be doing. "But where the hell are those files?"

We stared hard at the wrecked room but nothing resembling a file caught our attention.

"Let's backtrack to the hall," said Tucker, "and try to work out what your husband must have done on his arrival home last night."

Outside the bedroom at the other end of the corridor I reflected: "Kim knew I was out for the evening but as he was back so late he'd assume I'd arrived home before him and he'd start looking for me straight away."

"Surely he'd be immediately diverted by all the mess?"

"No, he'd already know the flat would be trashed. He'd commissioned Mrs. Mayfield to trash it."

Tucker said with mild astonishment: "Does Mother Mayfield have an occupation whenever she's not flitting around like a witch on a broomstick?"

"She's a psychic healer."

"No wonder the medics blanch when they hear the words 'alternative medicine'!"

"Tucker, I assure you this woman's no laughing matter! If you'd heard Nicholas reading off the information on his computer—"

"Say no more, I get the picture. Let's have another shot at visualising what Kim did. He comes into the hall, he calls your name, there's no reply—"

"—and he goes into the living-room to check the answering machine," I said, welcoming this known fact with relief.

"Is he still carrying the files?"

"Yes, he's keen to read them."

"Okay, he takes the files to the living-room—" Tucker led the way back down the corridor as we retraced Kim's footsteps "—and he plays back the message on the answerphone—"

"—and he learns where I am. He's still keen to read the files but he's even keener to rush off and rescue me, so—"

"—he shoves the files into the first temporary hiding-place he can think of. After all, if you're going to be returning to the flat together he won't want them lying around to catch your interest... What's in this room here?"

"My junk. But his junk's next door. Maybe—"

"No, too obvious."

"Not necessarily. At this stage he doesn't know that I know the files exist. So—"

"—let's check."

We stared around at Kim's junk for several seconds but no bilious-yellow file demanded to be noticed.

"I think we're on the wrong track," said Tucker at last. "This is a man in a hurry. He's in the living-room by the telephone and he wants to rush out of the flat—wouldn't he just ram the files into the nearest available hidey-hole?"

"Yes, but—"

"How tall is he?"

"Just over six feet. Why?"

"If I were Kim Betz, trying to hide files from my wife who's several inches shorter than I am, I'd stretch up and shove the files on a high shelf so that they'd be out of her sight unless she was standing on a chair. Where are the high shelves you can't reach?"

"In the kitchen."

Once more we started to move down the cor-

366

ridor but a second later we stopped dead. Beyond the front door, which I had deliberately left open earlier, one of the lifts was halting in the lobby, and as the passengers emerged I heard a familiar voice exclaim: "Well, look at that! It seems I won't be needing a locksmith after all—although of course I'll pay you for your time."

In horror I whispered: "It's Kim."

"Stall him," muttered Tucker, and vanished towards the kitchen.

My feet carried me down the corridor in the opposite direction. Taut with dread I re-entered the hall just as Kim crossed the threshold with a man who I assumed to be the locksmith.

Behind them was Mrs. Mayfield.

VII

I nearly passed out. My heart was racing and my legs felt weak. It seemed amazing that I should remain conscious.

"Carter!" Kim did not seem particularly surprised to see me. He did not seem particularly upset either. The exclamation was wary but not hostile. "Well, I did wonder if you might be here early," he said with the kind of charm one uses to gloss over an awkward social situation, "but I thought last night you were too exhausted to be here quite as early as this! May I introduce Tom Callan, who's Mrs. Mayfield's local locksmith?"

"You can go now, Tommy," said Mrs. Mayfield placidly as she glanced into the bedroom and observed the disorder. "I'll talk to you later... Dear oh dearie me! *What* a nasty feel this flat's got! Quite uninhabitable I'd say, and fit only for laying out

367

corpses—and talking of corpses, Kate dear, you're looking peakier than ever, poor little thing, it really is sad to see someone deteriorate so fast, but they can do wonders for people now in mental hospitals, so I hear, for those who survive long enough to get there... Ah, here's the lift, back again! Bye-bye, Tommy! No, don't close the front door, Jake, just get what you came for and we'll be off. I don't believe in hanging around a place like this unless I'm really hard up for entertainment."

Amidst my horror I was trying to dream up a delaying tactic, but I found all I could do was exclaim feebly to Kim: "How dare you bring that woman here!"

Kim sidestepped my anger by making an irrelevant reply. "She knew a locksmith who wouldn't keep me waiting for hours."

"Well, if you were really so keen to get into the flat, why didn't you just use her copy of your key? I figured you wouldn't be here early because you wouldn't want to give away the fact that she had the means to trash the flat last night, but if you're now too desperate to care—"

"Don't be silly, dear," said Mrs. Mayfield, still very placid, "or I'll think you've teetered over the brink into persecution mania. Of course I didn't wreck your flat and of course I don't have a copy of his key! Go on, Jake, don't let her delay you, get what you want and then we'll—oh, my goodness me, what a lovely young man! Hullo, dear, who are you? No, wait a moment, I know who you are! You're the temporary personal assistant who's all too personal and not quite so temporary!"

Kim junked the charm and spun to face me. "What the hell's he doing here?"

"Helping me uncover your lies!" I shot back but my voice shook.

"Christ, if you two have spent the night here together, I'll—"

"Calm down, Jake," said Mrs. Mayfield, taking charge of the situation. "Be sensible, there's a pet. The way this place is now no one would want to have sex in it unless they were necrophiliacs—or perhaps coprophiliacs... What's that nasty smell?"

I said to Kim: "Get that woman out of here." I was trying to work out if Tucker had had time to find the files and hide them somewhere else. I had hardly been expecting him to reappear so quickly.

"Pull yourself together!" Kim was still livid with me. "At least Mrs. Mayfield was generous enough to offer me hospitality for the night after you'd kept me out of here!"

I forgot Tucker. I was too busy welcoming the strength generated by a rush of rage. "My God, are you trying to tell me you spent the night under the same roof as this woman? And now you're accusing *me* of unacceptable behaviour?"

"Shut up! You damn well gutted me by the way you carried on at that Rectory! Thank God Elizabeth was finally home by the time I got to Fulham—I had to talk to her, I was so bloody upset, but if you think for one moment that she and I—"

"Sour milk," said Mrs. Mayfield who by this time was well on her way down the corridor to the living-room. "A real smell of decay if ever there was one, almost as bad as dead flowers. Who was it that wrote that beautiful line: 'Lilies that fester smell far worse than weeds'?"

Turning my back on Kim I raced after her into the living-room. "Get out of my flat, you bitch! I won't have you invading it like this!"

"Oh, don't be so silly, pet, you're behaving like a two-year-old. Yes, there it is—sour milk on the kitchen floor! Well, there's only one thing to do, isn't there?" She emerged from the kitchen and started heading for the balcony door. "This flat needs airing."

I opened my mouth to yell: "NO!" but nothing happened. I could only back away until I was pressed against the wall. By this time Kim and Tucker were facing each other across one of the upturned armchairs and Mrs. Mayfield was within six feet of the windows.

But Tucker shot in front of her to guard the balcony door. "Hey, wait a minute!" he said to us all in the friendliest of voices. "I think Mrs. Mayfield's got this right by staying calm, so why don't we all follow her example, lighten up a bit, maybe even have some coffee? Would you like some coffee, Kim?"

"I'm Mr. Betz to you, sonny!"

Tucker's mouth hardened but he persisted in pushing the line which would propel me into a windowless room. "Carter, you wouldn't mind fixing some coffee, would you? But keep the kitchen door shut so we're not all overpowered by that sour milk!" As he spoke I knew he had realised I could escape from the kitchen into the utility room and from the utility room into the flat's corridor, a move which would give me a clear run to the front door, but before I could even begin to overcome my panic, Mrs. Mayfield was saying reprovingly to him: "Well, that's not a very gentlemanly suggestion, dear! Telling a lady to shut herself up in a smelly room? Your mother couldn't have brought you up properly! No, Kate needs some fresh air—look at her, she's almost green. Come along, Kate my pet—you just step out onto the balcony with me and I guarantee you'll be transformed in no time!"

"I'm sorry, Mrs. Mayfield," said Tucker courteously as I started to shudder, "but I've got no head for heights and right now I can't take the idea of any outside door in this flat being opened."

Mrs. Mayfield paused to gaze at him. "What did you say your name was, dear?"

"I didn't, but it's Eric Tucker."

"Eric! What a lovely name! You should have been a blond, dear, like all those gorgeous Vikings, but never mind, I've always had a weakness for redheads, and I'm not the only one who's partial to them, am I? What was the name of that woman who kept you for a while, the brunette who was all face-lifts and couldn't live without a toy-boy in her life?"

Tucker went ash-white.

Mrs. Mayfield turned sharply to Kim. "Get what you came for. No more delays. I feel time running out."

Kim went into the kitchen. I heard a cupboard door open and then slam shut. "Bloody hell!" He hurtled back into the dining-area, where I was pressed as if glued to the wall, and shouted at me: "Where did you put them?"

Instantly Tucker abandoned the balcony door. "Are you really so inadequate," he said furiously, planting himself right in front of Kim, "that you can't treat your wife with the respect she deserves?"

Kim was so stunned, so overpowered by amazement that a junior male should address him in such a fashion, that for once he was unable to slam back a violent reply. He could only say in stupefaction to Mrs. Mayfield: "They've found those papers. They've put them somewhere else."

"Yes, dear," said Mrs. Mayfield, who now had an unimpeded path to the window. "I was wondering why Young Lochinvar had taken his time in coming out to meet us—not exactly a shrinking violet, are you, Eric pet?" As she spoke she was crossing the floor.

"But Elizabeth—"

"Don't worry, dear, I'm sure he'll soon tell us where they are." Pulling the lever which set the sliding mechanism in action, she heaved open the balcony door. "Come along, Kate," she said as a chill wind immediately blew through the room. "Don't take any notice of those two boys striking macho poses. Out you come, dear, to take your breath of air."

"Freeze, Carter!" Tucker shouted, and pushing Mrs. Mayfield aside he rammed the door shut again.

"Jake," said Mrs. Mayfield to Kim, and her voice was quite changed. "Get a knife."

I suddenly realised I had left the wall and—in defiance of my will—moved closer to the windows; I was now standing by the end of the dining-table, and behind me Kim was returning to the kitchen. I heard the sound of the cutlery drawer opening but I was unable to react because I was in such a state of terror that part of my brain had closed down. I was like those victims of ineffective anaesthesia who remain awake during their operations but are powerless to communicate with the staff in the operating theatre.

"Put the knife to her throat and bring her over here to the window."

"Elizabeth—"

"Do as I say," she insisted, and added a sentence in German. It was something about "the boy." Make the boy think—make the boy believe... My memory of German cut out.

"Mr. Betz," said Tucker, who had left the door again in an automatic attempt to reason with Kim, "please put down that knife, sir. Believe me— it's not a good idea." I realised then that he understood no German and did not grasp how he was being manipulated. I knew Kim would never harm me. But Tucker didn't know and I was unable to tell him. My vocal cords were no longer operating.

"Do as I say, Jake," said Mrs. Mayfield, slipping back into position by the door and playing the dominatrix for all she was worth to make Tucker think she had the power to reduce Kim to a robot. "Always do as I say. If you do as I say, you'll be all right, you know that, don't you? So just do as I say and bring her over here."

My right hand was grasped and twisted up behind my back. It was hardly a delicate manoeuvre but he could have been much rougher. "Tucker!" I managed to whisper, desperate to reveal the charade, but then I felt the knife graze my cheek and the power of speech deserted me again. It took me several seconds to realise that Kim was holding the blunt edge of the knife against my skin, but by the time this truth dawned I was so frightened by the balcony door that I could only gasp for air.

"Now, Eric my love," said Mrs. Mayfield, "you're going to produce those papers." She pulled the lever again and the balcony door groaned as it shifted down the groove. Once more the wind blew across the room and this time it felt icy. As Kim propelled me closer I gave my first scream.

Tucker darted forward but stopped; he was now believing he dared not try to rescue me in case Kim took leave of the last of his senses.

"Okay, cool it," he said in a rush. "The files are still in the kitchen."

"Get them. Or the girl goes out on the balcony."

Tucker hesitated but when I screamed again he returned to the kitchen at once. Kim swivelled to watch him, and this meant I swivelled too. Almost sobbing with relief that I was no longer facing the void beyond the balcony rail I saw Tucker open the door of the oven and pull out both the yellow file and the large brown envelope.

"That's more like it," said Mrs. Mayfield satisfied. "Put them down on the table. Jake, you can let Kate go now. Sorry about the little act with the knife, dear," she said to me as she slipped back effortlessly into her cosy suburban persona, "but your young man's ever so lively, isn't he, and I didn't want him starting a fight. There! No harm intended and no harm done! Now, pet, why don't you go and shut that door just to show us what a brave girl you really are? Or are you still afraid that once you get to the threshold of the balcony you'll see that rail and—" She stopped.

I stared at her. Once Kim had released me I had been unable to stop trembling and now she too, I saw, was visibly unnerved. She was losing colour. Her rouge stood out starkly on her plump cheeks and her moist lips seemed bloodless.

I suddenly realised that Tucker also was transfixed and that Kim had halted, the knife still in his hand.

They were all looking past me, and when at last I too turned to face the living-room doorway I saw Nicholas Darrow standing stock still on the threshold.

VIII

He was formally attired in a black suit with a black stock and an old-fashioned clerical collar; I supposed he was dressed up for the religious ritual he had planned to conduct at nine. On his chest he was wearing a substantial gold crucifix suspended from a thick gold chain. The sheer size of the crucifix was unnerving. I found my gaze was irresistibly drawn to it, but a second later I realised that its impact was jacked up by the fact that it was Nicholas who was doing the wearing. The full power of his personality had been unleashed. He was no longer just a pale, bony item with mouse-brown hair and dishwater-grey eyes who favoured casual clothes. He was as riveting as a great actor who makes a long-delayed entrance and captivates the audience instantly just by raising an eyebrow. The very air around him seemed charged with a hyped-up magnetic tension. Long-limbed, lissom and languid, he radiated a mesmerising self-confidence and authority.

He made no effort to speak but merely stood there, framed in the doorway, as he surveyed the scene and made his deductions. He was quite calm. Then as if satisfied that his entrance had had the maximum impact on everyone present, he strolled gracefully into the room. Not for the first time I was aware of the fluent, almost liquid quality of his movements, and I was aware too that on this occasion there was a heavy sexual edge to each one of them. It was still not a sexuality which appealed to me; I found it much too hypnotic and dangerous, but I could see all too clearly now why Alice was enslaved. It then occurred to me how amazing it was that such a man had chosen to operate within the staid Church of England, an organisation which even today would demand strict standards in his private life, and the next moment I understood why he had been so keen at the start of our talk at the Rectory to emphasise the checks and balances which kept his ministry on the rails. He was an honest man who had faced up to his capacity to leave a trail of devastation in his wake, and he knew a keg of dynamite could only be safely stored in well-guarded premises.

Casually he glided around the upturned furniture. Sinuously he eased shut the balcony door and flicked back the lever to fasten it. Then coolly he said to the woman he had never met: "The party's over, Mrs. Mayfield. It's time to go."

I wanted to punch the air and cheer myself hoarse.

But unfortunately my euphoria was premature.

IX

"Well, well, well!" said Mrs. Mayfield, finally finding her tongue. "No prizes for guessing who *you* are! It's Nicky, isn't it? Or at least that's what one lady calls you, the lady who's giving you so much trouble at the moment!"

"Spare me the psychic parlour-tricks," said Nicholas bored. "I've seen them all before." Picking his way through the broken ornaments which littered the floor he began to move away from the window.

"Don't you come over all high and mighty with *me*, my love! I know things about you which you wouldn't want these nice people to hear!"

Nicholas drifted closer to Tucker and said to him: "For your information, Eric, let me point out that Mrs. Mayfield's behaviour is typical of a corrupt psychic. She affects to recognise me by psychic power, but in fact she would have known by this time that I'm involved in the case; Kim would have told her. She would also be familiar with my name; I have a reputation in the world she inhabits, and I'm sure she's heard I'm getting divorced. Because of this she feels it's a safe bet to assume either my wife or some other woman is causing me difficulty, and as my name's Nicholas it's an even safer bet to assume the lady in question calls me Nick or Nicky." Wandering past Tucker he circled the table to my side. I was gripping one of the dining-chairs to stop my hands shaking.

"You're all right now," he said, looking straight at me. His grey eyes were brilliantly clear, so clear that they seemed almost blue. "You're all right."

I nodded. When he said I was all right I *knew* I was all right. There was no doubt in my mind, and when he briefly covered my hands with his I found I could let go of the chair.

"Eric," he said, "come and stand by Carter for a moment to help her feel quite safe."

"You shouldn't have let Nicky touch you, Kate," said Mrs. Mayfield sharply. "That man's a rapist."

Nicholas naturally paid no attention to this fantastic accusation. Moving on around the table to

377

Kim he said: "I think it's time you put down that knife." But Kim's knuckles only whitened as he increased his grip. He was sweating.

Nicholas looked back at Mrs. Mayfield. "Tell him to put it down."

Mrs. Mayfield just smirked. "He's not yours, dear," she said. "He's mine." And as Kim transferred the knife to his right hand in order to wipe the sweat from his forehead with his left, she added abruptly to him: "We're leaving. I don't care for the company your wife keeps."

Immediately Nicholas said to Kim: "You don't have to go. There's a choice."

"Don't listen to him, pet," said Mrs. Mayfield, as Kim transferred the knife back to his left hand. "All clergymen are such liars. The rubbish they talk about a convicted Jewish criminal! It shouldn't be allowed."

Nicholas paused, looking her up and down. Then he said casually: "Let's hear you say his name."

Mrs. Mayfield turned away. "Come along, Jake dear. Off we go."

At once Nicholas said strongly: "You do have a choice, Kim. Never doubt that there's a choice. And never doubt that if you choose to stay I'll give you every possible support."

Mrs. Mayfield swung back to face him. "Leave him alone, you bastard! He's mine, *mine*, MINE!"

"He's not yours, Mrs. Mayfield. You're lying over and over again and you're lying because you're frightened. In fact you're so frightened that you can't even say the name of—"

"I'll do a deal with you," she said. "You keep the girl—I'll leave her alone in future—but I keep the man."

"I don't do deals, Mrs. Mayfield. I follow a man

who never did deals, and it's in his name that I'm ordering you now to leave this flat, leave it at once and leave it on your own."

"Fuck you!" shouted Mrs. Mayfield, but she was moving towards the door. "Fuck you and curse you!" Then suddenly she was rushing back, spitting at him and screaming: "Curse you, curse your wife, curse that fat bitch you keep—"

"Lord Jesus Christ," said Nicholas rapidly, somehow keeping his voice level, "protect me, protect Rosalind, protect Alice—"

"Who's fucking frightened now!" jeered Mrs. Mayfield, after automatically stepping backwards as if in revulsion. Stepping forward again she added violently: "And he won't protect you, you know! You're going to sicken! You're going to rot! You're going to—"

"IN THE NAME OF JESUS CHRIST," declaimed Nicholas, blasting the attack apart by jacking up his power to a new level, "LEAVE HERE AND NEVER RETURN!" But although Mrs. Mayfield recoiled and although she was temporarily speechless, she still managed to spit at him again and suddenly Nicholas seemed to run out of energy. "Lewis!" he shouted. "Help me escort Mrs. Mayfield to the front door!"

Mrs. Mayfield found her tongue. "Calling in the cavalry, dear?" she taunted, but she was backing away from him. I was just thinking numbly that she had at last conceded defeat when she turned and came face to face with Lewis in the doorway.

"Oh, for God's sake, woman!" he exclaimed in disgust. "Stop making such a pathetic exhibition of yourself!" And to Nicholas he added: "What a very common, vulgar female—and how boring women are when they resort to four-letter words!"

Mrs. Mayfield turned scarlet with rage. Then all hell broke loose as she flung down her handbag and attacked Lewis head on.

X

I find it hard to describe what happened next but I must try. I must try because I was ultimately responsible for it. It was my idea to go to the flat early without seeking advice from the experts. It was my idea to take Tucker with me. It was my note to Alice which brought Nicholas and Lewis hurrying to protect me from the worst-case scenario, and my talk of clergymen to the car-park attendant which enabled them not just to leave their car in the garage but to gain admittance to the building. Afterwards I kept saying to myself: "If I hadn't done this..." and: "If I hadn't done that..." Once one starts saying "if" one can speculate interminably. I did indeed speculate interminably after it was all over, and the speculation proved to be a most effective form of mental torture.

All I can do now is state the facts. Mrs. Mayfield flew at Lewis. He was taken by surprise, I saw that, and I saw too—we all saw—that although he recovered quickly she was suddenly endowed with abnormal strength. Nicholas said later that some people can summon up a huge adrenaline rush to perform feats they could never achieve in ordinary circumstances, and I was immensely relieved he was able to come up with that scientific explanation; I was immensely relieved I could say rationally that having witnessed the clash of two exceptionally powerful personalities, the clash decked out and hyped up by their conflicting world-views, I had then witnessed someone gripped by a huge surge of adrenaline. Yet still I feel there was something about these abnormal events which lay far beyond the boundaries of any rationalist's vocabulary.

Lewis had a heavy, thickset frame but she shoved him against the wall so hard that he slid sideways, lost his balance and fell across an upturned chair. Nicholas was there in a flash but Mrs. Mayfield, undeterred, attacked him as well. Nicholas was at least six feet tall, with a strong, lean build, but she felled him. He scrambled up at once but she moved in again and he was forced to wrestle with her to keep on his feet. Meanwhile Lewis was trying to get up but he was apparently disabled by pain. It was then that Tucker left my side and rushed into action.

Mrs. Mayfield saw him coming. "Jake!" she shouted, and added a brief sentence in German which I was long past being able to interpret.

Kim moved abruptly forward. I moved too then, wanting to grab his arm and pull him back, but I was too late; everything happened so quickly and there was no time. Time had run out for all of us in that scene, and besides, it's only in dramatic representations that violence is lengthy and elaborately choreographed. In real life violence is usually just a short, sharp, shattering mess.

Mrs. Mayfield finally flung aside Nicholas with a huge display of force.

He cannoned directly into Tucker.

And Tucker, no longer wearing the jacket

which might have protected him, reeled straight into the path of the knife which Kim had so stubbornly refused to discard.

PART FOUR

EMBRACING THE CHAOS

The word integrity itself has two meanings. The first is "honesty"... We have to be honest in facing our limitations, in facing the sheer complexity of the world, honest in facing criticism even of things which are deeply precious to us. But integrity also means wholeness, oneness, the desire for single vision, the refusal to split our minds into separate compartments where incompatible ideas are not allowed to come into contact.

✳   ✳   ✳

An undivided mind looks in the end for an undivided truth, a oneness at the heart of things. And this isn't just fantasy. The whole intellectual quest despite its fragmentation, despite its limitations and uncertainties, seems to presuppose that in the end we are all encountering a single reality, and a single truth.

JOHN HABGOOD
Confessions of a Conservative Liberal

FOURTEEN

The urgency of the crisis takes over the present moment and demands attention and action.

DAVID F. FORD
The Shape of Living

I

All I can remember now are the fragments, as if Mrs. Mayfield's unnatural force had exploded out of the dark to shatter my memory to pieces. It was like a bomb atrocity: destruction by fragmentation, thousands of pieces hurtling away from the centre at thousands of feet per second. Then after the blast came the long silence followed by the despair that the pieces could ever again be reassembled into a pattern which had meaning and value.

II

The knife went in below the shoulder.

Lewis made all the phone calls, including one to the doctor who worked with Nicholas at the Healing Centre. Too shocked to speak I knelt down by Tucker, but Nicholas was already there; he was gripping Tucker's hand and saying: "Hold on. I've got you. Just hold on." Tucker was still conscious. I heard him say: "It's like a war, isn't it? I'm a front-line casualty," and as I began to cry, Nicholas slipped off his cross so that Tucker could clasp it.

384

I heard Tucker whisper: "Say a prayer, Nick. I can't think of the words." Then Nicholas prayed, although I cannot now remember what he said; all I can remember is thinking that a man was dying and it was all my fault.

But Tucker held on.

III

He was in the intensive care ward at the hospital for twenty-four hours, a fact which meant no one but his family could visit him. I was far beyond tears by this time. Other things were going on, most of them excruciatingly painful, but the only person I could consistently focus on was Tucker. After a while it occurred to me that this wordless concentration—this other-centred, self-forgetting—was a form of prayer. I had tried praying in words. I would have done anything to try to save him, and even an irrational endeavour such as prayer seemed more endurable than nothing, but all I had been able to produce was a boardroom speech which reduced the entire activity to bathos.

Yet that night, very late, when sleep was something other people did in another universe, I sat by the window of my Rectory bedroom and looked for a long time over the rooftops as I listened to the silence of the City. And as I waited, my whole being focused on willing Tucker to live, I experienced a feeling of minds all flowing into one another and I knew that somewhere beyond all the fragmentation was an immense, indestructible unity. That was when I realised that my focus on Tucker was a form of prayer. It was as if, in the mansion of my consciousness,

385

I had stumbled into a huge hall which connected every room in the house, and in the centre of that hall was a white-hot core of energy which seized my agonised thought patterns and transformed them, with a single burst of light, into an irresistible force.

I instinctively squeezed my eyes shut to protect them, and as the image of the mansion faded I saw my consciousness as just a droplet in the river of multiconsciousness, and I knew the river was flowing steadily towards an unending sea. I wondered how I could make myself heard above the roar of the water, but the next moment I knew there was someone on the riverbank. He came down into the river and he walked upstream towards me, and as my consciousness slipped gears again, losing the image of the river, I knew I was back once more on the corner of Paternoster Row as my unseen companion, unarmed but unassailable, rolled back the darkness of the Principalities and Powers.

I said to him: "If Eric Tucker dies, help me live with the guilt without going mad." But then it occurred to me that this request was very self-centred, focusing on my own uncomfortable feelings and hardly dwelling on Tucker at all, so I added: "No, forget about me, just concentrate on him." And I added: "Please," as an afterthought, although what I was doing talking to this psychological construct as if it were a person was quite beyond my power to rationalise.

Paternoster Row faded. For a second I saw the streets of the City forming a pattern like a vast spider's web, and as I stared I saw that one of the threads of the web was damaged, spoiling the beauty of the design. And the next moment I was exclaiming to my companion: "Oh, let me help you fix it! Whether Tucker lives or dies, let me help you make it all come right!" And then the molten core at the heart of my multiroomed mansion burst with light again before subsiding into a steady, hissing white noise which I recognised but could not identify.

I woke up. The hiss was rain, hurling itself against the pane and streaking the rooftops of Egg Street, but beyond the darkness the sky was pale as dawn broke at last over the City.

At nine o'clock that morning Gilbert Tucker phoned to say that his brother was out of intensive care and expected to recover.

IV

After that I cried for a whole day. I was still at the Rectory. Nobody seemed to mind. So was Alice. Nobody seemed to mind that either. I was not constantly attended but I knew I was always within reach of people who cared what happened to me. I had no desire for twenty-four-hour attendants anyway. I was too preoccupied with my own personal version of Niagara Falls.

"I can't understand it," I said to Val Fredericks, the doctor who worked with Nicholas. "Anyone would think Tucker had died! Why am I crying like this?"

"There's often a lot of grief in our lives which we suppress because it's too painful to deal with. Perhaps Eric's brush with death threw open the hatches which you'd battened down for so long."

"I didn't think I'd suppressed anything," I said, opening another box of Kleenex.

"Maybe that was the problem," said Val.

387

V

The next day the tears finally stopped. I went out, hiding my swollen eyes behind a pair of dark glasses borrowed from Alice, and bought some make-up. It was a Saturday, so I also kept my appointment at the hairdresser's. Afterwards I bought a new suit. Two of the Healing Centre's "Befrienders" had performed the saintly task of clearing up my flat and packing a suitcase of clothes for me, but they had packed the wrong outfits and I was still unable to face returning to Harvey Tower to retrieve the right ones.

I felt better once I was smartly dressed with my hair styled, my face made up and my nails manicured. At a florist's I bought a dozen muscular red tulips which conjured up an image of masculine vitality. Then I took a cab to the hospital to see Tucker.

He had a room to himself but unfortunately he was not alone when I arrived. A female in the early stages of old age was present, the lioness guarding her mauled cub. She had golden hair, the result not of chemicals but of red hair turning white, and a plump figure togged up in the fashions of thirty years ago. As I entered the room she gave me a sharp, shrewd, snobbish, judgemental look which indicated that she recognised me as a typical specimen of modern womanhood and found me very seriously wanting.

"Mrs. Tucker? Good afternoon," I said, falling back upon the iron courtesy which I used to trim the claws of scratchy clients. "I'm Carter Graham."

"How very kind of you to call, Mrs. Betz," she said in the sort of voice middle-class women use in the presence of anyone whom they deem "common," "but unfortunately Eric isn't up to seeing visitors at present."

"He's well up to seeing this one," said the invalid in the bed.

"Darling, you know the doctor said only one visitor at a time—"

"Do me a favour, Mum, and find a nice vase for those flowers Carter's brought."

Mrs. Tucker pursed her lips and patted her Mrs. Thatcher hair-do to make sure everything was standing on end beneath the lacquer. "Two minutes," she said to me, "and that's all. He's still very unwell." And leaving me no time to reply she swept from the room.

Tucker sighed. There were shadows beneath his eyes; his pallor was marked; his extreme languor hinted that he had a fever; his left forearm was hooked up to a drip. Still clutching my tough tulips I sank down in the chair by the bed and somehow managed to say: "I'm so sorry for everything. I'm so very, very sorry."

"Hey, that's my line! I wanted to apologise for making such a mess of looking after you... Are you all right?"

I nodded, scrabbling in my bag for Alice's dark glasses, but my eyes were so full of tears that I could no longer see what I was doing. Abandoning the search I hid my face from him by sniffing the flowers, but I only succeeded in shedding a tear onto the most macho tulip in the bunch. Beyond the muscular red petals, all standing stiffly to attention, the black stamen had a hard-edged, pumped-up look.

"Ms. G, stop making love to those fleshy floral numbers, stop feeling guilty and just listen for a moment. I'm glad you're here. I've got to talk to you about what Mrs. Mayfield said to me."

"Mrs. Mayfield!" Forgetting my tears I finally raised my face from the tulips. "For God's sake, what's there to say? That woman was all lies and phoney ESP!"

"Maybe most of the time, but she got me right. I did live off that woman she described. It was back in my twenties and I was such a mess then, it's hard to describe what a mess I was, but—"

"Tucker, you don't have to talk about this—"

"Oh yes, I do! Listen, I lived with women and I lived off women because I was so damned arrogant and so damned deluded that I thought I was some kind of literary genius who was too grand to work for a living—God, how pathetic it all seems now, but that's where I was, that was the kind of life I was living, and of course it all went wrong and I wound up homeless and penniless on Gil's doorstep—couldn't go to my parents, I was too ashamed, and my other brother had long since washed his hands of me—"

"But it's so easy to make mistakes in one's twenties!"

"These weren't just mistakes. My entire way of life was a cataclysmic balls-up which destroyed my self-respect and made a lot of people, including myself, very unhappy. But when I was thirty and wound up broke on Gil's doorstep, I finally started getting my act together. Gil said I had to have a reliable way of earning my keep, a way which would allow me some self-respect, and that was when I did my first round of office-skills courses— I didn't want to, I thought secretarial work was just for women and wimps, but Gil was implacable. He said: 'You're a spoiled, pigheaded, self-centred, immature bastard, but do you really have to be a sexist bastard as well?' So I borrowed the money from him to do the courses, and I stayed with him rent-free and I washed dishes in the evenings at a Covent Garden restaurant to earn some pocket-money. Then I worked in the West End as a secretary full time—I had a dirt-cheap room in Lambeth, and gradually I shaped up and grew up—and it was all because of Gil, all because of the brother I'd despised for being gay, but when the chips were down he cared enough to stand by me, and that kind of caring makes you think, it makes you believe you might possibly be more than a pile of shit, it makes you hope and strive for better things, it gives you courage.

"So I turned my life around, thanks to Gil—but no, it wasn't just thanks to Gil, because beyond Gil was...well, never mind all that. No, wait a minute, *I* mind, what am I doing not calling a spade a spade just because you're an atheist? I'm such a bloody coward sometimes, but listen, here's the way it really was: I turned my life around by the grace of God through Jesus Christ and the power of the Spirit, as Christians say—and now you can laugh just as much as you like, but—"

"I'm not laughing," I said.

"—but all I can tell you is that's the best way of describing what happened. Then I got a book published—and another—and in the end I could afford to adopt this pattern of doing office-work part time instead of full time, and I moved out of my Lambeth dump into a neat little pad in Fulham, just one room, but there was a tree outside the window, I loved that tree, and then...

"Well, last year I had a relapse. Gil says the spir-

391

itual journey's often a bumpy ride, and I hit a bump—although 'bump' is hardly the word to describe the married model with expensive tastes who—well, all I need say is that I wound up dead broke and homeless again on Gil's doorstep, but I've got over that now, I've got my finances sorted out and I pay Gil rent and when my next book's published I'll get a room of my own again and have another shot at living happily ever after.

"Well, Ms. G, that's all I have to say, but I had to say it because truth matters, doesn't it, and I'd like to think I would have been truthful about my past anyway in due course without Mrs. Mayfield forcing my hand. But you and I hadn't reached the stage where we could have swapped pasts, had we, and probably we never would have done, since you're all bound up with someone else, so this scene between us now—this scene now—it's like—it's like—God, I'm going fuzzy, my brain's closing down, but I must finish what I want to say—"

"This scene now—"

"This scene now's like a moment out of time, but when you remember me in future I don't want you to think: 'What a gigolo, what a shit!' I want you to think: 'He was an honest man who told the truth,' and then perhaps there's a chance you'll remember me without wanting to wipe the memory from your mind."

All I could do was weep.

Mrs. Tucker returned to the room and evicted me.

Back at the Rectory I destroyed yet another box of Kleenex.

And Kim? Where was he while all these tear-drenched scenes were going on? Whereabouts in the wasteland created by the explosion was the split-off fragment which contained him?

Directly after the stabbing I could focus only on Tucker, but once Nicholas had left with him in the ambulance Lewis and I hurriedly searched the flat. The police were present by that time, but all the questions had had to wait until Tucker was on his way to hospital.

We found Kim in the small bedroom where his junk was stored. When we entered the room we saw he was sitting on the floor with his back to a packing-case, his arms clasped tightly around his knees.

All he said was: "If I move I'll disintegrate."

As Nicholas's colleague, Val Fredericks, joined us Lewis said to Kim: "Our doctor's got the medicine which'll keep you in one piece," and Val, taking in the situation at a glance, said strongly to the police who were trying to crowd into the room: "Stand back, please—this man is clearly ill."

So the police withdrew, and as Lewis knelt down by Kim and Val opened her black bag for the hypodermic, I watched from the threshold, my fingers clinging to the frame of the door. I found myself staring at Val, whom I had not met before, and trying to visualise her working in partnership with Nicholas. She was a woman in her thirties, plump, with carelessly dyed short blonde hair, large gold earrings and no make-up except for scarlet lipstick with a high-gloss finish. Beneath her red anorak she was wearing an off-beat combination of a formal white blouse with denim dungarees. It may seem bizarre that I paid so much attention to Val at that harrowing moment, but I found it easier to look at her than to look at Kim's contorted form and distorted expression.

"If you could just slip out of your jacket—"

"I can't move."

"Lewis will hold you. He'll stop you splitting."

"He can't."

"Yes, I can," said Lewis, and gripped him hard.

This sort of dialogue continued for over a minute. Both Lewis and Val were so patient and kind while all I could do was shiver with revulsion and rage.

"Carter," said Lewis at last, as if he could feel the whole range of my violent emotions, "would you mind waiting in the passage, please?"

As I withdrew I heard Kim whisper: "I didn't mean to kill that man."

"He's not dead."

"Then why am I being given a lethal injection?"

I stumbled into the shower-room, far from all the windows, and waited, panting and shuddering, for the ordeal to end.

A second ambulance eventually took Kim to a mental hospital in south-east London. Val went with him in the ambulance and so did two of the police, but since by that time he was unconscious they never had the opportunity to question him.

Lewis and I stayed on at the flat to be interrogated at mind-numbing length by their colleagues.

And Mrs. Mayfield? What happened to her?

She vanished. Well, she would, wouldn't she? When Tucker fell she must have paused only to pick up the files from the table before slipping down the corridor, gliding into the lift and flitting away across the podium to lose herself among the rush-hour crowds streaming out of the Barbican tube station.

The police wanted to question her but she was never found. The house in Fulham turned out to be rented to an organisation with a box office number in the Cayman Isles, and she left no forwarding address. No charge card issued in the name of Elizabeth Mayfield was ever used again, and no further cheques were written on the one modest bank account which was uncovered. So swift and so complete was her disappearance that the police assumed she must have had a parallel life somewhere else in London, a trick which would have enabled her to withdraw at any time into her other identity, and despite extensive enquiries she was never traced. Her groups were questioned but had no information to offer, and no investigation proved that they had been engaged in illegal activities.

Nicholas made various entries on his computer and left the file open. "She'll be back," he said. "She'll resurface in that other identity, but I'll pick up her trail from the victims she's bound to leave behind, and one day our paths will recross."

I phoned a friend who specialised in criminal law to check that Mrs. Mayfield had committed no offence in the flat, but even a charge of inciting Kim to threaten me with a knife fell flat when I had to admit the threat had been a fake with no intent to cause harm. My friend thought any attempt to charge Kim with Tucker's wounding would fail too, since the witnesses could only testify that it had been an accident. There had been no criminal intent. It was not an offence for a man to remove a knife from his kitchen, use it in a bout of play-acting and later be too mesmerised to put the knife down when the scene so suddenly exploded into violence. Besides, Kim's mental breakdown meant that any action against him would be most unlikely to succeed.

"The truth is," I said to Alice, after explaining the legal position, "it was Mrs. Mayfield who was responsible for the mayhem. It was she who refused to order Kim to put down the knife after he started behaving like a zonked-out zombie, and she who shoved Nicholas at Tucker and sent Tucker reeling into Kim."

"But if no charges can be brought against her," said Alice puzzled, "why should she embark on this total disappearance?"

I thought this was a good question and posed it to Nicholas. He thought it was a good question too.

"It makes one wonder if she was involved with a crime after all," he said, "despite her usual habit of operating just within the law. But what was the crime, who was the victim and where did it take place?"

"Murder? Sophie? Oakshott?"

"Those are the obvious answers, but are they the right ones? Let's see what Sophie's inquest reveals."

I need hardly add that thanks to Mrs. Mayfield,

the files which had driven me to endanger
Tucker's life were never seen again.

VIII

The next fragment which whirled away into the
dark contained my job at Curtis, Towers.

It was painfully ironic in retrospect to remember
the enormous energy Kim and I had put into dis-
tancing ourselves from Sophie's death by resorting
to unprofessional behaviour. All our stupid
cover-ups were exposed in the end because I
could not cope with any more lying evasions. I
talked to the Oakshott police. I told them
everything. Bizarrely—and this was the crowning
irony—they decided I was just a sweet little
piece of blonde fluff who could not be blamed for
suffering a hysterical reaction after uncovering
a dead body in a sinister house surrounded by
spooky woods; the chief inspector was very
fatherly towards me and at one stage even patted
my shining blonde head as I hit the Kleenex. With
Kim he would have undoubtedly been as tough
as nails, but Kim was still in hospital, still unfit
to be questioned.

Naturally I had wondered if Kim could be
faking the breakdown in order to avoid the
inevitable interrogation, but Val said firmly that
it would have been impossible for him to fool the
experts at the Maudsley Hospital.

Sophie's inquest turned out to be a non-starter
as the coroner adjourned it until Kim proved fit
to testify, but my newly acquired friends among
the Oakshott police disclosed indiscreetly to me
that there was no evidence of foul play. The
pathologist thought the injuries were entirely

consistent with the theory that Sophie had accidentally fallen as the result of turning her ankle and snapping the heel of her shoe; apparently there were impressions in the carpet near the top of the stairs which encouraged the verdict of accident.

However, even though the inquest was adjourned, the death had created a great buzz of speculation in the Oakshott community, and the local newshounds were soon sniffing around so noisily that the sound of their snuffles reached London. It would be hard to exaggerate the joy of the media when some bright young spark noticed that the interesting death at Oakshott involved the same people as the ones involved in an even more interesting stabbing at the Barbican less than twenty-four hours later. A media mass orgasm was soon afterwards achieved when it was realised that the stabbing had taken place in the presence of not just one but two clergymen, both of whom were famous in a field which the Church of England preferred to cloak in secrecy.

After that my fate was sealed, and Kim's too. All the dinosaurs, whippets and fluffettes in the City were reading about the Square-mile lawyers who had hit the bad-time buffers at ninety miles an hour. Not even the Governor of the Bank of England could have saved our jobs after this media-fest, and the Law Society was certainly not going to bother, particularly when one of those loquacious Oakshott policemen happened to mention to some fiery newshound with a penchant for scorched earth that Kim and I had been messing up a potential crime scene.

While the *Evening Standard* was selling out after work on every London street corner, I was talking again to the City police, who by this time had conferred with their Oakshott brethren and decided to recheck all the witnesses' statements relating to the stabbing. Obviously they must have been keen to nail Kim on some charge or other but no new evidence emerged which gave them a hope of obtaining a conviction.

I must stress that the police gave us a fair deal. It was the members of the press who washed us up. There is no crime yet called media-mauling, but all I can say is that there ought to be. No one found out about the alleged poltergeist or Sophie's ghost, but as soon as the police began to hunt for Mrs. Mayfield there was talk of psychic healers and wild speculation about why the clergymen had been present when Tucker was stabbed. Soon everyone was thinking that Kim and I had gone berserk as the result of killing Sophie by black magic, and that the saintly Mrs. Mayfield's heroic attempt to heal us had been interrupted by a couple of shady clerics spouting an antique form of religious nutterguff which had sent everyone fruity-loops.

To be fair I must admit that not all the media were in hock to infotainment. There was one scholarly article saying that many New Age healers were worthy people, and that some of the New Age tenets, such as concern for the environment, were both intellectually and morally respectable. But no one stood up for Christianity. The authorities at Church House, the headquarters of the Church of England, preserved an arctic silence, and to fill the vacuum the press printed some ferocious criticism which emanated from within the Church itself. Various theologians declared that the Church's involvement with exorcism was intellectually untenable, while the religious radicals bellowed that any bishop who kept an exorcist on his staff ought to have his head examined. Lewis remarked drily that as every diocese now had an exorcist to deal with paranormal pastoral problems, the queue of bishops lining up to have their heads examined would stretch halfway down Harley Street, but I knew he was furious at the enormous distortions of the truth which were now taking place and the hostile spotlight which was being shone on St. Benet's.

The stupid part was that I had never thought of either Nicholas or Lewis as being exorcists. I had merely seen them both as efficient, experienced professionals who were offering a high-quality pastoral care. Lewis was officially retired and so could be written off by the authorities as an elderly eccentric, but Nicholas was lambasted by his embarrassed trustees, blasted by his archdeacon and hauled before his bishop for a suitably severe reproof. The problem, I soon realised, was not that he was an exorcist; his ministry was approved by the bishop and he acted as a consultant to several other dioceses. The problem was that by failing to prevent a case going horribly wrong he had made all the disastrous publicity possible. The Church did not care at all for one of its exorcists hitting the headlines, and after the media-mauling I could quite understand why.

"How dare the press imply that Nicholas is an incompetent nutter!" growled Lewis, who was by this time crosser than ever. "What ignorant impertinence! The truth is that to work successfully in the ministry of deliverance you need to be exceptionally sane and well-integrated!"

I finally allowed my bewilderment free rein. "But

surely Nicholas doesn't believe all that exorcism stuff? I mean..." I attempted and failed to make the leap into an alternative world-view. "God, Lewis, he wasn't really trying to exorcise Mrs. Mayfield, was he?"

"No," said Lewis shortly.

"But in that case what was going on?"

"He was trying to control and expel a very dangerous woman who was using the darker mysteries of personality in a way which was deeply destructive."

"Yes, yes, yes, but—"

"I messed things up by picking the wrong technique to assist in ejecting her. These people are often so puffed up with pride that ridicule can be an effective weapon, but I must face the unvarnished truth here and admit I underestimated the dangerous levels of tension which were present. When the ministry of deliverance goes wrong it can go very wrong indeed—which is why no one should attempt it without proper training by an expert."

"Obviously, but I'm still at sea, I don't understand this foreign language you talk. Is exorcism—"

"Exorcism is a tool for dealing with a certain pastoral problem which occurs in the borderland between religion and psychiatry. It's very rarely used for treating people but it can still be helpful when treating places. Much more common is deliverance, a lesser rite, but most clergy, even clergy with healing ministries, tend to shy away from deliverance for fear of bringing their ministries into disrepute. The ministry of deliverance is very much the ugly twin sister of the attractive ministry of healing."

"You mean it's really just for eccentrics."

"No, of course I don't mean that! Do pay attention, Carter, and try to hear what I'm saying instead of just jumping to emotional conclusions as women so often do—"

(Five minutes were lost here in futile sexist jousting.)

When the discussion was finally resumed, Lewis said: "The popular view of the deliverance ministry has almost no relation to what actually goes on, but sound, respectable, unobtrusive work in this area is being done by sane, sensible, first-class priests such as Nicholas who work with doctors. If you were to read *Deliverance*, an excellent, down-to-earth modern handbook for exorcists edited by Archdeacon Michael Perry, you'd find—"

"I bet. But listen, why didn't Nicholas exorcise Mrs. Mayfield instead of just trying to expel her?"

"You can only exorcise people who feel so oppressed that they come to you begging for help to relieve their torment—and even then exorcism may not be the correct solution. Mrs. Mayfield is without doubt an evil woman, but if she wants neither healing nor deliverance we can do nothing but keep her at bay when she makes open assaults on our ministry. The person who really needs deliverance here," said Lewis, watching me closely, "is your husband. He needs to be delivered from the oppression arising from his connection to Mrs. Mayfield, the connection which has warped his personality and resulted in his breakdown."

I ignored this. In embarrassment I demanded: "Are you implying Mrs. Mayfield's the Devil?"

I felt it was one thing to believe in evil forces—even a single supreme evil force—but quite another to believe that force was a person, the protagonist of so many religious horror-stories.

"Mrs. Mayfield," said Lewis firmly at once, "is most certainly not the Devil—or, to use another metaphor for this aspect of reality—she's certainly not the chief among the Powers of Darkness. She's a human being made in the image of God, just as we all are, and as such she should be prayed for, but as she's sufficiently open to the Devil to be able to do his work with ease, we're usually too busy praying for her victims to pray for her as we should."

I could make no sense of this statement. "Skip the religious language and tell me this: what's wrong with her?"

"A doctor might describe her as a psychopath of the most destructive type, combining this profound personality disorder with a pathological taste for inflicting damage on those she chooses to exploit."

"Fine. Why couldn't you say that in the first place without resorting to religious language?"

"Because ultimately medical language has no vocabulary for talking about evil. It can only describe the symptoms."

I retreated into a baffled silence, but it contained no hostility.

One of the reasons why I was increasingly willing to talk to Lewis, despite his tiger-thumping inclinations, was that no matter how rude I was as I struggled to expand my world-view to cover my recent experiences, he never flinched and always tried to serve up what he called "the unvarnished truth." This was why, when I read in

one of the tabloids that Mrs. Mayfield had con-
trived to vanish from the flat by borrowing the
Eastern mystical trick of making herself invisible,
I went back to him and said irritably: "I can't figure
out this paranormal stuff at all. How can I tell
what's nutterguff and what isn't?"

Lewis was quite unfazed. Promptly he said:
"Study the subject. Remember that the majority
of paranormal cases have normal explanations,
and try to learn the patterns formed by the cases
which don't fall into this category. And keep an
open mind while maintaining a healthy scepticism."

I liked this display of good sense. Cautiously
I said: "I remember you told me earlier that
being psychic isn't the same as being spiritual."

"Is Mrs. Mayfield knocking at heaven's gate?"
he retorted drily, and when I smiled he added:
"Psychic gifts are often a handicap because they
encourage pride and arrogance, and in order to
get to grips with life you need to see yourself
absolutely as you are, warts and all. If you can
do that, then you have a good chance of discerning
the kind of life God's designed you to lead."

I immediately decided he was huffing and
puffing about a problem which any intelligent
person could solve without too much trouble
at the start of adult life. "Well, I know exactly who
I am and what kind of life I'm supposed to be
leading," I said, "so I don't have to go through
any introspective time-wasting."

"Sincere congratulations! So who are you?
Why did you really marry that husband of yours?
How have you managed to get yourself into such
a tight corner that you're dispossessed from
your home and reduced to camping out with

strangers? And how are you going to cope in a situation where your money and success have proved powerless to help you and where even your smart car is now just a lump of metal in a garage?"

There was a long silence before I said: "I'll get over this. I'll pull myself up by my bootstraps." And when Lewis said nothing I added obstinately: "Okay, I've lost my bootstraps, but I'll get another pair." It was only when he still remained silent that I said uncertainly: "Won't I?"

"It may not actually be bootstraps that you need."

We sat looking at each other until at last I said: "I'm frightened about my job."

"Frightened you're going to lose it?"

"I know I'm going to lose it."

"Then what's frightening you?"

"I'm frightened I won't mind."

We thought about that for a while. Finally I said: "I don't know what that implies. I feel I don't know anything any more. In fact I feel I know less than nothing."

"Now you're really beginning to make progress," said Lewis.

IX

I lost my job.

The articles of partnership at Curtis, Towers provided for those unfortunate circumstances when a partner behaved in a manner unbecoming to a lawyer, and no eminent legal firm could wish to retain a partner who had not only blundered as I had blundered at Oakshott but had witnessed a lurid stabbing, hobnobbed with an exorcist and featured in the tabloids as a scandal-prone *femme fatale*. Moreover the Law Society were already considering whether they should officially censure my Oakshott conduct, and any partner who fell foul of the Law Society was always in line for liquidation. I could not be fired as if I were a mere employee, but I had no trouble picturing the other partners voting to line me up for the golden handshake.

The only redeeming feature of the mess was that my competence as a tax specialist was unmarred, and that my crucial mistake lay not so much in my stupid behaviour as in the fact that I had been found out. (In this respect my situation resembled Nicholas's.) However as most of my partners had probably also suffered from bouts of stupidity in the past, I suspected they were even now shuddering in sympathy for me, a state of affairs which suggested the golden handshake was likely to be substantial.

When the time came to terminate me, the chief dinosaur declared that my partners extended their "fullest sympathy" over the "personal nature" of my ordeal, and regretted that, given the "difficult circumstances," I might not be "entirely happy" at the prospect of remaining at Curtis, Towers. It was everyone's "most earnest and sincere wish" to be generous to me in my "time of trial," and in order to settle this most unfortunate matter as "speedily and discreetly" as possible, the partners were willing to cede me more than the required sum laid down in the articles of partnership.

The chief dinosaur continued to grind out this sick-making pompoguff for some time, but the message was already clear. If I went quietly, my bank account would be considerably expanded by the fruits of my partners' good-will; but if I put them all to the trouble of prising me loose they would screw me financially as far as the articles allowed and probably top off this brutality by bad-mouthing me to the next set of people who invited me to join a partnership. Or in other words, if I fell on my sword I would not only save myself from being murdered but ensure myself of a generous eulogy at the funeral.

It was nice to think we were still maintaining the traditions of Ancient Rome in our modern version of Roman Londinium.

I fell on my sword.

Afterwards I knew it was not without significance that I remained dry-eyed as I walked away for the last time from that office in Bevis Marks.

But I still felt gutted to the core.

X

Kim was still officially at Graf-Rosen; it was considered not ethically correct to terminate a colleague while he was in hospital, but I had no doubt the appropriate financial package was being drawn up.

While all this upheaval was unfolding, Tucker left hospital and was whisked away by his doting parents to convalesce at their villa on the Algarve. On the day I fell on my sword a postcard bearing a picture of an idyllic Portuguese seascape arrived for me at the Rectory. Tucker had written: "Greetings, Ms. G! I'm already bored with swilling Portuguese plonk. Drink a tankard of the Widow for me at the Lord Mayor's Cat! Thanks for those tulips. What an erotic vision of femininity they conjured up! Yours still stimulated, E.T. (No quips about extra-terrestials, please.)"

Having obtained the Algarve address from his brother I bought a postcard of St. Benet's and wrote: "Just joined the ranks of the unemployed. Heading for the Lord M's C. Will Swill. *Re* tulips: I don't get it. They were the most macho flowers I've ever seen! Yours baffled, C.G."

As I dropped the card in the nearest postbox I wished I too could have a holiday on the Algarve, but I knew I was still a long way from gaining a respite from my troubles.

I was becoming increasingly disturbed by the thought of Kim.

FIFTEEN

And as modern psychology and psychoanalysis have stressed, many of our life-shaping secrets are ones we are not even conscious of—they are repressed, forgotten, denied and deposited in the unconscious.

DAVID F. FORD
The Shape of Living

I

The trouble was that I could not now think of my marriage without being assaulted by a wave of unbearable emotions which I felt quite unable to handle. Rage that Kim should have been deceiving me on such a huge scale, coupled with horror at his disastrous involvement with Mrs. Mayfield, were followed by grief that my love had apparently been a grand illusion, coupled with a violent, unforgiving self-disgust that I should have made such a devastating mess of my personal life. I began to think I was going through emotions similar to those which a man must experience after castration: an overwhelming shame, an all-consuming humiliation and a marked loss of confidence and self-esteem.

I was coping with the collapse of my career at Curtis, Towers by telling myself, with justification, that the disaster was survivable. But I had no idea how to cope with the collapse of my marriage. I found such a failure impossible to process mentally; whenever I started to think of Kim, my mind would shut down in less than twenty seconds. The memories of the final scene at my flat were unendurable.

It was obvious that his final frantic attempt to regain his files meant that I had by no means heard the whole story of his past. It also seemed plain that Mrs. Mayfield's willingness to help him conceal it must mean that the rock-bottom secret involved her in some way. But beyond that point my powers of reason and logic refused to work. I was still too traumatised by that scene when Mrs. Mayfield had called the shots and Kim had acquiesced in her attempt to brutalise me. How could he have stood by while she reduced me to a speechless, panic-stricken wreck? I accepted that the stabbing of Tucker was an accident; I accepted that the charade with the knife had seemed the best way to get Tucker to disclose where the files were; but I could not accept any behaviour which had permitted Mrs. Mayfield to scare me out of my mind.

I could only conclude he had never genuinely loved me, and that conclusion, making a mockery of my judgement, my discernment, my perspicacity, my common sense, my good taste—indeed my whole grasp of reality—was devastating to me. I felt he had rewritten the past and trashed the happy memories we had shared.

Nicholas tried to tell me that Kim had been in the opening stages of mental breakdown and so not responsible for his final actions at the flat, but I refused to listen. I still thought Kim was faking the breakdown to gain time to plan how he could best survive the disasters of Sophie's death and Tucker's wounding. Nicholas also said that Kim might well still love me but that Mrs. Mayfield had so subjected him to her will that by the end of the scene at the flat he had had no will of his own. However, I refused to listen to this theory either, since it failed to correspond to my knowledge of Kim as a tough customer, and when Nicholas tried to reason with me I cut him off.

I could not cope with Nicholas by that stage. I could not now cope with the memory of him as an exorcist, unleashing the power of his personality to grapple with forces which terrified me. Or perhaps the truth was I was recoiling from the sexuality which was keeping Alice in thrall to him and which any woman who valued her sanity would do better to avoid. I distrusted men who had such power over women. I distrusted men who had power. I distrusted men. I was awash with distrust, battered and broken by it. I felt I would never be able to trust any man again.

"How about me?" said Lewis on the day

Tucker's first postcard arrived from the Algarve. "You can't possibly feel threatened where I'm concerned! After all, I'm just a dilapidated old tiger-thumper—what could be more reassuring than such a familiar and pitiable stereotype?"

I laughed but was unconvinced. Lewis had told me that he wanted to visit Kim in hospital.

II

Nobody suggested that it was my moral duty to visit my husband. Nobody talked about my moral responsibilities as a wife. But Val kept in touch with the doctors at the hospital, Nicholas kept in touch with the senior chaplain there, and now Lewis was talking of keeping in touch with Kim himself. The more I tried to escape from the reality of my shattered marriage, the more my new companions seemed to be quietly drawing my attention back to the husband I was unable to confront.

"The chaplain's told Nicholas that Kim's well enough now to receive visitors," Lewis said, "so I thought I might drop in for a word or two. After all, I was the one who established the rapport with him at the Rectory."

I said nothing.

"You remain our primary client," said Lewis after a moment. "Never doubt that. But the trouble is that Kim is so inextricably bound up with your case that we can't just 'split him off,' as a psychologist would say, and pretend he doesn't exist. We have to try to integrate him into the healing process."

I still said nothing.

"Kim has no family," persisted Lewis, "and his

411

friends are now giving him a wide berth because mental illness is the modern equivalent of leprosy, so I could be useful in alleviating his inevitable feelings of isolation. Besides, Mrs. Mayfield's abandonment of him could create a dangerous vacuum. We don't want more passing Powers taking up residence in his personality— they could be even worse than the ones introduced by Mrs. Mayfield."

But again I was unable to make sense of the foreign language. "Wouldn't it be simpler just to write him off?"

"Christ never wrote anyone off. And he had a particularly good track record with the mentally ill."

"I'm not interested in Christ," I said. "I don't believe what you believe. I only believe in what I can perceive with the aid of my five senses."

Now it was Lewis's turn to be silent. I sat there with him in the kitchen. I sat there with this clergyman in the main kitchen of the Rectory. I sat there in a situation which even as recently as a month ago would have seemed inconceivable, and every one of my five senses told me the scene was real, just as every cell of my rational brain told me I was being cared for with infinite patience. I looked over my shoulder; the door of the room was closed but it was as if someone had come in. As I covered my face with my hands I felt someone sit down beside me, but of course that was Lewis, moving around the table to offer me the box of Kleenex. Through my fingers I could see the box, see his square old hand, covered with age spots, but as the tears blurred my vision the hand began to seem younger, smoother, tougher, brimming with energy, vibrating with power, bursting with light.

I wanted to touch it but I was too frightened of hallucinations and of breaking down beyond repair. I knew then how frightened I was, and what frightened me most of all was the chaos of a world which my five senses could not reduce to order.

My unseen companion urged: "Start naming the names!" I heard him clearly, inside my head, so I knew he was present; I knew he had come through the closed door of the room; I knew he was separate from Lewis although at the same time mysteriously fused with him. "Start naming the names!" he urged, and I knew that if I could name the names I would reach my destination, whatever that was, just as I had reached St. Eadred's vicarage after my long journey across the City through the dark.

"Bevis Marks," I whispered, "Houndsditch, Bishopsgate, Moorgate, Lothbury, Aldermanbury, Cornhill, Threadneedle Street, Poultry, Cheapside, St. Martin's Le Grand, Paternoster Row, Ave Maria Lane, Amen Court..."

Someone said: "You're going to be all right, Carter. You're going to be all right," and of course it was Lewis's voice which I heard.

But the person beyond the voice was not a dilapidated old tiger-thumper at all.

III

A long while later I said to Lewis: "I can't stand there being no order. I'm so frightened of the chaos."

"It's like being thrown into the deep end of a swimming-pool, isn't it?" said Lewis casually. "The rules that apply to life on dry land no longer apply.

413

You're immersed in water, a substance which has the potential to drown you. If you're not accustomed to swimming every instinct tells you to yell in terror and grab the rail at the side of the pool, but in fact this isn't the way to deal with the problem. You have to make the problem no longer a problem by embracing it—you have to let go of the rail and launch yourself out on the water because once you're swimming, playing by the water-rules instead of the land-rules, you find the water's stimulating, bracing, even welcoming. So by embracing the chaos instead of shunning it you've opened up a whole new dimension of reality."

I pushed this picture around in my mind for a moment but could only say: "I feel more like an earthquake victim than a swimmer. I feel I could cope better if only I had a patch of firm ground to stand on."

"What would the patch look like?"

We started to speculate about what would make me feel more secure. Lewis suggested that I might be missing the comforting routine of the office but I said no, it was a relief not to be battered, blitzed and brutalised daily by the demands of a top job. He then suggested that I might be missing the comforting surroundings of my own home, but I just shuddered. Finally he suggested I might be missing the comforting presence of a husband, but at that point I just reached for the Kleenex again.

However, before I could get as far as shedding a tear I heard myself say: "If only I could understand why I've wound up like this, the chaos wouldn't seem so chaotic. Perhaps my 'patch of firm ground' is just a mental state where I can look at the chaos and see a pattern of meaning."

"Sounds promising."

"You asked me questions the other day which I couldn't answer. Why did I really marry Kim, how have I wound up camping out at a rectory—"

"I remember."

"Well, I can think of more questions. Why have I been so in thrall to the dream of becoming a high flyer? Why have I devoted myself to a fanatical lifestyle which is as strict as the fanatical lifestyle required by a fundamentalist religion? I feel as if I've been brainwashed about how I should live—about how much sex and money and power I should have in order to achieve salvation. I feel as if I've been conned all the way along the line."

"No salvation?"

"Well, I'm hardly living happily ever after, am I, even though I've sweated and slaved for years to do everything this fundamentalist religion said I ought to do. So obviously my world-view needs changing, but how do I do it? And how do I recognise a world-view which will be liberating and life-giving instead of oppressive and soul-destroying?"

"Those are certainly big questions. But you've made enormous progress just by asking them."

"So what are the answers?"

"Your next task is undoubtedly to find out."

"You mean I have to answer all these questions myself?"

"Yes, in the sense that it's your spiritual journey, no one else's, but no, in the sense that you won't have to take this journey without guides. I suggest the first question you might try to answer is why you were prepared to make such sacrifices to be a high flyer—and if you're going to take a look at your unconscious drives you might like to have a word with Robin."

Robin was the Healing Centre's psychologist. I must have looked unenthusiastic for Lewis added quickly: "He's good at giving people encouragement in this sort of situation, and as counselling's a short-term process, designed to get people in trouble back on their feet quickly, you needn't fear you're heading for years of analysis."

I toyed with the idea of Robin. Finally I said: "I'm so desperate I'll try anything. But will this mean I won't get to talk to you any more?"

"Of course it won't mean that! Robin and I will complement each other. He'll help you uncover the information you need about your past, and then you and I can discuss what meaning and value can be attached to it so that the present makes more sense."

"But if you're going to cosy up to Kim, won't there be a conflict of interests?"

"I'm only going to visit Kim as a sympathetic acquaintance. I'm not going to counsel him."

I was unable to stop myself saying: "I wish you'd give up the whole idea."

"Don't you at least want firsthand information about what sort of state he's in? The Maudsley will report to you, of course, whenever you care to approach them, but you're not their patient and their views are inevitably going to be coloured by what Kim tells them. So if you bear this in mind, doesn't it seem a good idea to sanction a scout to make a reconnaissance?"

With dread I had to concede that it did.

IV

Robin, the psychologist and counsellor at the Healing Centre, was a man of about forty-five, very tall and thin with horn-rimmed glasses, a campish air and a florid taste in ties. I was surprised to see he wore a wedding ring. It took me more than one session to realise that Robin himself did not find his marital status surprising at all.

He was adept at giving the impression that he sympathised with me entirely on every emotional level I had ever imagined and quite a few that I hadn't. Beneath this faintly nauseous professional caring he was sharp as a needle and nudged me skilfully into some interesting insights. These I appreciated, and gradually I came to respect him, despite his trick of talking in italics as if to stress the sincerity behind his professional manner.

"Of course I'm not a *Freudian*," he said after I had completed the trip through my past. "In my counselling role I'm more interested in the *here and now* instead of remote history, but sometimes connections *pop up*, as it were and simply *demand* to be noticed...like this business of your mother telling you not to cry when your father lost the *cat*. And like—gosh, now I'm *really* reaching for it!—the fact that your real name's Catriona, a word beginning C-A-T. Am I being *completely* fruity-loops, as you would say, or is this rather *more* than just a curious little coincidence?"

I heard myself say: "My father calls me Kitty. I was his Little Kitty," I said, "and he lost me. He let go of my hand and he let my mother take me away and all my mother said afterwards was: 'Big girls don't cry.'"

V

"My mother never cried, never," I said in a later session, "and after she remarried she used to say angrily to me: 'You can't possibly be unhappy, you've got so much to be thankful for!' So I wasn't allowed to be unhappy, it didn't happen, and I never cried, never. But not crying didn't mean I felt happy and after a while I got angry. I thought: I'll show her! I'm going to escape into a world she only sees on telly and I'm going to drive the kind of car James Bond would drive and I'm going to live in a place like you only see pictures of in magazines and I'll be so bloody rich I'll be able to have ANYTHING I WANT, and I'll show them all—I'll show not only Mam and Ken and those two stupid girls but *him* up in Glasgow—I'll show them all I can live very nicely without family, thanks very much, and then I'll be really happy because I'll never again have to pretend to be happy when I'm not.

"And in the end, I said to myself, in the end I'm going to marry the exact opposite of *him* up in Glasgow, I'm going to marry a man who's hugely rich because I know it's only money that counts, and if *him* in Glasgow had had money he wouldn't have spent his life in the betting-shop trying to win a fortune and he wouldn't have let go of my hand and we'd all be together still and I'd be happy.

"So it all seemed so clear, you see, it seemed so obvious that you had to be very successful in order to make lots of money, and having lots of money was the only way to control what happened to you, it was the only way to survive all the bloody mess everywhere, the mess generated by all the people who couldn't make money. God, I can't tell you what a mess it was when I was little, living from hand to mouth, never knowing when the bailiffs were coming—yes, it was chaos, *chaos,* and the chaos was vile, it was terrifying, it was absolute bloody hell.

"But I found my way out of all that, didn't I? I was saved by my brains—and by my determination never to wind up like my mother. Never, never, never, I said to myself was I going to marry a man like my father who would destroy my trust and rob me blind and lie to me over and over again! No way was *I* ever going to wind up trashed like that, I told myself, because once I had money I'd be safe, I'd be secure, I'd have everything under control, I'D BE HAPPY.

"I had this life-plan. I loved my life-plan, loved it, and I followed it to the letter. I got the education, I got the professional qualification, I got the jobs, I got the red Porsche, I got the dream-home in the sky, I got—oh, so much money, I can't tell you!—I got power, I got control, I got ORDER. No more chaos. And at the end of all that I even got the man of my dreams, so everything was perfect, perfect, perfect... although, of course, life was quite a strain, I was always working so hard, never having time for...well, for just living a normal life, just simply *being.* I mean, there was really no time for anything except achieving my goals on schedule and working my life into a statement which said to my parents: 'Fuck you for not loving me properly, fuck you for all the mess which made me miserable...' It was almost like an act of revenge. Well, I suppose it *was* an act of revenge... But of course it was also the road to happiness, and I wanted happiness, lots of it, it was owing to me.

"Sometimes I did wonder if I was happy. Sometimes when the City bastards were bloody to me, sometimes when all the hard work seemed too much to bear. But I couldn't be unhappy, could I? My life-plan was guaranteed to bring me happiness. The guarantee was cast-iron, blue-chip, fail-safe. I was so rich and so successful—how could I be other than happy? As my mother would have said, I had so much to be thankful for, and big girls don't cry.

"But sometimes I think I wanted to cry. Sometimes when it all seemed more of a strain than I could bear... But I never did cry, except when my last lover left me. That was so painful that I couldn't help crying, but I only cried for less than a minute and after that I filed the memory away, I wiped it, it was as if it had never happened. I soon put my life in order again, believe me. I always had everything so absolutely under control, and that's how I succeeded in winding up with the perfect job, the perfect home and the perfect husband."

I stopped speaking. Robin said nothing. He always knew when to keep his mouth shut.

Then I broke down and began to weep again for everything I had lost.

VI

At another session I said: "My job wasn't without its satisfactions, but it nearly killed me. It was

420

as if I was obliged to lie every day on a beautiful, luxurious sofa which was actually a rack in disguise. And I'll tell you something else. I liked my home, but it was spooky being so far from the ground. Do you think Mrs. Mayfield was able to sense that? Sometimes now I think she didn't have to plant in my mind the horror of the Big Fall; she merely had to exploit an ambivalence which was already there."

"That's certainly an interesting thought."

"It was strange, wasn't it, about the disorder which kept breaking out in my flat? Of course I don't believe in all that poltergeist rubbish, but it was odd how the disorder coincided with the unravelling of my personal life. It was as if the flat was a mirror reflecting the gathering chaos."

"A mirror...yes, that's a good simile."

"And I'll tell you an even odder thing: my telescope was never damaged. I mentioned my telescope to you, didn't I?"

"You did, yes. Are you able to say why the telescope was so important to you?"

I said carefully: "It was like a link to a parallel world. I knew there was another world out there but I couldn't connect with it as I slaved away in my daily life. When I was looking through my telescope...well, I used to look at the stars and sunsets and the patterns of the city lights and feel such a sense of wonder and awe... There was never any room for those sorts of feelings when I was working. Do you think I was just being sentimental? After all, I was only looking at an urban landscape, wasn't I?"

"When we listen to music all we hear are vibrations in the air. But of course we get more out of music than mere vibrations."

I felt sufficiently encouraged by this observation to confess: "I love the City! People think it's ugly compared with the glamorous West End, but I love the way it refuses to die. No matter how many catastrophes devastate it, it always springs back to life."

"So you're saying it's not just an urban landscape. It's a powerful image of regeneration."

"It's a symbol of the power of life." I thought about that statement. Then I said: "But it's more than a symbol. It *is* life—*real* life." I thought some more and was able to add: "But I could only make contact with it when I looked through my telescope."

"But then you were called down from your ivory tower, weren't you?"

"Called down? I was evicted! The Powers kicked me out onto the street and smashed me up!"

"But you made it to Fleetside."

"Just! Yes, I did."

"So the Powers didn't have the last word."

"Not that time. There was something else waiting for me down on those City streets, something else waiting down there in real life."

"And what was that?"

I glanced at my watch. "Luck," I said. I revolved the strap on my wrist. "Let's face it, I've been pretty damn lucky, winding up at St. Benet's and receiving all this top-quality care. Otherwise I might have gone mad, but of course I know now that Sophie's ghost was just a bereavement phenomenon and that there was no poltergeist, just that arch-cow Mayfield playing tricks. All the same...it was strange how the telescope was never damaged, wasn't it?"

"Very strange," said Robin.

VII

"Hey!" wrote Tucker on the back of his second postcard from the Algarve. "I'm tired of quaffing Mateus, adorning the pool and getting myself fit. (You should see my forearms!) To please my mother I'm now sporting a short haircut and no beard. To please my father I listened yesterday without interrupting while he expounded on his latest theories about the Witan (Anglo-Saxon pow-wow place). To please myself I've been indulging in primal screams. What's new? I'm trying to get the parents to instal a fax here but we can't work out how to do it in Portuguese. Yours banjaxed, E.T. PS: Poor old Nick, being unmasked as an exorcist! Has he had any Hollywood offers yet?"

VIII

"Kim seemed far from well," said Lewis, "but he's sure the chief problem now is the drugs—apparently the doctors are still trying to get the cocktail right. He didn't want to talk much but he was keen to learn how you were."

I felt queasy. "Did he ask whether I was going to visit him?"

"Yes, but I explained that you too had problems to work through, and he seemed to have no trouble accepting that you weren't up to visiting him at the moment. What upset him was the news of your departure from Curtis, Towers."

I felt queasier than ever. "What did he say?"

"He asked me to tell you that he was very, very sorry and that he just hoped you'd be able to forgive him one day for dragging you into such a mess."

"I don't want to hear any more," I said, and walked out.

IX

"...and so there I was," I said to Robin, "standing in the kitchen of my mother's house in Newcastle, and telling her she shouldn't put so much salt in the stew because I didn't want to wind up with high blood pressure, and she said: 'What do *you* know about cooking—you can't even cook a decent breakfast!' So I said: 'You're damn right I can't—I've got better things to do with my time, thanks very much!' And we had another row—all my Christmas visits seem to end in a row and it's nearly always about food because she keeps on cooking things which I don't want to eat."

"How difficult!" said Robin, exuding sympathy, but he added: "Food has a tremendously *symbolic* quality, I often think."

"But surely food's just fuel!"

"Fundamentally, yes, but sometimes it symbolises *nurture* and *care* and a sort of *wordless love*."

"My stomach's about to heave. If you're saying these ghastly, high-fat, high-cholesterol meals are her weird way of saying 'I love you,' you couldn't be more mistaken!"

"Couldn't I?"

"Well, no way does this woman love me! I was just a millstone round her neck after she left my father, and I'm sure she never wanted me around after she remarried. She was always mean to me—why, she never even let me have another cat! If I'd had a cat of my own to replace Hamish, a real cat instead of that slobbish hunk of fur my stepfather chose for my half-sisters, I wouldn't have minded not being loved by my parents. My cat would have loved me instead."

"Animals are very good at giving unconditional love."

"Well, never mind that, forget Hamish, let me explode this nauseating theory of yours that my mother cooks as a way of saying 'I love you.' The truth is she cooks for one reason and one reason only: she has to fuel that dreadfully dull man she's now married to."

"I wonder why she did marry that dreadfully dull man."

"Obviously she was suffering from a violent reaction to my father's lethal charm!"

"No other reason?"

"What other reason could there be?"

"*Was your stepfather ever nasty to you?*" Robin had dropped the italics. That meant we were nearing another stretch of white water in our counselling canoe, but although I peered ahead I was unable to spot the rapids.

"Nasty to me?" I was exclaiming scornfully. "Ken? He wouldn't know how!"

"He didn't abuse you? He wasn't cruel?"

"Don't be funny, he's not the type!"

"You'd be amazed how many different types of abuser there are," said Robin quietly. "Many of my clients were abused in some way by their stepfathers."

"Okay, so I didn't have an awful stepfather! But that was just the luck of the draw, wasn't it?"

"Was it?" said Robin. "But there was no draw, was there? Your mother chose him."

I opened my mouth but found I was quite unable to reply.

X

"Hey, Tucker! (I refuse to address you as E.T.) Soon I'll be able to send you a postcard moaning about *my* parents. I've decided to take a fresh look at them to see if my previous assessment needs updating; that cunning Robin has whetted my curiosity and now it's insatiable. Alice is going to come with me. She's hardly ever been north of Watford Gap so this will be like a polar expedition for her. I thought I could face my mother more easily if Alice was there to talk about food. Does *your* mother try to stuff food into you all the time? (Note my tact in sending this card in an envelope so that she can't read it.) Keep swilling that PortuPlonk. Cheers, C.G. PS: I was most interested to hear news of your forearms."

XI

"Kim's feeling much better," said Lewis. "They finally got the drug cocktail right."

"Oh."

"He was certainly more chatty—we had the most interesting talk about that film *Days of Wine and Roses* which I'm sure you're too young to remember."

"Ah."

"The bad news is that the senior chaplain's starting to take a dim view of me, even though I've assured him I'm simply there as a visitor. As Kim refuses to have anything to do with the members of the chaplaincy team, it's naturally galling for them when I sail in and talk to him for half an hour... Did you see Val this morning? No?

The latest medical word on Kim seems to be favouring the diagnosis that he's merely a normal man who'd reached the end of his tether—in other words, they're saying he's not a psychopath and not suffering from some long-term illness such as schizophrenia. That's good news, of course. If it's true."

I finally managed to rouse myself. "The doctors still think he's not faking the breakdown?"

"Apparently."

"But do you think the doctors have got it right?"

"I've no idea. I'm not privy to their discussions, but I'll tell you this: although this mental breakdown may be genuine, his basic problem—how to live outside the world of Mrs. Mayfield—is spiritual. And so far as I know that problem hasn't been addressed at all."

I shuddered and turned away.

XII

"Sweetheart, Forgive me writing, but I just want to say I LOVE YOU, you're still the most important thing in my life, and once I'm better we're going to work this out, I promise. KIM."

XIII

"This steak-and-kidney pudding is marvellous!" exclaimed Alice to my mother three days later. "It's much better than my own recipe. How very kind of you to go to so much trouble to give us such a delicious meal—you must have been slaving over that stove for hours!"

"Oh, it's no trouble!" said my mother, very

427

casual, but despite her downcast eyes I knew she was deeply gratified.

XIV

"Hey, Tucker! My family are slavering at Alice's feet. I'm surfing along in her wake and wondering if it's all a dream. Tonight I plan to have a serious conversation with my mother. This is unprecedented. Drink a glass of PortuPlonk for me and pray I don't go fruity-loops. C. G."

XV

"Oh, Katie!" said my mother as Alice watched television with my stepfather in the back room and I helped with the washing-up, "I do like your friend, what a nice lass, I always wanted you to have a friend like that, what a lot you missed out on because you were so busy working, you were always such a loner.

"What I want to say, love, now I've got you on my own, is that I'm sorry things aren't working out with your husband, but it's only a few months since you married, isn't it, and the first year of marriage is often very difficult—well, I should know, what with your father always in the betting-shop and Ken always watching telly—not that there's anything wrong with watching telly, of course, but sometimes I think it's a bit dull.

"Why did I marry him? Well, what a funny question! He had a good job, didn't he, with the Electricity, and I knew he was steady and decent, I knew he'd look after us—which was more than I could say for that Rob I was also seeing, but you probably don't remember Rob because I mostly kept quiet about him. Anyway I made the right decision because Ken's been a much better father than Rob would have been, and I had to think of that, didn't I, especially after all you'd been through.

"I knew Ken would be kind to you because when I told him how much you'd cried after your father lost Wee Hamish, his eyes filled with tears and he said: 'Poor little lass!' That's why we eventually did have another cat. I didn't want another, I was so exhausted all the time when the girls were little, but when the girls were finally at school I said to Ken: 'All right,' I said, 'I give in, get the cat,' so he went and chose Squashy, but the girls took over Squashy at once, didn't they, so you still didn't have a cat of your own, and I knew you ought to have one that was specially yours, like Wee Hamish, but I was going out to work again by then so that you girls wouldn't go short of anything, and life was just one thing after another, and somehow I never could face that extra cat.

"So what I want to say, Katie, now that I'm talking about Squashy, is that I'm sorry I didn't get that extra cat for you. I can see now I was being selfish, not making that extra effort, and I know you always resented it. I knew you always felt you were short-changed."

When she stopped speaking there was a long silence before I managed to say: "But I wasn't short-changed about the things that mattered."

"Well, just so long as that's all straightened out," she said, busy scouring a saucepan, "that's fine... My goodness, Katie, are those tears in your eyes? Well, we can't have that, can we! Remember what I always said: 'Big girls don't cry'—although sometimes I think I was really talking to myself when I said that. When I was going through the bad times, you see, I often felt that if I ever started crying I'd never stop, and if I was to break down you'd be taken into care, and...well, never mind that, it didn't happen, did it? I married Ken and everything came right and every day I think how much I've got to be thankful for. Always count your blessings, Katie! It used to make me so cross when you wouldn't do that, but now perhaps you can look back and...well, you did have so much to be thankful for, didn't you? You really did..."

XVI

"Hey, Tucker! Greetings from Glasgow. Alice is shopping in the smart part but I'm about to head for the dark side."

I paused, my pen poised above the card.

The seconds trickled emptily away, but then I thought of Tucker saying: "Truth matters," and I remembered Kim telling me lie after lie.

Gripping my pen hard I wrote: "My father's in jail for theft. Being on the dole didn't give him enough money for gambling. He'll be out in September—which is just as well as this is the worst prison he's ever been in. It's a long story and not one which can be told on a postcard. Just be thankful for your own father, wittering on about the Witan in glorious, sun-drenched Portugal. C.G."

XVII

"I'm going to make it this time," said my father. "I've got a feeling in my bones. Okay, I know you've heard me say all that before but *this time I really mean it.* Yes, I know you've heard me say that before too, but this time when I get out I'm going straight, I swear it, because if I wind up in a place like this again I'll make sure I get carried out feet first in double-quick time.

"But you don't want to hear me talking like that. Are you all right, sweetheart? How's my wonderful girl? How's the best daughter in the world? Now, I want to hear all about this husband of yours—I need to be convinced he's good enough for my Kitty! When I get out I'm going to buy you a really good wedding present—I don't want your husband thinking I'm a loser just because Lady Luck deserted me and I wound up in a tight corner. After all, I could have made it big if only—but you don't want to hear me say that either. I've said it too often before. I know what I do wrong, as I said to the new chaplain only the other day.

"'I know what I do wrong so all I need now is one lucky break!' I said to him, but when he just sighed I said: 'But I do get lucky sometimes! I've got this daughter who's the best girl in the world. There's luck for you!' So he pretended to be interested and said: 'How often does she come to visit?' but when I told him: 'Every Christmas without fail!' I could see he just thought that was pathetic. He said gloomily—just like a bloodhound he looks—he said gloomily: 'Would you like me to pray for her?' So then I lost patience and said: 'What for? She's not going to visit me more often. She's busy making bloody millions and she's just got herself a husband. She won't come near Glasgow till I'm out of here and she can pretend to her man I'm employed.'

"Then the chaplain makes his great blood-hound face look even gloomier and says: 'Maybe I could thank God that at least you have someone who's important to you,' so then I get so pissed off I tell him: 'Sod it, my girl's hardly in my life at all, God knows why she ever comes here, she never forgave me for losing her cat when she was six years old.'

"Well, you won't believe it, but this interested him. He twisted his awful bloodhound face into a strained expression as if he was constipated and he said: 'Have you ever said you were sorry?' and I said sure. 'I said it was Lady Luck playing me false,' I said, but he just mumbled: 'I hear that's not the way it's done at Gamblers Anonymous.'

"Well, I didn't like him nagging me like that— they're not supposed to, you know—so I snapped: 'Don't you bloody preach to me, I've heard it all before—"Accept responsibility for your actions" and all that—but how do I say to my girl: "Yes, I was solely responsible for losing your toys and Wee Hamish?" What man can face his beautiful daughter, the only good thing that's come out of his fucking stupid life and admit straight out that he's nothing but a fucking mess?' But the chap-lain just said: 'If she can suffer the wrong you did, you can apologise for it.' Bastard! They're not meant to do that, you know, they're not meant to, it's called 'Being Judgemental' and the social workers all say it's wrong. So I just told him: 'Fuck off—and fuck your prayers and preaching too!' And then the next morning in the post...

"Do you suppose you came because he prayed you would, Kitty? But no, that's not possible, is it? You must have decided to see me well before Old Bloodhound flapped his chops."

I said: "Yes, but last night I wanted to chicken out."

"But you didn't chicken out!" he exclaimed shining-eyed. "You came!"

"There are things I have to try to understand, things I—"

"Kitty, I'm sorry it was all such a mess. I'm sorry I made you lose your toys. I'm sorry I lost that wee cat you loved so much. And above all I'm sorry I lost *you*—but it wasn't because I didn't love you, Kitty, it wasn't because I didn't care—"

"Sure."

"You don't believe me, but Kitty, if only you knew what it's like to be hooked into something which makes you destroy all that's good! It's like—well, it's like being drafted into an army led by someone like Hitler or Stalin, and the people in command—the Powers-That-Be—keep forcing you to destroy things. I know that sounds as if I'm refusing to accept responsibility as usual, but Kitty, I fight and fight against those Powers, I really do, it's not as if I don't try—"

"Dad—"

"It's the Powers, you see, it's the Powers! They're so strong, so—well, never mind all that, I don't look for understanding or forgiveness anyway, not after being such a fucking awful father to you, but I'm sorry, I swear I am, for losing your toys and Wee Hamish, and meanwhile—"

"Oh Dad, Dad, Dad—"

"—meanwhile I just want to say this: I LOVE YOU, sweetheart, you're still the most important thing in my life, and once I'm out of here I'm going to make amends to you, I promise."

He stopped. With an enormous effort I drew breath to respond, but when I finally looked straight into his bloodshot blue eyes words failed me because all I saw was Kim, looking back.

SIXTEEN

The issue at stake is the whole shape of living. To attend to that when we are being overwhelmed is no easy matter. But it is hard to imagine any adequate way of coping that does not try to answer the big questions about life, death, purpose, good and evil.

DAVID F. FORD
The Shape of Living

I

"Hey, Ms. G! I'm seriously concerned about your mammoth excavation of the past. This is tough stuff. Why take it on now when you've got so much else on your plate? I'm sorry about your father but I appreciate your honesty with me. I've lit a candle for you in the local church. (RC, but when the chips are down the Pope doesn't count, as Henry VIII said long ago.) No news here. To my amazement I find that boredom's not a terminal condition. E. T. PS: I'd come home but my parents would both have apoplexy and I couldn't stand the guilt."

II

"So?" said Robin, in his office at the Healing Centre.

"I can't begin to describe the emotional depths I've plumbed. I feel pie-eyed, zonked and banjaxed."

"I suspect that describes the situation rather well."

We paused, snug in our counselling bubble, and considered my journey into chaos.

"However," I said at last, "I'm still alive, aren't I?"

"Very much so."

I breathed deeply, savouring my survival, before I admitted: "It was a useful trip to make."

"You've found a firm patch of ground where you can take your stand?"

"I've found a little piece of scorched earth where I can rest with my life-support machine, yes."

"Progress can come in all shapes and sizes."

"Apparently it can." I had to breathe deeply again before I was able to add: "I'd got it wrong. The problem wasn't that my parents didn't love me. It was just that they were stupid about showing it and I was stupid about understanding them. So the great act of revenge which has consumed my adult life was misconceived."

"Well," said Robin vaguely, "it's an ill wind that blows no one no good. At least you got a good education and had a lot of fun with that Porsche."

"Yes, but—" I broke off, scrabbling for the right words, but only wound up saying: "I feel I've crucified myself for years for nothing."

"Profound insights can often leave one feeling

435

devastated but remember: when one's devastated one's unlikely to view the situation with detachment."

"Well, I can see there were genuine benefits from all that hard work, but I still feel like a sweater unlucky enough to have been washed on the all-white cotton cycle, and now that my motivation's been exposed as a grand illusion, where does that leave me?"

"In a position to work out a more authentic existence, a life more in touch with your real self."

"Oh, spare me the psychobabble! Do you seriously think I can cope with the future while I'm being disembowelled by the present? Now, listen to me. I think I've got a better grip on the mother-problem because I can see she's essentially benign—which means I'll no longer want to bite her head off whenever I see her. But tell me what the hell I'm going to do about..." I tried and failed to stop my voice trailing away.

"Isn't he benign too?"

"Oh, he's much worse than that. He's doting. Adoring. A total nightmare. I can't cope."

Another silence ensued as we breathed quietly in our counselling bubble, insulated from all the chaos.

At last I said: "I always vowed I'd never marry a man like my father. So why in God's name did I marry Kim?"

"We're all more in the grip of unconscious forces than we realise, but perhaps when we talk about this further—"

"I don't want to talk about it further," I said, and beat the rapidest of retreats from his consulting-room.

III

"Kim's very much better," said Lewis. "He's in group therapy now. Val says the doctors are very pleased and are sure he'll be leaving the hospital sooner rather than later."

"Sorry, Lewis. Can't cope. Pass."

IV

"Ms. G, I've decided to risk giving my parents apoplexy and come home. I talked to Gil last night. He says he'll fly out here to calm them down provided that I do nothing stupid as soon as I hit London. I was so grateful that I offered to pay his fare out of my anorexic bank account, but he said no, he has no problem borrowing money from his friendly gay bank manager. Sometimes I think it must be almost worth being gay for the contacts one gets. I'll send further details of my return later. Meanwhile my forearms salute you! E.T."

V

"Are you all right, Carter?" said Alice.

"I've no idea. I've forgotten what 'all right' feels like."

"I know how traumatic it was for you up in the north. Actually I don't think Robin should have encouraged you to go while you're still struggling with the Kim disaster."

"It's all connected."

"So you keep saying, but—"

"I thought I married Kim because he fitted the right profile in my high flyer's life-plan, but while I was up north to find out why I chose to fly high in the first place I uncovered this truly revolting Oedipal dimension which makes me want to throw up... Or did I uncover it? Maybe I've finally gone insane."

"Dearest Carter," said Alice, passing me her ginger cat who had been imported from her Clerkenwell flat, "give Redford a massage while I make some soothing hot chocolate and wheel on the comfort cookies—"

"Just wheel on the Scotch!" I barked. "Let me hit the bottle in the biggest possible way!"

But Alice merely smiled and made the hot chocolate.

VI

"I know I couldn't talk about my father when we were in Glasgow," I said later to Alice as the ginger cat purred on my lap like a muffled high-tech drill, "but he started out very bright. He was working class but he was a scholarship boy and he got a white-collar job. Then the personality disorder kicked in and gambling took over his life."

"That doesn't sound like Kim," said Alice.

"But supposing Kim too is the victim of a personality disorder which makes him as vulnerable to Mrs. Mayfield's sex industry as my father is to gambling?"

Alice swirled her hot chocolate around and around in the mug. "What you're really asking is whether Kim is a victim or a villain."

"What I'm really asking is whether the marriage can conceivably have a future."

"What do the professionals say?"

"Damn all. Obviously they have their opinions,

but equally obviously they want to avoid influencing me when I'm in a vulnerable state."

"I'm sure they believe they're acting in your best interests—"

"I'm sure of that too, but all this reticence is driving me crazy. I've got to figure out how to deal with Kim when he comes out of hospital, and how can I do that if everyone's being too professionally correct to offer me an honest opinion?"

"How do you feel about Kim right now this minute?"

"Nauseated. And if I receive one more letter from him I'm going to climb every single wall in this flat..."

VII

"Sweetheart, This is just a line to say I'm thinking of you, I really miss you, I love you. I know you're still too traumatised to write and I accept that I can't see you just yet, but I wonder if you could come down here and have a chat with my psychiatrist instead? He's keen to discuss with you the possibility that you and I could go into therapy together to try to straighten out the marriage, and—"

I stopped reading and shredded the letter with shaking hands.

VIII

I was sitting at the table in the dining area of the Rectory flat on the following evening when Nicholas came up the stairs to see me. I was paying some bills. Alice went to the Harvey Tower flat twice a week to pick up the mail and check that everything was in order. I myself was still unable to face going there.

Alice was completing her caretaking duties that evening by visiting her flat in Clerkenwell, so I was alone except for Redford, the ginger cat, who was curled up on the dining-chair next to mine. Redford confined himself to the attic flat because he was frightened of James, the Rectory tabby, who patrolled the lower floors.

"It occurred to me that I hadn't had the chance to speak to you for some time," said Nicholas. "Is this a convenient moment or should I come back later?"

I pushed away the bills. "Have a seat." Scooping Redford onto my lap I started to massage him again. There was something very comforting about moulding all that thick fur over the curves of those elegant feline bones.

Nicholas was wearing blue jeans and a blue clerical shirt; he looked tired and pale and not in the least sexy; the wattage of his personality was turned down low, so low that it was hard for me to remember the mesmerising star of the deliverance ministry who had told Mrs. Mayfield the party had ended. He still moved gracefully but the grace was shot through with exhaustion, and when he sank down opposite me at the table he seemed barely able to haul one long leg over the other in the effort to look relaxed.

"I was wondering," he said, "if there might be something you wanted to talk to me about."

"Not particularly," I said, irritated by the thought that Alice might have been worried enough about me to nag him into a display of pastoral care. "God, Nicholas, you're such a workaholic! Why should you be dealing with a client at this hour?"

Equably he said: "It seemed like a good opportunity. And I've been so weighed down with the fall-out from the Mayfield fiasco that I'm afraid I haven't been as attentive to you as I should have been."

"I'm okay," I said, knowing I wasn't but knowing too that I did not want to talk to him.

We sat for a moment in silence as I wondered for the umpteenth time whether he was sleeping with Alice. I hoped for Alice's sake that he was, but I had my doubts. Alice had mentioned to me more than once how important it was for him to keep himself "spiritually fit" and I knew he saw his "spiritual director," who was a nun, twice a week without fail. Would a nun approve of Nicholas having sex with Alice? No. Would Nicholas lie to the nun about it? No—unless he was desperate, a state of affairs which was by no means unimaginable, even though he was a clergyman. Could I ask Alice if she and Nicholas managed to get together occasionally in the Rector's first-floor flat now that she was staying in the house? No. Alice was not the kind of woman who would let her hair down over champagne at the Lord Mayor's Cat and discuss whom she had or hadn't screwed that week. Alice cared too much about Nicholas to discuss the intimate details of her relationship with him.

I respected this attitude and never pressed her for information, but somehow this modest, dignified, old-fashioned silence made me feel more annoyed with Nicholas than ever. His divorce was still on hold because of his elder son's drug problem, and the family all met for therapy once a week at some ghastly counselling centre in the West End. Alice was still waiting, still being a saint.

I thought that the least she deserved was some sex now and then to cheer her up, but paradoxically I was aware that I would have respected Nicholas much less if he had been game for a screw because I would have considered such behaviour to be a rampant exploitation of Alice's patient devotion. So as far as I was concerned Nicholas was in a no-win situation. I would have damned him if he did but now I was damning him that he didn't. The whole convoluted mess made me simmer with irritation whenever he cruised into view.

Meanwhile Nicholas was saying: "I was wondering if you wanted to discuss Kim."

"No, thanks." I was now sure that Alice had expressed her anxiety about me and galvanised him into being pastoral, but this thought merely made me feel more annoyed than ever.

Eventually he said: "I know you prefer to talk to Lewis, but I was worried in case you felt Lewis was currently a little too close to Kim."

This was true but I decided straight away not to satisfy him by admitting it. "Lewis is fine," I said. "Anyway I talk to Robin as well."

"Yes, but there are areas where Robin can't go because they lie beyond his remit as a counsellor. There are questions of forgiveness which could come up. Questions of repentance. Questions of how to make sense of suffering and chaos. Ultimate questions."

"Uh-huh." I stopped massaging Redford in order to look ostentatiously at my watch. "I hope Alice gets back soon," I remarked. "There's a TV programme she wants to see."

"May I just ask one more question?" said Nicholas, taking the hint and rising to his feet.

"Are you angry with me for losing control over that scene with Mrs. Mayfield?"

That startled me. Automatically I said: "But it wasn't your fault—you were succeeding in getting her to leave without Kim. It was Lewis who blew it, not you."

He shook his head. "I should never have summoned him. It created that two-on-one situation which drove her into a corner."

"Then why—"

"I lost my nerve. She was so very powerful psychically and when she cursed Alice—"

"Yes, that was vile."

"—it finally undermined me. But Carter, although I lost that round to Mrs. Mayfield I can still work to redeem the mess she left behind—which means I have a powerful motive to help you in any way I can."

I nodded and murmured my thanks. But when I made no further response he said good night and went downstairs.

IX

"I shouldn't have reacted to Nicholas like that," I said fiercely when Alice returned from Clerkenwell. "I know he wants to help me. I know how able and experienced he is. I really should have made more effort to talk to him."

"You're upset. Upset people can't make efforts."

"Well, it's about time this upset person did! Look, Alice, why don't you start the ball rolling here—why don't you help me get my head together by telling me what you're secretly thinking about Kim?"

443

"Oh, but Carter, I'm not a professional!"

"That's why I'm asking you! Obviously I haven't quite enough nerve to face the professionals yet, and I need a dress rehearsal with a non-professional to help me along."

"But I don't know where to begin!"

"Answer just two questions: one, do you think this marriage can be saved? And two, do you see Kim as a victim or a villain? Okay, now shoot from the hip and don't pull the punches—I'm all set for a bumpy ride..."

X

"I'd like to think that the marriage could be saved," said Alice, "but there's an important question which the men seem to have ignored. How do you really feel about having children, Carter? Do you just want them in order to meet the goal listed in your life-plan, or do you want them for themselves? If you really do want children and Kim really doesn't, then the marriage may be beyond saving—but it may be beyond saving anyway, since he's been so busy destroying your trust.

"And talking of children, how did Sophie endure that childless marriage after Kim's infidelity had ensured she was sterile? I suppose she loved him so much that she convinced herself her love would redeem him—and like all abused women she got so brainwashed by the situation that she came to think the abnormal was normal, something to be adjusted to, something to be accepted... But I'll tell you one thing that doesn't add up here, Carter: Kim's story that Sophie had a love affair.

444

"I can imagine her turning to someone else if the marriage became unendurable, but I believe if this had happened the marriage would have ended. Sophie was high-principled; she wouldn't have wanted to live a double life. I know I can't be sure I'm right about this, but all I can say is that when I heard the story about the love-letters my reaction was: no, I don't believe that.

"But if there were no secret love-letters, what was in that mysterious brown envelope? The divorce file isn't really important, is it, because Sophie's lawyers have copies of the letters there and Kim only took the file because he couldn't bear to miss the opportunity to find out what she'd said, but that brown envelope...well, I suppose we'll never know what was in it, not now, because even if he tells you, how do you know whether to believe him? I think your situation's a nightmare, Carter, and if I were in your shoes I couldn't handle it, couldn't cope with a serial liar—I'd go mad with never knowing where I stood and the marriage would be absolutely unworkable.

"But having said all that... Well, I can't help believing Kim really does love you. I remember how he looked at you on the night of the dinner-party—and incidentally, he was very sweet to me then, you know. He needn't have been but he was. And maybe he *is* some sort of victim—maybe his parents really were ghastly and he was justified in hating them. I hated my mother for years before I visited her last summer and discovered she wasn't an ogress after all but just a middle-aged house-wife who hit the sherry too hard when faced with the child she'd abandoned all those years ago... I was just so lucky to have that great-aunt who brought me up, just as Kim was so lucky in the end to get that British stepfather who helped him do well. I turned out pretty weird after that upbringing but even so I think I'm finally getting my act together. So maybe Kim too turned out weird in lots of ways—and maybe you were the person enabling *him* to get his act together, just as Nicholas was the one who enabled me to change *my* life.

"It's awful not knowing where the truth lies, isn't it? It seems to me that even if the marriage can't be saved you've still got to find out the truth— not just to stop yourself going mad but to be fair to Kim. How strange—I started out by seeing him as a villain, and yet now I seem to have ended up on his side. I hope Mrs. Mayfield's not brainwashing me long-distance! Of course I feel angry with him for putting you through such hell, but at the same time...well, I did like him when I met him. In fact to be absolutely honest, I thought he was rather super..."

XI

I went downstairs to see if Nicholas had retired to the Rector's flat, but he was still in his study on the ground floor. He was writing a letter by hand. It seemed odd to see the pen between his fingers when the computer lurked behind him, but Alice had told me he often replied by hand to correspondents who sought spiritual advice.

"I'm still being a workaholic, aren't I?" he said guiltily when I appeared in the doorway, and immediately capped the pen.

"I didn't mean to interrupt." I hovered uncertainly on the threshold. "I just wanted to say I'm sorry I froze you out earlier. I'm truly grateful for all your help."

446

He seemed relieved by these statements. After inviting me to sit down he said: "I know I haven't been much use lately."

"Well, you could certainly be of use now." I posed to him the questions I had asked Alice. "I've got to know what you think," I said, "or if you can't tell me what you think, I need some hints and suggestions about how I can get my head together. I can't just go on guessing in the dark when my marital future's on the line."

He seemed to find this opinion reasonable. "If you're ready to listen," he replied willingly enough, "I'm ready to talk. The only problem is that you may not be able to hear what I have to say—in which case we'll fail to connect and I'll still be no use to you."

"I'll take the chance," I said, and privately vowed to suppress my current annoyance with him in order to benefit from his professional experience.

XII

"You ask if the marriage is still viable," said Nicholas, "and I think it could be—provided, of course, that Kim levels with you about the past and disassociates himself from Mrs. Mayfield.

"But let me just make my position clear about divorce. As a priest I certainly believe that life-long marriage is the ideal to aim for, but I believe too that we're imperfect people living in an imperfect world and our inevitable failures should be recognised instead of denied. If a marriage is dead, I think it's better to face that fact and seek a divorce. There are Christians who would disagree with me about this, but I would

447

point out to them that Jesus' teaching on divorce isn't so clear-cut as is often supposed. What's far clearer is that he thought there were times when applying the law strictly could result in injustice, while a more compassionate approach could revitalise blighted lives—and I'm inclined to apply that attitude to the problem of broken marriages. But as Lewis is always telling me, I'm just a wishy-washy Church of England liberal, and there are priests older and wiser than I am who are made of sterner stuff.

"What I'm trying to say, Carter, is this: if I suggest your marriage could be viable, I won't be making the suggestion because I'm ideologically opposed to divorce. But how likely is it that the marriage is viable? One can't deny it's taken some terrible knocks, but marriages do recover from even the most catastrophic blows, and this one may recover too.

"I think it's important to remember that you've only been married for a few months. That's not long. Maybe the marriage just needs more time to assimilate all the traumatic baggage which is being brought into it from the past. And there's one big psychological advantage in giving Kim a second chance: if the marriage still fails, at least you'll be able to tell yourself you did all you could to resurrect it—whereas if you end the marriage now you'll never be entirely sure whether it might have been saved, and this ambiguity could lead to guilt and depression.

"But everything I've just said about trying again depends on Kim's desire to turn his life around and make a fresh start. Assuming the desire's there, your response becomes crucial, so obviously the next question is: can you forgive him for what he's done?

"As a priest I've come to believe forgiveness is one of the most difficult and complex of the spiritual issues which people have to wrestle with. Let me say straight away that no one should try to forgive Kim on your behalf. You're the one he wronged and you own the suffering resulting from that wrong. If Kim made a confession to me and expressed a genuine desire to repent, I could offer him forgiveness for the wrong he's done to God by behaving as he has, but he'd still have to remake the relationship with you. If he were a believer and could feel he 'stood right with God' as the result of his confession, he'd be well-placed psychologically to translate his repentance into effective action, but even if you eventually said: 'I forgive you,' those words would mean little unless they reflected your actual feelings. Forgiveness can't be turned on like a tap, that's the truth of it. It's not a matter of will-power. Forgiveness is ultimately a gift from God, but as you prefer not to think in theological language I'll just say: to forgive and be forgiven is a form of healing, but the healing dynamic can't always be accessed by the powers of reason and logic. We certainly need to forgive in order to stay healthy, but it can be the hardest of goals to attain.

"Is Kim a villain or a victim, you ask. But really all that matters is that if he genuinely repents he's eligible for forgiveness and a fresh start. So the biggest question right now has to be: does he genuinely repent? And that's a question we're not yet in a position to answer..."

XIII

"So if Kim regrets what he did," I said flatly, "I'm to forgive him, and—bingo!—the marriage becomes viable. Is that what you're saying?"

"By condensing my words into that bald statement you've lost all the nuances. But yes, if we're talking in shorthand, resurrection and renewal can follow on from repentance and forgiveness."

"So a man's allowed to crash around doing what he likes and the woman's supposed to be a saint and put up with all manner of crap for ever provided that he says sorry every now and then?"

"I think if you take a moment to go back over what I've said, you'll find—"

"What bloody male-orientated rubbish!"

"—you'll find that repentance involves far more than glibly saying one's sorry. Repentance means—"

"Okay, so Kim's got to promise to do better! But how the hell can I ever trust him to keep his promise?"

"Maybe if you saw he was genuinely repentant—trying hard to turn his life around—the idea of trusting him might not seem so inconceivable."

"But I don't want to see him!"

"Surely at some stage you'll want to give him the chance to level with you? Surely it's vital that you should find out the whole truth? If you were to visit him at the Maudsley—"

"You're out of your mind," I said, and walked out.

XIV

"Nicholas drove me up the wall again," I said to Alice. I was in such a state that I could hardly speak, and when I did manage to spew out some more words I was unable to censor myself. "He delivers all this stuff about me forgiving Kim and making the relationship viable, but he seems to have no idea how bloody offensive this is to me after watching what he gets up to in his private life! Damn it, there he is, giving you a hard time and apparently repenting of nothing, while you keep forgiving him when you should be kicking his teeth in!"

"But Carter—"

"And how does he have the nerve to tell me my marriage is viable when he's busy telling you— on his good days—that his own marriage is over? Why can't my marriage be over too? Why can't I go off and find happiness with someone else, just as he has?"

"Carter dear, you must see Lewis—you're so upset that you're getting everything mixed up—"

"If I see another clergyman tonight I'll go berserk!" I shouted, but Alice, with admirable determination, was already buzzing Lewis on the intercom.

XV

"I can't help thinking these persistent failures with you must be very good for Nicholas," mused Lewis. "The ego of a successful healer does need to be deflated on a regular basis, but since he's supposed to be good for you and not vice versa, that comment is hardly relevant."

We were in the main kitchen on the ground floor and I was sitting slumped at the table while Lewis was padding around making tea. Reflecting the lateness of the hour he was wearing an ancient

451

claret-coloured dressing-gown over faded green pyjamas. I had apologised for disturbing him, but when he had taken the interruption in his stride I had remembered Tucker's remark that some people found chaos stimulating.

"If I continue to think of Nicholas I'll burst a blood vessel," I said. "So why don't you yourself tell me what you think of those questions I posed him?"

"You want the unvarnished truth?"

"What else?"

"Very well, let me see if I can avoid inciting you to new heights of wrath. At least I have the advantage that my wife's now dead and I'm not contemplating a trip to the altar."

"I know I should blot Nicholas's private life out of my mind when I'm talking to him, but—"

"My dear," said Lewis, "why on earth should you? If a priest's private life is in disarray, it's going to affect his work and muddy the pastoral waters. How can it be other than an upsetting distraction for those who require help with their own private lives? Now, sit down, take some deep breaths and relax with your tea...can I give you some whisky on the side?"

"You can do anything you like, Lewis, so long as you stop calling me 'my dear.'"

He sighed and trundled off to retrieve the whisky bottle.

XVI

"First of all," said Lewis briskly, "let me tell you that you're asking the wrong questions, and if Nicholas wasn't in a sub-standard state as the result of trying to cope with his complicated private life, this fact would be as clear to him as it is to me. At present we have no way of knowing whether the marriage is viable because we have insufficient information—so forget the marriage for the moment, put it on ice. The real question you should be asking is whether any relationship between you and Kim is remotely possible. Could you, for example, meet him and utter the words: 'How are you?' I think it would be very difficult for you even to get this far, but I think too that I can come up with a motive which would encourage you to try. However, I'll get to that in a minute. Let me just explain why your second question's also a non-starter.

"'Is Kim a victim or a villain?' you ask, with a touching faith that a clear-cut answer is available, but it's perfectly possible for him to be both. He could well be a victim of that Nazi past and those unpleasant parents, but he could also have chosen later of his own free will to do evil things. I must tell you straight away that I don't go along with this pathetic modern habit of blaming all one's wrong-doings on a difficult past and refusing to accept responsibility for one's actions. In my opinion such a fudging of the truth does the soul no good at all.

"The real question here, you mark my words, is not whether Kim's a victim or a villain. It's whether or not he's a psychopath. The doctors at the hospital have concluded that he's not, and as I said to you in one of our earlier conversations, that's good news—if it's true. Personally I prefer to keep an open mind in this sort of case; I think it's safer, particularly when severe spiritual illness is present. And let me just say, in case you've been too influenced by those

Hitchcock films you like so much, that the typical psychopath isn't an axe-swinging murderer! The truth is you've probably met dozens of psychopaths in the course of your work because they often do wonderfully well in big business; they flourish in an amoral environment. They need never get into trouble with the law, particularly if they're clever, and they can be very attractive to the opposite sex—although no relationship lasts long. And now I see you're about to remind me that Kim was married to Sophie for over twenty years! But how long was that marriage a going concern? How soon after the wedding did he start to be unfaithful to her?

"Now, we're talking here of a serious personality disorder which is notoriously difficult to treat. If Kim's *not* a psychopath—if he knows the difference between right and wrong and can empathise with other people sufficiently to be able to form genuine relationships—then it would certainly be possible for him to reject Mrs. Mayfield, embark on a new life and work with you to save the marriage. But if he *is* a psychopath, we're looking at a much bleaker prognosis, and I doubt if the marriage could survive no matter how strenuously you made a habit of forgiving him—as Sophie did for so many years. Of course with the grace of God anything's possible, and I don't want to say that psychopaths can never receive any degree of healing, but the main problem, from your point of view, would be that Kim wouldn't be the man you thought you'd married. In fact Roman Catholics might well say you were entitled to a nullity in such circumstances... But let's put the marriage firmly back on ice, where it belongs at present, and refocus on the question of whether any relationship with Kim is now possible.

"I said a moment ago that you'd need a strong motive even to say: 'How are you?' but the motive does exist and it's this: you've got to find out, once and for all, what kind of a man he is and what he did in the past because if you don't find out you'll be so haunted by an obsessive desire to speculate that you could wind up with serious problems. I also think that only when we know the full story will we really be in a position to judge whether or not he's a psychopath.

"Let me add that you don't have to see him at the Maudsley. (Nicholas was wrong to suggest this.) Kim does want to see you, but not, I think, when he's in circumstances which suggest he's weak and powerless. If I'm reading between the lines correctly, he's relieved that you don't want to visit him at present. So it seems to me that the best solution is for you both to meet at the Healing Centre after he's been discharged from hospital, and then you can talk to him in the presence of others who'll help you discern where the truth lies."

He stopped speaking and for a moment we were silent as I digested his advice, but finally I asked: "You've been seeing him regularly. I respect the fact that you're keeping an open mind, but how has he actually seemed to you?"

"I was afraid you'd ask that," said Lewis.

XVII

He poured us some more tea and added another tot of whisky to my glass. "The problem is I have to be careful to respect the confidentiality rules here," he said. "I did start my visits to Kim as a mere sympathetic acquaintance, but we struck up more of a rapport than I anticipated and the fact that I'm a priest now definitely features in the relationship. (I'm afraid the chaplaincy team were right to suspect me of trespassing on their territory.)

"However, although I can't say much about my conversations with Kim, I'd like to underline my original opinion that he's spiritually sick. As I see it, his personality's become so warped by his commitment to Mrs. Mayfield's world that he's become morally desensitised—he's reached the point where wrong-doing fails to arouse normal, healthy feelings of guilt. I say this not as the result of my recent conversations with him but as the result of his past behaviour to you and Sophie, and this personality damage explains why it's difficult to judge whether or not he's a psychopath; in my view he's capable of behaving like one even if, technically, he doesn't meet the medical definition of the condition.

"I have to say he's always charming now whenever I visit the hospital, and I often think—hope—certainly pray—that I'm getting somewhere with him, but at the same time I have to be very careful not to be tempted to make assumptions that simply aren't true. The seamy explanation for all the charm is that he's trying to manipulate me in the hope that I'll further his cause with you. I do want to think well of him, but I'm still gauging the extent of the damage to his personality, and I need time for the survey to be completed.

"And talking of manipulation, I must confess that I still have my doubts about this breakdown of his. It's a subject we've never touched on in our conversations, so I'm still free to voice an opinion, and my opinion, frankly, is that the breakdown couldn't have been more convenient. It allowed him to avoid the police while they were establishing there was no forensic evidence to prove either that Sophie was murdered or that he was the murderer, and when they were finally allowed to tiptoe into the hospital to talk to him in the presence of a doctor, it ensured the questioning was low-key. Also, the breakdown virtually guaranteed that any charge relating to Eric's injury would be dropped, and when you eventually discuss that final scene in your flat it will enable Kim to say to you: 'I'm sorry, but I was out of my mind and not responsible for my actions.'

"I can see you're trying to calculate how likely it is that he's fooled all the doctors, but the first thing to remember is that he might not have done; when a group takes some time to reach a verdict, this usually means there's at least one dissenting voice. The second thing to remember is that Kim's a clever man with exceptional lying skills. It would be difficult for him to deceive the doctors, but not, I think, impossible.

"Well, my dear—well, Carter, I have to end by saying I could be wrong to be so suspicious. I do get things wrong, of course. The first thing I said to Nicholas years ago when I was training him to use his psychic gifts properly was: 'Look in the mirror and say to yourself: "I CAN BE WRONG!"' So I must now say 'I CAN BE WRONG,' but one thing at least I can add with confidence: Kim desperately wants to be reconciled to you. This desire, I'm convinced, is genuine, and perhaps it steers us closer to the unvarnished truth of the situation than all these unpleasant suspicions I've been voicing..."

XVIII

After a tormented night I went to see Val in her office at the Healing Centre to request stronger sleeping pills, and in less than a minute I found myself confessing that Lewis's suspicions had given me insomnia.

"Listen," said Val kindly when I ground to a halt, "dear old Lewis is a great priest in many ways, and I'm sure we're all grateful to him for his past influence on Nick, who's truly exceptional, but Lewis has no medical training; he just thinks that his stint as a chaplain at that mental hospital thirty years ago gives him the expertise to diagnose the mentally ill and issue all kinds of dubious comments. He should never have said what he did to you! I must have a word with Nick and get him to rein the old boy in.

"Yes, I know Lewis did stress to you that he could be wrong, but that's exactly why he's so naughty! He seems to think that if he repeats the words 'I CAN BE WRONG' often enough, this will make it all right for him to adopt his favourite role—the maverick—and spout all kinds of wacky theories. You should hear him holding forth on the causes of homosexuality! But as I'm gay I'm naturally going to be seething.

"The trouble is that when people get old they tend to become exaggerated versions of themselves—well, I don't want to biff Lewis too hard; I'm sure I'll be exaggerated as hell by the time I'm nearly seventy, but in Lewis's case the exaggeration is having the effect of converting him from an eccentric maverick into a loose cannon. Look at the way he blew the end of that scene in your flat when Eric got stabbed! All right, I know Nick's determined to take responsibility—'the buck stops here' and all that—but let's face it, what actually happened? Lewis blasts along, gives Mayfield an earful that no woman in her right mind would stand, least of all a lethal old vixen addicted to mayhem, and wham! The whole scene explodes with disastrous results. Gil Tucker was absolutely incandescent when I met him later at the hospital—I've never seen him so angry, but of course he and Lewis have been at daggers drawn for years over the gay issue.

"But I'm digressing. Or am I? No, I'm not—I think you *should* understand all that about Lewis so that you can put his evaluation of Kim in the right context. The common-sense, down-to-earth truth is that the doctors at the Maudsley jolly well know which end is up. They've been working with Kim now for some time and he's made excellent progress—so excellent that he'll be discharged soon, although I'm sure the doctors will want him to continue as an out-patient for a few months to guard against a relapse. Certainly my instinct is to trust their judgement. But I would say that, wouldn't I? I'm a doctor.

"Okay, let me put the old professional blinkers aside for a moment and admit it *is* possible to fake illness successfully. Any doctor who's read up Münchhausen's syndrome knows that, but if I were faking mental illness I wouldn't try to do it at the Maudsley, which is stuffed with experts on mental health. Yes, the doctors *were* divided for a time about the diagnosis—but that's not uncommon, particularly in this sort of case. Kim seemed genuinely ill to me after the stabbing, and in fact I thought he was showing signs of schizophrenia, but I'm not a psychiatrist and I hope my ego isn't so big that I can't acknowledge my limitations. When the Maudsley doctors finally reached agreement I for one had no trouble accepting their expert diagnosis—and Lewis shouldn't have had trouble either.

"Sorry, I didn't catch what you said—could you...oh yes, you think it's unlikely that a tough-guy like Kim would crack, but try this scenario; it's the one Nick and I favour as it's consistent with both our disciplines.

"As we see it, Kim had a difficult upbringing which left deep fissures in his personality, but thanks to the benign British stepfather he was able to paper over the cracks and move on to function well in adult life. This meant one could meet Kim and get to know him well without realising that his personality was actually quite fragile.

"Our theory is that when he became mega-successful and began moving in an exceptionally high-powered world, his personality, always frag-ile, began to crumble under stress and he resorted to various ways of keeping it glued together. But unfortunately using sex as a cure for deep-seated emotional problems is no more a long-term solution than drink or drugs are—the sufferer just comes to need a bigger and bigger fix.

"Nick would say Kim was worshipping the wrong gods when he went down this self-destructive route and that he needed a different world-view in order to repair the damage. Now, there are many ways of looking at Christianity, but from a medical point of view I feel it's about integration, about developing and ordering the personality in such a way that you live the richest possible life. (I'm talking about real Christianity now, of course, not the genteel, bloodless Christianity which the media love to slag off.) It's interesting to me as a scientist to see how— okay, I can sense you're thinking this is irrelevant, but I promise you it's not. I'm chugging back in a straight line to Kim.

"The Christian process looks like this: you centre yourself on the concept of a loving, creative God, and if you're centred correctly, this alignment somehow produces visible beneficial results—it enables you to turn outwards to help other people while at the same time it balances you inwardly so that you can fulfil your human potential. It's a very *healing* process, particularly for those who aren't well integrated.

"Our theory is that Kim picked the wrong form of healing for his emotional problems, and that Mayfield finally shattered his fragile personality. However, with the right medical help there's no reason why the personality shouldn't be reassembled, and with the right spiritual help alongside the right medical help Kim could well be on his way to a new life and a much healthier existence.

"Oh, and talking of mental health, can I just state firmly that Kim's not a psychopath? The sociopath (to use the modern term) can't relate to people properly, but Kim seems to relate to you—yes, I know he did a lot wrong, but his emotions seem to be normal here, they're the sort of emotions which husbands who love their wives do display. Frankly I think Lewis's nightmare that Kim could be a super-cunning villain is way over the top and doesn't fit the clinical picture of Kim at all.

"Does the marriage have a future? Well, I think you should take a look at Kim in a controlled environment with other people present—at least dear old Lewis got *that* right! At the moment all your fears and anxieties are clubbing together to promote a horrific image which probably doesn't have much connection with reality, and if you were to see him again you might well be pleasantly surprised and enormously relieved. Whether the marriage is ultimately viable remains to be seen, but I do hope the two of you can make it back together again because personally I think marriage is a great institution. I just wish the Church sanctioned it for gays..."

XIX

"Right," said Robin when I kept my appointment with him that morning at eleven o'clock. "I can see you're now strong enough to grapple with the reality of Kim's approaching discharge from hospital. But unfortunately I can't answer these questions you're posing about his true nature and the future of the marriage because they require from me some kind of psychological evaluation, and as Kim and I have never met, any opinion I might put forward about his psychology is professionally worthless. But what I can do, if you like, is to highlight some areas which you might find helpful to consider.

"Okay? Fine. The first area I'd like to focus on is Kim's early life. You said he seemed to hate his parents, but this is fairly unusual. Even if one's parents drive one to drink there's usually, in

462

normal people, a deep connectedness which jus-
tifies the old saying 'blood is thicker than water.'
In fact a person can feel this deep connectedness
even with the most frightful parents, so if Kim
shows no sign of connectedness, this could be a
marker of abnormality.

"The second area I'd like to focus on is his sex
life. There seems to be a discrepancy here—and
I'm not talking about the impotence which led
him to seek Mrs. Mayfield's help many years
ago; I find it plausible that although his guilt about
Sophie reduced him to impotence he eventually recovered. I'm talking about the discrepancy
between the sex life he must have been leading
directly before he met you and the sex life you
and he have shared together. In Mrs. Mayfield's
group he would probably have participated in a
wide range of activities on both sides of the traditional line which marks the perverted from
the normal, yet you've told me that apart from
the last time he made love to you he was very
straightforward in bed; you said what a relief that
was to you, and of course I quite understood
because in this era of no-holds-barred sex-romps
the most degrading behaviour is passed off as
normal, particularly on the singles scene. I do a
lot of counselling with casualties in that area.

"But what was the real explanation behind
Kim's restraint with you? I find it odd that he's
been so unadventurous. Maybe stress did affect
his sex-drive, just as he says, but macho men love
to show off their macho skills. Which reminds me:
what exactly was it about that final bedroom
scene which enabled macho man to show off
his skills at last?

"And this leads me to the third area I'd like to

focus on: how does Kim see you? What do you represent to him? We know he loves you, but is this a realistic or a romantic love? I must say at once that romantic love is commonly found among all types of extremely normal people, but from a psychological point of view it does involve a distortion, a projection on the beloved of qualities which may not be there at all. Is Kim seeing a projection or is he seeing the real you? He may be sincere in saying he loves you and it may be the real you that he loves, but if he's in love with a projection, that could cast a dubious light on the situation, particularly when one remembers that the dark side of romantic love is neurotic obsession.

"The fourth area I'd like to focus on is Kim's talent as a liar. Lewis fastened on this but seems not to have considered that there are different types of liars, some normal and some abnormal. At one end of the range are the people who tell a fib every now and then, usually so as not to hurt someone or to smooth over an awkward social situation. In the middle of the range there are both people who lie because they can't cope with some particular reality and people who lie because they can't cope with reality in general. And at the extreme end of the range there are abnormal people for whom lying is a way of life—they lie for fun, they lie to get what they want, they lie because truth is unimportant to them. What kind of a liar is Kim?

"We know he's been lying to cover up certain facts, but this isn't unusual; many normal people do this, particularly respectable people who slip up and then can't admit to others that they're in a jam. But Kim's lying seems more extensive. In order to live a double life with Sophie for years he must have developed a talent for lying to the back teeth. Does this talent indicate abnormality? Maybe this still doesn't put him in the same league as the sociopath Mrs. Mayfield, for whom lying is clearly as natural as breathing, but it could nonetheless represent a substantial problem.

"I point all this out as an alternative to the two current explanations of Kim's behaviour: the explanation that he's a sociopath and the explanation that he's normal but temporarily sick. It's possible that he's not a sociopath yet not normal either; the Maudsley doctors would be right to diagnose no serious mental illness, but even so the word 'normal' wouldn't stretch far enough to cover him. This is where the concept of spiritual sickness would become particularly relevant, but I'm not qualified to talk about that. Suffice it to say that in the shadowy borderland between the mad and the bad, there are cases which orthodox medicine finds difficult to treat and heal.

"And talking of shadowy borderlands, the final area I want to focus on concerns a point which the priests don't seem to have picked up: the death of the blackmailer after falling under a train. There are cases which show it's possible to will someone to death—the evidence is clear among tribes such as the Aborigines, and cases have also been reported in the Western world. It's like an inverted form of prayer; instead of wishing people well, you wish them ill. It works on the power of suggestion, and human beings are very suggestible. Is it possible that Mrs. Mayfield took care of both the blackmailer and Sophie for Kim by willing them to death? Far-fetched, you say?

Out of the question? But think of your own vulnerability to Mrs. Mayfield's suggestions! In high-stress circumstances even the most balanced and sophisticated people can be brainwashed into acting out of character, and I think it's interesting that Mrs. Mayfield should be attracted to such a malign form of mind control; it certainly makes one wonder what Kim's been getting up to during all the years of his association with her.

"Well, those are the areas I want to highlight, the areas which I think might repay further reflection as you sort out your thoughts. All that remains for me to say is that I do think you need to know the whole truth about Kim in order to make the right decision about the future, and you won't uncover that truth by keeping your distance from him. How would you feel about seeing him here at the Healing Centre so that we can all give you a helping hand? It strikes me that you have nothing to lose by doing that and everything to gain—but of course the final decision must be yours and yours alone..."

XX

That evening a fax arrived at the Rectory. After giving details of his flight home that Friday Tucker added: "...and I'll be arriving two hours after St. Gilbert leaves for the Algarve to pacify the apoplectic parents. Is there any chance you can meet me at the airport? I've long yearned to be conveyed from Heathrow to the City in a scarlet Porsche driven by a very cool blonde, but if this dream is destined to remain unfulfilled, please leave word at the information desk. Meanwhile I live in hope. By the way, just as I'm

466

about to leave I find an American neighbour who has a fax! Why didn't I realise earlier that a Yank would be unable to live without the right technology? The PortuPlonk must have addled my brain, but I'm sure a few Porsche fumes will quickly reverse the damage. Yours resurrected, E. T."

XXI

I saw him as soon as he emerged from Customs. He was pushing a trolley stacked with suitcases and duty-free shopping bags, and his white jeans were topped by a vivid green polo shirt. It was very hot in the terminal, even hotter than it was outside. The torrid summer of 1990 was finally shifting into top gear.

I was wearing a pale blue sleeveless dress, skimpy, very plain and made of some wonder-fabric which never creased, not even when the temperature made linen look like corrugated iron in less than five minutes. My small shoulder-bag was as white as my high-heeled sandals. I wore no jewellery apart from my wedding-ring; my necklace of white beads was valueless. I was made up very carefully to look as if I wasn't made up at all.

Tucker's dark hair seemed much redder and I wondered if this signified an overdose of sunlight, but he was not noticeably tanned. Perhaps I was just more aware of that red-haired gene of his which would make prolonged exposure to a hot southern sun undesirable. I noticed at once that he had lost weight. The chunky look had been replaced by a streamlined physique which killed all resemblance to an overgrown cherub. As he had warned me, he was cleanshaven; Mrs. Tucker's conservative tastes and maternal demands had resulted in the disappearance of both the lusciously hirsute Bohemian who had tended me at St. Eadred's Vicarage and the dramatically pale Pre-Raphaelite invalid who had been languishing in the hospital bed. He looked fit, taut and tough.

When he saw me he smiled.

For one long moment I forgot how to breathe.

Then I nearly passed out amidst the onslaught of an unprecedented sexual desire.

SEVENTEEN

We do not need to drown in what overwhelms us.

DAVID F. FORD
The Shape of Living

I

"E. T., I presume."

"All ready for the Close Encounters, Ms. G! What's this?"

"My hand. I thought you might want to shake it."

"But don't I get to kiss the air on either side of your head?"

"I had no idea you got your kicks out of kissing air, Tucker. Don't you find it rather insubstantial?"

I was, of course, on autopilot, hardly aware of what I was saying. Only the experience of many business meetings when I had perfected the art of staying ice-cool and glass-smooth in searing circumstances was now preventing me from liquefying into a white-hot mess. All the nerve-endings in the pit of my stomach were rippling. My heart was beating hard enough to bust a valve. I was stupefied. In fact I was shocked to the core.

It is one thing to like a man a great deal, to appreciate his particular brand of sexuality and to indulge in some dead-pan bantering which appeals to one's sense of humour. It is quite another to encounter that same man and want to rush straight to the nearest bed. However the next moment lust had been overtaken by fright. I told myself I was retreating from my marital disaster into a fantasy. I told myself the disordered feelings were merely reflecting my disordered life. I told myself that whichever way one cut the cake I was grabbing the nutty slice. But no matter what I told myself I knew I now had a far more serious problem than feeling compelled to sob against a male chest.

Meanwhile Tucker was saying casually: "You're looking good!" And he smiled again.

"Thanks. You too," I said in my crispest voice, and glanced down at his duty-free shopping bags. I found myself gazing at them as if I had never seen a duty-free shopping bag before.

"It's really good of you to meet me like this!" he exclaimed, very friendly. "Can I buy you a drink before we start out?"

I murmured a monosyllable indicating substantial confusion.

469

"You're not keen on a drink-drive situation? Okay, let's postpone the booze till we get back to Fleetside."

I remember thinking that whatever happened I had to avoid the vodka martinis.

We set off to the car park. I asked politely after his health and he said he was fine. He asked politely after my health and I said I was still in one piece.

"And what a piece!" he said with a touch of his old flirtatiousness, but then without allowing me time to reply, he started to talk about his parents, their villa and his convalescence. This smoothly crafted stream of chat took us all the way to the car park's pay-machine.

"...and so all I did was swim and exercise as much as the doctor recommended. Nothing else to do. Couldn't write with the parents twittering around. Couldn't think of anything except what might or might not be going on in London. Couldn't talk to the parents about anything—I told them I was too traumatised, but fortunately Gil had long since given them a sanitised version of events... Hey, Ms. G, if only you'd waited instead of shooting in front of me like that, *I* would have paid for the parking!"

"Forget it—just give me a mega-drink when we hit the Vicarage," I said, but at once began to speculate fearfully about the contents of the duty-free shopping bags.

I was still trying to work out what excuse I could give to avoid all alcohol when Tucker was diverted by the sight of my Porsche.

"That car," he said, "gives the sin of covetousness a whole new dimension."

"Nice, isn't it?" I managed to issue a casual apology for the lack of storage space but when I slid behind the steering-wheel I was in such a state that I could hardly fit the key in the ignition. Meanwhile Tucker was stowing his hand-luggage in the minuscule boot and sliding his cases into the cramped area behind the front seats. A moment later he had scrambled into the passenger seat and slammed the door.

There was a silence which seemed to last a full minute but was probably no more than five seconds. Then he said—and his whole manner was quite altered: "Carter."

I dared not look at him. Instead I looked at the ignition key, deep in its narrow slot.

He said in a low voice: "I know I've been droning drivel to spike the tension, but you mustn't think I've forgotten you're going through hell and you mustn't think I just dragged you out here so that I could get a free ride home. I really need to see you—talk to you—help you in any way I can... Are you all right?"

"Fine," I said at once. "Fine. If I seem slightly brain-dead it's because I'm just so...well, so relieved to see that you're fully recovered and looking so...well, so..." My voice trailed away.

"Yes." The single syllable wrapped up the whole situation and sparked a moment of word-less communication in which a number of emotions surfaced. I still did not dare to look at him, but I heard him say in that quiet, level voice: "There's one other thing you mustn't think I've forgotten, Carter. I haven't forgotten you're married."

I covered my face with my hands.

"That's why I didn't call," he said. "That's why I just sent postcards. That's why I agreed to go to the Algarve. Even I, dumb as I've been about women in the past, could see that you were so bruised by all the marital chaos that the last thing you needed was to deal with me when I was toked up on testosterone. Gil spelled it all out to me when I was in hospital but he didn't have to. I work at St. Benet's. I know that the one thing that's absolutely taboo is to mess with the vulnerable people who seek help there."

I let my hands rest on the wheel. "What did Gil say?"

"He said: 'The marriage could still work out. If it doesn't you need to be sure that's no fault of yours. Her needs come first here, and if you forget that it's abuse.'"

"So you remembered."

"So I remembered. And I'm still remembering, but I had to come back, Carter. When I read between the lines of your postcards and realised how tough things were, I called Gil and said: 'Look, I'm a big boy now. I'm coming home to be a mature adult and if you don't like it you can sod off.' 'Give me your word you'll do nothing stupid,' he said, 'and I'll sod off anywhere you like,' and that was when I begged him to sort out the parents. He was due to visit them for a weekend anyway— he always does when they're out there. No services at St. Eadred's on a weekend, of course. It's a Guild church like St. Benet's."

I suddenly found it much easier to speak. "But why were your parents working themselves into such a snit?"

"They're still recovering from the shock that I nearly snuffed it and they've convinced themselves they'll have no peace until they've steered me into a radically different lifestyle. My father says he can get me a job teaching history at a prep school in Winchester, and my mother says she knows a nice girl who—well, when she started telling me I had to stay on at the villa to meet the Grantly-Pattersons who were arriving with their unmarried daughter at the weekend... Carter, I couldn't cope. I was going fruity-toots."

"Fruity-loops," I said, finally managing to look at him.

"I think I prefer fruity-toots," said Tucker. "It's perkier."

At that point we laughed, and afterwards I found I was no longer frightened of being destroyed by another melt-down. The sexual desire was still there but I was calm because I was no longer afraid he would exploit it. Control had been restored to me. A safe space had been created in the middle of the emotional minefield. For the time being at least I was preserved from bad decisions, unwise impulses and flea-brained behaviour which would leave me feeling even more trashed than I felt already.

At last I said: "I'm so glad you're back, Tucker. But it's still such a war zone."

"Relax, Ms. G! Your trusty PA is here to give you moral, repeat *moral*, support."

I finally succeeded in launching us on our journey to the City.

III

We talked little on the journey because I said I

needed to concentrate on the task of driving in heavy traffic, but as soon as we reached the Vicarage we retired to the kitchen, a huge, dreary room which looked out on a blackened wall, and I began to relax. By mutual consent we passed up the vodka and opened a bottle of Chablis which Tucker found in the refrigerator. He also found various items from the food department of Marks and Spencer, the collection thoughtfully acquired with dinner for two in mind.

"St. Gilbert's been at work again," said Tucker. "He'll soon have to wear a neck-brace to support the halo." Lighting the oven he started to read the instructions on the back of a package containing Cumberland pie.

We were alone in the house. Gil had two lodgers, both theology students at King's College in the Strand, but the long vacation had begun at London University and the students had returned to their homes in the provinces.

While the food heated and I talked, the white wine disappeared, accompanied by liberal amounts of Perrier water, and by the time Tucker had finished cooking some vegetables, we had made the decision to switch to claret. "I know the weather's really too hot for red wine," said Tucker, "but Gil's an oenophile. His friendly gay wine merchant gives him amazing stuff at a huge discount."

We ate. To my surprise I found I was hungry, and we both agreed that there was something very comforting about Marks and Spencer's transformation of basic British fodder into a home-grown *haute cuisine*.

After the main course we sampled some cheese as I continued to bring him up to date with all that had happened; fortunately, as I had now levelled with the police, I could even tell him about my ordeal at Oakshott. As a trained listener he never bombarded me with his own views and never passed judgement either on me or on anyone else, but eventually I found that this faultlessly professional behaviour made me want to scream with irritation.

"Tucker, unless you put your cards on the table in twenty seconds and tell me what you really think," I yelped at last, "I'm going to send you straight back to the Algarve to Ms. Grantly-Patterson!"

Tucker was most alarmed. "But when I did my listening course, courtesy of the Acorn Trust, I was taught—"

"Hey, you're a great listener, the best, but right now I don't want a St. Benet's Befriender, I want a PA who's not afraid to dish out some hard-headed opinions! So lay them on the line right now by telling me (a) what you think goes on with Kim, and (b) what the hell I should do next."

"I love it when you (a) and (b) me, Ms. G. Coffee?"

"Yeah, and make it sugarless, black as pitch and strong enough to make an elephant levitate."

He laughed, delighted to be reminded of our office dialogues—and delighted too, perhaps, to see me finally regaining my equilibrium despite the stress of telling my story.

Then he began to talk.

IV

"I'm sure you'll make the necessary allowances for my prejudice," said Tucker, "but to be honest, I thought Kim was a bastard. When he said: 'I'm Mr. Betz to you, sonny,' I wanted to shove my fist straight into his face, and when he stuck that knife into me I wasn't too pleased either. But if I can now make a big effort to move beyond these obvious comments, I have to admit my first impression of him was that he was formidable, a real corporate bruiser. I've seen a number of corporate bruisers during my adventures as a PersonPower International serf, and I'm sure I have far more experience of this type of male than any of the St. Benet's crew.

"Now, don't get me wrong—I'm not saying Nick, Lewis, Robin and Val are naïve, but the trouble is that the Healing Centre deals primarily with the damaged. It's just the same with a conventional medical practice. Most healthy people never go near a doctor, so the doctor's experience is primarily with the unwell.

"I think this syndrome lies at the root of what's happening here—I think this is why every opinion you've received about Kim from the St. Benet's crowd misses the mark. These people are great at what they do but they're used to clients who could never even begin to function at Kim Betz's level. I doubt if a real boardroom barracuda like Kim has ever swum into their orbit before.

"Carter, surely the point about Kim is that he's a survivor on the grand scale? Whatever happened to him in the past he survived it brilliantly, so brilliantly that he became a very high achiever. I'm sorry, but I just don't believe Val and Nick's theory that Kim has a—quote—'fragile' personality. That man's about as fragile as an iron bar. You and I both know that high flyers don't survive year after year in the heart of the City jungle unless they're ten times smarter and tougher than anyone else on the block. How come a barracuda never winds up bitten in two? Because he always bites before he can be bitten.

"And what does this mean? It means Kim's capable of doing just about anything which will enable him to survive. He doesn't have to be a psychopath. He'd know the difference between right and wrong, but when the chips were down morality would just become an irrelevance.

"I don't see him having any problem about leading a double life during the marriage to Sophie. If we assume that Sophie was an early version of the trophy wife who gave him the image he needed, I can see him being satisfied with her for years without loving her in the least. The satisfaction wouldn't include sexual satisfaction, but that wouldn't bother him—he'd slip into a double life as easily as I used to slip into that swimming-pool every day at the villa. Of course the VD disaster would have rocked him, but he'd smooth that over and go on as before. I mean, this is a real bruiser we're talking about, a real barracuda! Survival's his business, and that's why in the end, when Sophie finally turned on him, he'd be prepared to go to any lengths to bust his way out of that tight corner.

"Do I think he killed her? Sure, why not? She'd fulfilled her purpose anyway, and now his taste in trophy wives had changed. Was he going to let her get in his way? Hell, no! And I'm sure he reacted in just the same way to the blackmailer. Do I think he killed this man? You bet. If anyone asks to be liquidated it's the fool who tries to blackmail Kim Betz. Oh, and incidentally I don't believe the story that he was blackmailed for years and lost a huge chunk of capital. Boardroom barracudas don't behave like doormats. They sharpen up their teeth and move in for the big bite. How do I explain the fact that Kim's nowhere near as rich as he should be? That's easy. He's still got the money he ought to have—less a few thousands to Mother Mayfield—but it's set aside in a numbered account in Switzerland in case he ever needs to make a quick getaway. Like father, like son.

"So much for Sophie and the blackmailer. Now we come to you. It's obvious you're the new trophy wife, designed to show all those other corporate bruisers that he can still cut it with a gorgeous blonde despite the fact that he's pushing fifty hard enough to break a wrist. But an additional bonus to Kim is your intelligence. I'll bet he got so bored with Sophie's ignorance of the legal scene, but now he doesn't have to be bored any longer—and better still, he doesn't need to waste time trawling elsewhere for sex. Life's suddenly vivid, vital, vibrant! He's really, really keen on this new trophy, so keen that he's jealous as hell when she acquires a heterosexual male secretary for a couple of weeks. But is he actually keen on you—*you*—Carter Graham?

"You've got to be kidding. The only person he cares about deep down is himself.

"All right, I've shot my mouth off, I'm frothing with jealousy, I'm sweating loathing from every pore. But before you dismiss me as just another novelist who's let his imagination run away with him, let me assure you that I know about people. I don't know how I know, but I know that I do know. Lewis thinks it's some *idiot savant* form of ESP. Nick thinks it's the creative spark batting around in the unconscious. But whatever the explanation I can look at people with X-ray vision whenever I'm booted up and ready to go.

"I'd just like to add a postscript by saying— or should I stop? Maybe I've handed out as much as you can take, and...okay, you want the postscript straight up with no frills.

"We all agreed my stabbing was an accident. We all agreed there was no way Kim could have foreseen that rapid sequence which resulted from Mother Mayfield's freak-out. Lewis, who speaks German, told me that Mrs. Mayfield did call to Kim for help at the end, but he'd barely had the chance to react when I came flying at him like a cannon-ball. So of course we were all going to think the stabbing was entirely accidental—there was no time for it to be anything else...or was there?

"The truth is there's an alternative scenario tucked into that scene, and you'll see it if you focus on Kim's behaviour during that dialogue between Nick and Mrs. Mayfield. Do you remember that he made no contribution to the conversation and seemed to be acting like a zombie? The St. Benet's crew, drawing on their experience of people with fragile personalities, leaped to the conclusion that he was in the first stage of a breakdown, but if you discard the theory that Kim's a fragile little flower, you start to wonder what he was up to. I think he held on to the knife not because Mrs. Mayfield had converted him into a tame robot but because he'd decided to do me harm if he was lucky enough to get the chance to make it look like an accident—and obviously the first step to faking an accident was to start behaving like a zombie.

"It's even possible that Mrs. Mayfield colluded with this behaviour in order to make Nick believe Kim wasn't dangerous. Maybe when she asserted to Nick that Kim belonged to her she was just hamming it up for the exorcist. After all, she and Kim started out as equal partners in that final scene—look how they worked together to get me to produce the files! That was quite a double act they had going there, and maybe they kept it going right up to the end.

"Remember, Kim had picked up the chemistry between us. He even suspected us of sleeping together, and if he really thought I'd made a successful raid on his trophy, I reckon he'd yearn to liquidate me. At the very least he'd yearn for the chance to give me a non-fatal stab.

"The truth is I think Kim's lethal, Carter, and regardless of what happens between us I think you should stay away from him both now and in the future. Or, as the typical author says to the long-suffering editor when queries are raised about the manuscript: 'I'm right and everyone else is wrong...'"

V

"You're very persuasive," I said, "but there's got to be a flaw in your theory. I can't believe I could have been involved with Kim for so many months without realising he was a monster."

"Why not? This man's an old hand at the double life and an accomplished liar. Just because you didn't cotton on to him straight away doesn't mean you were dumb, Carter. It just underlines how formidable he is to take in a woman like you."

"Yes, but—"

"Okay, there *is* a flaw in my theory that the stabbing was intentional, and if I'm honest I've got to admit it. Can you remember what happened after Nick told Kim to put down the knife? Kim transferred the knife from his left hand to his right and used his left hand to wipe his forehead. Then he transferred the knife back to his left hand again."

"So?"

"The point is that if he'd been waiting, poised for the opportunity to attack me in a way which could be passed off as an accident, he'd have kept the knife in his right hand, wouldn't he? He'd have wanted to be ready to strike."

"But he was," I said, and my voice was horrified. "He's left-handed."

VI

After a long silence I said: "You've certainly spun a nightmare scenario appropriate for a writer of fiction. But something tells me real life isn't as colourful as that."

"But truth is always stranger than fiction! If a novelist can imagine it, you can bet someone's out there doing it—and in even more glorious Technicolor!"

I did not answer. I just stared down into my empty coffee-cup.

Finally Tucker said: "Have we reached the point where you deliver your own verdict on Kim?"

"Believe me, I'd like nothing more than to make up my mind but I don't see how I can do that without knowing what it is he's trying to hide."

"So what you're saying is—"

"I've got to see him. That's the one thing Nicholas, Lewis, Robin and Val all agree on, and I'm sure they're right. I've got to excavate this truth."

"At the Healing Centre, in a safe, controlled environment?"

I ran my fingers through my hair in despair. "But can't you see? Such a meeting would be worse than useless! This is where your view of Kim as the boardroom barracuda fuses with the Kim I know, and I can tell you that he'll never reveal the whole truth now unless he and I are on our own. He's fought too hard to conceal this information for it to be anything less than dynamite, and if you think there's any hope that he'll confess everything meekly in front of a bunch of witnesses—"

"But what are you going to do?"

"See him on his own, of course."

"You're fruity-toots," said Tucker appalled.

VII

My plan, which had been steadily evolving during my interviews with the Healing Centre's personnel, was in fact a model of reason and logic. First I would write to Kim with apologies for my long silence and say that now I was feeling better I was anxious to give him a helping hand, even though I was not quite ready to resume married life; would he like me to pick him up in the Mercedes when he was discharged from hospital?

Lewis had told me that Kim was willing to live at the Oakshott house while I made up my mind about the future. In a startling but characteristically moral move, Sophie, who had gone to great lengths to deprive him of the house at the time of the divorce, had restored the place to him in the new will she had made afterwards. Apparently she had reasoned that having made the statement that he had deserved to lose the property, she should acknowledge at her death that the house had been acquired solely with his money.

"...and after suggesting the pick-up from the hospital," I was explaining to Tucker, "I'll offer to drive him to Oakshott. In my letter I'll make it all seem perfectly natural, so natural that he'll never suspect he's being set up for truth-extraction—I'll say: 'This way you'll not only get your car back immediately but I'll have demonstrated that I want to be constructive about the future. Hoping you find this suggestion helpful, darling—thinking of you constantly__'"

"This plan stinks."

I was exasperated. "So what do you want me to do? Give you a rose to smell?"

"What's the name of that old movie—the one where the cool blonde is all alone in the isolated house with the husband who can't wait to strangle her?"

"Very funny! Look, if you think I'm going the whole way to Oakshott, you're nuts. I'm going to bail out long before then, and if you'd only listen quietly instead of whinnying like a whippet—"

"Wrong verb. Horses whinny. Whippets whine."

"Oh, stop trying to edit me, I'm not a manuscript! Damn it, Tucker, what's your problem? You think I can't handle corporate bruisers? You think I've never squared up to one of these guys before? Hell, in the past I've twisted every tooth from a boardroom barracuda with one hand tied behind my back!"

"Oh my God," said Tucker in an actor's aside. "The next line's going to be: 'My penis is bigger than yours is.'"

"Now just you listen to me—"

"No, just you listen to *me*, Ms. Graham! If you think I'm going to let you put this crazy scheme of yours into action—"

"But you haven't yet heard the whole plan! Now calm down and stop yelping—and while you're doing that, why don't we stop drinking black coffee? We're so wired now that we could generate enough electricity to floodlight St. Paul's."

"How about some Scotch?"

"That's the first sensible thing you've said for some time."

He mixed two modest Scotches and filled both glasses to the brim with water.

Then we resumed our battle.

VIII

"Please try to bear in mind," I said, "that this is a thoroughly rational plan made by someone who has a legally trained mind and who is now bored with her temporary role of helpless, water-logged fluffette. I'm rising like a phoenix from the ashes."

"I'm getting confused with all these creatures which are roaming around," complained Tucker. "We've had whippets that whinny, toothless barracudas and now, for crying out loud, we've got an ashy phoenix! Can't we just put them all in the nearest zoo and focus on how you survive your husband?"

I ignored him to resume my presentation. "Let me just remind you of a couple of things," I said. "First of all Lewis has been busy convincing Kim that he—Kim—has to level with me if the marriage is to have a future, and I believe Kim himself will come to see this is the only way forward—provided that he and I can be alone together when confession time comes around. Second, it's vital that Kim should think I'm one hundred per cent sincere instead of ambivalent as hell—otherwise I'll get nowhere. And that's why the meeting mustn't seem engineered in any way; it's got to flow naturally out of the situation and what could be more natural than that he should want his car transferred from Harvey Tower to that ghastly house at Oakshott? It's also natural, believe it or not, that I should offer to give him a helping hand when he comes out of hospital. The truth is we've been very close very recently, and if I now make this gesture of goodwill via a letter in which I call him 'darling' Kim's not going to find it unbelievable. The word 'darling' is a carrot, of course, leading the donkey on to...okay, okay, let's keep animals out of this. I'll just stress that although the marriage has taken some terrible knocks, marriages do recover even from the most appalling blows (someone said that to me the other day—was it Nicholas?) and since Kim's apparently keen for the relationship to recover, he'll want to believe I'm keen too. Are you with me so far?"

"Uh-huh. You turn up at the hospital, you present him with the car-keys and he drives you to a deserted spot in the Surrey Hills where he—"

"Could you save this plot for one of your

novels? Kim and I drive away from the Maudsley but he's not at the wheel—I am. How can I be sure he won't want to drive? Because according to Val, who's checked with the doctors, Kim's on a cocktail of drugs which makes driving out of the question. So I offer to drive, a move which puts me in total control—"

"When do you bail out?"

"At the Reigate exit of the M25."

"The M25? Surely that's miles out of the way!"

"Yes, but the point is that there's a hotel near the Reigate exit at the top of the hill, and I'm going to take him there for lunch—we did that once before, very successfully, when we drove into the country for a weekend spin, so there'll be a sentimental memory to make the diversion look completely natural."

"And over lunch you excavate the truth?"

"Exactly. In a public place with other people present. Then after I've extracted the truth, *no matter what the truth is*, and *even if I decide he's a blameless victim who deserves a reconciliation*, I'll pull the plug on the meeting so that I can discuss the results with the St. Benet's team. I'll tell him I just can't face that house at Oakshott—that'll be true enough—and then I'll bail out by driving away in my own car which I'll have brought down the night before and left in the hotel car park. Kim can always get a taxi to take him the last few miles to Oakshott, and meanwhile I'll be racing back to the City as fast as a bat out of—okay, forget the bat. But this is a foolproof scheme, can't you see? Raise any objection you like, Tucker, but I can't believe there's a single one I won't be able to answer..."

IX

We sipped our Scotches and argued back and forth for some time.

"Something will go wrong," said Tucker obstinately. "You'll run out of petrol on a sinister, woodsy stretch of the M25."

"Not if I've filled the tank beforehand. And anyway, why should Kim instantly want to harm me when he's so keen for a reconciliation?"

"He could be faking the desire for a reconciliation in order to get hold of you. Listen, I think you ought to be wired for sound. Then if anything goes wrong—"

"Forget it. This barracuda has a built-in radar system which is constantly scanning the horizon for signs of danger, and if he has any suspicion at all that I'm not playing straight with him his radar screen will fill with blips. I'm already planning to wear a clinging tank-top and skin-tight stretch-pants so that he can see I'm concealing nothing."

"Lucky Kim. But surely the police should be involved? After all, they must have their suspicions of him, and once he leaves hospital they're bound to welcome the chance to give him a real grilling, particularly since the inquest into Sophie's death will now be reconvened."

"Do you seriously think Kim would be unaware of a bunch of stray males hanging around the hotel and trying to eavesdrop on our conversation?"

"But if you don't tell them what you're up to, aren't you guilty of obstructing justice? If Kim killed Sophie—"

"I don't think he did. I don't think he killed her either accidentally or on purpose."

"What makes you so sure?"

"Reason and logic. If he was responsible for that death I believe he would have removed the body and dumped it somewhere so that it wouldn't have been discovered for a while. Then no one would have been able to tell exactly when she died and his alibi with Warren Schaeffer would have looked a good deal healthier."

I paused but when he said nothing I added: "I'm sorry, Tucker, but I just don't believe he's the villain you think he is. I can't imagine myself ever trusting him again, but he's my husband and not so long ago he made me very happy. In some sense, some very real sense"—I stumbled but recovered—"this slice of the chaos is just between him and me. I don't believe I'm in the middle of a Hitchcock murder film, and I don't believe I'm in the middle of one of your adventure novels either. I think this is primarily the story of a talented late-twentieth-century man who dined with the Devil and then found himself stuck with a bill which bankrupted him. I think it's about the false gods we worship in our society and about the price we pay when we flush our morals down the john. I think it's about...well, never mind all that."

I paused again, needing to drum up some strength before I could add levelly: "The legal situation's simply this: I'm not obstructing the police by concealing information; I've already told them all I know. I'm not perverting the course of justice by scheming to prevent Kim's crimes (if any) coming to light; if he admits to anything criminal I'll inform the police afterwards. Meanwhile it's not a crime to refuse to be wired for sound and it's not a crime to fail to tell the police that I'm going to have a serious talk with my husband. I'm not breaking the law, I assure you. My hands are clean."

There was another silence before Tucker said quietly: "But don't you understand, my darling, how worried I am about your safety?"

I stood up and said: "It's time to go."

X

"Sorry, I blew it. Wipe that endearment."

"I assure you I'm not fluffing out just because—"

"Carter, you're not proposing to keep this plan from Nick and Lewis, are you?"

"Of course not!"

"But do you really think they'll allow you to go through with it?"

"What's all this about 'allow'? Since when have I needed any man's permission about how to run my life?"

"Oh my God! Listen, sweet pea. The feminist nutterguff is as cute as Shirley Temple singing 'The Good Ship Lollypop,' but it's totally irrelevant here, can't you see that? Good friends are going to want to protect someone they care about, regardless of whether that someone's male, female or hermaphrodite... Are you really leaving now?"

"Yes, all this gender-talk's making me nervous. But many thanks for dinner—and for listening—"

"Are you okay to drive?"

"Sure." I had suddenly realised the sexual temperature was rising so fast that I had to make a quick exit before I reached the point of liquefaction. By this time I was in the hall. I reached out to raise the latch on the front door, but it seemed to be trapped by a security lever. Feverishly I struggled with the mechanism.

His hand slipped past me to push the lever upwards. For a second his forearm brushed mine and his free hand slipped around my waist as he stood behind me. I felt him kiss the nape of my neck but all he said was: "Bon voyage."

I gripped the hand at my waist very hard. Then I let go, wrenched open the door and blundered outside into the heavy, humid night air.

God knows how I ever made it back to the Rectory.

XI

"I hear what you say about wanting your conversation with Kim to be private," said Nicholas carefully after breakfast the next morning, "and I take your point that this private conversation will be conducted in a public place, but since many unpleasant scenes do erupt in public places, perhaps Eric's right to raise the issue of security."

It was a Saturday, and as the Healing Centre was closed Nicholas was in no rush. We were in his study at the Rectory, and Lewis was also present. The morning was very hot; the windows were open to air the room but since the City was deserted on weekends, Egg Street was eerily silent. Neither of the men was in uniform, a fact which made them look more individual, more off-beat and, in Lewis's case, younger and racier. Nicholas wore a blue T-shirt over his loosest pair of jeans, while Lewis was wearing an open-necked white shirt, sleeves rolled up, and a scruffy pair of dark trousers.

I responded to Nicholas's comments by saying: "I'm sure Kim won't harm me."

"I'm equally sure the doctors wouldn't discharge him if they thought he was dangerous," agreed Nicholas readily enough, "but nevertheless after that disaster at your flat I'm very conscious that a scene can start innocuously yet end by swinging right out of control."

"Better safe than sorry," said Lewis, allowing me no time to argue. "We can provide you with a bodyguard—there's a nice little firm in Stepney which we use when we counsel battered wives and the husbands take umbrage."

"And this could dovetail neatly with your plan," added Nicholas, following on so smoothly that I still had no chance to speak. "The bodyguard would be waiting at the hotel and could keep an eye on you during the conversation. When you stand up to go, the bodyguard could make himself known to you and you could introduce him to Kim as a chauffeur hired to complete the journey to Oakshott. This move would ensure that Kim doesn't make a scene when you leave."

"An excellent idea!" said Lewis, completing the seamless two-hander.

They turned to look at me expectantly.

I wanted to take an obstinate line, but in the clear light of day and unfortified by a liberal indulgence in wine, I felt rather less insouciant than I had felt during the dinner at St. Eadred's Vicarage.

I agreed to hire the bodyguard.

XII

"Everything's falling neatly into place," said Lewis that evening after his final visit to the Maudsley to see Kim. "He was extremely pleased

491

by your offer to deliver the Mercedes and enormously cheered when I gave him your letter—after he'd read it he told me to say he quite understood that it would take time to get the marriage back on its feet again and that meanwhile he wouldn't expect more from you than the lift to Oakshott... I had to tread carefully, since I know you're bailing out at Reigate, but my conscience is clear on that score because I know this is all part of your genuine effort to explore whether the marriage is still viable. When are you taking the Porsche down to the hotel?"

I said: "I've changed my mind about that. I don't want the Porsche to be sitting in the car park when we arrive because Kim will immediately recognise it and realise I plan to bail out, so I'm picking up a hire-car and driving it down tomorrow evening. Tucker will follow in Gil's car and bring me back."

Lewis said after a pause: "I hope young Tucker's not intending to involve himself any further in your plan."

"He accepted a ban from the scene once he knew about the bodyguard."

The conversation ceased but Lewis made no move to indicate I should leave. We were in the area of the Rectory's ground floor known as "the bedsit," a pair of interconnecting rooms which Lewis had colonised some years ago; his bedroom was in one half of the area, and his sitting-room was in the other. Both rooms were crammed with old-fashioned furniture, photographs of his daughter and her family, religious pictures, icons, a mini-altar, masses of hi-fi, and floor-to-ceiling shelves of books, vinyl records, tapes and CDs. The air was strongly infused with various smells; I could identify not only cigarettes and whisky but the air freshener which the cleaner managed to spray whenever she tricked her way in to dust any exposed surface and reintroduce the threadbare carpet to the vacuum cleaner. I was sitting in an armchair on one side of the sitting-room fireplace and trying not to sneeze. Lewis had just lit a cigarette and we were both nursing glasses of whisky-and-soda. Although his expression was benign, the coolness with which he had spoken of Tucker had put me on my guard, and I was reminded of that poem about the fly which had so graciously been invited into a spider's parlour for purposes which it had utterly failed to anticipate. Uneasily I shifted in the battered old leather armchair.

"Last year Eric started coming here to talk to me every now and then," Lewis remarked at last, "but in fact I haven't seen him on his own since that evening when we went on to Clerkenwell to dine with Alice and I met you for the first time. I suspect that at present he's confiding only in his brother."

"I understand you and Gil don't get on."

"We have our differences. However, I'm sure Gilbert is a good enough priest to realise that he's too emotionally involved with his brother to be able to give him the kind of spiritual counselling which Eric would seem to need at this time."

"Obviously this is all to do with the fact that Tucker and I are good friends, but—"

"That's a subject which Eric apparently doesn't want to discuss with me and so it's none of my business. What *is* my business is this meeting between you and Kim. I want it to go well. I want you to be in the best possible position to make the right decision about your marriage, and that position's not likely to be achieved if Eric's tempted to act out in real life a storyline which he would be much wiser to confine to the pages of one of his novels."

"Lewis, I don't know what you're implying, but—"

"My dear Carter, you know exactly what I'm implying! Don't insult both our intelligences by playing the ingénue!"

"But this is just wild speculation! You can't have a clue what's been happening between me and Tucker!"

"No? I think you asked him, just as you've been asking all of us, to give you an opinion on the current crisis, and I think I can imagine all too clearly how he would have responded. It's extremely traumatic when a man finds himself powerless to protect a woman who's sought his help, and I'm sure Eric blames himself—even hates himself—for emerging from the scene as a victim instead of a hero. But he doesn't want to hate himself. He'd much rather hate Kim instead. It would be far easier, far more comforting and infinitely more satisfying."

He paused for me to comment but I was unable to speak.

"His sense of failure, I suspect, is one of the reasons why Eric feels driven to help you at present," continued Lewis at last. "It's not the only reason but it's an important reason. We won't speak of the other reasons." And when I remained silent he added briskly: "It would be natural in the circumstances if Eric chose to demonise Kim. But unfortunately this very forgivable psychological reaction is going to make what he

494

says about Kim unreliable—and you don't need the marital waters to be muddied in that way, Carter. You need them to be crystal clear."

This time the silence lasted a full twenty seconds. It was so quiet in the house that the ticking of the clock on the mantelshelf seemed abnormally loud.

"Just bear all that in mind when you meet Kim on Monday," said Lewis. "It's very important that you meet the real Kim then and not someone else's psychological projection."

I lost my nerve. "Do you think I haven't realised that?" I stormed at him, although I knew I had been blind to the dimension of reality which he had exposed. "What do you think I am— some kind of brain-dead bimbo bombing along in hormonal overdrive?"

"I think you're a vulnerable woman," said Lewis, not turning a hair. "I think too that deep down you know this, and it's making you very frightened. But Carter, if you accept your vulnerability instead of denying it you'll be much better equipped to deal with Kim on Monday— it'll make you more in touch with your emotions and in consequence more perceptive, more aware of what's really going on."

"What a put-down! How you have the nerve to tell me I must be a vulnerable female in order to make two and two equal four, I just don't know!"

"You misunderstand. I said you should recognise your vulnerability because to do so will make you less vulnerable."

I swallowed, again unable to speak.

"And anyway," said Lewis, "if I have to choose between political correctness and the unvarnished truth, you know very well what choice I'm going to make. Carter, you can certainly be forgiven for not trusting any man at present, but as a Christian I have an absolute commitment to truth. Trust *that*."

My eyes filled with tears. I stood up and stumbled away.

XIII

"Hey, Tucker—"

"Ah, I was hoping you'd phone! Come on out and have a drink!"

"My liver's keen for a quiet life. Listen, I'm calling to say I've decided to make my own way back from Reigate tomorrow after taking the hire-car to the hotel. The train journey won't take long."

"But wouldn't it be easier if—"

"I don't think so."

"Why the change?"

"Got to psych myself up. No distractions."

"But seriously, is there nothing I can do?"

"Light a candle for me somewhere."

"But I've been doing that all day! St. Eadred's is a mass of well-ordered little flames!"

"Oh Tucker..."

"Let me bring you back from Reigate tomorrow. Let me take you out for a non-alcoholic drink tonight. Let me—"

I hung up and started to cry.

XIV

He called back straight away. "Sorry," he said, "but I'm just so concerned and I keep remem-

496

bering something Edmund Burke's supposed to have said. It's not in any of his writings but there are several versions of the quote around, and the one I like best is—"

"Edmund who?"

"Burke. The politician. Don't tell me you missed out on the entire eighteenth century in addition to a huge chunk of Victorian literature!"

"What's the sound-bite?"

"'All that's required for evil to triumph is for good men to do nothing.'"

I managed to say: "I'll call you as soon as I get back to London after seeing Kim," and without waiting for a reply I again ended our conversation.

XV

"Sweetheart!"

Kim was walking towards me. I was at the hospital. It was eleven thirty on yet another brilliant summer morning. I was wearing slimline navy-blue stretch-pants, a hot-pink skin-tight tank-top and the small silverish cross which I had borrowed from Nicholas's collection on the night of my meltdown. Kim was wearing a red sports shirt, complete with black designer logo, fawn trousers and his latest watch acquired on a recent trip to Switzerland. He was carrying a suitcase; his devoted PA Mary Waters had been to the flat soon after the disaster and packed some clothes for him to wear at the hospital.

"Hi," I said, sounding as awkward as a teenager on her first date.

I had spent some time wondering whether or not I should kiss him. I thought I probably

497

should, so as not to arouse his suspicions, but on the other hand a willingness to kiss after all we had been through in recent weeks might have seemed even more suspicious. However, when the moment came, the choice was taken out of my hands. Dumping the suitcase he flung wide his arms and enfolded me in a hug. There was a kiss but it was planted somewhere around my left ear. No chance was given for me to kiss him. I moved from being swept into his arms, crushed against his chest and released in the space of five shuddering seconds.

"This is really good of you," he said. "I can't thank you enough. And sweetheart, before we go a step farther let me say how very, very sorry I am about all the disasters, but I'm going to make amends and turn my life around, I swear it... How's that kid?"

"Kid? Oh, you mean—"

"Tucker. Now that I'm better I'm going to write to him to apologise. Is he fully recovered yet?"

I spotted the trap. "I believe he is," I said, speaking as if I had only heard news of Tucker through other people. "He's been convalescing on the Algarve."

"So Lewis said. Lewis! My God, what a man! Okay, let's go, there's so much to talk about... Where's the car?"

"Street-parked around the corner."

We set off, he steaming happily out of the hospital without a backward glance, I aware of no emotion except a queasy surprise. What startled me was how well he looked. I had expected him to look more haggard.

"You seem pretty fit," I heard myself say.

"Well, it may sound strange, but the enforced

rest really did do me good—and I benefited from time without alcohol as well."

"So you're feeling well?"

"Great!" he exclaimed buoyantly, smiling at me. "That's why I feel so sure I can get on top of this situation. Lewis said—ah, there's the car! Wonderful—I've missed my Merc! Where are the keys?"

"Keys?"

"Well, I can't drive without keys, can I?" He was laughing at the absurdity, his face radiant with the pleasure of being a free man again.

"But Val Fredericks said your medication didn't permit—"

"Oh, forget the medication! The nurses weren't checking on me as I was about to be discharged, and since I wanted to be bright and sharp for you I flushed the pills down the lavatory."

"You flushed the—"

"Sure, good riddance to bad rubbish... Why, what's the matter?"

"Well, I really think I ought to drive—after all, you're still convalescing—"

"Nonsense, if I'm well enough to be an outpatient I'm well enough to drive a car! Come on, sweetheart, let's have those keys—I can't wait to get going!"

Knowing myself outmanoeuvred I mutely did as I was told.

EIGHTEEN

Almost any aspect of life can give rise to over-powering desires. Eating, drinking, health, exercise, physical appearance, sport, sex, drugs: those are just a few of the areas directly to do with our bodies which can give rise to compulsions and addictions that fundamentally affect our whole lives.

DAVID F. FORD
The Shape of Living

I

I was trying to think clearly, but my thought processes, the ones which dealt with imagination and resourcefulness, appeared to have closed down. My fingers were so stiff that I could hardly fasten my safety belt.

"It won't take long to hit the A3," Kim said, starting the engine. "We just have to head west through Clapham."

"But Kim, I was planning to drop down to the M25 and—"

"The *M25*? What do you want to go there for?"

"Well, you see—well, the truth is—well, I had a surprise planned. I thought we could have lunch at that hotel by the Reigate exit. I thought—"

"That's a great idea," he said, pausing to smile at me before he angled the car away from the kerb, "and I like the thought of going back

500

to a place where we were so happy, but not today, okay? Today I just want to get home."

"Home!"

"I'm sorry, what am I saying, of course it's not home, is it, but in some ways that house still feels like home, particularly as I now own it again—"

"Kim," I said, "darling, I don't want to be tiresome about this, I really don't, but I just can't stand the thought of going back to that place, not after what happened."

"I thought of that," he said seriously. "I discussed it with my psychiatrist, and we both felt it would be therapeutic for you to go back and see what a beautiful peaceful place it really is. You don't want to have to carry around a terrible memory of a dead body in a creepy house, and this way the memory gets to be exorcised—as Lewis would say. God, I must tell you about Lewis. That is one hell of an extraordinary man."

"Look, please don't think I don't want to spend some time with you—I'm keen to talk, but I'd really, truly prefer it if—"

"Okay, I'll level with you," he said. "I've got a surprise planned there. I fixed it with Mary, and she's organised champagne and smoked salmon sandwiches. As you've made this generous gesture of turning up with the car, I thought the least I could do would be to offer you a treat on our arrival!"

"Ah. Yes. Well, that would certainly be a treat—and one which I never anticipated—"

"That's the point about surprises!" he said cheerfully. "One doesn't anticipate them! Now sit back and relax, sweetheart, and let's just enjoy being together again..."

We drove off into the traffic of Denmark Hill.

II

I did think of insisting that he drop me at the nearest tube station, but I knew that once I had acted in a way which he could interpret as a rejection, my attempt to appear benign about the marital future would be washed up along with all hope of learning the full truth about his past. I did think too of requesting a stop at a petrol station; under the pretext of using the lavatory I could sneak off to the garage payphone to report the complete failure of my plan, but there was no guarantee that the payphone would be near the lavatories and the risk of Kim becoming suspicious was too great.

As far as I could see, the choice was stark: either I went on in the hope that I could achieve deliverance from all my tormenting speculations, or I bailed out and settled for living in torment. The only reassuring feature of this searing situation was my conviction that Kim would never harm me so long as he believed the marriage could be saved. So provided I did not make some asinine remark such as: "Reconciliation? You've got to be kidding!" I hardly needed to fear that I was about to drink my last glass of champagne.

I told myself that I was rationally satisfied by this sane, sensible conclusion.

But the trouble was I still felt irrationally scared out of my skull.

III

"Now, I want to hear all you've been doing, sweetheart," said Kim, "but right now there are

502

certain preliminary things I want to say so please excuse me if I hog the conversation for a moment.

"First of all I want to stress how glad I was that you found sanctuary at the Rectory and were even able to share a flat there with that nice girl Alice. (Haven't forgotten that sexy uniform of hers!) It made a lot of difference to me to know you were being cared for properly after all you'd been through; I'd have worried myself sick about you otherwise. Oh, and of course I understood why you weren't able to face seeing me or writing letters. You needed time to heal too, Lewis explained all that, and anyway I'd have been no fun to visit when I was drugged to the eyeballs.

"I know it must seem now as if I've never been ill, but I really did get to the end of my tether. That final scene with Mrs. Mayfield...all that business about the balcony... I felt—but I'll get to that later. Suffice it to say that I knew I couldn't cope with the aftermath of the stabbing—I'd been under stress for too long and my brain just closed down. I confess I did fake a few symptoms of schizophrenia in order to get admitted to hospital, but it was the only way I could cope with reality by that stage. The Maudsley doctors soon realised that the schizophrenia was faked, but they recognised that I did have genuine problems— which is why they're keen for me to continue as an out-patient even though I'm now basically okay. Well, I don't mind going back there for a chat every couple of weeks! After all, I can always drop out, can't I? And I could see that promising to be an out-patient was the best way to extricate myself from that place once I'd decided I'd had enough.

"Anyway, there I was, not mad but definitely

well beyond the end of my tether, when Lewis arrived for his first visit. I was so addled by the drugs that I could only say: 'I don't get it—why are you here?' But he answered straight away: 'My job's to turn up from time to time to signal that no matter what happens you don't have to face it alone.'

"Then suddenly my memory clicked and I understood. Did you ever see that film *Days of Wine and Roses*? No, you'd have been too young. Well, Jack Lemmon plays a man who's sliding down into the dark—into alcoholism, it was, but he couldn't admit it, he was in denial. Down and down he went but finally he hit rock-bottom and ended up dead drunk in jail. He came to, hung over and humiliated, feeling like death was the softest option available, and then this stranger turned up. It was a very powerful moment, because of course the stranger was the man from Alcoholics Anonymous who had stopped off just to be there and share the pain.

"Lewis and I didn't talk much at first. I was feeling too ill. Then the doctors altered the drug cocktail and I felt better, talked more. At last I got sufficiently interested to say: 'I'm sure there are different types of job in a corporation the size of the Church of England. What's your speciality?' And he just said straight out: 'I'm a retired exorcist.' Need I say that after that I was hooked?

"We talked about Mrs. Mayfield. Funnily enough I couldn't discuss her with the psychiatrists. Well, there were a lot of things I couldn't discuss with the psychiatrists, but I could talk about Mrs. Mayfield to Lewis because he not only knew all about her but he understood the whole damned scene—he knew it was for me the equivalent of the alcohol which brought down the character Jack Lemmon played in the film. At one stage I said: 'How are you able to talk about her as if she's someone you've known for years?' and he gave such an interesting answer. He said Mrs. Mayfield represented what he and Nicholas Darrow might have become if they'd dedicated their own gifts to the Powers instead of to God.

"We had a long, long talk about the Powers. We discussed the nature of evil. Lewis said the problem of Auschwitz, which is so famous for its evil past, is that it encourages people to think evil only exists in certain places, whereas the reality is that evil's everywhere. 'Evil is in every place where lies are told in preference to truth and deceit is a way of life,' said Lewis. 'Evil is in every place where human beings are manipulated and debased and abused. Evil is a spiritual sickness,' said Lewis, 'and we're all vulnerable to it, all of us, no one's immune.' God, he was amazing! He didn't care that what he was saying was unfashionable. He wasn't afraid that I'd laugh at him—but I didn't laugh because I could relate to what he was saying. I told him about the evil I'd experienced when I was growing up and how it had led to this quest to gain power over the Powers... He understood it all, of course. He understood it just as well as Mrs. Mayfield. Yet he'd survived by travelling such a very different road.

"Well, I don't want to play down the help the doctors gave me. They were great, treating me with kindness and respect. But Lewis... I felt he was reaching into areas of experience where they couldn't go, and yet it was in these areas that I most needed help. He...well, he gave me hope.

When he understood me so well, I came to trust him, and when he told me I could still turn my life around no matter what I'd done, I thought: if he believes that, then I believe it too.

"I did say: 'Supposing I'm not forgivable?' but he said: 'Everyone's forgivable,' and when I asked about Hitler he answered: 'Hitler's not on record as having faced up to what he did and regretted it before God.' Then he started talking about free will giving us all the option of rejecting God, but at that point I didn't want to be side-tracked because it was his last visit and time was running out. I said: 'Okay, I accept that your God will forgive me if I face up to what I've done and say I'm sorry, but to be honest,' I said, 'I'm more interested in my wife than your God. How can I make her forgive me for screwing up so badly?'

"Well, Lewis isn't a man to mince his words. 'You can't force her to forgive you,' he said, 'but if you can come clean about your past in order to establish a spirit of truth in your marriage, you can show her in no uncertain way that you've rejected the lies generated by Mrs. Mayfield. And meanwhile I'll be praying that you'll be healed of this way of life which has smashed you to pieces.'

"Then he added something about Christ—God—whatever—and left. What a man, never afraid to say what he thought and never fazed by anything I said! And when I remembered how well he knew his way around the spiritual scene I asked myself: 'What have I got to lose by following his advice about telling Carter the whole truth?' And it was then that I was finally able to say: 'Yes, I've gone down the spiritual drain, it's no longer any use pretending otherwise, but I really do want to crawl back up.' I suppose I must have reached that moment in *Days of Wine and Roses* when Jack Lemmon goes to his first AA meeting and succeeds in announcing: 'My name is so-and-so and I'm an alcoholic...'

"So that's where I am, sweetheart, and forgive me for monopolising the conversation, but I felt I just had to explain everything to you so that you'd know where I was coming from. I'm primed to confess, I swear it—but not before I've whipped up some Dutch courage with champagne..."

IV

I managed to make some encouraging comments, but I was quite unable to decide whether or not I believed in his new desire to treat Lewis as a spiritual guru. I found I was too confused to make this assessment, too disturbed by his admission that he had manipulated his way both into and out of hospital—or was he just saying that to boost his self-esteem and convince both of us that he had retained some sort of control over his situation during the breakdown? I knew he had a horror that I should see him as weak and powerless.

Making a new effort to distract myself from my anxiety I began to tell him about my visit to the North with Alice, but I found he had already been informed of my travels.

"Lewis was upset," he remarked, "because he let the cat out of the bag when he said you'd been to see your father—he didn't know you'd never told me that your father was in jail... So we've both had our secrets from each other, haven't we,

Carter? And maybe there's more stuff you've kept quiet about too, stuff you regret now and wish hadn't happened. I never asked you too closely, did I, about your sexual past—I figured that as you wanted to settle down it would be stupid of me to become obsessed with it. You see, *I* let *you* start again with a clean slate! I loved you enough to forgive you anything—still do, if there's anything recent which needs forgiving...but Lewis said that if I were wise I'd just drop the subject of Tucker or else you'd get annoyed by my reluctance to believe there was nothing going on."

"How well Lewis put it."

"I'm sorry, but if you think I can't tell when some long-haired kid finds you attractive—"

"Tucker's thirty-five."

"Yes, but he's obviously never grown up. I know that type. Women would find him attractive because he'd always be up for a screw, but—"

"Kim, I'll say this once and then I don't expect to be obliged to say it again: I have not been to bed with Eric Tucker. I stopped bed-hopping years ago when my self-esteem improved to the point where brain-dead behaviour no longer seemed essential to my well-being."

A second after completing this speech I remembered that Kim himself had started off in my life as a one-night stand, but before I could draw breath to shudder he had apologised and was starting to chat idly instead about the routine of his life in hospital.

V

By the time we reached the A3 he had finished his descriptions of the doctors, the nurses, the

508

other patients, the tests, the therapies and the drugs, but was lingering over his account of the meals and the socialising.

"I decided to have no visitors except for Lewis," he said. "It was a matter of pride—I didn't want anyone to see me in that setting."

"Any word from Graf-Rosen?"

"I had a formal letter of sympathy, but of course they're just waiting for me to get well enough to be sacked. The letter said I could take as much time as I liked to recuperate."

"Kiss of death." Time was the one thing no one in demand was allowed.

"Well, it got my adrenaline going. I spent many happy hours planning how I could kick them all in the balls by nailing a better job elsewhere."

"That's the spirit!" I said encouragingly, but I wondered how employable he was now that he was nearly fifty and had a history of mental breakdown. When he asked about my departure from Curtis, Towers I did not tell him that the answerphone at Harvey Tower had already recorded messages from headhunters, anxious to talk to me. I merely outlined how the chief dinosaur had coaxed me to fall on my sword.

"Bastard!" said Kim, and removed his left hand from the wheel to caress the inside of my right thigh.

I never flinched, but even while I was grappling with my physical distaste I was aware of a terrible sympathy dawning for him. For a high flyer there were few things worse than having a question mark placed over one's long-term future.

I heard myself say: "Darling, I'm really sorry you've had to go through all this."

"I'll be okay," he said simply, "just so long as I still have you."

At that point I felt so choked up, churned up and messed up that I even ceased to worry that I was now heading for Oakshott at eighty miles an hour.

VI

As we approached the Oakshott exit of the A3, I finally nerved myself to say: "I suppose Mrs. Mayfield hasn't been in touch?"

"No, it's clear she's dumped me. And the group hasn't been in touch either. All that's completely finished as far as I'm concerned," he said, and when I was silent he added with a passionate sincerity: "You've got to believe that, Carter, because I swear it's the truth!"

"How could I not believe you after all you've told me about your talks with Lewis?" I said at once. "Of course I believe you!"

But did I?

We reached the Oakshott exit and he swung the car off towards the woods.

VII

"Beautiful, isn't it?" said Kim as he turned the car into the drive of that horrible house which I could now clearly see was built in the handsome style of a between-the-wars architect; with dread I realised that on this second visit I was going to take in far more details, thus ensuring the place was more firmly etched than ever in my memory. I was now noticing the immaculate garden. The front lawn, smooth as green baize, appeared to be weedless. All the borders were bursting with blooms. Even the sinister trees looked as if they harboured nothing more harmless on this occasion than squirrels—and the squirrels would be the red kind, the nice-natured, shy-mannered little tree-rats which always looked so cuddly in those classic storybooks for pre-schoolers.

"I made sure the gardener was kept on after Sophie's death," Kim was saying. "Gardens quickly go to pieces if they're not looked after."

I managed to rouse myself sufficiently to say: "Probate can't have been granted yet—did the lawyers raise any objection when you said you wanted to stay here for a while?"

"Are you kidding? They couldn't wait for me to move in and protect the place from burglars and vandals! Sophie's brother objected at first—he's inherited the contents of the house—but he was quick to see the argument for having the house occupied... Now, come along inside"—he halted the car on the gravel sweep in front of the main entrance—"and let's set those traumatic memories to rest once and for all. The cleaning woman gave notice, but Mary organised a firm to do a make-over only the other day so everything should be looking good..."

I slowly emerged from the car. Despite the fact that I knew there were other houses nearby I could not see them; I felt as if I were marooned miles from anywhere.

Kim was opening the front door, moving forward swiftly to turn off the alarm. "Okay, first things first!" I heard him say cheerfully. "Let's find that bottle of champagne!"

With enormous reluctance I followed him into the circular hall and saw again the long curve of the staircase as it snaked up to the gallery of the floor above. The sheer luxury of all that chandelier-crowned wasted space reminded me not only of the money Kim had made in the past but of the mystery attached to the money he claimed to have lost. I might have dwelled on this thought for longer but suddenly I was so busy trying to avoid looking at the spot where Sophie's corpse had lain that no coherent thinking was possible at all.

"Want to use the cloakroom?"

"What? Oh...yes...but I know where it is," I said, and immediately found myself reliving the moment when I had vomited into the lavatory on the night Sophie had died. I began to veer towards the cloakroom door but stopped when I realised that I had no desire to relieve myself and no desire to let him out of my sight. I found I had to be sure there was no tampering with the champagne, and although I knew this reaction was paranoid I found I was quite unable to eliminate it.

"I've changed my mind," I said, following him towards the kitchen. "I'm all right at the moment."

"Me too. No, wait a moment, I'll be handling food so I ought to wash my hands. Funny how hygienic one becomes in hospital! Have a seat at the table here, sweetheart—I'll be right back."

I waited until I heard the cloakroom door close across the hall and then my paranoia ensured that I slipped after him to listen to his activities, but only normal, water-sloshing sounds reached me. Speeding back to the kitchen, my heart thudding uncomfortably, I was sitting at the table by the time he returned.

"Look at that—Sophie's gardening clobber's

still here!" he murmured in irritation as he moved towards the refrigerator, and following his glance I saw again the flat wooden basket, now containing not only the gloves and secateurs but the straw hat, draped over one edge. The contract cleaners, evidently wanting to leave the table uncluttered, had fought shy of removing the hat and basket from the scene but had dumped the gear on the floor behind the back door.

"I'm sorry," Kim was saying rapidly as he saw the expression on my face, "I should have made sure that such an obvious reminder of that traumatic night was well out of sight, but I'm afraid I forgot. Well, let's face it, I probably chose to forget because whenever I think of that night my head starts to ache. In fact I feel as if I might have a headache coming on right now, but I'm sure it'll go away when I've knocked back some champagne... Did Lewis tell you about my headaches?"

"No."

"First of all I thought Mrs. Mayfield was causing them long-distance, but when I said that to my doctors they just thought I was round the twist—I mean, even more round the twist than I was already—so I shut up. They did do tests, just to make sure there was no brain tumour, but when nothing showed up they wrote the headaches off as a stress symptom."

"But why should you think Mrs. Mayfield was being malign towards you?"

"I wondered if she'd come to the conclusion that I was now more of a liability than an asset... But let's forget all that for the moment and enjoy our treat. Ah yes, here they are—smoked salmon sandwiches, made by Mary first thing this morning and dropped off here along with the vintage Moët! Shall we take it all into the living-room?"

The curtains had been closed in the living-room when I had seen it before, and I was struck now by how light it was in the heat of the day, its long windows facing a terrace beyond which another shaven lawn lay shimmering in the sun. Glossy chintzes in autumnal colours covered the sofas and chairs, and the carpet was the colour of those exotic mushrooms which gourmet food departments sell at rip-off prices. The whole room reeked of the stultifying good taste which the southern English have spent generations cultivating. Even the oil paintings depicted scenes guaranteed not to give offence, and I suspected that these yawn-inducing heirlooms had been inherited by Sophie; Kim's interest in modern art was nowhere in evidence. A multitude of other valuable knick-knacks, ranging from the antique clock to the pair of silver fruit-baskets, also whispered "CLASS" with sibilants which hissed. I decided I loathed the house more than ever.

"It's hot in here, isn't it?" said Kim, after filling both our glasses and replacing the champagne bottle in the ice-bucket. "I'll open the French windows."

"Maybe we could sit on the terrace?" Despite all the windows I was finding the room increasingly claustrophobic.

"We could," he agreed, "but I think it would be too hot for comfort. It'll be all right in here once we get some air circulating."

Once the French windows were open I did feel better; at least if things went wrong I had unimpeded access to an escape route. However, Kim

514

seemed to be having no difficulty in sustaining his role of friendly host, and there was no hint that the scene might take a disastrous turn. I decided that although anxiety was excusable fear was unjustified; firmly I told myself I had to stop being so neurotic.

"Sandwich?"

"Thanks." I took one and looked at it. I even nibbled a corner of the brown bread before putting the sandwich on my plate and reaching for my glass of champagne. "Here's to us both," I said. "May we each make a full recovery from the hell of the last few weeks."

"I'll second that!" he said fervently, and we drank. When we came up for air we both sighed, and as we laughed at our identical reaction I felt for the first time that the Kim I had loved was still there, still alive beneath all the wreckage. I was even tempted to write off my attraction to Tucker as an infatuation born of stress.

"You're already looking quite recovered!" Kim was saying, smiling at me. "I like that outfit...but why are you wearing a cross?"

I was startled but said simply: "Lewis gave it to me."

"Ah... Did anyone at that place try to convert you?"

"No. Why?"

"I wondered if, after all that flirting with the enemy, the enemy had tried flirting back."

"They cared for me even though I was a stranger. They were committed to truth when I was drowning in lies. They gave me hope even though I wanted to despair. If that's flirting there ought to be more of it around."

He smiled at me again. "After being befriended

515

by Lewis I assure you I feel the same way... And talking of Lewis and his fondness for the 'unvarnished truth'—"

"Is this where we embark on a Cluedo-style exercise to find out who did what to whom in the library?"

"Well, at least there's no library."

We failed to laugh this time; the tension was now too great, and as I abandoned all thought of eating I started steadily sipping champagne.

VIII

"I'll start at the beginning," said Kim, "and confirm that I was born in Cologne and that my father was a Nazi lawyer, but although he sent a lot of men to their deaths he wouldn't have wound up at Nuremberg. The men he condemned were all German soldiers who'd got into trouble. He was a judge who wound up presiding at courts martial."

"You mean he didn't know Hans Frank at all?"

"He knew Frank but he didn't work for him in Krakow. What happened was this: at the beginning of the war my father was working in the *Volksgerichtshof*, known as the VGH, which was the highest Nazi court for political crimes—it was part of Germany's normal legal system in that those who appeared before it were arrested and prosecuted in the normal way, but the trouble was Germany moved from being a constitutional state, based on the rule of law, to being a police state where oppression was the only means of ruling. So the VGH quickly became corrupted. There was no right of appeal, no trial by jury and

516

certainly no impartiality, as the judges were committed Nazis. And the people lucky enough to be acquitted weren't set free—they were just turned over to the Gestapo and sent to concentration camps.

"My father didn't approve of this procedure because he disliked the fact that the police authority wasn't put under the control of the law, and he thought the Gestapo should be subject to the judiciary. Well, there was no changing the system but he did manage to change his job. He wrote to Frank to ask for a helping hand and Frank arranged for him to go to Poland to do courts martial; the system required a professional judge to preside with two soldiers. However, I rather doubt if my father enjoyed this either since his function was to be disciplinary rather than judicial and a high number of executions had to be ordered... No wonder he took to drink after the war! I think he was just ploughed under by all those disastrous events which wrecked his career and destroyed the law as he knew it. Yes, he was a Nazi, and yes, he should have been able to foresee the mayhem, but it's easy for us to say that with the wisdom of hindsight, isn't it, and my father certainly wasn't alone in failing to foresee the horrors when he joined the Nazi party in 1929 in pursuit of his dream of a better Germany... It's strange, but since I've wound up ploughed under myself I find I have a good deal more sympathy for him—or so I said to my psychiatrist during one of our interminable sessions centred on my past."

"But if your father wasn't a war criminal—"

"We still took the rat-run to Argentina—that was all true—but it wasn't because he needed to evade the prosecutors at Nuremberg. We went because my father couldn't bear to stay in a wrecked Germany and he had the money and the contacts required to escape."

"But in that case, why did you float the story that he was a war criminal?"

"I needed a plausible reason to explain why I could be blackmailed, and a criminal father hyped up the credibility factor." He reached for another sandwich. "You're not eating, sweetheart!"

"I'll get to it in a minute. So you invented the blackmail story about that Jew who had been with you on the ship to Argentina—"

"Yes, that was all a fiction. I've never been blackmailed about my Nazi origins."

"But you were blackmailed about something else."

"I was, but as I felt I couldn't tell you the truth I had to come up with an alternative explanation."

"And you felt you had to disclose the blackmail to explain your lack of capital?"

"I did feel the need to explain that, but in fact what drove me on to invent an alternative explanation was that I was afraid Sophie would tell you the truth. I discussed the situation with Elizabeth—with Mrs. Mayfield—"

"Wait a moment. When I first asked you about Mrs. Mayfield, you said she was just someone you didn't see any more."

"I was certainly estranged from her—we'd quarrelled over my decision to marry you. But after Sophie succeeded in meeting you face to face I felt I just had to have Mrs. Mayfield's help in controlling the situation and I called her the next day."

"I'm surprised Mrs. Mayfield chose to help you! Why not simply let Sophie bust up our relationship?"

"For various reasons she didn't want the true story about the blackmail coming out. I'll get to that later. Anyway—"

"—anyway, you and Mayfield cooked up a plot to defuse Sophie if she tried to spill the beans. But weren't you afraid right from the start that the beans would be spilled?"

"Yes, but there was more than one type of bean, wasn't there? When Sophie first heard I planned to remarry she said you ought to know that I'd been unfaithful to her from the beginning and had even destroyed her chance of having children. *That* was the disclosure I was fearing in the run-up to the wedding."

I began to understand. "You mean in the beginning you thought Sophie wouldn't spill the blackmail beans?"

"I knew she wouldn't. She'd told me she hadn't been able to bring herself to discuss the subject of the blackmail with anyone, even that local clergyman of hers. She'd found the subject quite literally unspeakable."

"So in that case—"

"—I was more than worried that she might succeed in spilling the infidelity beans, but I thought I could survive that; I thought that if the worst came to the worst I'd be able to convince you she was just out of her mind with jealousy. I also thought she'd back off after the wedding because she'd always claimed her aim was to prevent the marriage taking place. However, to my horror I found she couldn't let the matter rest after all."

Even before he had finished speaking I was remembering Sophie's conversation with me in the supermarket. "She felt more strongly than ever, didn't she," I said, "that God wanted her to make a new effort to dish up the truth—and this time she was going to speak the unspeakable."

All he said in reply was: "When she told you to ask me about Mrs. Mayfield, I knew the writing was on the wall."

"And that was when you got together again with Mayfield. Was it she who came up with the next plan?"

"Yes, she thought it would be a better tactical move if I didn't wait for Sophie to spill the blackmail beans but went ahead and pre-empted the true story with the fiction. She thought you'd be more likely to swallow the fiction if it appeared to be dragged out of me in the form of a confession, so she got Mandy Simmons to stage that phone call—"

"—and then afterwards you and Mayfield slogged away at the task of convincing me Sophie was certifiable."

"Well, we had to destroy her credibility!"

"Sure." I ran my tongue around my lips as if to soften them up for pronouncing the crucial sentence. "So why exactly," I said, "were you being blackmailed?"

Finishing his glass of champagne he stood up and began to roam around the room. He could no longer look at me.

At last he said: "It was a sex-mess." Halting by the window at the far end of the room he stood staring out over the tranquil garden. "Before I go any further," I heard him say, "I want to make it clear that I've been very happy with

520

you, and I don't want to live now as I lived in the past."

"Fair enough," I said. "I appreciate the compliment. But just how the hell did you live in the past?"

He returned to the ice-bucket on the coffee-table and poured himself another dose of champagne.

IX

To help him along I said in my calmest voice: "Of course I'd realised Mrs. Mayfield's groups mainline on sex."

But he seemed untroubled by this statement. "The groups' activities are well within the law," he said. "But the big advantage of them is that Mrs. Mayfield makes sure they're secure. There's never any trouble with blackmailers."

"How often did you—"

"I never went back to the group after I met you."

"But that night—the night when you said you went to say goodbye—"

"I didn't go. The story that Mandy and Steve were trying to get me back into the group wasn't true. I just floated it to make it more plausible that Mandy should phone me. It would have looked odd if she'd called out of the blue."

"Then what were you doing on the night you were supposed to be saying goodbye to the group?"

"I was with Mrs. Mayfield. I thought it would be politic to take her out to dinner at a nice restaurant—and no, I didn't take drugs that night! If I seemed woolly when I got back it was only because I'd had a lot to drink and I was dead tired."

I made no comment but pushed the conversation forward by asking: "How often did you see the group when you were married to Sophie?"

"Hardly at all—you've misunderstood what was going on. I've only been involved with a Mayfield group twice, and on both occasions my involvement lasted no more than a year. Mrs. Mayfield prescribed the groups as therapy, not as long-term recreation."

"How did you actually meet this woman?" I was trying to keep my tone neutral, as if I were a lawyer questioning a client about some ethically dubious facts. I reckoned this approach would be the most likely to produce good results. Now was not the time to sink into my customary verbal abuse of Mrs. Mayfield.

"I met her just as I originally told you," he said. "I happened to see her card in that Soho bookshop. But as I admitted at the Rectory, this meeting took place much earlier than I'd previously disclosed and she was living in Lambeth then, not Fulham. When we met I was only four years into my marriage, but Sophie had found out about the sterility, and by that time my guilt was so great that I was unable to perform either with her or with anyone else. Well, I didn't mind not sleeping with Sophie, but I certainly minded not being able to make it with other women—"

"I bet." I found myself unable to stop the neutral mask slipping.

"You're thinking I'm callous, aren't you, but don't jump to conclusions! I was very fond of Sophie. However, we never hit it off in bed so after the VD disaster she was more than happy to switch off her sex life—and who can blame her for that? I certainly didn't. And I didn't want to leave her. She was still exactly the kind of wife I needed at that time, and anyway... I felt justified in living with her." He paused as if reconsidering this sentence and realising, as I did, that it was off-key.

I nailed the neutral mask back in place. "Justified?" I repeated, careful to sound non-threatening, but he seemed to have trouble working out how to explain himself. At last he said: "She gave me the well-run, beautiful home I should have had—the home I did have before my parents emigrated and went to pieces. Sophie had such taste and class and style." He hesitated again but added abruptly: "A woman like that was owing to me after all I'd been through with my mother."

"Could Mrs. Mayfield understand that?"

"Of course. But don't forget that when I first consulted Mrs. Mayfield, the topic under discussion wasn't how I could renew my sexual relationship with Sophie but how I could get going with other women again. It wasn't until years later, when my marriage finally broke down as the result of the blackmail, that Elizabeth—Mrs. Mayfield—advised me to marry again in order to get my personal life into a safer groove. Until that time she'd quite understood that Sophie had to stay in my life."

"Did Mrs. Mayfield have a wife in mind for you?"

"Yes, that was the second time she directed me to a group for therapy. The woman was already a member."

"God, not Mandy!"

"No, she was already married to Steve."

"And did you decide straight away that the bride-to-be was unsuitable?"

"I knew she'd be unsuitable even before I saw her," he said drily. "I certainly wasn't going to get permanently involved with any woman hooked on group sex. However, because Mrs. Mayfield had helped me at the time of the blackmail I felt I couldn't dismiss her suggestions about marriage out of hand. I played along with her plan for a while—until I met you and drew the line."

I heard myself say very casually, as if attending to a barely relevant thought which had just chanced to drift into my mind: "I suppose Mrs. Mayfield never fancied marrying you herself? After all, you're much the same age as she is, aren't you, and if you met her when you were a lot younger—"

He raised an eyebrow to convey sardonic amusement. "Mrs. Mayfield has long since figured out that the last encumbrance she needs is a husband!"

"But how did you feel? If she were to ditch that grey wig, which I suppose she thought gave her a passing resemblance to your description of a frumpish Sophie, and if she were to tog herself up in black satin with plenty of cleavage—"

"Well, of course I screwed her," he said. "That was all part of the treatment when I first sought a cure for impotence. But marriage? Good God, no! Can you seriously imagine me marrying anyone who has that kind of suburban accent?"

"Lucky I learned to talk acceptable English then, wasn't it?" I said, automatically attempting to conceal my horror with humour, but I was hardly aware of what I was saying. On some level of my mind I believe I had faced the possibility that he had slept with Mrs. Mayfield. But I had never faced the possibility that he might consider her worst flaw was her accent.

Meanwhile he was saying casually: "One can't pretend accents don't matter. Well, as I was saying—"

"You screwed Mrs. Mayfield."

He suddenly became aware of my true reaction, the reaction which implied criticism. Moving away from me again he wandered over to the silver fruit-baskets and checked one as if he were looking for tarnish. "After my impotence had been overcome," he said levelly, "Mrs. Mayfield sent me to a group—that was the first time I went. She said it offered a way in which I could get my full confidence back by using a variety of women." He put down the fruit-basket. "I didn't sleep with her again," I heard him say. "We both had other fish to fry, and besides...it was a question of power. Mrs. Mayfield would never have wanted to give me that much control on a continuing basis."

I found this plausible but still had to ask: "What about the night before the stabbing when you bedded down at her Fulham house?"

"By then I was quite definitely not Mrs. Mayfield's flavour-of-the-month. Nothing happened."

There was a silence.

"Well, as I was saying"—he had clearly decided to skate away fast from this awkward topic—"the first time I sampled the group was when I was recovering from impotence, but after a while I got bored and wanted to drop out. I thought Mrs. Mayfield might be annoyed, but she explained that this kind of group therapy usually had a limited time-span and all that mattered was that I was now fully cured. She then said"—he paused to gulp down some champagne—"she then said she had a much more interesting group for me to sample, a group which would engage me mentally and spiritually as well as physically, and would I be interested in giving it a try. So I said: 'Fine—tell me more about it,' and the first thing she said was: 'Well, it's not really a group. It's a society.'"

I drained my glass and at once reached for the bottle in the ice-bucket. "A secret society?"

"Very secret. Sweetheart, I hate to admit I lied to you about this, but—"

"You were up to your neck in the occult," I said, and at last began to believe I had never really known him at all.

X

"The word 'occult' has unfortunately acquired a very pejorative meaning," said Kim fluently. "Naturally you're going to be alarmed in case I've been involved with a bunch of socially inadequate weirdos who believe fairies live at the bottom of every garden, but surely you can accept that a man of my intelligence isn't going to dabble with anything which doesn't chime in some way with reality? Mrs. Mayfield recommended the society to me because she knew how interested I was in harnessing and mastering the Powers. Well, how close to reality can one get? The Powers had smashed up my early life and haunted me ever since! Of course I longed to know how I could control them."

He paused as if expecting me to argue with him but I could only wait numbly for him to continue.

"The occult," he resumed smoothly at last, "is a word referring to a system of hidden truths, known to a few. The more you know, the better placed you are to control and manipulate reality for your own benefit because the system provides a spiritual empowerment by means of an expansion of consciousness. The Powers are essentially Spirit but exist as archetypes in the unconscious mind, so if you expand your consciousness you can encompass them, subjugate them and use them for your own purposes... In other words, what I'm really talking about is a modern version of the old Gnostic heresy which the Christians have spent so much energy trying to liquidate in the past. No wonder Mrs. Mayfield always sees Christians as the enemy!"

"No wonder. Are we talking witchcraft here?"

"Certainly not! Strict occult practice is quite different from either respectable Wicca rituals or the witchcraft fantasies peddled by the ignorant media. Genuine Wicca practitioners are concerned with nature and the environment—with natural forces. We're interested in the cosmic, in the different levels of reality which exist beyond this world altogether. Wicca practitioners are basically uninterested in Christianity, whereas the Gnostics...well, Gnosticism and Christianity are like two brothers who shared a nursery but fell out in adolescence and have been enemies all their adult life. They both had a common bond in mysticism, and in the early centuries there were actually Christian Gnostics and Gnostic Gospels, so you can see what a confused philosophical melting-pot it was, but after Christianity got hyped up on dogma—"

"Forget all that. Just get back to brass tacks. What did this occult society of yours actually do?"

"The first point to grasp is that this isn't a spiritually undeveloped group focused primarily on hedonism. This is a serious society using sex as

527

a mere tool to open up the mind to spiritual enlightenment."

I somehow managed to stop myself saying: "Oh yeah?" but it was becoming increasingly hard to maintain anything resembling a neutral professional manner.

"There are different kinds of Gnostics," said Kim, "and many forms of Gnosticism. Some Gnostics starve and deprive the body in order to open up the mind but some Gnostics choose to indulge in every sensual experience available. But in the end the body's of no importance. So long as you have the right spiritual knowledge—the right 'gnosis'—you're on course for salvation."

"Uh-huh. And what do the Christians have to say about that?"

"Oh, they're very sentimental! They believe the body is the temple of the indwelling Holy Spirit and as such should be treated with reverence!"

"You're saying they don't approve of sexual abuse."

"I—"

"That's sentimental?"

"What I meant was—"

"Sure. By the way, I'm getting sceptical about your alleged non-use of drugs. I'd have thought drugs were essential in this kind of mind-expanding get-together."

"I repeat: we're not talking about mindless hedonism here. This is a serious society dedicated to spiritual enlightenment, and no matter what may go on in lesser occult societies I can tell you that Mrs. Mayfield is very opposed to drugs being used."

"Because she's keen to operate within the law?"

"Another important reason is that drugs always wind up affecting sexual performance—if not in the short-term, then in the long-term. Look at the havoc alcohol can cause! I'm not saying I've never seen drugs taken at the meetings, but the serious spiritual seekers will prefer to get high on their own adrenaline. Mrs. Mayfield always says that the chemicals the body manufactures are far more potent than anything a chemist could concoct in a laboratory."

"Cheaper too. But let me ask you this—and I apologise if it seems a dumb question: what's so bloody spiritual about all this sex, with or without drugs?"

"The theory is that you satiate the body to keep it quiet. Then the mind is liberated. The unconscious is opened right up, and all the archetypes become accessible, moving in patterns which can be understood and mastered—"

"I'm sorry, can you just run all that past me again?"

"Forget it. All you need to understand is that the society gave me a map in my quest to stitch up the split in my consciousness."

"What split?"

"The one the Powers were always trying to get through to destroy me. I always felt so dislocated...alienated...restless... But the society helped me, it gave me an intellectual framework to operate in, it made me feel more in control of the Powers—"

"Just by having sex?"

"Well, of course there was more. There were psychic procedures, rituals—but I'd better not go into detail. I've taken a vow of secrecy, and you wouldn't understand anyway."

"But are you still an active member?"

"Not sexually active, not since we met. But I'm still a member because I've never been able to work out how to sever my links without suffering reprisals. Lewis says the people at St. Benet's would give me every support, but—"

"Why wouldn't the members of the society just accept your resignation?"

"Because I'm too damned important to them! I not only look after the society's finances but I bring in rich contacts, people who have considerable power and influence. If I try to resign I'll be subjected to heavy psychological pressure, and although I'm attracted to Lewis's offer of help I don't feel strong enough right now to cut myself loose."

"Would they try to blackmail you?"

"If you mean in the strict legal sense of extorting money, no. As you just said, Mrs. Mayfield aims to keep within the law."

"But does she always succeed? What about all this sex?"

"I promise you children are never involved. Mrs. Mayfield screens out the paedophiles."

I found I dared not pause to ask myself if he was telling the truth. Nor could I pause to ask him about other illegal activities. I could only blurt out: "Don't the other members object if you don't take part in the sex-stuff?"

"They believe I'm going through a phase and they've decided to allow me a certain amount of leeway. Mrs. Mayfield's told them the problem's my marriage but it'll inevitably break up."

"God... But if you abstain, don't you miss out on all that mind-expansion which turned you on?"

"To be honest, I'd lost interest in that even before I met you. And after I met you, of course, all I wanted to do was abstain."

"So while the sex-stuff was going on, you just—"

"Watched."

I found I had to press him again about the activities; I had to test his veracity by probing further. "But what did go on? Just what were these sexual rituals?"

His self-control cracked. In a sudden burst of despair he exclaimed: "Sweetheart, surely all you need to know is that I've been faithful to you since we met? Surely all that matters is that I've never, never involved you in any sex which isn't thoroughly acceptable and normal? Okay, I know that on that last occasion I let out the throttle, but everything was still on the right side of the line, wasn't it—although to be honest I did feel afterwards that I'd gone too far. I've got a horror of doing with you anything which would trigger the wrong memories and make me relive some of the shit I waded through with those people—"

"Yes, I see. Yes, I understand." My self-control was cracking too, and in an effort to maintain my grip on it I backed down from demanding graphic information. Instead I said shakily: "If you saw Mrs. Mayfield regularly at these society meetings, even after we were married, you've been lying in saying you were estranged from her."

"No, it was the truth—we weren't on speaking terms. I did see her but there was no communication."

"But if she's the boss and you're the finance manager—"

"She's not the boss. She's a consultant. The

chief executive is someone else, and she advises him. He's the one I report to at the inner circle meetings, not her."

"Excuse me... Did you say 'inner circle'?"

"I meant the management committee. But Carter, when I contacted her to ask for her help in defusing Sophie, I assure you it was the first time we'd been in direct communication since my marriage. So when you first brought up the subject of Mrs. Mayfield, I really did feel justified in saying: 'Oh, she's someone I don't see any more'—all right, I admit I couldn't have said anything else then, since I didn't want you to know about the society, but—"

Unable to bear this hair-splitting I interrupted: "How much did Sophie know?"

"We had a big showdown at the time of the blackmail. I admitted my involvement in the occult and told her about my association with Mrs. Mayfield, but I didn't go into detail about the society and I gave the impression that both the involvement and the association were recent."

I was confused. "But you still haven't told me what this blackmail was all about! Did one of the members try to blackmail you about your behaviour at the meetings—the general meetings where the sex-stuff went on?"

"No, the actual incident which gave rise to the blackmail had nothing to do with the society and nothing to do with Mrs. Mayfield."

I felt more confused than ever. "Then what was it all about?"

"It arose out of a hobby I used to have."

Seconds slipped by. At last I said: "Hobby?"

He drank a third glass of champagne straight off but afterwards muttered: "God, I'd better go easy on the drink! I'm forgetting I'm not used to it." Abandoning his glass he moved restlessly to the far end of the room again before saying: "In the end I found I couldn't control the Powers after all—they bloody nearly destroyed me. I suppose that was when I became disillusioned with the society; I was already disillusioned before I met you." The tension emanating from him by the time he finished speaking was so acute that I could almost hear the air crackle.

"Kim—"

"I had this hobby," he interrupted, staring out of the window. "I'd had it all my adult life. I had it long before I met Mrs. Mayfield, and I kept it up until the time of the blackmail. It was just something I did occasionally, not often, just every now and then—I was like a drinker having a binge, seeking refuge in something which would relieve the tension and ease the split in my personality. To be honest it worked better than the occult practices, better than the sex therapy groups, but Mrs. Mayfield always said I had to try to find an alternative way to heal the split because the hobby was too damn dangerous. And she was right."

I tried to speak but failed. I could only listen as he added: "It was such a shock. I never thought I'd ever be blackmailed because I was so discreet, so careful."

I put out a shaking hand. I raised my glass and drank. Only then was I able to say neutrally, the model lawyer handling the client with kid gloves: "And the hobby was—?" I paused, waiting.

"I liked to screw men," he said, and after that there was a silence which lasted for a very long time.

"You'll note I used the past tense," he said at last, still not looking at me, still staring out over the garden. "All the sexual methods I was driven to use to try to integrate myself—to try to heal the split in my personality and make me feel less dislocated—that whole way of life became redundant when I met you. That's why I'll do anything to keep you, anything, even make this very painful and difficult confession."

I answered: "I see." But I barely knew what I was saying.

Rapidly he said: "What I used to do was this: I'd spend the evening in London, pick up someone in a gay bar and...well, it was nothing, just a brief anonymous episode. And let me make it clear that I'm not a homosexual. I like to live with women, I like to make love to women, I've never had any doubt about my sexual orientation. Screwing men was just something I did to jack up the adrenaline and blot out the dislocation—in fact I often felt the activity didn't have much connection with sex. It wasn't desire that switched on the adrenaline. It was rage."

"Rage?"

"Yes, but that's all gone now, along with the dislocation. Never mind that. Let's focus on the blackmail."

"The blackmail, yes—"

"What happened was this. Around two and a half years ago my luck ran out and I picked up a man who happened to be a very professional extortionist. I then compounded my bad luck by making a big mistake: I went back to his flat. Normally I always hired a room in a cheap hotel, but on that occasion I was at the other end of Soho, the man said his flat was in the next street and I just thought: why not. He did tell me he worked in the security business, but I assumed he meant he was some kind of guard. Bloody stupid of me. It turned out he had a shop which sold all kinds of surveillance equipment and his bedroom was stuffed with micro-cameras, the kind you can't see unless you're looking for them with a magnifying glass. I was using a false name and I thought I was carrying no identification, but as I said, this was a real professional.

"My clothes for the evening were off the peg—no Savile Row gear for that particular game—but I was still wearing my handmade shoes from Blaydon's, and when I was in the lavatory the bastard checked all my clothes, realised he'd hit pay-dirt with the shoes and noted the maker's name. Then the next day he went to Blaydon's and spun some story about how he'd met me at a party and admired my shoes and I'd told him to visit their shop in St. James's—he couldn't quite remember my name, but... Of course Blaydon's had no trouble identifying me from his description, and he had no trouble milking them of the information which enabled him to track me down. Three days later I received a letter which said... But you can guess the gist. God, I've got to have another drop of champagne even though I've now had my half of the bottle—I'm running out of courage. How about you?"

"No more at the moment, thanks."

"I mean are you still there, still hanging in?"

"Apparently." Making an enormous effort I tried to help him along by adding: "I'm grateful to you for being so honest. I really admire your guts."

"You're the one with guts, I think." He attempted a smile before refocusing on the narrative. "Well, the next disaster was that Sophie found out. He sent her a couple of photographs to show me he meant business. His big threat was to fax the pictures to all the members of the board of my last company... I was scared shitless, demented with anxiety. Of course I paid up to keep the bastard at bay while I worked out what the hell I could do, but eventually I swallowed my pride and went to Mrs. Mayfield. That was more of an ordeal than you might think. She'd always condemned the hobby as too risky and I'd sworn to her that I'd given it up."

"Was she angry?"

"Furious. But I knew she'd have a strong motive to help me out—I was too valuable to the society to be allowed to go down the tubes. When I asked her what the hell I was going to do she said straight away: 'You're going to get lucky again. I see him lying on a railway line.'"

"Are you trying to tell me—"

"The next day we went into action. I managed to find my way back to his flat. Then once we had his address Mrs. Mayfield made contact, put a curse on him, predicted his death on a railway line and finally called the society together to visualise and will the death into being."

"You're making this up."

"I knew you'd say that, but all I can tell you is that influencing people by the power of the group-will is a psychic procedure which the society regularly practises—"

"As a matter of fact the St. Benet's psychologist told me there are cases recorded of people being willed to die."

"You can will people to do almost anything if you go about it in the right way." Suddenly and most unexpectedly he shuddered. "It was bloody odd in the flat during that final scene," he said. "I believe the reason I went to pieces as the scene progressed was because I felt Mrs. Mayfield was threatening me."

"You? But it was me she was trying to drag onto the balcony!"

"That was what was ostensibly going on. But I began to feel she was saying to me: 'I can break your wife in pieces and I can break you too!' Remember what I said earlier? When I was telling you about my headaches I said I was worried that after this latest bout of trouble Mrs. Mayfield would decide I'd finally become more of a liability than an asset."

"But at the end of that repulsive scene at the flat she made it clear to Nicholas that she wanted to keep you!"

"Well, of course she didn't want me to fall into the hands of the enemy and spill my guts out about the society! But she was bargaining with Darrow as if I was just an object, wasn't she? Somehow that seemed to reveal all her malevolence towards me—I *felt* all her malevolence, and then it was as if I really did become just an object, subhuman. I couldn't do anything, couldn't even put down that knife—and I certainly couldn't react fast enough when Tucker cannoned into me... Carter, I know you must have wondered if I deliberately harmed that man, but believe me I didn't want any more trouble at that stage. Supposing he too had died by accident—and so soon after Sophie? How would that have looked to the police? Anyway, I didn't want to kill Tucker, I just wanted to take a swing at him. But that stabbing...it was really Elizabeth's fault for mentally zapping me like that—and I know she did zap me, I know she did... And when I started getting these headaches I thought: bloody hell, she's got the society exercising the group-will to make me think I have brain cancer, and then I'll want to kill myself, I'll want to go back to that flat and go out on that balcony and—"

"Kim—"

"Okay, okay, I'm being neurotic, I'll stop. The doctors say I don't have brain cancer. Fine. But if Elizabeth's decided I'm expendable, she could still get to me. Why else should she have hammered away about the balcony if she hadn't wanted to demonstrate—"

"Kim, it was me she wanted to wreck, not you! And besides, I don't see why she should feel you'd become expendable. Surely—"

"She skewered that image of the balcony into my brain, I absolutely felt it going in—"

"No, I'm sure you're imagining that. Listen, Lewis will help you, I know he will—he helped me live with that image of the balcony. I still can't go to the flat, but at least I can sleep at night and I'm not afraid I'm going to hurl myself out of the nearest upstairs window."

But he could only shudder. "How typical of Elizabeth," he said, "to choose the image of the big fall to zap us. Every high flyer fears that."

I realised that he had stopped calling her Mrs. Mayfield but I realised too this was a sign of his stress and I knew I had to steer us both away from the subject of the balcony. "I assume the blackmailer did die on a railway line," I said, "but how did the information reach you?"

"The society has its contacts. We asked to be informed of all the fatalities on the Underground. The man was dead within two weeks of hearing Elizabeth's curse and prediction." He wiped the sweat from his forehead as he spoke and I knew we were still on shaky ground. I tried to move the narrative on.

"And this was two and a half years ago, you said. So you weren't blackmailed for years and years."

"No, I originally told Sophie that because I saw at once it was a good way to explain my lack of capital. I knew by that time the marriage was doomed and I'd have to declare all my assets when the divorce settlement came around. I could have blamed my loss on the crash of '87, of course, but it might have seemed implausible as the market recovered so well."

"Where did the money go if it didn't go to the blackmailer?"

"Mrs. Mayfield and the society. I thought it was money well-spent. I would have done anything to ease that dislocation, but of course Sophie didn't understand. When we had our big showdown after the blackmailer sent her the pictures I did try to explain how my hobby, my involvement with Elizabeth and my membership of the society were all part of my search for healing and integration, but she couldn't cope, didn't want to know. That was when I realised we'd reached the end of the road."

Enlightenment hit me so hard that I never stopped to censor myself. I said: "She junked you, didn't she? It wasn't you who decided you'd had enough of the marriage—it was quite the other way around!"

Sweat broke out on his forehead again. I watched him wipe it away, and as I watched, I wished, too late, that I had been less blunt, less ready to hit him with an unpalatable reality.

"Elizabeth said it was all for the best," he answered levelly at last. "That was when she advised me to marry a woman she would choose for me, and to indulge my hobby only within one of the groups, in a controlled setting, with people she'd personally vetted. But the trouble was I wasn't interested in pursuing my hobby in a tame setting where I couldn't get a charge out of being a loner on the prowl. To appease Elizabeth I did agree to attend the Wapping group, but I kept the connections there heterosexual, wasn't interested in doing anything else, so the group didn't actually solve anything."

"What about the society?"

"I certainly couldn't be a loner on the prowl there and the sex was all ritualised anyway... Well, as I said, I did try to explain it all to Sophie—I really didn't want to lose her even then...and I hated the thought of losing my home... I just loved my home... But Sophie drew the line. She said I deserved to lose everything I had. She said I'd destroyed her love, her trust, her respect. She said I was—" He broke off and covered his face with his hands. I heard him whisper: "But of course I couldn't tell you all that."

"Of course not." I was sweating myself now. My tank-top was clinging wetly to my back.

"Then at the end of that disastrous year I met you. Salvation had finally arrived, I saw that at once, but as soon as Sophie heard I wanted to remarry she hit the roof. 'You're not fit to marry anyone,' she said. 'No woman should be allowed to risk being deceived as systematically as you've always deceived me. I'll continue with the divorce,' she said, 'but I'm going to spin it out for as long as possible in the hope that the girl comes to her senses and realises just what kind of a man you really are.' She was absolutely implacable. I was appalled. Then just as I was thinking the situation couldn't get any worse—"

"—she started trying to communicate with me."

"Can you wonder that in the end I turned back to Elizabeth, who hadn't been speaking to me since I'd become involved with you? I was at my wits' end, so terrified of losing you—"

"You must have felt very tempted to kill Sophie."

"Yes, but listen, Carter. I know I had a huge motive, but *I didn't do it*. If I'd killed her...well, for a start, I wouldn't have left the body lying around. I'd have buried it in the Oakshott woods or dumped it in the River Mole so that no one would have been able to tell later exactly when she'd died."

"I know. I finally figured that out. But aren't you going to tell me Mrs. Mayfield rang her up, predicted her death and ordered your occult pals to will Sophie to fall down the staircase?"

He somehow managed to smile. I suspected this was because he was relieved beyond measure to learn I did not suspect him of killing Sophie. "It's a natural conclusion for you to jump to," he said, "but there wasn't time. It was only on that final afternoon that we realised you'd be determined to see Sophie, and she was dead that same evening. To have any psychic success with a group-will coupled with the power of suggestion, you need at least a week and probably longer."

"So Sophie died by accident?"

"I'm now sure she did, yes, because Lewis tells me the police have uncovered no evidence of foul play and I think a stray nutter would have left some evidence behind... But you can see, can't you, how horrified Elizabeth must be by this latest fiasco of mine? The last thing she ever wants is trouble with the police." He squeezed his eyes shut for a moment before saying in an abrupt change of subject: "Damn it, I thought the drink would stave off the headache by relaxing me, but I'm in such a state that the alcohol's having next to no effect."

"Do you have any special painkillers?"

"One of the doctors gave me a prescription this morning but I was so excited by the thought of seeing you that I decided not to delay my departure by going to the hospital pharmacy... I'd better get some painkillers from upstairs. Sophie always kept Anadin in her bathroom cabinet." He moved as far as the door before turning to look back at me. "Are you okay?"

"Yep. More or less. Still hanging in."

"You're not going to run away, are you?"

"Not yet. There are a couple more questions I want to ask."

"About what?"

"About the blackmail."

"Well, I can't imagine what else there is to say, but...okay, wait, just let me dose myself with Anadin." He disappeared.

Immediately I reached for my glass and wondered how I could have absorbed so much horror yet still be conscious.

I was aware of the urge to bolt, but the compulsion to complete my quest for the truth was now far stronger than my fear. Every word he had uttered implied how desperate he was to win me back, and so long as he believed I was open to the possibility of a reconciliation, I was sure he would not harm me.

As I took another gulp of champagne I tried to focus on the unsolved mystery of why I represented salvation to him—such salvation that he was even prepared to embark on a high-risk confession to save the marriage. But I not only failed to understand why I solved all his problems; I failed to understand exactly what these problems were. I had ample evidence of warped behaviour, but what was generating it? All I could tell myself was that only someone profoundly unintegrated could have wound up leading such a distorted and bizarre private life. "Distorted" and "bizarre," of course, were in this context euphemisms for "obscene" and "revolting." I tried to beat back my repulsion in the name of detachment, but that proved impossible. I was this man's wife. I was standing in Sophie's shoes.

I suddenly thought: how I wish she were here to help me! And when I began to think of her with all my familiar guilt and grief, I found myself empathising with her more vividly than ever. I was now shaking with the shock she must have experienced when she had seen those photographs of Kim with his blackmailer—and as the word "blackmailer" reverberated sickeningly in my mind, I suddenly heard Tucker say: "Do I think he killed the blackmailer? You bet. If anyone asks to be liquidated it's a blackmailer who gets in Kim Betz's way."

As the memory drove through my brain like a clenched fist I realised that Tucker's hunch about the brevity of the blackmail episode had been correct. My memory blazed on. It was unstoppable. "Boardroom barracudas don't behave like doormats. They sharpen their teeth and move in straight away for the big bite," I heard Tucker say, and suddenly I found I understood why Mrs. Mayfield could have come to see Kim as expendable. The double disaster of Sophie's death and Tucker's stabbing had drawn too much attention to him, and the police might easily become too interested in his past.

I now realised I had been so traumatised by Kim's revelations, so intent on responding in a manner which concealed the full extent of my horror, that I had ceased to listen with an ear fine-tuned to distinguish truth from falsehood. Automatically I refocused on the story he had told me about the blackmailer. Did I believe the man had fallen accidentally under a train? No. Did I believe the man had committed suicide? No. Could I really brainwash myself into believing that Mrs. Mayfield and her occult gang had willed him to death after softening him up with the power of suggestion? Well, possibly, since Robin had assured me there was scientific evidence that such things had happened, but the trouble was that I could also remember Lewis saying that in nine out of ten allegedly paranormal cases the normal explanation was the correct one. I could also remember Nicholas talking of Occam's razor: the theory which is most likely to be true is the one which has been stripped of all its fancy trimmings.

If a blackmailer died much too conveniently what was the most likely explanation? And when a blackmailer was murdered, who was most likely to be the killer?

I did not bother to answer that last question. I merely gulped down the last of my champagne and decided that this was neither the time nor the place to complete my quest for the truth. I also decided that I should leave before I lost my nerve entirely and betrayed that the marriage had no future.

At that point it occurred to me that he had been gone for rather longer than I had anticipated.

"Kim?" I called, moving into the hall. "Kim, are you all right up there?"

There was no reply.

I paused, forcing myself to review the state of play, but I could see no reason why his attitude towards me should have undergone any dangerous change.

"Kim?" I called again, but still there was no response. I went on standing at the foot of the staircase—until it dawned on me that I was standing where Sophie's corpse had lain. I jumped violently. Then, still convinced that Kim could have no idea of the emotions which were now boiling away behind my rigorously composed façade, I slowly began to mount the stairs.

XIII

I reached the landing. At the top of the stairs a gallery flanked by banisters skirted the drop into the double-decker hall and passed various closed doors. At the end of the gallery one of the doors stood open, and as I drew cautiously nearer I saw beyond the threshold the thin glare of strip-lighting streaming from a place which I deduced to be an interior bathroom. Memories of modern hotels provided me with an instant picture of the layout: one entered the bedroom, one found the interior bathroom immediately on the left or right, and one walked past the row of closets opposite into a large sleeping area. In a house of this vintage the bathroom would have been a later addition, carved out of the master bedroom.

I paused on the threshold, but as the insertion of the bathroom had made the room L-shaped I could not see all of the sleeping area.

"Kim?" I said again. "Are you all right?"

No answer came. Maybe, having lost his tolerance for alcohol, he had passed out. It seemed a plausible explanation, so plausible that I decided to risk inching forward so that I could see the part of the room which was hidden from me.

I inched. Sweat was gluing my tank-top to my back again. My mouth was quite dry.

The moment I was far enough into the room to see that the sleeping area was empty, he slipped out of his hiding-place in the closet and slammed the door.

The key turned in the lock.

Then he leaned back against the panels and looked at me with unnaturally expressionless blue eyes.

NINETEEN

Anyone who does anything bad or criminal will of course want to conceal the fact, and secrecy is essential to deception, hypocrisy and other ways of misleading people.

DAVID F. FORD
The Shape of Living

I

I knew at once I must show no fear of any kind. As the experts on big fish say, blood in the water can trigger a feeding frenzy.

In a split second I had my reactions ordered: a sharp exclamation of justifiable shock, an exasperated reproof and a crisp return to the matter in hand. In another split second the scene was launched.

"Damn it, Betz!" I said crossly. "What the hell are you playing at? You nearly gave me a coronary!" Turning my back on him I tramped furiously across to the window and glared out over the garden as I tried to control my breathing. A pant or two after an unpleasant shock was excusable; continued panting had to be eliminated. Spinning to face him again I demanded: "Did you find the Anadin?"

He did not answer. He had removed the key from the door and was tossing it lightly as if it were a coin.

I knew this tactic. It was the silence-blanket.

Silence can be unnerving, particularly at a business meeting where talking is always expected. The antidote, naturally, is noise. Talking must at once ensue. The topic is unimportant. What matters is to show indifference to the intimidating behaviour.

"Oh, do stop playing with that key!" I snapped irritably. "Either put it back in the lock, for God's sake, or put it in your pocket. If you want to talk up here behind a locked door, that's fine, I don't care, I suppose you're afraid I might run away, but as I told you quite truthfully downstairs, I've no intention of disappearing (a) because I haven't yet had my share of the smoked salmon sandwiches, and (b) because I'm expecting a lift to the station in the Mercedes when the time comes for me to go. So forget all thought of me scurrying away through those godawful woods and let's get down to planning our future together—or are you feeling too knackered for that at present? If you want to have a nap I can easily wait, finish the sandwiches, make myself some coffee—"

"No, I'll keep going," he said, deciding it was time to grab control of the conversation. "I took the Anadin and I'll be better in a minute."

"Then I don't understand what we're doing up here. Can we go back downstairs?"

"Not just yet." He pocketed the key and moved into the bathroom. I heard a tap running and when he emerged he was sipping a glass of water. I recognised this tactic too. It usually appears at a business dinner when one's rivals are half-dead with tension and swilling alcohol as if it were lemonade. One then appears with a glass of water to signal not only that one's in total control of the situation but that one's will-power is sufficient to make every other person in the room look like a broken reed.

"Water!" I exclaimed. "Just what I need! Is there a second glass?"

Suddenly he laughed. "My God, you're a cool customer!" he exclaimed, relaxing as he leaned back against the bathroom door frame. "I couldn't have handled that rough ride better myself!"

"Well, now that we've got that little game over and you've had the pleasure of seeing me 'act tough,' as you always put it, can we talk about the future?"

"I didn't think we were quite through with talking about the past. What were those questions you said you wanted to ask me?"

"Questions. Ah yes," I said, heart lurching as I scrabbled around in my mind for a subject unconnected with the blackmail, "I was so busy recovering from my near-coronary that I quite forgot I was going to ask you about the stuff Mrs. Mayfield ended up by swiping. Was the divorce file as innocuous as you said it was, and what was really in that brown envelope?"

He answered willingly enough: "As far as I could gather from my quick skim, the divorce file really did seem to be bland—I told you the truth about that at the Rectory. Either Sophie didn't tell her lawyers the worst stuff or else she told them off the record at a meeting."

"And the brown envelope?"

"That was the dynamite. It contained copies she had taken of her letters to you, but the crowning irony was that I never stopped to read them. As soon as I saw the first letter saying 'Dear Miss Graham' I knew all the contents of the envelope had to be destroyed so I pressed on right away back to London."

"So when Mrs. Mayfield swiped both the envelope and the file—"

"It was an essential safety measure. She knew I'd told Sophie I was a member of an occult society, and she knew Sophie could connect me with the real blackmailer." He started to wander around the king-size bed to put down his water on the bedside table. "And that reminds me," I heard him say. "Talking of the blackmail—"

"Yes, a terrible subject," I said rapidly. "Let's draw a veil over the whole damn nightmare."

"But when you said downstairs just now that you had a couple more questions to ask, you weren't thinking of the missing files, were you, sweetheart? It was the blackmail you had in mind," he said, and when he turned abruptly to face me I knew my careless disclosure that I still had questions to ask even after he had completed his story had been a very big mistake. I now realised he had lured me upstairs and applied the searing psychological pressure because he had felt driven to find out how far I believed him.

"So," he said, taking care to give me an agreeable smile, "what exactly were the questions you wanted to ask?"

I had wanted to know where the blackmailer had been killed and how the fall onto the line had occurred, but there was no way I was going to ask either question when he and I were alone together in an isolated house behind a locked door. "Well, on reflection," I said in my most matter-of-fact voice, "they're not so important as the questions about the files. I was only going to ask"— there was a horrible moment when my powers of invention deserted me, but two harmless questions popped into my mind in the nick of time—"about Sophie," I said briskly. "When she received the blackmailer's photographs, was that the first time she knew of your 'hobby'?"

"Yes, I'd never discussed it with her. Of course she accepted I'd have a sex life elsewhere after we stopped sleeping together, but she would have visualised it in terms of a few occasional utterly monogamous relationships."

"With women?"

"Of course. The idea that I would have connections with men would never have occurred to her. Did you have another question?"

"Only about the VD. Did you get it from a woman or—"

"From a woman, yes, but you can be sure that after that episode I always used condoms, so you needn't start worrying about your health. I've been practising self-preservation since long before the age of AIDS."

I fell silent. A wave of empathy for Sophie was washing over me again and bringing a tightness to my throat. I thought of how much she must have loved Kim to stay with him after he had destroyed her hope of having children; I thought of how hard she must have worked to sustain the marriage by blotting out all thought of his inevitable infidelity. I thought of how her love had enabled her to forgive him—until she was finally blasted and brutalised by the truth which emerged from the blackmail. I knew one could argue that she was a masochist with low self-esteem who had been mad not to cut her losses and leave a dead-end, pain-streaked relationship; that would have been the tough-minded feminist position. But I was standing now in Sophie's shoes and I knew life was neither so simple nor so clear-cut as the activists needed to believe. When you love someone you long to trust them. When you love someone you yearn for the relationship to come right. When you love someone forgiveness is easy, patience is natural and hope becomes a way of life. How easy it is to endure too much suffering and lose sight of the place where the line against abuse has to be drawn! And as these truths swept through my mind I felt outraged by how this man had used and abused his trophy wife year after year so that he could have the marriage which would jack up his image, enhance his career prospects and guarantee the upmarket home which he felt was owing to him.

I said suddenly: "You didn't treat Sophie as a person." I was quite unable to stop myself saying this. Nor was I able to stop myself saying: "You treated her as an object in the most self-centred way imaginable, and in doing so you demeaned and degraded her. If that's the road to self-realisation as defined by Mrs. Mayfield and the members of your occult society, then they're as evil as the Nazis who destroyed the innocent people who got in their way."

His eyes widened.

Instantly I guillotined the rush of revulsion and backtracked. "Sorry," I said, "I got carried away there for a moment, but I'm not blaming the man you are now, the man you've become, the man you are with me. I'm blaming Mrs. Mayfield's influence on the man you used to be before you decided to break with her and get out of her world."

He did not answer immediately. He just stood

looking at me with those cool, expressionless blue eyes while my heart banged with fear, but at last he said neutrally enough: "Sophie was all right. She could have walked out at any time. She had her own money." His glance shifted to the cross at my throat. "I wish you'd take that thing off," he said. "I don't like it."

"I thought Lewis had made you sympathetic towards Christianity!" I said lightly, trying to ease the tension, but he merely answered: "I don't like you wearing something which reminds me of Sophie and I particularly don't like you making offensive remarks about the way I treated her. I was always courteous, generous, kind and considerate. It wasn't my fault that the blackmailer destroyed the marriage by dumping those photographs on her."

I saw at once that he had parted company with reality. With nausea I remembered my father, refusing in the past to accept responsibility for his actions and blaming all his failures on Lady Luck. "You're absolutely right," said my voice without a second's hesitation, "and I apologise for being so stupid. I suppose I was just having a moment's emotional reaction from all the revelations, but darling, don't let's talk any more about the past! All my questions have been answered now and I have nothing else to say—except, of course, that I truly admire your courage in confessing everything. You've really restored my love and respect, I can tell you!"

"Great!" he said at once, the barracuda finally moving in for the big bite. "Let's celebrate! Why don't you take off rather more than just that cross?"

I took a step backwards and found myself pressed against the wall.

I had given myself away. That single reflex, born of revulsion, had betrayed me. Desperately I willed myself to cover up the error by another casual remark, but I was too frightened now to dissimulate. No words came.

He said with that same empty look in his eyes: "You're not coming back to me, are you?"

My voice said: "Jesus Christ." But the name was not being used as an expletive. I was silently screaming for help. "Jesus Christ," I said again, my fingers clutching the little cross, and suddenly I saw that these words could be interpreted as yet another display of exasperation. The next moment I was demanding ferociously: "Look, buster, are you out of your mind? Do you honestly, seriously believe I'd go to bed with you here, not just in Sophie's home but in *Sophie's bedroom*? God, I can't believe I'm hearing this!"

"All right, all right!" His expression changed. The emptiness vanished. It was as if he were slipping in and out of two different personalities, and as I saw again how unintegrated he was, I realised how much damage remained to be healed despite his weeks in hospital. "I'm sorry, sweetheart," he said, and to my huge relief I saw he even looked shamefaced. "That was very insensitive of me, but I just feel so strung up over this whole business. I'm not myself at all."

I had a brainwave. "Is now the time, perhaps, to take that medication you passed up this morning?"

"So long as you're here I'm not taking anything which affects performance. Carter, what I really want now is—"

"I don't blame you. And talking of sex, darling, I was very touched when you said you didn't want our relationship to be tainted with all that other stuff, but you needn't be afraid our last session was too much for me—I really was telling you the truth afterwards when I said I thought it was a great expression of our love for each other, so obviously we're all set for the best of bedroom futures—and talking of the future, do let's discuss what we're going to do once you're fully recovered..." I was frantically trying to keep him talking while I worked out how I could escape, but no plan sprang to mind. My despair increased. I had to struggle hard to listen to him.

"Well, I thought a lot about this in hospital," he was saying, obviously reassured by my vision of an adventurous sex life in a future where we were still married, "and I've come to the conclusion that our best bet is to relocate to the States. Despite all that's happened I'm sure I can still get a job there—you can always make it in New York if you've got what it takes, and my American friends are influential enough to fix the visa problem so that we can get our green cards. I was thinking we could fly over, make a reconnaissance, look at top-grade apartments—"

"Won't that kind of relocation cost rather a lot of money?" I said, spotting a topic which was certain to prolong the conversation—although how I was managing to sustain any conversation at all I hardly knew. "I concede we're not on the breadline, but aren't you talking megabucks here?"

He just smiled at me. He had the intensely self-satisfied air of someone who has just pulled off a first-class con-trick. I had seen my father look like that on those rare occasions when he had backed a horse which had won against long odds. "I can see the time's come to tell you something I've never told a soul," he said, by this time almost vibrating with delight. "Now I'm *really* coming clean with you, sweetheart! I've got a secret stash in a numbered bank account in Switzerland, and I assure you we're currently in a position to relocate anywhere we damn well please..."

III

"Ah!" I said. No acting skill was required to sound stunned. Once again I was gripped by the memory of Tucker's chilling speculations.

"If there was one thing I learned from my father," said Kim, still deep in self-satisfaction, "it was the importance of having a secret stash so that if and when disaster struck one had the means to start again."

"Ah," I repeated, and somehow managed to pull myself together sufficiently to add: "Very wise."

"I wasn't entirely truthful earlier when I said the missing money went to Mrs. Mayfield and the society. I did make regular payments to Mrs. Mayfield, but I paid no money to the society. I gave them my professional expertise without charge instead and brought in some moneyed new members, so—"

"—so they gave you a free ride. I see. And since you weren't paying a blackmailer for years—"

"—I was able to salt away a good portion of my salary. As Sophie had her own money we never needed to work closely together on our financial affairs, so she never knew what was going on."

"Neat."

"Yes, but just as I was patting myself on the back for having my financial affairs in ideal order, the blackmailer turned up and wreaked havoc. You can see clearly now, can't you, why Mrs. Mayfield became so disenchanted with me? I'd passed up her advice to abandon my hobby—with the result that I'd involved her in a serious mess. I then refused to marry the woman she wanted me to marry and rejected her advice again when I took up with you. Taking up with you led to Sophie going on the rampage—which in turn led to not just one but two brushes with the police. In other words I became a walking disaster—and it all began with the blackmail."

"Yes, I do see—"

"And can you also see more clearly now why I kept going with the society? It was because I thought that so long as I was useful to it neither Elizabeth nor anyone else would take action against me. But of course that was before Sophie's death involved me with the police. I suspect now that Elizabeth decided I was expendable when I turned up on her doorstep on the night Sophie died. That was why she was so malevolent to me next morning at the flat—that was why she took such care to skewer the image of the balcony into my brain—"

"But I'm still sure it was only me she was gunning for!"

"Well, I'll certainly be in her sights now! For God's sake, she's gone on red alert, ditched the Fulham identity—"

"Have you really no idea where she's gone?"

"That's what the police asked when they were

finally allowed to ask me a few soft questions, but all I could tell them was that although the house in Fulham was used for her activities as a healer, I always suspected it was more of an office than a home. The only reason she was there on the night Sophie died was because I'd left a series of desperate messages on her answering machine."

"It's weird how she's managed to disappear—"

"She may have disappeared but she could still be willing me to self-destruct—and that's why I want to go to America as soon as possible. If I do there's a chance Elizabeth will just write me off; there's no fun in terrorising people if you can't see the results."

"But how can you inform her you've gone abroad if you don't know where she is?"

"The society's chief executive would know."

"Did you tell the police about him?"

"God, I don't want to give those people an extra reason to liquidate me! Isn't it enough that Elizabeth's worried about me shopping her to the police?"

"But I can't quite see why she's getting her knickers in such a twist," I said, my brain finally going fuzzy after all the brain-battering stress. "If Sophie died by accident and Mrs. Mayfield had no part in the events at Oakshott that night—" I broke off, remembering—too late—that Mrs. Mayfield had been helping Kim conceal a lethal truth long before Sophie died. Panic swept through me as I realised I had taken the path which led straight to the abyss. "Well, never mind all that," I said, the words tumbling out of my mouth. "The only important thing from my point of view is that you want to get right away from that woman. Now, darling, let's turn to the future again, let's—"

"You know," he said, "don't you."

My scalp crawled. "Know?"

"About the blackmailer. You've guessed the real reason why Elizabeth's afraid of me spilling my guts out to the police."

"Obviously she wants to protect the society."

"I'm not talking about the society."

My heart gave an extra thud. "Kim, let's just forget the blackmail, put it right behind us—"

"No, it's got to come out into the open now that you've guessed."

"But all I want, I promise you, is to draw a line under the past and focus on the future! So far as the blackmailer's concerned—"

"I killed him," he said.

IV

I was so frightened now that I could hardly breathe. How I managed to respond in less than five seconds I have no idea but I heard myself say: "I don't blame you. I'd have done the same thing myself in those circumstances."

"So I was right!" he exclaimed, and suddenly his eyes were moist with adoration. "I thought you'd take that line but I had to wait till I was sure. You're just like me, aren't you, sweetheart? So I'm not just telling you because I have to—I'm telling you because I want to. After all, if you're still committed to the marriage even though you've guessed what really happened to the blackmailer—"

Without hesitation I said: "Of course I am."

"Then I can trust you completely, can't I?" He was so relieved he even laughed before adding: "I was always so worried that the truth would undermine your feelings for me."

"No way! So what did happen to the black-mailer?"

Swiftly he said: "Elizabeth and I worked out a plan. She did offer to psych him into falling under a train, but of course I said I couldn't risk failure; psychic powers are a long way from being reliable, and she knew that as well as I did."

Futilely I wished I was wired for sound. "You're saying she was an accessory before the fact."

"Right."

"So much for her desire to operate within the law!"

"The blackmailer created a major emergency—she knew I was determined to get rid of him so she decided she had to get involved to make sure I got away with it. Quite apart from the fact that I was too valuable to the society to be cut loose, the last thing she wanted was the police arresting me for murder, putting my life under scrutiny and uncovering my occult connections."

"That makes sense, particularly if some of the occult activities were illegal."

But he chose to gloss over this comment. "It took us a while to work out the right plan," he said, "but we agreed from the start that I would kill him here in this house; all those micro-cameras made it too dangerous to kill him at his flat. Sophie had gone away to recover from the shock of finding out the truth, so we didn't have to worry about her. The real problem was what to do with the body. Unfortunately it was winter—the February of '88, a few months before you and I met—and although I wanted to bury him in the woods, there was no way I could have dug a grave in the frozen ground without a pneumatic drill. I did wonder if I could just leave him in the woods but Elizabeth said no, it would be better if we could cover up the fact that he'd been murdered because the police never close their files on a murder case and we both wanted to put the disaster behind us."

"But what on earth did you do?"

"I invited him down here. I promised I'd pay him an enormous sum if only he would hand over all the other photographs and the negatives—I even said, oozing desperation and appeasement, that if he agreed to end the blackmail I was willing to celebrate by partying with him afterwards. I knew he'd never be able to resist that, and I was right. He was so vain he thought I still fancied him and so hooked on the menu I was offering that he had to come back for more.

"I killed him in the shower in the end. It seemed best to do it in a place where any mess could be sluiced away and there were no clothes to be stained. I slammed his head against the wall and while he was still semi-stunned I strangled him. Then I put his clothes back on, wrapped him in a blanket to lock in any tell-tale fibres and stowed him in the trunk of my car.

"By that time it was eight o'clock. Sophie hadn't taken her car with her—she'd gone by plane to her friends in Scotland—so I left my car at the house and took her car to London. When I reached Soho it was crowded and I felt sure no one would notice me. I let myself into his flat with his keys, went through his files and removed the evidence which related to my case. (Of course he'd retained a set of negatives, the bastard!) All the files of his victims' photographs were arranged in a very businesslike way, and he even had the accounts stored on his personal computer. Black-mail in the age of technology! Disgusting.

"When I was sure there was nothing left in the flat to connect me with him I drove back to Surrey. By then it was very late. There's a valley near Oakshott, the Mole valley, and Sophie and I had often walked there on weekends in the early days of our marriage, so I knew it well. I'd remembered there was a cart-track leading up to a bridge over the railway which runs through that cutting, and I knew there would be nothing around, least of all a cart, at that time of night. I drove up the track, reached the bridge and heaved him onto the line—fulfilling Elizabeth's prophecy, of course, but it was the prophecy which had given me the idea.

"I knew the train might not destroy the physical evidence that he'd been murdered, but I figured that once the body was smashed up, some overworked pathologist would write the death off as a suicide and not bother to waste more time on the case. Elizabeth was prepared to give me an alibi for the night in question, but it was never needed because the police never found anything to connect me with him. I burned the evidence I'd recovered from the flat, I burned the blanket I'd used to wrap the body, and as a safety precaution I even traded in my car. I was safe—but we didn't get that closure of the file we'd been hoping for. The train failed to crush the appropriate parts, the pathologist did his work properly and the inquest produced a murder verdict.

"Was this just bad luck for us? No, we should have foreseen what happened. The trouble was that as we wanted to create the possibility of suicide I didn't remove the evidence of his identity, and as soon as the police went to his flat and found evidence of the thriving extortion racket, they were never going to believe he wasn't murdered.

"At that point the big problem for us was Sophie. Fortunately she never knew the blackmailer's name so she had no way of connecting me with the story in the local paper about the murdered man found on the railway line, and as the police kept the lid on his activities while they were pursuing their enquiries the word 'blackmail' didn't come up at the inquest. But of course Sophie, not knowing the man was dead, was still very worried about what he was going to do next. In the end I told her that I'd taken steps to give him a final pay-off, that I'd found out he had other victims and that with luck he'd now leave me alone and move on. Sophie seemed to accept this; we were living apart by that time, going for the two-year separation, and she said it was just as well we had to wait for a divorce because otherwise the blackmailer might see it as a fresh chance to pressure us and renew his demands.

"I was very relieved when she made this comment, of course, because it showed she didn't suspect the truth. But when you came on the scene I started to feel nervous about the blackmail all over again. I wasn't too surprised that Sophie never suspected me of murdering him—she'd lived a sheltered life in that plush Surrey ghetto, and she wasn't exactly streetwise. But *you*! You were never going to believe that a successful extortionist would vanish obligingly into the blue after striking gold! So I wasn't just worried about Sophie giving you the true story about the blackmail and revealing my hobby; I was worried that you'd wonder what the hell had happened to the blackmailer. Even though the press coverage had been minimal I thought you might have a look at the newspapers for February 1988, the month I'd supposedly made the last payment and see what kind of murders had been going on in London and Surrey—and if you did that I was sure the item in the local paper about the murdered man on the railway line a couple of miles from Oakshott would hit you between the eyes.

"Well, now you can see how important it was that Elizabeth and I should destroy Sophie's credibility and feed you the false story about the blackmail to pre-empt Sophie's version. And in case you're wondering all over again—no, neither of us killed Sophie. The very last thing I needed was an in-depth police investigation into my private life, and anyway by the time our attempt to destroy Sophie's credibility failed I had a motive the size of a mountain. Of course I wasn't going to kill her! I went to Oakshott to make one last all-out attempt to talk her into keeping silent, and I'd drummed up a new strategy, a strategy which I still think would have worked: I was going to grovel, beg for mercy and swear not only that I'd repented but that my repentance was all due to my new marriage. Then I was going to ask her if her attempts to break up that marriage could really be morally justified—and I think she'd have backed down at that point, I think she would, because breaking up marriages, let's face it, isn't a Christian occupation, particularly if one of the partners is trying to embark on a better life. I should have adopted this strategy long ago with Sophie, I can see that now, but the trouble was I just couldn't bring myself to grovel, I was too bloody angry. However, since I had my back to the wall I had no choice but to abandon my pride and pull out all the stops...except that in the end I didn't have to, did I, because she died. *But I didn't kill her!* The situation was quite different from the one involving the blackmailer because Sophie was ultimately a moral woman amenable to reason, whereas the blackmailer... No, there's no comparison.

"I've no regrets about killing that bastard, none whatsoever. He was truly the scum of the earth, and what does it matter anyway if there's now one homosexual less in the world? You know, Carter, I'm the first to say Hitler was a villain, and of course I've always been totally opposed to his treatment of the Jews, who are human beings just like us; I would never normally defend him, but between you and me, in the privacy of these four walls, I think he had the correct idea about homosexuals. I think in future, when science is more advanced, they should be recognised as mutations and genetically engineered out of the human race... Ah, now I've offended your liberal principles! I've gone too far and need to be reined in—isn't that what you're thinking, sweetheart? Okay, I'll backtrack! I know those sentiments are dead wrong and I promise you I'm really totally opposed to any form of eugenics, but that blackmailing bastard put me through such hell that it's hardly surprising I sometimes wish all homosexuals could be eliminated."

"Of course," I replied at once, but found I could say no more.

I had suddenly received a horrible insight into why he was so obsessed with me.

"How brave and resourceful you were!" I said when I could speak again. "I'm sure I could never have matched your nerve!"

"Oh yes, you could!" he said dotingly. "We're so alike—as you yourself often used to say when we first knew each other."

Trying not to think of my father I managed to answer: "I knew there was something uncannily familiar about you, but I thought the familiarity was due to the fact that we were both outsiders in England, both high flyers, both worshipping the same gods in the same temple."

"There was more to it than that!"

"Yes, I realise that now," I said, thinking how I had unconsciously seen in this powerful, successful man who loved me the idealised version of the man whom my inadequate, neglecting father had never been able to become. I saw then exactly how obsessed I had been to make good this loss for which I had never been allowed to grieve, and the insight was rendered all the more devastating by the result of my obsession: all I had done was marry a man who was just as emotionally inadequate as my father—and just as ready to neglect my true needs.

Meanwhile Kim was still luxuriating in his satisfaction with me. Rousing myself I heard him say: "Our personalities are mirror images of each other—the difference in sex doesn't matter."

The horrible insight deepened but I only said: "I'm not sure I quite understand."

"Remember how I said I felt so dislocated before I met you? That was because I felt part of my self was missing—separated from me in some way—and this seemed to create a split in my consciousness which kept crying out to be stitched together."

"I remember. So the reason why I'm so attractive to you is because—" I paused, just as a lawyer should, not wanting to lead the witness.

"Isn't it obvious?" he exclaimed in triumph. "Wasn't it clear how much you turned me on whenever you were tough as nails? I know you're wholly heterosexual—and of course as a heterosexual myself I couldn't live with any other kind of woman—but deep down you're *just like a man*! You're the missing part of myself which I've never before been able to find..."

VI

"As I told my psychiatrist only last week," Kim was saying with enthusiasm, "I no longer feel as if something's missing, because this mirror image you present somehow manages to unify me and heal the split in my consciousness. I'm not sure how this miracle works in psychological terms, but—"

"Excuse me," I said clumsily, and my voice sounded a long way away, "but I have to go to the bathroom."

"—but the fact is that as soon as I saw you I knew you were perfect," he declared, not listening. "The way you picked me up in that airport lounge! I thought: here's this beautiful, sexy girl and she's *just like a man*! For months you only showed me your feminine side when we were alone together, but that was okay, that was fine, because I knew that beneath the femininity lay the hard masculine core of your personality—

567

your true self—and that one day, if I waited long enough, you'd come right out to meet me. And one day, sure enough... Well, when we had that row—when you finally switched on your true self and showed me your masculine side—my God, I was knocked out, I'd never felt so turned on in all my life, and I knew then, without any shadow of doubt, that you'd never wind up reminding me of my bloody whore of a mother who was forever nauseating me with all her feminine flirting and flouncing—"

"I won't be a moment," I said, stumbling into the bathroom. "I'll be right back."

But the next moment the vomit was rushing up my throat and for the second time in that terrible house I found myself physically racked by revulsion.

VII

He was very kind. He seemed to think his murder confession had been too much for me after a surfeit of champagne on an almost empty stomach, but my collapse sprang primarily from the devastating knowledge that he had never known or understood me, just as I had never known or understood him. Haunted, even enslaved by our troubled pasts, we had been chasing fantasies which did not exist, and as we had moved together through our sinister hall of mirrors, the false images had merely multiplied to deceive us further and lead us on into a life unconnected with reality.

The reality was that I was a woman. My masculine persona, adopted long ago to help me survive in a cut-throat world dominated by men, was just a hyped-up expression of my masculine side, the side which my true self recognised but to which it assigned no predominant place in my personality. I accepted that this side provided the masculine traits which had enabled me to fashion my hyped-up professional persona, but I had never doubted that my feminine side was in the driving-seat of my personality, and perhaps it was this very confidence in my femininity which had enabled me not only to ape the men without inhibitions but often to ape them tongue in cheek.

Tucker had always understood that. But *this* man—this man who wanted to live with a woman who he thought was just like a man—this macho man who feared and despised in others what he had unconsciously feared and despised in himself—this promiscuous loner who felt so threatened by homosexuals that he had to brutalise them periodically to keep his fears at bay—this corporate bruiser who used and abused people without hesitation to further his own ends—this board-room barracuda who committed murder without regret—this serial liar who systematically cheated everyone who trusted him—*this* man was someone who could not only never understand me but could never see me as I truly was. He was obsessed by someone who didn't exist. It was pointless for him to swear that he loved me. He simply wanted me in order that he could function more smoothly. I was merely an object which promised to make his private life more manageable. I was to be used—and no doubt later abused if I dared to be so feminine as to have a child. Our marriage had been an illusion from start to finish, and indeed our whole relationship, constructed to fill each other's darkest needs and obsessions, had been a *folie à deux* on the grandest of scales.

All these thoughts flashed through my mind as I struggled with the physical manifestations of my revulsion, but when I had finished being sick there was no time to think further about the marriage. I had to concentrate with every ounce of strength I still possessed on the task of play-acting in order to survive.

"Have some water," he was saying sympathetically, handing me his refilled glass.

I drank, pressed my burning forehead for a moment against the cool, rose-coloured tiles of the bathroom wall and finally managed to straighten my back.

"Feeling better?" he said, moving much too close to me.

"Yep." I was trying to decide what I should do if he slipped his arms around my waist, but I thought he would probably allow me more time to recover before he pursued his sexual inclinations again.

"There's a trace of vomit on that cross of yours," he said suddenly. "Let me take it off." And before I could react he had jerked the cross hard, breaking the fragile clasp and pulling the chain from my neck.

"Kim, for God's sake!" I exclaimed, too unnerved to censor myself, but he only said: "I just couldn't stand looking at it any longer," and he dropped the cross in the wastepaper basket. "I'll tell you what I'd like to do now if you're feeling better," he said, smiling as he turned back to face me. "I'd like to take you to one of the other bedrooms, somewhere quite empty of my past here with Sophie, and then—"

He told me what he wanted to do to celebrate our reconciliation, but I ceased to listen. All I knew was that my one chance to save myself had finally arrived; all I knew was that he was going to unlock that bedroom door.

VIII

He led the way out of the room. As he stepped into the corridor and turned to put an arm around me I halted abruptly on the threshold and said: "I must get the cross. Sorry." Then I feinted a retreat but immediately, while he was off guard, I doubled back, charged past him and began to race hell for leather around the galleried hall to the stairs.

"Tucker!" I shouted at the top of my voice, to give the impression that a bodyguard had been hidden nearby all along—and suddenly I realised there was someone in the hall below.

A woman was moving smoothly from the kitchen towards the living-room. She wore a plain dark red suit with a wide-brimmed straw hat, and she was carrying the flat wooden basket which had been abandoned in the kitchen on the night she had died.

For a moment she glanced up at me but the brim of her hat ensured that her face remained in deep shadow.

Then she moved on out of sight into the living-room.

IX

I knew my disordered brain was projecting the image, and I knew why I was seeing what I saw.

571

I was in Sophie's house and Sophie's suffering had been repeatedly dominating my thoughts. If my brain was now reacting to intolerable stress again, what could be more natural than that I should see her in her own home, where every room held such strong memories of her presence? Yet I still found the sighting a shattering experience.

Shock had jerked me to a halt at the head of the stairs, and the next moment Kim was grabbing me. His grip was savage. He had realised how far he had been deceived.

I screamed and screamed as I struggled in his arms, but now I no longer needed to pretend there was help nearby because someone really was there, rushing to my rescue. I heard footsteps racing across the hall—not Sophie's footsteps; Sophie had made no sound and she had not been running. At first I thought the footsteps were a hallucination but then I realised Kim had heard them too; he was swivelling sideways to look down into the hall, and as the shock made him relax his grip I shoved him hard, so hard that he lost his balance and cannoned into the banisters.

A second later someone hurtled up the stairs and shot in front of me.

In stupefaction I recognised Tucker.

X

As Kim scrabbled to recover his balance and I lurched back with a sob of relief against the wall, Tucker planted himself between us and said strongly: "Forget the next accident, Mr. Betz—it isn't going to happen!" Glancing back at me over his shoulder he demanded: "Do you want to go or stay?"

"Go."

"Right. We're leaving. Precede me down the stairs, please, in case he tries to attack you again." He swung back to Kim who was now standing upright and breathing hard. "You want to make something of this? You want to land a punch so that I can call the police and get you locked up? You can bet your life they'd be salivating if they knew you'd attacked me a second time!"

Kim lost his nerve. After spewing out a string of obscenities he shouted: "What do you think you're doing, breaking into my house and hurling threats at me like a bloody lunatic? Just who the hell do you think you are?"

"*Retribution!*" yelled Tucker, but I grabbed his hand before he could be drawn again into violence, and tugged him back towards me.

To Kim I said: "He's right. Injure him a second time and no one'll believe it was an accident." I began to grope my way down the stairs. Black spots danced before my eyes and for a moment I thought I might pass out, but Tucker grasped my arm and steered me safely past the last step.

I looked back. Kim had not moved. He was very still now, his face pale and expressionless. As our glances met he said: "You lied to me," and I answered straight away without regret: "Yes, I did."

"But I trusted you!"

"You've been brutalising people who trusted you for years. Why shouldn't you be finally dosed with your own medicine?" I began to move unsteadily towards the front door.

"Well, don't kid yourself there's anything you

573

can do to touch me!" he shouted, suddenly unable to control himself a second longer as his personality once more began to disintegrate. "There's no forensic evidence!"

I stopped. I turned. I faced him. Then I said so clearly that Tucker would remember every word when the time came to talk to the police: "You're wrong. If the pathologist did the autopsy so thoroughly that he realised the mangled corpse was murdered, he'll have found the man had sex before he died, and they'll get you on the DNA."

"Oh no, they bloody won't!" yelled Kim. "I used a condom!"

There was a moment of silence as jolting as a high-volt electrical charge. Then Tucker said urgently: "*Run*, Carter!" and jerking me forward with him he flung wide the heavy front door.

XI

We rushed to the Mercedes, parked in front of the house, but I saw at once there was no key in the ignition.

Tucker said swiftly: "My car's beyond the gates."

But the drive seemed very long.

"You can make it!" urged Tucker as my pace flagged. "Keep going!"

I tore up the gravel beneath my feet again. The sun was blazing down so fiercely that my body felt as if it were on the brink of dissolving. I heard myself gasp: "He'll figure no one knows we're here. He'll kill us and bury the bodies in the woods."

"Fat chance. I've got a book to finish."

I tried to laugh, tried to cry but wound up just panting for breath. There was a stitch in my side. My lungs were hurting.

"I'll carry you," said Tucker, catching me as I stumbled.

"The hell you will!" I staggered on.

We reached the gates. "No sign of him," said Tucker, looking back, but then such an unnerving thought struck him that he stopped dead. "Could he be getting a gun?"

I shook my head, bending double to ease the stitch as I halted beside him. "He's never mentioned owning one—and if he did—it would be in London—and not here." My gasps for breath provided a bizarre punctuation.

Tucker exclaimed exasperated: "I wish you'd let me sweep you off your feet!" but I just whispered: "Sorry. Not sweepable."

"Why not? A spunky heroine should always wind up swept. If we were back in WWII—"

"Stuff that. Here's Kim."

We hurtled past the open gates and when Tucker steered me to the left I saw the dirty white Ford parked less than twenty yards away. But my relief was rapidly displaced by fear.

"Tucker, the Mercedes will bust that heap apart! It'll be like Jaws closing in on a goldfish!"

"We'll hide." He flung open the passenger door.

I fell inside and within seconds he was starting the engine. The interior of the car was oven-hot. I wanted to faint but there was no time.

"Where—"

"Let's get out of this road and into the next.

Then we'll keep our eyes peeled for an empty garage."

We rocketed away from the kerb and bucketed down the sedate private road like a hot-rod from hell. The tyres screeched as we rounded the corner at the end, but Tucker braked abruptly and we began to peer up the driveways, he looking to the right and I to the left.

"There!" I shouted.

He slammed on the brakes, thrust the car into reverse and backed up to take a better look. At the end of a hundred yard stretch of gravel a two-car garage yawned emptily beside another interwar house.

"Go for it!" I cried, but Tucker already had his foot pressed hard down on the accelerator. Shooting up the drive we reached the garage in seconds.

"Keep down," muttered Tucker, slumping in his seat after angling the driver's mirror to ensure he still had a view of the road.

We waited, no longer able to talk. I was counting the seconds and had just reached twenty-eight when Tucker said suddenly: "There he goes. We've done it."

"Thank God," I whispered, again wanting to faint but again knowing that fainting was an unaffordable luxury, and struggled to focus on the next stage of the ordeal.

XII

"He'll backtrack when he realises he's failed to catch us," I said. "Let's stay right where we are till we see him return."

"What makes you so sure he'll head back after

he realises he's lost us?" demanded Tucker at once. "What would *I* do if I were Kim Betz? I already know an independent witness has heard me acknowledge I'm a murderer. I must know my marriage is finally washed up. I'm bound to realise in no time that my life in England is no longer viable, so—"

"He'll take the rat-run," I said unsteadily, "just as his father did. He'll head for Heathrow and take the first plane out to a country where there's no extradition treaty."

"Where's his passport?"

"At Harvey Tower—unless he asked his PA to bring it to Oakshott. He was already planning to go abroad."

"Not straight away, surely?"

"After we were reconciled. But if he now plans to take the rat-run, he'll want more than his passport—he'll want the crucial papers, and they must still be at the flat among the stuff he kept in his junk-room."

"What papers?"

"The papers relating to his Swiss stash. Tucker, he's got to go back to Harvey Tower, got to— there's no way he can vanish into the blue without first going back to the City..."

XIII

"We need a phone," said Tucker when we had agreed that my theory was the most plausible possibility on offer, "and something tells me that if we start knocking on doors in this neighbourhood, the paranoid rich will refuse to let us cross their thresholds. Let's go back to the house."

"You're nuts! If Kim returns—"

"As soon as he realises he's lost us he'll drive on to London."

"But you can't be sure of that!"

"He doesn't have the time to come back here, Carter. Every second counts now." He started the engine and began backing the car out of the garage.

"But couldn't we drive into the village and find a payphone?"

"The house is nearer than the village." He reversed the Ford into the road and shoved the gear-shift forward. "I'm going to call Nick," he added. "If we call the local police we'll be bogged down for hours in long explanations, but Nick knows the top brass in the City police and he should be able to cut through the red tape to ensure Kim's intercepted at the Barbican... Can you save time by writing down the number of the Mercedes for me?"

My bag was still at the house but in the glove compartment I found both pen and paper. I had just jotted down the number when we reached the gates.

"Supposing he locked up before he left?" I said worried.

"He'd have been too distracted." Tucker swung the car up the drive.

"But supposing he comes back after all and sees—"

"He doesn't know this is my car, and you can keep watch from the hall once we get inside. We can always escape out of the back if we have to."

We found the French windows still open. Picking up my bag from the coffee table I moved as if in a dream back to the hall to keep watch while

Tucker made the call. I knew Sophie was near even though I could no longer see her. I thought of her as I stared through my unshed tears at the front lawn.

I heard Tucker explaining the situation succinctly to Nicholas. When the call finished I made no move but continued to stand by the window.

"I'm all right," I said to Tucker as he moved to my side, and before he could touch me I repeated fiercely: "I'm all right."

He said gently: "Come and sit down for a moment in the living-room."

"No, I can't wait to get out of this house." I began to heave open the front door but stopped when I remembered Sophie again. "We must lock up," I said. "She would have wanted her home to be protected from vandals and burglars. It's something we can do for her." So we closed and bolted the French windows before we left. I kept whispering: "Sophie!" to myself and wiping the tears from my eyes.

"Did he kill her?" said Tucker when we finally returned to the car.

"No. He just cheated and lied and brutalised her and said afterwards he'd treated her with kindness, generosity and consideration." Anger helped me to get a grip on the tears. Once I was sitting in the car I found a tissue in my bag and began to mop myself.

"But he killed the blackmailer," said Tucker, sliding behind the wheel before adding: "Did provincial police forces really have access to DNA testing back then?"

"I doubt it. I'm not sure that even today's scientists can do a DNA test on semen. I think they can only do it on blood."

"Then I'm surprised Kim didn't query your DNA fantasy!"

"He was out of control, not thinking straight. And maybe he knows even less about new forensic techniques than I do."

Tucker said no more but drove to the nearest pit-stop on the A3 where he insisted on buying me coffee and a doughnut. The caffeine gave my brain a boost; the sugar provided some much needed energy. Finally I was able to ask the big question. It was: "How on earth did you manage to be in the right place at the right time?"

"I always knew he'd grab control and rip up your well-ordered little plan."

"When did you give up waiting for us at the hotel on Reigate Hill?"

"I never went to Reigate. I drove straight to the hospital and followed the Mercedes from the beginning. It was easy at first in the slow-moving traffic, but although I lost you on the A3 I was sure by then you were heading for Oakshott."

"How did you find out the address?"

"As soon as I reached the village I found the church, stormed the Vicarage and asked the vicar's wife for help—I also used her phone to let Nick know what had happened."

"And when you got to the house—"

"I skulked around in the garden for a time. All those trees provided perfect cover, and since the French windows were open I had a clear view of the two of you in the living-room. I was alarmed when you eventually disappeared, but when the neighbour turned up seconds later I figured you were safe for a while—obviously Kim wasn't going to harm you as long as she was there. It was when she came out again that I started to worry, but then a very odd thing happened. This woman looked across the lawn, saw me standing among the trees and gestured to the French windows as if to say: 'Do go in!' but she didn't call out to ask who I was or what I was doing. She just moved around the side of the house and...Hey, what's the matter? What did I say?"

I said numbly: "There was no other person in the house."

"Of course there was! I saw her go in and I saw her come out! She was wearing a dark red outfit with a straw hat and she was carrying a flat wooden basket, the kind my mother uses when she's gardening—"

I finally succeeded in fainting.

XIV

After I had recovered consciousness I was offered a free cup of tea by our anxious waitress but I settled for a glass of water. Tucker then insisted on carrying me from the restaurant to the car, so just as I achieved my desire to faint he achieved his desire to sweep me off my feet. Quite what that proved and to whom I was too dazed to decide, but he seemed to find the experience satisfying and I was groggy enough to be glad of the ride, so this excursion into feminist pre-history was not without its rewards. Tucker was wearing a pale green shirt, almost entirely unbuttoned, but instead of the Essex-man medallion which so often accompanies this free-wheeling sartorial style, he wore a small, discreet gold cross. It was made even more discreet by the fact that it was half-buried in the dark red hair which ran in a tapering line from his chest to his navel. He was also

581

wearing blue jeans, the weathered pair which had faded in interesting places, and although my capacity for sexual response was by that time as non-existent as that of a mass-produced doll, I was vaguely aware that in another time and in another place I might have found myself turning tigerish. The trouble was I could neither imagine another time nor picture another place. Pinned to an agonising present I was too pulped to do more than endure the damage I had suffered and wonder if I would ever recover.

"What a fluff-out!" I muttered as he arranged me on the front seat of the car.

"Relax—lie back and think of England!" he said kindly, as if I were a Victorian maiden being initiated into an upper-class breeding programme, and proceeded to drive me straight to St. Benet's. I did manage to tell him he had seen Sophie's ghost, just as I had, but he only said: "Do you really want me to drive into the back of a truck?" and added that I should avoid all conversation until later in order to rest. At that point I passed out again, this time because I was exhausted, and when I awoke I found the Ford was halting in the cobbled forecourt of the Rectory.

They all came to meet me. I was vaguely surprised by this mass turn-out by the Healing Centre's senior personnel; I supposed they thought I was some sort of emergency case, but I was feeling better by this time and no longer afraid that I might behave like a water-logged fluffette. Eventually I managed to say to Nicholas: "Did the police get there in time?" and Nicholas answered: "Yes, they did," but he created a small pause before he added: "It's all over now, Carter."

Then I knew, with emotions almost unbearable in their intensity, that Kim's final rat-run had turned out to be very different from the one he had always planned.

XV

The police were waiting for Kim at Harvey Tower but they allowed him to go up to the flat before they made their presence known. He paused in the podium lobby to pick up the spare keys, which I had long since returned to the porters' desk, and remained unaware that the plain-clothes man in the basement car park had already alerted the patrol cars to the arrival of the Mercedes.

He opened the front door when the police rang the bell, and he appeared willing to talk to them, but as soon as they followed him into the living-room he opened the balcony door, supposedly to let some air into the stifling flat, and when he darted outside they were not quick enough to catch him. He ran the length of the wrap-around balcony to distance himself from his pursuers, and then outside the bedroom where I had so often loved him so much, he scrambled over the rail without a backward glance and plunged thirty-five floors to the concrete far below.

PART FIVE

TOWARDS HEALING

I hope it has begun to emerge from what I have been saying that faith in God can actually be a liberating thing, a breaker down of barriers, a refusal to accept fragmentation as the last word, a stimulus to look beyond our own relative, partial, blinkered standpoint, an encouragement not to be frightened and overwhelmed by mysteries beyond our understanding, a promise held out to us that truth is one, and truth is great, and will prevail.

JOHN HABGOOD
Confessions of a Conservative Liberal

✳   ✳   ✳

In our bewildered, painful, often despairing world there is still the presence of one who comes, who calls, who gives life and light and healing, who is revealed to us in the simplicity of childhood and in the awful desolation of suffering. And as of old, those who respond to his call and allow him to expand their own horizons of meaning, discover in experience who he is.

JOHN HABGOOD
Making Sense

TWENTY

What healing can we hope for in our suffering?
The longing is for something magical, the quick
fix, the miraculous touch or medicine, the dra-
matic release. And occasionally the miracle does
happen. But it is clear too that... God is not a
God of quick fixes and easy, instantaneous solu-
tions.

DAVID F. FORD
The Shape of Living

I

"She killed him," I said much later when I was alone with the two priests. "He kept getting these headaches and he said she'd skewered the image of the balcony into his brain. She terminated him."

"Of course she did!" agreed Lewis. "Her hold over him was demonic, she'd already caused his personality to disintegrate, and she finally pushed the self-destruct button."

I turned to Nicholas who was still silent. "He wasn't the suicidal type," I insisted. "He was a survivor. He would have worked out that he was most unlikely to be convicted of the murder of that blackmailer—there was no knock-down forensic evidence, and I doubt if he would have been convicted on Tucker's testimony of what was said in that hall. Prosecuting counsel would only have had to show that Tucker and I were attracted to each other—a fact amply demonstrated by Tucker's presence at the scene—and then Tucker's evidence would have become suspect. Kim would have hired a top QC to ensure an acquittal and then gone on to fight another day in the States. I tell you, if it hadn't been for that arch-cow he'd be still alive!"

Nicholas said carefully: "We can't ignore Mrs. Mayfield's role in Kim's tragedy, but this is a complex case and it may be that his decision to kill himself had more than one cause. One has to consider—"

"I don't have to consider anything," I said. "She killed him. Case closed."

II

"She killed him," I said to the psychologist. "She skewered the image of the balcony into his brain and I'll bet she also got that bloody society to will him to death!"

"You're saying you believe Mrs. Mayfield took a malign line," said Robin.

"Damn it, I don't just 'believe'—I *know* she did!"

"Of course it's very important, when we feel we're drowning in chaos, to find certainties which can keep us afloat."

"What's that supposed to mean? Are you saying I'm just proclaiming this fact—repeat, *fact*—to cheer myself up?"

"I think there can be little doubt that Mrs. Mayfield had a disastrous effect on Kim."

"You concede she willed him to death?"

"I concede it's not impossible. But right now I'm more interested in you—your grief, your anguish, your struggle to cope with this tragedy—"

587

"All I want is someone to believe me!" I shouted, and stormed out of his consulting-room.

III

"She killed him," I said to the doctor. "She willed him to death, brainwashed him into it. It wasn't suicide. It was murder."

"Well, whichever way you cut the cake it was a tragedy," said Val, "and tragedies are very distressing for those involved."

"No, don't start talking to me as if I'm unhinged! I'm thinking clearly, rationally and logically, and what I want is some kind of acknowledgement that Kim was finally destroyed by that bloody woman! In my opinion he died of evil!"

"I have every sympathy for that point of view," said Val at once, "but since evil isn't a listing in the medical dictionary I can't serve it up to you as part of a professional opinion."

"Then give me your professional opinion about why Kim should have committed suicide!"

"Well, Carter, I think we have to take on board the fact that he'd been in a mental hospital for a few weeks, and—"

"But he wasn't suicidal in hospital!"

"No, but that might have been because he never lost hope of achieving a reconciliation with you. That hope was helping him to get better quickly, but when everything went wrong, the fragility of his mental health meant that he didn't have the resources to—"

I cut her off and walked out.

IV

"He was murdered by that woman Mayfield," I said to the police. "She willed him to death, programmed him to self-destruct. There have been cases reported in scientific journals. Aborigines can do it. This is murder, not suicide."

The two policemen exchanged meaningful glances before the older one said to me kindly: "Of course this is all a big ordeal for you, Mrs. Betz. We can come back later, if you'd prefer."

There was a long silence.

Then I nodded and they went away.

V

"How are you doing, Ms. G?"

"Fine."

"Just thought I'd check in."

"Thanks."

"You don't mind me phoning, do you?"

"Not at all."

"Anything I can do to help?"

"I don't think so, thanks."

"Any chance of seeing you?"

"It's a bit difficult right now."

"I'm sure it is. You'll let me know, won't you, if there's anything I can do."

"Of course. Thanks, Tucker," I said, and hung up before I could start to cry.

VI

"I've made you a chocolate mousse to tempt you to eat," said Alice. "There's something so comforting about chocolate, I always think, and the mousse will slip down so easily you'll hardly be aware that you're eating. Do give it a try!"

I managed three spoonfuls. "Alice, you do think Mrs. Mayfield killed Kim, don't you?"

"Of course. Would you like a spot of cream to help the mousse along?"

"No thanks. Alice, she did kill him, didn't she?"

"Definitely. And it was easier for her, wasn't it, because he wasn't mentally strong. He mightn't have been the type to commit suicide when he was well, but that day must have been so stressful for a man who was still sick—why, the confession alone must have been such a strain, particularly since he so much wanted the marriage to come right—"

I abandoned the mousse and bolted.

VII

After those interviews I decided to think no more about the manner of Kim's death. Obviously it was less upsetting to let other people work out how and why he had died, and as soon as I reached this conclusion I felt much better. I also realised I was now free to detach myself emotionally from the mess and embark on a familiar exercise: reducing the chaos to order with professional efficiency.

In the immediate aftermath of the death the police continued to be kind to me, but Tucker and I were interrogated for a long time about the events at Oakshott. By mutual consent we never mentioned the ghost; when I said that Kim had caught up with me in the gallery I did not explain that I had been brought up short by the sight of

590

Sophie in the hall, and when Tucker told the police about his decision to enter the house he merely said he had been unable to endure the suspense of waiting a second longer. The police were painstaking in their pursuit of detail not only because they needed to close their file on the blackmailer's murder but because they were toying with the idea that Kim had been responsible for other unsolved homosexual murders committed in London over the past few years. However, the links with these murders were never proved, and I myself did not believe they existed. Kim's "hobby" had been dangerous enough; I could not imagine him choosing to make it still more dangerous by committing murders which were unnecessary to his survival.

The media got the wrong end of the stick once again and decided I had called in the police to stop Kim committing suicide. Various theories for the suicide then circulated: he was the victim of an exorcism which had gone wrong, he was a drug addict who had despaired of kicking the habit, he had leaped from the balcony while under the influence of LSD. (The coroner later panned all these theories but no journalist seemed to take much notice.) Meanwhile the police, anxious to pursue their investigations in peace, said nothing about the information which Tucker and I had given them, and neither Tucker nor I had the slightest intention of giving a press conference. The media yammered away both after the death and at the time of the inquest, but fortunately on each occasion the news moved on swiftly and so did the reporters.

The inquest itself, neatly choreographed by the coroner, produced the inevitable verdict that

591

Kim had committed suicide while the balance of his mind was disturbed. As soon as evidence was given that he had been spending time in a mental hospital, the verdict was a foregone conclusion, although his doctors insisted heatedly that there had been no reason to regard him as a suicide risk.

Long before this the lawyers had carted away all the papers in Kim's junk-room in order to explore every aspect of his finances, and I had discovered that under his will I had inherited all his real and personal estate—which included not only the house at Oakshott but the Swiss stash, numerous stocks and shares, and a substantial bank balance. Whatever problems I had to face in the immediate future, money was not going to be one of them.

Tucker phoned regularly, and I saw him at the inquest, but I found I was still unable to face meeting him on my own. Fear of intimacy, fear of making another catastrophic mistake in my private life, hung over me like a pall, but although I was aware of this additional legacy from Kim I recoiled from dwelling on it. It was easier just to toil on with the task of reducing the chaos to order, so although I told Tucker there would be a time later for socialising, I did not say when "later" would be and he took care never to pressure me by asking.

Then finally, after the interviews with the police, after the media blitzes, after the sessions with Kim's lawyers, accountants, colleagues and bankers, after the inquest had delivered the formal verdict on the death, Kim's body was released by the authorities and I found my next task was to organise the funeral. That was when my emotions crawled off the ice, where I had dumped them, and began to defrost. That was when I realised that the role of the efficient businesswoman could no longer be sustained. And that was when I knew I was face to face at last with the ordeal of trying to come to terms with what had happened.

VIII

"A cremation, of course," I said to Lewis, "and no religious service."

I was still feeling grateful to Lewis for supporting my belief that Mrs. Mayfield had killed Kim, but my gratitude quickly faded as he failed to approve this proposal about the funeral. He merely smoothed the skirt of his cassock and remained silent for a moment.

We were in the vestry of the church. Lewis did have an office in the Healing Centre but he spent much of his working day in the main part of the church as he attended to stray callers, the organisation of the services and the numerous other items of ecclesiastical business which Nicholas was too busy to deal with. The vestry desk was crowded; Lewis was, as usual, smoking a cigarette; in the distance the organist was practising, and the music provided comforting evidence of the church's stable weekday routines.

Lewis said at last: "Kim was not uninterested in religion. I would definitely classify him as a seeker."

"He conned you. At the end he was so anti-Christian that he tore the cross from my neck."

"That was certainly significant. However—"

"He was depraved. Obscene. Evil."

"True. But—"

"He was a murderer!"

"Yes, but immediately after his death, wasn't it very important to you that Mrs. Mayfield's part in his destruction should be underlined?"

I stared, sensing he was trying to throw me a lifeline. After a moment I said: "Go on."

"I think that despite all that had happened your first instinct was to try to hold on to your memory of the Kim you had loved—the real Kim—by keeping him separate from the other Kim, the demonic Kim, the man who terrified you at Oakshott and who (you now clearly feel) deserved all that was coming to him. And I think the only way you found you could do this was by pushing the idea that Kim—the real Kim—had been destroyed by Mrs. Mayfield. You'll remember I supported this theory. I supported it even though we don't know for certain whether or not she was willing him to kill himself; all we do know is that in his weakened mental state he became obsessed with the lethal image of the balcony."

I made a huge effort to grasp what he was saying. "You mean you supported me because—"

"—because it was your way of saying there were two Kims, and I believed this to be a genuine insight into what was going on. Let's take the incident when he tore the cross from your neck. Was that the real Kim, who (as he told you) was disillusioned with Gnosticism and who (as he told me) was beginning to feel Christianity might have something to say to him? Or was it another Kim altogether? Was the man who tore off the cross a manifestation of Kim's true personality, or was he manifesting the subpersonality which Mrs. Mayfield fostered and controlled, the subpersonality which expanded to such a size during those final scenes that it crushed the true personality to pieces?"

There was a long silence.

"If you want no religious service," said Lewis at last, "then of course your wish should be respected. You're the widow. But who is it who deserves no religious service? Mrs. Mayfield's 'Jake'? Or the real Kim who saw you as symbolising the escape which he wanted to make from her world?"

All I could manage to say was: "You're splitting hairs."

"No. Just pursuing the unvarnished truth."

I fought hard to maintain my equilibrium. "You knew him," I said when I was sure I could keep my voice level. "What do you think he would have wanted?"

"Well, we know what he wanted when he left hospital, don't we? He wanted forgiveness. He loved you and was willing to embark on a very difficult confession because he wanted the marriage to go on."

"But he didn't love me! He radically misunderstood the kind of person I really was!"

"That's true. But nevertheless he experienced a love which he believed was genuine, and this love made him long for forgiveness and reconciliation."

"Yes, but—"

"Love is the most powerful integrating and healing force on earth," pursued Lewis, "and Kim believed not only that he loved you but that this love would prove the pathway to salvation. His beliefs were misdirected, but nevertheless he was still involved with a certain spiritual dynamic, and this was why he was so receptive to my visits. The dynamic—the spiritual cycle—consists of sin, repentance, forgiveness, redemption, resurrection and renewal. That's the Christian pattern, and that was the pattern he was reaching for."

After several seconds spent groping for a reply I muttered: "But he still wasn't a Christian."

"No, but real Christianity is about counting people in, not drawing a line to keep people out— as the Gnostics do when they declare their special saving knowledge is only available to a few. Carter, I'm not denying Kim had committed himself to a corrupt form of Gnosticism which had been designed by evil people for evil purposes. All I'm saying is that in the end he wanted to reject that and start again because after he met you what he wanted to believe in was the primacy of love and the need for forgiveness. Those two things point to a very different path to salvation—and when I say 'salvation' I mean integration and healing."

I tried to process this information, tried to make sense of it, tried not to feel that I was being led into a minefield where one false step might blow me to pieces.

"Kim was on a journey," said Lewis at last. "He was derailed in the end because the Powers were still in possession of a major section of his personality, and in the crunch he wasn't integrated enough to withstand their overwhelming pressure to fragment, but I believe he was finally on his way from darkness into light. I'm not suggesting that there should be a full Christian burial service, but I think a brief acknowledgement of his spiritual struggle for a new life might not be entirely misguided."

I was unable to speak.

"An opening sentence," said Lewis. "A reading. The Lord's Prayer. A silence of perhaps thirty seconds for private prayer. A blessing. The whole thing need take no more than five minutes."

I had a sudden picture of Kim. But it was not of the barracuda who had terrified and revolted me at Oakshott. It was of the playful dolphin who had been so happy with me on our honeymoon.

Tears filled my eyes as Lewis said: "It would symbolise that the Powers never have the final word—and symbols are so important, always pointing beyond themselves to truths which aren't easily expressed in words... What do you think, Carter? Could this perhaps be a more appropriate way forward?"

I nodded and stumbled away.

IX

I allowed Nicholas and Alice to come with me to hear Lewis conduct the brief service at the crematorium. I realised eventually that I needed Alice, who had such a comforting personality, and I felt I could hardly tell Nicholas to get lost when he volunteered to accompany her. The only other person whom I allowed to attend this very private funeral was Gilbert Tucker. He phoned to ask if he could be present, though he did not say whether he was representing his brother or whether he was merely signalling the concern he had felt for me ever since I had wound up at his vicarage on the night of the melt-down.

I found I was glad to see him. He reminded me of my unseen companion who had steered me through the darkness, although when I saw Gil again he seemed just another priest in uniform, just another clerical carer with well-honed professional skills.

There was no sign of my unseen companion as we gathered in the chapel, but during the opening sentence I knew he had somehow slipped in because light began to stream through the darkened neural pathways of my brain.

Lewis said, quoting St. Paul: "'For I am persuaded, that neither death, nor life, nor angels, nor principalities, *nor powers*, nor things present, nor things to come, nor height, nor depth, nor any other creature, shall be able to separate us from the love of God...'"

A wave of emotion overwhelmed me as I finally started to grieve.

X

I have no clear memory of the rest of the service but afterwards I managed to say to Gilbert Tucker: "Please try to explain to your brother that I thought I understood everything but now I realise I understand almost nothing, and while I sort out the mess I don't want to hear him slagging off Kim as he did that other time. That'll only make me more ripe for a head transplant than ever."

Gil said: "He realises that now," and when he had given my hands a comforting clasp he added as if we were discussing some exotic item of food which had to be kept at the right temperature in the refrigerator: "Don't worry about Eric. He'll keep."

"Tell him the phoenix will eventually rise from the ashes," I said impulsively, but afterwards I wished this sentence had remained unspoken.

I knew the thought of another relationship still terrified me.

XI

It was noon when we arrived back at the Rectory. Normally Alice would have gone to the kitchen to prepare the informal weekday lunch which the Healing Centre's staff were welcome to attend, but on that day the task had been delegated and she came upstairs to the flat with me instead.

After I had fixed myself a vodka martini and she had poured herself a glass of wine we sat down together on the sofa. "Thanks, Alice," I heard myself say. "Thanks for everything." Then I started to guzzle the martini.

When I came up for air Alice said cautiously: "Do you feel awful, not so awful or really and truly frightful?"

"I've no idea, I'm too banjaxed to know. All I do know is that unless I dig up some answers to all the unanswered questions soon, I'm going to go nuts."

"Questions about Kim?"

"Questions about everything. Lewis did help me by suggesting the monster at Oakshott was reflecting a malign subpersonality which was eclipsing Kim's real self; that made me see that a funeral service for the Kim I'd loved was still possible, and as the funeral service was obviously...obviously—"

"Obviously right," said Alice.

"—obviously right, yes, Lewis must have hit on some sort of truth. But what exactly was this truth he hit on? I mean, how does one explain what happened to Kim in medical and scientific terms?"

"Can't one just say Kim had a nervous breakdown and leave it at that?"

"But 'nervous breakdown' isn't a scientific term. It's a metaphor."

"I don't really understand about metaphors," said Alice, "but surely, from a common-sense point of view, it's all quite simple?"

"Is it? But how does one explain someone like Mrs. Mayfield? How does one explain evil? And if God exists, why doesn't he just zap the Powers and—but no, I can't cope with God. All I know is that I've somehow got to stop myself being so frightened of repeating the experience with Kim that I wind up a hermit chained to a rock, and unless I understand what's happened how can I guarantee there won't be a rerun?"

"Well, if you did wind up chained to a rock, I bet some gorgeous St. George would soon ride along and rescue you!"

"Sister, forget St. George! I couldn't cope—I'd cling to my rock and scream at him to go away!"

Alice sighed, but probably not at the thought of a sexy St. George rescuing a woman from a dead-end situation; her loyalty to that ditherer Nicholas was indestructible. With sympathy she said: "Well, of course, I'm just an ordinary person, not intellectual or anything, but the way I see it is this: Kim was damaged in his childhood and couldn't heal himself. Mrs. Mayfield damaged him further because she enjoyed having power over people and didn't care whether they got damaged or not. Kim's damage had already made him sick, and because Mrs. Mayfield made the sickness worse he eventually killed himself. Why do you have to translate all that into scientific language?"

"Because I must have the basic facts interpreted by someone qualified to give an opinion! Supposing I bought a very expensive car and it broke down soon afterwards. I couldn't just say: 'Oh, it broke down because it's a lemon!' I'd want to take it back to the garage and stand alongside the mechanic when he looked at the engine—I'd want to be told by the appropriate expert, using the appropriate technical language, exactly what had gone wrong."

"Well, I know I'd never understand what the mechanic said," responded Alice, "so I'd just ask for the car to be repaired under the warranty."

"I envy you. But would you *never* want an explanation for why things go profoundly wrong?"

"For evil, you mean? But evil just *is*! It's like an elephant—difficult to describe but we all know it when we see it and there's no point in asking why it exists because it just does."

"But we don't all know evil when we see it," I said at once. "Lots of very nice people in the 1930s thought Hitler was wonderful. And how do you explain Hitler?"

"He was a freak, like Stalin and that Chinese man who was always taking great leaps forward. But you can't explain freaks any more than you can explain evil. They just happen, like elephants."

"But why does God let them happen?"

"Oh, we can't possibly know the mind of God! Our brains are too small."

"Then why didn't he make them bigger? Surely God wouldn't be so inefficient as to give no comprehensible explanation?"

"What's efficiency got to do with it? God's ways aren't our ways—but look how spectacular his ways are! Look at the skies and the stars and the mountains and the seas and the animals and the fish—"

I thought of my dolphin. Then I drained my glass and said: "I don't care about all that. I just want an explanation, and if God can't come up with one he can get lost."

"It's people who get lost, Carter."

"Then why the bloody hell can't God send someone to find them?"

"I sort of think he already did."

"But Kim stayed lost," I said, and went away to shut myself in my bedroom.

XII

When Alice eventually came to check that I was resisting the urge to bang my head against the wall, I said: "If I'd loved him as he wanted to be loved I might have saved him." I was sobbing so hard I could barely speak.

"Oh Carter, no—you mustn't blame yourself—"

"But I'm responsible, aren't I? It wasn't Mrs. Mayfield who killed him after all. I killed him by rejecting him and giving him nothing left to live for."

"Carter, you didn't kill him. He killed himself. And he did that because he was sick and Mrs. Mayfield had driven him mad."

"But if I'd loved him as he wanted to be loved—"

"Carter, this man was a murderer! He did terrible things for years and years and years—"

"Yes, but that wasn't his true self! If the evil other self could have been amputated—evicted—

whatever—then I might have saved his true self by loving him. If I'd agreed to a reconciliation—"

"How could you possibly have done such a thing? Kim had crushed your love to death with all his cheating and his lies! How could you ever, ever have trusted him again?"

"But if I'd somehow managed to forgive him—"

"Forgiving him is one thing. Forgiving him and going on with the marriage by living a lie, pretending the love still existed even though it was dead, is something else."

"But I did love his true self! If that was still there, buried under all the evil, then perhaps if only the evil could have been shovelled off—"

"Yes, I understand what you're getting at, but bearing in mind what happened at Oakshott, how can you blame yourself for recoiling from a reconciliation either then or now? And if you can't blame yourself for that, how can you blame yourself for the suicide?"

I had no answer but felt no better. "I can't bear to think of those scenes at Oakshott!" I burst out, starting to cry again. "If I go on remembering how much I hated and feared him then, I'll go mad too, I swear it, I'll never get over it, never— which is why I've got to focus on the real Kim, the man I once loved—and yet if I do that I'll go mad too because then I'll have to blame myself for not loving him enough, not agreeing to a reconciliation, not being strong enough to save him—"

"Carter dear—"

"Oh God, I'm so messed up, I can't believe how messed up I am, but if only I could get some kind of a rational, logical handle on what really happened I feel there's a chance I might stay sane—"

The doorbell rang as Val arrived to pay a lunch-time house call.

XIII

"I've got to understand what happened," I said to Val after Alice had left us alone together. I had mopped up my tears, consigned the sodden tissues to the wastepaper basket and mixed myself a second vodka martini. Val had declined my offer of a drink but showed no sign that she disapproved of my self-prescribed tranquilliser. "In law," I said, "a case may look a mess, but once you interpret it from a legal point of view and apply the correct legal principles the problems become comprehensible and the mess can be overcome. So please—give me the medical, scientific explanation of what was wrong with Kim! Then I'm sure I'll be able to sort out the mess and get on with my life."

"That sounds like a positive attitude," said Val, trying to be encouraging but only succeeding in sounding wary. "However, medicine can't always provide clear-cut answers, and scientific theories are often far more speculative than the non-scientific members of the public are willing to believe."

"But what's the final medical verdict on Kim? There must be a final verdict!"

"As I understand it, the hospital's in-depth inquiry into why Kim killed himself shed no additional light on the evidence given by the doctors at the inquest. The psychiatrist in charge of the case remains convinced that Kim's release from hospital wasn't premature."

"But it must have been!"

"The psychiatrist defends himself by saying this second breakdown was entirely due to the extreme stress involved in the confession, and he blames Lewis for encouraging Kim to go down this route when he was in no fit state to do so. Lewis, on the other hand—"

"—says the men in the white coats are round the twist."

Val sighed. "Everyone gets upset when a case ends tragically," she said, "but the hard fact is that not all tragedies are avoidable. Personally I wouldn't want to condemn dear old Lewis here because I believe he did valuable work in befriending Kim, but I do see the psychiatrist's point of view. He'd been led to think you were just going to drive Kim to Oakshott, have a sandwich or two and enjoy a friendly conversation which would bode well for the marital future. That was a very different script from the high-stress confrontation which actually took place."

"So the doctors never secretly revised their diagnosis that both the suicide and the initial breakdown were due to stress? They still honestly believe there was no pathological illness and no serious personality disorder present?"

"I know why you're asking those questions," said Val. "It's because the man you described in those final scenes appeared to be behaving like a sociopath. But when a personality fragments under extreme pressure, all kinds of subpersonalities, normally suppressed by the ego, can erupt out of the unconscious and grab control of the mind. Of course anyone who commits murder without remorse has a serious problem, but personally I still don't feel I can label him a sociopath, someone disconnected from normal emotions. We know he felt guilt about Sophie; we know he cared deeply for you."

"But surely he must have been in some sense mad?"

"He was certainly disturbed but he remained lucid, he wasn't suffering from hallucinations and he wasn't suicidal when he was in hospital. I don't actually think he was mad at all until right at the end when his personality shattered to pieces on that balcony."

"So what the hell was going on?"

"Well, if I were to say he was bad but not mad I'd be making a judgement which a doctor isn't qualified to make. I can't say: 'He was a corrupted man who couldn't bear the burden of his sins.' That's not a medical diagnosis. One could treat the medical problems caused by this spiritual malaise, but as for the malaise itself... No. The scientific, medical language stops here. All I can say is that this case was definitely one for the priests..."

XIV

We were silent for a moment. Outside it had begun to rain, and I watched the drops spatter across the windowpane as a gust of wind swept up Egg Street from the south. I was aware of Val's stillness, the concentrated quality of her attention, and I wondered if, in the uncharted borderland which lay between sickness and health, I was traversing an abyss which I was too terrified to allow my eyes to see.

"Then was I to blame," I heard myself say

606

numbly, "for forcing Kim into this high-stress confrontation?"

"But you didn't force him, did you?" Val said at once. "He was burning to tell you everything in the belief that this would save the marriage. If the blame belongs to anyone it belongs to Lewis, but on the other hand I'm sure Lewis was right to believe Kim had to level with you— by that stage you couldn't have gone on with the relationship without learning the whole truth. No, the real problem was that it was the wrong time and the wrong place for the confessional."

"But that really was my fault! I didn't intend to wind up at Oakshott, but I certainly insisted that I meet him on his own as soon as he left hospital!"

"But we all knew of this plan of yours, didn't we? So the fault was ours for not talking you out of it! Carter, the truth is we've all made mistakes in this case, so don't crucify yourself by taking on all the guilt. That would certainly be the road to neurosis—which reminds me: Robin said I was to tell you he had a cancellation at four-thirty this afternoon, and if you wanted to drop in for a word he'd be very happy to see you."

I thanked her and agreed with relief to be there.

XV

"I can certainly offer you an opinion resembling a diagnosis if you feel this would be helpful," said Robin when I saw him later in his consulting-room at the Healing Centre. "Now that the marriage is unquestionably over I can be more frank, but I must warn you that my opinion may not be as satisfactory as you think."

"Why not?"

"Reality isn't always something which can be committed to paper, analysed, tied up in pink ribbon and filed away neatly in the correct drawer of the filing cabinet."

"All I'm looking for is a professional opinion which is reasonable and logical—"

"Reason and logic are useful tools, but human beings are so mysterious, so very much more, it always seems to me, than the reasonable, logical sum of their mental and physical parts... And don't forget that as I never met Kim what I say will inevitably be speculative. Scientific accuracy? No, I'm afraid that won't be possible. But would you be prepared to look at an impressionistic sketch?"

"Anything's better than nothing!"

"Then let me start with those questions I raised for you to consider earlier. Some of them turned out to be more important than others, didn't they? I was interested to hear that Kim showed signs of being more benign towards his father, more forgiving. It sounds as if his psychiatrist did some effective work on that front even if he never got to grips with some of the other problems... But we have to remember that Kim was only at the beginning of being treated. Several months of out-patient therapy might have made a big difference to him.

"I was certainly right to call attention to the enigma of his sexuality. His most obvious problem, it seems, was that he reached adult life with a poorly integrated sexuality, and the part he couldn't adjust to was split off and repressed. Am I saying he was a closet homosexual? Not necessarily. Without interviewing Kim in depth it really is impossible for me to reach any kind of firm conclusion, but if you pushed me hard enough I'd say he sounds more like a maladjusted heterosexual than a homosexual. Wasn't he bisexual, you ask? Not in my opinion. The evidence suggests that he was strongly attracted only to women and that the motivation behind the homosexual episodes was more akin to the motivation underlying rape—which is primarily about violence, not about sex. Cases like this illustrate that sexuality is a far more complicated subject than a lot of people think, and that all the conventional sexual categories are really only broad generalisations which can be seriously misleading...

"But for clarity's sake, let me add this: let me theorise that Kim hated and feared the unintegrated part of his sexuality, and this hatred and fear was projected onto homosexuals whom he then abused; it would have been a way of ridding himself not only of self-loathing but of great psychological discomfort. He talked of easing a dislocation, didn't he? Yes, I see him as someone who never came to terms with his feminine side and so despised any man who didn't fit his definition of the macho male. Why was he like this? We don't know. Possibly his father always insisted on him being very tough—while at the same time his mother made certain aspects of the feminine repulsive to him.

"The dislocation would have set up a fault-line in his personality and under stress this fault-line would rupture, propelling him into the incidents which formed his 'hobby.' No, I don't see his personality as fragile but I do see it as fractured; that's not quite the same thing. He was certainly tough enough to paper over the fracture most of the time, but the trouble is that the more we repress unwelcome feelings and the deeper we bury them in our unconscious minds, the more likely those feelings are to erupt eventually in very disagreeable forms.

"Kim's remark to you that his 'hobby' seemed to have more to do with rage than with sex supports my theory that the homosexual episodes had nothing to do with his basic sexual orientation. I see him as an angry man, angry with his parents for not fulfilling his emotional needs, angry with Sophie for making him feel guilty, angry even with the professional success which gave him so much yet couldn't give him the satisfaction he was still seeking when he got involved with Mrs. Mayfield's occult society—and in the end perhaps he was angry that he ever got involved with Mrs. Mayfield in the first place. If his feelings for you were genuine he would have been angered by the trouble he was having disassociating himself from both her and her world."

Robin paused. I supposed he felt it was time to check that his "impressionistic portrait" was not affecting me too adversely, but I was already feeling better. It helped to have the baffling pieces in the jigsaw of Kim's personality slotted into a pattern which made sense. I felt I was beginning to have a firmer grasp of Lewis's idea that the personality of the real Kim had been invaded and poisoned by a malign subpersonality, and by spelling out the psychological distortions which had grown upon Kim's true self, Robin was helping me to visualise a metaphorical cancer of the mind, a spiritual cancer, which had in the end proved terminal.

"Go on," I said. "Do you, in fact, think his feelings for me were genuine?"

"It certainly sounds as if they were—although, as you came to realise, he was projecting onto you an image which didn't match your reality. But as I explained to you before, this is not uncommon behaviour when people are in love, and as it turned out, you were projecting an image onto him too... Can you see now what was going on?"

"Oh yes," I said, and although I tried to keep my voice light and ironical I was unable to stop the bitterness creeping in. "I was projecting onto Kim the image of an idealised father, the father whom my real father had failed to become, the father I always felt was owing to me—although that projection was too painful ever to admit."

Robin nodded, refraining from comment, allowing me my moment of grief. Finally I was able to say: "But if Kim and I were projecting false images onto each other, surely the relationship was a grand illusion?"

"Not at all. The images weren't entirely false, were they? You did have this masculine persona and Kim was indeed a version of the man your father had the intelligence to be. Of course Kim misread your persona—and as you chose not to see his resemblance to your father you couldn't judge how accurate the resemblance was—but these projections were mere distortions of reality, not total inventions. I suggest that the fact that you were projecting these images onto each other just means you were romantically in love, but romantic love can often precede a successful, reality-based relationship."

"But if Kim was attracted to me because of my

masculine persona, surely this means—" I broke off, too confused to put my doubts into words.

"It seems clear that Kim was primarily attracted to you for all the obvious reasons connected with your femininity," said Robin without hesitation. "I doubt if he'd have been interested in a woman who didn't appeal first and foremost to his heterosexual taste. But the big bonus to him—the bonus which made you unique—was that this masculine persona of yours had the power to call forth the feminine side of his personality which he had repressed. Now, this masculine persona's like a radio which you operate instinctively, adjusting the volume for each situation; the volume can be turned right up, but most of the time when you're not at the office it's just a background hum. Kim detected the persona straight away, he said, when you picked him up at the airport, and my guess is it fulfilled such a need in him that he could always hear it, even when you had the volume turned down low."

"And when I turned it up high—"

"He would have been bowled over. But even when he wasn't bowled over I believe the background hum would have had an important effect on him; I believe that whenever he was able to discard the role of shark and play the dolphin with you, he was indulging the feminine side of his personality, and this unprecedented freedom to be more fully himself would have made him feel more integrated; he would have experienced this as some kind of healing."

"So that was why he felt the time was right to give up Mrs. Mayfield and her various 'cures'!"

"Exactly. But I'm sorry to say," said Robin with a sigh, "that there were two big flaws in this potential happy ending—and this is where we face your dread that if only you'd agreed to a reconciliation you and Kim might have lived happily ever after (assuming, of course, that he escaped a murder conviction). The first big flaw—"

"This must be where we also face the fact that the masculine persona isn't the real me."

"I'd prefer to say this is where we face the fact that the romantic love you both shared was unlikely to develop into a long-term reality-based relationship. Your masculine persona doesn't accurately mirror the masculine side of your personality—it's a hyped-up distortion aimed at helping you survive in a man's world. Could Kim ever have adjusted to this reality once it impinged, as it inevitably would have done, on his romantic illusions? Your experience when you told him you wanted children leads me to say: probably not. His attraction to you was too bound up with this mask of yours, but if your journey was leading you out of a masculine world into a feminine one the mask would have become redundant and a key feature of the relationship would have been displaced. My guess is that when that happened Kim would soon have started searching elsewhere for another woman who could keep him stitched together, and something tells me you wouldn't have been as willing as Sophie to put up with an unfaithful husband."

I shuddered but merely said: "And the second flaw in the potential happy ending?"

"This is even more of a marital chiller. In the end, contrary to what Kim appears to have thought, I believe he would have felt compelled to return to his 'hobby.' Carter, it's a safe bet to say that even if you'd been the woman he thought you were, you alone could never have provided Kim with a long-term answer to this problem— the healing you provided wouldn't in the end have been enough because the roots of the compulsive behaviour hadn't been treated. Kim would have needed a great deal of therapy to bring the behaviour under control—indeed in my view he would also have needed to turn himself over to what the members of Alcoholics Anonymous call a 'Higher Power.' How interesting that he could identify with the part Jack Lemmon played in *Days of Wine and Roses*! He was not without self-knowledge, it seems, and certainly not without intelligence, but he needed professional help on a massive scale. Mrs. Mayfield, I need hardly add, would have been no use to him at all, quite the contrary; she would have made him worse by encouraging him to replace the 'hobby' with other deviations, all of which would have failed to solve the problem."

"Could Kim ever have been cured?"

"In these cases 'cure' isn't the favoured word to use, but he might have achieved a remission which would turn out to be permanent. The danger of relapse would always be there but with the right support he'd be all right."

"Like a recovering alcoholic in AA?"

"That's it. And as I said, the right support would be crucial. Ideally a priest would be working alongside the doctors, and there'd need to be a caring community, praying regularly—"

"But why?"

"Well, medicine doesn't have the complete answer to this type of problem. Doctors—even a psychologist like me—can offer a great deal of help, but in the end when we start to use phrases such as 'turning oneself over to a Higher Power' or 'accepting Jesus Christ as Lord' we're really venturing beyond the boundaries of our disciplines. We can justify these phrases by saying that they're both referring to an integrating principle and that integration equals salvation, but nevertheless...no, I think it's healthy to admit we don't have all the answers, healthy to admit that in this kind of case the priests should always be working alongside us to reach the parts the medical textbooks fail to touch..."

XVI

"How guilty should I feel about all this?" I said after a prolonged pause spent surveying this portrait of Kim. I was unsure how far Robin would respond to this direct question, since he preferred to help me uncover the answers to my questions myself, but he answered willingly enough: "It's normal to feel some degree of guilt when one's marriage fails, and that's not unhealthy. It's the obsessive, morbid forms of guilt which cause trouble."

"I wasn't thinking of the failed marriage. I can see now it would never have worked out." I hesitated before confessing in a rush: "I'm still feeling so guilty because my confrontation with him triggered the suicide."

Again Robin seemed to realise he could help me best by offering a frank reply. "It's also normal for those closest to someone who commits suicide to experience guilt," he said at once, "but don't forget that a suicide can have multiple causes, and in this case I think it would be more in keeping with reality if you allowed Kim some responsibility for his actions. Remember that he was seriously disturbed as the result of a way of life he had embraced long before he met you, and you were neither responsible for that chosen way of life nor for the damage he suffered in the remote past. You were also not responsible if, thanks to Mrs. Mayfield, he became neurotically drawn to see the balcony as an invitation to self-destruct."

"That's true." I began to be conscious of relief.

"Don't forget either that suicide can be an act of aggression," added Robin, startling me. "It's an act which lashes out not only against the world but against the nearest and dearest. If Kim had punched you in the face, would you have been tempted to assume that your broken nose was your fault?"

"Certainly not... But isn't one supposed to turn the other cheek when one's on the receiving end of aggression?"

"The subject of forgiveness does of course come up," said Robin, becoming cagey again as he reverted to a more oblique approach, "but you need time, Carter. Profound emotional responses to a crisis or tragedy can't be worked out swiftly by means of reason and logic. Other areas of the brain have to come into play, and they may not be immediately accessible."

"But I want to sort everything out *now* so that I can get on with my life! Can't you tell me how to press the right psychological button which will allow me to forgive Kim for wrecking me and forgive myself for allowing the wrecking to happen?"

"Definitely questions for the priests."

"Robin—"

"I'm sure that with the help of Nick or Lewis or both of them, you and I can uncover the right way forward."

"That's not good enough!" I said exasperated. "If I can't work out my response quickly by means of reason and logic, then you must give me the appropriate psychological principle to apply!"

"That would be no use. This is a response you have to feel, Carter, not intellectually grasp. Reason and logic are fine but you need another tool here to open up the area of the mind which deals not in words but in symbols and images. After all, forgiveness is rather more than just a three-syllable word, isn't it? It's a concept, a vision, an experience."

"So what's the tool?"

"Well, have you ever thought of going to our regular Friday healing service? Sometimes the laying-on of hands unlocks the psyche and allows the mind to make powerful connections which—"

"I'm an atheist," I said, finally losing patience with him, and terminated the session.

XVII

In the reception area outside Robin's consulting-room I found Alice talking to Nicholas, who was extracting a Coke from the vending machine. The hands of the clock on the wall above the reception-ist's desk pointed to five-thirty, and a fresh detachment of Befrienders was arriving to cater for the stressed-out City workers who were leaving their offices and feeling in need of sympathetic listeners. On Thursdays the Centre was open until eight.

"Carter!" Alice hurried towards me. "Nicholas wondered if you wanted to have a word—I was telling him about the questions you wanted answered, particularly the one about evil."

I felt extremely annoyed. I was already ruffled by Robin's refusal to carry our conversation into the areas I wanted to discuss and by his banal suggestion that I could be helped by a religious rite which meant nothing to me. The last thing I wanted at that moment was to be incarcerated with Nicholas, who always managed to set my teeth on edge. I also felt Alice had breached my confidence by reporting my distracted outpourings to him.

"I'm sure Nicholas is much too busy to talk to me now," I said flatly. "Some other time, perhaps." I turned away but immediately saw Tucker on the other side of the glass doors which stood at the Centre's main entrance. I had forgotten he worked on the Thursday evening shift. "I'm sorry," I said, swinging back to face Nicholas. "How rude that sounded! Yes, could we have a word, please?" And with my back turned to the main entrance I moved quickly past him into his consulting-room.

I had never been in this room before. Robin was the person I talked to at the Healing Centre, and my conversations with Lewis and Nicholas had taken place more informally at the Rectory. As soon as I walked in I saw to my horror a large painting of a snooty blonde with a glassy stare and a steel-trap mouth. I could hardly believe my eyes. My jaw sagged. Automatically angling the chair so that I would not have to look at this chilling mess of oils, I sat down facing an ancient but smartly dressed teddy-bear who was sitting incongruously on top of the long, waist-high bookcase beyond the desk.

"God, you're an odd man, Nicholas!" I said before I could stop myself.

"I know I should take down that portrait," he said rapidly, and it was the first time I had ever seen him embarrassed. "Of course I'll take it down when the divorce is finalised, but Rosalind's not just my wife—she's my oldest friend. We met before we even got to kindergarten."

"How sweet."

"Well, I can see you disapprove, but—"

"Nicholas, it's not the slightest concern of mine how you choose to adorn a wall of your office—or the top of your bookcase. Is that the bear you both played with in the nursery?"

"Oh, he's on his way out," said Nicholas more rapidly than ever. "I want to give him away to the right person but the right person never seems to turn up."

"I wouldn't mind a bear," I said moodily. "The bailiffs took my toys away when I was six—but I didn't come here to whinge about my childhood. Can we get down to business?"

"Of course," said Nicholas, almost gasping with relief. "Alice mentioned—"

"Yes, can you make it clear to Alice, please, that when I have a private conversation with her I don't expect it to be repeated?"

"I'm sure Alice didn't mean to upset you, but—"

"Forget it, what's one small indiscretion when I'm floundering around in shit creek and trying to understand not only how I got here but how the hell I'm going to get out? Now listen to me— put some steel into that clerical collar of yours and give me some straight answers to the following questions: how do you explain someone like Mrs. Mayfield? Was Kim a hundred per cent evil at the end or wasn't he? If he was evil, was he beyond redemption? Is forgiveness of evil actually possible? And what do you have to say about evil anyway?"

To give credit where credit is due I have to record that Nicholas never batted an eyelid as he faced this stream of verbal gunfire. But to my acute irritation he only answered with a sigh: "I'm afraid these aren't such easy questions to answer as you might think..."

XVIII

"Evil is a very emotive word," said Nicholas. "Of course it refers to something which is all too real when we encounter it, but it's very easy, by using emotive language, to make evil seem slightly *un*real, something 'other,' something which exists 'out there' and can be kept at arm's length while we all get on with our ordinary lives. There's a strong urge in us to disarm it in this way because the reality is so difficult and so frightening that our natural inclination is to run away rather than confront it. It's only when our lives are invaded by evil that we realise it's not at all like the lurid fantasies in stylised Hollywood horror movies. Hannah Arendt, who wrote about the Eichmann trial, coined the phrase 'the banality of evil,' and that seems nearer the mark to me than all the lurid fantasies in the media.

"The trouble is, you see, that evil isn't just 'out there,' along with the witches in funny clothes and the Dracula look-alikes. It's among us all the time. A little lie here, a little cheating there, a little self-centredness somewhere else—and then suddenly all those little moments latch onto each other to present a cluster of evil and we come face to face with a monster. But the monster's not sporting fangs and wearing a black cape. It's wearing a cardigan and calling itself Mrs. Mayfield.

"But the terrible truth is that our everyday 'shadow' sides—our wrong actions and unchecked weaknesses—produce people like Mrs. Mayfield. She couldn't operate in a vacuum. She feeds on our flaws, and our flaws in turn are fed by her needs.

"So where does Kim fit into all this? He did evil things, there's no doubt of that. But he himself was bruised and twisted by other people's evil— by the evil of the Nazi culture—and that's where we get into an area which the media, in their fascination with demonic stereotypes, are all too ready to overlook. Evil isn't just a matter affecting private individuals. It affects entire cultures. It's global. And being civilised is no defence because evil isn't confined to people who know no better. The Germans were highly cultured and civilised yet they produced Auschwitz. And let's not forget that concentration camps were invented by the British at the height of their imperial splendour.

"The sheer pervasiveness of evil means we're all bruised and twisted by it in some way or other, so who are we to reject a fellow victim just because he happens to be rather more damaged than we are? How tempting it is to label Kim EVIL and cast him out, ejecting the evil by saying it takes place within someone 'out there' beyond the pale—how comforting that would be! But Kim was one of us. He was 'in here' and not 'out there,' and that's why we have to try to avoid using him as a scapegoat and projecting onto him all our own hidden flaws, psychic damage and secret fears.

"But how do we deal with him as 'one of us' and not as a monster beyond redemption? I think we have to try to see him as a real person, the man who expressed to Lewis his longing for forgiveness and the chance to turn his life around. To see him in this way is not to excuse the wrong he did. It's to make him more accessible, easier to understand and, ultimately, easier to forgive and let go.

"Robin outlined to me earlier his psychological portrait of Kim, but although I would go along with what he said there's always the danger, with such portraits, that the weird is emphasised at the expense of the normal. I'd like to provide a counterpoint by stressing Kim's normality. He had a job he enjoyed, he led a typically busy urban life, he wanted a wife he could love, he felt guilty about the wife he had treated badly, he liked a nice home, expensive cars, good food and wine, dinner-parties, travel, swimming... How normal it all sounds, doesn't it? Of course he had his hang-ups about the past (don't we all!) and he had a serious problem with promiscuous sexual behaviour, but one can understand why the doctors decided this man was not pathologically ill but just in need of rest to heal the stress and therapy to iron out the hang-ups.

"And I'm quite sure both the rest and the therapy were helping him. But the real problem was that Kim's way of life, with a little lie here and a little infidelity there, had led him to Mrs. Mayfield who had converted his moral weaknesses into a moral decay which rotted his personality. This sounds as if I'm putting all the blame on Mrs. Mayfield, but we mustn't forget it was Kim who chose to associate with her; he deliberately chose to embrace a milieu which was actively opposed to truth, decency, unselfishness, compassion, trust, hope and love.

"Now, human beings must have access to these things or they become deformed. Lies, degradation, selfishness, callousness, deceit, cynicism and exploitation may seem very exciting when they arrive coated in various forms of self-indulgence, but they have nothing to do with lasting happiness or integration or fulfilling one's potential as a human being.

"In other words, when a person chooses evil like that he or she has to unchoose it in order to set out on the road to healing. Otherwise the spiritual sickness will only continue, and the psychiatrists might heal the symptoms only to discover that far worse symptoms had broken out to take their place.

"Ideally a psychiatrist and a priest would have worked together on Kim's case, each complementing the other. The primary illness was spiritual, but his long-standing psychological problems fed and nurtured it. And he was acutely aware, wasn't he, of his need for healing? It was his search for healing which drew him deeper and deeper into the world of Mrs. Mayfield; it was his hunger for integration which drove him to join that occult society which only succeeded in keeping him dislocated and divided. He was a spiritually sick man who made wrong choices—yet even so he was still one of us, still human enough to recognise in the end that he'd taken a wrong turn, still human enough to long to begin again and find redemption through love.

"His true self wasn't evil, you see. He was deeply alienated from his true self, he was trapped in an inauthentic existence, but...Carter, you're looking very dissatisfied! What have I done wrong this time?"

"Do you realise," I said, feeling almost demented with irritation, "that you—a clergyman—have spent several minutes talking about evil, sin and morality, and yet you've never once mentioned God? Damn it, even Robin mentioned Jesus Christ and Robin's not a clergyman at all!"

"I thought that perhaps as you were an atheist—"

"Of course I'm an atheist, but you might at least mention God! What the hell do you get paid for? And why didn't you mention Jesus Christ either?"

"Well, sometimes when an atheist has no personal experience of Christ, it's wiser to—"

"Who says I've had no personal experience of Christ? If your Christ is all he's cracked up to be, do you really think he's incapable of making himself known to an atheist like me?"

"On the contrary, I know it happens all the time, but—"

"Well, then! What's your problem?" I was on my feet and awash with the urge to smash something—preferably the portrait of Ms. Snootykins. I wondered if Alice knew it was still there but suspected that she would have no reason to go into Nicholas's consulting-room and that the staff at the Healing Centre all liked her too much to inform her of the interior decoration.

Curbing my urge to commit an act of vandalism I grabbed the teddy-bear from the bookcase and said to him strongly: "It's time you turned your life around, Mr. Bear, and started out with a clean slate in the company of someone who knows better than to keep you hanging around gathering dust on top of a bookcase." I patted his little pair of jeans and his T-shirt embroidered with the words "ST BENET'S." Then I dumped him on the desk. "This animal's too good for you," I said to Nicholas. "Unless you pay him a great deal more attention very soon he's going to get up and walk." And having eased my irritation by delivering this barbed prophecy on Alice's behalf, I swept out of the consulting-room.

Outside I cannoned straight into Tucker.

TWENTY-ONE

There comes a point where the questions change. Then we no longer ask about how to avoid a particular suffering or even why it is happening to us. Instead, all our resources are focused on how we might come through it, and our ultimate question becomes: what is it for? The basic trust is that suffering, evil and even death do not have the last word about life.

DAVID F. FORD
The Shape of Living

"Ms. Ashy Phoenix, I presume."

"Oh my God—"

"How are you doing, Ms. Ash?"

"Badly, but I'm trying to improve."

"Gil told me the funeral was—"

"I don't want to talk about it."

"I lit an extra candle for you this morning."

"Ah, Tucker..."

"I've temporarily shelved the novel in order to light candles for you. I've become an arsonist fixated on wax. Whenever I see a wick I'm immediately seized by this ungovernable urge to—"

"I hate to interrupt you when you're on the subject of ungovernable urges, but aren't you supposed to be befriending people?"

"I'm befriending you, Ms. G."

"Yes, but—"

"I'm going back to the salt-mines next week to give my bank balance a make-over. Let me take you out to lunch tomorrow with my last twenty-pound note."

"I seem to have given up eating."

"Oh, it's fun, you'll like it!"

"Tucker—"

"Okay, forget lunch, how about a tankard of the Widow at the Lord Mayor's Cat? I can't believe you've given up champagne!"

"I—"

"Think about it. Call me," he said, and veered away to give the receptionist a hand as two drunken yuppies started to wail that with the loss of their jobs their lives had ended at the age of twenty-two.

I groped my way back to the Rectory.

On the ground floor's hall table I discovered some letters addressed to me and realised that Alice had been back to the flat that afternoon to collect the post. Among the usual bills and junk mail I found a letter written on prison stationery. My heart sank. My first reaction was to shove the envelope deep into my bag but then I found I had to know what my father had said. Dumping my bag on the table I extracted his letter and broke the seal.

"Sweetheart," my father had written, "let me say straight away that I'm not asking for money. I just want to tell you how great it was to see you so unexpectedly. You looked beautiful. I felt so proud. I should have written before but I didn't like to in case you thought I wanted something. Then the other day the chaplain said: 'How will she know what you're thinking if you don't tell her?' so I'm hoping you won't be cross if I write to tell you this: I'm thinking I can't wait to get out of this place. I'm thinking I'm never coming back here. I'm thinking it's only the thought of you that keeps me going. Please send me a postcard to let me know you're okay and not annoyed with me for bothering you. I love you, sweetheart. I want to turn my life around, I promise. Take care, DAD."

I muttered a curse and rammed the letter back into my bag, but before I could begin the long climb up the stairs to the attic flat the front door of the house opened as Lewis returned home from the church.

"How are you?" he said neutrally.

"In dire need of a triple vodka martini."

"Excellent! I feel like drinking too. Let me take you to the Savoy."

I was so startled by this lavish invitation that I was at a loss to know how to decline it. Then it occurred to me that a complete change of scene might do me good and that I had been so rude to so many people that day that a touch of politeness now would hardly go amiss. "Thank you," I said, but knowing nothing of Lewis's financial situation I felt obliged to add: "We can go to a local wine bar if you'd prefer."

"I detest wine bars," said Lewis acidly.

"Oh good." I assumed that this lofty dismissal of plebeian watering holes hinted at the presence of a private income.

After he had changed from his cassock into a clerical suit, we set off for the Savoy in his car. In keeping with the anti-luxury bias of his calling, this heap was a very noisy, very old Volkswagen Beetle but he drove it as if it were an Aston Martin. By the time we had parked on Savoy Hill I felt more in need of a drink than ever.

In the main lounge we settled ourselves at a corner table which afforded us privacy, and a waiter immediately arrived to take our order.

"Two pussyfoots, please," said Lewis before I could draw breath to speak, "and two ham and cheese sandwiches on white bread, not toasted—and make sure the cheese is very mature Cheddar."

"Hey, wait a minute!" I exclaimed stupefied, but the waiter was already speeding off into the distance. Swivelling to face Lewis I demanded outraged: "What's going on?"

"It's time you rested your liver, my dear, and it's certainly time you ate something nutritious. Take Uncle Lewis's advice, be a good little girl and don't even think of throwing a tantrum."

I said: "I don't believe I'm hearing this."

"I enjoy buying attractive women pussyfoots," said Lewis complacently, "and since I'm sure you wouldn't want to deprive an old man of a little innocent pleasure, why don't you abandon the feminist fury and tell me how you've been getting on?"

I did think of walking out but the chair was too comfortable, and the Savoy, enfolding me like a luxurious fur coat, was too soothing. It occurred to me that I had been through hell that day but I was now being offered a little visit to heaven to help me along.

I stayed.

IV

"It wasn't Nicholas's view of evil which drove me up the wall," I explained in between bites of my sandwich. "I found that convincing in its own modern, liberal way, but it didn't strike me as being spiritually robust and when he failed to mention either God or Jesus Christ I just wanted to slap him. Was I being unreasonable?"

"Absolutely not!" said Lewis.

"And anyway, how can a clergyman talk of evil without mentioning the Devil?"

"How indeed! But if you want spiritual robustness couched in good, old-fashioned religious language, I'm without doubt your man."

"Great! So was Kim totally evil or wasn't he? Did that subpersonality you mentioned earlier mean he has to be classified as evil after it took him over? Could the subpersonality ever have been evicted or was it there for ever, and if it was there for ever, could he have got it under control and lived a normal life? Robin approved the parallel with a recovering alcoholic and said—"

"Well, if we're going to bandy metaphors and analogies around," said Lewis, starting to enjoy himself, "let's go all the way and talk of a mind infested by demons. What does this strange phrase mean, you ask? I'll tell you. When I say 'demons' I don't mean amusing little creatures with horns and tails. I mean psychic entities, forces which flow directly from the malign archetypes which lurk in the collective unconscious of the human race—but psychological language is so often lugubrious, using twenty words when one will do, and the one word which will do nicely here is 'demons.' So let's use it.

"Similarly when I say 'infested' I don't mean that amusing little creatures with horns and tails were swarming over Kim's personality like an army of lice colonising a head of hair. I mean that those psychic entities, the demons, took root in him by latching on to one of the subpersonalities which lay buried in his unconscious mind, and dragging it to consciousness so that ultimately the subpersonality was able to take control of the ego. (We all have a variety of subpersonalities but usually, if our minds are working healthily, we're unaware of them.) Well, here again you have the psychological language huffing and puffing to say something which the old-fashioned religious language expresses in three words: demons infested him. Let me just add that the psychological language doesn't 'explain away' the religious language or vice versa. They're simply two different ways of describing the same spiritual landscape.

"You want me to be spiritually robust? Then let me give you robustness *par excellence* by saying that demons are the Devil's cohorts! You might well have heard this blood-curdling phrase used in Scotland when you were a little girl, because Scots Calvinism is very strong on hell and the Devil. Without tangling again with psychological jargon, I can tell you that the Devil is the dark, messy side of creation. (Jung got it slightly wrong when he said the Devil was the shadow side of God.) Eventually God will reach the point in his creation where he'll bring the dark, messy side under control, but meanwhile we're staggering around in all the mess and being mangled by the demons—or, as Kim would have said, by the Powers, the Powers of Darkness. In short, we're being mangled by evil. But we don't have to be destroyed by all this terrifying chaos. And by hooking ourselves up to the Light instead of the Dark we don't have to become evil ourselves.

"Got it? Are you with me so far? Well done— we've reached the point where we can say that Kim, by hooking himself up to the Dark instead of the Light, paved the way for his own demonic infestation. But let me now make one thing crystal clear. His true self, which was crushed and battered but still there under the poisonous and bloated subpersonality, was not evil—repeat, *not evil*. It couldn't be. That's because our true selves are made in the image of God, the image of the benign force which created us. What Kim needed was deliverance from the infested sub-personality which had corroded his soul—he needed deliverance so that his true self could have the chance to regain its rightful place in the centre of his personality.

"So Kim wasn't totally evil. But did he do evil deeds? Of course! Murder is hardly in the same league as earning a parking ticket. And while considering his evil deeds we can't overlook his appalling abuse of Sophie and the acute mental suffering he inflicted on you as he destroyed your trust. There's also the matter of all the homosexuals he picked up before he met his nemesis. Can we read between the lines of his confession and deduce he was into sado-masochism? Maybe—and no, that's not incompatible with the blackmailer wanting to come back for more. You wouldn't believe what gluttons some masochists are for punishment! When I was a chaplain at that mental hospital all those years ago...but I mustn't digress.

"Can we excuse Kim by saying he was sick? Absolutely not! Whether he was sick or not is a matter of medical—or possibly legal—definition, but we shouldn't use sickness here to obscure the issue and let him off the hook. You don't catch spiritual sickness like a common cold anyway. It's the result of bad decisions, not bad luck. I've met young people who come to the Centre in dire distress and moan: 'But it wasn't my fault, it was just my bad luck that the Ouija board did this, that and the other!' Stuff and nonsense! What were they doing messing around with the Ouija board in the first place? If you mess with the occult, the occult will mess with you. If you live by the sword you die by the sword...and so on and so on.

"But let me return to Kim. Was he beyond redemption? Certainly not! No one is, because thanks to the love of God, the grace of Our Lord Jesus Christ and the power of the Holy Spirit— the Forces of Light which can outplay the Powers of Darkness—we can reactivate our true selves, no matter how maimed and mangled they've become, and achieve healing.

"Could Kim have been cured? At St. Benet's we draw a distinction between a cure and a healing, and the example of the recovering alcoholic illustrates that even when a permanent cure can't be guaranteed a very high degree of healing is still possible. But in spiritual terms we have to remember that perfection, in the form of a total cure, isn't available to us in this life; no matter how far we manage to become our true selves we're always vulnerable to sin and temptation. But the point is: *we don't have to be destroyed by our vulnerability*! Spiritual health can be recaptured, nurtured, maintained and buffed to a high lustre to ward off all those soul-poisoning demons—and yes, of course priests should mention God to atheists! They should mention every member of the Trinity! Atheists not only expect that but long for it because it gives them the chance to spring passionately to the defence of their own beliefs! Atheists are such *religious* people, I always feel...

"Anyway, where was I? Oh yes, healing Kim. Well, some Christian healers would have just waded in and commanded the demons to come out of him, but I don't work that way. I prefer the deliverance rite to be very carefully prepared, and with someone like Kim I feel there has to be a long lead-in period in which the healer gains the confidence of the sufferer, first of all simply by being there and offering sympathy. One prays for the sufferer as much as possible, day by day, and hopes that the opportunity for offering deliverance will come, but it's no good forcing the pace.

"I know I got somewhere with Kim. I didn't get as far as I would have liked, but I got the message of hope across and I believe I convinced him that he could succeed in embarking on a new life if he rejected the Devil and turned to Christ. (Translation: if he'd rejected Mrs. Mayfield's false attempts to heal him and embraced the correct integrating principle.) If that had indeed happened, then he would have been on the road to recognising the demons and longing for them to be cast out. (Translation: ceasing to be 'in denial' and facing up to his problems in order to conquer them.) Then the rite of deliverance would have been appropriate; it would have ratified the progress already made and taken the healing forward into a new stage. Rites and rituals are very important, as I've said to you before. They take over the task of expressing truth when mere words are inadequate.

"Following the deliverance rite, Kim would have needed a great deal of aftercare, not only from a psychiatrist and a priest but also from a Christian community who could enfold him with love and provide the necessary framework for his new life. Love is very important in this sort of case, because the sufferer has usually been deprived of it at a crucial stage of life—indeed you can argue that all addictions are fundamentally attempts to find the peace and ease and happiness which genuine love provides.

"This leads me to tackle the question which I know tormented you even though you knew this man had done terrible things: could your love have saved him? Well, that question should really be: could you have saved him if you'd played the last scenes at Oakshott differently, submitted to his advances, and entered into a relationship where you would have been constantly lying to suppress your fear, anger and revulsion? Carter, no one could have expected you to follow such a course, even if your motive was to assist his healing—and besides, since healing has to be built on truth, not lies, you actually wouldn't have assisted his healing at all. Quite the reverse. If you'd faked a reconciliation, my guess is he would have washed his hands of the healing process, gone off to New York as he planned and then resumed his old habits when the marriage inevitably broke down. And let's be honest about this: could you really have played those last scenes at Oakshott differently? I think not.

"Perhaps it might help you if I point out that healing's usually a team effort. You made your vital contribution to Kim's healing when you came into his life and showed him that a well-integrated, far happier existence was still possible for him, but even if Kim had lived and continued with the healing process, it might not have been in your power to help him further. God used you to show him what salvation could look like. But others might have been chosen to travel with him along the future road to health and wholeness.

"So (I can hear you thinking) this vain old boy thinks he was personally chosen by God to lead Kim along the primrose path to heaven! He thinks he had the case sewn up and now can't resist patting himself on the back for the healing he's sure he would have achieved! Not so. The part I played in Kim's healing might also have been near its end, and even if it wasn't—even if I *had* been called to go further—I might not have had the case sewn up. And even if the case had ended well, I could have claimed no credit because I myself wouldn't have healed him. The healing would have come from Christ the Healer, working either through me or in spite of me. Christian healers always have to remember that, because pride is an occupational hazard and one needs to fight against it day in, day out...

"Well, at least Kim doesn't have to cope now with either me or the white-coated wonder-boys at the hospital. He's with God and God will do what's necessary to heal him—oh, and death isn't the end, of course. That's so obvious that I hardly like to mention it, but young people get such strange ideas into their heads nowadays and you're young enough to be no exception. People don't understand either that death is a part of life, and in a life lived as a journey there must be many endings and beginnings...and of course God told us what he thought of endings and beginnings when he gave us Easter. You're going through your Good Friday, Carter, but never forget that we look back at Good Friday in the light of Easter Day.

"Well, the next question you want to ask, of course, is—but no, you're looking a little white around the gills, perhaps you didn't realise that my spiritual robustness would be quite so robust! Can I offer you another pussyfoot?"

"Thanks. I'll have it with a double brandy on the side."

He flagged down the waiter, ordered another round of pussyfoots and to my fury substituted Perrier water for the brandy.

V

"Lewis!" I got the order cancelled by accusing him of intolerable bossiness and saying one pussyfoot was more than enough for anyone, but he was unabashed.

"Think of me as what I believe is called a Personal Trainer, keen to keep you fit!" he said brightly. "No, don't waste your breath on further protests! Aren't you anxious to know what your next question's going to be?"

"If I say yes, you'll smirk and boast: 'I knew you'd never be able to resist your feminine curiosity!' And then I'll feel obliged to slap your face and storm out."

"Goodness me, how exciting! But as I'm wearing my clerical collar let me avoid goading you into acting out this charming fantasy and tell you instead about your next question. You're going to ask—"

"I know what my next question's going to be, thanks very much, and the one after that—and even the one after that. I'm going to ask: why did I have to go through this hell? What's it all been for? And how do I make it all come right?"

Lewis promptly launched himself into his reply.

VI

"The first thing to realise," said Lewis firmly, "is that God never wills suffering but tries always to

637

redeem it. Suffering's the dark side of the creative process, as I said earlier, but the true artist can never stand it and can't rest till the mess is fixed. Sometimes suffering is brought on us by our wrong actions—as I pointed out when I mentioned the people who dabble with Ouija boards—but even then suffering can be quite disproportionate to the sin, so priests should always think hard before they surge into the pulpit and thunder out: 'We reap what we sow!' Indeed suffering is often random and not the result of any wrong action at all.

"Let me say next that I think you did the right thing when you tried to work out why you married Kim—what part your upbringing, lifestyle and world-view played in making you Mrs. Betz. By putting yourself under the microscope in this way, you've learned something you didn't know before—and that's definitely a step forward on the spiritual journey where our first task is to know ourselves as well as we can in order to grasp what we can potentially become.

"So there you have one positive result, one redeeming feature, of this negative experience. And there'll be others if you now align yourself with God by rebuilding your life in the best possible way. The rebuilding will give meaning to the tragedy, the meaning which will transform it and, in the end, redeem it. It's meaningless suffering which destroys people, but if you can find meaning in this suffering you've endured you'll be on course for a healing which will enable you to forgive Kim, forgive yourself and move on to live and love again.

"All right (I hear you thinking), that's a choice little piece of clerical optimism, but what's the old boy really getting at? I'll tell you. You have to use your new knowledge, so painfully acquired, to help you realise your true self and embark on your correct destiny. Realising your true self (the one God designed) and fulfilling your correct destiny (the one best suited to the design) is the road to true happiness, of course. Happiness doesn't lie, I assure you, in being what other people think you should be in order to satisfy the fashionable whims of a transient society.

"Please note that I'm not—repeat, *not*—suggesting that you're now inevitably obliged to give away all your money and go to India to work for Mother Teresa. It may be that you're still required to go on as a high-flying lawyer and continue to earn—what's that nasty word?—megabucks. Money is neutral; it's what you do with it that counts. The big question you have to answer is: is this the real me or would I be more myself if I became a different kind of lawyer—or if I worked in a different field altogether? If so, earning megabucks may not necessarily be a priority in your new life.

"Take Eric Tucker, for example. He'd love to earn good money as a writer, of course, and I hope he will some day. But the important thing is that he's doing what God's clearly designed him to do and he's doing it in a way which allows him to keep his integrity. How pitiful to be a mere story-teller, some people might say, but we can be called to all manner of work, even to jobs which the majority (but not God) would consider trivial. I read once about a man who loved his job as a lavatory attendant so much that his lavatories were a wonder of cleanliness and beauty—no, I'm not joking! I'm saying that man was called to be a lavatory attendant, and God was no doubt delighted by his splendid response. Even lavatory attendants have their part to play in God's amazingly varied creation.

"So what I'm saying, Carter, is this: if you can rebuild your life to chime with God's purpose for you, you'll find the Powers don't have the last word—you'll find crucifixion really is followed by resurrection. You'll find too that not only Kim's death will be redeemed but also the work of the Powers which engulfed him, because your new life—which will benefit not just you but those you meet—will be shaped by your new knowledge, the knowledge which has arisen directly out of the suffering you've had to endure. All things can be worked by God into his creative purpose, that's the unvarnished truth of it, and there's no darkness so dark that in the end it can't be penetrated and subsumed by the light... But remember: *you must act*! You can't sit back and wait for redemption to drop into your lap! As Eric quoted to me the other day: 'All that's required for evil to triumph is for good men to do nothing!' Dear me, I suppose that should be 'good *people*' nowadays, shouldn't it? I fancy I can almost hear Edmund Burke revolving in his grave..."

VII

There was a prolonged pause. Gradually I became aware again of my surroundings: the plush furniture, the thick carpet, the drone of conversation, the waiters flitting hither and thither, silent as moths, and, far away in the River Room, the golden evening sunlight glowing beyond the long windows which faced the gardens of the Embankment. Finally I said: "How do I rebuild my life?"

"Don't panic! God hasn't demanded a thirty-page business plan and given you a twenty-four-hour deadline! At present your major task is simply to improve your physical health, which is why I've been nurturing you with a pussyfoot instead of those disgusting vodka martinis."

"But you said I had to act!"

"Improving your health *is* an act. While this improvement is in process, take one day at a time and concentrate on the people you meet. Listen to them very carefully and give them your full attention."

"Why?"

"Because you need to know what God has in mind for you, and he often communicates with us through other people. So does the Devil too, which is why you'll need help as you struggle to work out what's going on."

I said in despair: "I'm no good at connecting with other people at the moment."

"All you're required to do is listen! No deep connection's required!"

"That's just as well, since I can't imagine ever wanting a deep connection with anyone again."

"That doesn't mean it'll never happen. It simply means your imagination's in bad shape." Before signalling the waiter for the bill he added: "Sure you don't want another pussyfoot?"

"All I really want is to get drunk."

"Quite so, but the danger of sinking regularly into an alcoholic stupor (quite apart from liver damage) is that you might miss an important communication from God. You didn't drink at the office, did you?"

"Never."

"Well, this is much more important than the office. If you're in an alcoholic haze, how likely are you to recognise the person whom God uses to lead you into the light?"

"I can't imagine being led anywhere by anyone."

"I led you here to the Savoy, didn't I?"

"Yes, but I thought I was going to get a vodka martini! How am I ever going to trust you again?"

He laughed before saying firmly: "When you wake up tomorrow morning after a good night's sleep and realise how pleasant it is not to be hung over."

That seemed to conclude the conversation. He paid the bill and we returned to his four-wheeled heap of German scrap-metal for the ride home.

VIII

"There's something I haven't mentioned," I said as he parked the Volkswagen in the Rectory forecourt, "and it's really bothering me. When am I going to stop seeing ghosts? I'm terrified I'll see Kim."

This time Lewis neither laughed nor made a quick retort. He merely said: "Let's have some coffee," and led the way into the Rectory's main kitchen. On my way through the hall I noticed that Nicholas was working late again in his study when he might have been enjoying some interesting moments alone with Alice. I did make a great effort not to dwell on his unforgivable lack of enterprise, but as usual when contemplating

Nicholas's private life I felt myself starting to seethe with irritation.

Meanwhile Lewis was saying as he made the coffee: "I can't promise you that you won't see Kim. But if there's no unhealthy guilt about his death and no strong desire to communicate with him, I doubt if he'll return to you as Sophie did when you saw her on the night of her death."

"But mightn't he still haunt the flat as a place-ghost?"

"If you permit us to perform our long-delayed blessing and spiritual cleansing of the flat, the odds against him appearing there as a place-ghost would be substantial." He placed the two mugs of coffee on the table and sat down opposite me.

"But do I really need to be present when you conduct this ritual?" I blurted out before I could stop myself, although I added at once: "I'm sorry to be wimpish but I'm so afraid of seeing him. It's why I still can't bring myself to go back there."

"There's no question of you being wimpish! Facing that flat again after all that's happened would be an ordeal even for someone who'd won the George medal, but it would be better if you were present when we did the cleansing. Give yourself a little more time. The strength will come, but it's no good forcing it."

"Do you think the house at Oakshott also needs to be—"

"Oh yes, I think so. I think Sophie needs help in letting go of her home."

I saw the chance to unravel another conundrum which had been baffling me. "When I saw her at Oakshott," I said slowly, "was it—" but I could not work out how to complete the sentence.

"It was certainly a different kind of ghost from the one you saw at Harvey Tower, but it's not entirely certain what kind of ghost this was. When you saw her, she seemed to be a place-ghost, performing the familiar routine of walking through the hall of her home. Yet when Eric saw her seconds later as she emerged from the house, she was more than just a place-ghost—more than a figure in something resembling a video replay—because she actively communicated with him by gesturing that he should go in search of you, and active communication with the living is the mark of an 'unquiet dead' ghost. This was Eric's second sighting, as you'll remember. On the first occasion, when he saw her go into the house, there was no communication and she could have been a place-ghost."

"So what's the solution to the mystery?"

"Paranormal mysteries don't always have clear-cut solutions. I suppose the neatest one is to say she was actually an 'unquiet dead' ghost in all three sightings, even though she only chose to communicate once. But...this could be wrong."

"Well, let me tell you what I think," I said, drinking some coffee and wishing it was vodka. "I think these paranormal explanations are all nutterguff and that every single paranormal event in this case was the result of either human intervention or ESP."

Lewis sighed and looked as if he were sharing my longing for an infusion of alcohol.

IX

"And what, may I ask, is ESP if it's not a paranormal phenomenon?" he demanded, finally succumbing to the urge to light a cigarette.

644

"Scientists believe in it. So it's a respectable theory."

"You mean some scientists believe in it. But why should your belief in ESP depend on whether scientists believe in it or not? Scientists can believe in all kinds of theories which are later proved to be nonsense—they're not infallible!"

"Yes, but—"

"All right, I'll allow you a blind faith in scientists since it seems to be such a popular cultural fad at present, but please note that no faith should be blind. Now tell me how you explain away all the paranormal phenomena in this case."

"Well, the incidents at Harvey Tower were clearly the work of either Kim or Mrs. Mayfield—apart from the first incident which was caused by the vibrations in the building—"

"What about the final incident?"

"Mrs. Mayfield let herself into the flat with the copy she'd made of Kim's key, continued the trashing and then waited for me to return from Oakshott. When I did, she was responsible for the violent opening and closing of the bedroom door—there was enough room for her to stand behind it. As for the ghost, it was a hallucination—it was kind of Nicholas to call it a sighting of a psychic reality, but I'd rather call a spade a spade."

"There are, of course, different types of spade... But do go on. How do you explain the curtains which moved even though the balcony door was closed?"

"Oh, they do that sometimes. It's very windy at the top of those towers, and air can be forced under the sliding door."

"And the flickering lights?"

"An electrical blip, like the TV coming on earlier when it should have been on standby."

"I see... But to return to Mrs. Mayfield: if she had her own key, why did she turn up the next morning with a locksmith?"

"Isn't that obvious? She wasn't going to admit to anyone that she'd entered my flat and caused criminal damage in pursuit of her vendetta against me. She wasn't engaged merely in discrediting Sophie by that time—she wanted to break up Kim's marriage by driving me mad."

"All right, let's move on from Harvey Tower to Oakshott. Are you saying you hallucinated again when you saw Sophie in the hall?"

"Of course! I was mad with stress and terror. Sophie was wearing the outfit I saw when I discovered her corpse, and that flat basket plus the straw hat were items I'd seen on the kitchen table that evening. Obviously what happened, when I had this second hallucination, was that my mind regurgitated those recent memories."

"A plausible theory! But how did Eric pick up this image?"

"By ESP."

"Good heavens, are you saying you transmitted the image to Eric and he received it long before you sent it? That really would be an unprecedented example of extra-sensory perception!"

"I hadn't forgotten," I said coldly, "that Tucker saw Sophie go into the house soon after I disappeared from the living-room to follow Kim upstairs; I hadn't forgotten Tucker saw her considerably earlier than I did. But my theory is this: long before I escaped from Kim and saw Sophie in the hall below, I'd been thinking about her. She'd been very present in my mind as soon as I entered that house, and she was even more present when I was locked up in her bedroom. I believe I transmitted this Sophie-image to Tucker before I actually saw her, and because he was so anxious about me he converted it into an apparently real person whose presence on the scene gave him the confidence to wait. However, his anxiety increased, and finally the image came again, this time in the form of someone who was encouraging him to enter the house. After all, he too was suffering from acute stress. I think we can allow him a couple of benign hallucinations based on the image I'd transmitted to him."

"That's most ingenious," said Lewis with what appeared to be sincere admiration.

A pause developed.

"Well?" I demanded annoyed. "Aren't you going to argue with me?"

"No, I think you should be allowed your own interpretation of these mysterious events, particularly since neither of us can provide a knockdown argument which proves the matter beyond all reasonable doubt."

"But—"

"I respect your interpretation," pursued Lewis, "because you've obviously thought hard before coming up with this theory which satisfies you. I'd say this was a positive step towards assimilating some of the more disturbing angles of this case."

"But supposing my theory's not true? Doesn't truth matter?"

"Of course it does, but since we see through a glass darkly there are inevitably going to be times when we're obliged to live with uncertainty. Only the narrow-minded think they know the truth about everything, and their certainty is usually a response born of fear."

"Fear of what?"

"Fear of disorder."

I busied myself by drinking my coffee. Eventually Lewis murmured mildly: "Talking of disorder...did you have any further thoughts about how your telescope managed to survive the chaos, particularly if Mrs. Mayfield was pursuing a vendetta against you?"

I swirled the coffee around in the mug. "What further thoughts are there to have? Wrecking the telescope was just something she didn't do. Why make a mystery out of it?"

"Well, even if it is a mystery," said Lewis comfortably, "not all mysteries have to be solved, particularly a low-grade mystery which has little significance. That sort of mystery can just be accepted and filed away."

"Right." I thought carefully before adding in my most neutral voice: "It's good to file away clutter. And one can always go back to the filing cabinet later in the unlikely event that one might want to give the clutter another look...some day...for some reason or other."

"A very sound attitude," said Lewis approvingly. "Very balanced and sensible."

Wanting to close our meeting on this harmonious note, I thanked him for the outing to the Savoy and rose to my feet, but I found I was unable to resist giving him a verbal biff for dragging up the subject of the telescope again. "You certainly sounded as if you 'knew the truth about everything' when you talked about God earlier," I remarked. "Does that mean you too are narrow-minded with a fear of disorder?"

"My dear," said Lewis, "I know very little about God. I was merely summarising for you part of a long tradition of wisdom. The best minds of Europe have been beating their brains out for nearly two thousand years to shape this tradition, and if you were to study it I doubt if you'd find it intellectually wanting."

Unable to drum up a smart reply I fell back on a mindless response. "Oh, stop addressing me as if we had an intimate relationship!" I snapped. "How would you like it if *I* called *you* 'my dear'?"

"I'd be charmed and feel at least ten years younger. Why don't you give it a try?"

I sighed, told him he was a feminist's nightmare and left him beaming as if I had delivered the most lavish of compliments.

X

That night Alice went to bed early but I lingered in the living-room while I reviewed all that had been said to me that day. It came as a most unwelcome surprise to realise that although I had a better intellectual grasp of what had happened to Kim my emotions were still in chaos. No matter which professional language one used to explain Kim's behaviour and no matter how well these explanations chimed with the reality I had experienced, I still felt as if my ability to love and trust had been slaughtered with a sledgehammer. I began to feel the comforting talk of a "real" Kim was illusory and pointless. All that mattered was that I had wound up trashed, and how could I forgive either the real

Kim or the monster for that? It occurred to me that I had forgotten to ask Lewis directly about forgiveness. I knew he had mentioned it some-where but only as something which would happen in the distant future as the result of rebuilding my life, and at that moment the idea of rebuilding anything seemed inconceivable. I felt too butchered.

Fleetingly I longed for a dose of Tucker's deadpan humour, but the next moment I was shud-dering at the thought of him. How could I be sure he too wouldn't turn into a monster? I felt I had had enough pain from an intimate relationship to last a lifetime, and as for sex... I could only recoil. I was sure I would never again be able to go to bed with a man without remembering Kim suggesting intercourse behind that locked door at Oakshott. In fact the very word "intercourse," crammed with images of emotional closeness, made me feel nauseous, and even the thought of hearing anyone saying "I love you" froze me to the bone. Love meant being trashed and being trashed meant horror, pain and nightmare.

Moving to my room I found my bag, extracted the letter from my father and tore it to pieces without rereading it. My father, with his con-temptible addiction, would now always remind me of the monster, addicted to his "hobby." I wanted nothing more to do with a man like that. He could rot for all I cared.

I knew that I was profoundly wounded, just as I now knew my intellect was powerless to save me from this emotional agony, but I could do nothing to heal myself. I had thought that by applying reason and logic to all the testimonies I had heard that day I would be able to rearrange my memories in a satisfactory pattern, a pattern I could live with, but all I had done was prove I was moving through a dimension of reality where reason and logic failed to run. I was being mangled by the Powers again, that was the truth of it. I felt as if some savage beast had sunk its teeth into my neck and was shaking me systematically before tearing me to pieces.

I was in such a state by this time that I could only slump down on the window-seat and clutch the new little cross Lewis had given me to replace the one abandoned at Oakshott. There were no words. I wanted to summon Lewis for help, but I was so shredded that I could not even summon the strength to use the intercom. All I could do was shudder and sob.

Then I thought of him saying at the Savoy: "You're going through your Good Friday, Carter," and the moment those words flickered through my mind my unseen companion slipped alongside me again, not to part the darkness this time—the darkness was too intractable—but to share the pain.

"I don't want you sharing it," I said. "I don't want anyone caring as much as that." But he knew about dereliction and despair, so he merely accepted the words, drawing them into himself and transforming them so that they became not a rejection but a cry for help. Then gradually, as he stayed on, the quality of the darkness too was transformed because the Powers were powerless to evict him, and in his silent presence, devoid of aggression, lay the strength which I knew would finally force them to let me go.

I said: "What exactly *is* this power you have?" but all I could hear was Robin talking of the integrating principle while Lewis was saying that love was the most powerful integrating force on earth—and the next moment I was with my dolphin again and I loved him and the monster was quite blotted out.

"Hold on to that dolphin!" cried my companion suddenly, and as I held on I knew that at that moment not one of the Powers of Darkness could have prised my fingers loose. Then he said: "You asked enough questions about evil. But you never asked once about love."

So I asked him to tell me about it, but of course his definition lay beyond words. He just went on sitting with me in the dark and taking the weight of my pain.

After a while I remembered how I had longed for a Rambo-type guard on the night of the meltdown but had received an unarmed guide. Now I had wanted an unarmed guide to part the darkness but had been given this passive sufferer. Whatever this image was in my mind, it was not generated by wish-fulfilment. I found myself theorising that he was not an auditory hallucination but, as Nicholas had put it, a psychic reality—although this psychic reality was obviously on a different level from all the paranormal rubbish—and the next moment I clearly saw how most instances of psychic phenomena were very low-grade experiences of no real value; they were merely items from a kind of junk-heap in the shallows of consciousness, leeches which could cling to a personality as barnacles cling to the bottom of a ship. But the deeper one moved into the oceanic depths of the mind the more profound the psychic realities became until one found at last in the very heart of consciousness—

My brain flaked out, but the complexity of reality hit me afresh. I started to marvel at all the mysteries of the mind beyond the area devoted to reason and logic, that neat little garden which I had so carefully preserved and tended. Yet reason and logic, I saw now, were not meant to be penned up in a neat little garden, and if I were to send them out to earn their living in the world beyond the garden fence they might one day enable me to say with a humility born of truth instead of an arrogance generated by my fear of disorder: "I'm confronting mysteries. I don't know all the answers. I must believe in order to understand."

I suddenly realised the darkness in my mind was breaking up. I held my breath, listening for my companion, but he had slipped away. Scrubbing the tears from my face I went to the kitchen, found the notepad which Alice used for her shopping lists and drew a dolphin on the top sheet of paper. Then I took the drawing back to the window-seat in the living-room and sat down again as I added a few more details with my pencil. My dolphin was now frolicking in a wide, wavy sea...

Or was he?

The next moment I was remembering Lewis saying: "Scots Calvinism is very strong on hell and the Devil," and at once I knew that this sentence had the power to reduce me to rubble again. I tried to dwell on the memory of Lewis assuring me that Kim was "with God" (whatever that meant) who would "do what was necessary to heal him," but the second this image formed in my mind of Kim being fixed by God, I knew there was no comfort for me after all in this idea. For how did God fix a person who had regularly behaved like a monster? Vile images of incineration scorched my brain. I found I had to pace up and down the room in a futile attempt to ease my distress. Once more I knew myself to be on the brink of despair.

Lewis had been right to assume I had picked up a certain brand of religious hearsay in Scotland. Memories of religious horror stories, acquired from one of my grandmothers, now surged to consciousness from some forgotten corner of my mind and told me that both "the real Kim" and the monster would without question be consigned by God to the fires of hell.

My fingers were still clinging to my dolphin but my horror was weakening their clasp. I needed to believe I still loved someone who had been worthy of saving despite all that had happened, someone who had always been present in my marriage and whom even the monster had been unable to destroy. This belief exonerated me both from the charge that I had committed a huge act of folly by marrying him and from the charge that I had connived at the wrecking of my life by welcoming a monster into my home; the belief made it possible for me to hope that I might one day be able to forgive myself for making such a mess of my personal life. I still couldn't imagine forgiving him for choosing a corrupt life which allowed the monster to wreck us both, but at least I could imagine forgiving myself. My self-esteem depended on me being forgivable, and I needed self-esteem in order to believe myself worthy of any kind of bearable future. Without that hope I could see myself sliding rapidly into breakdown.

However, the religious horror stories suggested that God would see only the evil deeds perpetrated by an entity called Kim Betz, and pass judgement accordingly. No distinction would be made between "the real Kim" and the monster because the evil deeds were too evil and the wrong choices too deliberate to permit the judge to take any but the hardest of hard lines—and this in turn meant everything Nicholas and Lewis had said about no one being beyond redemption had been just clergyguff designed to cheer me up. The truth was "the real Kim" had been worthless and I had been merely a pathetic bag of hormones so desperate for marriage and motherhood that I'd ended up with an obscene villain.

Painful tears, now fuelled by physical weariness and emotional exhaustion, sprang back to my eyes, but I found I was no longer grieving for my shredded self-esteem. I was grieving for my dolphin, for the love which I had tried to hold on to but which was now being ripped from my hands. I couldn't bear to think of him being burned. I wanted him to be saved and healed and kept in a safe place where he wouldn't have to suffer. I couldn't endure the thought that he had escaped at last from the torments of the Powers only to be tortured by that terrifying judge waiting for him on the far side of the grave.

I told myself fiercely that I refused to believe in God but that failed to shift the image of the implacable judge from my mind. Then I told myself I refused to believe in Christianity, but I had a horrible feeling it was all true, even the ghastliness of life after death when one fell into the hands of a sadist. The tears were now streaming down my face as the Powers made their final devastating assault on me, but just as I was about to cry out to my unseen companion: "Why did you desert me? Why have you gone away?" I heard the stairs creak as someone crept up to the landing outside the front door of the attic flat.

XI

My first thought was that it was Kim's ghost. I had been remembering him so vividly amidst such agonising emotional stress that I felt his return as a psychic presence was almost inevitable. Then I remembered that the footsteps of ghosts made no noise; Sophie's approach had been soundless as she crossed the marble floor of that hall in Oakshott. That meant my late-night visitor had to be a living person and this in turn meant the visitor was either Nicholas or Lewis, but whoever it was, why was he tiptoeing up the stairs on the wrong side of midnight?

I decided that this was a mystery but not a mystery which I should be too afraid to solve. Brushing the tears from my face again I called sharply: "Lewis?" and at once the creaking stopped as Nicholas called back in a low voice: "No, it's me."

When I opened the front door I found he was holding the teddy-bear in his arms. "I was going to leave him outside with a note," he said awkwardly as I boggled at this outstanding example of eccentric behaviour. "I'm sorry I disturbed you."

"But why on earth are you abandoning that poor animal here?"

"I suddenly realised you were the owner he's been waiting for. You liked him but weren't sentimental."

"You mean you're giving him to me?"

"Consider it a gesture symbolising my gratitude."

"*Gratitude?*"

"I've been wanting to thank you for some time."

"Wait a moment, let me make sure I've got this right. You, Nicholas Darrow, are thanking *me*?"

"You've been extraordinarily helpful to my ministry ever since you came to stay here—in fact my spiritual director says you're a real gift from God."

"She's got to be kidding!"

"No, Lewis and I may have been sent to help you, but it's clear now that you've also been sent to help us. I've been shown that I can't split my private life off from my professional life and pretend this has no effect on my work as a healer, while Lewis has been shown that modern women aren't all as intolerable as he wanted to believe they were. So I really do think it's time that at least one of us said thank you."

I opened my mouth and shut it again.

He held out the bear.

Accepting it wordlessly I cradled it in my left arm as I ran the fingers of my right hand distractedly through my hair. The scene was faintly reminiscent of a Victorian melodrama where the wronged woman, complete with illegitimate child, turns up on the doorstep of the cad who has ruined her and mutely hands over the innocent result of their doomed union.

"I was going to give him to you tomorrow," said Nicholas, "but suddenly I had this feeling that I had to bring him upstairs tonight." He paused before adding: "I get these feelings sometimes."

Cautiously I said: "ESP?"

"Not necessarily. In this case I probably felt concerned because of something Lewis said earlier—he was speculating that you might have been influenced when you were young by a particularly severe strand of Christianity which can be upsetting to many people, particularly at a time of bereavement—"

"You'd better come in," I said, and pulled the front door open wide.

XII

"Lewis said you had a good talk together at the Savoy," said Nicholas, ambling into the living-room and parking himself in front of the unlit gas fire. "He didn't go into detail; no doubt he felt most of the conversation was confidential, but when he theorised that Calvinism had played a part somewhere in your cultural background, it occurred to me that you might not quite understand that Calvinism isn't the only form of Christianity on offer. There are—and have been almost from the beginning—many Christianities, but this is much less peculiar than it sounds because no great religion is an unchanging monolith. If it flourishes, it's bound to be diverse and dynamic—which means the basic truths will stay the same but they'll always be subject to reinterpretation as time passes and the world moves on... I'm sorry, you're probably too tired and stressed to connect with all this right now, but—"

"Don't patronise me." I placed Mr. Bear in the best armchair, adjusted his legs to a sedentary position and propped him up with a small cushion so that he was sitting alertly on the edge of the seat. "The law too expresses basic truths," I said, "and the law too is diverse and dynamic, subject to reinterpretation and remodelling as time passes and the world moves on. You think I can't understand the concept of development?"

"No, no," said Nicholas hastily, "of course not. Then you'll understand that sometimes a theological belief—a latecoming variant on some traditional theme—can become obsolete. Or it may survive but become unfashionable—or even intellectually untenable. Or it becomes not actually wrong but superseded by an idea which is closer to being right. An outsider might find all this dynamic evolution chaotic, but—"

"—but there are careful rules about updating."

"Exactly. Well, what I'm trying to say is that in Christian theology the concept of judgement hasn't remained unchanged. Many people do still favour the idea of hellfire and damnation, but although I respect their veneration of a certain past tradition, I can't go along with it."

"But who are you to chuck out tradition?"

"I'm not chucking it out. I'm just choosing to emphasise an older, more biblical tradition. And I'm not alone. I'm just reflecting modern research and scholarship."

He finally decided to sit down. Perhaps he felt he needed some extra seconds to work out what to say next. "A lot of the talk about hell isn't very scriptural," he said apologetically as if he feared I might consider him personally responsible. "A lot of the images of damnation only go back to the Middle Ages, and I doubt if Jesus would have favoured those medieval scenes of torment which show a Grand Inquisitor tossing people into the flames. Jesus seems to have been more interested in speaking clearly about a shepherd who went out of his way to search for a lost sheep...and that brings me to the story I wanted to tell you about the sheepdog trials."

He paused again, and suddenly I realised he had ceased to irritate me. I sat down opposite him. He was quite still now. He had one leg crossed over the other and had interlaced his long fingers which he was now watching intently. In a flash of understanding which mesmerised me, I knew he was psyching himself up. He was like a mountaineer manoeuvring himself into position by a series of elaborate, high-risk moves to rescue the damaged climber wedged helplessly in the rockface. Indeed his concentration on this intimidating task which required all his skill was now so great that within seconds I was no longer seeing the classic image of the mountaineer which symbolised the fight against adverse forces; I was remembering how I had watched the Wimbledon championships on television and seen the extreme concentration shown by a great tennis player who, after four sets riddled with errors, clawed his way back to level-pegging in the final set before miraculously raising his game to win the match.

"Surely the truth is this," he said to his interlaced fingers. "You can't talk about judgement without talking about justice—and justice is the other side of love. If we love someone we want justice for them. We don't want them to be treated unfairly; we want them to be treated with love and understanding. People so often think of judgement as something severe, but a great judge will weigh up the good points as well as the bad; a great judge will see that *real* justice is done—

or so my father said once in a sermon he preached about some sheepdog trials."

He unlocked his hands and began to examine his thumbnail as if he had never seen it before. Each word was now being carved laboriously from his vocabulary. I could almost see him sweat over the choosing and the extraction. I could almost hear him pant over the extreme effort required to form each sentence. Yet the sentences when they emerged were smooth and fluent, spoken in a calm, unruffled voice.

"You know what I mean by sheepdog trials, don't you?" he said. "They're open-air exhibitions of the skills dogs show when herding sheep, and the judge has to decide which dog is the most skilful. Well, once upon a time, my father said, a man and his small son were on holiday in the Lake District and they saw a sign directing them along a road to some sheepdog trials which were being held on a nearby hillside. The little boy said: 'Oh, I'd like to see a trial!' so his father agreed to take him, but when they arrived at the scene the little boy was very disappointed. He said to his father: 'But where's the jury? And where's the judge in the black cap, like the judge at the Old Bailey who sentences murderers to hang?' (This was long before the abolition of capital punishment.) Then the father had to explain that it wasn't that kind of trial. No dog was going to be condemned to death or sentenced to prison. Every one of them was there to be affirmed and valued and encouraged, and if some of them didn't come up to the mark they were always told they were welcome to come back later on when they had learned how to be more skilful."

My eyes once more filled with tears but even

as I dashed them away Nicholas looked straight at me and said simply: "Kim will be all right now, Carter. He'll be shorn at last of Mrs. Mayfield's 'Jake,' because in the end we all belong to God, not to the Powers, and God is like the judge of the sheepdog trials, not like the judge in the black cap at the Old Bailey. So mourn for all the happy times you and Kim had together, grieve for all the suffering you both had to endure, but then have the courage to let him go to be loved and healed by his maker—because nothing in the end can separate us from the love of God, nothing, of that I'm quite sure."

He stood up suddenly, not waiting for my reply, but instead of moving to the door he walked to the window, drew back one of the curtains and stared out into the dark night. "Yet sometimes it's not so easy to let a spouse go, I realise that," I heard him say. "No matter how much went wrong with the marriage there was still that profound commitment in the beginning, and how very sad it is, isn't it, to be forced to witness the painful death of so many cherished hopes and dreams."

There was a long, long silence.

Then I rose from my chair and moved to his side to comfort him.

Twenty-Two

In his brief ministry Jesus did his best to give short-term help in healings and feedings. But the thrust of his teaching was to get at the roots of evil and suffering, and his message of the Kingdom of God was about a healing which involved love, trust, compassion, forgiveness, and radically inclusive hospitality. He faced the fact that that sort of healing can only be offered by those who embody it, whatever the cost.

DAVID F. FORD
The Shape of Living

I

As we stood looking out over the moonlit church, Nicholas was finally able to say: "It's not that I don't love Alice. But I've needed time."

I told him I understood. I also told him I was sorry I had been so rough with him in the past whenever the subject of his private life had slithered into our conversations.

"But it was good for me to hear what you had to say!" he answered at once. "That was what my spiritual director found so interesting. You always spotted my weaknesses and rooted them out for me to look at."

"I was bloody rude... Do you still love Rosalind?"

"I still miss her. The real problem is that I've never before had to live without her being in my life. She's like the sister I never had."

"Ah."

"I realise that sounds a trifle strange, but—"

"Not at all. As it turns out, I married a man who was like the father I never had. Probably there are loads of people out there who marry either to replicate a family relationship or to create a version of one which never existed."

Nicholas said simply: "You loved Kim, didn't you?"

There was a pause before I was able to answer: "I certainly found I didn't want him lined up for the long roast." Then after another pause I said: "I loved the man he might have been." But finally I could say: "I loved the man he managed to be with me for a little while before his past dynamited him and Mrs. Mayfield's 'Jake' came between us."

"You're talking of the real Kim."

I nodded before blurting out: "But I've been so tormented that he might have been just a worthless illusion conjured up by a pathetic thirty-something past her sell-by date."

"No, he was real. I caught a glimpse of him on the night of Sophie's death when he came to the Rectory. He said: 'I wanted Carter to love me for the man I really was, deep down, the man I now feel I can claim and become.' Do you remember him saying that? And he added: 'I wanted to keep her quite separate from that other person, the shit who'd mistreated Sophie and messed around in the world of Mrs. Mayfield.'"

"I remember... But how did you know he was telling the truth?"

"Because I saw his statements rang true for you. You were hostile and sceptical towards him but at that point I could see from your reaction that something very real had been disclosed."

"But how did you know my love for him hadn't been wiped out altogether by those final nightmare events at Oakshott? Most people would just assume I was glad to be shot of him after all that... *I* thought at first I was glad to be shot of him after all that...so what made you so sure there was still some love left that you clambered up here with that bear at half-past twelve in the morning to reassure me that this man, whom ninety-nine people out of a hundred would have judged a complete villain, wasn't due for the long roast?"

"As I told you once, I leave judgement to God. He's the only one who knows the whole truth about any of us."

"Yes, but—"

"You and Kim had some happy months together, didn't you, both before and after you were married? When a marriage ends catastrophically, one tends to focus on the catastrophe but after a while the memories of love resurface...or so Rosalind seems to have found."

"God, are you saying—"

"My marriage ended catastrophically. My fault. It still makes me ill to think of it. But we did love each other once and that can't be rewritten—no catastrophe can rewrite it."

"No?"

"No, because love, as the Christian mystics said, is the Great Reality. And my father admired a non-Christian philosopher called Plotinus who used to say that nothing that really *is* can ever die. So perhaps one can say that despite all that went wrong in your relationship with Kim—despite all the deceptions which created such *un*reality and illusion—there was still something there which was intensely real, something worth remembering, something which enriched your life by making you more fully yourself. And some day, maybe a long way off, maybe sooner than you imagine, you'll think to yourself: yes, I'd like to take another look at that Great Reality, if I'm ever lucky enough to encounter it again."

Tentatively I said: "And you got lucky sooner rather than later."

"Too soon. That's why it's all been so difficult."

"I suppose there's no chance that you and Rosalind—"

"No, we can't go back. But I've come to hope we can be friends again instead of embittered strangers. I've accepted now," he said, standing up and moving over to his bear, "that I can't stay stuck in the past, the past which ran all the way back to the nursery and my earliest memories of Rosalind. I've accepted that I've got to let it go." But as he stroked the bear's black-thread mouth with his index finger, he was unable to stop himself heaving a huge sigh.

"Relax!" I said drily. "I'll look after him for you, but when does someone else get to look after that portrait in your office?"

"I'll take it down to Rosalind this weekend." He sighed gustily again.

I bit back an acid comment and said mildly instead: "If you both agree you have to move on, why has the divorce got bogged down?"

"Rosalind feels she can't cope alone at the moment with our elder boy's problems."

"But you're not going to vanish into thin air after the divorce! And how old's this child anyway?"

"Nineteen."

"*Nineteen?* Good God, Nicholas, if he's old enough to get married, die for his country and vote, he's old enough to do without Mum and Dad breathing anxiety all over him! Boot him out of the cradle, give away the babyfood and for God's sake get on with your lives!"

Nicholas finally managed to laugh. "There you go again, telling me exactly what I need to hear!"

"Then that's a fair exchange, isn't it? You've certainly told me what I needed to hear."

I thought those remarks would conclude our conversation but he suddenly became very still, as if an important idea had occurred to him but he was unsure how to slide it into the conversation. At last he said: "You had a catastrophe once before in your life, didn't you?"

"Did I?"

"When the bailiffs came and your parents split up."

"Oh, that! Past history. I've got it all sorted now."

Nicholas seemed not to hear. "By the way," he said, "before we leave the subject of catastrophes, let me just ask you this: do you now think that Kim could have been helped to gain control over his addiction and achieve a better quality of life?"

"Yes, I do."

"You believe now that no one's beyond redemption if they repent and want to start afresh?"

"Yep."

He turned away, glancing at his watch before murmuring: "One needs to pray very hard for such people, of course. Prayer underpins our whole ministry here at St. Benet's. Praying's such an important act." Unexpectedly he swung back to face me. "Shall I say a prayer to round off this conversation?"

It seemed right to seize this chance to show respect for him after all my rudeness, so I listened politely while he said a few words asking God to look after me and added a brief request that Kim's soul should rest in peace. He even included a prayer for my family, a gesture which I felt was hardly necessary, but I kept my mouth shut and let him finish. When it was over he made no comment on what had been said but glanced at his watch again and remarked that he needed to catch some sleep in order to be wide awake for the weekly healing service, due to take place in a few hours' time.

"Couldn't you give it a miss for once?" I said, somehow resisting the urge to tell him again what a workaholic he was.

"I could, since the healers on duty don't have to be priests, but I'm reluctant to miss the service when I need healing as much as anyone else who'll be present."

"You mean you get the healing too?"

"The healers always lay hands on one another. We may be physically fit but none of us is perfect. We all carry damage and pain around with us in some form or other."

I said: "I hope the magic works for you today."

"There's no magic. Just Christ the Healer. He's always there." Patting his bear one last time he murmured: "Goodbye, old friend." Then he said good night to me and left the flat without looking back.

I fell into bed and slept. There were no nightmares, and when I returned to consciousness I found I had slept for a long time. It was almost ten o'clock. For a while I lay in bed and thought of Nicholas talking of the sheepdog trials, but although tears filled my eyes again they were tears of relief. I found I could think of my dolphin and know I was remembering something real, something which cast light on all the darkness and altered the quality of my memories so that they became bearable. But I still could not imagine ever wanting to risk embracing such a reality again.

On my way to the kitchen I paused to give the bear a proper assessment. In the light of day he was looking more haggard, but he had a striking pair of glass eyes and an appealing air of world-weary wisdom. Peeking under his new clothes I discovered that although he was threadbare in places his joints all moved, and I was sure he had been very beautiful in his youth, far more beautiful than my cheap floppy number who had disappeared into the bailiffs' van long ago.

When Alice came upstairs five minutes later to check how I was, she found me sitting in an armchair with the bear on my lap.

"I noticed him earlier!" she exclaimed at once. "What's he doing up here?"

That Nicholas certainly needed lessons in how to communicate with his fiancée. Quashing the familiar surge of irritation I managed to say mildly: "Didn't Nicholas tell you? He's given him to me."

Alice was beside herself with excitement. "He

has?" Evidently the symbolic meaning of the gesture was all too plain to her.

"Yeah, he's finally crawling out of the nursery and saying goodbye to all his old playmates... Hey, why didn't you tell me that little what's-his-face Darrow is a full-grown hulk of nineteen?"

"I assumed you already knew!"

"Nicholas never talks about his kids."

"That's because he feels guilty that he was never around much when they were little, but of course when he and I have children it'll be different."

"Are you honestly sure you want to marry him, Alice? I mean, excuse me, I do like him now, but let's face it, any middle-aged man who makes a symbolic gesture of giving away his teddy-bear has to be quite seriously peculiar."

Alice exclaimed laughing: "We're all peculiar in some way or other!" and looked radiantly happy. She even picked up Mr. Bear and gave him a hug.

I decided she was clearly in the grip of the Great Reality.

I also felt more determined than ever to avoid skewering myself in this way again.

III

I wandered over to the church later to light a candle. Perhaps I had been impressed by Tucker's dedication to melting wax for me, but I lit a candle for Alice and hoped she would now speedily become the second Mrs. Darrow. Having completed this task I then read every request on the prayer notice-board nearby. I had done this before when I had ventured into the church out of curiosity. I had found it comforting to be reminded that I was not the only person enduring a fraught time, and now I browsed for some minutes among the slips of paper written by or on behalf of those in need. My wandering gaze was eventually arrested by a message requesting prayers for David, a drug-addict, currently in some rehab centre but no doubt at risk of relapse when he emerged.

I stared at the message. The word DAVID, printed in capital letters, seemed to dance before my eyes, and the next moment I was remembering Nicholas talking of catastrophes, asking me if I believed Kim could have been helped, praying inexplicably for my family. My memory, locked into replay, suddenly spun into total recall. Lines of dialogue flashed by, some blaring, some muted. "I loved the man he might have been... I loved the man he managed to be with me for a little while," I heard myself say of Kim, but now I was thinking of my father, and a second later Nicholas was telling me: "Nothing that really *is* can ever die... No catastrophe can rewrite it."

Catastrophe! What a very elegant word that was for such gut-wrenching horror and pain.

"You had a catastrophe once before in your life, didn't you...do you believe now that no one's beyond redemption...one needs to pray very hard for such people... Praying's such an important act..."

Lewis elbowed Nicholas aside in my memory.

"You have to use your new knowledge so painfully acquired... You'll find the Powers don't have the final word..."

"DAVID!" shouted the capital letters on the notice-board.

"*You must act!*" yelled Lewis in my head.

I stepped forward. That was an act. I took a prayer-slip from the box on the table below the board. That was an act. By the box was a pencil and I picked it up. That was an act. Then I wrote: "Please pray for DAVID GRAHAM who needs help with a gambling addiction," and that was the most important act of all.

As I pinned the note to the board I found myself saying soundlessly to Kim: "I couldn't do this for you while you were alive, but I can do it for someone else and remember you as you'd want to be remembered." And as I framed those words I knew I could do those things because love was the great reality and nothing that really *is* can ever die.

I was still standing there, still staring at my message and wondering if Tucker had ever heard of that philosopher Plotinus, whom Nicholas had quoted, when a hand touched my arm.

I turned, and found myself facing Val.

IV

"You're looking better!" she said approvingly.

"I had nine hours' sleep."

"Followed by breakfast?"

"Don't expect miracles!"

"Am I being guilty of false optimism?" she said laughing. "Or am I only guilty of hope?" And before I could reply she added idly: "Coming to the healing service?"

"Well—"

"Oh, do come! You'll give me moral support—I'm one of the people doing the laying-on of hands today, and I always feel nervous beforehand."

I said evasively: "Nicholas was telling me that the healers don't have to be priests."

"That's right, anyone can have a go. Nick says that's because we're all connected—we're like islands in an archipelago, he says, all joined together below the surface of the sea...ah, there *is* Nick—excuse me, I must just have a word with him..." She skimmed away.

I turned to make my escape but immediately bumped into one of the Befrienders who had taken up a position by the door to greet the people who were beginning to arrive for the service.

"You're wise to be here early!" she said smiling after we had exchanged apologies for the collision. "We're always packed out on Fridays!" And somehow I found myself unable to tell her I wanted to leave.

I decided to wait until she was too busy to notice me as I slipped away.

V

I was halfway through reading the prayer-slips for the second time when someone exclaimed behind me: "Carter!"

It was Robin. He was looking summery in a pale blue suit, a pink shirt and a flowered tie which looked as if it had been excavated from a drawer untouched since the 1960s. "I was *hoping* I might find you here," he said, falling back into his old trick of speaking in italics to convey an impression of limitless empathy, "although *of course* I would have understood if you'd felt it was all *too much* at present. Personally I find that by Friday lunchtime I can *either* attend the service *or* collapse in a *dishevelled heap*, and since I can't *bear* being dishevelled the service *always* seems the most sensible option… Shall we find a couple of seats before the *madding crowd* tramples us underfoot?"

Finding myself powerless to say no, I mutely followed him down the aisle.

VI

I found it difficult to grasp the words of the service, impossible to analyse them. I was so struck by the fact that I was seeing another dimension in the lives of the people who had befriended me, and dimly, like a very stupid person grasping at last that two plus two equals four, I realised that I was seeing not only the symbols which expressed my friends' beliefs but the framework which supported their ministry; I was witnessing not the enactment of nebulous fantasies but the manifestation of a living reality, practical and down to earth, which permeated each day from beginning to end.

I remembered how not so long ago I had wondered what Nicholas was doing behind the closed door of his study at an early hour of the morning. Now I knew. He was not just reading the Bible and praying. He was following a discipline which focused him and made it possible for him to realise his full potential. He was lining up his centre with the integrating principle at work in the universe, the principle which was ultimately stronger than the drive to fragment. He was tapping into the powers of light which would allow him to live dynamically, surfing the chaos, splitting the darkness, serving his creator by serving others again and again and again.

The words of the service continued to slip through my consciousness like grains of sand through a wide-meshed sieve, but the gestures and movements of the principal participants resonated in my mind until my heart felt as if it were bursting with emotions I could not name. Gradually, as I watched Nicholas and Lewis in their professional roles, the clerical uniforms blotted out their individuality and smoothed them into symbols, pointing beyond themselves to truths which I sensed but could find no words to express.

Then I focused on the two women who were to join them in the laying-on of hands that day. One woman was a Befriender whom I did not know but as I turned my attention to Val I saw she was no longer just the casually dressed doctor who was so familiar; she seemed now to be reflecting an image of what a truly successful professional woman could be—not rich by my standards, not hacking her way to the top of a hierarchy to satisfy the demands of an ambition which resulted from unconscious psychological drives, but being herself, being whom she was supposed to be and doing what she was supposed to do in order to connect with others both for their benefit and for her own. And in this new definition of success which she was presenting to me I glimpsed the unknown self which I was still struggling to uncover, the self I had suppressed in order to achieve those goals I had so carefully listed in that life-plan which had been so deeply unreal.

I still did not know what I was going to do with my life, but I was sure now that I would find the right way forward. There would certainly be no more squeezing myself into a pattern of soul-shredding toil which allowed me no time either to think or simply to be. I did not have to prove myself to anyone any more. I no longer had to pay my parents back for my past pain. There would be no returning to the world of Curtis, Towers, the world where I had been sweating my life away, yet I knew I could still use the experience I had gained there. The past would not be wasted; instead it would be adapted and transformed.

I saw then that my marriage too did not have to be considered a write-off. The brief reality I had encountered with Kim could form a spring-board which I could use to transcend all the grief and failure, but that was a future still too hard to imagine in detail; I could only grasp it as a theoretical possibility while at the same time wondering how it could ever become a practical reality when I felt permanently maimed, unable to trust, unable to connect with anyone in a close relationship, unable even to touch those who had saved me and cared for me. Alice had put her arm around me after the funeral but when I had struggled free she had not attempted the gesture of comfort again. Gil Tucker had grasped my hands at the crematorium but I had withdrawn them as soon as politeness permitted. Touching reminded me too painfully of Kim grabbing me at Oakshott, the demonic Kim, Mrs. Mayfield's "Jake." I had wondered since then if in my terror I had exaggerated the danger of him killing me once my revulsion had become apparent to him, but I knew that rape would have been on the cards, and how could I be sure that once the violence had exploded between us he would have stopped short of murder? The real Kim would never have killed me, I was certain of that, just as I was certain that at the end of our time at Oakshott it had been the demonic Kim in control.

With a shudder I experienced again the terrifying moment when he had laid his hands on me, and at that point I knew I could never go up to the altar-rail to be touched. I wanted to believe we were islands in an archipelago, all joined together below the surface of the sea, but I knew it had to be untrue. My connection had been severed. I was grateful to Nicholas for enabling me to remember the real Kim with love, but I could not imagine ever recovering from the demonic Kim who still had me in that powerful grip.

Yet I knew I wanted to go up to the altar-rail. The sight of the doctor and the priest standing side by side had such a powerful impact on me that I could not stop looking at them. Even more powerful was the impact made by all four healers when they laid hands on one another in acknowledgement of their own need for healing, and most powerful of all was the moment when they moved forward to await the approach of the congregation.

I had to glance away. I could only stare down at my clenched hands as I knew myself unable to take part in that ritual of connectedness, and the next moment I realised with shock that my cut-off state was nothing new. I had been isolated for years by the unhealed wounds which had severed me from my family, prevented me from making close friends and driven me to blot out the inevitable pain of loneliness by living only for my work. I had feared intimacy for a very long time; I had feared having my trust broken, my hopes cast down and my love laid waste, and this fear had driven me into a sterile existence where any loss of control over my well-ordered servitude was seen as a threat. It was a wonder I had ever brought myself to marry Kim, I could see that now, although of course I had been driven on by the demands of my life-plan and the unconscious need to love the man my father might have become. Yet even though I had indeed come to love Kim, I had so often been unable to stop withholding myself in the most private moments of our life together. Then in another terrible flash of enlightenment I saw what he and I had had in common: we had both been loners who, estranged in childhood from our parents, had had trouble connecting with people on an intimate level; we had both been people who had longed for love but who had only been capable of giving a maimed love in return.

Seeing in myself the sickness which had destroyed Kim, I was so horrified that I nearly passed out. But simultaneously I knew I could now understand the decision which had led him into the world of Mrs. Mayfield. Loneliness, alienation, isolation and despair—what would one not do to be healed of such searing diseases? I saw that I too had dabbled in desperate remedies: I had tried drink, I had tried sex, I had tried structuring my existence so tightly that I had had no time to think, but none of those strategies had brought healing... If I hadn't started "flirting with the enemy," God only knew what ideology I might ultimately have embraced.

I whispered to Kim: "I understand now," and with that sentence forgiveness became no longer just a meaningless three-syllable word but a concept and a vision which I would eventually be able to experience.

Then as I reflected on the diseases which arose from being estranged from others and cut off from one's true self, I heard Nicholas say in my memory: "Without love human beings wither and die," and I knew how crucial it was that I should find healing. I could not go back to my past isolation. The Powers would merely move in to annihilate me. I had to rejoin the archipelago, but how could I when I was so powerless to find salvation by my own efforts?

I went on staring down at my fists, my whole body rigid, my throat tight with an unbearable pain, my eyes blind with tears, until at last I became aware of Robin rising to his feet. I heard him whisper: "Are you going up?" but when I shook my head he accepted my refusal and began his journey along the central aisle.

I thought of Nicholas saying that Christ the Healer was always present at this service. He had come to meet me in Robin, I was sure of that, but it had made no difference because in the end I had been too cut off to respond. I knew then that no one could help me. I was drifting away from the archipelago into distant waters, and by this time I had gone too far to be brought back.

The row emptied as others followed Robin up to the altar-rail. Then I became aware that someone was standing in the central aisle at the row's end. I looked up. It was Tucker.

He said nothing. He did not even smile. He simply held out his hand.

I told myself I was unable to move. But I did. I gripped the chair in front of me and I hauled myself to my feet. I still did not see how I could possibly reach him but I started edging clumsily along the row. It seemed to take such a long time to get to the last chair. I thought Tucker would become impatient and move on. But he waited. He never moved. And I reached him.

As I stepped into the central aisle I stumbled but he gripped my hand and steadied me. That was when I knew I would be rescued. I could no more recoil from his touch than a drowning swimmer could have recoiled from a life-line. I was going to make it to the altar-rail. I could believe that now. I was going to get there. I was very sick but I was going to get well.

I was too dazed to work out if one could choose the healer one wanted. At the top of the aisle one of the Befrienders whispered: "Dr. Val's free," and Tucker led me forward, he led me all the way there, and when he let go at last Val's square work-manlike hands seemed to shimmer with light as she stepped towards me.

She said a prayer but I could not hear it. The sea was making too much noise. Then as she laid her hands upon me amidst the roaring waters, I knew I was once more joined to all the islands in the archipelago, for my unseen companion had rebuilt the shattered link to bring me home.

VII

Someone had a box of Kleenex. Someone always did at St. Benet's. One of the Befrienders slipped forward to take care of me as I groped my way back to my seat. Robin had already returned. The box appeared from somewhere and Robin fed the tissues to me one by one. I had no idea what had happened to Tucker. My tears made it impossible for me to see far in any direction.

There was a hymn at the end of the service but

I merely sat and waited for it to be over. Reality had been reduced—or rather, expanded—to a succession of wordless images. I had realised how light the church was. Light seemed to be streaming all over everywhere. The little islands of the archipelago were basking in a sparkling sea. I could see that seascape so clearly, and even the city air of that hot day in late summer seemed as clear as if it had been funnelled through an invisible filter. I took deep breaths, closed my eyes and pictured myself luxuriating on a white-sand beach beneath a brilliant blue sky.

"Carter?" said Robin as if from a long way away.

"Yeah."

"How are you feeling?"

"Yeah," I repeated incoherently, and tried to focus on what was happening. The service had ended. The principal participants had processed down the aisle and were saying goodbye to the departing congregation at the back of the church. There was no sign of Tucker.

I struggled to my feet just as Val detached herself from the throng and came to join me.

"Carter!" she exclaimed warmly, but when I saw her wait, careful not to intrude on my personal space without an invitation, I put an end to this very proper professional reticence by hugging her. Then I hugged Robin. There were no words. As I staggered down the aisle Lewis saw me and ploughed through the crowd to my side.

"Carter?"

"Yeah," I said a third time, and patted him gratefully on the chest before moving on. Nicholas was looking at me over the heads of a crowd of admirers, all female, but I merely blew him a kiss and flailed my way outside. In the little churchyard the flowers were blooming and the ancient headstones cast almost no shadows. Screwing up my eyes in reaction to the blazing light I saw Tucker sitting on the churchyard wall.

He scrambled to his feet, hands in his pockets, every professional boundary nailed carefully in place.

"Thanks, Tucker," I said when I reached him.

"My pleasure, Ms. G."

"Sorry I was too banjaxed to enjoy our trip to the altar just now."

"We could always try a rerun some day."

I smiled and held out my hand. "Do you still want to buy me lunch?"

Our hands clasped.

Leaving the churchyard we began to walk up Egg Street to London Wall.

VIII

"Of course I realise I've got a long way to go," I said as we sat in the self-service restaurant of the Barbican Arts Centre and ate our salads. "But I'll keep going to the healing services and I'll keep talking to the St. Benet's people, so whatever happens next you can be sure I won't fade away like some Victorian maidenette."

"The word 'maiden' is sufficient," said Tucker sternly, "although possibly if the maiden were under three feet tall, poetic licence would allow you to—"

"Can it, Tucker, I'm not a manuscript!" I barked, but we were already snuffling at the thought of a maiden midget.

We were sitting at one of the windows which looked out on the fountains playing in the artificial lake, and across the water the church of St. Giles Cripplegate, risen from the ashes of the Blitz, like so much of the City, had a bleached look as it baked beneath the sun. Some people were sitting at tables outside on the terrace, but mindful of Tucker's red-haired gene I had suggested we stayed in the shade. At the far end of the lake, flowers and greenery trailed from the balconies of Gilbert House, the apartment block jacked up on pillars four storeys high, and the splashes of colour softened the straight lines of the Barbican's uncompromising concrete modernism.

Because of his imminent return to office serfdom Tucker was short-haired and clean-shaven again, but to cheer himself up he was wearing not only a patterned shirt, predominantly the colour of egg yolks, but his favourite pair of white jeans, clean as a couple of whistles and bearing a fake designer label which he had sewn upside down on the back pocket. He had been undoing a button on the shirt every twenty minutes. I calculated that by four o'clock it would be open to the navel.

"If you're determined not to play the wilting maiden," he was saying, "it's lucky I'm not wedded to a vision of you languishing on a chaise-longue amidst a froth of Victorian lace."

"If you can picture me lying on a chaise-longue in a froth at Harvey Tower, your imagination's even better than I thought it was! Incidentally, I'm going to sell that flat but only after an exorcism has allowed me to spend at least five minutes on the balcony laying a wreath for Kim and smashing the arch-cow's hex to pieces. I don't want to live in an ivory tower any more."

"No more tuning in to reality via your tele-scope?"

"I intend to live in the thick of reality. I shan't need my telescope then."

"How do you get in the thick?"

"I have to keep plugged into the celestial grapevine to await instructions, but I'll tell you this: I'm going to revolutionise my lifestyle."

"Oh God, does this mean you'll axe the Porsche?"

"No, I've decided every woman must be allowed one luxury, even if she opts for a life without megabucks."

"I was sort of hoping *I* could be your one luxury, Ms. G."

"You can be my *cher ami*," I said, "but that's not a luxury. It's an essential."

"I feel as if I've been awarded the Nobel Prize for Literature! But does a *cher ami* get to drive the Porsche?"

"Only if he's extremely *cher*."

"How do I make the grade? Of course I'll go to work full time—if Anthony Trollope could pro-duce masterpieces just by writing for a few hours before breakfast while holding down a job at the Post Office, who am I to whinge about working full time in the salt-mines?"

"I don't want you to be Anthony Trollope. I want you to be Eric Tucker."

"Fine, but if you think I'm ever again going to put myself in the position of being kept by a rich woman—"

"How do you know I'm going to be rich? How do you know I don't intend to give all Kim's money to the Healing Centre?"

Tucker boggled but recovered sufficiently to

say: "Okay, assuming you're going to be penni-less—"

"Not quite penniless. I think I may be able to find a little loose change to start a coin-breeding programme."

"Well, whatever your financial status *I must get a proper job* or our *amitié* will be on the rocks in no time flat!"

"Oh, stop talking like a middle-class southerner who was raised on Victorian values!"

"I *am* a middle-class southerner who was raised on Victorian values!"

"You're also a City slicker accustomed to hacking it in 1990s London—oh, come on, Tucker, get real! Pay your way, just as you're doing now with Gil, and I'll pay mine. Do you think I want to be kept any more than you do? And do you seriously think I'm no better than a bedwardly-mobile fluffette who rates a man's genitals according to the size of his bank balance?"

I had expected him to smile but he just looked at me with grave dark eyes and said soberly: "We're talking of primitive emotions, the kind which cultural trends cover up but don't change. You're the one who has to get real here, Carter."

"Well, if it's realism you want, let me tell you that I don't expect any future relationship to be easy and I don't expect it to be perfect. I just want it to be right."

Then he did smile. "Well, if you've got the faith and hope—"

"I must have. I've torn up my life-plan."

"—and I've got the—"

"—skill to teach me how to live dynamically, we'll be fine. But only if you stay Eric Tucker and don't try to be Anthony Trollope." I pushed aside my plate and stood up. "Is it too hot to walk to St. Paul's?"

"Your *cher ami* would willingly escort you through a burning desert!"

"That's more like it! I got worried just then when you started bleating about money. Don't you know that a *cher ami* is by definition incapable of being kept? He wouldn't be *cher* if he sponged."

"I get the picture. I'm to be a non-sponging, non-Trollopian, 1990s man who's equally happy either driving a Porsche or running around in Lycra shorts with a feather duster."

"Running around in—"

"Okay, forget the Lycra shorts."

"Forget the feather duster! That sounds much too wimpish! Just be yourself, but remember that a *cher ami* never caterwauls about money to his widowed sizzlerina and never makes her regret being rich."

"I'm beginning to see all this as an epistolary novel by Richardson," mused Tucker. "Instead of *Clarissa* we'd have *Catriona*. 'Cher ami,' the beleaguered heiress would write to her lovelorn swain—"

Before he could discover I had no idea who Richardson was I said hastily: "Talking of Catriona, I'm changing the spelling of my name. I've decided that Carter as in President Jimmy is too masculine so I'm going to become Carta as in Magna instead."

"Why not go for a real change and become Magna as in Carta? And while we're on the subject of names, are you ever, ever going to call me Eric?"

"You sound like someone asking a girl if she's ever, ever going to lose her virginity!"

"You mean we're talking about a real life-changing commitment here?"

I laughed and clasped his hand again. All I said was: "Let's go to St. Paul's."

IX

I told him I wanted to retrace the route I had taken on the night of the melt-down; I wanted to see it bathed in light. So we walked along the podium to Aldersgate Street and headed south to the junction with London Wall.

As we rounded the bend into King Edward Street, we saw the Cathedral sweltering ahead of us as it erupted from the summit of Ludgate Hill, its dome ash-grey against the steamy blue sky, its gold cross shimmering as if liquefied by the sun. We wandered past the shade of the trees in Postman's Park, past the roses in the ruins of Christ Church Greyfriars, and all around us I seemed to hear the ancient names of the City streets vibrating in harmony as if celebrating their resurrections from the Plague, the Fire and the Blitz.

When we reached the corner of Paternoster Row I said to Tucker: "I want to send a post-card to my father, and I thought the Cathedral might have one which will say to him without words that the Powers are survivable."

"When's he due for release?"

"Very soon."

Then Tucker asked me to tell him more, so we went into the gardens of the Cathedral churchyard and sat beneath one of the trees as I talked of my father's troubled life. "I believe that with the right healing process he could be helped," I said. "I believe now that even the worst addictions are treatable."

"I understand. So—"

"I wouldn't expect a cure," I said quickly. "I'm not stupid enough to expect miracles. All I'd hope for would be for him to have a better quality of life—a way of living which would keep him out of jail and enable him to connect better with people."

"But wouldn't that indeed be a miracle?"

"You think it's too much to ask?"

"No, no, I didn't mean that—I think you can ask for anything, even a cure. What I meant was that miracles come in all shapes and sizes."

"Well, whether a miracle's possible or not, I must act," I said fiercely. *"I must act."*

"All that's required for evil to triumph—"

"Exactly. I couldn't save Kim," I said rapidly, "but I've learned from that death. I've learned that no one's beyond redemption. I've learned that if you can love someone, even someone very emotionally damaged, that can make a vital difference to them if they want to get well." I had to pause there but after a moment I was able to add in a level voice: "I loved my father once. I disconnected myself from that relationship but I didn't stop loving him, I know that now, because I was always looking for an idealised version of him. I thought I'd found that in Kim, but I was wrong. All I'd found was a damaged man who was just as bad at making real connections with people as my father was."

I paused again. It was peaceful sitting there in the shadow of the Cathedral. I was no longer aware of the tourists and the roar of the distant traffic. I could only see Tucker's hand entwined with mine. "I couldn't save Kim," I said again, "but I know now how I can help my father. And if my father can be helped just a fraction— just the tiniest fraction—then Kim's tragedy will have meaning and the whole bloody mess of the last few months will begin to look a little different."

Tucker said: "How old were you when you disconnected yourself from your father?"

"Six. That was when the bailiffs came for the last time. That was when he lost Hamish, my cat." I revolved the memory slowly in my mind. "Sometimes," I heard myself say, "sometimes I think I don't want kids because I'd never want any child of mine to go through what I went through when my parents split up."

"But they wouldn't, would they? You'd make sure they never did."

I pondered on this but could only say in despair: "When one thinks of all the pain and suffering in the world it's illogical and irrational that anyone should want to bring new life into it! Why do you think people want kids, Tucker?"

"Beats me, Ms. G. But then I always hanker to do crazy things which kick reason and logic in the teeth."

"Honestly?"

"You bet. And having kids kicks the Powers in the teeth too, doesn't it? Since they want to wipe us out, we beat them when we reproduce."

"True." I suddenly felt better. "And talking of kicking the Powers in the teeth—"

"Let's go and choose that postcard for your father."

Wandering on through the churchyard we reached the massive West Front where tourists were sitting on the steps like roosting pigeons and watching the red buses toiling up Ludgate Hill. Inside the Cathedral the air was stuffy but felt cooler than the air in the sun-baked streets. For a brief moment I glanced down the nave at the vast, glowing interior. Then I moved to the postcard stands grouped near the entrance.

"Is your father religious?" enquired Tucker after we had inspected the conventional views of the dome and moved on to the close-ups of the ceiling mosaics.

"Not in the least."

"In that case let's rule out the shots of angels. How about a picture of Holman Hunt's *Light of the World*?"

"Good try, but he's not turned on by Jesus." I revolved the stand restlessly, then heard the rasp of my breath as I saw what I wanted. The next moment I was plucking the card from its slot.

I was looking at the famous photograph of St. Paul's taken in 1940 as the German bombers blasted the City apart. Beyond the blackened ruins in the foreground, beyond the billowing smoke, beyond all the brutal destruction wreaked by the Powers of Darkness, the dome of the Cathedral, untouched and radiant, was eerily illuminated by the fires which raged beneath that pitch-black night sky.

"*Yes!*" said Tucker at once when I showed the picture to him.

I bought the card. My fingers were trembling, and I felt so overwhelmed that I had to ask him to sort out the right coins from my change-purse. Scrabbling blindly in my bag afterwards I muttered: "I can't find my pen."

"Here," said Tucker, finding it for me, and slipping an arm around my waist he steered me to the nearest row of chairs. By the time we sat down my fingers had stopped shaking but were as mobile as lumps of lead. Clumsily I wrote on the back of the card: "When you come out, I'll be there." Never had seven commonplace words been harder to commit to paper. I had to pause afterwards to take several deep breaths. Then I wrote: "I want you to visit London to meet my new friends."

At that point Tucker had to take charge of the card before my tears rendered the message illegible, but five minutes later I was at last able to write: "It's okay now about Hamish. I know you're sorry you lost him. All my love, KITTY."

XI

With the card safely tucked in my bag to await a stamp, we began to walk up the long nave, across the marble floor, past the rows of chairs and clusters of tourists, towards the great golden mosaics glittering high on the recessed walls by the transepts and on the vaulted roof of the choir. I had visited the Cathedral as a sightseer years ago when I had first arrived in London, but I had forgotten how enormous it was, how overpowering in its magnificence, and for a moment, as I glimpsed ahead the huge mosaic showing Christ as ruler of the world, I wondered what the carpenter from Nazareth would have thought of such lavish grandeur. But I did not wonder for long. I knew now that the Cathedral was representing the richness of life, and I knew too that in the heart of that life Christ would always be there, parting the darkness, saving the lost and healing the broken as he triumphed again and again and again over the forces of disintegration and decay.

"Hey, Tucker—"

"Yes, Ms. G?"

"Why doesn't God just zap the Powers and get on with it?"

"You might as well ask why I don't toss off the perfect novel in twenty-four hours! I mean, this is a big creative project we're talking about here—cosmologically speaking it's only just got going!"

"I still don't see why the Powers are unzappable."

"It's because they're essential to creation. You can't create without making messes and generating chaos and blundering down blind alleys and crawling back up again—you can't create without those efforts which end in disaster, because it's the disasters which show you how to get things right. That's why every disaster during creation is potentially redeemable—it's because without the disasters the creator could never complete any worthwhile project."

"But why can't God create more efficiently?"

"Because creation's not about efficiency, it's about love. It's about shedding blood, sweat and tears to make the thing you care about come right. It's about enduring the shadow side of creation and using it so that in the end everything can be brought into the light... Why are you suddenly looking so anxious?"

"I'm finally facing up to the fact that you're not only better educated than I am but much smarter... Have you ever heard of Plotinus?"

"The philosopher? The Neo-Platonist who had such a profound influence on Pseudo-Dionysius?"

"That settles it. I'm going to have an inferiority complex."

"Well, I suppose that's less trouble than having a baby, but I bet it's not half as much fun."

"Listen." I was busy processing his information about creators. On the south side of the Cathedral the light was streaming through the long windows onto the floor of the dome ahead of us as we wandered on down the central aisle. "Listen—"

"I'm listening, Ms. G."

"—since the God-project's so big, what can one human being matter?"

"In the perfect novel every word matters. In the perfect painting every fleck of paint matters. In this amazing cathedral every grain of marble matters." He smiled at me before saying: "In the creation which tops all creations, *you* matter, Carta-with-two-As."

"And you, Eric."

For one long moment I thought of my old isolated life when I had been incarcerated in my tower and peering through my telescope at a world which had lain beyond my reach. Then as we paused at last beneath the dome and turned to face each other, I knew that all the happiness I had ever wanted was waiting for me in a matchless reality I had barely begun to explore.

AUTHOR'S NOTE

The Right Reverend and Right Honourable Lord Habgood of Calverton, the author of the quotations which precede each part of this book, was the Archbishop of York from 1983 to 1995.

Dr. David F. Ford, the author of the quotations which precede each chapter, is currently Regius Professor of Divinity at the University of Cambridge.

I wish to thank the Very Reverend Alex Wedderspoon, Dean of Guildford, for his sermon about the sheepdog trials.

A NOTE ABOUT THE AUTHOR

SUSAN HOWATCH was born in Surrey in 1940. After taking a degree in law, she immigrated to the United States where she married, had a daughter and embarked on a career as a writer. In 1976 she left the States and lived in the Republic of Ireland for four years before returning to England. She lived in Salisbury—the inspiration for her Starbridge series of novels—and now lives in London.